ECSTASY'

It was a despicable
innocents.

He, Charles, was the son of the most depraved
woman in France. She, Bonne, was the girl-
wife to the wickedest man in the land, the Satan-
worshipping De Giac. And now this youthful
pair had been thrust into bed together by their
infinitely corrupt elders.

But it turned out to be quite glorious.

"Oh, my Bonne," said Charles, and kissed her.
Then suddenly the transition from boy to man
was easy for him, and with his body ready for
love, he went to the joyous place between
Bonne's thighs and set up the slow, strong,
harshly sweet rhythm he had heard of but
never before known. And the girl, unafraid at
last, raised her lips, her breasts, her hips to
him, abandoning shame and moving with
Charles toward the heaven they both longed
for. . . .

**Bonne was to be the first but far from the last
of—**

THE
KING'S
WOMEN

THE
KING'S
WOMEN

DINAH LAMPITT

A SIGNET BOOK

SIGNET
Published by the Penguin Group
Penguin Books USA Inc., 375 Hudson Street,
New York, New York 10014, U.S.A.
Penguin Books Ltd, 27 Wrights Lane,
London W8 5TZ, England
Penguin Books Australia Ltd, Ringwood,
Victoria, Australia
Penguin Books Canada Ltd, 10 Alcorn Avenue,
Toronto, Ontario, Canada M4V 3B2
Penguin Books (N.Z.) Ltd, 182–190 Wairau Road,
Auckland 10, New Zealand

Penguin Books Ltd, Registered Offices:
Harmondsworth, Middlesex, England

Published by Signet, an imprint of Dutton Signet,
a division of Penguin Books USA Inc. Originally published in Great Britain by
New English Library.

First American Printing, December, 1993
10 9 8 7 6 5 4 3 2 1

Printed in the United States of America

*For Charles Purle—with admiration
and affection.*

Acknowledgments

My sincere thanks are due to Monsieur Bernard Juguet of the Auberge Reine de Sicile in Saumur who helped me pursue some original and fascinating research on Jehanne, to Carlo Demetriou who started as a translator and ended as a friend, to Zak Packham who walked with me in the steps of Charles de Valois and patiently filmed the entire journey. Thanks, too, to Erika Lock for typing the manuscript, to Anna Foinette, my superb secretary, to my friend and agent Shirley Russell, and to Geoffrey Glassborow and Peter Jeffrey, always there when they are needed.

Cast of Characters

THE ROYAL FAMILY

Charles VI, mad King of France, Charles's nominal father.

Isabeau of Bavaria, Queen of France, Charles's mother.

Louis, their son, the Dauphin.

Marguerite, his wife, daughter of the Duke of Burgundy, future wife of Richemont.

Jean, the second Dauphin.

Jacqueline of Hainault and Bavaria, his wife, future wife of Duke Humphrey of Gloucester.

Charles, Count of Ponthieu, future Dauphin and King of France.

Marie d'Anjou, daughter of Yolande, Charles's future Queen.

Louis, their eldest child, Dauphin and future Louis XI of France.

Margaret of Scotland, his wife, the Dauphine.

Catherine, Charles's sister, future wife of Henry V.

THE DUKES

Louis, Duke of Orléans, Charles VI's brother, Isabeau's lover.

Charles, future Duke of Orléans, Louis's legitimate son.

Jean the Fearless, Duke of Burgundy, leader of the Burgundians.

Philippe the Good, his son, future Duke of Burgundy.

Jean, Duke of Alençon, friend of Charles and Jehanne.

Jean, Duke of Brittany, brother of Richemont.

Charles, Duke of Lorraine, future father-in-law of René d'Anjou and lover of Alison du May.

THE HOUSE OF ANJOU

Duke Louis II.

Yolande, his wife, frequently Regent, Duchess and Queen of Sicily.

Duke Louis III (Jade), their son.

Marie d'Anjou, their daughter, Charles's future wife.

René d'Anjou, their second son, future Duke of Lorraine and Bar, Grand Master of the Priory of Sion.

Isabelle of Lorraine, Duke Charles's daughter, René's wife.

Marguerite d'Anjou, René's daughter, future wife of Henry VI of England.

Charles, Count of Maine, Yolande's third son.

Yolande, Yolande's third daughter.

MYSTICS

Jehanne Darc, La Pucelle.

Nicolas Flamel, Grand Master of the Priory of Sion.

The Cardinal of Bar, acting Grand Master during René's minority.

Guy and Jacques, twin brothers, Astrologer Royal and Abbot.

COURTIERS

Arthur de Richemont, Earl of Richmond, brother of the Duke of Brittany and future Constable of France.

Jean, future Count of Dunois, the Bastard of Orleans.

Robert le Maçon, the Chancellor.

Pierre de Beauvau, the Seneschal of Anjou.

Hardouin de Maillé, *grand maître* of Charles's household.

Lady Jeanne du Mesnil, Charles's governess.

Hervé and Jean du Mesnil, Lady Jeanne's sons.

Tanneguy de Chastel, former Provost of Paris.

Guillaume d'Avagour.

Jean Louvet, *président* of Provence, Chancellor of the Exchequer, father-in-law to the Bastard.

Pierre de Giac

Bonne (born Jeanne de Naillac), his wife.

Georges de la Trémoille, future Duke of Sully.

Catherine, his second wife, widow of de Giac.

Pierre de Brézé, Seneschal of Anjou and Poitou.
Agnès Sorel, his mistress, also mistress to Charles and former lover of the Dauphin, La Dame de Beauté.

THE ENGLISH

Henry V of Lancaster.
Henry VI of Lancaster, his son by Catherine de Valois.
John of Lancaster, Duke of Bedford, Regent of France, Henry V's brother.
Anne, daughter of Jean the Fearless, first wife to John of Bedford.
Humphrey of Lancaster, Duke of Gloucester, Regent of England, Henry V's brother.
The Earl of Warwick, Governor of Rouen.
Sir John Fastolfe, officer, the basis for Shakespeare's Falstaff.
Sir William Glasdale, commander of the garrison in les Tourelles.
Lord John Talbot, commander at Orléans.

OTHERS

Count Bernard d'Armagnac, Charles d'Orléans's father-in-law.
Jacquetta of Luxemburg, early love of Richemont, future wife of John of Bedford.
Catherine of Luxemburg, her sister, Richemont's third wife.
Robert de Baudricourt, garrison commander of Vaucouleurs.
Bertrand de Poulengy, a soldier.
Jean de Metz, a soldier.
Jacqueline Sarrazin, Yolande's principal Lady.
Jean d'Aulon, Jehanne's squire.
Louis de Coutes, Jehanne's page.
Gilles de Rais, follower of Jehanne, a future child sex murderer.
Jacques Coeur, a wealthy merchant.
La Hire, a French mercenary commander.
Alison du May, loyal servant of Yolande, future mistress of Charles, Duke of Lorraine.

Prologue

It was a strange quirk of fate. At the precise moment she threw a winning hand, the Queen went into labor. There before her on the marble table top lay two dice, their white inlay each showing six, while simultaneously deep in her swollen body came that faint sharp pang Isabeau knew so well.

With an almost imperceptible sigh, the Queen of France indicated her win, cried, "Voilà," and chose to ignore the fact that her eleventh child had started on its journey into life.

The other players noticed nothing, only the dwarf looking up slyly as a muscle twitched involuntarily in Isabeau's cheek. "Bravo, ma Reine," he squeaked in his high unearthly voice. "You have beaten us all yet again."

The Queen looked at him with dislike. "Get out you little freak, you bore me." Then added in a softer voice, "Philippe, Jean, you may stay to attend us," nodding in the direction of the two young fops who made up the rest of the gambling school, smiling her bright smile, drawing her full lips back to reveal small white teeth, before finally standing up.

Her velvet gown, stitched over with a thousand pearls, flowed round her distended body so cleverly that it was almost impossible to tell Isabeau was pregnant, let alone at the end of her time. She was half Italian, half Bavarian, but in looks the Queen's Germanic blood had been sublimated by the vivid colors of the south. Her hair was long and so black that occasionally it seemed to have an almost violet shimmer, while her eyes were brilliantly alive, flashing whenever she spoke, the deep liquid brown of topaz. But the radiant beauty which had been hers when she had been the fourteen-year-old bride of fifteen-year-old Charles VI of France, was systematically being eroded by Isabeau's appetites.

Standing up now, short in stature despite her high-heeled wooden shoes, the Queen contemplated just one more act of naughtiness before she went to her lying in.

"You boys," she said, looking at the brothers Jean and Philippe Vallier, "you pretty little dandies, pour me some wine and kiss me with your sweet rosy mouths. At once now, do you hear?"

It was a game they had all played before and the rules were always the same. First they must go to the Hall of Rosewater, where stood braziers from which rose the pungent scents of oriental perfumes from Damascus, making the senses of all who inhaled them reel; and there they would settle the goddess of pleasure on cushions and massage her, embrace her, do whatever she wished.

But today Isabeau only required that her garments be loosened and her back rubbed and when Jean slipped his hand beneath to fondle her enormous but wonderful breasts, he was firmly slapped away.

"You do not want love, ma Reine?" he whispered into her ear, from the lobe of which swung an emerald as big as an eye.

"No, a mother cannot be wanton."

The twins exchanged a glance, understanding what she meant, and wondering whether they should send for the Queen's ladies.

Isabeau read their minds. "It's not coming yet. You can take me to my chamber in half an hour. Now please me, you sweet young creatures."

And that was how the royal midwives finally found her, summoned by an anxious Jean who had slipped away unnoticed while his brother expertly ministered to Isabeau's whims.

"Madame, you must come with me," said Mère Jacques, marching up to where the Queen lay in ecstasy. She was the most senior of them all, the woman who had delivered Isabeau's last four children: Marie, Louis the Dauphin, Jean and Catherine. "No more playing. You must give birth to your child."

No other woman in the kingdom would have risked being so direct, no other woman approaching the Queen would have dared show brown rotting teeth and a plain stern face with no hint of cosmetic artifice.

Isabeau looked up lazily from her cushions. "Is it you, you old witch? I should have known you would come to spoil things."

"The sooner you get shot of it the sooner you can return to your games," Mère Jacques answered grimly.

"Damn you," said Isabeau, but she allowed the twins to heave her to her feet and pass her into the midwives' care, before tottering off on her high heels toward the Queen's private apartments.

Watching the great shape with its accompanying party of hens as it disappeared into the depths of the palace, Philippe grinned slyly at his brother.

"I wonder who fathered it?" he said in a whisper.

"It wasn't me," answered Jean. "You?"

"Very unlikely." Philippe lowered his voice even further. "Even less likely than the King."

The twins nudged each other, laughed silently, then went off in pursuit of further diversion.

Three hours later, the time now being two in the morning, Isabeau, with a grunt, delivered a sickly boy into the world. Mère Jacques, believing the old wives' tale that in its first few moments a newborn always resembles its father, scrutinized its features with a hard stare. But apart from the fact that she had never seen such a hideous baby in her life there was nothing to reveal who had sired the poor thing. It resembled neither Charles VI of France, who had once been so beautiful but who had now degenerated into a hopeless lunatic, nor his exquisite brother, the Duke of Orléans, the Queen's most favored lover. In fact it resembled nothing but a hobgoblin, with its bald head, big nose and staring eyes.

"What sex is it?" asked Isabeau, wearily, from her great bed.

"A boy, Madame," answered Mère Jacques, and briskly sponged the infant's eyes and nose with a damp cloth to try and make it look a little more presentable.

"Pass him to me," said the Queen, not with obvious maternal feeling but more with the interest she always reserved for any new pet that joined the royal household.

"Mon Dieu, he won't be famed for his looks!" she exclaimed. "What a creature! Where is the Lady Jeanne du Mesnil?"

"Here, Majesty," answered the lady-in-waiting who had already been chosen to act as the new baby's governess.

"Stand where I can see you. Now see to it that the boy has enough silver plate and linen, and furs to keep him warm." Isabeau heaved herself up in the bed a little and drank a deep measure of wine. "And tell my chief astrologer to cast omens for the child. I think he's going to need them with that face."

Jeanne du Mesnil curtsied and put out her arms to take the new Count of Ponthieu from his mother, and Isabeau—after dropping an absent-minded kiss on the infant's brow—handed him over with a sigh of relief.

"Now I shall sleep. In the morning send the musicians and my new singer to me, they can cheer my lying in."

She closed her eyes and leant back on her fine lace pillows, thus dismissing all but those who were assigned to wash and perfume her body after the birth.

In the arms of Lady du Mesnil the Count of Ponthieu, swathed in so many layers of swaddling that his ugly little face was hardly visible, stirred and his mouth opened to yell.

"She's coming, your nurse is coming," soothed the governess as, after dropping a reverential curtsy to the Queen, she briskly carried the infant to the royal nursery where Jeanne Chamoisy, the wet nurse, already waited, naked but for a clean linen shift and shivering with cold as a result.

As soon as it had been finally discovered that the Queen was in labor, the woman had been fetched from her bed, stripped and scrubbed hard, to ensure that her working-class breasts would be fit to feed a member of the royal house of Valois. But its newest addition had no doubt. As Jeanne bared her nipple and held the baby to it, he took the flow greedily.

"He sucks well," said Jeanne the governess, who knew the wet nurse from the time of the Queen's last confinement when the Princess Catherine had also been fed by her.

"Poor little thing," Jeanne Chamoisy answered without thinking.

"Why do you say that?"

"Well, he's not a pretty child, is he? Not like Catty."

Jeanne du Mesnil looked down at the infant face, half obscured by the large sensible breast nourishing it.

"I can't see who he resembles."

"No," answered Jeanne, and the eyes of the two women met and held for a second.

"The maids will bring the prince to his cradle when you've finished feeding him. Then you may retire for four hours, unless he cries of course, in which case you will be sent for," said Jeanne the governess, suddenly very business-like.

"Yes, Madame."

"Now I shall go and see that all is prepared." And the lady-in-waiting bustled from the room to the apartment where the two royal cots stood in readiness, and gave instructions to Lady Suzanne Rion to straighten the hangings of the one about to receive its new occupant.

The cradles were beautiful, a work of art in themselves: made from Irish fir trees, the rich wood embellished with gold and copper, the Queen's arms—the Wittelsbach device, the emblem of the royal house of Bavaria—carved proudly at their head for all the world to see.

"Just the Queen's arms," thought Lady du Mesnil reflectively. "Why not those of France?"

Was this, she wondered, Isabeau's way of covertly telling the world that her latest child was the fruit of her affair with that most elegant of princes, that formidable womanizer, Louis d'Orléans? These days the couple could not get enough of one another, delighting in each other's company, or so it was said. And though both may have other lovers, as they most certainly did, it was claimed that these counted for nothing, that together the Queen and her brother-in-law had found a passion so sweet and rare that nobody else could ever matter again.

Jeanne du Mesnil's mind went to the child's nominal father, the King of France, confined to his quarters in the palace, sometimes lucid, sometimes raving, covered with dirt. She felt a moment's pity for the monarch, once so respected, now brought so low, seized by madness a full eleven years ago. She also felt a wave of compassion for Isabeau who in the past had loved him greatly but who, because of her husband's lunacy, had progressively become the most debauched woman in the known world, nicknamed Queen Venus because of her wild way of life.

And now there was another infant to add to that un-
healthy excitable bunch of siblings who were the royal children of France.

"Poor little thing," she said, echoing Jeanne Chamoisy's
words, then turned as the sound of feet behind her heralded
the arrival of the newborn prince.

"His Highness, Monsieur le Comte, is asleep," said the
Lady Marie de Barrois importantly, and handed the minute
bundle into Jeanne's care.

How gently she laid him in his cradle of Irish wood, how
softly bent to take another look at the small face, smoothed
out by sleep, how tenderly tucked him beneath a coverlet
of fur to protect the babe against the raw February night,
as cold as any yet in the bleak winter which held France
in its bite in that year of 1403.

PART ONE

▨

YOLANDE AND ISABEAU

One

The most extraordinary thing about the palace known as the Hôtel St. Pol was its chaotic character. No overall plan encompassed the building's collection of individual mansions or *hôtels*, rich and extravagant though each was. And no grand design had overseen the way in which these lavish dwellings were linked together. Instead, a sprawl of gardens, courtyards and fountains, quadrangles, cloisters, passageways and galleries, to say nothing of a menagerie, formed the connecting links between the various great houses, the whole being termed the King's lodging, his domain, the household where he lived in his twilight world of madness.

Yet to that frenetic group of young people who were the mad King's offspring nothing could have been more exciting than that hotch-potch of a place where wild unhappy beasts paced tetchily in cages, and aviaries of exotic birds beat their wings against imprisoning mesh. Here was havoc, a maze, a pit of shadows where one could get dangerously lost, a place of sunshine where exuberant fountains gushed and splashed at every corner.

Within this crazy network of mansions lay the Hôtel du Petit-Musc, and it was here that the royal children dwelled. Once it had belonged to their uncle, the decadent, naughty Duke d'Orléans, but now he had gone and the house had been given over to them, principally that they might keep to themselves within its walls and not force their unwanted attention on the adult population of the Hôtel St. Pol.

Altogether there had been eleven of them but now only two remained, Catherine and Charles, aged six and four respectively. Their elder brothers, the Dauphin Louis, and Jean, Duke of Touraine, still lived in the palace, of course, but they were ten and nine years of age, already betrothed and no longer considered children, able now to command their own private apartments.

As to the rest of the brood, the first had been a boy, Charles, who had died in infancy; then had come Jeanne, who had met the same fate. The first child to survive had been Isabelle, who had married King Richard II of England when she had been less than nine years old, and he already thirty. Another Jeanne had followed, this one to live and marry the heir to the Duke of Brittany when she had been little older than her sister. A Dauphin, Charles, had been born next and he had lived eight years before an untimely death. Then, in close proximity, there had been two little girls, Michelle and Marie; Michelle promised as the future bride of the son of Jean the Fearless, Duke of Burgundy, Marie to be given to God, destined from the cradle to become a nun in return, or so it was hoped, for her mad father's return to sanity. But the sacrifice had been in vain. The child still pined in a convent while the King verged between phases of wild exhilaration—a mood in which he could be highly dangerous—and desperate depression. When these times came he would lie in the dark, refuse to eat, to wash or be washed, becoming filthy and thin, covered with lice and excrement.

Louis, the present Dauphin, had followed the two daughters, then had come Jean, and finally Catherine and Charles, Count of Ponthieu, the third boy to bear that name, it being the custom to name a living child after another dead sibling. And all the while the King had slipped further into madness, inheriting his mother's unbalanced tendencies, loathed by the wife who once had loved him, served sexually by a string of prostitutes, their frequent visits organized by the Queen herself.

But on this November day of 1407, Charles VI of France was reasonably rational, ready to receive a visit from his remaining children, and was washed, shaved, and properly dressed for the first time in months. And even while he allowed the royal barber to trim his hair, the Lady Jeanne du Mesnil was threading her way through the lower gallery which ran in the direction of the river Seine and the gardens that went down to the high wall above the water's edge, turning right into a fountained courtyard which lay before the Hôtel du Petit-Musc, then staring up at a first-floor window.

"Are you prepared inside?" she called, then shivered as the chill autumn wind rustled the leaves that crunched, shriveled and decaying, beneath her well shod feet.

"Coming," shouted a little voice in reply, and Jeanne smiled as she made her way to the stout wooden door set in an archway which served as the mansion's main entrance, only to see it swing open before she even got there.

The children who stood in the doorway, hand-in-hand and breathing a little faster as the raw cold air bit at their nostrils, could be seen to be brother and sister through one distinguishing feature alone, for each of them bore the long Valois nose that no amount of new blood introduced into the family seemed able to eradicate.

In the boy's case this nose was not only long but thick, dominating his small plain face and giving him the ridiculous comic dash of a cheerful elf. Yet nature had not been completely cruel to this ugly imp for a pair of candid eyes, the translucent greenish shade associated with clear water and streams, looked with trust on the face of his beloved governess, while a thick cap of russet hair crowned a surprisingly well-shaped head.

The girl was very different, beautiful in the slanting pointed way of a cat. Tilting dark brows, in extreme and exciting contrast to her hair, which was deep gold and hung, thick and heavy, about her face, rose above eyes that had absorbed every shade of the color blue. In one light they could have been described as harebell, in another hyacinth, in yet another, sky. And in her case the long nose was thin and elegant, sensual somehow, an attribute above the wide feline mouth.

Jeanne du Mesnil smiled. "Monsieur le Comte, Madame la Princesse, are you ready to visit His Grace the King?"

"Is he quite well?" asked Catherine anxiously, her slanting brows meeting in a sudden frown.

"Much recovered," Jeanne replied soothingly, and put out her hand to Charles, who hung back, shivering despite the small fur-lined mantle he was wearing.

"What is it, mon cher? Are you cold?"

The four-year-old shook his head. "No. It is just that His Majesty my father makes me so nervous."

Lady du Mesnil compromised between her duty as governess and saying what she actually thought.

"It will tire His Grace if you stay long so this need only be a short visit, Monsieur. Simply congratulate the King on his return to health and pay him your respects."

"Will you be there?" Charles continued in the same vein.

"I shall remain in the antechamber, not far away. Now come along."

But it was with reluctant steps that the two royal children made their way out of the courtyard, through the gallery that ran the length of the menagerie where the big cats stirred fitfully, past the round tower and finally into the King's great hall, deserted except for two young gentlemen who crouched over the fire warming their hands.

The couple looked up as the three people entered, and made slight, somehow mocking, bows. Lady du Mesnil inclined her head grandly and stalked past with her charges, Charles turning to look back over his shoulder.

"Who are those men, Masher?" he whispered, using his own special nickname for her, a name as near as he had been able to get to Madame Chérie when he had first learned to speak.

"The taller is your brother-in-law the Duke of Brittany's brother. He is an Earl—but an English one. The other is his aide."

"An English Earl?" repeated Charles in surprise. "How?"

"In a complicated way," answered Lady du Mesnil. "Now come along, you cannot keep the King your father waiting."

But Charles hesitated a further moment, staring at the young lordling, wishing that he could be even a quarter as handsome as the elegant creature that now sprawled in its chair, holding its pointed shoes to the fire, and winking a careless eye at the small child regarding it.

"What is his name?" Charles breathed noisily.

"Arthur de Richemont, which is pronounced Richmond in English. Can you say that word?"

"Reechmoond," answered the Count of Ponthieu, not concentrating.

The Earl, hearing him, rose and bowed again. "Greetings, my Prince," he said, grinning broadly.

The poor child, aware of its ugliness, flushed unbecomingly, unable to take his saucer eyes from Richemont's beautifully proportioned face, seemingly molded around the cheek bones; a face above which grew a shining crop of hair dark as night, yet with lights in it, lights the shade of mulled wine, of log fires and winter sunsets. This same hair, cut straight round his head, the very height of fashion, would have curled had it been allowed to grow but one inch longer.

Lady du Mesnil swept a curtsy. "Monsieur le Comte is already late for an appointment to see the King, Monsieur."

Richemont bowed elegantly, once more winking a glittering blue eye as his head came down level with that of the little boy's. "Indeed? Let me not keep him, Madame."

Then he smiled and Charles saw the Earl's pupils deepen in color, changing from ice to jewel blue, while a distant rose bloomed and died in Madame du Mesnil's cheeks.

"Au revoir, Monsieur," the child said cautiously.

"Au revoir, my Prince," answered Arthur de Richemont as he turned and sauntered casually back to his chair, thus showing that the sons of the late Duke of Brittany considered themselves almost on an equal footing with those of His Majesty the King.

"And this day," thought Charles, as his small feet carried him, quaking, across the stone floor of the King's private chamber, "mon père *is* majestic."

For the King sat still in his high chair, observing the world through his pale mad eyes, which at the moment showed no hint of the unrestrained behavior that could suddenly grip him during one of his more rational phases.

"Well, well," he said as they drew nearer, "if it isn't my pretty Catherine with her lovely face. Come kiss your papa, chérie," and he held out his hands to her.

The girl obeyed, trembling violently as she approached the royal seat, but her father merely bent low and kissed his daughter on both cheeks, not looking frightening at all.

"I'm here too, Sire," ventured Charles in a nervous voice.

The King ignored him, pulling Catherine onto his lap, twisting her golden locks round his fingers and dropping innumerable kisses onto her head and brow. Charles had a brief glimpse of his sister's terrified face before it was hidden by a veil of their father's white hair.

"I'm here, Sire," he tried again.

The King paused in mid-kiss, peering round suspiciously, his eyes suddenly narrowing.

"Who are you?" he said, for the first time looking directly at the child.

"Charles, Sir. Your youngest son."

The monarch's eyes narrowed even further. "Ah, the bastard! Come closer. Let me have a look at you."

Very alarmed, the boy managed a few more nervous steps toward the high chair.

"Mon Dieu!" exclaimed the King, starting back in surprise. "What a terrible face. She should have kept her eyes away from gargoyles when she carried you. Which of her freaks was your father I wonder."

Charles gulped miserably, unable to answer.

"You see, they think I don't know," Charles VI continued to the room in general. "They think I don't know what goes on—but nothing escapes me, my little damsels of the night make sure of that."

The child stared at him uncomprehendingly while somewhere in the background one of the Monarch's Gentlemen cleared his throat noisily.

"For she's a great and terrible whore," roared the King suddenly, simultaneously standing up, so that Catherine went crashing to the floor, where she lay for a moment, stunned. "She fornicates with them all; dwarves, pimps, astrologers, pretty boys—all of them have known her. And my brother too. Didn't you realize, you little bastards, that your uncle is sharing your mother's bed?"

Startled by the sudden noise, Catherine burst into floods of tears, crawling to where her brother stood trembling, a small cowed figure, and throwing her arms round him, then remaining unnaturally still.

"And now there's another member of her filthy brood," the King screamed, stepping down from his dais, the saliva which flecked his lips spraying as he spoke. "She had a baby twelve days ago and thought she'd keep it secret by giving birth in her love nest. But she didn't fool me. My pretty doxies told me all about it. It was another boy but it died soon after it was born. And the silly trollop thinks I don't know. What a joke!"

And with that the King began to rock with uncontrollable laughter, clutching his sides and bunching his cheeks, looking almost jolly as a result.

Charles stood stricken, aware of his sister's ice-cold body, of his own stabbing fear, of the fact that the King's Principal Gentleman had left the group of male courtiers and was now advancing toward his sovereign.

"Sire," he was saying soothingly as he approached, "Sire, do not distress yourself. Let me accompany you to your chamber. Why don't you rest for a while? Or perhaps take some refreshment? Shall I send for Lady du Mesnil to remove the Count of Ponthieu and the Princess?"

"No," snarled the monarch, turning like a whip. "No, no, no. I'm having a good time." And with that he snatched from its scabbard the jeweled dress sword which the Gentleman wore buckled round his waist, and whirled it over his head.

"Help!" shrieked Catherine, coming out of her frozen state, and, scrambling to her feet, dragged Charles to the furthest corner of the room where they stood huddled.

"So you want to play, my pretty bastard?" shrieked the King in a ghastly parody of fatherly love and, continuing to slash the sword through the air, charged to where the two children had pressed themselves against the stone wall.

"Ah, it's the hobgoblin," he exclaimed, stopping short before Charles and crouching down to stare into the child's face. "I swear I have never seen anything like it. It's not human, this changeling. I wonder, might it look better if I cut off its ears?"

In the distance Charles heard the whole group of male courtiers start to move cautiously forward.

"What do you say?" the King persisted. "Shall I improve you, gargoyle?"

"No, Sire, please," answered the boy in stark terror and then, to his shame, began to scream at the top of his voice.

Without turning to look at the party of people creeping up on him, the King suddenly hissed, "If one of you comes near I shall kill the Queen's spawn now," and he put the point of his sword to Charles's throat.

The boy was dimly conscious that his sister had lost all color and was slumped against the wall like a lifeless doll, that Madame du Mesnil's frantic face had appeared in the doorway, that beside her stood young Richemont and his companion. Then he closed his eyes, thinking he had arrived at the moment of death.

"Catch," called a sudden cheery voice, and peeping through almost closed lids Charles saw that the Earl had rushed into the room and was throwing a ball to his companion even while they darted about.

"Catch yourself," said the other, sending it back.

"Catch as catch can," replied Richemont nonsensically, and with that cavorted to where the King stood, still holding the hapless boy at bay.

"A turn?" asked Richemont pleasantly, showing the King the ball.

"Out!" screamed the monarch. "Get out!" and he started forward, menacing the Earl with the swishing sword. What Charles saw next was so quick that he was never quite sure afterward that it had actually happened. A toe of one of Richemont's fashionable pointed shoes was momentarily in the King's path and there was a crash as Charles VI went flying, hitting the ground heavily then lying where he fell, eyeing the world malevolently. In a second his Gentlemen had surrounded him and those who lifted him up were also those who were strong enough to hold his arms by his sides and wrest the sword away.

"Quick," said Richemont. "It's time for you to go," and he snatched up the Count of Ponthieu, swinging the child off his feet, then turned to Catherine. "Give me your hand, Madame, and let's be on our way."

Relief, gratitude, sudden end to danger, made Charles turn his sad little face into the Earl's youthful shoulder and weep harder than ever.

"Stop at once, Monsieur," said Richemont briskly. "These clothes were a present from the English King, my stepfather, and I don't want them ruined by your snot."

"Thank you for saving me," whispered Charles. "You were so brave."

"Brave, nothing," came the nonchalant reply. "I simply felt like playing ball."

"And that was all?"

"All," said Richemont as he handed the boy over to his governess.

"My grateful thanks, Monsieur," said Lady du Mesnil as she took her charges from the young man's care. "I trust we will be seeing more of you at court now that you have returned from England. Perhaps then we can give you some token of our appreciation."

"Who knows?" answered Richemont casually. "I have no plans at present. I might stay and then again I might not."

"Well, God speed you whatever you decide."

"Au revoir," said Charles to the departing figure.

"A ton service," replied the Earl, then smiled and was gone.

In contrast to the Hôtel St. Pol the Hôtel Barbette was small, but it was here, amongst its gracious reception rooms and light airy towers that Isabeau of Bavaria—Queen Venus—had chosen to dwell, rarely visiting her husband's palace and, when she did so, only with reluctance.

It was also here that thirteen nights earlier, on 10th November 1407, she had given birth to her twelfth child, a boy, Philippe, who had lived only a day. If people conjectured about the paternity of her other children, particularly Charles, about this latest there could be no doubt. Her blatant affair with the Duke of Orléans was public knowledge, the couple appearing to glory in their flagrant liaison. But then, of course, for the charming Duke adultery was nothing new.

It had been his pleasure in the past to have the walls of the gaming rooms in his various châteaux hung with portraits of his many mistresses, then invite their husbands to dine with him and admire the works of art.

High-born ladies, clad only in their nether garments, were often seen being bundled from bedrooms when fathers and husbands had come unexpectedly to call. Wives of others suddenly became suspiciously pregnant, particularly the noble Yolande d'Enghien, whose son Jean was presently being brought up in the Duke's household, publicly known as the Bastard of Orléans. And now the fantastic prince had formed a dissolute passion for his sister-in-law, a passion which she returned in full.

Seeing Isabeau lying on a decorated couch, her black hair loose about her shoulders, a fortune in emeralds glittering at her white throat, Louis d'Orléans felt a thrill of lust as he bent to kiss her and caught a momentary glimpse of her tremendous breasts, supported on their ivory busks, the biggest and firmest he had ever come across in all his years as a womanizer.

"You are beautiful, ma chérie," he whispered.

"But not yet churched," she answered warningly, referring to the ceremony of ritual cleansing by priest after childbirth.

"More's the pity," said Louis with a cynical smile that always made his mouth disconcertingly crooked.

"Indeed," she replied, a voluptuary to her fingertips and as eager as he was to share his bed once more. "But the birth was bad and the child weak. I must recover my strength."

"Certainly you shall," said the Duke, pouring himself a goblet of wine. "So now let us consider other delights. Are we to dine privately?"

"We are."

"Thank God," he answered, slipping off his long-toed shoes. "This has been a difficult week. I'm in no mood for company."

"There will be a few friends present, my brother for one."

Louis raised a fine eyebrow. "Give him enough food and drink and he'll ask for nothing more. As for anyone else, I shall ignore them."

"How churlish!" remonstrated Isabeau, but she was laughing, totally enamored with this cultured and intelligent man who delighted as much as she did in every pleasure of the flesh. "Tell me why?"

"Burgundy," replied Louis shortly.

"You have seen him?"

"Worse! I had to kiss him! That terrible cold snake's skin lay beneath my lips for a second. Mon Dieu, I thought I would vomit where I stood."

The Queen frowned slightly. "And that is all which has made you out of spirits?"

Louis hesitated for a second, thinking, then said, "No, ma Reine. The death of our son has, of course, cut me to the quick."

"He was very small," Isabeau answered quietly. "Poor tiny child."

The Duke d'Orléans nodded. "A tragedy."

But somehow it was hard to believe that the elegant rake who had scattered his seed so widely could find it in him to mourn a dead infant he had not even seen. Nor did Isabeau labor the point, afraid that he might ask her about Charles, the secret of whose paternity was not known even to her. For she had, by her own judgment, been even more naughty than usual at the time of his conception, drinking too much and allowing familiarities with those she would normally have spurned. Even the King had lain with her once at the relevant time, the final coupling they had shared, so that now whenever she looked at the hideous child, she felt a guilty hatred, furious that he had come along to torment her with memories of the past.

As if he was reading her mind Louis said in a whisper, "But we have Charles."

Isabeau hid her face in her wine cup. "Yes. Now tell me more of Burgundy."

D'Orléans looked dour. "My beloved cousin? He is as repellent as ever."

"But has good reason to hate you."

"He is jealous of me if that is what you mean."

"He covets your lands and your power most certainly. But obviously he did not take kindly to your ravishing his wife behind a tapestry, particularly at such a great reception."

The Duke smiled wickedly. "What a marvelous sensation that was. All those people assembled, the noise and the heat, and myself like a satyr, lunging at her for all I was worth just out of sight."

"You're depraved," said Isabeau.

"Yes, so I am," replied Louis, and they laughed together, at one in their love of sexual excess.

"And she was always considered such a good little woman," the Duke added when he had calmed somewhat. "Such a modest, well-behaved creature. I wish you could have seen Jean's face when he found out. When he came calling on me and saw her portrait in my collection."

Just for a moment Isabeau looked serious. "But it brought about a blood feud, that little fornication of yours."

The Duke winked a glittering eye. "Yes, I suppose it did."

And it was true. Though Jean the Fearless, Duke of Burgundy, had envied his cousin's wealth, territories, and position as unofficial Regent of France, it had taken his wife's infidelity to push him over the edge into open warfare against the Duke of Orléans.

"It was worth it though," added that most dissolute of men. "It was so exciting."

"You obviously preferred coupling with her to our diversions," snapped Isabeau, angry now.

"Not at all," answered Duke Louis earnestly. "The woman has such meager dugs."

And that pleased Queen Venus, inordinately proud of her vast bosom, aware that the young fops of her court laid wagers as to whether it was the largest in all France.

"Truly?" she said, casually regarding her nails.

"Truly," answered Louis, very serious.

"Then it is I who have pleased you most?"

"More than any of them."

They were at peace, as near to being in love as was possible for two such debauched beings. And because of their high spirits and frivolity—their dead son already forgotten—the supper party went well, the musicians playing bravely, the food sumptuous, the wine fine and clear, the spices thrown on the brazier heady and intoxicating.

Throughout, Isabeau, her breasts bond tightly to stop her milk flow but her bosom bedecked with jewels to make up for the lack, lay on her great couch, clapping her hands for her servants, flashing her dark eyes at her lover, masterminding the proceedings perfectly though only thirteen days from her travail. Yet finally even this glutton grew tired and with a further clap of hands announced that she was ready to retire for the night. But still the last to leave her side was the Duke of Orléans, bending over to kiss her first on the fingers, then full on the lips.

"Recover soon," he said, fondling her, then bowed impressively before making his way to the antechamber where his equerries and servants waited to escort him home.

"It is freezing hard, your Grace," said one, holding open a fur-lined mantle which he had been warming by the fire.

"Then we had better return at speed," answered the Duke, pulling on a stout hat and thick gloves. "Cold round my extreme parts has never favored me."

His Gentlemen laughed automatically, each of them chosen for his discretion and humor, then the party made its way out into the bitter night.

In the palace courtyard the horses sparked their hooves on the cobbles while d'Orléans's torchbearers came running round from the kitchens, their flares already ablaze.

"Are we ready?" he called to them carelessly.

"Yes, your Grace."

"Then let's away."

The little troop, small this evening as the Duke had been dining incognito, turned out of the great wooden gates of the Hôtel Barbette, which creaked closed and were bolted behind them, into the dark rat-infested streets of Paris. Here narrow alleys led one from the next in a confusing labyrinth, and the gables of the houses leaned toward one another, shutting out even the smallest glimpse of moonlight. In the doorways of the churches bundles of rags moved and heaved where the beggars slept, only the occasional whiteness of a rolling eye revealing that a living creature lay there.

D'Orléans raised a scented handkerchief to his nostrils, loathing the stench of the filthy streets. And so it was, with his face almost buried in fine linen, that he did not see a company of twelve horsemen detach themselves from the shadows and follow him into the Rue du Vieil Temple, nor did Louis hear them for the sacking tied on the hooves of their mounts. In this way the Duke of Orléans came face to face with his murderers at the very last second, and both he and his small band of riders were taken completely by surprise.

"God's mother!" he called out. "Who are you?"

But there was no answer as one of the masked men swiftly raised a club and crashed it down on the Duke's unprotected head. Without a sound Louis d'Orléans fell into the gutter where he lay among the filth he detested so much.

"You lecherous prick," hissed an anonymous voice, "now it's your turn."

Then the Duke vanished beneath a welter of men who rained blow after blow on him, hacking off his right hand at the wrist and cleaving his skull open with a cut that ran from one ear to the other.

His servants, hopelessly outnumbered, fled into the night with no more than a second's hesitation, leaving that most elegant of princes, the great lover of his day, to die alone, coughing blood, his brains mingling with the slime of the cobbles and no priest to ease his passing.

In the charming confines of the Hôtel Barbette his mistress, Queen Isabeau, stirred in her sleep as she dreamed of him, unaware that he was gone and that nothing would ever be the same again for herself and her pathetic brood of hapless children.

Two

The April storm rolling up the river Maine was signaled for almost an hour before it reached the castle. First the sky darkened to slate, matching the color of the seventeen huge and looming towers which were the fortress's main defences, then it deepened even further to a shade like that of the wild plums which grew in profusion on the clustered fruit trees of Anjou. Finally, as night fell and the sky took on a dusky hue that would last till dawn, the tempest arrived overhead and crashed into life above the winding streets of the walled city of Angers, lying beneath the castle's foot.

Lightning splintered the sky like cuts from a knife and accompanying thunder snarled, the noise echoing through the fortress's many courtyards and shaking the timbered houses of the town. Citizens who were still abroad on such a menacing night hurried home, their clothes kilted above their knees, avoiding the unpleasant debris which coursed over the cobbles as torrents of rain set the narrow streets awash.

On the battlements of the castle, looking out to where the river foamed far below, dark and frantic in the wind and rain, a cloaked figure pulled up its hood for protection but remained silently standing despite the driving bolts of water. For several minutes it stayed like this, then drew back its head in exultation, obviously enjoying the elemental thrill of such a superb display of nature's savagery. A laugh rang out, light yet deep, an exciting sound, then the woman tipped her face upward to bathe it in fresh cool rainwater. Yolande, Duchess of Anjou and Queen of Sicily, was allowing herself to get soaked through, and relishing every moment.

The Duchess was not truly beautiful in the accepted sense but possessed a powerful attraction which transcended conventional prettiness. Tall, supple as a bow, enjoying an athlete's body with slight hips and a taut slender waist, only her breasts, neat and firm, surprisingly well-shaped and not in the least small, saved Yolande d'Anjou from having a mannish and somehow daunting frame.

But her face was a different matter, for here an array of features combined to make her so arresting that people mistakenly believed her to be one of the loveliest women in France. A hawkish nose was the one flaw in a fine-boned countenance dominated by a pair of magnificent eyes. Green was their color, the green of a cave's shallow water, of tigers' orbs, of jade from Cathay, of ripe and succulent gooseberries. All these shades were there and more, for her pupils were surrounded by a sunburst of one green, and her irises another, darker. And dark, too, were the lashes that protected these brilliant eyes, darker than the cinnamon hair which waved about her head and shoulders, curling and full, speaking of the Spanish blood that flowed so densely in the Duchess's veins.

But though her nose might be masculine, Yolande's mouth was assertively female, full-lipped and red, even without the rouge she applied. An interesting mouth, both proud and passionate, with an underlying air of determination and purpose. Yet there was something sensual in the way she held it now, slightly open, drinking in the rain, and laughing to herself at her own strange behavior. A fascinating woman at all times and even more so at this moment of total privacy.

Or that was how it seemed to the one other person eccentric enough to be out in such a storm, enjoying it almost as much as the Duchess herself. Walking along the battlements in his soft close boots, playing a boy's game in the raindrops, Arthur de Richemont nearly fell over the edge as his eyes alighted on the Suzeraine, the lieutenant-general, the thirty-one-year-old acting head of the house of Anjou, standing with her eyes closed, reveling in the rain as if she were half her actual age. Just for a moment he stood watching her, his lively face lit by a sudden smile, before he cleared his throat and said, "Pardon me, ma Reine. It did not occur to me that anyone would be out here on such an evil night."

Yolande jumped visibly and just for a second the youth saw her hand move swiftly toward her capacious sleeve.

"So she carries a dagger when she is alone," he thought, half amused, half respectful. "A wise precaution in these troubled times."

"Who is it?" the Duchess hissed angrily, and Richemont was subjected to a furious glance guaranteed to wither a man where he stood, from a pair of eyes hard as emeralds.

"Arthur of Brittany, Earl of Richmond," he replied formally, fighting her fire with a little of his own.

"Oh, Richemont," she said, relieved, then laughed, adding, "I should have guessed."

"Why, Madame?"

"Because only you could be so foolish as to walk about in thunderstorms."

"But in good company," Richemont answered without malice, and made her a small bow.

They stood staring at one another, assessing each other's qualities and faults. In the seventeen-year-old Earl, Yolande saw a boy whose pedigree was, to say the least, both varied and exciting, a fact which, in her view, accounted for his somewhat erratic behavior. For there were signs about him already of political opportunism, of running with the hare and hunting with the hounds, not admirable characteristics admittedly but greatly mitigated by his enormous charm.

Richemont's father had been Jean the Valiant, Duke of Brittany, old when he had married the boy's mother, Jehanne of Navarre, but still capable of siring the seven children which she had borne him in rapid succession. None the less, on his death Jehanne did not mourn him long, but seduced and won the King of England, the widowed Henry IV of Lancaster. Then, having entrusted her sons to the care of the Duke of Burgundy, Jehanne had set off for England with her two baby daughters, several nursemaids, and a large train of other attendants.

Thinking of this as she looked at one of the Queen of England's sons, Yolande d'Anjou smiled in admiration. Richemont's mother personified the very type of woman that Yolande admired above all other: a woman capable of taking hold of her own destiny and bringing it round to advantage, a woman in control not only of her own fate but also that of others.

Almost exactly a year to the day after her marriage to Henry of England in 1403, Jehanne had sent for her second son, Arthur, and persuaded his stepfather to invest him with the title Earl of Richmond. In this way the likeable boy had begun his practice of having a foot in both camps, swearing on oath to his liegelord, Henry IV, while remaining a true Breton.

Yolande smiled again, "I'm beginning to get wet," she said.

Richemont shook his head. "Just one moment before you go in, Madame. It is so rare to catch you alone."

Before she could frown, the young man went on one knee before the Duchess, splashing into a huge puddle and thoroughly soaking his hose. A lesser woman might have laughed but Yolande stood still, calmly letting Richemont pay her homage, her face unreadable in the gloom.

"What an incredible creature," thought the Earl. "Not only wife and mother but also in complete control of her husband's domain while he fights abroad."

A wicked idea occurred to him and he bent his head to hide his scampish face. But it was a fact that Duke Louis II of Anjou had spent so much time overseas, battling to regain his kingdoms of Naples and Sicily, that he had scarcely had more than a handful of years at his wife's side, scant time to be a husband, let alone father children. And Yolande only had three offspring, two sons and a daughter, in marked contrast to the productive Isabeau who had at one time produced babies at almost yearly intervals.

Yet it was not in the traditional female roles alone that the Duchess of Anjou excelled, for she was also the powerful leader of a mighty province of France, a strong administrator whose every action and thought was for the good of her duchy, yet a clever woman who disguised the fact of her total control by wisely taking counsel with her husband's advisers, so contriving to make some of her ideas appear to come from others.

"You are remarkable, ma Reine," Richemont burst out in a moment of youthful enthusiasm. "Beautiful and clever, a powerful combination of assets."

Yolande put up the dark wing of an eyebrow, the only clue to being lost in thought that keen observers had ever noticed, and regarded Richemont in silence. Finally she said, "Do you play chess, Lord Earl?"

"It was His Majesty your husband who taught me, Madame."

The Duchess of Anjou looked genuinely surprised. "Was it? I had forgotten that. When did he do so?"

"Not long after I returned from England, ma Reine. When I made my way here from Paris."

"About the time that Orléans was assassinated?"

"Yes."

They were both silent, thinking of the terrible consequences of the violent death of Louis d'Orléans, crushed in the gutter, his severed hand tossed carelessly down beside him. Nearly three and a half years had passed since that night but despite the mad king's forgiveness of Burgundy, who had freely admitted being behind the killing, it now seemed as if France was on the brink of civil war. Count Bernard of Armagnac's eleven-year-old daughter had married Charles of Orléans, the dead Duke's son. His only wish to avenge the murder of his lifelong friend, Armagnac constantly urged his elegant and poetic son-in-law to challenge the Duke of Burgundy to a fight.

In the midst of this uncertainty the royal children, abandoned by their lunatic father and dissipated mother, continued their life in Paris, a Paris now preparing itself to be torn by conflict. Isabeau, wavering between fear and greed, frequently changed sides between Burgundy and Armagnac, the place in her bed once occupied by Orléans now filled by a series of foppish young men, the periods when her husband was lucid, less and less frequent.

As if they shared a thought, Yolande said, "It was fortunate you left when you did," while Richemont started to say, "I must rejoin my brother soon. He will require my services if there is going to be a war."

The Duchess smiled ironically. "Your brother of Brittany? Or your stepbrother of England?"

"I am a Breton first and foremost, Madame," Richemont replied hotly. "And it is there that my loyalty lies."

Yolande did not answer, merely straightening even further her long lean back. Eventually she said, "Loyalties will come and loyalties, I fear, will go, if the threatened bloody conflict takes place."

"I hope I'll be no turncoat," the Earl stated solemnly.

The winged black brow rose again. "Who knows? Now I am going in. Goodnight, Richemont."

"Goodnight, ma Reine."

He bent to kiss the thin hand suddenly extended toward his and could not help noticing how strong the bony fingers were beneath his lips.

"Madame ..."

The Duchess turned in the arched doorway leading to her apartments. "Yes?"

"May I accept your challenge to chess before I leave Angers?"

There was a second's pause before Yolande answered, "I did not realize I had challenged you. But yes, we shall play tomorrow. You may join me after I have dined."

Richemont bowed low. "I count the hours."

Yolande laughed, and the husky exciting sound haunted the young Earl constantly for the rest of that night.

The people of Paris suffered an epidemic of plague during that warm spring of 1411, the stench of death from the streets almost equaling the smell coming from the King's apartments in the Hôtel St. Pol, for he had once more sunk into deep depression and lay in the dark amongst his own droppings, disease-carrying flies continuously buzzing round his filthy, matted head.

To keep his children quiet and calm in these appalling circumstances was a nightmare that came daily to haunt Lady du Mesnil, these days bringing up Charles almost single-handed and, in looking after him, having to care for Catherine at the same time. For the two children clung to one another pathetically, crying a great deal if they were separated. The young princess mothered her brother in a way that wrung Jeanne du Mesnil's heart, and the governess would wonder in her bleaker moments whether it might not be better for the young couple if they were to contract the fatal disease now raging, and slip peacefully out of such a tortured world.

Life at court had not been made easier for anyone by the fact that the Dauphin Louis, now aged fourteen and married to Marguerite, daughter of the Duke of Burgundy, Jean the Fearless, had discovered not only marital sex but extramarital as well. With a profligacy clearly inherited from his mother, the boy, frequently inebriated, could think of nothing but pleasure and indulged himself in every variety. No woman was safe with him and age did not deter him from trying to seduce any female with whom he came into contact. Only the extremely old, the extremely young, and the hideous, were exempt from his hot-eyed pursuit. As to his brother, Jean, the Duke of Touraine, only a year younger and also recently wed, it would seem that he was very little better.

All this made the task of keeping Catherine and Charles out of trouble more difficult, as it was both Louis's and Jean's delight to make the little ones drunk, then roar with laughter as they staggered and fell over. And an appeal to Isabeau was out of the question. She had taken herself off to the Hôtel Barbette where she literally locked the troubles of the world out and a string of youthful lovers in. In a plethora of increasing sexual adventure and drinking, the Queen of France passed her days pleasurably enough.

Despite all this intrigue lessons for the youngest royal children had to go on. As was the custom, it differed widely between the sexes. For though both Charles and Catherine were learning to form their characters, it was he who already owned a Latin grammar, not very well thumbed, and a book of psalms. Catherine, on the other hand, was being given instruction on how to sew and embroider, spin, sing and accompany herself on the harp, and develop a beautiful expression, looking straight in front of her and neither frowning nor laughing over much. Both of them, however, were learning to play chess, and Charles's teaching also extended to backgammon. And today they sat poring over the chessboard while Jeanne du Mesnil engaged Marie de Barrois in conversation.

"Will this threatened civil war take place, do you think?" Lady du Mesnil whispered anxiously.

"Oh, it will come all right," Marie murmured in return. "I know so—and I'll tell you how. Ma chérie listen, I came across the Tarot cards belonging to Valentine Visconti the other day—quite by accident you understand—and—"

"Where did you find them?" interrupted Jeanne, most interested.

"She had left them in a hidden drawer, of which I knew the whereabouts. It was in a desk in the apartments she once occupied, that is before the Queen told her to leave."

Adult as the two women were they none the less looked at one another and tittered. For it was not the fact that Valentine Visconti had been the lawful wife, and widow, of Louis d'Orléans which had enraged Isabeau so much she had sent the Duchess into exile, but really that the Italian woman had had a wonderful figure. Slim and elegant, Valentine had been able to eat whatever she liked without gaining an ounce of superfluous flesh, whereas Isabeau was fast disappearing into a flounder of fat. Furthermore, the Duchess of Orléans had been gracious and had despised excess in everything. Indeed Valentine had possessed the capacity to reduce Isabeau to silent tears of fury and frustration. It had been hardly surprising that, with Orléans gone, Isabeau had accused his widow of bewitching the King and had exiled Valentine to Blois for the rest of her time, which had, in fact, been barely two years.

The truth of the accusation was simply that the Duchess had had in her possession a set of Tarot cards, cards which had been in use in her native Italy since the thirteenth century, and which she had eventually become expert in reading. The King, in his lucid moments, had enjoyed looking at them, hearing from Valentine's own lips the story and meaning of each one. But now the Duchess was dead, her cards long forgotten, and it was left to Marie de Barrois, having unearthed them again, to triumphantly produce them from a bag attached to her belt and put the pack on the table.

"What strange symbols," said Lady du Mesnil, picking one up and looking at it closely. "A woman sitting blindfold upon a beach, a sword in either hand. What can it mean?"

Marie shook her head. "I don't know. But it has a sinister look somehow."

Jeanne glanced to where her two charges sat rapt, engrossed in the chess game for which Charles, young as he was, already had a fondness and the signs of some talent.

"I wish I knew what would befall them."

Marie's voice lowered to a whisper. "I have learnt this much. If you think of the subject, then shuffle and cut into three with your left hand, a strong impression of their future should be visible."

Jeanne looked at her sidelong. "But can you interpret what you see?"

"We could try to do that together."

Lady du Mesnil gleamed with excitement. "Then let us proceed."

She picked the cards up rapidly, shuffled with vigor, then

cut deeply into three packs, muttering, "What will befall the Princess Catherine?" as she did so.

Lady de Barrois turned the decks over and the two women looked with some uncertainty at the cards revealed. One showed a crowned, cloaked King, seated on a throne, bearing in his hand a mighty sword; the next, a Queen, similarly seated but with her bare feet paddling in the sea, an elaborate cup in her hands; the third, a rider, bearing a laurel-crowned stave in his hand, a crowd also bearing staves jostling around him. Underneath were words written in Italian.

"What do they say?" asked Jeanne.

"The King of Swords, the Queen of Cups, and the Knight of Wands."

"And what does it mean?"

"Perhaps that Catherine will marry a king."

"If so, a warlike one," Lady du Mesnil put in with a certain bitterness. "And what of the knight?"

"That is one card I do know," Marie answered quietly. "It means betrayal."

"Betrayal!" said Jeanne breathlessly. "But of whom and by what?"

Marie shook her head. "I don't have enough skill to answer that. Unless *you* can guess its meaning."

"I wouldn't like to. I only hope it doesn't foretell treachery to Catty."

"Or hers to another," breathed Lady de Barrois, looking to where the ten-year-old's beauty shone in the gloom of the vaulted room. But Jeanne did not hear her, concentrating as she was on drawing cards for Charles. This time three women came up, a fair-haired empress sitting out of doors, her diadem crowned with stars, an orb of majesty in her hand; a plainly gowned girl wrestling with a dog-like creature; a blue-robed priestess, a sphere on her head, a white cross on her breast, and a sickle moon at her feet, sitting between two pillars, one bearing the initial B, the other J.

Once again, Jeanne du Mesnil asked, "What are these?"

"The Empress, Strength, and the High Priestess."

"Three powerful creatures!"

"Each bearing great virtues."

Jeanne picked up the card depicting the priestess. "I wonder what the initials B. J. stand for."

"Jesus? Jerusalem? Who knows?"

"And the B?"

Marie shook her head. "I have no idea. But at least the cards are a good draw for Charles."

"Should one take them literally? That he will know three extraordinary women?"

"Yes," Lady de Barrois answered, her eyes twinkling. "Let's say he will, and that it is a very good omen indeed."

"He'll need all the fair fortune he can get," his governess replied quietly.

"Check," called Charles from the corner.

"You little pig," shouted Catherine in answer. "I cannot make a move."

"As I planned," Charles went on triumphantly. "Mate!"

"No quarreling," said their governess automatically, but was smiling as she went to help them pack away the board and pieces, before taking them to the Hall in the Hôtel du Petit-Musc, where the two young people would dine alone except for their loyal servants.

"Check," said Richemont, unable to conceal his delighted smile.

"Ah!" answered Yolande and leant forward over the board, moving a candle closer in order to throw more light. Illuminated thus, every feature of her face was thrown into stark relief, an effect enhanced by the fact that the Duchess's hair was pulled back into a taffeta turban, so there was no softness about her. Like this, with her eyes hooded by their heavy lids, her resemblance to a bird of prey was marked. The hawk's nose threw a harsh shadow and her pupils, when she finally looked at him, glittered with intensity.

Richemont felt himself attracted and repelled simultaneously. No other female of his acquaintance could ignite the hot stir of passion yet freeze him with fear lest he should fall out of favor and become her enemy. In that moment he knew, even though he was not yet eighteen and in many ways inexperienced in the ways of the world, that Yolande was the most disturbing woman he would ever meet in his life.

"Your turn, I think," said the Duchess and Richemont saw that while he had been staring at her she had captured his attacking knight with a surprise move from her bishop.

He laughed in sheer amazement. "You are a master of the game, Madame."

"I was taught by my father," Yolande answered simply, the words conjuring up a vision of a young Spanish Princess, laughing in the high hills of Aragon, running free, riding hard, beside her sire, King Juan.

"My name in Spanish is Violante, did you know that?" the Duchess went on.

"I think I have heard it," Richemont answered slowly. "Does it mean violent?"

Yolande laughed, putting back her head like a man and showing white teeth. "Of course not, that is naughty of you. It is the word for violet."

"So that is why you chose such a color for your turban. It suits you well."

She was pleased, there was no doubt of it. The strong features relaxed and the green gaze sparkled. "Thank you, Monsieur. I have been somewhat short of male flattery recently." Despite her acute mind, the Duchess felt herself warming to his exuberant charm.

"A great pity for a woman of your beauty," Richemont went on gallantly.

There was a momentary silence while Yolande's unforgettable eyes looked at him, an unreadable expression in their depths.

"You must never spoil yourself, Richemont," she said eventually.

"What do you mean, Madame?"

"Don't become a fawning fop, living to give and receive empty compliments."

He felt a thrill of pure annoyance. "That is very far from my thoughts. I am sorry you regard what I say so poorly. I think perhaps I should retire. Please excuse me."

And with that the young man swept to his feet, but a strong hand reached over and covered his before he could make another move.

"Lord Earl, please sit down, and kindly remove that frown. It spoils your looks. If I have said anything to offend I apologize. It is only because I am fond of you that I am concerned for the sort of person you will become in the future."

Richemont remained where he stood. "You may have

concern, ma Reine, but it would appear you have little trust."

Yolande's face softened visibly. "Of course I have trust. That is why I do not want to be disappointed."

Aware that he was probably making a fool of himself, Richemont protested wildly, "I will never disappoint you. I would rather die."

She laughed her husky laugh. "Don't do that, mon ami. No woman is worth the sacrifice."

To his enormous surprise the young man suddenly found himself on his knees before her. "But you are no ordinary woman, ma Reine. You are a goddess in comparison with others." And he passionately kissed the clasped fingers that lay in her lap.

Yolande stared at him in amazement, shaking her head a little then, snatching her hands away, took his face between them.

"Richemont, control yourself. I do not look to arouse such emotion."

What it was about her touch that triggered off tears, he did not know. Perhaps such tenderness made him think of the mother he still missed, or perhaps it was because the Duchess seemed usually so remote; whatever the reason, Richemont wept, silently and bitterly. For a moment Yolande d'Anjou did nothing, then, without a word, gently pulled his head into her lap and stroked his hair.

"I love you, ma Reine," said Richemont through his tears. "I swear to be your liegeman. I will serve you always."

Yolande laughed softly. "You are liegeman to King Henry of England and also to your brother of Brittany. I could not ask you to spread yourself further."

"Do you mock me?" asked the sobbing boy.

"Not in the least," answered the Duchess soothingly, then bent to kiss his brow.

It was all he needed. In a burst of passion, hot as the blood that throbbed through his veins, Richemont turned his mouth to hers and kissed her, his tears wetting her lips with salt.

"I love you, I love you," he repeated fervently, as he snatched his mouth away then covered her lips once more.

And in being so close to her he sensed the moment, virgin though he was, when her body relaxed and she exchanged kiss for kiss with him. But then she tensed again and pushed him away, still kneeling on the floor at her feet.

"Enough, Richemont, enough," she said. "Go to your quarters."

He gave her a broken look. "I have offended you."

Yolande stood up from her chair. "No, no. Go now. We'll speak no more of it."

The Earl got to his feet. "Obviously I shall leave tomorrow. May I see you to say farewell?"

Yolande turned away so that all he could glimpse was the rise of her dark brow.

"I shall be with my Council all day."

"Then must we part without a word?"

She turned to look at him, her face expressionless. "No, that would not be right for an ally and friend. I shall dine early. You may come to say goodbye after that."

Richemont bowed stiffly, suddenly very aware of his tear-stained face and the terrible thing he had done.

"Thank you for being so civil to me, Madame. I apologize!—"

"I don't wish to discuss it," she cut in fiercely. "Goodnight, Richemont."

"Goodnight, ma Reine," he answered, and snatching at the threads of his dignity bowed again and left her alone, staring out of the narrow window to where the river flowed far below.

Three

The Queen's new gown had been made from Genoese velvet studded with pearls, the skirt flowing in soft pleats caught up at the side by a golden and jeweled hook to reveal a glimpse of stockinged leg. The bodice, high and tight, was a miraculous feat of engineering acting as a platform for Isabeau's breasts, which today had been bathed in poppy juice, rinsed in rose water, and buffed with ivy and camphor, even the nipples subtly painted with essence made from red berries. On her head she wore a vast conical head-dress called a hennin; expensively made of gold brocade and over a yard high, it was covered with precious stones, the veil from its pointed peak hanging over her shoulders and half-way down her back.

On another woman all this magnificence would have been dazzling, enough to ensure the illusion of great beauty, but on the Queen it was grotesque. For no amount of clever draping could now disguise the fact that she was growing enormously fat, no stout wooden busks conceal the truth that her breasts should have been hidden away years ago, no clever work with paint box and brushes mask her sagging jowls and double chin.

Crouched at her feet like little gray spiders, her sewing women shivered in awful anticipation that one of them would give a cry of horror as they looked up at the vast obscene figure that loomed above them.

"Well?" said Isabeau, turning slowly, eyeing them half in challenge.

"Superb, your Majesty," answered Flore, the Queen's most senior seamstress.

"Umm," responded her mistress, and once again stared at herself in the mirror held by two of her waiting women.

She was at the stage of her life when secretly she knew that she was becoming revolting, that her youthful good looks were vanishing forever, yet still she lacked the will-power to do anything about it. And today, when a new handsome reckless lad was to present himself, messenger of Yolande d'Anjou, Isabeau felt uncertain, her hands flying to her bodice in an attempt to cram her breasts within.

"Which one of you made this?" she screamed, as the tight-fitting top stubbornly refused to accommodate the extra girth.

"Madame, Madame," answered Flore soothingly, standing up. "The busks are meant to give support. The dress was not designed to wear the bosom concealed. But if your Majesty would prefer I could cut in laces."

Just for a moment Isabeau looked pathetic and the seamstress was vividly reminded of the terrible old trollops of Paris still plying their trade though no man had hired them long since.

"I thought perhaps I might appear immodest," the Queen answered slowly.

Thinking of the children who relied on her money in order to eat, Flore said, "Her Grace the Queen always looks the height of fashion. A little provocative perhaps, a trifle daring, but this is the style that suits Madame. Let the dull gray women of this world cover themselves. The Queen of France is not one of them."

Isabeau turned to her delightedly. "You really think so?"

"Truly, ma Reine."

"Then you shall be well rewarded. Lady de Lyon, see that this woman is given an *écu d'or* for her services."

The lady-in-waiting bobbed a curtsy, simultaneously shooting Flore a look which needed no words.

But perhaps the deceit was worth while, for the Queen, seated at her dressing table a few minutes later, radiated happiness and excitement as she vigorously applied her tongue scraper, her ear pick, and finally her paint. Freshly made up like this she imagined that the beauty she had once possessed when she came to France from Bavaria as a fourteen-year-old bride still shone as brightly. And the illusion was heightened even further by the lighting of candles in her receiving room, all advantageously placed, as dusk fell over Paris. In such a flattering gloaming, Isabeau and her jewels gleamed and sparkled. The Queen was obviously ready for a new love affair.

She had expected the Duchess of Anjou's messenger before dark but as it was torches blazed outside the palace and in the corridors, and extra candles had been brought to the Queen's apartments, before the noise of a horse's hooves crunching the cobbles sounded distinctly from the courtyard below. For no reason Isabeau was reminded of the last night she and the Duke d'Orléans had had together three and a half years before, and the merry din made as he and his party left the Hôtel Barbette. Unwanted, a solitary tear escaped her right eye and ploughed through the powder on her cheeks, forming a canal. A nervous feeling overcame her and without realizing it Isabeau found herself reaching for her wine cup, but before she could even drink a voice from the shadowed doorway made her almost spill its contents over her new gown.

"Gracious Queen, I bring you salutations from Madame Yolande, Queen of Sicily, Queen of Naples, and Duchess of Anjou," said the unseen visitor.

Hastily gathering her wits, Isabeau called, "Come in, come in," and hoped her lip rouge had not smudged.

The door opened wider and a draught blowing down the stone passageway outside made every candle in the room flicker and bend before returning to its usual strength. Dimly, Isabeau could see that a dark shape had entered and now knelt bowing before her.

"Who are you?" she said, half afraid of the silent way in which the stranger paid her homage.

"An admirer, ma Reine," said a muffled voice, and with that the man threw back his mantle and rose to his feet, laughing to himself at some private amusement.

To say that he was handsome would have been an understatement for an incredible young man stood in front of Isabeau's high chair, all long lean limbs and golden hair. His eyes were frightening: a fierce wild blue with some dark shadow in their depths; but the Queen could not see that, dangerously attracted to the stranger who was now looking at her boldly, licking his lips with a wolfish tongue.

"I had heard you were beautiful but not like this," he said, apparently unafraid of reproach. "I am your ardent admirer, Madame."

Once again the candles dipped and Isabeau was glad of the momentary respite as she suddenly drenched with sweat, a feeling of feverish desire sweeping her enormous frame. Hardly able to speak, she found herself whispering, "What is your name?"

"Pierre de Giac, sweet Queen. The man born to serve you."

And when he said it she knew that it was true, knew that a lover had come who could once again mean something to her.

Attempting nonchalance, Isabeau asked, "What is your message from the Queen of Sicily?"

"She greets you as one monarch to another and orders me give you this," and with that Pierre bowed again and produced a rolled and sealed parchment from within his cloak.

"I shall read it later," Isabeau answered, waddling down from her high seat. "For now it is *my* turn to give you orders."

"Whatever they are I shall obey them to the letter," Pierre replied fulsomely, and taking her hand raised it to his lips. They were strangely cold, bloodless almost, reminding Isabeau of the dank touch of a reptile.

Slightly disturbed, she none the less said, "I command that you sup with us and that you spend the night as my honored guest."

De Giac's eyes blazed like torches. "If I had my way, Madame, you would repeat those instructions every day that I have left on earth."

"You are very bold, Monsieur," Isabeau answered, wishing that she were not so drawn to this extraordinarily insolent creature.

"In the sight of such beauty only a eunuch could be anything but," Pierre whispered in return.

The Queen looked at him sideways, about to tell him that he was an idle flatterer, then saw that he meant it, that her age and her fat did not deter him at all.

"I find you very forward," she answered. "I should have you whipped outdoors for a saucy fellow."

"But you won't," answered Pierre, his look dangerous. "For it is decreed that you and I will love as no couple ever have before."

He was so close that she could feel his breath upon her, smell the heavy scent on his body, exciting as a drug. Isabeau pursed her full lips.

"That remains to be seen, young man."

"I shall love you tonight, never fear. It is foretold."

"By whom, pray?"

"I cannot say that," de Giac answered, smiling.

Isabeau shook her head, uncertain quite how to handle the situation but forgiving much of Pierre's bad behavior because of his thrilling looks and ardent manner.

"Will you take wine, Monsieur?" she said by way of changing the conversation, and before he could reply had clapped her hands for her servants, who came and went as discreetly as always.

De Giac drained the cup they brought thirstily and held it out for more, his sleeve falling back at the wrist as he did so. A flash of gold caught Isabeau's eye and she saw that he wore a thick bracelet, its clasp formed by the representation of a pair of horns, a triumph of the goldsmith's art, each one surmounted by a small twinkling diamond.

"What a handsome adornment," she said curiously.

Pierre turned to look at her, his crazy eyes suddenly alight. "I am never without it. It shall be cut from my body when I die."

The Queen shivered, thinking of the fate of her lover, of how he had been savagely struck down, his right hand hacked from his wrist, probably while he still lived.

"Don't say that," she breathed, aware that suddenly she was as cold as ice.

"Why not, ma Reine? It is true."

"It reminds me of something I prefer to forget."

"Of Monsieur le Duc d'Orléans?" de Giac answered, uncannily correct. "They say he was a Satanist and his severed hand had been guided by sorcery."

"That's a lie!" Isabeau exclaimed. "He was interested in all forms of love but that is the only resemblance he had to a follower of Satan."

"Love," said de Giac with a cynical smile, "is merely a part of what the Prince of Darkness offers. There is also wealth and power. But it is true that an uninhibited delight in sexual extravagance is probably the best gift of all." His expression changed. "You should join his entourage, ma Reine. You with your wonderful body, built for ecstasy."

In a flash, Isabeau saw it all. A Devil worshipper was in her presence, a man who equated her with Astarte, the great nature goddess, fruitful and voluptuous.

"You ..." she hissed shudderingly, "you are a Devil's man."

De Giac's eyes smoldered. "Yes. I am his sworn henchman. I have signed a pact with the Dark Master himself."

Isabeau found herself gripped by a terrible fascination. "What were its terms? What did you offer and what did you get in return?"

"I have pledged him my right hand. It is his to do with as he wills. In exchange he has made me the greatest lover in France. Women would kill to receive my favors. He has also promised me gold and power—but these gifts are yet to come."

The Queen stood staring in disbelief. "Mon Dieu! Is this really true?"

De Giac smiled. "Speak not of God, ma Reine. My dark Prince has sent me to you, to satisfy you as no man has ever done before, not even Louis d'Orléans. And in return ..."

"What?"

"You are to raise me high, help me in my search for riches and supremacy."

Isabeau found that she could not speak, enraptured by the presence of evil so tangibly close to her.

"And if I do?"

"I shall be yours."

As he said this Pierre's lips parted in a lupine smile and the Queen found herself quivering with sheer raw lust.

The cruel smiled broadened. "Come to me, ma Reine," de Giac said slowly, then without another word drew her toward the great draped couch which stood close to the crackling fire.

It could not but be noticed that Yolande, Queen of Sicily, Duchess and Regent of Anjou, was unusually silent during the council meeting held that month of April 1411 in the great hall of the castle of Angers. This hall, restored and rebuilt after a fire in the 1130s, lay along the top of the cliffs over the river Maine, commanding a devastating view for any *Conseiller* whose attention might momentarily wander. And today, with the river running in high spring spate, it was Yolande's eyes which turned toward the one large window, her hawkish profile slightly averted, her eyelids drooping a little.

With a sense of shock the Seneschal, or Steward, of

Anjou, the Lord de Beauvau, seated near to her high chair of state, realized that his royal master's wife was not attending. For to him Yolande was almost masculine in her capability and courage, her grasp of state affairs rivaling that of her husband, and the sight of her behaving like a moonstruck girl, daydreaming and paying scant attention, was not one he relished at all.

With a note of asperity in his voice, de Beauvau cupped his hand over his mouth and whispered, "Is all well, ma Reine?"

Yolande started noticeably, then collected herself. "Yes, thank you, Seneschal." She raised her voice. "Gentlemen, I have just recalled a matter of great urgency to which I must attend at once. Lord Chancellor, if you would be good enough to preside over the rest of the meeting."

Everyone stared at her aghast. It was unheard of for the Regent to depart before the end of the Council's session, yet that was precisely what she was doing. With a swish of her heavy skirts, embroidered in silver with a design of strawberry leaves, Yolande got to her feet, bade a polite farewell to the gentlemen present and without another word left the great hall, its occupants staring after her.

"Well, well," said le Maçon, sitting down.

The Seneschal looked knowing, his great face creasing into a thousand lines. "She's missing her lord I dare say."

"I suppose so, though if she caught someone saying as much the consequences would be dire."

"Yes. She always puts on a convincing show of being self-sufficient."

"The trouble is she thinks like a man," answered Robert le Maçon slowly.

"Not all the time," contradicted the Seneschal, looking like a grizzly bear as he shook his head and his long brown hair fell from beneath his high-crowned hat and swung about his face.

"What do you mean?"

"Today the lady was far away, in a dream, not contemplating the Council at all."

"An unusual occurrence." Le Maçon smiled. "But who knows? Perhaps she was planning the next move in a campaign so secret that none of us is yet privy to it."

"Perhaps," answered Beauvau, winking a round brown eye.

Robert glanced at him in silence, then got back to his feet.

"Gentlemen, as the Regent is otherwise engaged I suggest that we reconvene the meeting for this time tomorrow."

There was a murmur of agreement and a shuffling of feet as the *Conseillers* of Anjou made their way to the huge oak door. A stone spiral staircase took them down from the first-floor great hall, out to where the entire complex of the fortress of Angers lay spread before them.

The original castle had been constructed in the beginning of the tenth century by Fulke the Red, but over the decades many alterations had been made so that now it stood a vast citadel, guarded by seventeen enormous towers, only the unscalable cliffs above the Maine left unprotected.

Fulke's first dwelling place had been rebuilt by St. Louis between 1228 and 1238 and it was Yolande's husband, Duke Louis II of Anjou, who had undertaken even further restoration and construction, so that now the fortress could be divided into two separate groups of buildings. Going in through the City Gate, the military and administrative offices, the gardens, pavilions and walkways, lay to the left; while to the right were the living quarters, all built round a large quadrangle known as Nobles' Court, access to which was obtained by means of a gatehouse.

Immediately opposite the gatehouse and built on the cliff's edge stood the great hall, these days high on the list of restorations that Duke Louis intended to make; to the right, joining the hall at a right angle, stood the King's Lodging, allowed to be so described by reason of Duke Louis including the title of King of Sicily and Naples amongst his many other honors. Adjoining the Lodging and filling the eastern corner was the new chapel that Yolande and her husband had ordered to be built especially for them; living and service quarters, including the kitchens, buttery and a high vaulted bakery, made up the other two sides of the square. The Duchess's private apartments lay in that part of the Lodging which adjoined the great hall, thus giving her a superb view over the river and the rolling countryside of the right bank.

But it was not to her rooms that Yolande now made her way. Instead, she crossed the space between the hall and the gatehouse and, passing through the entrance, walked toward the City Gate, then turned just short of it and climbed a steep stone staircase set in the huge battlements. Here, between the castle's outer curtain wall and an inner retaining wall, where St. Louis had built ramparts, Yolande had asked the gardeners to create a pleasure garden and vineyard for her on the resultant terraces.

High above the city, protected by the massive towers, each one three stories high, their huge foundations sunk deep into the moat, Yolande could wander amongst her herbs and flowers, her fruit trees and grapes, away from the world in every sense. Each day, whatever the weather, she could come to look at and enjoy the change in nature's colors, sweeping away the snow if necessary, feeding the birds which nested in the trees year after year. Fish swum in an ornamental pond near by and in a shady arbor stood a stone seat where the Duchess could rest when the sun was at its hottest. And now she went to it and sat down at once, pulling her mantle tightly around her and shivering. Yet it was not altogether the coldness of that bright raw spring day which made Yolande d'Anjou tremble where she sat, but rather the fact that she, as a woman not as a Regent, was in turmoil.

It had been her father, hard as leather and a tough capable ruler, who had personally supervised that part of Yolande's education dedicated to life and the humanities. And it had been he, Juan of Aragon, who had explained to his daughter that a disciplined person leading a disciplined life would be he—or she—who came out the victor in every situation. Juan had also taught her that two of Christ's messages should most seriously be taken to heart: "As you sow so shall you reap," and "Cast thy bread upon the water and it shall be returned after many days."

"What do they mean?" the ten-year-old Princess of Aragon had asked.

"Simply this. If you sow a bad crop, which is a hidden way of saying do bad things, bad things will be done to you. If you sow a good crop, however, good things will happen. Do you understand?"

"I do," Violante, as Yolande had been called, had said seriously. "But what of the other?"

"That is somewhat complex. The casting of the bread is a way of describing what you put into life, whether it be in relation to other people or simply to events. The re-

turning is the richness that will follow as a result of all the
positive things you have done, however intangible."

"Father, are you saying that people who take little action
are rewarded by leading empty lives?"

"In a way, yes."

"But what about the people with no money and no hope,
how can they cast their bread?"

"Very easily," King Juan had answered. "It has nothing
to do with riches, it is the richness of the soul that I am
talking about."

The child had understood most of it, the girl had put the
ideas into action, the woman knew them to be true. Yolande had tried hard to sow a good harvest, to give herself
generously to husband, children and subjects, to cast her
bread fruitfully. And the person who had emerged from
this way of life had been self-controlled and highly intelligent, a woman who could never deliberately be unjust or
cruel unless she thought that ultimate good would follow.
In this way Yolande had put down uprisings by the use of
force, had presented a stony face to the enemies of Anjou,
had ruled in her husband's stead as a powerful Regent. But
now, in the privacy of the Queen of Sicily's garden, this
strong personality wept.

The easy thing would have been to send Arthur de
Richemont away without seeing him again, and the reason
the Duchess had given herself for not doing so had been
that he was the brother of her ally, the Duke of Brittany.
On its northern border Anjou had Brittany as its neighbor
and it was important for the duchy to keep cordial relations
with that house. Thus the ruling families were on friendly
terms, and to dismiss the Duke's younger brother without
a farewell would have been inexcusable. This is what the
Duchess told herself, knowing all the while that it was not
true.

In reality, the reason why she could not bear him to go
without seeing her once more was far more dangerous. For
all her discipline, for all her desire to live according to the
strict rules she had set herself, Yolande was still only thirty-
one years old and full of the warm rich blood of Spain.
Her marriage to Duke Louis, arranged by their respective
fathers, was as successful as any partnership of that kind
could be. As a bride with no choice in the matter of husband, at least she and Louis had become friends, united in

their efforts to do the utmost for the Duchy of Anjou. But Yolande had never felt the thrill of real passion until last night, when a virgin boy had put his lips on hers and showered her with the hot wild tears of love.

In this agony of mind, the Duchess sat alone in her private garden wrestling with a conscience which seemed to be deserting her, and a physical longing not helped by the fact that her husband had been away at war for some considerable while. For the sensual side of her admitted that it wanted Richemont, longed to lie down beside his shapely young body and teach him all it knew about love and, perhaps, in that very teaching learn something itself.

"Oh, mon Dieu, mon Dieu," Yolande said aloud. "What shall I do?"

And this was no empty cry for the poor creature meant it, torn between her natural instincts and the knowledge that to commit adultery was sowing the seeds of a bitter harvest indeed. But finally it would seem the Duchess came to some sort of decision for she stood up, her back in its usual straight line, and determinedly paced right round her floral domain before descending the stone steps and returning to the King's Lodging.

Yet here she was tortured by doubt again for on reaching her vaulted bedroom, the fire already blazing in the big stone hearth, Yolande kicked off her shoes and flung herself onto the bed, crying as she had not done for years. Finally, though, every tear was shed and she stood up dry-eyed, then plunged her face into a basin of cold water until all traces of her recent despair had vanished. Crossing to her desk, the Duchess picked up her quill pen and scratched a note.

"My dear Richemont," it said. "I think it would be better if we did not meet for some while. So let me bid you farewell in this letter and wish you all joy and happiness in your future life. My greetings to both you and your brother. Yolande."

Now that she had made the decision she seemed determined to act on it, loudly ringing a bell for her servants, sealing the note with hot wax into which she pressed a mold bearing her device then, almost with a sigh of relief, handing it over to her principal lady, Jacqueline Sarrazin, with the instruction to deliver it to the Earl of Richmond where he resided in the Guests' Lodging. This done, Yolande sank down on a stool in front of the fire and stared moodily into the flames.

Inside the vaulted chamber the light grew dim as the sharp April afternoon deepened, and a shower flirted over the walled city, throwing a rainbow above the Maine. Birds in Yolande's terraced gardens preened their feathers in clear drops of fresh water, and a blackbird boldly chanted his song for the darkening day. But she saw and heard none of it, sinking her chin deeper into her cupped hands, seeing in her mind's eye a vision of her father and knowing that he had been right.

"As you sow, so shall you reap," said Yolande into the shadows. "Oh, God, help me please."

Into this dense silence, punctuated only by the Duchess's occasional sigh, came the far distant clamor of sound and, almost in disbelief, she raised her head to listen. Distantly but distinctly came the noise of hurrying feet, almost running, and two voices raised in disagreement. Yolande recognized with a great surging of blood that of Arthur de Richemont.

She could never remember being more grateful than at that moment, filled with love and tenderness, longing for the beautiful boy to throw open her door and demand to see her, which a minute later he did. Behind him, Yolande could spy Jacqueline Sarrazin, scampering to catch up with him, red in the face with annoyance.

Before anyone could say a word the Duchess raised her hand. "Jacqueline, I will deal with this so please go and regain your breath. I would like to speak to Monsieur Duc alone."

Staring somewhat, the panting Lady Sarrazin retraced her steps down the stone-flagged corridor, turning once to look over her shoulder to where Richemont still stood in the Duchess's doorway, Yolande fixing him with an icy stare.

"What is the meaning of this?" the lady-in-waiting heard her mistress say before she went out of earshot.

Turning to check that he could not be overheard, Richemont whispered urgently, "I had to see you, Madame. I could not go without being with you once more. Have me whipped if that is your will but please let me speak to you for a moment."

Yolande stood back from the archway. "Come in," she said, and her voice could have frozen the river.

Visibly shaking, Richemont took a pace or two forward.

"Well, close the door behind you. Or do you want all the world to hear what you have to say?"

"No, no, Madame," he answered nervously, and wheeled to pull the heavy oak door shut. When he turned back again, Richemont saw that the Duchess had gone to stand before the fire, staring into it and holding out her hands to the flames.

"Forgive me," he said miserably.

"It is I who need that," she answered softly, her tone entirely changed.

He took a further step toward her. "What do you mean?"

"That I am glad you came, and that it is wrong of me to feel so."

The boy could not believe what he was hearing. "Glad! You say you are glad, ma Reine?"

"Yes," she said, and turned to look at him. In wonderful disbelief the Earl saw that her eyes were lit from within, glowing with such warmth that he was drawn to stand beside her.

"You are *not* angry at all," he said in astonishment.

"Only with myself."

"Then why did you look at me so furiously just now?"

"Because the door was open and I wanted no one to witness the Queen of Sicily making a fool of herself."

Still Richemont shook his head, totally bewildered. "What am I to think, ma Reine?"

Yolande took his face between her hands, her eyes almost level with his because of her exceptional height.

"That I have fallen in love with you, poor idiot that I am. I am old enough to be your mother and, as for you, you should have been married years ago. But none of that changes the fact that I love you."

Richemont did not wait another second, full of a virgin's wonderful desire. Almost roughly, he drew the Duchess into his arms and poured kiss after kiss onto her mouth, her eyes, and her neck, even daring to kiss her breasts on the outside of her heavy gown. But it was she who eventually loosened the fine stuff till it slipped to the floor about her feet, and it was she who gently led him to her beautiful bed, decorated with woven hangings of green and silver.

"You are virgin still?" she asked quietly, her face soft now that the heavy coil of hair had been loosened and lay upon the pillow.

"Yes, ma Reine."

"Why?"

"Because I was waiting for you."

"Why really?"

"I was betrothed when I was a boy to a woman many years older than I was. Poor thing, she was so frail and decayed that her skin seemed stretched over her skull like a mask. She died long before the marriage could take place and by then the situation had changed at home and no other match was arranged for me."

"But that doesn't explain why, at seventeen, you are still innocent."

Richemont smiled a little sadly. "Perhaps it was true that I was waiting for you, ma Reine. I wanted the first time to be so wonderful that I hung back from strumpets and whores."

"Then I shall make it memorable for you," answered Yolande quietly, and drew him to her, guiding his every move until instinct took over and the boy kissed and thrust and changed position as if he had been making love for years. It was exquisite for them both, the difference in their ages irrelevant as they mingled and became one. Over and over again, Richemont took the Duchess for his own, claiming her with that part of him which penetrated her deepest mysteries.

Exhaustion alone brought their exquisite coupling to an end, after a night whose secrets only those who truly love can learn. And then, before they slept, the young Earl kissed every part of Yolande d'Anjou before he finally lay silent beside her.

In the darkness before dawn, pierced only by the flame of a solitary candle, she stayed awake, staring at the perfect face so near to hers, noticing the sweep of his black lashes, the gleam of lights in his cap of hair. She was aware at that moment that Richemont was flawless, truly the most exquisite creature ever born.

"I love you with all my heart," whispered Yolande, then she rose, slipping on a long loose robe and going to her desk. Once again she picked up her pen and wrote him a letter.

He found it in the morning when he woke alone and stretched out to hold her, his hands grasping the rough parchment instead of her soft warm body. With a sinking heart, Arthur de Richemont read aloud what Yolande d'Anjou had to say to him.

"My darling," he whispered in horror to the empty room. "I want you to know that you are all that could be desired as a lover and I envy the woman who will one day be your wife. It was with great sadness that I left you asleep but knew that it was better I did so. Secrets have a way of being discovered and I could not bear either of us to be in disgrace. Leave my room by the hidden door behind the tapestry depicting Spring, go down the staircase and you will find yourself in Nobles' Court. Go from the castle today and join your brother quickly. Tell no one what transpired between us. Last night I gave you my heart. It is yours always, Yolande."

With a groan of despair, the Earl put his head in his hands. At seventeen years of age it seemed to him that his life had come abruptly to an end.

Four

The worst had happened. As everyone had anticipated, Charles of Orléans and his warmongering father-in-law were arming their men. The challenge to Jean the Fearless was expected daily, the dark hour of civil war was at hand.

In the teeming alleys of Paris where the shadows of the houses blotted out the daylight and fresh air never penetrated, the inhabitants, crammed together in noisome proximity, prepared to defend themselves. Built on the right and left banks of the Seine as the City was, the entire right bank had been surrounded by a protective wall during the reign of Charles V, and this was now put into good repair. Enclosed within these ramparts there loomed to the west the fortress of the Louvre, once a royal residence but considered gloomy by Isabeau and her husband, while on the eastern side towered the Bastille. Yet there was none who held out much hope for the citadel should an invading force make a strong attack.

Outside the encompassing wall, standing on the Left Bank, was the University of Paris, granted its charter in 1215 and housing some twenty thousand students, hailing from all over Europe as well as every part of France. Here Latin was spoken as the common language and because of this the autonomous borough which housed the university buildings was known as the Latin Quarter. By contrast, on the right bank was the commercial part of the city, administered by a Provost, where each individual trade could be found in its own particular area.

At la Cité were gathered the apothecaries; goldsmiths and money changers were based on the Grand Pont; the butchers near the Grand Châtelet; mercers close to the Rue

Saint Denis; the bankers and money lenders, known as Lombards, near the Rue Saint Martin. Only the booksellers, scribes, parchment sellers and illuminators traded in the Latin Quarter where, indeed, lay most of their custom.

There were also many markets in the overcrowded city, each specializing in one thing: herbs could be obtained from the quayside at the Isle de la Cité; eggs and flowers on the Petit Pont; sausages from the market near Saint Germain l'Auxerrois; bread in the Place Maubert. Alongside these stood shops, all with brightly colored signs: des Trois Visages, du Pied de Boeuf, du Chat qui Pêche, and many others equally jolly.

Every day before first light, when the gates of Paris opened, peasants came in from the country to buy and sell, alongside them the traveling jongleurs and mountebanks, the hawkers and traders, the couriers carrying urgent messages from one part of the country to the other. And with this daily increase the population swelled to bursting point, and all crammed within the odorous and confined space of a fortified city.

To go out into the bustling streets always meant, for better or worse, that there was a sight to see, and today was no exception. A group of mountebanks, accompanied by two jongleurs, were playing the fool in the square outside the house with the sign of the Eagle, a crowd already gathering to watch.

To Isabeau, reclining in a litter borne by two stout horses, it was a wonderful excuse to pause in her journey, reluctantly undertaken as it was. For the time had come, as duty insisted, when she must leave her pretty château and go to the Hôtel St. Pol, to see her children and glance in the direction of the King. This chore alone was enough to put the Queen into a bad mood but today there were additional troubles. Menstruation had not been easy for her since puberty but now, with her childbearing days done, it had become agonizing. So painful indeed, Isabeau had been forced to swallow an extra dose of ground emeralds and potable gold, the only things in the lady's opinion which alleviated her sufferings.

But this was not all. Pierre de Giac, who had proved to be a sensational lover, delighting in his own depravity and introducing the Queen to strange rituals in which nudity was all important and smoking black candles threw flick-

ering light on their exotically mingled bodies, had finally
returned to Anjou. Not only that, with the threat of civil
war he had been unable to give Isabeau any reassurance
as to when he would return.

"You cannot go," she had sobbed. "No one could satisfy
me after you."

"Many men will, Madame," de Giac had answered, his
lupine smile twisting his handsome face. "You will dance
the jig with a thousand men, that is your destiny."

"How do you know?"

Pierre laughed soundlessly. "My Dark Master has told
me all of this and much more. Will you not join me in his
service?"

"Of course not," Isabeau had answered, but not with as
much conviction as usual, wondering if she too could barter
even greater riches and sex with any man she chose, in
exchange for one of her hands.

Yet these ideas were not in her mind as she watched the
buffoons through a parting in the curtains of her litter. Instead she thought what glorious creatures they were with
their painted faces and croaking voices, barracking the
crowd even while they tumbled and jumped. And the spec-
tators obviously shared her view for they roared their approval and threw coins onto the cobbles beneath the
mountebanks' feet. It was at this point that one of their
number dressed in a black gown like a student from the
university came to the forefront.

"Good people," he called, launching into his sales pitch,
"good people of Paris, threatened you may be by outside
forces, dying you might be of the plague, but all of you can
be protected from this and more by buying one of my
magic amulets brought all the way from the court of the
Khan of Tartary. With these incredible charms you will be
safe from attack, seen or unseen. And in addition to this
mystical protection I can also guarantee to save you from
any ailment. Watch in awe, citizens, as I give a demonstra-
tion of the healing powers of the enchanted water drawn
straight from the legendary golden spring of Damascus.
This liquid can cure you of anything, from the pox to palsy
and pimples. So, by buying both, you can not only protect
yourself from danger but be immune to all illness into the
bargain."

The mountebank paused, looking straight across at the grandly draped litter.

"I see that we have a great lady amongst us. What say you to these magical properties, my Dame?"

"Keep him away," hissed Isabeau to the captain of her escort, and drew the curtains so tightly that she was only left a peephole. But even this obscured vision did not stop her from seeing what happened next. Out of the crowd, advancing toward the mountebank with a pitiful expression on his face, came one of the saddest sights she had ever set eyes on. A boy of about twelve, a small thin starveling of a creature, with a hunch on his back and gangling limbs desperately in need of flesh, was coming forward. The Queen of France watched in amazement as the child stepped in front of the salesman.

"Can you cure me?" it said in a tired, somehow lifeless, voice.

The mountebank stroked his chin. "Well . . ."

"Oh, please, sir, please," the wretched whine went on.

"But can you afford it, sonny?"

"I have no money," the boy replied pitifully, on the verge of tears.

"Then I am afraid I cannot help you. Unless someone in the crowd . . ."

Again he looked straight at the litter and the captain, his horse pressed close, whispered through the drapery, "Don't give him anything, Madame. This is a well-known trick."

"But I'd like to see it," Isabeau retorted, and slipped money into the captain's hand.

He looked doubtful but none the less called, "My mistress says you are to cure the boy," and flung a sparkling coin at the mountebank's feet.

The man grinned, picked it up, tested it between his teeth, then slipped the money into an invisible pocket.

"Well, lad, it would seem you have a patron, so we mustn't disappoint the lady, must we? Kneel down in front of me."

The wretched child stole a glance toward the litter and Isabeau saw dark hollow eyes, one of them half closed, swelling up from a recent blow. For the first time in her life she felt genuine pity.

"Go on, child," she called, her voice muted and mysterious through the swaying fabric of the drapes.

The boy obeyed, kneeling down, his head bowed in an attitude of utter resignation. Isabeau found that she was holding her breath as the charlatan produced a stone bottle from deep in his gown, drew the cork, and poured some water into the palm of his hand.

"Pull back your shirt," he ordered, and the boy heaved at his terrible rags, exposing the hump for all the world to see. Isabeau craned her neck, morbidly fascinated by freaks, especially this one for whose cure she had paid.

"Now, pay attention," called the mountebank to the crowd, every one of whom already was. "I shall rub a little of the enchanted water into the hunch and wish it away."

"It's a trick," the captain repeated. "Look carefully, ma Reine, and you will see that the mountebank uses *two* boys. One of them is concealed somewhere at this very minute."

In her excitement Isabeau almost drew back the shielding curtains but remembered in time that it would not be discreet to do so. Instead she widened her peephole a fraction more and saw that the hunchback was now rolling round the cobblestones as if in some great and mortal agony.

"Watch the table, Madame," the captain whispered. "Now, do you see?"

And indeed she did. It had been done so quickly that it was almost impossible to pinpoint the moment when the changeover took place, but as the hunchback rolled by the crude table used during the act, another child rolled from underneath the concealing black cloth, the original disappearing beneath; all this action concealed by the mountebank, who let off a puff of smoke from a long-necked vessel at exactly the appropriate second. The crowd, who had noticed nothing, pressed forward as the "cured" child stood up.

"But it's the same boy!" breathed Isabeau, unable to believe her own eyes.

"Twins, I expect, Madame," answered the captain. "They usually use children who are almost identical."

"How clever," Isabeau said in wonderment. "I think they deserve their money."

And that indeed was pouring in as the onlookers jostled round the mountebank, begging a bottle of his miraculous cure-all.

The captain made to take his place at the head of the

column, calling, "We'd best be off, ma Reine. The show is over."

"One moment," the Queen called back. "I have an idea."

And what a good one! Even before he had left, Isabeau had been mulling over what present to send to Pierre de Giac, what novelty might capture his frenzied imagination, and now she had found the answer. For where the Queen was fascinated by freaks, her favorite being dwarves, de Giac actually collected them. With what enormous enthusiasm had he described for her his assortment of cripples, giants and midgets, all used as participants when he celebrated the Black Mass, and with what cynical power had he insisted that Isabeau's dwarves were present when he made love to her, saying their presence gave him additional strength.

"At home I always have at least two voyeurs, if not three," he had informed her.

"How disgusting!" Isabeau had answered, but secretly the idea had excited her.

And now here was a young hunchback, gloriously misshapen but with a face that might turn out to be comely when all the dirt and bruising were gone. Impulsively, Isabeau put her hand through the curtains and took the captain by the arm.

"Mon Capitaine, kindly go to the mountebank and offer to buy the hunchback."

"What!" exclaimed her escort, certain he had heard incorrectly.

"Go and buy the hunchback."

"But he won't sell him, Madame. The boy is part of his act."

"I have made up my mind to own the child," Isabeau answered determinedly. "And the mountebank will sell all right. Offer him this," and without another thought she plucked a ring from one of her fat fingers and thrust it into the captain's hand. He stared in astonishment, seeing a ruby bright as a cherry winking at him in the sunshine.

"But, Madame, surely ..."

"Do it!" answered the Queen through gritted teeth.

The captain knew that tone, knew that it was more than his future was worth to protest further. Staying on horseback, he directed his mount through the crowd to where the charlatan was selling bottles as quickly as he could pass them over.

Watching from her hiding-place, Isabeau saw every stage of the bargaining and smiled in triumph when the man, having gasped at the sheer size and quality of the ring, nodded his head in agreement. A few minutes later, having assured himself that the last of his customers had straggled from the square, the mountebank produced the hunchback from under the table, cuffing the poor wretch about the head as he did so.

"But I can't leave my brother," the child was sobbing. "Please don't send me away."

"Shut up, you little monster. A rich lady has bought you and you should be grateful. You are to serve her well, do you hear?"

The healthy twin, alarmed by the commotion, hurried over and also started to cry, the noise becoming so unbearable that Isabeau was forced to put her hands over her ears.

"Tell them to stop that terrible din," she shouted from within her litter. "Say that I will go now, the bargain unstruck, if they are not silent at once."

"Do you hear that, snivellers?" said the mountebank, knocking the boys' heads painfully together.

They nodded and began to weep silently, a more pathetic sight unbelievable.

"I'll take them both," Isabeau announced by way of putting an end to it. "The strong one will make a useful servant. And I want no argument from you, charlatan. That ring was more than enough for the pair of them. So hand them to my captain at once. He will go with them to the Hôtel Barbette and see that they are fumigated."

"The Hôtel Barbette?" said the mountebank, slipping down on one knee. "Oh, Majesty, what an honor."

"Rubbish!" snorted Isabeau. "Now, for the love of God let us be off. I have wasted enough time on this escapade as it is."

And with that her bright little cavalcade made haste over the cobbles leaving the two dirty urchins staring tremulously in the direction in which the Queen had gone.

It was a brave sight as the army of Charles, Duke of Orléans, marched out from his capital city and headed eastward, following the line of the great river Loire. Beside Charles rode his fearsome father-in-law. Short, squat, his hair cut so close to his head that it was a mass of bristles, his small eyes regarding the world ferociously, Count Bernard d'Armagnac was a creature whose very look rung the knell of doom for civilization. And it was not revenge for the murder of his friend d'Orléans that was really the nub of this matter but something far less honorable and fine. The truth was that Bernard wanted power, wanted to seize the sword of state for himself and would fight to the very feet of the mad King's throne in order to get it, aware as he was that if he did not make a move first, Jean the Fearless of Burgundy would surely do so.

As far as these two mighty magnates were concerned this war was really a show of strength, winner taking all, including the realm of France. For the rightful King, that wreck of humanity who simply refused to die, they had no feelings other than to wish him swiftly gone, his sons with him. So it was with these terrible ideals, the leaders of both sides lusting for riches and supremacy, that the civil war which was almost to ruin France began. And what hope was there for a country the reins of whose government lay within the terrible grasp of a lunatic and a libertine?

The Armagnacs had white for their favors, and white ribbons tied upon their escutcheons and standards which bore the slogan, "This is Justice!", a hollow cry indeed. But as they passed through the villages of Sully and Gien, each built round the foot of its formidable château, the peasants turned out to stare at the jingling cavalcade, white pennants fluttering in the brisk breeze blowing from the river. Some gave a cheer, little knowing that they were about to be plunged into a conflict so dark that it would take years for them and their poor country to recover from its savagery.

In the council meeting of the Duchy of Anjou, the news that the Duke of Orléans had finally mobilized was received in silence, nobody stirring for several minutes as the fact sank in. Then it was the Seneschal, big and gruff and forceful, who rose to his feet and said, "Majesty, my Lords, gentlemen, this situation is potentially dangerous to the province. I propose that we send extra men to our borders."

"But at the moment there is no direct threat," answered Yolande from her high chair.

"Indeed, ma Reine. *At the moment* there is none. But civil war is exactly what it says. Bands of soldiers can very soon be reduced to bands of brigands, terrorizing the countryside. It is my view that the Seigneurs of Burgundy and Armagnac are capable of fighting anywhere the fancy takes them and a poorly protected border will be considered as an open invitation to maraud."

The Duchess nodded, saying nothing, and the Seneschal sat down, watching her as she contemplated her reply. He thought that she had got very thin since the spring, the bones in her face almost visible and the skin over them stretched tightly, giving her a delicate transparent look.

"In fact," considered the Seneschal, "Madame Yolande looks far from well. She is doing too much."

But the Regent's voice when she finally spoke was as confident and in control as ever. "My Lords, it is my view that the Seneschal is right. I suggest that archers are sent to all our vulnerable posts for there is no way in which we can tolerate an invasion of our territory, nor can we allow Anjou to participate in the battle between the Dukes of Burgundy and Orléans."

The Chancellor, Robert le Maçon, gave a dry laugh and called out, "For Orléans read Armagnac. Young Charles would never have issued a challenge if his father-in-law hadn't worn him down like a stone."

Yolande permitted the interruption, fond of her Chestnut Chancellor as she thought of him, everything about le Maçon being that color, from his cropped hair to his large and elegant shoes.

"Be that as it may, my Lord, the challenge has been issued and accepted, the war has begun. And in the case of civil strife other parties can easily get drawn in as you well know. Yet let me state clearly it is not my wish to see Anjou taking sides."

"Fine words, my lady, fine words," whispered Robert. "But just you wait till one or other of them upsets you, then we'll see."

"Did you say something?" Yolande enquired politely.

"No, Madame, I was simply clearing my throat," answered the Chancellor, and bowed from the waist to where she sat in the chair of state.

"Then in that case I would ask you, Chancellor, Seneschal, gentlemen, to listen to my messenger, Pierre de Giac, who has recently returned from Paris and can apprise us of the latest situation there."

From a seat at the back of the hall de Giac rose, taking in the assembly with a single sweeping look.

"My Lords, first of all may I give you greeting from the sovereign lady of France, Queen Isabeau."

From out of sight, somebody gave a hearty chortle and the Seneschal, who once again was observing the Duchess, saw her lips twitch at the corners.

"That gracious Queen," de Giac went on, his piercing eyes angrily raking the crowd, trying to identify the offender, "fears for the future of France and has striven to maintain peace between the two sides in this conflict."

"Can't make up her mind which would be the better bet, eh?" replied the same hidden voice.

"Gentlemen, please!" Yolande interrupted sharply, raising her eyebrows and looking round.

"Shall I continue, Majesty?" De Giac was staring directly at her.

"Please do. Let the man have a hearing in peace, my Lords."

"There will never be peace for a Satanist," the unknown speaker countered.

"That's enough," roared de Giac, "come from your hiding place, you son of a whore, and let me thrash the liver out of you."

Yolande, unusually pale to start with, went the color of a lily, wondering if there could be any truth in the accusation of devil worship. "This behavior is unforgivable," she said in a terrifying whisper that was far more effective than a shout. "Seneschal, clear the assembly. And let those who make mock of the Ducal Council by using it to slander and threaten be warned."

Only de Giac looked unperturbed as the Lord de Beauvau growled, "Out with you now," and lumbered to the doorway where he remained standing until everyone had filed out, everyone that is except for Pierre. Standing up, proudly displaying an extremely short tunic with long trailing sleeves which he had obtained in Paris, so short indeed that it barely concealed a formidable black codpiece, de Giac sauntered casually in the direction of the chair of state. Hardly moving his head, the Seneschal glanced over to Yolande, brows raised in a secret signal, and she nodded imperceptibly.

"No further," said de Beauvau. "You are dismissed too. Off you go, Monsieur."

"But I must speak with the Duchess."

"She will see you tomorrow. Goodbye, Monsieur de Giac."

It was useless to protest, the Seneschal was almost as broad as he was long and his resemblance to a bear did not end with his massive frame and mane of brown hair. For now his lips drew back from his strong, rather yellowish teeth, in a smile which somehow resembled a snarl.

"At what time shall I attend her?" asked Pierre as insolently as he dared.

"One of Madame's ladies will let you know."

"Then I'd best say au revoir," de Giac called to the silent figure in the high chair, and made a fulsome bow.

Yolande nodded by way of acknowledgement but did not say a word and there was nothing left for him to do but leave the great hall and head for the Guests' Lodging, which is what Pierre reluctantly did.

"Tell me, Lord de Beauvau," said Yolande softly as the fashionably dressed young man disappeared from view, "does he truly celebrate Black Mass?"

"I'm afraid so," answered the Seneschal, approaching the chair of state and helping the Regent down. "Come, Madame, you look tired. Let me escort you to your Lodging," and he gave her his arm.

She smiled gratefully and as they emerged into the daylight de Beauvau was struck afresh by the Duchess's fragility and the whiteness of her skin.

"Excuse me, ma Reine, but I believe I know you well enough to ask if you are presently in good health," he said gently.

Yolande looked nervous, the first time that the Seneschal had ever seen such a thing, but answered, "I am, yes. But I must admit to being exhausted. I have been sleeping badly this last week or two."

"Then get to bed now, have an early night, please rest. Madame, you are very precious to us all, you know."

"How good you are, Lord Seneschal," the Duchess replied, but de Beauvau had the oddest feeling that the Suzeraine was thinking of something else.

They had been crossing Nobles' Court while they spoke and now had reached the doorway leading to the King's apartments.

"Goodnight, ma Reine," said the Seneschal, kissing her hand.

"Goodnight, my Lord," she answered, then smiled and hurried in through the arched doorway. But once inside and hidden from view Yolande's entire aspect changed. Her hand flew to her throat, her lips trembled, her eyes glassed over as tears welled down her colorless cheeks.

"Oh, mon Dieu, what shall I do?" she muttered, trembling as she unsteadily climbed the spiral staircase that led to her private apartments. "What will become of me? How can I emerge from this with any honor left?"

For the fact was, and there was no escaping it, that there had been no monthly flux from her body since the night she and Richemont had spent together. And there were other signs too: her breasts were tender, the smell of certain food gave her a feeling of nausea, in fact everything pointed to her having conceived the Earl's child during those ardent hours they had spent together.

In other circumstances Yolande would have been proud to have borne a baby created in such ecstasy, would have faced the world boldly and without shame. But she was no ordinary woman, no peasant girl who could bring up a love child in the security of her family. She was the Queen of Sicily whose husband had been away fighting to regain his lands, and so could not possibly be the father of that fragile thing growing within. A royal husband, too, who would be humiliated beyond measure to learn that his wife had spent the night with a boy of seventeen who had succeeded in making her pregnant.

The situation was desperate in its terrible implications, yet despite it all Yolande knew for certain that she could never drink those evil substances made to procure an abortion, would rather leave Anjou for ever than damage Richemont's child. Weeping pitifully, the Duchess blindly made her way to her bedroom and lay down in the brightness of that late afternoon.

She must have slept straight away for when she next opened her eyes the pinkness had gone from the day and her room gleamed red. Suppressing an involuntary sob, Yolande got up and went to look out of the window.

The sun hung like a fireball above the river, which flowed the color of life's precious blood, while the distant hills were scarcely visible for a haze of damson. The sky was lucent, festooned with strips of cloud, bright banners of gold and rose engraved against its vivid blue. The cross on the spire of the Abbey of St. Nicolas, built amongst the verdant pastures of the right bank, suddenly gleamed as it caught the rays of the sun, while in the fishing village upstream a silver-scaled catch, just being hauled ashore, glittered like rubies. Yolande drew breath at the sight of it all and unconsciously her hand went to her body, almost as if she could transmit to the child the glory of such an evening.

A loud knock on the door had the Duchess turning rapidly, rubbing her face with a dampened handkerchief lest the tell-tale signs of tears still lingered. But the effort was in vain, for her principal lady hurried in, peered at her, then said anxiously, "Ma Reine, you look ill. Have you a headache?"

"Yes, yes," Yolande lied desperately. "I am really not well at all. Could you help me prepare for bed, Jacqueline?"

"But of course, Madame. Would you like me to send for your physician?"

"No!" answered Yolande, a shade too quickly. "That will not be necessary. If you would fetch me a cool drink I shall retire immediately."

Lady Sarrazin stood hesitating. "There is just one thing, ma Reine . . ."

"And what is that?"

"An unexpected visitor has arrived who has most particularly requested an audience with you. He says that he is going off to fight, that he has joined the Armagnac cause and must see you to say farewell."

Even before she had asked the question Yolande knew the answer and had sat down on the bed in order to prepare herself.

"And who might this visitor be?" she asked, her voice expressionless.

"Monsieur the Earl of Richmond, Madame. He came an hour ago and is presently in the Guests' Lodging."

The Duchess looked at her wearily. "I do not feel like receiving visitors tonight. Perhaps you could get word sent that I cannot see him."

"But I did that once before, Madame, and he forced his way in, do you remember?"

"Indeed I do," answered Yolande and turned her face away.

"Well, I'll see to it he won't be getting up to those tricks again!" Jacqueline replied briskly. "Now, Madame, let me help you undress. Shall I light a fire in case it gets cold in the night?"

Yolande nodded in silence, the words going round in her brain. Cold in the night! It hadn't been cold when Richemont had held her. It hadn't been cold when he had made love to her, mingling his body with hers. It hadn't been cold when he had given her the child she now carried in her womb. And yet he was here, under the same roof, and she must send him away without setting eyes on him, the one person who had filled her heart with the love it constantly craved.

As the door closed behind Jacqueline Sarrazin, bustling off to get the things her mistress had asked for, the Duchess, with a mighty effort of will, dragged herself to her desk and sat there, picking up a pen, thinking that she seemed to do nothing but send letters to Richemont when all she wanted was to hold him in her arms.

"Oh, I love him, how I love him," she said to the blank stone wall as she started to write.

"My dear Richemont," Yolande began, wishing she were able to put, "My dearest love."

"It is more than kind of you to visit me at Angers but, alas, I feel it would not be wise for us to meet on this occasion. I pray that God will be with you now you are taking up arms for the Armagnac cause and that you will return safely to your brother. Sincerely your friend. Yolande R."

Sending him away to war without a word was a vile thing to do, she knew it well, but what other alternative was there if she was to protect his child, herself and, above all, the baby's father, the Earl of Richmond?

Even as she put her seal into the wax Yolande could imagine his face, so flawless and so vulnerable, as he read those cruel words. Would it kill his love for her? she wondered, prepared to take that chance. For her husband, Duke Louis, was due to return early next year and by that time all trace of lover and child must vanish.

Slowly, the Duchess rose from her desk and seemed to fall the distance to her bed, stretching herself full length and closing her eyes. But as Lady Sarrazin returned, Yolande made one final effort, sitting up and holding out the letter.

"Jacqueline, I have scribbled a note for Monsieur the Earl. Be sure that he gets it straightaway."

"Shall I tell him you will see him tomorrow, Madame?"

"Say nothing. I think perhaps he might be leaving soon."

If Jacqueline guessed anything of the truth she did not show it, merely taking the sealed document and leaving the room as bidden, not even waiting to help the Duchess undress and put on her shift. But when she returned a quarter of an hour later, the letter safely delivered to the Earl, she saw that her mistress had managed to prepare herself for the night and was now fast asleep, lying amidst her shining coils of hair, the pillow still damp with Yolande's newly shed tears.

The guests, what few of them there were that night, had dined in the great hall in the King's Lodging, together with the Lords of Anjou staying on to attend the next day's reconvened council meeting. Noticeably, the seats at the high table where the Ducal family usually sat were empty, the Seneschal presiding from his chair, two places down from that of Duke Louis.

Out of courtesy the Lord de Beauvau had placed Pierre de Giac on the high table, though somehow contriving to be too far away to speak to him. But with Arthur de Richemont he had done the opposite, seating the lively young man immediately on his right, obviously in the hope of an amusing evening. But in this the Seneschal was to be disappointed, for Richemont hardly uttered a word, staring at his plate, on which the food lay untouched, seeming lost in a fit of deep depression. Nor did the Earl stay to hear the singers, come to entertain the company at the end of the meal. Instead, with a murmured apology to the Seneschal for his silence and an excuse that he was suffering from a pain behind the eyes, Richemont rose, bowed, and left the great hall.

It would seem, however, that he was not the only one of the guests so afflicted, for shortly after Richemont's departure de Giac also got up, blamed the fatigue of traveling, and likewise departed.

"No stamina these youngsters," growled the Seneschal.

Robert le Maçon raised an eyebrow. "Perhaps, perhaps not. More likely de Giac has gone to confer with his Dark Master; and as to Richemont, I suspect he is in love."

"I should hope so indeed. I cannot think why his mother did not find him a good match years ago."

"Too busy finding her own, I shouldn't wonder," answered le Maçon, and the two men laughed.

But though the Chancellor was right about Richemont, who sat moodily before the fire in the Guests' Lodging wondering whether he dare try to enter Yolande's apartments by the hidden staircase, about de Giac he was wrong. That young man had, in fact, merely walked round the battlements in order to get some air before he retired, at the same time mulling over the possible reasons why Richemont was behaving in such a strange manner.

So it was with particularly cruel delight that he returned to see the subject of his deliberations sitting quietly in front of the fire in the chamber leading from the great hall in the guests' quarters. Staring at the back of the Earl's neck, Pierre in a flash guessed part of the truth. The little upstart lusted after someone in the castle of Angers. De Giac smiled his wolfish smile and sent a prayer to his demonic master that he would get at the truth and thus have a hold on the Duke of Brittany's pretty brother.

"Good evening," he said softly, bowing low. "I hope I do not disturb you, my Lord."

Startled, Richemont turned round. "Oh, it is you, Monsieur de Giac. No, no, I was just getting warm before I went to bed."

"May I join you for a while?" Pierre was bowing again, his smile reassuring.

"Please do."

There was silence as de Giac took his place at Richemont's side on the low wooden bench pulled before the hearth and stared at the flames which since his arrival had suddenly seemed to glow a deeper shade of red.

"I left early because there were too few ladies dining tonight to suit my taste," said the newcomer eventually, breaking the stillness.

"Were there?" answered Richemont, surprised.

Di Giac grinned knowingly. "Ah! You obviously had eyes for only one—and *she* was present."

"As a matter of fact you're wrong," replied the Earl, wondering even as he spoke what could possess him that he was being so blatantly reckless.

Pierre said nothing but winked, his pupils molten in the firelight. Richemont had the extraordinary feeling that he would get drawn into de Giac's eyes and drown in them. He stared at the other man transfixed, quite unable to move.

"Not there, eh?" answered Pierre, the sound deep in his throat like a tiger's purr.

Richemont heard a disembodied voice saying, "She doesn't want to see me. That's why she kept away."

"Really, how foolish of her. Women can be very stupid sometimes."

The distant voice answered, "But she isn't. She is the most brilliant woman in France."

De Giac stretched, seeming to grow in size like a serpent, and Richemont fought to recover his slipping senses.

"Now who can you possibly mean, I wonder?" Pierre whispered, but his smile said it all. He knew everything, though how, Richemont could not guess.

"That I'll not say," the Earl answered abruptly, standing up. "I've revealed too much already. I'll bid you goodnight, Sir."

"Pleasant dreams," smiled the other. "Let's hope the lady changes her mind tomorrow. But then she probably will. She's an unpredictable creature as far as her personal life is concerned."

Richemont did not stop to challenge that remark, only too glad to get away from de Giac's consuming presence and hurry to his room, where he stripped off his clothes and lay on top of the bed, suddenly too hot despite the chill stone walls of the castle.

He must have slept lightly, for the first call of a blackbird, leading the chorale of sweet voices which welcomed the dawn, had him wide awake instantly. In that early-morning air, Richemont shivered, realizing with anguish that he and Yolande had spent a night under the same roof but not together.

"God help me, there is nothing left but to respect her wishes and go," he muttered out loud. "But if only I could understand *why*."

Yet staring helplessly out of his narrow window toward the King's Lodging gave him no answers and it was with a heavy heart that the Earl dressed, collected his few things together and went down to the stables to fetch his horse. That dark beast at least was glad to see him and Richemont slipped his soft boots into the stirrups almost with a sense of relief to be getting out. Without turning back he made his way across the stable yard toward the Country Gate.

The castle had three entrances: the City, the Country and the Water Gates. This last, for those who traveled by way of the river, consisted of a protected mooring bay, but the City and Country gates led into the fortress direct, each guarded by a drawbridge and portcullis set between two close and forbidding towers. The Earl of Richmond shivered as he waited in the shadow of the vaulted passageway while the clanking drawbridge lowered to let him pass.

Once through and across the moat there was another wooden bridge to be negotiated before the Earl found himself facing the open countryside, the golden hills in front, the city of Angers behind, and to his right the gurgling river, rushing green and cool in the dawn light. It promised to be a beautiful day, the haze just lifting from the slopes and the sun still veiled by mist.

Richemont reined in his horse for a moment and stood looking about him, seeing the distant roofs of the Abbey of St. Laud catch the light, the sound of its bells ringing for Prime clear in the fine morning air. The trees of the right bank were already beginning to shimmer slightly, long before the heat of midday, and the smell of summer, of grass, of roses, of ripening apples and plums, made the breeze heady as wine.

With a sigh, Richemont turned his horse southward and would have cantered off had not a distant cry from the direction of the castle mingled with the sound of abbey bells. The Earl's heart quickened its pace so violently that he thought it might burst through the padded chest of his doublet, but peering into the distance dashed his hopes. Pierre de Giac was making his way across the wooden bridge, his falcon hooded on his arm, calling out as he came.

It was too late to pretend he hadn't heard. With an air of resignation, Richemont braced himself for another encounter with that unnerving creature who had so recently guessed the secrets of his soul.

"A lovely morning," de Giac was shouting pleasantly as he hurried toward the Earl. "May I inquire in which direction you are traveling, Monsieur? Perhaps I could ride with you for a while."

Much irritated, Richemont said briefly, "I'm going south, to join the Count of Armagnac."

"Ah, then I shall accompany you a little of the way," de Giac replied.

Constrained by politeness, the Earl nodded his head and managed a smile, though actual words seemed to stick in his gullet. So it was in silence that they covered the first few miles, a silence broken by de Giac who gave an elaborate yawn and said, "Forgive me, my Lord. That woman was insatiable last night. I can't remember when I felt so exhausted."

Even at the words a feeling of dread began to rise in Richemont's throat. "Insatiable?" he repeated dazedly.

De Giac pulled at his horse's mouth. "But of course! Don't *you* find her so?"

The Duke stared at him uncomprehendingly. "What are you talking about?"

"What or who? My good friend, I speak of the delightful creature whose pleasure it is to play love games with the likes of you and me. That eager slut who simply cannot resist a young companion while her husband is away fighting his interminable wars."

Richemont wrenched his horse to a standstill. "What are you saying?"

"My dear fellow, I'm saying that I spent last night in bed with the Duchess Yolande who pleasured herself with me until daybreak."

The Earl was off his mount in one move, grabbing at de Giac's legs and pulling him out of the saddle, the falcon rearing in alarm.

"You lying son of a whore, don't soil her name by speaking it."

"But it's true," gasped Pierre, struggling to his feet.

"If it is I'll kill you," answered Richemont, and crushed his hand round the other man's throat, squeezing until de Giac's face began to turn from red to blue.

It was then that a sudden and agonizing pain ran through

the Earl's fingers, forcing him to release his hold and so allow Pierre to struggle free. Richemont heard his adversary mutter, "Thank you, Master," before de Giac whirled round on him, a dagger in his hand.

"Now beg for mercy you senseless little prat," he hissed. "Beg for your life, knowing I have no intention of sparing it."

"I'll not beg anything from you," spat the Earl. "Kill me if that's your will and become the most wanted man in France, for my brother of Brittany will seek revenge, you can rely on it."

"And how will he know the identity of your killer?"

"Through his court astrologer who sees everything and, or so it is widely believed, is in league with the Devil."

The words went home for de Giac hesitated and in that second Richemont wrenched at the other man's arm and seized his weapon.

"Now it should be your turn to beg," he snarled, "but for the fact I have decided not to kill you. For if it is true that you and she are lovers I would rather spend my life working against you both."

De Giac smiled cynically. "So be it. I put my faith in him whom I serve. I have no fear of you, Richemont. And neither has she. When she gave her body to me she had already forgotten who you were."

It was said so convincingly that the Earl of Richmond finally believed and tasted the bitter bile of hatred. "Then by God I'll give her cause to remember in the years that lie ahead," he answered quietly. "And so too you, de Giac. Look for me behind every shadow, as well may she."

"And in turn," whispered the other, his eyes blazing, "I curse you, Richemont. I call on my Dark Prince to see you damned."

And with that the Devil's man mounted his horse at speed and galloped away toward the hills without looking back.

Five

The day did not start well. Rising early, as was her custom, the Duchess and Regent of Anjou had at once felt so weak that she had been forced to go back to bed, where for an hour she had lain tossing uneasily, thinking about her problems and seeing no easy solution to any of them. Every worry she had of course was dominated by the fact that she was now almost five months pregnant and still had no plan prepared to deal with the situation. That she must go away and secretly give birth, putting the baby out to foster parents, was obvious, but as to where and to whom she simply had no idea. With an ominous feeling of disaster, Yolande finally swung her long thin feet onto the cold flags of the floor and hurried to perform her ablutions.

The garderobes in the castle of Angers drained into the moat which, in turn, was cleansed by the river. The Duchess had also seen to it some while ago that wooden seats replaced the old stone ones. Thus sanitation in the fortress was of reasonably high standard and Yolande had even gone so far as to provide a garderobe conveniently near the banqueting table in the great hall for the comfort of those dining.

The Regent herself owned a large wooden bathing tub, lined inside with thirty ells of common cloth and decorated above with a canopy of red Malines. But this morning Yolande did not bathe, simply calling for a pail of water to be heated over the kitchen furnace and brought to her apartments. When this arrived she duly stripped and washed before dressing privately, without the assistance of her ladies.

Through long years of riding and exercise the Duchess's

body had remained muscular and strong and, as with her other three pregnancies, there was as yet no obvious outward sign that she carried a baby. But *she* knew, was conscious that her abdomen had by now started to swell, already rounding to a child, and the fear that a sharp-eyed servant, particularly Lady Sarrazin, might notice a change in the Regent's physique had Yolande dispensing with her women's services more and more. Yet she was aware that even this change in routine might give rise to comment. The Duchess was caught in a trap of which she was only too well aware.

The fashions of the day, however, particularly those gowns which floated straight down from the bust, were of enormous help. Yolande had seen to it that the up-turned collar and very long trailing sleeves which were part of that particular style were embroidered in bright and different colors, or covered with pearl drops and gems, to attract the eye away from her figure. But yet all these wiles would be of little purpose by the late autumn when her pregnancy could no longer be concealed.

The Duchess had calculated, knowing the date of conception as she did, that the child was due at some time during the Twelve Days of Christmas and a vague idea that she might go away, giving the excuse that she must keep her Christmas elsewhere, was just beginning to form at the back of her mind. Yet there could be one fatal twist of fate that would ruin not only her tentative plan but her entire life: if Duke Louis were to return from the fighting earlier than anticipated she would be finished and could resign herself to being banished to a convent for the rest of her days, branded both adulteress and whore.

Richemont's child, as Yolande could surely have predicted, was already strong, she could tell that by its frequent movement. Her third baby, René, had been similar, in contrast to the first two, Louis and Marie, who had not moved much and who had both been born quiet and docile. Much as she despised the idea of having favorites, the Duchess secretly admitted that of the three of them it was René, with his bright jewel eyes and quick beautiful smile, who was the one she loved the best. But this baby, sired by the flawless Earl, must be the child Yolande would hold dearest of all even though she could never give it public acknowledgement. With a sigh, the Regent, fully dressed now, her face freshly painted, went to the window to look out at the day.

Every morning at first light the three entrances to the fortress were opened so that the town folk and visitors might enter with their wares, accompanied by those wishing to have audience with the Duchess. From her vantage point, Yolande could see the Water Gate already busy with fisher people, amongst their bright colors the black habits of the Benedictine monks of the Abbey of St. Nicolas, founded on the right bank by Duke Fulk Nerra in 1010, and the equally dark vestments of the sisters of the Abbey of Ronceray, built by the same Duke some fifty years later. The members of both orders would cross the river daily to buy and sell in town, and every week the Abbots of the various houses would communicate by letter or visit to the Regent. Bracing herself for the hours that lay ahead, Yolande smoothed her hands over the front of her dress to check that it still hung flat, and left her apartments with a resolute step.

She had broken her fast with bread and honey, washed down with a pitcher of verjuice, a combination of sour fruit juices, and would not eat again until dinner, which was served at noon. At this meal Yolande would see her children for the first time that day and would, if her appointments permitted, remain with them until they retired for the night. But now, before the pressures of duty began, the Regent crossed Nobles' Court and headed off in the direction of her private garden.

The September weather was still very warm and the Duchess at once made for the shaded paths in which to stroll, looking about her with enormous pleasure at the harmonious blendings of color, the bursting beds of lily, rose and lupins; violet, poppy and heliotrope; all their combined perfumes filling the air with a delicious heady scent which was ecstasy to inhale. Here, too, were the Duchess's herbs: coriander, sage, mint and dittany; musk leaves and southernwood adding their aromatic smell. Beyond lay the fruit trees and, on a whim, Yolande went to pick herself an apple, crunching her strong white teeth into its crisp skin.

Why she chose that moment to look down into the walkway running many feet below, the Regent never knew. But look down she did, only to see a couple struggling brutally, reduced in size by the distance but still clearly grappling

with one another. Just for a moment the Duchess thought
they might be embracing lovers, for one was male and the
other definitely female, but realized a second later that this
was not so, for the man delivered the girl a blow that rang
out to the terrace above like a cracking whip.

Without thinking of her physical condition, Yolande
acted immediately. Shouting, "Stop at once, do you hear?"
she rushed for the steep stone stairs cut into the battlement
wall and began to hurry down. Inside, her baby leapt wildly
in response to its mother's quickened heartbeat, and it was
with gasping breath that the Duchess of Anjou reached the
bottom of the steps and started to run.

She doubted that the man had even heard her, so intent
was he on his victim. For having knocked her to the ground
he was now kneeling over the girl, tearing brutally at her
clothing. Thus with his back turned and attention distracted
he did not see Yolande approaching like a fury. Not till
the point of a dagger pricked the nape of his neck was the
attacker even aware that anybody so much as stood behind
him.

He made to thrust backward to wrench his assailant's
arm but was stopped by the blade delicately entering his
flesh and his own warm blood gushing thickly.

"If you move again I will kill you, have no doubt of
that," said a hissing voice, which trebled in strength as it
added, "Guard, guard! Come at once in the name of the
Regent of Anjou."

Then there were running feet and heavy-fisted hands and
soldiers who did not care how they handled a man in order
to drag him upright. Ever afterward the attacker remembered a tall woman, white-faced with rage, casting upon
him a pair of eyes that smoldered in her face like molten
emeralds.

"Take him to the dungeons and send for the Seneschal.
The man is a worthless wretch," Yolande ordered furiously,
then, very gently, put down a hand to help the hapless
victim to stand.

"Why did he do it?" the Duchess asked in a much qui-
eter voice.

"He wanted me there and then, my Lady," whispered
the girl. "He said the trees would hide us from view and
tried to rape me when I refused. He is a trader like myself,

a pork butcher, and is far more base than the beasts he slaughters. He has been pestering me for weeks."

"I see. And you are . . . ?"

"Alison du May, Madame. My father is a vegetable vendor in the town."

"And you have come to sell your wares here at the castle?"

Quick as a flash and with a glint of her usual mettle, the chit answered, "My vegetables, aye. But not the goods he wanted. I would need a higher bidder than he." And a wink fluttered and went like the flight of a butterfly before her glittering silver eye vanished behind a bruise.

Despite the girl's cheekiness, the Regent laughed. "Indeed? Now you'd best come with me. I think my physician must look to those cuts and grazes before you go home."

"*Your* physician?" exclaimed Mademoiselle du May, staring and astonished. "I thought you were somebody important when you called out the guard. And I'm obviously right!"

Again Yolande smiled. "I am the Duchess of Anjou."

The girl fell on one cut and bleeding knee and raised the Regent's hand to her bruised lips. "And you risked yourself to rescue me? Then you are a very great lady indeed. I offer you my life, Madame." And with that the girl solemnly made the sign of the cross over her heart and kissed Yolande's hand three times to represent the Trinity.

Those bringing petitions to the House of Anjou were given audience in a large chamber in the King's Lodging, situated exactly a floor below Yolande's private apartments. Here, views of the sparkling river could be glimpsed through the leaded windows and in the brightness of this particular morning the room was full of little lights and quivers which danced over the walls and lit the Regent's bony face with interesting planes of shadow. In such a dazzle her profile looked dark and imposing, her eyes full of glinting reflections and enigmatical depths. So much so that Yolande's private secretary, Roger de Machet, old now and fading into a delightful shade of gray rather than growing wrinkled, swept into the room and stopped short, the academic gown which he always affected to wear rippling behind him like a stream.

"Majesty, you are as beautiful and fine as an angel this morning," he said in wonderment.

"Thank you," answered Yolande, without a hint of annoyance or vanity. "How good of you to tell me." She looked down at the list that already lay on the desk before her. "Now, who have I to see today?"

"The Abbess of Ronceray is here to report to you on the foundlings, Madame, and Brother Xavier is come to bring greeting from the Abbot of St. Nicolas. Prior Paul is also in attendance to speak about the hospital. Other than that we have the usual petitioners—neighbors' grievances, a suit for breach of promise, all things that can be referred to the courts. But there *are* two boys here . . ."

"Boys?" repeated Yolande, raising a dark brow.

"Yes, ma Reine. They arrived at the Country Gate at daybreak and said they were looking for Monsieur de Giac. They told the guard they had been given to him as a gift from Queen Isabeau."

Yolande stared in astonishment. "What?"

"They did have a letter with them, Madame. It lies on the desk before you."

Yolande looked down, identified the parchment, then ripped the seal open without hesitation.

"Well, well," she exclaimed, but did not read aloud, leaving Machet to study her mobile features in silence, lit by the swift gleams of the river light as they were. Eventually, Yolande said, "Bring the children in. I will see them first."

Machet bowed. "Certainly, ma Reine."

A moment later he re-entered the room leading the two boys by the hand, and as Yolande rose to greet them she gasped at the fact they were identical, though one sadly misshapen and lame.

"How did you get here?" she asked at once, her business-like manner hiding her pity for the poor wretches, clearly doomed to a life of degradation if Isabeau and de Giac had their sordid way.

"We have come from Paris, Madame," answered the whole one, obviously a beautiful child beneath his layers of grime. "We were bought by the Queen as a gift for her friend, Monsieur de Giac, and she sent us here to Angers to join his household."

"But while we were traveling," put in the hunchback, "the man who was escorting us vanished, horse and all, so we walked the rest of the way. It was not always easy because there are bands of soldiers everywhere."

The Regent nodded silently. The ferocity of the civil war had grown worse and though she still had not officially taken sides, her sympathies were leaning more and more toward the Orleanist cause. And Yolande well knew that the time was fast approaching when she must declare her intent as to which faction the house of Anjou would follow. With an effort, she focused her attention on the twins.

"You walked, you say? It must have been a long journey."

"It was," the boys chorused together, and the Duchess saw that both had bleeding feet bound up by tattered rags.

"Well, you have arrived now," she said, and smiled. "So, tell me your names."

"I am Guy," answered the hunchback, "and this is Jacques. We have no other name because we were born in a ditch and left for dead by our mother."

"At least that is what the mountebank told us."

"The mountebank?" repeated the Regent, frowning.

"We were working for him in the streets of Paris. That is where Queen Isabeau saw us. We amused her, I think, and she thought we would be suitable to enter the household of Monsieur de Giac."

"Yes, I'm sure she did," murmured Yolande with a small and bitter smile.

"We can sing," Jacques went on, "and I can dance, and Guy can juggle really well."

"Good," answered the Duchess, "that is very good. Now you must go with Monsieur de Machet who will see to it that you are scrubbed down and given clothes and food and that your feet are tended to. Then I will decide what is to be done with you."

"But what about our new master?"

Yolande straightened her long back. "He is not here and I do not believe you would suit him after all. You will remain in my protection for the moment."

"Are *you* a Queen as well?" asked Guy, round-eyed.

"Amongst other things. But I have two boys of my own, though younger than you are, so I do not lack understanding. I will make sure your future is a good one."

They smiled simultaneously, those two sweet faces, and Yolande found herself thinking that this must indeed be a day of miracles and that, perhaps, she was acting as guardian angel to both them and to Alison du May.

Since the building of the hospital in Angers, the Hôtel-Dieu St. Jean, in 1175, the scope of its services to the people had continued to increase and be delegated. Originally run by laymen, it was now administered by the Augustinians, and patients of every country and every religion were given welcome, except for incurables, lepers and foundlings. The orphans, the bastards, and the unwanted were the responsibility of the Abbey of Ronceray, where the children were fed and clothed by the sisters, many staying behind to take the veil. Though some of the boys went straight to the monastery, others were sent out into the world to learn a trade or go into service. Similarly, the incurably ill and the lepers were housed in the leper hospital of St. Lazarus, which lay midway between the Abbey of St. Nicolas and the hospital, outside the walls of the Doutre, the nickname given to the populated quarter on the right bank, its name simply meaning "the other side."

Though the Abbot of St. Nicolas had not been visiting the Regent personally, his representative Brother Xavier, who supervised the musical life of the monastery, had gladly carried back a letter from the Duchess asking that the twin boys who had so unexpectedly arrived into her care should be accepted as pupils at the abbey school. And as the sun had dipped behind the hills sheltering St. Nicolas in their comfortable folds, one of the boats used by the monks had drawn up to the castle's landing-stage to take them away.

Yolande had personally gone down to see them off, her heart anxious for them as they climbed fearfully into the craft waiting to take them on the first stage of their new life. Fortunately Brother Michel, who had been in the world a husband and father, had come to fetch them.

"I hear you both sing," he had said cheerfully. "Is that right?"

"We did," Guy had answered, "but not monks' songs."

Michel had grinned in amusement, an old soldier before he had taken the cloth. "Well, never mind that. They say that a man who can sing a street song can sing any song in the world. Brother Xavier will soon have you sounding like angels."

"I can juggle too," Guy went on, leaning his hunched back against Michel's stout arm. "Will that be of any use?"

"Certainly," the soldier monk answered gravely. "Do you not know the story of the Tombeur de Notre-Dame?"

"No," chorused the twins, unaware that the boat had cast off and was heading gently up river.

"Well, about two hundred years ago in the monastery at Clairvaux, an acrobat became a monk ..."

The boat had reached midstream and was gliding out into the golden mellowness of that September evening.

"Yes?" Their voices were growing slightly distant.

"He wasn't very good at book learning this monk, coming to it rather late, unlike your good selves, so he did not know what service to render Our Lady."

"What happened?" This from Jacques, his voice almost fading away. Yolande strained her ears to hear Brother Michel's reply.

"He went into the chapel at night and secretly performed his best tricks before her altar ..."

"Yes?" Their voices were a whisper on the breath of the evening.

"And the monks who had gone to spy on him saw the Virgin herself come down from where she stood and mop his brow with the edge of her mantle. Now what do you think of that?"

They were gone, it was dusk, the soft late summer day had slipped into twilight. From the right bank where lay the Doutre, the Abbey of St. Nicolas, the leprosarium of St. Lazarus, the Hôtel-Dieu St. Jean and the fishing village of Reculée came the sounds of evening: voices raised in song, the splash of oars as boats pulled into the riverbank moorings, a distant bell breaking through the mist that had started to rise like swansdown.

Yolande had turned on her way back, half-way up the steep path, and looked across the river at the undulating countryside, the water meadows, the sweep of plum-colored hills beyond. The lake, on the banks of which St. Nicolas was built, glittered and flashed in the dying rays of the sun, then subsided, dark and silvery as a sleeping serpent. Just for a moment, caught up in the glow of that dying September day, the Duchess of Anjou had felt at peace with herself—and then her unborn child had leapt within. Unable to control her tears, Yolande had sunk down on one of the

stone seats built at intervals along the steep path, and put
her head in her hands.

She had not seen the limping figure of Alison du May
coming painfully toward her, was not aware of her presence
until the girl's voice said, "Please don't cry, ma Reine,"
and the Regent felt someone kneel at her feet.

"I could not come to see you earlier," the girl's voice
went on. "I had dinner in the kitchen as you ordered and
then I fell asleep. But I could not leave the castle without
thanking you. You saved my life, Madame, and once again
I offer you mine in return. I swear to be your liege woman
of life and of limb."

It was such a strange version of the oath of allegiance
that Yolande laughed despite everything.

"I mean it," Alison persisted. "I would die for you. Let
me serve you, however humbly."

Yolande had looked at the swollen face, the tangle of
flaming hair, the bruised eyes and sore limbs. "You're in
earnest, I think, though it is difficult to read your expression when it is somewhat concealed."

Alison had smiled at that and just for a second there had
been a flash of the amusing redheaded beauty which lay
beneath her temporary disfigurement.

"I swear I mean it. I want nothing more than to be your
servant."

Yolande had gently cupped the battered face in her
hands. "But what about your parents? You live with them,
work at your father's trade. What would they say?"

"They would be as honored as I," Alison answered
quietly.

Yolande had gazed out over the darkening river, touched
by the girl's sincerity, and then the little miracle that she
needed so much took place. Alison had suddenly put a
gentle hand on Yolande's stomach, an act daring enough
to earn her a whipping, and the two women had looked at
each other straight in the eye.

"I know," Alison whispered.

"How?"

"That I can't tell you. It was as if the world was suddenly
clear, everything surrounded by a sharp edge of light. And
in that moment I knew you were with child, Madame."

"Did you also know its paternity?"

"No, but that is not important. I have been sent to help,

I am certain of it. Something took me by the hand and led me to you, ma Reine. I will take care of everything."

"If you are going to blackmail me I shall kill you," Yolande answered bitterly, and then regretted ever speaking so, for the girl collapsed into fierce burning tears that seemed an agony to shed.

"I ... could ... never ..." Alison gasped, then silently wept.

Yolande had reached the nadir of her existence. Shame for her love of Richemont, despair that she had heard nothing from him, fear for her future, had combined, then, in a moment so bleak and dark that she truly wished to die.

"Help me, Alison, help me," she had cried, and put out her hand, the mightiest woman in France humbled and brought low at last.

And now, Duchess Yolande knelt in her private oratory, giving thanks to God for the blessing that this strange and oddly beautiful day had brought her. She had been sent a friend in the unlikely form of a nineteen-year-old peasant girl, sworn to secrecy before leaving the castle, and gone now to ask her parents' permission to serve the Regent of Anjou, a permission that in no circumstances could possibly be withheld.

"Cast thy bread ..." thought Yolande. She had saved two boys from a lifetime of corruption and had been rewarded by the arrival of a loyal heart.

With a contented sigh, Yolande rose to her feet and went to the window to look out at the night. On the Doutre lights glimmered and a glow to the left of the walled quarter showed that Compline was being heard in the Abbey of St. Nicolas. In the lazar house a few candles flickered as the last of the afflicted lay down to sleep.

"I pray their peace lasts," the Regent said aloud. "I pray that Anjou is spared the war, I pray that France might one day be re-united as a whole. God help me, I will do all I can to bring that about."

As if she were going into labor, the Duchess's body was gripped by a sudden thrilling contraction and in alarm she put a hand to her baby.

"Be still," she whispered, "be still."

But the child created by the midnight heat of herself and the Earl of Richmond refused to rest.

Six

November 1411, and the Eve of Martinmas, the festival of winter's beginning. In the duchies of France, as in the capital itself, all thoughts began to turn toward the great Christian festival that lay ahead, though the people of Paris as a corporate entity anticipated no pleasure to come, for now they knew the bleak deprivation of being conquered. Jean the Fearless, Duke of Burgundy, had taken over their city.

Every night the mighty bell of Notre-Dame rang curfew at eight and most of the common folk were only too glad to get off the streets and hide in their houses. Death being the reward for not openly supporting Burgundy, the citizens wore Burgundian red favors on their hoods and caps, keeping a spare set of white hidden in readiness lest the Armagnacs should arrive unexpectedly. But in the privacy of their houses they ground these favors beneath their heel, hating Burgundian domination, only the University having struck some kind of bargain with the omnipotent Duke.

To add to the general suffering of the populace, provisions were in short supply, the countryside now being under heavy attack from bands of armed men who had gone past the point of differentiating between friend and foe and snatched anything they could find for their own consumption. What goods there were made their way into the hands of the rich, the only people who could afford the hideously inflated prices demanded.

But while her wretched subjects drew near to starvation, Isabeau, Queen of France, fatter than ever, recklessly organized banquets and balls, and thought of the Twelve Days of Christmas with enthusiasm, planning a Feast of Venus with all such an event implied, for herself and the Duke of Burgundy.

She had found it extremely pleasurable to welcome Jean the Fearless to her bed, the fact that he had murdered her lover, Louis d'Orléans, some four years earlier forgotten. When challenged on this point by one of her ladies, Isabeau had protested furiously that she had given herself to the Duke because it was politically expedient to do so.

"I hate him. I did it for the people of Paris," she had answered—but it had been a lie. Burgundy, with his haughty face and long aristocratic nose, excited her as much if not more than most of her lovers because of the very fact he *was* an enemy. A case of forbidden fruit tasting sweetest, Isabeau supposed. Yet she missed the depraved de Giac, taken from her side by the duties of war, thinking that the greatest Christmas gift she could have would be for him to arrive unexpectedly. Meanwhile the Queen prepared for the culinary and sexual excesses which lay ahead by ordering twenty-four new gowns, twelve for day and twelve for night, to be made especially for the forthcoming celebrations.

In the castle of Angers, in stark contrast to her gleeful and overblown kinswoman, the Duchess of Anjou looked ahead to the impending festivities with what could only be described as a despairing hope; hope that the plan she and Alison du May had devised together would work, despair that her entire future lay in jeopardy and might be shattered by the smallest error.

There had been a great deal of comment amongst the ladies of Yolande's suite concerning the sudden training of Alison for the role of fully fledged lady-in-waiting, this apparent favoritism causing a considerable amount of jealousy. For though having to admit that the girl was beautiful enough, with a head of rich red hair, a satin skin and lovely crystal gray eyes which in certain lights could appear almost silver, no one could deny her humble origins. To make matters worse she spoke with a peasant's accent and was considered beyond the pale by most of the Regent's servants. Yet it was obvious that the Duchess had taken to her and frequently called upon the girl to perform duties which Lady Sarrazin, for one, felt were way beyond the dignity of such a common little creature. But if any of the unkind whispers reached the ears of the Duchess it was obvious that Yolande chose to ignore them.

She had spent the autumn busily, giving herself little time to think of the terrible situation she was in, her principal task being the marriage arrangements for her two younger children. In a way, the fact that the Duchess was expecting a child had had a bearing on her determination to see their future settled, for lurking right at the back of her mind was the idea that they might be left without either parent. If Duke Louis were to be killed fighting and she to die giving birth, at least they would have their parents-in-law to care for them.

The least of her concerns was Yolande's first born, young Louis. He stood to inherit all the massive kingdoms and lands belonging to Anjou: Sicily, Naples, Hungary, Majorca and Sardinia, as well as, through his mother, Aragon and Valencia. There was also the Kingdom of Jerusalem, a purely titular honor but one going back a long way indeed. In infancy, Louis had been betrothed to Katherine of Burgundy, a daughter of the Duke, now residing at Angers, being brought up as a member of the Regent's family; an arrangement about which, as the civil war worsened, Yolande felt more and more uneasy.

For her second son, René, the Duchess had entered into negotiations with the house of Lorraine. The present Duke had no son and on his death his son-in-law and heir would succeed to the Dukedom. As to her daughter, Marie, the Regent had settled on Queen Isabeau's third son Charles, Count of Ponthieu, as a future bridegroom for the girl, a match with no apparent potential at all.

"And yet," thought Yolande tapping her chin with the feather of her goose quill pen as she finished the last of her correspondence, "who knows?"

The boy's brothers were, if rumor were correct, as corrupt and decadent as their mother. It might still turn out that neither of them would make old bones, that the throne of France might indeed pass to the third son, still too young to have been led astray. And on the day of his betrothal it was arranged that the boy would be removed to Angers to be educated by his future parents-in-law, thus escaping the Queen's amoral clutches.

"An investment for the future, perhaps?" murmured Yolande to herself.

With a flourish she signed her last letter, addressing it to His Grace Charles, Duke of Lorraine, then dripped the hot wax on to seal it, pressing in a die bearing her double device of kinship with both the houses of Aragon and Anjou. This done, Yolande leaned back in her chair and silently ran over the course of events which would begin on the following morning and end early in January.

At first light all was prepared for her to leave Angers on an official visit to the Lord of Lorraine, the intention of such a meeting to finalize arrangements for the handing over of René to his care. Traveling with the Regent there would be an unusually small party, quite literally only the men of the armed escort and one lady-in-waiting, namely the newcomer, Alison du May. The Duchess was already aware that there was gossip about this, that Lady Sarrazin was both slighted and angry but no longer had any choice.

Leaving Anjou, the party would head eastward along the banks of the Loire until it reached Orléans; there, it would leave the river and continue east to Troyes, and from that place enter the province of Bar. From Bar they would cross the border into Lorraine, a Dukedom not dependent upon the Kingdom of France. In this way Yolande would, when she had reached her destination, no longer be on French soil.

In many of the principal towns in their territories the Duke and Duchess of Anjou owned houses referred to as *Les Maisons du Roi de Sicile,* and in some cases these houses belonging to the King of Sicily had been built in the provinces of Anjou's allies. It was for this reason that in the Duchy of Lorraine, a few miles outside the capital city of Nancy, the King of Sicily, better known as Duke Louis II, owned a modest manor house, Le Manoir du Haut-Pin. How simple, then, for the Regent's party to make its way to the Manoir, and once there for the Duchess to be taken mysteriously ill.

On the face of it the plan seemed feasible. A hint that Yolande's sickness might be plague would keep everyone away, courtiers and servants alike. Yet how, even with the faithful Alison in constant attendance, could a baby be kept secret when it was finally born? How could they avoid some scullion hearing its distant hungry cries?

Yolande shook her head, still unable to see how things could be managed yet, at the same time, feeling a marvel-

ous thrill of joy that she would soon be holding Richemont's child in her arms, putting it to her breast and feeling
it suckle. If only, she thought, she could keep the baby
and have the pleasure of watching it grow, become like its
beautiful father. But that was not possible; for the sake of
all concerned foster parents must be found and the child
settled with them.

Yet how could she bring herself to part permanently with
Richemont's seed? He had left the castle of Angers in the
dawning and ridden away to war, it was possible that she
might never see him again. Surely God would allow her to
keep something of the man she loved to cherish in the cruel
and lonely future, she thought, as she rose slowly from her
desk.

The trouble was that though he hated and despised her, he
could not get the woman out of his mind, nothing could
blot Yolande from his thoughts. Richemont had gone to
join the Armagnacs, offering his services, fighting like a
savage on every occasion they had met the opposing troops
of the Duke of Burgundy, and still the ghost of her would
not leave him.

In the way of soldiers, the unspoilt boy had gone drinking
and whoring and been a boy no more, manhood coming
suddenly and bitterly in the thick of inglorious battle. But
then Paris had fallen into the hands of the Burgundians,
and Count Bernard d'Armagnac had been thrown into dis-
array. Wisely, he had disbanded his younger men for the
Christmas festivities, telling them to return to him refreshed
early in the new year when they must fight with renewed
vigor. Then the Count had gone off to counsel with his
seasoned campaigners as to the wresting of Paris from Burgundian hands.

But bad news had awaited the Earl of Richmond when
he had walked into his brother's apartments on the evening
of his return to Brittany, for in Duke Jean's hand had been
a letter from their mother, Jehanne of Navarre, Queen of
England.

"Our stepfather the King is dying of leprosy," Jean had
said briefly, and had risen to embrace Richemont, giving
him the fraternal kiss on both cheeks.

"I'll go to her," Arthur had answered at once.

"She says she will see no one, not even us. She is duty

bound to remain with her husband and he can no longer receive visitors."

"Oh, mon Dieu!" Richemont had exclaimed, then had burst into tears, a strange reaction and one which had made Jean suspicious that more lay behind it than grief for a dying stepfather, even though Arthur was the English King's sworn liegeman.

"Come, come," Brittany had said gently. "It is a tragedy, I know, that such a brave man should come to so terrible an end."

"Forgive me," his brother had answered. "I am very tired. I will be myself in a moment."

They had always been closely and inexplicably linked, utterly different though they were. For Jean was small and dark, with cynical eyes, black and glistening as olives, a total contrast to his beautiful sibling. Yet mentally there was a bond between them that nothing could break and, as if he could look into Richemont's mind, the Duke of Brittany had at that moment guessed his brother was in the aftermath of an unhappy love affair.

"Ah, well," thought Jean, smiling to himself, "we all have to do it," while aloud he said, "Perhaps it would be of benefit if you *did* visit England this Christmas despite the circumstances. Even if you cannot see our mother the change might do you good."

Richemont had suddenly looked so vulnerable and young that, tough as he was, Jean of Brittany had felt a tug at his heart. He had leant forward from his high chair and ruffled his brother's hair.

"Go on, cross the Channel, forget her, whoever she is. You can take some money from the treasury for expenses. I'll authorize it. Whatever happens, you can enjoy yourself amidst the younger people."

"Including our stepbrother, Prince Harry?"

"Yes, even including him," Jean had answered, smiling.

"Then I think I will not go after all."

"Why?"

Richemont had repaid the compliment by ruffling Duke Jean's hair in his turn. "I like and trust the man about as much as you do, my Lord."

"And he would put you off going, eh? Then if you won't visit England what can we do to lift your spirits?"

"Perhaps I'll disobey orders and return to the fight."

Jean had shaken his head. "No, that would be counter-productive. Armagnac wants his men rested and mettle-some when it comes to taking Paris. Yet how I wish that he and Burgundy would soon see sense and stop this bloody conflict before it is too late."

Richemont had stared. "What do you mean exactly?"

Jean had taken two goblets of wine, already filled, from a nearby table and passed his brother one, sipping his deli-cately, relishing each drop, whereas Richemont downed the contents of his glass in one.

"Is it not obvious?" Jean had asked, half smiling still.

Arthur had frowned. "No, not to me."

Britanny sighed. "Think, little brother, think. Just let our stepfather of England die, which event both you and I know privily is not far away now, and I'll wager that either Armagnac or Burgundy, possibly both, would be prepared to make an alliance with that beastly little warmonger Hal, in return for troops. God's guts, Richemont, they are tear-ing each other apart only to let the real enemy of France in through the side door. Let our stepbrother once get the crown of England on his unlovely pate and we'll be at war, mark my words."

"And would you side with him?" Richemont had asked quietly.

"I'll leave that to traitors," Jean had answered coldly. "Brittany is my main concern. Let Henry Bolingbroke's son set one foot on my territory and I'll kick his arse so hard he'll cross the Channel without a ship."

Richemont grinned, "And I'll kick it with you. I've al-ways detested him. His mouth is unbelievably obscene."

"Red as a rosebud yet the shape of a scimitar."

"The lips of a violent sensualist."

It was Jean's turn to grin. "No, you don't like him, do you." He had taken hold of his brother's sleeve. "Listen, Arthur, if total war lies ahead then who knows when we may next celebrate the Twelve Days together? So let us make this one memorable. You shall have all the help you need but the actual planning for this particular feast will be entirely in your hands. I'll give you until the Eve of Christmas to transform this court into a place of total plea-sure. Now, what do you say?"

Richemont hesitated, still tinged with sadness.

"Well . . . ?"

"I might do it badly."

"Nonsense. Besides, ..." Jean had added slyly, "... if there is a lady somewhere who has played you false, imagine how envious she will be when news of Brittany's great festivity reaches her ears."

"She wouldn't think like that," Richemont had answered, almost to himself. "That sort of thing would be beneath her dignity. But in other ways, alas, her pride is not so great."

"Then to hell with her," Jean had answered, rising from his chair and going to stand by his brother. "It's not worth torturing yourself over that kind. Put it down to experience."

Arthur had looked at the Duke, shorter than he by a head. "The trouble is I loved her and still can't get her out of my thoughts."

"You need a wife," Jean had answered briskly. "Let me find you someone who can bring a sizeable dower and is a good sturdy breeder."

"You might as well at that. For certain, I'll never marry for love."

"Who does?" Jean's sardonic face had creased. "The trouble is you are a romantic, Richemont."

Arthur had turned away. "Perhaps, perhaps."

Sensing his brother's misery, Brittany had dropped his teasing tone. "Well, what's the answer to my suggestion? Will you mastermind the Christmas revels?"

His brother rubbed a hand across his eyes and straightened his shoulders. "It will be a pleasure."

The Duke of Brittany had clasped the Earl of Richmond in his arms. "Good then, now get about your work. It is already 24th November and time has a terrible way of passing quickly."

Richemont bowed and kissed his brother's hand. "I know it does, Sir. Though recently, for me at least, it has dragged."

"Forget her—that's an order," Brittany answered gruffly, and with that turned on his heel and left the room.

In the cold bright darkness of the morning of 25th November, St. Catherine's Day, devoted to virgins and lacemakers, Yolande d'Anjou, heavy with child, and Alison du May, whose virginity could not be vouched for, left the castle of

Angers and headed eastward away from the river Maine toward the Loire. At the head of the column rode the captain-at-arms, followed by seven horsemen, then came the horse-drawn litters bearing the two women, and finally another ten armed riders. This was considered a modest turnout for an official visit and many queried the fact that the Regent of Anjou had not taken more waiting women and servants. And yet her answer to this question had made very good sense.

"In view of the civil war," she had announced at the last council meeting Yolande had attended before leaving, when she had handed over the reins to her Chancellor, Robert le Maçon, the Seneschal, Pierre de Beauvau, having gone to Italy to join Duke Louis, "I do not intend to move across France with a vast horde of people. A light traveling column is all that is required. I can obtain other servants when I reach Lorraine."

There had been a general rumble of agreement because, in truth, the Duchess was right. It *was* more sensible not to attract too much attention when making a journey of some considerable distance across warring territories.

"And yet," considered le Maçon, his chestnut eyes narrowing slightly. "And yet . . ." And he had looked the Duchess up and down, thought his thoughts, and held his peace.

But this morning in the cold, his face pale in the flickering torchlight, he had kissed Yolande's hand as he bade her farewell and stared appraisingly at the pretty upstart du May, taking a shrewd guess as to why this cheerful young peasant should have been chosen to go to Lorraine and not one of the other high-born ladies.

Alison had seen him looking at her. "Is my head-dress on crooked, my Lord?" she said, very pertly in his view.

"It must be gratifying," he had murmured in reply, "to have risen so high so fast. There are those who say you have your eye to the main chance, Madamoiselle."

"Then let them pee in their own boots." Alison had flushed angrily.

Le Maçon had smiled his slow smile. "Don't make enemies, my girl. You might just possibly upset the wrong person."

"I am loyal to the Duchess and you can tell them that. I would give my life for her."

"Let's hope you are never called upon to do so," the

Chancellor replied smoothly and turned to help the Regent into her litter. She was carrying a child, he felt sure of it but he, too, had his loyalties and nothing on earth would ever induce him to say so to another.

"God speed, ma Reine," he said as he kissed her hand once more.

"I thank you," she answered without looking him directly in the eye.

And now both he and the castle were left behind and Yolande sat silently in her litter, pulling her fur coverlet higher and thinking of the birth that lay ahead before she would ever see Angers again.

Seven

It was Christmas Eve 1411 which, in accordance with the Julian calendar brought in by Julius Caesar himself, was celebrated on 5th January, Christmas Day being the Feast of Epiphany on the 6th. The name Epiphany, or so it was said, came from a Greek word meaning manifestation and was the day when the Christ child had been revealed to the Magi. It was also the day when all the world celebrated Christ's birthday and was the time for great festivity.

In the castle of Angers, the kitchens were ablaze with the light of fires and candles as the cooks and scullions prepared the Epiphany feast. This evening, it being a fast, only fish was to be served but the serious work of preparing tomorrow's enormous banquet had begun hours since.

The Great Pie, consisting of a mixture of small game— peacocks, pigeons, herons, cranes, chickens, capons and geese, to name but a few—was being prepared, its vast hood of pastry already rolled; swans were being cased in paste and baked; three boars' heads, already smoked, were now being glazed and decorated; neats' tongues were in the oven; boars, calves, kids and pigs were turning on the spits; a fresh ox was being doused in herbs; while two great cauldrons of frumenty to go with the venison—the eggs, cream and saffron bubbling thickly together—were suspended above the fire by sturdy hooks.

In the great hall of the castle the plain fare of tench, eels, pikes and gurnet, ling, hake, herrings and barr, to say nothing of the mountainous plates of shrimps and shellfish, glistening with oysters and boasting mussels galore, was ready on the table. And as the Chancellor bade the min-

strels play, wine cups were raised; Christmas had formally
begun.

Yet one face was missing from the feast. The Duchess of
Anjou was not present, still enjoying her state visit to
Charles, Duke of Lorraine, with whom, no doubt, she
would be keeping a most merry Twelve Days. In her absence Yolande's health was drunk, as it would be every
night of Christmas, particularly heartily on New Year's Eve,
celebrated on 11th January, and Twelfth Night which fell
on the 17th.

"I wonder," said the Duchess with just a hint of acerbity,
"if they are drinking my health at home—or if they are too
busy feasting and have already forgotten about me."

"You shouldn't say those words, Madame," answered
Alison, who sat opposite her at the far end of a trestle
dining-table, the firelight throwing dark red shadows on her
hair. "That could never be the case. But then I think you
know that well and are just feeling a little sorry for
yourself."

"You are very familiar, you know," retorted Yolande,
with no real anger.

"That is because I love you, ma Reine, and have no
desire to see you depressed. After all, we have arrived here
safely; we were not attacked by war parties on the way; the
Duke of Lorraine believes you may well have the plague
and is leaving you alone; and the master cook and scullions,
to say nothing of the cleaning women, are terrified to come
near you. I would have thought our plan had succeeded
admirably."

After a moment Yolande nodded, stretching out her
hand toward the girl. "You are right, my dear. And it can
be no fun for you being cooped up here with me, virtually
living the life of a prisoner."

"I owe you everything," Alison answered simply. "I am
your creature and will serve you all my days. I enjoy caring
for you."

"With no thought for yourself?" Yolande's tone was
mildly teasing.

Alison lowered her eyes, the candlelight concealing her
flushed face.

"Even as a child, ma Reine, I believed that one day I
would leave the streets of Angers and become a grand lady,

living in a grand house, with a great man to love me. It was more than a belief, in fact, for sometimes I actually thought I could see a vision of that future. I confess I *did* snatch at the chance to help the dream come true by offering to serve you, but that in no way diminishes my loyalty. That is all I have to say."

"I'm sorry," answered the Duchess, humbled. "It was wrong of me to speak thus."

"Thank you, Madame." Alison raised her glass. "I drink to the future of all present, including . . ." She lowered her voice to a whisper, " . . . the baby."

Yolande smiled sadly. "Poor little thing. I will try to do my best for it."

"And so will I when I go in search of the foster parents."

"You must be very careful in your choice, Alison. Everything depends on you selecting them wisely."

"I will choose them as if I were you yourself, Majesty."

"If only I could go looking with you," the Regent answered with a note of despair. "But the risk would be too great."

"It would indeed. I shall pretend that it is I who have sinned and am desperate to hide the proof of my adultery . . ."

Yolande flinched but Alison, cheerfully unaware, went on speaking.

" . . . then I can tell them with authority how well they must care for the child for whose keep, of course, they will believe I pay."

"And they will be well paid," the Duchess added earnestly.

Alison left her place, going to stand by the Regent and putting her arm round the other woman's shoulders.

"Please trust me, Madame. I promise to find a couple who will love the baby as if it were their own."

A tear ran down Yolande's cheek. "Yes, Alison, please try hard. For the sake of the child and its father we must give it a good home."

"Its father . . ." Alison whispered to herself, conjecturing about his identity for the millionth time.

"I wonder where he is now," the Duchess went on, another tear joining the first. "And if he ever thinks of me."

The Eve of Christmas in Brittany, and Duke Jean and his court sitting down to a feast *par excellence,* all the fruits

the sea could yield up served before them, every superb
dish their emerald coast could provide laid on gleaming
platters, fancifully decorated to delight their gaze, crammed
onto the many trestles packing the great hall.

Only the master of ceremonies himself, Arthur, Earl of
Richmond, seemed not to be tempted by the banquet and
sat drinking much and eating little, worrying his brother
who from time to time shot him inquisitive glances down
the length of the high table.

"So he is still in love," thought Jean, and wondered yet
again who might be the object of Richemont's affections.

The Duke had taken the trouble to place his brother
next to Jacquetta of Luxemburg, Jean of Luxemburg's
thirteen-year-old daughter, with the hope that she might
awake a spark of interest in him, though at the moment
Arthur was showing no sign of life, gazing off into space
and nervously turning the gold ring he always wore on his
little finger.

The girl on the other hand, or so Jean thought, was more
than aware of her companion, her beautiful eyes, which
always seemed to have a flicker of amusement in their
depths, hardly leaving Richemont's face.

"Oh, come on!" hissed Duke Jean, wishing he could influence events.

But for once the Earl of Richmond did not pick up his
brother's thought processes, almost unaware of the girl who
sat beside him, his mind too full of images of Yolande,
wondering how she might be spending her Christmas Eve—
and with whom!

" . . . completely naked."

The words startled Richemont back to the present and
he frowned at Jacquetta in surprise. "What did you say?"
he asked abruptly, not really caring if he was being rude.

"I said that if you don't talk to me soon I shall take off
my clothes and dance upon the table completely naked.
That might arouse your interest at least."

He smiled despite himself. "Yes, I think it probably
would."

"Then shall I?" She seemed serious.

"No, no. It would shock the other guests."

"And you, would it shock you, my Lord?"

"I don't imagine so. I consider myself a man of the
world."

Jacquetta smiled knowingly. "Of course. I forgot. You are a member of the licentious soldiery. Have you slept with dozens of women?"

"Hundreds," answered Richemont, finally entering into the spirit of the conversation. "I've had more women than you've had nightmares, as they say."

The girl clapped her hands together. "How wonderful! I love experienced men."

"I take it from this that you are not married?"

"Not yet, but heavily betrothed. I shall be a bride next year. He is hideous, by the way, and I shall shut my eyes when I have to go to bed with him."

"That's a pity for you."

"Don't worry," Jacquetta lowered her voice to a mutter. "I intend to have many lovers to make up for it."

Richemont laughed, suddenly amused, and further up the table Duke Jean heaved a sigh of relief and finally started to concentrate on his meal.

"And you, you are the gallant Earl of Richmond are you not? And not wed either."

"No, I was betrothed when I was a boy to a woman many years older than I, twenty-five to my eleven in fact, but she died."

"Before consummation?"

"Yes, you cheeky chit."

"That's a pity, you could have learnt much from her."

"I think not, she was very frail and tragic."

"*I* would like to learn from an experienced man," said Jacquetta, giving Richemont a look that made him go warm.

"You should be careful to whom you say that."

"I *am* careful to whom I say it, I assure you."

"I really think we should change the topic of conversation. Tell me about your family."

Jacquetta gave a knowing smile. "I take after my aunt, of course, my mother Marguerite d'Enghien's sister, Yolande. Despite being married she had an affair with the late Duc d'Orléans and bore him a son, known as the Bastard of Orléans. Have you met my cousin?"

"Oh, yes, I know the Bastard well. He is close to his half-brother Duke Charles d'Orléans."

"I hear he has connections with the house of Anjou."

"What do you mean?"

"Just connections."

She pulled a face and said nothing more, leaving Richemont with the awful feeling that the handsome Bastard, young though he was, might be one of Yolande's lovers.

"Are you all right, my Lord?" For the first time Jacquetta's voice had lost its provocative undertone.

"Why do you ask?"

"You're sweating suddenly."

"It's just that I am hot. If you will excuse me I think I'll go out for some air."

"I'll join you," Jacquetta answered instantly.

Richemont rose and gave a bow, "Please do."

"Gladly," she said, and inclined her head.

It was politeness only, he cared nothing as to whether the forward minx walked with him or not. So it was with a feeling of slight annoyance that Richemont caught his ducal brother's eye and saw a hint of a wink before Jean studiously looked away. But despite his irritation, Arthur of Richmond offered the girl his arm and was surprised how good it felt as her little bosom brushed against it. For the first time, as they left the great hall and stepped out onto the paved walkway that ran along the lower battlements, he looked at her properly.

Jacquetta was so stunningly beautiful, her presence in a room being almost an insult to every other woman there, that Richemont wondered how he could possibly have ignored her for so long. Her figure was small, delicate, as befitted her extreme youth, but the breasts, though tiny, were both shapely and lovely, while her eyes were particularly wonderful, an unusual shade, like the wild violets that grew in profusion throughout the woods of Brittany. To crown her perfect features, Jacquetta's hair, which Richemont could glimpse beneath her fashionable head-dress, made of soft padded rolls of material decorated with cut out leaf shapes, was a glorious shade of gold.

"Well, you've looked at me at last," she said.

"Yes."

"And?"

"You are a very beautiful girl."

Jacquetta gave a laugh. "But you don't really care for me."

Richemont felt embarrassed. "I didn't say that."

"You had no need. Your mind has been elsewhere all the evening as, indeed, has mine."

Not knowing how to answer, the Earl merely stared at her.

"You see I can read you," Jacquetta went on, tucking her arm more firmly through his. "I, too, have been crossed in love."

"Really?" Richemont was astonished at such frankness.

"Yes. I was taken to England when I was eleven and there fell in love with John of Lancaster. Do you know him?"

"Casually, yes."

"Then you will be aware of how magnificent he is."

"Well . . . yes."

It had never occurred to Richemont that his middle step-brother, full brother to Prince Henry, was anything out of the ordinary. But Jacquetta was not waiting for a reply.

"Of course we will never be allowed to marry. As I have already told you my father has chosen someone else who is politically more expedient. But that will not stop me loving John for the rest of my days."

The Earl gazed at her. "That is very much how I feel," he said quietly.

Jacquetta's lovely eyes took on a speculative expression. "Would I know the lady?"

"I doubt it. But even if you did I should not tell you who she was."

She laughed prettily, and squeezed Arthur's arm. "How discreet you are! I am such a gossip I simply cannot keep a thing to myself. How would you like to come to my apartment for a chat? My sisters are still at the banquet."

Richemont gazed in amazement, wondering exactly how to interpret the remark and, as if to leave him without doubt, Jacquetta stood on tiptoe and rapidly kissed his cheek.

"We orphans of love might just as well comfort one another," she whispered. "I meant it when I said I liked experienced men."

The Earl had hardly been celibate since he had parted from Yolande, determined to pay the Regent back in her own coin, and this new adventure had every prospect of being delightful even though the girl was rather young.

"Madame, you honor me too much," he answered, tightening his hold on her.

"And honor me you certainly shall," answered Jacquetta without a moment's hesitation, and kissed him again, but this time full on the lips.

It was one of the best Christmas Eves that the Queen of France could remember. Not only did the fish and wine for supper promise to be of the highest quality but, since Martinmas, she had discovered the Duke of Burgundy to be an even more exciting lover than she had at first imagined. Fearing Armagnac may attack at any time he had taken to keeping his boots on in bed, a variation which both thrilled and delighted Isabeau. So much so, in fact, she had plans to attend her Feast of Venus, planned for Twelfth Night, as booted and spurred as he.

Conversation, too, on this particular 5th January had proved stimulating, for Jean the Fearless had arrived that morning with a witty young man, twenty-nine-year-old Georges de la Trémoille, son of one of Isabeau's former lovers. In order to remind herself of the father she had invited the son to her chamber for an hour or two, with excellent results. With so many capable men around her the Feast of Venus looked fraught with possibilities!

The one blight to the Queen's enjoyment had been the fact that the necessary evils of Christmas, the obligations to attend Mass and to see one's children, could not be avoided. She had sighed deeply as the young people had come trooping into her presence, complete with wives in the case of Louis the Dauphin and Jean, Duke of Touraine. These two were now fifteen and fourteen respectively, behaving more badly than ever, Louis as promiscuous as his mother and furious that he must restrain himself under the eagle eye of his father-in-law, the Duke of Burgundy. As if to annoy his elder brother, Touraine, in contrast, had chased every female in sight, reducing his young wife, Jacqueline of Bavaria, a large ungainly girl with a red face, to constant and copious tears.

"Be quiet!" Isabeau had thundered at the creature, to whom she was close kin. "Turn a blind eye, do you hear me? That is the duty of all royal wives."

"And in your case obviously of royal husbands too," the

girl had dared to retort, and had received a smarting blow round the head for her temerity.

In the midst of this chaos, Catherine and Charles, she having recently celebrated her tenth birthday, he approaching his ninth, sat quietly together playing chess. Earlier in the day, one of the Queen's Ladies had offered them food and drink, which they had gladly taken, but since then they had made as few demands as possible, anxious to keep out of the domestic dramas erupting all around them. Yet even this discreet behavior could not guarantee their safety when, after leaving for a light midday repast, Isabeau returned sparkling with wine.

Charles now knew that he hated his mother, dreaded the moment when her gleaming dark eyes would alight on him. He was no longer too young to understand her taunts about his ugliness, nor the murmured whispers that he was a bastard, son of the man he had once thought of as uncle. In his wilder moments the wretched boy cherished the idea of his mother silently dropping dead at his feet while he muttered some deep and heartfelt curse. And today was no exception. As Isabeau came into her receiving hall on the arm of Jean the Fearless, Charles took his sister's queen, squeezing the chess piece hard in his hand and whispering "I wish this were my mother."

The Queen took her place in her great chair—great in every sense as it had now been especially widened and strengthened to accommodate her bulk—and stared round the room. The Count of Ponthieu shuddered, then looked away as Isabeau called, "Catty, come here, ma chérie. I want to talk to you."

Thankfully, Charles bent his head over the chessboard, hoping that nobody would notice him while, her eyes cast to the ground, Catherine silently made her way to where their mother sat.

"My sweetheart, you are so pretty," Isabeau was saying, heaving her daughter onto her knee. "How can it be that such a beauty will be the last one to leave home?"

"What do you mean?" Catherine had forgotten to be ingratiating in her obvious surprise.

"Simply that you are the only one of my children whose marriage I have not yet arranged."

From where he sat, Charles began to listen hard.

"And the strangest thing about it ..." Isabeau went on

" . . . is that you are the best looking of them all. So what do you make of that, daughter?"

"That you must be saving me for the greatest prize," Catherine answered pertly, and there was a roar of approval from everyone in the room, particularly la Trémoille who slapped his leg and shouted with laughter.

He was a fat young man, barely of medium height, and had enormous buttocks, thighs and genitals, none of which were concealed by his tight party-colored hose, over-short doublet, and scanty codpiece. As with many fat people he insisted on wearing the latest fashions regardless of the fact that they did not suit him. But Georges's face was pleasant enough; round, with an easy smile and lazy light brown eyes which twinkled as he talked. He also had a cutting wit and was dagger-sharp in conversation. The Dauphin and Duke of Touraine hung on his every word, while Catherine and Charles found him amiable and not unkind.

Now he remarked, "You have a clever daughter there, ma Reine. Made in your mold if I may dare to say so."

Isabeau, who was occasionally capable of making jokes against herself and who, this afternoon, felt buoyant with drink, glanced down at her enormous body and said, "But a smaller model, let God be praised," and once again the entire company broke into laughter.

"And what of the Count of Ponthieu?" drawled Georges, voicing the very question that Charles longed but did not dare to ask himself. "Are we to presume that Madame has found him a bride?"

"I did ask one of the gargoyles if it would like to marry him," Isabeau answered merrily, casting her eyes round for further cheap approval, "but it refused. I have, therefore, been forced to enter into negotiation with the Vestal Virgin of Anjou."

The Duke of Burgundy gave a growl. "Don't speak of her so lightly. A betrothal to the Angevins is always worth having. There is a great deal of wealth in Anjou, believe me."

"What is a Vestal Virgin, Mother?" asked Catherine, starting to wriggle from Isabeau's lap.

"A pure untouchable woman," answered the Queen, snorting slightly. "The sort of woman, indeed, who would make an ideal mother-in-law for an ugly little boy."

Charles, still gallantly staring at the chessboard, felt his blood rise, aware that everyone in the room was looking in his direction, staring no doubt at his bulbous nose and big mouth, some with pity, others not. With great self-control in one so small, the child did not give the Queen the satisfaction of even glancing in her direction.

"Wouldn't she, Charles?" Isabeau called out loudly.

He did not move.

"Charles, do you hear what I am saying?"

Still he made no response, aware that his mother was working herself into a fury.

"Come here, you little wretch, or I'll give you a beating," she shouted in exasperation.

And it was then that the unhappy boy knew exactly what he must do to win this particular game. Looking over in the direction of the Duke of Burgundy, he said politely but distinctly, "My Lord Duke, I think my mother is speaking to you."

There was chaos as the courtiers shrieked with genuine amusement, the jester actually falling onto the floor and rolling about in ecstasy. But even while they did so, Isabeau rose from her seat and bore down on the child like a vengeful mountain.

For a fat man, Georges de la Trémoille moved very fast, jumping to his feet from where he sat on a cushion and placing his body, diminutive in comparison with Isabeau's but sizeable by any other standard, between the Queen and her son.

"How wonderful it must be," he said loudly, "to be dam to both beauty and wit. For indeed, Madame, that gift you certainly have in your two younger children. One so fair and the other so ready with his tongue, it must be a blessing that many a mother would envy."

She stopped in her tracks, looking at la Trémoille suspiciously, wondering if he was mocking her. But his twinkling eyes were wide and ingenuous and the smile on his jolly moon face was disarmingly full of admiration.

"Well said," put in Burgundy, bored with upheaval and anxious to rest before the evening's entertainment. "An amusing child." He stood up, jerking his eyebrows several times in the direction of the now uncertain Isabeau. "Well, I'm to my chamber for an hour or so. Adieu."

He nodded to the company and left the room, passing

Charles's chair and giving the boy a pat on the head which practically rendered him senseless.

"So you like chess, mon Prince?" said de la Trémoille, squeezing with difficulty into the place recently occupied by Catherine.

Charles looked up slowly, his steadfast eyes taking in the details of Georges's face, the buzzing in his head caused by Burgundy's hand dying away.

"I do enjoy playing certainly, but before we speak of the game may I say thank you for saving me from a beating," he murmured.

"Saving you?" Georges repeated guilessly.

Charles said nothing but flicked his eyes in the direction of his mother who, now the Duke had gone, was beginning to yawn pointedly.

"Ah!" said Georges, his jolly gaze bright. "Think nothing of it, Monsieur. Call it a service for Christmas Eve."

"Very well, I will. But, my Lord, I want you to remember that I am in your debt. If ever I can grant you a favor . . ."

"I shall most certainly call on you," de la Trémoille answered, and smiled so knowingly that the Count of Ponthieu believed the man really meant it.

Jacquetta of Luxemburg was certainly ready for love, pulling Richemont close to her as soon as the heavy door of her chamber had swung to behind them, then opening her mouth wide beneath his hard and demanding kisses. But afterwards, in the soft aftermath of lovemaking when he held Jacquetta in his arms, Richemont thought of Yolande and knew the guilty despair that only one who truly adores another can ever experience. He saw himself as a villain, dishonoring his brother's guest, betraying the woman with whom he would be obsessed until his death. But had she not played him false, had she not used him as something little more than a stallion?

"What's the matter?" asked Jacquetta sleepily.

"I was thinking what a wicked wretch I am."

"Don't do that, please. I made you go on when you would have stopped." She sat upright, the firelight gleaming on her skin, turning it the color of morning. "But the odd thing is my heart still loves John even though my body wants yours."

Richemont smiled despite his teeming thoughts. "You

little witch, you have the gift of reading my mind. For I love that woman, though I wish to God I could shake myself free of her."

"What exactly did she do to you?" Jacquetta asked curiously.

"She betrayed me with another."

"Oh!"

And it was as well that the shadows in the room hid Jacquetta's secret smile as the irony of the situation slowly dawned upon her.

It was growing late and the simple fish meal that Yolande d'Anjou and Alison du May had enjoyed together had long since been cleared away by Alison herself.

As in every house that the King-Duke owned a small permanent staff kept the place running all the year round, reinforced by a great body of servants who traveled with their royal master when he went to stay in one of his many homes. But on this particular occasion the Queen Duchess had brought no other retainers, which the servants who ran the Manoir du Haut-Pin considered a blessing in view of the fact that Madame might well have the plague.

Every day the master cook and his scullions came in and prepared the food, while the cleaning women worked throughout the manor house, leaving the top floor where the Duchess lay ill to the good offices of Madamoiselle du May. And every evening, instead of sleeping round the fire, they left the Manoir and stayed with relatives to lessen the chance of contracting the illness. Only Jacqui the pot boy, kind-hearted but born stupid, remained behind to protect the place at night.

"Bonne nuit," he called now through the dining-room door, doing his final rounds before sleeping.

"And to you," Alison called back, she and Yolande having abruptly ceased to speak on hearing his approaching footsteps.

"Oh, and Jacqui . . ."

"Yes?"

"Don't lock up yet, I shall be going for a short walk before I retire."

"Very good, Madame. Is the Duchess any better this evening?"

"No better, no worse," Alison answered. "Thank you for inquiring. I shall tell her you did. Bon Noël."

"Bon Noël," the boy replied cheerfully, and the two women heard him move away toward the kitchens.

"*May* I go for a walk?" Alison asked now. "Once I have helped you prepare for the night?"

"As long as you make it a short one. It's very cold out there."

"I promise to be quick. It's just that fresh air helps me to sleep."

"You can borrow my fur mantle."

So it was that Alison du May, protected from the bitter weather, did not worry as she saw the dark sky begin to shed its burden and the first great flakes come down softly, covering the black earth with a delicate sprinkling of fine powder.

Looking out of her window the Duchess, too, noticed the snow start to fall and hoped that Alison would not be long, partly because she was concerned for the girl's safety, partly because being alone was such a strange sensation.

With a sudden lurch of her heart, Yolande realized that it must be almost the first time in her entire life that she had experienced solitude. A protected child, a young bride, a Queen, a mother, a Regent, she had always been surrounded by people. And now here she was, an island, alone in an ocean of quiet, the only other person near her a slumbering kitchen lad. With a deep sigh, the Duchess left the window and going to her bed lay down on it fully dressed, momentarily closing her eyes.

It was the silence that woke her, deep down from a wonderful sleep, every care she had forgotten and soothed. But as she came to wakefulness Yolande knew that the situation had reached its conclusion, that nothing could ever be the same again, that the end of nine long months had arrived. In the unearthly quiet of a snow-filled night she had, at last, gone into labor.

The Duchess of Anjou, King Juan's brave daughter, faced birth as she did everything else in her life, with fierce determination. When her first child, Louis, had been born she had been twenty-three years old, strong as oak but supple as willow, yet that had been eight years before and there had been two other births in the gap between.

"Alison," she called out loud, as she took stock of the

situation and prepared herself for onslaught. "Can you come to me?"

But there was no responding movement in the close blackness of the house and Yolande guessed at once that she was alone, that her pretty Lady was still out, lost somewhere in a white wilderness.

"So," she said aloud, "we are solitary, my babe, you and I. Come easily then, and do your mother no harm."

Then the Queen-Duchess eased herself into the position that gave her most comfort, breathed deeply but gently, and waded into the sea of birth, fearing nothing.

The Queen of France lay face down on a heap of scattered cushions in that exotic place in the Hôtel St. Pol known as the Hall of Rosewater, inhaling the rare fine smoke from the braziers and the musky perfume that floated everywhere. To say that she was annoyed was an understatement, for Christmas Eve had turned out to be a disappointment after all.

Isabeau had returned from Mass, hoping for light relief after the ordeal, only to find Burgundy so drunk that he had been fit for nothing but to stagger to his bed, while Georges de la Trémoille was suddenly nowhere to be found. Furthermore, Isabeau's other occasional partners all seemed mysteriously about some private business of their own and so, in a mood for love, she had found herself alone.

There had been nothing for it but to make the best of a bad situation. Snatching a handful of spice, especially brought from Damascus and said to have an extremely powerful and exotic effect, the Queen had made for the hall and thrown all the substance onto the braziers. And now, indeed, the benefits could be felt. Isabeau smiled as she began to drift off into a dream into which the flame of every candle dipped to half its full strength. At that moment it seemed to her a bare body climbed onto her back and hands slid beneath to knead her great breasts, hands that belonged to Pierre de Giac himself.

It was nearly midnight and still the swirling snowflakes fell from a black velvet sky, confusing the landscape utterly so that no landmark looked the same as it had done an hour earlier. What had begun as a simple walk round the Manoir's formal garden and into the meadows lying beyond had become a desperate trek to find the way home. Gasping for breath, Alison resolutely turned her back against the wind, shielded her eyes with her hand, and attempted to get her bearings.

As its name suggested the manor house stood high, an ancient and majestic pine tree its landmark. But this tree, like all the others, must be glistening with diamonds, no longer standing out as something to head towards. The lights of the house, too, would be dim by now as Jacqui always doused the candles and torches before bedding down for the night.

To Alison's left lay an expanse of white which appeared to have no end, while to the right the only discernible break in the snow fields was a clump of trees. In front of her the same pale blanket spread on again, and it was with more desperation than hope that she decided the only way to turn was into the wind, blinded by the driving flakes as this would make her, to try to pick up the direction in which she had come. Unable to see a single step before her, Madamoiselle du May wheeled round and bravely began to struggle along.

The flicker of a flare was so unexpected and so quickly gone again, a point of light brief as a firefly, that Alison dashed her hand across her eyes, wiping the snow from her lashes, convinced that she was seeing a mirage. But then the sight came again and she began to hurry as best she could through the drifts which by now almost reached up to the calves of her legs.

"Help," she called, her voice blanketed by the dense night. "I'm over here."

The torch flashed once more and suddenly she saw a dark shape, a man leading a horse, the poor beast struggling through the snow as best it could, was coming towards her.

"Help me, please help," Alison called again.

It was impossible to see his features in the wild conditions but a tall shape loomed directly up to her, putting an arm round her shoulders to steady her against the blowing drifts.

"I take it you're lost?" said a pleasant voice, muffled by the folds of the stranger's hood.

"Yes. I'm trying to find the Manoir du Haut-Pin."

She felt him stiffen in surprise. "But that's the Duchess of Anjou's home! Is she not lying there sick with the plague?"

"She is, yes, she is, and I am most anxious to get back to her. I am her Lady, the only one who tends to her."

Tight against her breast, she felt him ripple with laughter. "Well, if you're a carrier I no doubt have caught the contagion."

"Who are you?" asked Alison, slightly shocked, staring up at the hooded face.

"Charles is my name, young lady. Now come on, take my hand, or we'll both get stranded."

It was a big friendly fist and Alison was glad to slip her fingers into its depths as the stranger with a touch of nonchalance contrived to lead her and the horse, while still grasping the flare, through the wildernesses which engulfed them.

And then, suddenly, there was the great pine tree raising its proud head bedecked with brilliants, and the dark shape of the house loomed, all draped in white.

"Off you go!" said her rescuer. "Get to your work—but take care."

She smiled and a long red curl fell from her bedraggled head-dress and for a moment caught in the fur of her mantle.

"A fiery one, eh?" he said, and briefly caressed the lock with his gloved fingers.

"Thank you for helping me, Sir," Alison answered, pulling away and running toward the great wooden door.

"What's your name?" he called over his departing shoulder.

"Alison du May."

"I'll remember that." His voice was distant, hollow. "Farewell."

Just for one luxurious moment as she got inside, Alison leaned against the heavy oak door to regain her breath before fleeing up the winding stone stairs to the top of the house. But no sooner was she through the entrance to Yolande's chamber than she saw the Duchess crouched by the head of the bed, her legs drawn up, her knees wide, and the top of the baby's head already visible.

"I'm here," shouted the girl, flinging herself forward. "I'm here."

But Yolande did not answer, pushing and grunting like the most primitive of peasants as she labored to bring her baby into the world.

"Come on," urged Alison, who had often seen birth in

the crowded dwellings of the walled city of Angers, and so was not afraid. "Heave him out, my Lady."

In that moment she had forgotten utterly that she addressed the Regent and had gone back to the patois of her youth. But Yolande only looked at her, wild-haired and wild-eyed, and sunk her chin onto her chest, rolling herself into a ball in order to push more strongly. And then it was not so hard. Alison put a delicate hand on either side of the head and turned it very gently, and a moment or two later a strangely appealing but very wrinkled face appeared.

"Another push," said Madamoiselle du May in a voice of command. "Get shot of him, come on, Madame."

It was done! The shoulders eased out one after the other and the little body almost dropped into Alison's waiting hands. It was a girl; Richemont had a daughter not a son.

As Yolande's head fell back onto the pillows and the eyes closed in her sweat-stained face, her servant tied a piece of string from her pocket around the cord, then cut it with her herb knife.

"What is it?" asked the Duchess, her voice an exhausted rasp.

"You have a baby daughter, ma Reine."

"Perfectly formed?"

"Perfect and strong, here."

And Alison passed the naked infant to its mother. She shouldn't have done it she knew, realizing how hard it would make the inevitable parting, but Yolande tore the covering shift from her breast and put the babe to suck. With that sensation, her milk began to come in, and she was transported to paradise, holding the tiny creature and feeling the flow like a magic fountain. Looking on, Alison shook her head, knowing how difficult this sweet ritual would make the Duchess's future.

"What will you call her, Majesty?" she whispered softly. "Have you thought of a name?"

"Oh yes, she shall be Jehanne after her father's mother."

"Her father," repeated Alison, wondering yet again who the man might be.

"Yes," answered Yolande, her voice scarcely audible. "Her beautiful father who has given me part of himself. A child that I shall cherish always, albeit from afar as destiny has decreed."

Eight

It was very strange. As Charles, Count of Ponthieu, had left the chapel of the Hôtel St. Pol after hearing Mass and walked back to the Hôtel du Petit-Musc, passing the aviaries teeming with rare and beautiful birds and the cages where the great beasts lay crouched, someone had brushed against him almost pushing him into the netting. A voice had whispered, "Jeanne Chamoisy, your former wet nurse, is coming to you with instructions which it is imperative you obey, Monsieur le Comte."

The child had wheeled around, frightened yet intrigued, but amongst all the people milling through the palace's maze of walkways it was impossible to know which one had spoken to him.

"Whatever is the matter?" called Lady du Mesnil over her shoulder. "Why are you lagging behind?"

"I have a stone in my shoe," Charles answered, and raising one leg removed his footwear and shook it. But while he did this he was thinking as quickly as any boy of nine could possibly do, wondering why the wet nurse, pensioned off now and living in a small establishment within the fortified walls of the palace, could possibly be giving him orders he must obey.

It occurred to Charles at this point in his deliberations that the Count Bernard d'Armagnac might be trying to enlist his help to free the city of Paris from Burgundy's iron fist, for civil war was still tearing France to shreds. Jean the Fearless, aided by soldiers sent from England, had kept the Armagnacs at bay only to discover that the English wouldn't go now that his need for them was not so urgent. Charles had heard the whisper along with everyone else that the Goddams, as the English troops were com-

monly known, would never leave, were only waiting for
Prince Hal to come to the throne of England and would
then wage war.

"Monsieur, come *on*," Jeanne du Mesnil called again. "I
want you home and ready to receive a guest."

"Who?" asked Charles innocently.

"Jeanne, your nurse, is coming to see you. Isn't that
good?"

The boy's spine tingled with apprehension. "Why is she
coming?"

"Really!" Lady du Mesnil replied sharply. "You know
she visits you every month. Don't you remember she was
ill last week at the time of your birthday? Well, now she
brings you your gift."

"How kind of her."

The answer came automatically but with it a strange leap
of Charles's nerves, a feeling of strain and power dizzily
combined. Somewhere, in a part of his brain of which he
had never before been aware, the child knew that something of vital significance would shortly occur.

And he was not to be disappointed; within the folds of
cloth that bound up his birthday present—a hand-carved
toy windmill with sails that actually spun around—was a
piece of folded parchment. Before Lady du Mesnil could
catch sight of it Charles thrust it into his sleeve and, across
the room, Jeanne Chamoisy raised her eyebrows in a question, to which the boy responded with a slight nod of his
head. Whatever the solution to the mystery, he thought,
this part of it was wonderfully intriguing and exciting.

But much to his irritation, Charles had to wait several
hours before he was able to read the mysterious parchment,
first having to entertain Jeanne with wine and spiced cakes
then, when she had gone, feigning extreme tiredness and
begging to go to bed, all of which took up valuable time.

"This is not like you," said Lady du Mesnil, as he
yawned. "You always grumble that you are being sent up
too early."

"Tonight is different," Charles answered grandly.

Yet this pretended fatigue nearly ran him into difficulties
as his governess, having tucked him in, went to take away
the bedside candle.

"Oh, Masher, please leave it," the child pleaded
anxiously.

"Why? You don't normally have a night light."

"I want to think for a while."

"Can't you think in the dark?"

The boy's face split into an endearing smile and Lady du Mesnil weakened, wondering as she often had before why such a pleasant child should have been born so very plain of feature.

"Why are you staring at me?" Charles's candid eyes were searching her face. "You're thinking that I'm hideous as a toad, aren't you?"

"Toads bear a gem in their crowns, did you know that?"

"No, I didn't. What sort of gem?"

"A glowing ruby. And that is what I was thinking; that you were a jewel. Now mull over your thoughts then go to sleep. Goodnight."

She bent over to kiss him and Charles once more feigned a yawn, feeling more devious and wicked than he ever had before, quite an exciting sensation in actual fact.

"Goodnight Masher," he answered in a sleepy voice.

She was gone and he lay still, listening for the sound of her feet descending the stone staircase that led to the floor below then, when all was quiet, cautiously sitting up and looking round. On his little desk lay the boy's Latin grammar into which he had thrust the mysterious parchment and, slipping out of bed silently, Charles padded across to it, opened the book at the center and drew out the paper.

On the outside of the letter, written in a thin tall hand, were the words, "Pour Monsieur le Prince Charles, le Comte de Ponthieu." Smiling with glee, thinking that he had never received such a thing in his life before, the boy broke the seal with stubby fingers.

"Monsieur le Prince," he read, "I send you formal greetings and heartfelt wishes for a long and happy life, and beg that you will regard the contents of this using the political acumen of which you will one day be capable.

"As you know, Monsieur, the Kingdom of France is now gravely threatened by civil strife, a strife which is destroying the realm. Yet, in the course of my studies, I have come to vital conclusions about this matter, which it is essential I impart to you without delay. Tomorrow, while Lady du Mesnil sleeps, Jeanne Chamoisy will come for you with the intention of bringing you to me. For the sake of poor

France I request you to do so. Your servant, Nicolas
Flamel."

"Nicolas Flamel," whispered Charles aloud, "the name
means nothing."

But this only added to the mystery of the entire affair.
A strange man had taken the trouble to write to him, a
nine-year-old boy with no power and none foreseeable either, to enlist his help to save France. The whole thing
smacked of lunacy and yet Charles felt certain that Jeanne
Chamoisy, to whom he was bonded for ever by the fact she
had fed him from her breast, would never involve him in
anything which could do him the slightest harm. Taking the
letter back to bed, the boy reread it twice more, then blew
out his candle, puzzling over the enigmatical phrase, "In
the course of my studies," until he fell asleep.

It was just as they rejoined the mighty river Loire at Mont-
geoffroy, having left it at Blois and headed across country,
that the bitter February wind, blowing harshly on this the
last day of the month, first hinted at the sting of snow.
Pulling their hoods down, the riders hastened their horses,
while the two women in the drawn litters snuggled their
fur coverlets to their chins. They had all of them left Anjou
in the bitter weather of Christmas time and now the royal
party was returning in conditions equally savage.

"Snow!" thought Yolande. "Is it destined that all the
fateful events in my life should be associated with it?" And
though the sensible side of her nature told her such things
were a mere coincidence, she could not help thinking that
the earth had often been covered with white when matters
of great importance had occurred.

Her first glimpse of her future husband, when she had
been taken to Saumur to meet both him and the woman
who was to become her mother-in-law, had been when the
beautiful countryside of Anjou was transformed by a covering of snow, glittering like diamonds in sunshine. Half-
closing her eyes, Yolande remembered Duke Louis as he
had looked on the day when she had seen him first: tall,
well made, with the long Valois nose, and lips that could
curl into a smile or just as easily look cruel and unrelenting,
he had been formidable even as a very young man. And
the years had done nothing to change that as lines had

appeared and his features grown in strength, his personality in power.

Her father, King Juan, had died when snow had come to the high peaks of Aragon and there had been a flukish flurry on Yolande's own birthday in July. But, most importantly of all, in the snow-filled dawning of Christmas Day Jehanne had been born, and Yolande held her daughter in her arms for the first time as she fed her.

She felt now, thinking back on the events of the last three months, that she had loved that child more than any of her others as it had taken her flow, and she still loved it, all the more fiercely and deeply since the Duchess had been forced to part with her newborn daughter.

Alison had been as good as her word and found a couple whose own child had been unable to take the first breath of life and had been buried unbaptized that same day. The woman, weeping and distraught when Madamoiselle du May had arrived, had put Jehanne straight to her breast and had become calm again.

"They are going to put it about she is their own," Alison had told Yolande on her return from delivering the infant to its foster parents.

"Did they ask many questions?"

"No, Madame. I simply said that I had given birth to a child I could not keep and would give them regular sums of money if they would adopt her."

"And will they be kind to her? Will they really love her?"

"I think she came as a godsend to them. The mother was beside herself with grief. I think she half believes Jehanne *is* hers."

Yolande had wept, jealous almost that another woman looked upon her daughter as her child, yet at the same time telling herself this was the best possible outcome.

"Please, Madame, do not distress yourself," an apologetic little voice had said then. "I will stay behind and act as Jehanne's guardian if that would make you happier."

Yolande had looked at Alison through gushing tears.

"But how could you? Where would you live, what would you do?"

Even that particularly naughty lady-in-waiting had had the good grace to go pink.

"Ma Reine, the Duke of Lorraine has invited me to stay

as his *Maîtresse en Titre*. If you agree to it I would very much like to accept."

The Duchess had laughed and cried simultaneously. "I am amazed. How can it be? Where did you meet him?"

Alison had smiled at her memories. "Madame, do you recall me telling you that a stranger rescued me from the snow on the night that Jehanne was born?"

"Indeed I do."

"Well, it was he, the Duke. And a few days later he sent me a message asking if you were free of the plague and, if so, could I meet him when I next walked in the gardens. To be blunt, ma Reine, we loved one another straight away and he took possession of me shortly afterwards."

"How shortly?" Yolande had asked, still laughing as she wept.

"An hour," Alison had answered matter-of-factly.

"Who am I to stand in your way?" the Duchess had replied, drying her eyes. "But if you stay you must promise to care for Jehanne and look after my other interests at the court."

"I swear it," Alison had replied in her usual solemn and dramatic manner.

"How neat," Yolande had thought looking at the girl's contented face. "Jehanne needed a guardian, Alison longed for a wealthy man, and Duke Charles was desperate for some beauty in his life. Now, in one stroke, all three are catered for." Fate had indeed played its usual cunning game.

Yolande smiled a little quizzically, guessing that in her litter Alison, who was returning home to take her leave of family and friends, was weeping over the temporary separation from the big handsome lazy nobleman who had fallen in love with her.

"Poor Duke Charles," thought Yolande, "or should I say lucky Duke Charles?"

For the head of the house of Lorraine had the misfortune to be married to Queen Isabeau's cousin, Marguerite of Bavaria, a woman who seemed in permanent contest with the Queen over which one of them could get fatter. And now he had the lovely Alison for his mistress and nothing would ever be as bad again.

"Happy ending," thought Yolande to herself, then added bitterly, "for some of us at least."

The royal travelers had parted with half their armed escort over an hour before, safely on home territory, needing an advance party to warn the inhabitants of the castle that the Regent would be arriving imminently. And now as they swept away from the Loire the remaining horsemen caught their first glimpse of the river Maine and a sudden distant view of the fortress standing proudly on the left bank. Simultaneously they put up a cheer and hearing them Yolande opened the curtains of her litter and looked out, her heartbeat suddenly racing as she saw again the castle of Angers.

And then she noticed something which made her draw breath. Even at this considerable distance the Regent could see that a pennant flew from the flagpole, flipping and flailing in the snow-filled February wind. Yolande went pale at the full realization of what that lively flag signified, for it was the sure sign that the Duke of Anjou was in residence and within the walls of the fortress awaited her arrival.

It seemed odd to Charles at first that his governess should have fallen asleep so deeply and so very conveniently too. Immediately after their supper of cakes and ale, just the two of them as Catherine had gone to visit the daughter of one of the Queen's ladies, a girl only a year older than herself, Lady du Mesnil had sat down in her favorite chair, closed her eyes—and that had been that. In what had seemed less than a minute she had been so soundly asleep that even though Charles had shaken her by the shoulder, fearing she might be ill, she had done nothing but snore more loudly.

The boy had decided then, a little more cunning as he was these days, that something had been slipped into her wine—only he had drunk the ale—and, indeed, when he had poured some into a bowl and his hound had lapped it up, it, too, had fallen insensible.

So this Flamel was obviously someone to be reckoned with, a man commanding a considerable sphere of influence, for only one of the servants could have drugged the governess's wine. With a feeling of tremendous apprehension, Charles went down to the receiving hall to await Jeanne Chamoisy's arrival.

It was dusk when she came, admitted by the porter, and

Charles saw that the nurse was carrying a fur-lined mantle and hood.

"These are for you, Monsieur," Jeanne said briskly. "Put them on. It is going to be very cold later."

Charles stayed where he was, small hands in fists. "What have you done to Lady du Mesnil?" he asked accusingly.

"What do you mean? What is wrong with her?"

"She has been drugged. I can't wake her up."

"It is better that she sleeps deeply," Jeanne answered soothingly.

"That's all very well, sleep is one thing, drugging is another."

The nurse gave Charles a penetrating look. "You are growing up, Monsieur. I think the Grand Master did right to send for you now."

The boy's brows rose making him look so funny that it was all Jeanne could do to restrain herself from laughing.

"Grand Master? Are you speaking of Nicolas Flamel, Madame?"

"I am, Monsieur Charles. You are about to meet one of the most important men in the world."

"But what is he Grand Master of? Who is this man, Jeanne? I must know."

"Monsieur Flamel is an alchemist and philosopher, a wise man and a benefactor. More than that I am not allowed to say."

"Then I shall ask him for myself," Charles answered determinedly, and with that took Jeanne's hand and allowed her to put on his warm clothing before they left the Hôtel and went on foot through the trellised rose garden, glistening with frost on such a bitter night, then threaded their way amongst the trees of the orchard that grew close to the palace's walls, finally coming to a halt at a tower which had a gatehouse perched on top of it. Now Charles understood Jeanne's concern about the cold: they were journeying to Nicolas Flamel by way of the dark and icy river.

A rowing boat was already lying to at the bottom of the three curving steps which led down to the water's edge, and as they stepped aboard Charles thought, almost absently, that it was strange they had not been challenged by the porter. But then this was obviously to be a night of surprises as their oarsman, huddled against the wind and concealed by his layers of clothing, struck out boldly for the Left Bank.

Charles made a wager with himself that the mysterious Grand Master lived somewhere near the University, deep in the heart of the Latin Quarter. Yet the house, when the boy finally came to it, was something of a shock. Grand Master or no, Charles had imagined that Nicolas Flamel would reside in some mean half-timbered place set in a dingy alley. But though he had been right about its proximity to the University, this house was large, with a sweeping courtyard in which a fountain played. Even in the flickering light of the torches that lit the entrance, Charles could see that this was the home of a very wealthy man indeed.

The interior, too, confirmed this fact. Beautiful tapestries hung on the walls, wooden carvings embellished the hall, while the huge fireplace displayed a moulded overmantel of dancing figures, both male and female. Charles stole a quick look at Jeanne's face and knew by her manner that she had been to this place before, that none of its grandeur was a surprise to her. But he was not prepared for her reaction when a man suddenly appeared at the top of the flight of stone stairs.

"I pay you homage," said Jeanne and made a reverence that would have been fitting for a man of the cloth.

Charles stared in amazement as the alchemist came to half-way down the stairs. He had expected someone old, white haired, but this creature was ageless, spare and sinewy, the bones of the face distinct, the eyes that looked out of it so bright they seemed almost colorless.

"Monsieur le Comte?" said the man, bowing slightly.

"Yes. Monsieur Flamel?"

"I am. Do me the honor, Monsieur, if you will, of accompanying me to my library," and with that the Grand Master held out his hand.

To say that Charles was drawn against his will would not have been quite the case yet at that moment the boy knew as he slowly ascended that he could not have refused even had he wanted to. Tilting his head back, Charles stared directly into those colorless eyes and saw there not only wisdom but great shrewdness.

"So you have decided to trust me?"

And the alchemist smiled, all the lines on his face suddenly etched in, confirming that he had indeed reached a considerable age.

"I think so," Charles answered cautiously and Flamel laughed, a curious rich sound that had a love of life in its depths.

Together they mounted the rest of the stairs and walked the length of a stone-flagged passageway into the room that lay at the end. Here a great fire glowed in the hearth, throwing its crimson light on the thousands of books that lined the walls, playing over the jars, bottles and retorts that stood on a table at the far end.

"Will you sit, Monsieur?" said Flamel and indicated one of the two chairs which stood on either side of the fireplace. "May I offer you some wine?"

Charles was tempted to ask if it was drugged but thought it too impolite, instead nodding silently and watching as the alchemist poured a dark red liquid into two silver cups. Slightly relieved that Flamel had taken some from the same jug, Charles sipped, relishing the pleasant taste.

"Do not be afraid," the alchemist said softly. "There is nothing in there to hurt you. I apologize for sending your governess to sleep but I assure you she will wake refreshed and well."

"Thank you," answered Charles solemnly.

"And now you will want to know, and rightly, who I am and why I have asked you here."

"Yes."

"I will begin if I may by telling you something of my past life . . ."

Charles nodded, attempting to look both wise and sensible.

"I am a Parisian, born in the city and proud of it. Educated here too, and starting my career in the Latin Quarter as a scribe, writing letters and documents for those who had not that skill. As you might well imagine, Monsieur, many interesting papers passed through my hands and through them I began to acquire knowledge of many different and fascinating things. And then one day I came across something which changed my entire life."

"What was it?" Charles found that he was listening intently.

"A book came into my possession with a strange and intriguing name." Flamel paused and took a mouthful of wine, and Charles noticed the gleaming eyes observing him closely. "It was called *The Sacred Book of Abraham the Jew, Prince, Priest, Levite, Astrologer and Philosopher to that Tribe of Jews who by the Wrath of God were Dispersed amongst the Gauls.*"

"Well, I think that is a terrible title if I may say so," Charles answered truthfully.

Flamel laughed his rich laugh. "It was terrible in every sense. I pored over that book for twenty-one years without being able to understand its meaning and then, one day, I met a Christian Jew in León and he told me the key to its mystery." The man's face changed, his features seeming to melt and reform into those of another even while Charles watched in profound amazement.

"I returned to Paris and put into practice all that I had learned and as a result achieved my first successful alchemical transmogrification."

"What do you mean?"

"I changed one substance into another."

Charles's mouth fell open. "Not lead to gold?"

Flamel's face flickered. "That is a question I cannot answer. Let me just say that the discovery enabled me to become a philanthropist, endowing hospitals and churches and giving alms to the poor."

"And is all this linked with your being a Grand Master?"

"In a way, yes. A great lady, a princess of Navarre who was also an alchemist, became my patron. She was the Grand Master of a secret order. When she died she passed that honor to me."

"And what is this order called?"

"You shall be told the name when you are a man. You will shortly meet the one who is to tell you and recognize him by the fact that his little finger is almost the same length as his fourth."

"Oh!" said Charles. "And how will *he* know the name?"

"Because it is already decreed that he will be the new Grand Master when I die."

The boy stared in astonishment. "Did you bring me here to tell all this?"

"No, there is more."

Flamel rose and, going to a large carved wooden desk, unlocked a drawer and took out a sheaf of papers, striking them with his fingers as he returned to his seat.

"These documents contain the story of your life, Monsieur. I have drafted them from the time of your birth. They contain what is called your zodiacal chart."

"I see."

"In them the path of your destiny is clearly shown. But I must warn you that we are all masters of our fate. Though greatness lies waiting for you it is up to you to follow its path."

The boy simply stared, unable to think of a word to say.

"You were born under the sign of the two Great Fishes and as a result will develop a complex character, secretive, elusive, and difficult to truly know. But these characteristics will be of enormous advantage to you in the difficult years that lie ahead. For the truth is, Monsieur le Comte, that if you follow the course which fate intends, it is you who have been chosen to become the future King of France."

Charles felt a shiver seize his spine and his eyes filled with tears of fear. "But how could such a thing come about? I have two brothers both older than I."

A faint frown crossed Flamel's misty features. "It would not be right that I reveal the answer to you. You are still too young to know. But hear this part well, Charles, I beg of you. You must fight to keep your birthright, you must claw your way tooth and nail to see this civil war over, and you must not stop until the English are driven from our soil. It is God's will that you do this because it is foretold that you, Charles the Victorious, will lead France out of decay to its rebirth."

The boy sobbed, trembling, overwhelmed by what he was hearing.

Flamel's voice rose. "*You* are the chosen one and you must fulfill your destiny."

"But I am small and ugly and nobody listens to me," Charles answered in awful terror.

"You will be helped, by many different people in fact. But there are three particular women more important than the rest. It will be up to you to accept what they can help you achieve."

"Who are they?"

"One is a tall queen, another virgin bringing a rose, and the third will be beauty to your beast."

Flamel's face began to change again and the boy saw the features of the alchemist reappearing. "I am tiring. The message is over. I shall be leaving Paris soon to escape the bloodshed. Charles, stay true . . ."

His voice died away and the Grand Master's eyes closed. "Monsieur Flamel?" said Charles anxiously. "Monsieur Flamel, please! There is much more I need to ask you."

But it was no use, the alchemist's clairvoyance was at an end and Charles found that he was simply looking at an old man asleep in a chair by the fire.

With a great sigh he got to his feet and stealthily went to pick up the papers which had fallen from Flamel's hand to the floor and now lay open on one particular page.

"Within Charles, whose destiny it is to bring about the birth of a new France, lie many men, each one a secret and extraordinary character. This child born on 22nd February 1403, may yet resist the greatness which could be his but, whatever the outcome, he is fated to die on—"

It was enough! The boy dropped the papers as if they had burnt his hands and rushed from the room and down the stairs, longing to be once more enfolded in the comfortable and loving arms of his nurse.

Even down by the Country Gate a handful of people had gathered in the cold to wave as the Duchess went into her castle, and as her litter swept beneath the arched entrance and through to Nobles' Court there was cheering. Yolande smiled and waved her hand, her closed face revealing nothing of her mental agony. Six weeks earlier she had given birth to another man's child and now she must face her husband.

"God help me," prayed the Duchess as the horses came to a stop.

He was there, standing on the steps of the King's Lodging, thinner than she remembered and somehow weathered, as if he had slept outside in conditions when a man should, by rights, be warm and comfortable.

"Ma chérie," he said, and the full mouth that could so easily betray his emotions smiled with pure joy.

"Oh, Louis, Louis," answered Yolande, and it was strangely comforting to feel him take her and then draw her close, not caring that they were in full view of the court. "I've missed you," she said, and it was true.

The Duke held her at arm's length again. "Let me look at you, just let me look."

Yolande braced herself, tilting her head and smiling, hoping that the evil of guilt was not written all over her face.

"You're pale," Louis said at last. "Was the journey bad?"

"Very," she answered, "but nothing compared to what you have had to endure. Oh, my dear, let's go inside out of the cold."

She had forgotten how reassuring he was, how warm and how kind. As she linked her arm through his, Yolande felt at peace for the first time in almost a year.

"All is prepared within," her husband was saying. "We shall sup alone, in our quarters, with only the musicians for company. Would you like that?"

Her heart sank at the thought, knowing what would follow in the bed-chamber afterwards, but Yolande smiled again and said, "I could think of nothing nicer to welcome me home."

"I've missed you desperately," Louis added in a lower voice. "It was a hard and bitter campaign—and a lonely one."

"But successful?"

He smiled. "Our territories are regained."

"So you are back for good?"

The Duke frowned. "No, I must return later this year to settle certain matters."

In a rush of emotion that she could not control, Yolande said, "Don't go away again, Louis. Don't leave me, please. I couldn't bear another time like this last."

He stared at her, astonished. "But everyone has been telling me how brilliantly you acted as Regent. Why, I almost felt my presence was no longer necessary. De Beauvau assured me that you handled the Council with the composure of a man."

Yolande pulled a face. "What a terrible compliment. I handled them like a woman let me hasten to assure you."

His big mouth widened. "Pardon me, Madame. I retract. Women are, of course, superior in absolutely everything. We men have only one useful function." And the Duke winked.

For no real reason other than the sheer relief of being with him, who was father and brother and friend all in one, Yolande laughed delightedly.

"That's better, my Lord. I'm glad to see that you have not lost your sense of proportion."

Louis pulled her hard against him. "Don't tease me too much or I will have to pay back your sharp tongue even before we've had our evening repast."

She shrank away, dreading what must inevitably take place between them, only wishing her poor tired body could be given time to recover properly from Jehanne's birth. Sensitive as he was to her after all their years together, the Duke sensed immediately that something was wrong.

"I wasn't serious, chérie. I can wait. After all, I've done without for almost two years."

The Duchess looked up at him. "No camp followers?"

"None. I was too tired anyway."

She waited for him to say, "And you?" but he didn't, simply escorting her inside and helping personally to remove her traveling cloak.

"It's good to be back," he said. "But I was sad when you weren't here to greet me. Didn't you get my letter telling you when I would be returning?"

"No, I must have already left for Lorraine."

The Duke looked at her, his pale blue eyes expressionless. "It was a long visit."

Inwardly Yolande cringed, wondering if he was hinting at something, but Louis merely added, "I hope it was worth it."

The Duchess took his hand between hers. "It was. René is set for a brilliant future there."

"And you and I, Yolande; have we a brilliant future too?"

"Of course, my darling," she answered, and this time forced herself not to flinch as his arms went around her.

Nine

It had always been the tradition at Isabeau's court that on the morning of May Day she and her courtiers, all dressed in green, would rise early and go to the woods to collect blossom, wash their faces in dew from the hawthorn tree, then feast and make merry until early afternoon when they would return to the palace and rest before the evening's May ball.

With uncaring resolve the Queen had insisted on this ritual being carried out in the face of war, pestilence and plague, determined that whatever the state of the country she would continue to sport in the woods with her friends.

"For, after all, outdoor lovemaking begins on May Day," she would say carelessly, shrugging a fat white shoulder. "Only a fool would miss that."

Every year this remark met with polite applause and laughter, particularly if Isabeau winked at a desirable gentleman as she said it. But this year, fluttering her lid at the Duke of Burgundy, the Queen was seen to bridle as he merely grunted by way of reply. The suspicion that he might be tiring of blubber and depravity crossed everyone's mind but they pushed such pessimistic thoughts away. Yet who could blame him if his mind was elsewhere?

Jean the Fearless had now ruled Paris for almost two years and the stirring of unrest from the ordinary citizens against his regime was daily becoming a more serious problem. Determined to get rid of the English but still needing a strong force to keep the Parisians beneath his domination, the Duke had armed the butchers under their leader Simon Caboche. At the same time as this, the University had decided on measures to reform morality, their more violent representatives, together with the butchers, the tripe sellers, the tanners, and all the other unsavory people who liked to think of themselves as vigilantes against sin, patrolling the streets nightly, setting about anyone who crossed their path.

A few weeks earlier the Caboche, as the murderous gang was known, had burst into the Hôtel St. Pol in the dead of the night, interrupting a grand ball given by the Dauphin, dispersing the dancers and sending the furious youth off to bed. Fortunately for Isabeau she had not been present, busy about her own affairs at the Hôtel Barbette, as she was one of the people specifically named by the University as needing to mend her ways.

And now it would seem that the consensus of opinion amongst her courtiers was that a May morn expedition to the woods might be dangerous, that the Caboche might strike by day, accuse them of immorality, and send them home humiliated—or worse!

"I'll simply go with a few loyal hearts in that case," Isabeau stormed furiously.

In the event, the morning being a fine one, a party of about twenty left through the city gates, their servants following behind bearing the food and wine that would make up the midday repast. In a swiftly moving cavalcade, the men mounted on their finest horses, the women on long-limbed palfreys, the Queen in a litter pulled by two mighty beasts, they went rapidly out of Paris to the pastures and meadows beyond. Here, sparkling streams gurgled, cutting through the landscape like silver threads, the dark emerald of the forest barely throwing a shadow at this hour, the carpet of wild flowers beneath the horses' feet a shining mixture of bluebells and periwinkles.

All clothed in green, the laughing courtiers sped through the dew-drenched dawn, bending low to avoid branches, the bells on the falcons that some of them carried—though this was far from a hunting party—jingling a brave accompaniment, the sound of a lark adding a melody, the whole sky-blue morning full of merriment and sound, the clack from the sails of a distant windmill a faint reminder that the less privileged were at work.

There was blossom everywhere, in the hedges, the fields, the orchards, and, seeing it, the courtiers hacked at the blooms, winding them round their necks and waists, bedecking their hats and hoods. This year of 1413 the petals

seemed whiter, more pure, than ever, almost as if nature
were fighting back against the blood and filth that spattered
the streets of Paris and choked the countryside half to
death.

But none of this laughing crowd saw that, indeed would
have looked blank if one of their number had pointed it
out, too intent on tearing the garlands down to enhance
their own appearances, Isabeau draping a great streamer
round a young man's neck, then pulling him playfully into
the trees and out of sight.

"This early?" whispered one of the grooms, nudging
another.

"Time means nothing to that great whore," answered his
companion. "And while she copulates, Paris is brought to
ruin."

"Something must be done," said the first man. "We cannot go on like this."

"Something will be done," murmured the other. "Revo-
lution is but a stone's throw away."

"Thank God."

Their words were drowned by a medley of sound as
every courtier that carried a musical instrument suddenly
began to play, serenading the Queen while she made love
out of doors. The birds flew off in fright at the noise, the
wild creatures hid themselves away. Once again, Queen
Venus had brought everything down to her own unspeakable level as she gasped and jerked in the forest with yet
another decadent young man.

On that same bright morning, just as the sun broke over
the river Maine, Yolande d'Anjou left the castle of Angers
and rode out alone toward the blossom-filled orchards that
lay on the right bank, just beyond the Doutre. Though it
was not yet fully light, the Duchess crossed the river at a
steady trot, over the Great Bridge which joined together
the merchant streets of Baudrière on the left bank and
Beaurepaire on the right, and was itself lined with shops,
though none of them open at this early hour. But though
she rode quickly, Yolande did not push herself too hard,
for she had only been riding again less than a month.

Her wish that her body could rest completely after the
delivery of Jehanne had been most bitterly refused by fate.
In that vulnerable time after a birth when it is so easy for

a woman to conceive again, she had done so. The ardor of a love-starved Duke Louis, just as Yolande had secretly dreaded, had resulted in another pregnancy and a baby girl had been born to them in December, eleven months after Jehanne had come into the world.

The pregnancy had nearly killed her and the Duchess could only thank God that she was naturally strong and resilient otherwise, she felt certain, the two travails so close together could have ended her life. As it was she had been far from well and the King-Duke had remained in Angers until after the birth of his child before considering it safe to return to his kingdoms of Sicily and Naples.

They had called the infant Yolande for its mother and the Duchess had fiercely dispensed with a wet nurse for the first three months, hoping that the pain of having to part with Jehanne might in some way be alleviated by nursing another. And, strangely, it had. Yolande had looked down at the contented baby feeding peacefully, and felt happier than she had for months.

So now there were five children in the castle—Louis, Marie, René, baby Yolande and Katherine of Burgundy, Jean the Fearless's daughter, still betrothed to young Louis despite the war. Secretly, Yolande was growing ever more uneasy about the girl, not really wanting to link the house of Anjou with the Burgundian cause, and casting around for any excuse to break the betrothal. But final decisions on this score had to be made by the Duke of Anjou himself and she could do nothing until Louis's return.

With a bright clattering of hooves Yolande's elegant mare left the bridge and turned toward the western heights overlooking the valley of the Brionneau, where lay the abbey of St. Nicolas. Here were housed the two other young people for whom she was responsible, Guy the hunchback and his twin brother Jacques, still at the abbey school and shortly to celebrate their fifteenth birthday.

With a swish of her long skirt in the grass of the meadow, Yolande entered the fields worked by the monks and called a greeting to the brothers already toiling. They smiled and waved back, always pleased to see the Regent, the Queen-Duchess who so wisely ruled her province in her husband's absence. In the abbey enclave, too, Yolande was warmly met as, indeed, she was by the Abbot, coming out of his lodging and standing on the steps to welcome her personally.

"You ride alone, ma Reine?"

"Yes, Abbot Dominique."

"Then one of the brothers will see to your horse. Pray come in."

The Abbot's parlor was still cool, the first trickles of sunshine coming through the open window splashing gold onto the stone-flagged floor. The smell of flowers filled the air and Dominique's face, sitting as he was with his back to the light, was full of dark hollows and gleaming planes.

"Not a handsome man," thought Yolande as she took a seat on the other side of his desk, "but curiously attractive with all those slanting facial bones."

"You wanted to see me, my Lord?" she said.

"Indeed I do, Madame, though I had not expected quite such an early visit."

"I have combined it with the task of collecting blossom for my lodgings."

"Ah yes, the first of May." The Abbot smiled away the pagan custom. "And no doubt you would like to visit Guy and Jacques before their lessons begin."

"I would, Father. And I presume that it is about the twins you wish to see me."

"Indeed yes." His dark profile gleamed in the sun's rays. "Jacques has recently told me he wishes to enter the cloister, that he has come to this belief of his own free will and believes he is now old enough to make such a choice."

"I see." Yolande raised a wing of eyebrow. "And what of you, my Lord? Do you think he is ready?"

The shadows in the Abbot's face shifted as he moved his head, silently considering the Regent's views on child oblates, in the past expressed forcibly to both himself and the Abbess of Ronceray.

"What I believe is beside the point, Madame. You are the boy's guardian and the decision rests finally with you."

Yolande leaned forward, her face earnest. "I have told you before, my Lord, that I believe it wrong to put a young child into the cloister before it knows anything of the world. I think that step should not be taken until the person concerned, be they boy or girl, is at least eighteen years of age."

"Not even to become a novice?"

"Not even that."

"But Jacques is not quite fifteen, yet still he longs to join our order. He says he has a vocation to do so."

"A vocation?" Yolande's mobile eyebrow rose again. "I shall have to speak to him." She changed the subject deliberately to the other boy. "And what of Guy, how is he faring? Does he also wish to enter the cloister?"

Abbot Dominique gave a delightfully small shrug. "Very far from it I fear. Frankly, ma Reine, the child is not cut out for either monastic or academic life. Guy sings divinely, still practices juggling, tumbles too, even with his crooked back. So I fear his ambition is very far removed from the pursuit of a religious life."

Yolande smiled more broadly than she had intended. "What can it be? A jester?"

"No, the study of the stars, Madame. Somewhere in his past the child was once given shelter by an astrologer, a magic man he called him. Now Guy is convinced this is his calling. Strange, is it not, that one brother has turned to God, the other to sorcery?"

"But surely," Yolande answered gently, "they are both in their different ways a quest for truth, for greater understanding of the hidden meaning of life."

Dominique shook his head ruefully. "With that I cannot agree, ma Reine. God is truth, there is no other."

Yolande nodded, saying nothing, knowing the moment when her liberal views might give offense.

"May I see the boys, my Lord?"

The Abbot rose to his feet. "They are probably preparing for their first lesson. Would you like them sent to you here?"

Yolande stood up also. "No, Father, I would prefer to walk with them in the grounds if that is agreeable to you. It is too fine a morning to be indoors."

"Indeed," answered Dominique, his face glowing as it caught the full sunlight. "I shall instruct the twins to meet you in the rose garden. The flowers are already in bloom and it is very pleasant to stroll there."

He made a solemn reverence, which Yolande returned, and went on his way leaving the Duchess to turn out of the great courtyard and walk down between the high hedges to where the flower-beds bloomed beyond the kitchen and herb gardens. Making her way to the stone seat set amongst the rose beds, Yolande sat down and closed her eyes in the sunshine.

She must have dozed momentarily for the next thing she knew was that a flower had been put into one of her hands and the twins, grinning cheerfully, were standing in front of her.

"Happy May Morn to you both," said the Duchess. "Do I find you well?"

"Yes, Madame," they chorused, and bowed formally.

"Come, sit beside me. Father Abbot wishes me to talk to you about your futures and I would like to do so as well."

She patted the spaces on either side of her and the twins sat, both looking at her expectantly. They had somehow contrived, even though they were identical, to grow less alike since she had seen them last. With a shock, Yolande realized that this must have been almost a year ago, kept indoors and forced to rest as she had been by her last exhausting pregnancy.

The beauty which had lain hidden beneath their layers of grime was now obvious, each boy being seen to have thick curling hair the color of cedar, streaked by the sun in places to a paler shade resembling oats. Their eyes were extraordinary, both a fierce piercing blue with an aureole of emerald green around the pupils. But there the similarity ended, for Jacques had grown straight and tall and slender, while little Guy, with his hunched back, had a round face and body that could never be anything but slightly comic.

"So," said Yolande, "you are soon to be fifteen."

"We believe that," answered Jacques, who these days was obviously very much in the lead. "The mountebank told us he found us in May and we were newborn then."

"Then you are still very young. Yet Father Abbot tells me you wish to enter the order, to become a Benedictine."

"Oh, yes," Jacques replied instantly. "I do. You see, I have had a sign."

"A sign?" Yolande drew her dark brows downward.

Jacques's brilliant eyes consumed her face. "A very simple sign, Madame. I was in the chapel, dusting it actually, and I heard a voice."

"Whose?"

"That I don't know. It simply told me that for the sake of France I must enter the abbey of St. Nicolas and one day in the future when Father Abbot is dead I will take his place."

"You saw nothing?"

"Only a brightness; the whole place was suddenly light as if the sun had burst forth. And the voice told me that when I was Abbot I would be called upon to help La Pucelle and must prepare."

"The virgin?" repeated the Duchess, frowning. "Surely you do not mean Christ's mother?"

"No, I don't think so because Mary is known to be the one who helps us, not the other way around."

"The voice meant somebody else," said Guy suddenly. "Somebody who is yet to come."

The Duchess turned to him with a smile. "And how do you know that?"

"I believe I have the gift of prediction, Madame, which is why I want to study the stars, to develop that art."

Yolande leaned back against the seat's hard stone. "Well, well, I don't know what to make of you two. I thought you would have pleasant uncomplicated lives when your time at the abbey was over and here you are throwing all my ideas awry."

"Let me leave the school now, ma Reine," Guy added urgently. "Let me live in the castle with you and study under Dr. Flavigny."

"But ..."

"Oh, please, Madame. I know he is old and was astrologer to your father-in-law before he became that of your husband, but why can't he be allowed to pass his knowledge on to me, who is so very willing to learn?"

Put in those terms the whole scheme sounded eminently sensible but still Yolande hesitated, feeling beholden, as adults frequently do when a child presents a good idea, to object.

"But I thought you wanted to be a singer and would eventually be attached to my household in that capacity," she said.

"Do you have something against astrologers?" asked Guy directly.

"I can't say that I have any particular belief in them."

"But in that you are singular, Madame. There are many others that do. And why could I not both sing and study the stars? I would have thought my chances of a place in

a noble household would have been doubled with those
two skills."

There was no arguing with the logic of this and the Duchess realized she had been put in a position of refusing the
boy's pleas for no better reason than that she did not altogether approve of them.

"Well . . ."

"Please, ma Reine. I promise I will study diligently and
you will be proud of me."

"And if you will let me enter the novitiate now," added
Jacques, "I can start getting ready straight away for the
coming of La Pucelle."

The Duchess frowned into her lap, not daring to meet
those two pairs of vivid eyes staring at her so imploringly.

"I will compromise," she said eventually. "Knowing how
changeable young people's minds are I will give you one
year to this day to see if you are still determined on these
courses. If you are I will grant my permission for you to
follow your chosen paths and on the day you celebrate your
sixteenth birthday your new lives will begin."

The twins simultaneously opened their mouths to object
and equally simultaneously closed them again. The Regent
of Anjou had given her ruling, to argue would be both
pointless and foolish. Moving at the same moment, the boys
stood up, considering the audience to be at an end.

"Thank you, Majesty," said Jacques, and kissed Yolande's long thin hand.

"Thank you," repeated Guy and, rolling himself into a
ball, turned joyous somersaults at her feet.

Outside the Hôtel St. Pol the people of Paris had gathered
in their thousands and wherever the courtiers scurried to
escape the sound, the cry of "Death to the foreign woman.
Death to the great whore," could still be heard. The downtrodden populace had risen at last, sickened by the brutality
of the Caboche, rebelling against Burgundian domination,
wanting their city back and the laughing-stock of a Queen,
the gigantic Bavarian, gone for good.

Crouching in her high chair, her face flushed and anxious,
Isabeau thought that perhaps she had made a mistake in
celebrating the recent May Day in her usual way. Talk of
her lewd behavior with yet another foppish young man had
somehow got back to the citizens and two days later they

had stormed the Bastille and released the prisoners, then come on to the palace, where they had burst into the Dauphin's apartments screaming that he must take over from his mad father and send both the Queen and the Duke of Burgundy away. Burgundian soldiers had quelled the riot on that occasion but now, two weeks later, to judge by the sound from the streets, the entire population had turned out and by sheer weight of numbers could prove unstoppable.

The Dauphin's apartments were tonight heavily guarded with extra troops and Isabeau, for her own safety, had been advised to leave the Hôtel Barbette and stay close to her family. Only the King remained oblivious of the threatened rebellion, lying in his apartments, shrieking to the walls that he was made of glass and no one should touch him lest he splinter.

To make matters more embarrassing and tense there was an official visitor to the court from the house of Anjou. The Duke's chancellor, Robert le Maçon, had arrived to further the arrangements for the betrothal of Charles to his master's daughter, Marie. And now he stood with everyone else listening to the highly vocal mob outside hurl insults at the Queen.

"Mon Dieu!" Isabeau felt desperate, furious that a new man on the scene should be hearing ill of her. "What lies! But then this rabble have crawled out of the gutter to come here. They do not truly represent the people of Paris."

Le Maçon looked up, his light brown eyes expressionless. "Wherever they have crawled from there seem to be a great many of them, Madame."

"Professional trouble-makers," she answered. "They want to overthrow law and order. They are anarchists every one."

The Chancellor nodded. "They certainly want to overthrow something. Listen to them now."

"Whore," came the distant cry. "Whore, whore, whore!"

"Such filthy language!" Isabeau pulled what she hoped was a disapproving face. "I am ashamed that my children are forced to hear it."

"But there is no other room we can take them to, ma Reine," put in Jeanne du Mesnil. "This is the safest place with all the extra guards on duty. And nowhere in the palace is out of earshot, believe me."

"It's disgusting," Isabeau went on, ignoring her. "The people of France sicken me sometimes."

"But you *are* their Queen," remarked Louis the Dauphin, grinning insolently.

He had reached that stage of drunkenness where reality had begun to elude him and was refusing to take the riot seriously, though his wife Marguerite, the Duke of Burgundy's daughter, made up for his lack of interest by screaming hysterically, partly because her father, very wisely, had taken himself off to an unknown destination, partly because she was utterly terror stricken.

"Shut up!" said her husband unsympathetically.

"But we might all be killed."

"Well at least if I'm dead I won't have to listen to you any more."

"Heartless wretch!" boomed Jacqueline of Bavaria unexpectedly, her large plain face red as a strawberry with rage. "You should not be so spiteful to her." She glared at the Dauphin and then added, "Monsieur," which ruined the effect.

"Mind your manners you ugly-faced bladder," he shouted in reply, at which Marguerite bellowed all the louder and the Duke of Touraine, Jacqueline's husband, not as drunk as his brother but well on the way, burst into a fit of hysterical giggling.

It was chaos, only the two youngest children behaving with any show of decorum while the rest screamed at one another and Isabeau, visibly sweating, kept repeating the words, "Oh, what will become of me? What will become of me?"

In the midst of this ridiculous scene Robert le Maçon suddenly lost his temper, bellowing, "Stop squabbling, the lot of you, do you hear?"

Everyone stared at him and in the silence that followed, the sound of the great wooden doors of the Dauphin's Lodging splintering apart fell like a stone.

"They've stormed the walls again," shrieked Isabeau. "Oh, God protect us, they're coming in."

And indeed the terrible noise of hand-to-hand fighting could be heard from the great hall as the Dauphin's guard struggled to keep the furious mob away from the upstairs chamber.

"Listen," said le Maçon urgently, addressing the drunken boy who stood swaying, obviously not in command of him-

self. "They're going to come in. There are hundreds of
them, your men haven't got a chance. Whatever you do,
agree to their terms, do you understand? Otherwise we
could all end up dead."

"Do what he says," Isabeau added hysterically. "They're
after my blood."

Somebody, somewhere, said, "They'll have a terrible
time finding it," and le Maçon quite literally did not know
whether to laugh or cry at the sheer outrageousness of such
a remark in these appalling circumstances. Beside him the
boy Charles stifled a giggle and the Chancellor stared at
him with suspicion.

"Keep quiet, for the love of God," he muttered, but the
child merely gave him an innocent smile as if he had no
idea what in the world was going on. Le Maçon, however,
remained uncertain and continued to gaze at him until the
sudden pounding of running feet on the stone stairs leading
from the hall wrenched his attention back to the current
and highly dangerous situation.

A terrible scream from someone standing right outside
rent the air, this awful sound followed by that of men close
by dying at the hands of others, the background to this the
dull thud of bodies falling to the floor.

"Prepare yourselves," hissed le Maçon. "Let none of you
make a move." And with that the wooden doors of the Dauphin's receiving room flew open to reveal a hefty raw-boned
fellow with a red face and enormous hands standing in the
entrance. "There they are, the fat whore and her bastard
brood. Let's kill the whole bunch of 'em," he bellowed.

In one move, le Maçon thrust the terrified Charles behind his back and stepped rapidly forward. "No," he
roared. "I command you in the name of Duke Louis of
Anjou to stay where you are."

"Coillons!" answered the other pithily. "Stand aside."

"By Christ I won't," answered le Maçon and, risking everything, stood directly in the revolutionary's path. "Now
listen to me," he hissed, "to touch one hair of their heads
is a crime the punishment for which is first torture, then
slow and agonizing death. And I vow that even if you were
to temporarily triumph by killing the Queen and her children, their cousin, Duke Louis, a prince of the Blood, remember, would march on Paris with his troops and put you
down like animals as soon as he heard the news."

"How could he?" answered the other, visibly shaken.

"Because the Duke has an army already with him in Italy, an army of Angevins who would rejoice to do his bidding if his family's blood were spilled."

The revolutionary's face suffused with rage. "So where does that leave us? What are we supposed to do? Bow the knee for ever to that whore's whelp Burgundy?"

"Burgundy must go, you are right in that," answered the Chancellor swiftly. "He is both usurper and tyrant."

"Fine words," the man said bitterly. "But they don't help us. All right, lads," he called over his shoulder, "take them prisoner."

"One moment more," pleaded le Maçon, his eyes molten in a face drained of color. "I swear on my solemn oath that if you will let these people go free I shall leave Paris at first light and go straight through France to Italy in search of my Lord of Anjou. And when I find him and tell him what has happened he will not fail you, I know it. He will drive Burgundy out of the land and set the people of Paris free."

The rebel leader glanced to his fellows crouching in the doorway like dogs ready to spring then wheeled round to look le Maçon in the eye once more. "That's for the future but there are two things the citizens insist upon immediately."

"What are they?"

"That that little sop," the man pointed at the Dauphin, "takes his duties as President of the Council seriously. All he can think about is whoremongering and drinking till he drops from excess. And second, the Queen's pretty boys go now and most of her ladies with them. It's time she learned to wipe her own arse."

"You're right," said the Dauphin suddenly, jumping up from where he had sat slumped in a chair. "She's a disgrace. And so am I. By God's precious blood you have taught me something tonight, good people."

The Chancellor looked at him sharply and saw that the boy had not only sobered up miraculously but for once was using his wits.

"Umm," answered the rebel leader, unconvinced. "Be that as it may, the undesirables leave Paris tonight. You'll be hard up for fornication, Madame."

Isabeau wobbled like a furious *blancmanger* but said nothing.

"And a good thing too," the Dauphin went on. "Now,

citizens, I beg you to go home, trusting that I will become a President worthy of you and will rule Paris wisely. Not only that; my Lord of Trèves will keep his word and go at once to seek Duke Louis's help."

"Let him swear it," rumbled someone from the doorway.

As if it had been prearranged, le Maçon raised a hand dramatically. "I swear upon my family honor with God as my judge and witness that I will do everything in my power to alleviate the sufferings of the people of Paris."

"So be it," answered the revolutionary leader. "But we'll take one of you with us just the same."

"So be it, indeed," answered the Dauphin. "Gentlemen, I am at your service. Would you like me for hostage or would you prefer to have my wife?"

He shot a malevolent look at Marguerite who burst into a further fit of weeping.

"She's Burgundy's daughter, isn't she?" called someone.

"Yes, she is."

"Then let her come. She can wait on us at table."

"Courage, chérie, courage," said the Dauphin and, patting her hand, tucked his wife's arm through his as he led her to the doorway.

"You cruel little pig," muttered le Maçon under his breath.

But it was Charles who called out, "You won't hurt her, will you? It's not her fault if her father is a beast."

Isabeau rose majestically from her high chair. "I will go. I will not risk the life of a young and innocent girl. Let *me* bargain with these men."

The rebels looked from one to the other. "Fancy a night with the big whore, lads?"

There was a general chorus of agreement and Robert le Maçon looked away, disgusted. No longer afraid, the Queen's eyes were glittering at the thought of what might befall her. Like Messalina of Ancient Rome, Isabeau was always willing to try a new experience.

"Go then," he muttered, deep in his throat.

"My brave Maman," added the Dauphin sweetly, and suddenly smiling, went to pour himself another drink.

It was only to be expected that no good could come from the promises of such a corrupt set of people. The single act that the Dauphin carried out was to barricade the Hôtel

St. Pol until it resembled a fortress under siege; while Isabeau, after a night of what she described as hard bargaining
with the rabble, could only complain of her health, swallowing yet another fortune in potable gold and ground emeralds in order to try and alleviate her symptoms. It was
the opinion of many in the know that she had contracted
the French pox from the common herd.

Only Robert le Maçon did as he had vowed and went
with few stops and little rest to seek out Duke Louis. But
in that he had been forestalled. As always when a state is
governed by extremes, the moderates make their voices
heard and deputations had been already sent to the royal
Princes—the Dukes of Berri, Alençon, Anjou and Orléans—begging them to rescue the people from the daily
bloodbath that life in Paris had now become.

Anarchy had taken over completely and nobody seemed
in charge any longer, day-to-day administration being in the
hands of the public executioner. Burgundy, fighting with his
back to the wall, authorized the Caboche to perpetuate
even greater atrocities and every day saw terrible deeds
savagely enacted on the people of Paris. The riff-raff had
snatched the law into their own hands.

This was the obvious moment for the Armagnacs to
swoop on the city and this time Count Bernard had the
strength of the royal Dukes behind him. On 23rd August,
the year being 1413, a combined force attacked, including
the army of Duke Louis who had traveled from Italy
through Provence, taking Paris completely by surprise.

It was all over by nightfall, the drastically outnumbered
Burgundians fleeing for their lives, the Duke included. But
yet Jean the Fearless had not lost his wits completely.
Going to the Hôtel St. Pol he had kidnapped his uncle, the
mad King, who had wet himself with fear, screaming that
he would shatter into a thousand pieces if the Duke so
much as laid a hand on him.

"I'm sorry, mon Roi," Burgundy had answered, swinging
his fist so hard into the King's face that there had actually
been a crunching sound. But this clever stratagem had not
lasted long. The victorious troops had gone in hot pursuit
and the lunatic, bellowing loudly, had been snatched back
again at Vincennes.

With the citizens set to clean up the streets and repair
the damage of battle, the Council of France, which included

the royal Princes, met with the Dauphin at its head to discuss the news that Jean the Fearless had fled to Flanders, part of Burgundy's enormous land holdings. Calls were made, then, for him to be banished from the land, no voice louder than that of Queen Isabeau. A fact noted with great irony by all those who heard it.

"She actually called him 'evil murderer'," wrote Duke Louis to Yolande. 'She who had so blatantly shared his bed. But other than her sickening hypocrisy all is well in Paris and I beg you to join me here as soon as you can.

"I have written formally to the Duchess of Burgundy breaking the betrothal between her daughter Katherine and young Louis. Please could you see to it that the girl is escorted back home as soon as possible. I no longer wish the house of Anjou to be associated with the Burgundians in any way whatsoever, and the quicker she is gone the happier I shall be.

"By the way, amongst the Armagnac forces occupying the city is the young Earl de Richemont whom I am sure you will remember with affection from bygone times. I played chess with him the other night and he asked particularly to be remembered to you. He said I taught him chess but that you taught him end game, whatever that might mean.

"Come soon, my darling, I miss you. Ever your loyal friend and husband, Louis."

He had added a postscript. "The Queen has arranged for the betrothal of Marie to the Count of Ponthieu to take place in December so please get here in good time for that."

Yolande had read the letter twice then thrown it on the fire. There had been no word of Richemont for over two years—and now this cutting slight! As vividly as if it had been yesterday she remembered the night of love they had spent together and the child that had been born as a result.

"If only you knew," the Duchess said aloud. "If only you knew what I have had to endure."

Then again came the nagging feeling that soon she must visit the Duke of Lorraine, at whose court Alison du May was these days happily enjoying the role of favored mistress, and make such a journey the excuse to see Jehanne once more.

Ten

It was almost impossible to believe that four months earlier the streets of Paris had been running with blood and the Hôtel St. Pol virtually under siege. Now, from the walls that bordered onto the Seine as far as the Town Gate, the mad King's crazy palace was *en fête*, decorated with what greenery and flowers the winter gardens could yield up. Pennants bearing the fleur-de-lis fluttered from every corner, mingled amongst them little banners made of red silk split into many points, known as oriflammes, the royal standard of France. Woven into this great display were countless other flags emblazoned with the coat-of-arms of the house of Anjou, together with the personal insignia of both Duke Louis and the Duchess Yolande.

The light from a thousand candles gleamed in the silver plate that had been polished and brought out for this special occasion; the tapestries, the dust beaten mercilessly from them, shone with bright colors; the minstrels, in shifts, played horn, rebec, gittern and flute; the stone floors, swept, soaped and scrubbed, were spread with clean sweet rushes mingled amongst dried and scented rose petals. And all this splendor and celebration in honor of the fact that that very morning in the cathedral of Notre-Dame, Charles, Count of Ponthieu had become betrothed to Marie of Anjou.

Swamped in a large green brocade cotte embroidered in gold with the arms of his countdom, the red-faced boy, cringing with embarrassment, had reluctantly asked the two tall and splendid people whom he now knew to be the Duke and Duchess of Anjou, for consent to have their daughter's hand in marriage. And then, even worse, on receiving the royal couple's formal agreement and with the Archbishop and all the court looking on, had been forced to endure the misery of repeating the question to the girl herself.

"And all *she* has to do," the wretched child had thought enviously, "is put her hand in mine."

He had experienced a strange feeling at that moment, looking down at the small docile hand which he was going to have to hold for years and years to come, aware that it belonged to a total stranger. In a way it had been quite pretty, plump and childish, with dimples where one day knuckles would show, none the less the emotion of it all had been too much for him and Charles, to his chagrin, had started to weep, then had sobbed at full voice, abjectly aware of the spectacle he was making of himself but unable to do anything about it.

Gazing around through a shower of tears, Charles had seen his mother mouth the word "Imbecile," and this had made him bellow all the more. To make matters worse, if that were possible, the girl, looking thoroughly startled, seemed on the point of tears herself.

In desperation, the Count of Ponthieu had cast about for some form of help; none from the stern-faced Archbishop nor the uneasy courtiers, or from his two brothers who were in hysterics and not bothering to hide it, and certainly none from the King, who had been washed and brought out especially for the occasion and was now picking his nose with great interest.

It was at that moment that the boy, in extremis, had caught the bright green eye of his future mother-in-law and much to his astonishment seen the lid slowly lower then rise again. Utterly amazed and far from certain whether the Duchess of Anjou was winking at him or merely twitching, Charles stopped crying and simply stared.

Seizing the opportunity of a moment's respite, the Archbishop hurriedly cleared his throat, pronounced the couple affianced, and at that precise second, obviously guided by some hidden signal, the bells of the cathedral pealed wildly. It was done, Charles de Valois and Marie d'Anjou were betrothed, and amidst a great deal of noise from the congregation the two young people had walked down the aisle and out into the bitter December day.

And now it was evening and time for the celebratory banquet and ball, held by custom in the King's great hall, wonderfully decorated and fine, sparkling with the corporate splendor of the most beautiful courtiers in France. Velvets from Genoa, rich stuffs from Damascus, and Persian taffetas vied with one another as the wonderfully gowned women swished past, leaning backward with hips thrust forward as was considered the stylish way to walk, high hennins and saddle head-dresses, swathed in yards of jewelled veiling, balancing precariously on their heads. The men meanwhile, not to be outdone, flaunted fur robes and pearl-sewn doublets, heavy gold necklaces gleaming with stones, glistening rings, jewelled belts and daggers, gigantic codpieces, winking brilliants, and hats large as platters decorated with gems.

In the center of the high table sat the Count of Ponthieu and his future bride, flanked by the Dauphin, taking the place of his father who had been locked in his quarters, and on the other side the Queen-Duchess of Anjou.

A hawk to Isabeau's pouter pigeon, Yolande had almost understated her ensemble in order to show off an emerald that had been passed down amongst the royal family of Aragon for over two hundred years. Clad in white, her simple gown utterly without adornment, the Duchess wore her hair pulled back starkly into a flat head-dress, its only decoration a wide band and the amazing emerald. The glittering stone danced and blazed and threw facets of light about the room, illuminating its wearer's eyes to such an extent that they too shone with the same color and intensity.

There was no doubt that Yolande was the most elegant woman in the hall and Isabeau, festooned in crimson velvet, her hennin five feet high, looming above all others and veiled with cloth of gold, felt overdressed. Adding to her discomfort was the fact that the logs burning in the two great hearths, each piece of wood the size of half a tree, had combined with the scented candles to produce such a great heat, the Queen had begun to sweat. Thoroughly ill at ease, Isabeau was very conscious of the fact that her heavily applied make up was starting to run and was dripping toward her nose.

Dwarfed by the overwhelming occasion the newly betrothed children, very small and solemn, sat in their places of honor in total silence. Charles, gorgeously dressed in a deep blue doublet embroidered with silver nettle leaves, silver hose on his thin little legs, looked exactly like an ornate goblin and felt both awkward and conspicuous. Marie, too, was obviously miserable, staring at her plate, seemingly incapable of speech.

"Oh, dear," thought the boy. "I wonder if she's always like this? Will I have to endure years of silence while she stares into her lap?"

"It's very hot," he ventured, but Marie did not reply.

Catherine, however, aged twelve now and more vivid and beautiful than ever, decided at this point to intervene. Leaning across the Dauphin, at whose right hand she was sitting, she slanted her eyes at the strange girl, saying pointedly, "Monsieur le Comte de Ponthieu plays chess superbly, Madame. Let it be hoped that you do so too."

"I don't," answered Marie in a quavering voice, her eyes still lowered.

"Dear me! Then tell us, pray, what are your interests?"

The wretched child, barely nine and an innocent babe in comparison with the children of the royal court, quivered slightly. "I do tapestry work, Madame."

Catherine smirked. "Really? How nice. I'm afraid I have always abominated working with my needle."

"Except for sticking it in," answered Charles instantly, aware that his ability to make a quick riposte was most gratifyingly increasing as he grew older.

Catherine flashed a feline smile. "Mon cher, how *sharp* you are!" She pealed with laughter into which the Dauphin, in his cups as usual, joined noisily.

"Good for you, Charles. Not as silly as you look, eh?"

"My mother believes," said Marie in a half-whisper, "that one should not judge people by their appearance."

"Well, that's as well!" answered Louis, and laughed all the more.

"You are *so* rude," muttered Charles, "that something awful will happen to you one of these days."

And then he remembered the prediction of Nicolas Flamel and went cold. But the Dauphin had not heard a word and was now busy staring round the room, saying, "Where the devil's Richemont? He told me he'd be here without fail. Can't leave his pretty whore I suppose."

Charles would have taken no notice, would have used this moment to attack his food, had something rather extraordinary not happened. Sitting next to him the Duchess of Anjou sighed, very softly but very distinctly. Covertly, the boy glanced up and saw that the beautiful bony face of the woman who was his mother-in-law elect had bleached as white as her dress.

They had by now reached the fourth and final course of the betrothal feast and the comforting sweet dishes that the boy loved dearly were being brought in from the kitchens: mountainous egg custards, puddings of honey and nuts, brightly colored jellies, succulent tarts, cakes, crustards and doucettes and, to crown all, a subtlety.

This night this particular confection, made from sugar and almond paste, was molded into the shape of a lover's knot entwined with the initials C and M, and as the subtlety was wheeled in before the assembled company there was a mighty cheer. Charles lowered his gaze to the tablecloth, noticing as he did so that Marie had gone bright red, and for the first time in his short life felt more sorry for someone else than he did for himself.

"Don't worry," he whispered, "it will all be over in another hour."

She said nothing, as usual, but he saw a flicker of relief pass over the face of Marie d'Anjou before she turned her head away.

She was, Charles thought, very far from beautiful, completely lacking her mother's style and charm, but the girl's features were pleasant enough even though she seemed to be a study in beige, hair, eyes and skin all very much the same shade. In many ways she reminded her future husband of a mouse, and not even the twinkling amusing sort that lived in the wild, but simply an ordinary domestic. The Count of Ponthieu sighed a little and wished that fate could have sent him someone rather more exciting.

"You must lead the dancing, Madame," Catherine was saying to the girl, obviously taking a delight in torturing a creature she considered an utter little simpleton. "It is your duty to open the ball."

"Oh, must I?" answered Marie, looking terrified. "Must I begin the dancing, Maman?"

The color had come back to Yolande's cheeks, Charles noticed, as she nodded and smiled.

"Yes, but it is Monsieur le Comte who will lead you out. You need not be nervous."

Every kindly streak in Charles's character rushed to the

forefront in his pity for the poor young dolt he was destined to marry.

"Come on," he said, "I will look after you."

That was the moment when nine-year-old Marie d'Anjou fell in love with him, she decided some time afterwards. It did not matter a bit that the boy whose wife she was eventually to be was the ugliest in the world, nor did it matter that she had only known him little over two weeks. What did matter was that his eyes were clear and true and were looking at her now as if she were made of glass and he must stop her breaking at all costs.

Marie's chest became constricted and her breathing difficult, while the color of her face went from rose to peony and back again in less than a minute.

"Merci, Monsieur," she said, and wished that she were as beautiful and bright as his horrible cat-like sister who at this very moment was giving her a supercilious grin.

"Don't forget, you are a good dancer," murmured her mother's voice comfortingly, but Marie gave a pitiful look as Charles rose to his feet and the minstrels struck up a slow melodious air while he bowed before his betrothed.

"There's a hole in your hose," whispered the Dauphin cruelly.

"I don't care," Charles replied with dignity and led Marie d'Anjou to the space in the middle of the hall.

It was not easy for two small people, both knowing that they were not very pretty nor, indeed, very interesting, to open the dancing together but it seemed only a moment or two before Duke Louis and the Queen had joined them, and then the Dauphin and the Duchess of Anjou.

"Your mother's very beautiful," said Charles, as the tall figure in white went past him, the emerald in her headdress catching the light and gleaming a million twinkling darts.

"I wish I was like her," answered Marie wistfully.

"I expect you will be when you're older," her betrothed replied stoutly, his gargoyle smile flashing across his face as he squeezed her hand comfortingly.

Love came afresh at that and Marie, tongue-tied once more, could think of nothing whatever to say by way of reply. So it was that conversation ceased and Charles, his liking for observation never more prevalent than tonight, saw what he could only think of as a grand arrival in the

arched entrance at the far end of the hall. Brilliantly
dressed in scarlet, a great black plume in his hat and a
diamond clasp on his shoulder, there suddenly appeared a
dazzling young man whom the Count of Ponthieu dimly
recognized as Arthur, Earl of Richmond, who once had
saved him from being viciously attacked by the King.

"There you are!" called the Dauphin above the din and,
smiling, Richemont began to thread his way through the
dancers.

The Count of Armagnac, no longer in the city, had left
a strong force behind him, aware as was everyone at court
that with the leprous Henry IV now dead and his son on
the throne, negotiations between the recently routed Duke
of Burgundy and the new English king were inevitable.
There was not an adult in Paris who did not fear future
retribution at the hands of Jean the Fearless should he ally
with the English, and Count Bernard was taking no
chances. His young strong supporters, of which Richemont
was one, remained in Paris like an occupying force.

"Monsieur," Arthur was shouting cheerfully, waving a
long lean arm and doffing his hat, so lacking in concentration on his whereabouts that what happened to him next
was more or less inevitable.

Weaving his way through the galloping dancers, now en-
thusiastically embarked on a trotto, the young man collided
so hard with a couple that he almost knocked them to the
ground. Charles's face took on a look of horror as he saw
that the woman was his future mother-in-law and her partner the Duke of Alençon. Bowing low in apology, Richemont had not actually noticed who they were until he
straightened. The Count of Ponthieu's eyes widened to
twice their normal size as he saw Arthur's face freeze and
the Duchess stiffen her back as a wave of ice ran between
the two.

For two and a half years, Yolande had endured a life of
misery since their last fateful meeting. While Richemont,
never able to escape her thrall, had known the bitter torment of hatred. And yet still, and both knew it at once,
their feelings were so strong they hardly dared touch. But
that was precisely what Richemont did.

Bowing low once more, he said, "Madame, please may I
make amends? If your partner will permit me to continue
the rest of this dance." And without waiting for a word

from either of them, Richemont pulled Yolande into his arms, almost roughly, and whirled her away. As always their eyes were on a level and as the Duchess's gleamed furious green fire so did Arthur's take on a lazy insolent expression.

"Still as beautiful as ever," he said with a drawl that grated on her like a scraping saw. "But I expect you've been told that many times since we last met."

She could hardly speak, sick for love yet hurt beyond measure by the terrible thing he was inferring.

"What do you mean?"

"What I say, Madame. That flattery must come as no stranger to a woman like you."

He longed to see her suffer and was glad when Yolande's body, so close to his own, shook from head to foot.

"If you mean what I think then by God's holy blood I shall strike you, here in public."

"Go ahead," answered Richemont, jeering. "I've been a soldier, I'm used to brawls."

The fact that they cared for each other so desperately was driving them on to even greater folly.

"Let me go," said Yolande, "I will not listen to this another minute."

For reply, the Earl squeezed her tightly against his chest. "Does this offend you, Madame? Do I not suit you any more? Have I grown too old for your bed perhaps?"

"You wretched creature," came her answer. "Yes, you do offend me. You have lost all the charm you ever had, Richemont. You have turned into a foul-mouthed blackguard."

"And you," he whispered back, "what have you turned into, eh, Madame?"

The wrenching push that separated them was covered by the fact that the trotto had doubled in pace by now, all the dancers stamping their feet wildly in time to the music. Taking advantage of the noise and total confusion, Yolande turned her back on the Earl and walked slowly away, tears transforming her eyes to green glass, while Richemont, a muscle in his cheek jumping uncontrollably, fought his way through to the Dauphin and burst into loud and somehow unpleasant laughter.

"I shall never speak to the whore again," he muttered

when he had quietened himself, aware that his entire body ached as if it had been dealt a hammer blow.

"What say?" asked Louis.

Lowering his voice out of respect for the Dauphin's wife, who had left her husband's side and hovered near by, Richemont murmured, "I said, let's go whoring."

Normally this suggestion would have been greeted with enthusiasm by the decadent youth, his prodigious sexual appetites as excessive as those of his dead uncle, Louis d'Orléans. But tonight the Dauphin shook his head.

"I'd better not. It is Charles's betrothal after all, and I am here *in loco parentis*, more's the pity." He peered into his friend's face. "Is anything the matter? You're suddenly drained of color."

Richemont attempted a smile. "Am I? It must be the heat."

Louis looked unconvinced. "I think not. Something's wrong, isn't it?"

Arthur looked grim. "I've seen a ghost tonight, if you must know. A woman I used to love has come back to haunt me, Monsieur."

The Dauphin brightened. "Really? Who is she?"

The Earl shook his head. "I would not reveal her identity for all of Tartary's treasure, not even to you."

Louis stroked his chin. "This gets more and more interesting. You sly fox, Richemont. You are the last man on earth I would have guessed to be hiding a secret love."

"Please forget it," Arthur answered abruptly, turning away with a movement almost of anger. "I simply can't bear to think or speak of her any more."

But even as he said the words his eyes slid to the high table and the place where Yolande d'Anjou sat alone, her immediate neighbors having left their places to dance. Louis, smiling quizzically, followed the line of his friend's gaze, saying nothing, his dissipated young face for once shrewd and knowing.

"Come," he said suddenly, "dance with my wife, stamp your feet, lift her in the air. It's an *estampie*."

The music for the wild dance which had originated in Provence filled the room and the Dauphin whirled away to find himself another partner so that Richemont had no choice but to pull the nervous Marguerite of Burgundy into his arms. Despite her timorousness she was a comely creature, well made and fair, her eyes a pretty shade of blue.

"Madame, please do me the honor," said Richemont, then without waiting for a reply picked the Dauphine up over his head, stamping his feet all the while. Even without looking round he knew that Yolande was watching him and clasped Marguerite all the harder, flirting shamelessly with his friend's wife and being rewarded by a sparkle suddenly appearing in her eyes in place of their generally frightened expression.

The inevitable had happened. Richemont, off his head with drink and the pain of hopeless love, had actually been mad enough to go to the Dauphine's room and climb onto her bed with her where, after some relatively innocent horseplay, the couple had fallen asleep in each other's arms. The Dauphin, however, returning to his apartments at dawn, had not considered it very amusing to find his wife, her clothing disarrayed, sleeping with another man and without waiting for an explanation had launched himself bodily at the pair. Fortunately, a surfeit of wine had impaired his judgement and he had missed the bed entirely, crashing onto the floor and knocking himself unconscious on the flagstones. This had sent Marguerite into a fit of giggling during which Richemont, deciding that discretion really was the better part of valor, had made an exit through one of the windows.

"Tell him he dreamed it," he called as he put one leg over the sill. "Please, Madame, don't let him discover the truth."

By this time the Dauphine was almost out of control and the last sight the Earl had of her, as he slithered the length of a drainpipe to the courtyard below, was bent double, clutching her sides, great tears rolling down her face. It was at that farcical moment that Richemont decided he liked her a great deal, certainly as much as Jacquetta though not as much as ...

In the harsh light of very early morning, Arthur pulled himself up sharply. It was fruitless, ludicrous, to go on in this way. He must put Yolande d'Anjou behind him for ever if he was to make any kind of life for himself. As long as he was possessed by her he would be fit for nothing and no one, his entire future depended on forgetting everything that had happened between them.

Bracing his shoulders, the Earl of Richmond marched to the nearest pump and put his head beneath it, relishing the sharp coldness of the water as he ritually washed away all thoughts of the past.

Eleven

They left Paris in the bitter cold of a raw February morning, all the world so bleak and gray that the city and the countryside beyond had neither form nor definition. River, clouds, landscape, all merged into one, the lines between them softened to a blurred smudge in the frozen wastes of a land transfigured by the iron bleakness of winter. In the colorless terrain the little cavalcade of horses and riders moved like a ribbon of color, a blob of bright paint running down an untouched canvas, gawdy in such stark surroundings.

At the head of the column rode Duke Louis of Anjou flanked by two of his most able young lieutenants, Hardouin de Maillé, brought up to serve the Angevin royal family and recently married in their presence, and Robert le Maçon, the Chancellor. Behind them came the men at arms, the Duchess Yolande, and the pair of young people whose betrothal had restored some of the spirit to a war-weary Paris.

Scorning a litter, the Queen-Duchess sat astride her horse, her long heavy skirt kilted to the knees, her arms around the body of Charles de Valois, who rode passenger in front of her. Similarly, Marie was cradled by Hugues de Noyer, who had accompanied the Duke from Anjou in order to join the Count of Ponthieu's service, the only familiar figure to Charles, Guillaume d'Avagour, who had served in the King's household and had now been commissioned to be Chamberlain to the Count.

Riding hard, the party headed westward toward the city of Chartres and late in the evening, just as the first bitter flakes began to fall, clattered in through the town gate beneath the brooding bulk of the huge cathedral of Notre-

Dame, coming to a halt in the Rue des Grenets where the Hôtel de Barrault, a mansion house already prepared for their visit, property of the Bishop, awaited them.

"Snow," thought Yolande as she entered the courtyard. "At memorable moments always snow."

And now as her future son-in-law took the momentous step of spending his first night away from home, a covering of white was settling on the roofs and cobbles.

"Come on, mon cher," she said quietly, looking at Charles, then saw that the child slept in the crook of her arm, his small fur-capped head snug against her breast.

"Poor little thing," she murmured. "What a wretched life! A madman for a father, a trollop for dam. What kind of happiness can he have had?"

The snow swirled more heavily, falling on the gargoyles jutting beneath the mansion's roof, obscuring the riders as they dismounted and took the sleepy children within. But Yolande paused before following them, letting the freezing dusk sting her face, relishing the moment of being solitary in the bitter night.

And it was then, dwarfed beneath the looming shadow of the cathedral, that a strange feeling suddenly swept her, chilling the marrow of her very bones. For it came to the Duchess with clear conviction that Charles, despite his puny size and nervous manner, had lying deep within him a potential for greatness, an ability for shrewdness and statesmanship that must be realized at all costs, and that hers would be the destined hand to mold this latent promise.

The Duchess shrank into the comfort of her cloak, her wild thoughts turning to Richemont and the springing hatred which had taken the place of their once fierce love. As she had left Paris that morning he had watched her from an upstairs window and just for a moment she had turned to look him full in the face, studying the perfect features, renouncing her lover even as she gazed at him. Seeing her stare, Richemont had stepped back into the room out of sight, giving her one swift expressionless glance before he did so.

At that moment they believed it was over for ever, that neither would ever see the other again. Wheeling her mettlesome mount, the Duchess had headed for the gateway, longing to be away from the place where so fine a feeling had been ultimately destroyed. And now in the icy evening a tear ran down her cheek and was gone, a single chilling epitaph for all that once had been.

"Oh, cheer up, do," the Dauphin said petulantly, his young face scowling and blotchy in the candlelight. "Come on Richemont I am truly sick of seeing you in the sullens."

But then he bit back the words as he saw to his amazement that Richemont was crying.

Getting up from his chair, Louis knelt before his friend, wiping away the tears with his own handkerchief, filled with so much tenderness and compassion that his heart ached. For the truth was that he loved the Earl, was in love with him probably, though he had never tried to express that emotion either by word or deed. Yet the fact remained that, given the choice, the heir to the throne of France would rather have spent his days in the company of Richemont than any other person on earth.

"Oh, Arthur," he said wretchedly, his face echoing all that his friend was suffering. "Please don't torture yourself any more."

"I can't help it," the young man answered, looking away. "I still have such strong feelings for—"

His voice ceased abruptly but the Dauphin, wisely, said nothing, asking no questions, positive that the cause of all this anguish was someone connected with the house of Anjou, if not the Duchess herself.

Eventually, he said slowly, "What is past is past, you know, and must be allowed both to die and be buried."

"I have already vowed it should be so," answered the Earl.

"Then why?"

"The ghost of her is not yet exorcised."

"I know little," the Dauphin said earnestly. "I am yet young and have been too busy killing myself to learn much. But one thing I am certain of. Time heals all things, there is no ailment, mental or physical, that its great slow magic cannot cure."

Richemont raised his head. "Then let the years pass quickly."

Louis trembled. "No, don't say that. Who knows what fate awaits us all? This is life's own sweet blood that we are spilling, these seconds are precious, every one."

"I welcome the passing of time," replied Arthur bitterly. "Let the days fly by until I am finally free of her."

But Louis only crouched close to his friend, shivering at the thought of the irrevocable march of destiny and all the savage events that might befall them in the years that lay ahead.

PART TWO

MARIE AND BONNE

Twelve

From his many journeys between Anjou and its Neapolitan territories, the Duke-King Louis had brought
back a formidable collection of treasures with which
to adorn his castle at Angers. Paintings and tapestries
brightened every room, mirrors reflected sparkling views of
the river and the changing colors of the landscape, the
Duchess and her ladies were dressed in clothes made from
rare and beautiful materials, while the aviaries rivalled
those of the Hôtel St. Pol in Paris containing, in addition
to all the exotic birds, a collection of doves and pigeons
which would circle the castle with a wild white beating of
wings before returning nightly to settle in their lofts.

On summer evenings the Duke's courtiers would stroll
amongst the gardens to the accompaniment of music and
poetry, the smell of rare and sumptuous perfumes filling the
air, shade thrown by fig trees and other plants not native to
Anjou. Indeed, a cultivated and cultured life was led by all
those lucky enough to live within the castle's precinct and,
in the midst of this atmosphere, the boy who had been
brought there less than two years earlier, thrived.

Charles de Valois had grown taller and filled out somewhat in that time. Predictably, his face had remained plain
but had lost its nervous apprehensive expression and developed an ugly charm all its own. His voice, too, now that
he was thirteen and pubescent, was dropping to a deli-
ciously husky timbre which was more attractive than anything else about him.

"That one will seduce women just by talking to them,"
Guillaume d'Avagour had said affectionately about his
young charge, and then added, "and I suppose when the
time comes we'll have to fix that up for him."

Hugues de Noyer had looked slightly askance. "But the Duchess would be furious. What about Marie?"

Guillaume had winked. "The Duchess would be the first to agree. She certainly won't want him cutting his teeth on her daughter."

"What an unbelievably vulgar phrase that is."

"But very true."

"Anyway, you won't have to worry about that for a year or two. Though I hear young Jean the Bastard's principal gentleman has been taking him to visit a certain high-born widow."

"Does Duke Louis know?" asked Guillaume, surprised.

"He arranged it in the first place. He wouldn't want his son's friend getting into bad company, now would he?"

They had both laughed at that, considering it an extremely civilized arrangement and far better than the early lifestyle of the Dauphin who, according to rumor from Paris, had contracted the *Croix de Vénus* and was far from well. For even Guillaume, sophisticated city dweller though he might be, was blossoming in Anjou as he never had before.

It was not just the beautiful countryside with its huge skyscapes and capricious rivers that was so captivating, but also the atmosphere in the town and castle of Angers itself. The walled city bustled with life, the street sellers calling their wares, the public fountains catching in the wind and showering passers-by with icy drops, the great bells of the cathedral of St. Maurice ringing out carillons, the stained glass windows, some of them dating from the 1180s, blazing like rainbows in the sunshine, the narrow streets crowded with shops, each with its own brightly painted sign, urchins playing on the cobbles.

Everywhere there was gaiety and noise as the populace bustled between the left bank and the Doutre, buying and trading, fighting and feasting, the black habits of the Benedictine orders adding sobriety to the vivid colors of the milling throng. And as if such a tangible zest for being alive was infectious, exhilaration seemed to have spread into the castle itself so that the children who dwelled there, quite in harmony with the cultured existence of their elders, enjoyed a carefree, boisterous upbringing, unusual in the somewhat formal times.

The leader of this merry set of young people was undoubtedly Jean, the fifteen-year-old Bastard of Orléans, il-legitimate son of the Duke who had been Isabeau's late lover, and half-brother to Charles d'Orléans, the present Duke. He had been betrothed to Marie Louvet, daughter of the *Président* of Provence, a few days after the betrothal of Charles de Valois and Marie d'Anjou and was, indeed, based in the *Président*'s household, though somehow con-triving to spend most of his time with the royal children.

Next in line came Charles de Valois, in his fourteenth year and truly finding his feet. In the two years since he had left Paris the boy had been taught to ride, swim and fence, and on fine evenings he and the other young males would shoot arrows in the butts on the riverbank. Yet most of all, the Comte de Ponthieu loved to read and study, by far the cleverest of all the children, with a brilliant mind already at work, and now playing a masterful game of chess.

Beside him young Louis d'Anjou, known as Jade by his family because of the intense green of his eyes, seemed almost slow-witted, yet this appearance was deceptive. A large, lazy, affable child with great feet and hands, Duke Louis's heir, though charming, was actually idle to the bone.

Next in the pecking order was poor Marie, simply by reason of the fact that she was now coming up for twelve years of age. Unfortunately her appearance had altered lit-tle since her betrothal, though the color of her skin had mercifully lightened so that her eyes seemed darker and therefore more interesting. But it was obvious even now that she would never make a beauty and Charles agonized over the fact that one day he would have to marry her. The first stirrings of sexuality were making themselves felt in his body and the boy knew already that he would soon become sensual, would cherish the company of lovely women and want to take them into his bed. And the thought of doing what his friend the Bastard did to the noble widow, and then afterwards so graphically described, to a girl Charles considered his little sister, a gentle com-panion who had taken the place of Catherine, frankly re-volted him.

By far the most interesting of the King-Duke's children, or so it was generally considered, was six-year-old René, a dark, saturnine child with huge eyes, so light a shade of brown they looked almost amber, set in a thin angular face. He had very unusual hands with long tapering fingers, quite extraordinary in a boy of his age. This large brood of youngsters from the house of Anjou was completed by little Yolande, aged two and a half, and Charles, Count of Maine, a baby of only nine months.

When the Duchess had departed from Paris in the bitter February of 1414 she had had only two principal aims: to irrevocably put away all thoughts of the Earl of Richmond and to mold the pathetic Charles de Valois into something like a proper child. The first had been difficult to achieve, costing her dear emotionally. But with her iron will Yolande had set about reshaping her life and, indeed, had achieved a kind of arid happiness, forcing herself to concentrate on her duties to her family and subjects and never allowing thoughts of love to enter her mind.

Fortunately, Duke Louis had not gone away to visit his distant territories again, and it had been inevitable with him at home that sooner or later another pregnancy would occur. In the late autumn of 1414, at the age of thirty-four, Yolande had given birth to her sixth child, a boy who had been named Charles in honor of the Count of Ponthieu but who was known to all as Maine, of which territory the infant was Count, in order not to confuse the two young people.

Despite her longing to see her fourth child once more, Yolande had firmly resisted, fearing that to do so might kindle painful memories of Jehanne's father. But news of the Duchess's bastard came regularly from Alison du May, now firmly entrenched as the Duke of Lorraine's mistress and already the mother of his baby sons. It would appear from these coded messages that the child was happy in its rustic existence, loved and cherished by her foster parents, good honest people of farming stock.

It was August 1415, hot and cloudless, the grapes swelling on the heavy vines of Anjou, the Maine and the mighty Loire, glistening with light, winding their way through the land like two sun-drenched lizards. The well-watered flower-beds of the castle bloomed with color, scenting the air with a heady sweet perfume, while in Yolande's terraced gardens trees threw a dappled shade. She could not remember a finer summer nor a more golden feeling of high harvest. All the world seemed in harmony with the lazy buzz of bees, the flutter and swirl of flirting butterflies, the splash of fish in the indolent river.

The Duchess pushed away the papers she was reading and stood up, her husband glancing toward her as she did so.

"I think I'll go down to the water. It's so hot in here."

Louis smiled at her absently. "You should send everyone away and swim."

"If I did would you come with me?"

"Yes. In half an hour or so."

"I can think of nothing nicer."

The devil that dwelt in her brain promptly told her that she was a fool, that nicer by far would be to swim naked with the Earl of Richmond and afterwards to lie in his arms beneath a willow tree and make love in the shaded sunshine. Resolutely, Yolande beat such torturing thoughts away.

"Don't be long," she said from the doorway and blew her husband a kiss before she made her way down to the river.

The castle's Water Gate and landing stage were protected by a fortified tower built out into the Maine itself. To the right of this were the unscalable cliffs on the top of which the fortress was built, but to the left, outside the actual walls yet still part of its land, a gentle bank swept down to the water. It was here that the butts were located and it was also here that it was considered safe enough for the children to swim. Yolande had been taught by her father and had encouraged Marie to learn the art, but the girl was afraid of water and preferred to sit in the shade sewing while her brothers and her betrothed splashed about.

Now, as she approached, the Duchess was somewhat surprised to hear her daughter call out, "Be careful. Maman is coming," and saw to her amazement that Jean, Charles and Jade were swimming stark naked. It was indecorous in front of Marie to say the least, but in a way Yolande was glad that there were no inhibitions between any of them.

"Get your hose on quickly," Marie was shouting, and Yolande deliberately slowed her pace to give them time.

Yet it was René, his dark looks burnished by the sun, who actually came to stop his mother catching the others unawares. Still only six, and unable to swim himself, he had been paddling and now ran barefoot through the grass to take Yolande's hand, winding his uncannily long fingers through hers.

"The boys are undressed," he said without embarrassment. "And Jean and Charles would be shy if you saw them."

"Then I'll sit here and talk to you till they're ready," said Yolande, and dropped down onto the grass, pulling her second son into her lap.

It was a moment she would remember all her life for later she saw it as the end of an era. But knowing nothing of this then, Yolande could only look about her and marvel at the day. A haze of beauty lay upon the hills and the water of the Maine was a clear blue gemstone; the houses on the Doutre bloomed like roses in the clear light, while the meadows and pasture lands, drawing water from the river, looked sharp and green in the rest of the sun-baked terrain.

The child on her knee enhanced the sensations of all she could see. With her arms wound around him, Yolande could hear the beat of René's heart, smell the body scent of him, feel the warmth of his skin. Burying her nose in his thick tangle of hair, sniffing its newly washed fragrance, licking his ear like a mother cat cleaning its young, the Duchess felt she was relishing her son like some delicious fruit.

"I shall miss you when you go to the Duke of Lorraine," she said.

"But that's in four years' time," he answered seriously, "and a lot can happen in four years."

"Indeed," Yolande replied thoughtfully and looking up saw that a flock of birds was flying between her and the sun, temporarily throwing a shadow.

The day changed color, tinged with the first fine thread of evening, and the boys appeared, dressed and respectable, grinning rather sheepishly.

"Madame," said the Bastard, and made the Duchess a bow, his white teeth gleaming in his tanned face and his black curls falling about his brows as he did so.

He was a magnificent youth, beautifully proportioned and immensely good looking, making Charles, his boon companion, seem thinner and plainer than ever.

"Take the others up to the castle, Jean," said Yolande,

handing René over to his care. "I am going to wait for the Duke. My Lord and I thought we might swim."

The youngsters giggled, even Marie, and Yolande knew they were wondering if she and Duke Louis might also bathe naked together. She kept a straight face, however.

"That's enough. Now, off you go."

They went, reluctantly, in a raggle-taggle procession, Jade loitering behind, not wanting to return indoors.

Very subtly the river deeps turned to sapphire, the sky darkened to claret, while the hills beyond were drenched in a veil of mulberry mist. Unnoticed, half an hour had passed and still there as no sign of the Duke.

Slowly, Yolande stood up, brushing the grass from her skirt, thinking that her husband had become so absorbed in his work he had lost all count of time. Disappointed she had not been able to swim with him, she started to make her way back to the castle, along the riverbank to the Water Gate and then up the steep path into the fortress itself.

Why she began to hurry she could not afterwards recall, but a sudden sense of urgency came over the Duchess of Anjou and she broke into a run, going quickly uphill, and finally rushing into Nobles' Court toward the King's Lodging. Even as she got inside and went up the spiral stairs that led to the receiving room, Yolande could hear voices and realized an unexpected visitor had come to the castle to see the Duke.

" ... Christ's Holy Wounds," her husband's voice was saying as she climbed, "this is a grievous day for France."

Suddenly afraid, Yolande swept the door open and gazed into the room in apprehension. Duke Louis and the visitor, who was caked with dust from riding at speed over the dry tracks of Anjou and looked fit to drop with fatigue, stood by the window, each of them grasping a wine cup. In fact, as the Duchess went in the stranger, obviously thirsty, was holding his out to be refilled.

"No," said Yolande, as the rider turned and attempted to bow, "that is not necessary. Simply tell me what has happened."

Duke Louis looked at her somberly and she thought she had never seen him so hollow-cheeked and gray. "That son of a whore Henry of England has landed in Normandy and is besieging Harfleur."

"Mon Dieu!" said Yolande, sitting down heavily. "What a blow for our poor country. Only just snatched out of Burgundy's thrall—and now this!"

"They're in league of course," the Duke answered angrily. "Burgundy would sell his grandmother if he thought it might improve his position."

"And the English King?"

"He's claiming France as his birthright by reason of his descendancy from Edward III."

Yolande poured herself a draught of wine and drank deeply. "What are we going to do?"

"A meeting of all the nobles and their armies is called to take place as soon as possible in Rouen," the messenger answered tersely. "There the battle plan will be drawn up."

"I shall bring my soldiers out of Provence," the Duke said quietly, almost to himself, "and march at their head to the Council of War. This tyrant must be stopped at all costs."

"But the country is so weak," put in Yolande, the messenger nodding his head in agreement with her.

"Every last man must fight," replied Louis harshly. "Every boy over sixteen must be called upon."

"Then ours are too young to go, thank God."

"Yes, but it will be difficult to restrain the Bastard. He'll be itching to join his brother."

"I shall stop him!" Yolande replied firmly. "I'll not have their young lives put at risk until it's absolutely necessary."

Throughout the rest of that summer and well into the autumn the couriers of the noble houses of France, carrying white wands as symbol of their office, rode furiously through the countryside bearing letters and documents setting up the great Council of War which, it was desperately hoped, would put an end to the greedy claims of the English King.

And even while this ponderous method of communication rumbled on, Henry of Lancaster, after terrible slaughter, took Harfleur and started to march north-east to Calais at the head of an army of six thousand men. But as he went, the flower of French nobility and their liegemen, organized at last, headed for Rouen.

They came from every corner of France: the Dukes of Alençon, Bourbon, Orléans and Anjou, the Counts of Armagnac, Foix, Etampes and Nevers, and the Earl de Richemont accompanied by his brother, the Duke of Brittany. From Paris came the senile Duke of Berri, the only uncle of the mad King left alive, to act as *Président*, the King, and his son the Dauphin, both being too ill to attend. And finally on 20th October, the Council of War was called into full session.

Clambering to his feet, the Duke of Berri spoke in the fluting tones of a child. "Gentlemen, let us negotiate with the English King. Let there not be one drop of French blood spilled while we are able to parley."

The Earl of Richmond was on his legs so fast it was obvious at once that etiquette and protocol and youth's respect for age had gone out of the window in the face of this terrible crisis.

"Coillons, Monsieur! Negotiation with a land-grabbing warmonger like him is out of the question. Henry of England is the kind who will stab you in the back while he shakes your hand. He is an unscrupulous villain and that describes him in the best possible terms. I know him of old. He is my stepbrother, more's the pity. And as such I hope it is I who deal him the death blow."

They stood up cheering, the noble lords of France, spoiling for a fight and full of justifiable fury at King Henry's rape of Harfleur.

"How many men has he got?" shouted Duke Louis of Anjou.

"Six thousand," answered Alençon, rising. "And they're tired, every one. Spies tell us they are a load of tatterdemalions; sick, feverish and some barefoot. They're ready for the taking. Who's with me?"

He raised his arms over his head and there was another huge cheer.

"How many men do *we* have?" called Bourbon.

"Nearly fifty thousand, and I've another twelve thousand in Brittany only waiting my signal to get on the move," answered Richemont's brother.

"I say we go for him now," cried Charles d'Orléans. "How far has he got on the march to Calais?"

"He's trying to cross the Somme and can't find a causeway."

"May he fall in on his arse," said Richemont and every-

one laughed while the Duke of Berri banged helplessly with
a gavel to restore order.

The Maréchal of France, Charles d'Albret, a seasoned
campaigner if ever there was one, spoke for the first time.

"Gentlemen, if we march at dawn tomorrow we can stalk
him all the way. There's nothing worse than looking over
your shoulder at an unseen menace. It will be a war of
nerves with the advantage to us. I agree with young
Richemont. This is an enemy with whom there can be no
parley. Let's strike now."

"No, no . . ." quavered Berri, but nobody paid any
attention.

"I'll back to Vannes and alert my men," said the Duke
of Brittany. "I'll catch you up on the way even if I have to
march all night."

"Then it is agreed that we leave at once?"

"I suggest we go tonight," put in Louis d'Anjou. "Surely
every minute is precious? We mustn't let him slip through
our fingers whatever happens."

The Maréchal who had taken charge, ignoring the impo-
tent Berri, nodded his head.

"If you gentlemen are willing I will give the order for
immediate mobilization. In that way we should be on the
move by midnight."

"I say we do it," said Alençon, and there was a huge
answering shout of "Oui."

"Death to the usurper," cried Richemont, his voice dis-
torted by all his pent-up emotion.

"Death to Harry of England," echoed Count Bernard
d'Armagnac. "Death to all who threaten the safety and
welfare of France."

It was an oblique reference to Burgundy but no one paid
any heed.

"Death to the English King," shouted the cream of
French chivalry in one voice and, as the Maréchal raised
his clenched fist in salute, left the Council chamber to prepare for battle.

Thirteen

They stalked Henry V of England for four days, a mighty ghost army of fifty thousand men constantly at his back. In a panic, the English King tried repeatedly to cross the river Somme but seemed to be thwarted at every turn. Finally, in desperation, Henry had no choice but to repair the causeway across the marshlands, his tired men felling trees and pulling apart deserted farmhouses to get wood. The English had waded up to their waists in mud to build that road, for the rain which had dogged them for days and which had started as a gentle drizzle had now turned into a blinding torrent.

On the night that the English army had gone safely across the makeshift road, the French had camped their mighty horde at Péronne, only six miles away from where Henry of Lancaster slept, and on the following morning the Bourbon heralds had ridden across and challenged him to war. The rose red lips of the Englishman, shocking somehow in his drained white face, had uttered the words of acceptance, and then Henry had continued to march on, waiting for that enormous shadow to reveal itself.

The weather had worsened, the mud had turned into a quagmire, and it was in these conditions that Maréchal d'Albret had decided to make a detour and pass the English, blocking their road to Calais irretrievably. So it was at Blangy that the two armies had caught sight of each other for the first time and the inequality of the fight had been made clear to both.

"We'll wipe him out," said Richemont, astride his horse, staring across to where the weary English had made camp.

"He asked for trouble and now he's got it," answered Charles, Duke d'Orléans. "His army's a wreck."

Behind them came the shrill excited neigh of the French destriers, the war horses, the finest in Europe, who tomorrow would be superbly caparisoned in their armor and adornments, ready to carry their riders into the fray.

"There's only one thing I fear from him," Richemont replied thoughtfully.

"And what's that?"

"His Welsh long bowmen, they are the best I have ever seen, magnificent marksmen and hard as nails every one."

"We'll mow them down."

"We must, because they are the strength of that grabbing bastard."

"Richemont," said Charles d'Orléans firmly, "we outnumber him five to one, six to one when your brother arrives with his extra troops. The odds are too great. He cannot succeed."

"Please God," answered the Earl. "Please God."

There was no sleep that night while the armorers worked at full pitch, their tools tapping away through the dark hours; the grooms inspecting every horse to see if it was fit to go into battle; the Archbishop of Sens, who tomorrow would fight with the French nobility, hearing confessions, shriving and absolving.

"I have sinned with the wife of another," whispered Richemont, on his knees, the floor of his tent damp with the mud beneath. "And I knew a man's betrothed before she went to her marriage bed."

The Archbishop said nothing, his oddly young face shadowed in the candlelight.

"I am a worthless wretch," the Earl went on, gulping away all the mixed emotions he felt at that moment. "But I *do* repent and pray only that I may be valorous in the company of my countrymen."

"In the name of Christ I forgive you your sins," answered the Archbishop quietly. "You are given absolution. If your soul is called to God this day then it will go shriven." There was no sound except for the steady beat of rain against the sides of the tent.

"Amen," said Richemont.

It was still raining at dawn when, after three hours' snatched sleep, the Earl rose to be dressed by his squire. Against his skin he wore a padded shirt to protect him from the weight of his breastplate, over which the squire slipped the Earl's *cote d'armes,* showing the chained and collared ermine of Brittany, together with the coroneted falcon of Richmond. The great helm with the family device above, Richemont carried with him as he went out into the damp morning to hear Mass.

They knelt in the mud to receive the sacrament and then, suddenly, it was time. With a swift leg up, the Earl was mounted on his handsome destrier, also wearing the crest of Brittany above its protective faceplate, its caparison sweeping the ground as it moved. Seizing the banner of Richmond from his squire's hand, Richemont took his place as the front line of the mighty French army formed up.

They were all there: Orléans, Alençon, Eu, to name but a few. Every Frenchman worth his salt that turned out to fight for his country—with three glaring omissions. Burgundy, obviously, was not present but, far more worryingly, the Duke of Brittany still had not appeared with his army, and though the Duke of Anjou's men were present, their leader was not. As they had left Rouen, Duke Louis had been seized with such an excruciating pain in his bowels that he had been forced to turn back.

Remarks of a cruel nature had been passed, of course, and to the Earl's chagrin it was now being whispered that his brother was using delaying tactics in order to avoid the confrontation which lay ahead. Almost as if to defy what was being said of his family, Richemont jostled his way to a place amongst the very front of the leaders.

Opposite, across the mile of what had once been a cornfield but was now nothing but a sodden pulp, the English army, what there was of it, stood ready. Narrowing his eyes, Richemont could make out clumps of bowmen breaking up the foot soldiers and the mounted. So his hated stepbrother was deploying his one strength cleverly. Yet looking down the line of the French, armored, prepared, three thousand banners, each denoting a noble house, waving behind the fluttering oriflammes, the Earl knew they were invincible.

The morning dragged on, the downpour giving way to drizzle, and still neither side made a move. An hour passed, two, three, possibly four, and then ridiculously, almost by accident, the battle began. French knights, still trying to have the honor of fighting in the front line, swelled its ranks so greatly that it broke. Seeing the French cavalry move forward, the English trumpets rang out, their counterparts responded, and the fight was on. Richemont, spurring his horse to full charge, momentarily glimpsed King Henry himself, sword in hand, holding his archers back until the last possible second.

The heavily armored destriers, slow in the mud, caught that first wave of arrows, some falling, and suddenly it seemed to the Earl that he was packed in too solidly by other riders. He realized then, though too late, that the French army was badly placed, hemmed in by trees on one side and the thick scrubland beneath the castle of Azincourt on the other. As his horse lumbered forward toward the English lines, going as fast as it could in the sucking slime, Richemont saw to his horror that the Welsh longbowmen had now produced pointed stakes and had made a wooden palisade in front of themselves.

The beautiful destriers, weighed down by their caparisons and sinking in the mud, charged on to their deaths, pierced to their faithful hearts by the vicious points of this makeshift barrier. In shock, the Earl felt his beloved horse founder beneath him and almost fell off, but then quickly scrambled up again ready to fight hand to hand. Maddened animals were everywhere, screaming in terror, knocking over the French knights as the frantic and injured creatures galloped wildly about.

"Oh, Christ help me," thought the Earl. "I mustn't fall."

But others had, lying on their backs, their armor too heavy to let them get up, the English slaughtering them almost casually where they lay.

"God's Holy Blood," screamed Richemont at the top of his voice, and turned to fight as he never had before, venting on the enemy his frustration that the most highly trained cavalry in the world had been brought quite literally to its feet by the sheer weight of its own numbers. There was mud and blood everywhere and complete chaos amongst the French as the English front line now moved from the defensive to the offensive position.

"You lousy bastards," Richemont shouted and his sword became an instrument of revenge as he killed frantically, horribly, without heed or mercy, in a frenzy of rage and despair.

How long he went on and how many lives he took, the Earl did not know, but a sudden cheer from the scattered and hapless French ranks brought him back from his delirium and he saw that a new contingent, bearing the banners of the Duke of Brabant, had arrived and were fresh, ready, and foolhardy enough to swing things in their favor. With a leap of his heart, the Earl took a breath, wiped his bloody hands on his sleeve and looked about him.

He stood in a circle of bodies, the ground beneath his feet dyed a sickly shade of ochre while a nearby puddle was completely filled with red water. Behind him, Brabant's men were coming hell for leather, but in front was a sight that made him retch. The French prisoners, huddled behind the English lines, were being slaughtered where they stood, like cattle, Henry of England, his obscene red mouth hard as a gash of blood, personally supervising this monstrous massacre. Without mercy, hundreds were being put to the sword, and the smell in the air was as acrid and foul as that of an abattoir.

All his violent dislike of his stepbrother welled like a mill race in Richemont's heart and he found himself mouthing a prayer that he might only get near enough to be the one to end the English King's arrogant life. And then, in the cold of that October afternoon, his wish was miraculously granted. The English regrouped and went at charge against Brabant and suddenly Henry was there, almost within his grasp, hacking and cutting with that awful controlled violence which the Earl so loathed in him.

"You!" shrieked Richemont. "You!"

And he careered toward his stepbrother, dripping weapon high. But he never got to him. Out of nowhere came a sword, sharp and cruel, its point and blade crimsoned and thick with blood. It seemed to the Earl of Richmond, then, that his entire life had been leading up to this one moment for now he faced its end for sure.

Slowly, almost with a terrible fascination, he watched the sword rise in the air and make contact with his forehead. And then came a pain so terrible that Richemont called for death. Blinded by blood, he heard the harsh sweet song of arrows and as he dropped to die a heap of other bodies fell on top of him, and all was darkness.

They stood in a desperate little group, knotted together by anguish, in the great hall of the castle of Angers, as the white-faced Duke of Anjou slowly walked through the door, back only a few minutes from his journey home from

Rouen. But they had already heard the news he had to tell from one of the swift white-wanded messengers who served them. Everyone knew, the Duchess, her three elder children, Charles, his friend the Bastard, the Seneschal, *Conseillers*, servants, that the mighty French army had been humbled by a scarecrow band and defeated ignominiously.

"And I couldn't be there," said the Duke without even greeting them, and wept publicly.

Nobody made a move, even his wife standing motionless, a hand on the shoulder of each of her two sons, watching in pitying horror as Duke Louis, of whose courage there could never be any question amongst these people who had seen him in battle, broke his heart that illness had prevented him fighting, and dying if necessary, with his fellow countrymen.

Eventually it was the Lord de Beauvau, the Seneschal, who said, "My Lord, I beg you not to distress yourself further. I pray you to be calm."

With a child's gesture, Louis dashed his eyes with his sleeve. "I arrived too late to fight but by God I saw the battlefield. Over ten thousand dead lay in the mud . . ."

Yolande drew her breath sharply but said nothing.

". . . and nearly every one of them French. When extra soldiers came from Brabant's army that bloody butcher Henry slaughtered every prisoner he had."

"I curse the monster," said someone softly.

"We have lost the flower of our nation."

"But how did it happen?" the Seneschal asked dazedly. "What went wrong?"

"The French army was too big and unwieldy for the area in which it fought. The horses were impaled on spikes and shot at with arrows. Then chaos followed as the oncoming riders fell over a mountain of dead men and beasts. It was carnage, total carnage."

"Did the Duke of Brittany betray us?"

"I think not. He and his men arrived in time to help clear the field and burn the bodies. I do not believe it was deliberate. But, of course, that is also being asked about me. Was I, Louis d'Anjou, a traitor to the cause?"

Yolande spoke for the first time. "No one who knows you will ever believe that and let your enemies whisper what they will."

The Seneschal said gruffly, "How did it end, my Lord? How was victory conceded to the Englishman?"

"The Maréchal d'Albret had been killed, the Archbishop of Sens also, the Dukes of Orléans, Bourbon and Alençon taken prisoner—"

"Not murdered?"

"No, no. They were taken after the devil's whelp knew he had won. At sunset it was over. As the sun went down he sent a messenger to parley and then he came himself. It was unspeakable. He gave us permission to bury our dead. But there were so many corpses that we ... that we ..."

The Duke broke down and Yolande, with her lips trembling, rushed to kneel by the chair into which he had thrown himself, his head in his hands.

"Oh, mon cher, mon cher, it is over now. Please feel no remorse. You did your best."

He looked at her with glazed eyes. "I must speak to you alone. There is something I feel I must impart."

"Let me have a few moments alone with the children," she whispered, "and then I will come to you straight away."

Half an hour later, puzzling over the complexities of life's twisting threads, the Duchess made her way to the private apartments she shared with her husband only to find that he was already seated in a chair by the fire, his boots and traveling clothes removed and soft shoes and a comfortable robe put in their place. His eyes were closed wearily but he opened them as she approached and, just for a second, Yolande saw death peep out at her.

"Oh, my darling," she said, full of tender love for this man who had fathered her children and who trusted so greatly in her capabilities as a ruler. "I have been worried for you. Tell me everything that occurred."

Louis shook his head, almost as if in disbelief. "I was ready to go, was just preparing to mount my horse when a searing pain shot through me. I felt my bowels and bladder were being burned out. Mon Dieu, Yolande, I never want to experience an agony like that again."

"I'm sure you will not," she answered soothingly, sitting at his feet on a low stool, taking his hand between both of hers.

The Duke looked at her so sadly that the Duchess could have wept. "Alas, sweetheart, I think you are wrong. A malignancy eats away at me and one of these days will become my master. That is why you and I must work hard in the time that is left to us to unite France against the usurper."

"But how can we? What can we do?"

"I believe that Count Bernard d'Armagnac should now be appointed Constable of France."

"But he is so cruel, such a vicious soldier."

"At least he and his men fought at Azincourt, whereas Burgundy lay low."

"He could hardly have come out of exile."

"He could have reappeared and signed a peace treaty with us all. No, I think the only course remaining is to rally behind Armagnac and prepare ourselves for further conflict."

"The messenger said Henry of England has already sailed from Calais."

"Oh yes, he's gone all right," the Duke answered bitterly. "But he'll be back. Mark my words, we haven't seen the last of him."

Yolande stared into the flames in silence for some while, before saying quietly, "Who else fought at Azincourt that I might know?"

"Orléans, Bourbon, Alençon, fat Georges de la Trémoille."

The Duchess smiled. "For a chamberlain to Jean the Fearless of Burgundy that was a brave act."

Louis smiled too. "I think, perhaps, he was afraid the Queen might banish him from her bed if he didn't rally to the cause of France."

"Indeed he *is* brave, having Isabeau for a mistress and Burgundy as a friend, but yet there is still something likeable about him."

"Georges is a rogue," Louis answered, "but an endearing one."

There was another intense silence during which the Duke began to stroke Yolande's hair, much as if she were a beloved cat.

"Did many of our friends die?" she asked at last.

"Too many to name. But have I told you about young Richemont?"

Beneath his hands, the Duke felt her tense and wondered at it.

"Has he been killed?"

"No, taken prisoner, though badly wounded I believe. Both he and Orléans were left for dead beneath a pile of bodies but were recovered by the English and sailed with the King. Henry will want enormous ransoms for them, of course."

"But at least they're alive," said Yolande joyfully, "that is something to be grateful for."

Louis patted her head gently. "There is very little left for us to rejoice about but, yes, I suppose it is something that Azincourt had a few French survivors."

It was almost midnight, the witching hour, before Yolande finally left her husband's side and, acting under compulsion, went through the dark of the sleeping castle to where the astrologer had his rooms. Eccentrically, and by reason of some ancient tradition the basis for which no one could any longer remember, the stargazers attached to the court always had their apartments in the left-hand part of the castle complex in one of the huge towers. Consequently, the Queen-Duchess was obliged to leave Nobles' Court, responding quietly to the challenge of the guard on gate-house duty, and walk the entire length of the mighty enclave in the darkness of that cold autumn night, the light from torches set in sconces at intervals along the walls insufficient to illuminate its deepest shadows.

Beneath Yolande's feet the leaves crackled and crunched, the death knell of the year, and she thought of all those who would never see spring again, and gave thanks that Richemont still had his life. In fact, she was dwelling on his fate even as she reached the ancient door leading into the tower and began to climb the stairs, so that somehow the Duchess was not surprised when Guy, his misshapen body not noticeable beneath the long robe affected by those who studied magic, met her in the entrance and said, "Those who survived the battle will return, Madame."

Raising one of her dark brows, the Duchess replied, "How did you know I was thinking about the prisoners of war?"

"Because Azincourt is uppermost in everyone's mind and it is obvious that while we must mourn the dead we must also be concerned for the living," he answered quickly.

"So it was just a shrewd guess."

The hunched shoulder rose crookedly as Guy smiled and spread his hands. "Partly, perhaps. But now my master awaits you, Madame. He felt you would come to him and is most anxious to unburden himself in view of all that has befallen France."

They climbed a few more steps, then went into the great round chamber where Dr. Flavigny sat at his desk, his white head nodding as he fought off sleep.

"Her Grace the Duchess is here, Monsieur," his apprentice called loudly, and the old man woke up, clambering to his feet to greet his noble visitor.

"Welcome, Madame, welcome. I pray you sit down by the fire. It is because of Azincourt that I believe I have to speak." Dr. Flavigny cleared his throat importantly. "Madame, the future King of France dwells even now within these walls."

Yolande stared blankly, not understanding, and Guy added softly, "It is true, ma Reine. Monsieur le Comte de Ponthieu is destined to inherit the throne in place of his two brothers and lead France to victory."

Yolande stared at him in disbelief. "Dr. Flavigny, the French have just suffered the most crushing defeat but yet you speak of triumph."

"It is destined in the stars, ma Reine, that Charles aided by La Pucelle can achieve just that."

"La Pucelle?" The Duchess frowned. "Who is La Pucelle?"

"That, Madame, I do not know," the astrologer replied. "The name came to Guy without explanation."

"But I've heard it before," Yolande said thoughtfully.

"From my brother, ma Reine," the hunchback answered. "He had a vision and entered the cloister that he might serve her."

"Then he knows who she is?"

Guy shook his head. "No, Madame, nobody does. But he believes, as do I, that she exists."

The Duchess stood up, her cynical attitude to such prophecies barely concealed. Yet going through the darkness afterward, alone in the black night except for the guards and the watchmen, Yolande found she was unable to shake off the strange feelings that the talk of La Pucelle had aroused in her. Was it merely bone weariness that had made the whole room seem to grow in dimension and a picture flash into her mind of an army, a small female figure at its head, marching beneath the oriflamme? Was it just tiredness that had made her experience, be it only momentarily, an inexplicable sense of pride and fulfillment?

Not understanding any of these things, Yolande decided that only time could answer her questions, and with a sigh entered the King's Lodging by way of the concealed staircase.

Fourteen

He had lived no kind of life at all yet he managed
to make a decent exit from it. In the Hôtel St. Pol
in Paris, almost two months after the ignominious
defeat of the French army at Azincourt, the Dauphin Louis
lay dying of syphilis. Alone but for his two physicians and
a priest, only a handful of his most loyal servants present,
he had been deserted by his family apart from his wife,
Marguerite of Burgundy.

Strangely, she who had so often wished him dead and
who had always maintained a healthy hatred for her youthful husband, now wept, not so much in sorrow but more at
the loss of someone she had known since she was a child.
She had been betrothed to Louis when she was seven, and
now he was leaving her for ever. Marguerite could do nothing but cry for the death of a man to whom she had, almost
against her will, grown both used and attached.

It was the second stage of the disease which was killing
the Dauphin, so that he lay swathed in white gauze to hide
his rash, his poor face invisible but for two holes allowing
him to see out and another pair, larger, for his nose and
mouth. To all appearances he seemed already dead and
could have been mistaken for a corpse, were it not for the
fact that his lids were raised and he was gazing painfully
toward the ceiling.

"Louis, please get better," Marguerite whispered pathetically to him from time to time, but her voice was drowned
by the solemn prayers of the Dauphin's confessor, while
her husband, responding to none of it, continued only to
stare heavenwards.

"He'll not last another hour," a member of his retinue

murmured to another, to which came the muttered reply, "The great pox never spares its victims."

"How dare you speak of pox," the Dauphine responded violently, grasping her dying husband's hand, her cheeks flushing in defiance. "It was the shock of Azincourt that killed Monsieur."

But nobody listened to her and Marguerite wept all the more for the fact that she was so powerless. Yet it was then, just as if he would finally agree with her at the very end of his life, that the Dauphin spoke his last words.

"Yes, it's true. Azincourt has speeded me on my way. It's because of Richemont's capture, I believe." He swivelled his eyes painfully to look at his wife. "If he ever comes back you are to marry him, do you hear?"

"Marry Richemont?" she said, dropping to her knees beside Louis's bed.

"Yes, you foolish little woman. That is my last wish." He squeezed the hand that still held his. "You've no sense and you're frigid but I believe you will do your best."

The fact that with his final breath he was, as always, scolding her, rent the Dauphine's heart.

"Did you love me at all?" she asked, the tears gushing freely.

He could not answer but just for a moment she thought she saw the flutter of a wink about one eye before they both slowly closed. The priest who had shriven Louis an hour before, giving him extreme unction, stepped hastily to the bedside.

"Monsieur le Dauphin, for the sake of your soul say these words with me. In te domine, confido, ne confundar in aeternum . . ."

But there was no response; the restless spirit of the heir to the throne of France had broken free. The Dauphin was dead and Marguerite of Burgundy, at the age of fifteen, was already a widow.

Before her fourth birthday, which fell on 6th January, Epiphany and also Christmas Day in the calendar followed by all the civilized world, Yolande d'Anjou sent a coded letter to Alison du May, requesting her to take a wooden toy—"One which moves"—to Jehanne.

"Then let me have word of her, dear Alison, please do. Does she grow fit and strong? And, above all, is she happy?

I torment myself frequently with the thought that I abandoned her to her fate, to a life to which she might not be suited. Despite your earlier letters reassuring me, please send me fresh news."

In February, on the eve of Charles's thirteenth birthday, Alison's answer duly arrived and Yolande took it to the privacy of her chamber to decode and study.

"Ma Reine," she read, "loyal greetings from your devoted servant. I apologize to you that I have not written sooner. The truth is that because of severe weather conditions I was unable to see Jehanne until the beginning of February but I am now pleased to report to you she is well, apart from the usual childhood complaints, and plays happily enough with what she believes to be her brothers and sister.

"The child is small but very sturdy, with dark hair and eyes, and a pleasant smile. She is not in the least shy and greeted me with enthusiasm though she had no idea who I was. She liked the wooden knights better than the doll I took her and spent a long time playing with them in the corner of the room while I talked to her parents . . ."

Yolande winced that the word "foster" had been left out but accepted that, by now, this sort of thing was inevitable.

". . . who said she was well behaved, had a charming belief in wood fairies and sometimes goes with the other village children to a certain tree known as the Fairies' Tree and there makes garlands, dances round it, and sings songs."

Yolande put the letter down, smiling to herself. It was a happy childhood, obviously, and carefree. Yolande thought of her daughter gamboling round a tree, flowers wound in her hair, holding her friends' hands, and for the first time was grateful that Jehanne was leading the innocent life of a country child, removed from the horrors of war and unaware of the danger in which France lay.

"I pray for my little girl's future," said the Duchess and, having read the letter to the end, locked the papers away in a secret drawer in her desk and turned her mind to that other child whose care was her concern, Charles de Valois.

Tomorrow the boy would be thirteen years old, and not long afterwards would be obliged, complete with an entourage of his own and accompanied by young Marie, to leave for Paris to take up his duties as the Dauphin's heir. But tonight he was to have formal audience with the Duke and

Duchess before the full Council of Anjou to hear what plans had been made for him. Going to the table where lay all her cosmetics and paints, Yolande rang a bell for Lady Sarrazin to come and attend her.

The Count was to be briefed in the council chamber, the old hall on the cliffs, and after this a celebratory banquet would be held with the new members of his household which would go on until well after midnight and thus run in to his birthday. In her future son-in-law's honor, Yolande dressed and prepared herself with care and, for this special occasion, wore soft green, a great ruby brooch sparkling high on her shoulder.

"You are wearing the colors of a wood fairy, Madame," Lady Sarrazin said whimsically, and Yolande smiled at the coincidence of her principal Lady's words.

Most of the *Conseillers* had arrived early and there was a scraping of seats as they stood up while Yolande ascended to one of the high chairs on the dais. Tonight a third chair had been placed in front of those of the Duke and Duchess and it was to this that Charles was led by the Duke of Anjou when they made their entrance a moment later.

"Gentlemen, be seated," Louis commanded, and there was a further clattering while all the great men of the province obeyed, taking their places expectantly, waiting to hear who had been chosen to form the Count of Ponthieu's first household.

The Duke stood up, clearing his throat, and immediately there was total silence.

"Gentlemen, I do not want to mar such a happy night as this by speaking of the tragedy of Azincourt. Let me simply say that the English King has renewed his suit for the Princess Catherine's hand and has announced his intention of returning to these shores if she and a dowry of two million crowns are not made available to him. The Council of France will not agree to such ridiculous terms and this can only mean that at some time in the future King Henry will come to invade us again. I speak of this simply to underline the fact that those chosen to protect and serve the Dauphin's heir must swear their utmost loyalty, for the Count of Ponthieu will be entering the world scene at a most dangerous and difficult time."

Louis laid his hand on Charles's shoulder and the boy

looked up at him, his eyes never more true and steadfast than at that moment.

"Charles de Valois," said the Duke solemnly, "do you swear to serve your country to the best of your ability, to take your place on the Council of France aware of the true dignity of such a body? Do you give your oath that you will do your utmost to keep foreign invaders from our shores and to quell internal troubles with a strong arm?"

"I swear it before God," said Charles, rising and laying his hand on the Bible that the Duke proffered to him.

"And do you also swear that if ever you should inherit the realm of France you will govern it as the true protector and champion of its people?"

"I do by God," answered the Count, his voice trembling.

"Then all is well," said the Duke seriously. His manner noticeably changed and became more business-like. "Monsieur le Comte, your household will be made up as follows: Robert le Maçon, Lord of Trèves, will be your Chancellor."

Charles smiled at the man, this night dressed in his favorite color of chestnut brown but with a crimson hat and decorations to give a dash of boldness. It had been he who had placed his body between Charles and the Caboche revolutionaries and, as such, had earned himself an honorable position.

"Jean Louvet will become *président* of the *chambre de comptes.*"

Glancing at the man who was the Bastard's future father-in-law, the Count saw a big bluff fellow in his late forties, handsome in a fleshy way. His mouth was sensual, or so Charles thought.

"Hugues de Noyer and Guillaume d'Avagour to continue as Chamberlains to Monsieur; Jean, the Bastard of Orléans, to take his place as a new Chamberlain."

The Count caught Jean's twinkling eye and both of the boys had difficulty in restraining a grin.

"Confessor to the Count of Ponthieu, Gérard Machet."

The tall cadaverous priest inclined his head to signify he understood that he must now leave the household of Duke Louis and travel with the boy to noisome Paris.

"And finally, and this by special request of Monsieur himself, Hunchback Guy as Personal Astrologer."

Gérard Machet sunk his bony jaw into his hand, obviously disapproving of this clash between theology and superstition, and there was a slight murmur amongst the more conventional members of the council. But the Duke ignored them. Astrologers were a part of life, dealing out medicine and political advice with equal ease. If Charles's difficult time in Paris could be alleviated by the presence of a soothsayer then Louis could see no objection to it.

"As soon as the winter is over and the ways are clear, Monsieur le Comte and his party will leave Anjou and take up residence in Paris. Gentlemen of his household, I ask you to make your arrangements to accompany him." Duke Louis smiled. "And now our business is formally at an end. The great banquet to celebrate the thirteenth birthday of the Dauphin's heir will shortly begin. I hope we will have the pleasure of entertaining each and every one of you on so joyous an occasion."

The *Conseillers* went with a will, having little enough to rejoice about in such troubled times, even the two youngest children of the household, little Yolande and the Count of Maine, being allowed to attend for a while. But throughout the happy occasion, the guest of honor found himself ill-at-ease, certain that the possibility of Nicolas Flamel being wrong about his future now seemed remote, that it truly was he who was destined to be the next King of France.

Staring moodily down the length of the table, Charles recalled yet again the words of the Grand Master.

"Three women will help you: a tall queen, a virgin bearing a rose, and the third will be beauty to your beast."

The tall queen could obviously be no other than the Duchess of Anjou, Queen of Sicily and Naples. She had already, in the two years that he had lived with her, been more than a good friend to him and, as much as one could love a great woman with a rapier mind like a mother, Charles did so. But the other two were a puzzle. Frowning deeply, Charles turned his mind to another of the alchemist's enigmatical phrases.

"You shall be told the name of the secret order when you are a man. You will shortly meet the one who is to tell you, and recognize him by the fact that his little finger is almost the same length as his fourth."

"Well, that didn't come true," thought the Count. "I didn't meet anyone like that at all. He was wrong."

Was it the will of God or a quirk of fate that at that very moment he happened to glance in the direction of

René d'Anjou, who was sitting opposite him? The child's extraordinarily large hands were spread out on the table-cloth before him, their very shape and contour enhanced by the white cloth embroidered in gold with the coat of arms of Anjou. With a gasp of amazement, Charles noticed for the first time that the boy's little fingers were anything but that, as long and as tapering as the fourth, a unique accident of birth.

The child realized he was being stared at and looked up. "What is it, Charles?"

"Do you know a man called Nicolas Flamel?" he answered, too surprised to be subtle.

There was a second's frozen silence during which René's brilliant eyes flickered then dropped and a shutter came down over his youthfully saturnine face.

"No," he said. "I don't."

But he was lying, there was no doubt about it. Even if he had not met the Grand Master, the name meant something to him.

The Count of Ponthieu leant forward, narrowing his eyes, but smiling all the while as if he had just heard a new and very amusing joke.

"Mon Dieu," he said quietly, "how foolish of me. I must be confusing you with someone else."

Just as Charles had guessed he would, René d'Anjou did not reply.

Fifteen

It was like going straight from Paradise to Hell. The royal party had left Anjou in June, riding past the gleaming rivers and through the rich vine-filled valleys, away from the sunshine and the luscious green of the bountiful land, heading north to Paris. Charles had turned his head for one last look, and had felt in that final glance that his two golden years of childhood had come to an end for ever, that nothing of the carefree magic he had known for the first time in the castle of Angers could ever come back again. And when he had seen the city of his birth once more his worst fears had been realized. It was even more terrible than he had remembered it.

Fires blazed round the outer walls of Paris, fires lit by the mercenaries of Jean the Fearless, for though the Duke of Burgundy might be skulking in Flanders, his cohorts incessantly pounced in lightening raids on the capital, inflicting as much damage as possible to both property and personnel. But even worse than this constant state of danger was the plight of the city's wretched people. Count Bernard d'Armagnac, now Constable of France, had been so determined to regain the fortress of Harfleur, manned by English soldiers left behind by Henry V, that he had levied a tax on the wretched population in order to raise the money to pay his troops. The suffering caused to a people already near to starvation had been enormous, and to make matters worse the Count's campaign had not succeeded. Harfleur remained in English hands.

Charles simply did not know which was more awful, the situation in Paris or the state of his mother, for during the years since he had last seen her, fat had consumed the Queen utterly. Isabeau now had nothing left that could be called a body, only a colossal bulk out of which rose a head, weighted down by the most enormous and extravagant kind of head-dresses. What there was of her neck was consequently foreshortened and thus Isabeau looked like two puddings, one, smaller, balanced upon another, enormous. At this size movement had become impossible for her and these days the Queen was dragged about in a wheelchair the width of a chariot.

Incredibly, this unappetizing woman still had lovers. Georges de la Trémoille, his ransom paid promptly and already returned from England, serviced her on a regular basis, a thought which had Charles's imagination wandering down strange corridors as Georges himself was now beginning to put on a serious amount of weight. Pierre de Giac, too, appeared from time to time, his eyes blazing wildly as he and Isabeau locked themselves away together for as long as a week. And when neither of those two was available, the Captain of the Guard offered himself as her stud. Even more amazingly, though no one would have believed it possible, Jean Louvet of Anjou trembled with lust when he first set eyes on the monstrous matron, secretly admitting to the Provost of Paris, Tanneguy de Chastel, that he found hugely fat women overwhelmingly attractive.

But her son thought her hideous and loathed it when Isabeau made a public display of affection, putting her over-painted face close to his and demanding a kiss. Near as Charles was at those moments, the boy could see the thick cake of her make-up and the place where her red lip paint had smudged and run. Everything about his mother repulsed him and if it had not been for the presence of the Duke and Duchess of Anjou in Paris, his *real* parents as the Count now thought of them, he felt he would have gone mad.

A further strain was added to the Dauphin's heir by the fact that the Dauphin himself was missing. Jean's wife, ugly Jacqueline, now Dauphine, may well have been a Duchess of Bavaria on her mother's side but her father was the ambitious Count of Hainault, a province which on its northwest border was neighbor to Flanders, a territory belonging to Burgundy and Jean the Fearless's present home. To say that the Duke and the Count were friends would not have been to state the case fully, they were like blood brothers and were political allies into the bargain. And now that

Jean had unexpectedly become the Dauphin it was Hainault's avowed intent to unite his son-in-law and Jean the Fearless and in that way see the Armagnacs off for ever.

And all the sudden and heavy responsibility of standing in for a missing brother who was the Dauphin of France had promptly fallen on the shoulders of a thirteen-year-old boy; a boy who wanted nothing more than to run away to Angers and resume his former peaceful existence within the walls of its castle. Charles, constrained by reason of Jean's absence to attend the meetings of the Council, where the noble lords sat arrayed in their velvets, felt that they looked on him as an intruder, as if he should have been in the company of tutors not bothering them with his unwanted presence, and hated every moment of it.

The summer of 1416, plagued by poverty and pestilence, passed thus, made worse by a heatwave during which Jean the Bastard and Charles, fearful to swim in the Seine because of the number of rotting bodies, both human and animal, floating therein, sighed for Anjou and the river Maine.

"Do you think we'll ever get back?" Charles had asked.

"Not unless the Dauphin returns to Paris soon," Jean had answered gloomily. "They seem to be relying on you to act for him these days."

"I feel sometimes that all this is a nightmare and that I'll wake to find I'm still in Angers."

"If only that were true."

"*You* may go," Charles had said loftily. "Don't think you have to stay here just because of me."

The Bastard's brilliant eyes had darkened. "I am your Chamberlain, Monsieur. I will serve you all my days as I have sworn. Now that my brother is prisoner in London's Tower it is you to whom I have pledged allegiance. I will remain by your side through thick and thin."

They had clasped hands and embraced and Charles had felt such a rush of fraternal affection that he had suspected yet again that both he and the Bastard had perhaps been sired by the same man.

For the rest of that noisome summer the Count had been sustained by Jean's loyal friendship, but never more so than when the Duchess of Anjou, pale to her mouth, had suddenly announced that she and the Duke must unexpectedly return to the Duchy.

"But why, Madame?"

Yolande had looked at him with such a serious expression on her face that the boy had felt himself begin to tremble.

"It is the health of Monsieur le Duc. I am afraid, Charles, that he is quite seriously ill."

The Count of Ponthieu had screwed up his ugly face to stop sudden tears.

"How is he ill? What do you mean?"

"Do you remember when my Lord could not fight at Azincourt? How he had a seizure on the way to battle and was in such pain that he could go no further?"

"Of course I do."

"Well now," Yolande said bitterly, "those enemies who accused him of cowardice will have to take back all they said. Monsieur is afflicted once more with that same agonizing pain in his bladder and bowels."

The tears had flowed then and Charles, throwing aside all decorum, had run to Yolande and flung himself into her arms.

"Does this mean you're going to leave me here by myself? Oh, my good mother, please don't go. I can't bear it."

It had been too much for her. The brilliant Duchess of Anjou, remembering another child she had been forced to abandon, had broken down and wept, and she and Charles had hugged one another tightly as the bitter tears fell.

Eventually, Yolande had controlled herself. "Mon cher, please realize that I *must* go with the Duke. We are obliged to return to Anjou and take up the reins of government. All must be prepared."

"For what?"

"For the possibility of my becoming Regent once more."

"But nothing's going to happen to him," Charles had sobbed despairingly. "It can't. He is my guardian, my father, the only proper one I've ever had."

Again, Yolande had not been able to answer, unable to voice her fears that her husband was now terminally ill, and Charles had wept hysterically, wanting reassurance, wanting to go with them, dreading the thought of being left at the mercy of his gross and greedy mother and her court of lovers and freaks.

"You will have the Bastard and your Gentlemen," Yolande had said, attempting to reassure him. "They will keep you company and look after you."

"But it won't be the same, Madame."

Yolande had hesitated, then added, "If I can possibly come back I will, but for the moment the family of Monsieur le Duc must remain together. And I am afraid, Charles, that means Marie must also return with us to Anjou."

Those words had been a relief, though the Count had been far too polite to say so. His future bride, hating the capital and her mother-in-law elect equally, had taken to sighing and sobbing at the slightest pretext, constantly bemoaning the fact that she had been forced to leave her carefree life in Angers to dwell in such a stinking hole as Paris, full of rats and beggars.

But if the Duchess had suspected what the Count of Ponthieu's true feelings were she had not said a word, and the next morning the royal family of Anjou, together with all their retainers and servants, had left Paris by the South Gate.

Duke Louis, suddenly old-looking, his full lips sunken and his strong nose pinched and thin, traveled in a decorated wagon, his wife and daughter sitting on either side of him, as Charles and his Gentlemen, on foot, stood amongst the falling leaves of autumn and waved them farewell.

"I shan't see him again," the Count whispered to the Bastard as the last of Louis's horsemen disappeared from view.

"But the Duke is only forty years old. Surely he will recover."

"I don't think so," answered the boy, and fell to wondering with a dull kind of anger at the extraordinary and haphazard whims of a destiny which allowed a lunatic hulk like his father to shamble about horribly alive while a vigorous and good man such as the Duke should already be under sentence of death.

"There's no justice in this world—or in heaven either come to that," said Charles miserably.

"You're right," replied Jean. "How can there be when men like my brother and the Earl of Richmond are confined in the Tower of London to rot away their sky-blue youth?"

"But surely Richemont's brother of Brittany is financing his return?"

"The rumor is that Henry of England doesn't want money for the Earl, that he prefers to keep him a permanent prisoner."

Charles looked at him in amazement. "Why, for God's sake?"

"The lousy pig maintains that Richemont betrayed his liegeman's oath to Henry IV by fighting for the French at Azincourt."

"He's not seriously claiming that Arthur should have fought on the English side?"

"Oh yes he is. That man is capable of more cunning and deception than any living creature I know."

"And he wants to marry my sister," said Charles in disgust. "It mustn't happen."

"But what other way out is there? The Lancastrian has set his heart on Catherine and now it seems nothing will deter him from getting her."

"He's never even seen her!" the Count replied angrily. "You know as well as I that she is simply a means to an end. Through her, Henry of England can get land and money. Why, I swear to God he'd marry a donkey if it were rich enough."

"I believe he is one of the most despicable men ever born," said Jean the Bastard with much dark feeling.

"I'll not argue with that," answered Charles, and on those sentiments the boys shook hands, as was their custom, and made their way back through the wretched stinking streets of Paris to the Hôtel St. Pol, glad only that the cold winds of autumn had come to kill the pestilence that had raged in the suffering city throughout the long hot summer months.

Sixteen

With Christmas over, invitations for the Count of Ponthieu's fourteenth birthday banquet became highly prized. It was to be held at the Château de Vincennes to which the Queen had removed her court, and rumor was rife that this would be one of the great events of the year 1417.

At fourteen the royal princes by tradition entered into man's estate, being obliged to take their places on the Council and assume certain important duties, though these had been thrust on Charles somewhat early by reason of the Dauphin's continuing absence.

News had reached the capital that the young man had now taken up residence in Compiègne, from whence his father-in-law, the Count of Hainault, sent messages to the Council of France that the Dauphin would not return unless accompanied by Jean the Fearless. Furthermore, the Count added, he would be coming to the capital personally to spell out to the Council the terms under which Jean the Dauphin would resume his duties. It was blackmail and everyone knew it but at the moment there was not a great deal that could be done. It was easier all round to stall for time and let the youthful Count of Ponthieu act in his brother's place, ignoring the fact that Charles was being overburdened prematurely.

In the gallery of gossip which was Paris, it was whispered that the price for the Dauphin's return, namely to be under Burgundian domination once more, might be too high to pay. It was further rumored that the Queen had been in secret correspondence with Jean the Fearless, that she was his hidden ally and was only waiting for the moment when he would return to Paris and her bed, boots and all!

But Charles knew nothing of this and on the day of his fourteenth birthday, there was a restless energy about the boy throughout the ride to the Château de Vincennes and the time in which he and his retinue prepared themselves for the festivities. So much so that the Count was in a mood of great elation when at four in the afternoon, everything eventually being ready, he and his Gentlemen made their way to the Great Hall and took their places at the high table awaiting the arrival of the Queen.

Much intrigued, Charles cast his eyes round the guests to see who was new on the scene.

Georges de la Trémoille had recently married. His bride, easy to identify because she was older than her groom, was a sandy-haired woman with a gap between her two front teeth large enough to house an *écu d'or*. She was also inclined to obesity and had large loose bosoms not entirely concealed by the open-work lacing at the front of her gown. Charles thought to himself that nobody was actually baring their breasts, as was becoming ever more fashionable, and then stared in surprise as he realized that one woman was.

A tiny thin creature with huge gray eyes set in a pale frightened but lovely face, a mass of dark hair pulled back and tucked into her head-dress, was revealing a surprisingly voluptuous breast, the corner of her crimson dress tucked back to show it. Yet how reluctantly and with what obvious distress, head down, eyes darting nervously, lips pressed tightly together as if to stop herself crying, did she do so.

"Poor little thing," thought Charles. "I wonder who she is."

But despite the fact he pitied her, the Count could not but feel a sharp pang of lust as he stared at her perfect shape, all gold and glistening with the cosmetics that had been applied to it. Then he could have died of shame as the girl stared straight at him, read what was in his eyes and looked away despairingly, as if she could have ended her life. At this moment, in a great flurry of trumpets, Isabeau's wheelchair appeared and both it and its mighty occupant were pushed to the head of the table, then silence followed as the Queen spoke.

"My Lords and Ladies, honored guests, tonight we celebrate the fourteenth birthday of our beloved son, Charles. Today the Comte de Ponthieu becomes a man . . ." Isabeau gave a merry but somewhat sinister chuckle. ". . . and may enter into a man's world. I ask you to stand and raise your wine cups in a toast to his health."

The words, "The Comte de Ponthieu," were on everyone's lips and Charles saw that his mother was floundering to her feet, gross beyond belief but still with a fluttering smile for de la Trémoille and de Giac, who had followed behind her chair and now took his seat at the trestle.

"My dear Madame de Giac," Isabeau swung her bulk in the direction of the stranger in the red dress, "would you do me the honor of sitting opposite my son tonight?"

Charles felt his jaw drop unattractively, hardly able to credit that de Giac had married, let alone such a sensitive soul.

"As Her Majesty wishes," the girl murmured and, rather reluctantly or so the Count thought, changed places.

In total silence, Charles stared at his plate, embarrassed and worried and, in the presence of Madame de Giac, highly charged with adolescent longing. Out of the far corner of his eye he saw the Bastard, wedged between two large titled ladies, looking appraisingly in his direction, and wished that his friend could somehow come to the rescue.

But immediate help was at hand with the arrival of mounds of food, the first course being served. Isabeau had obviously spared no expense or effort as a boar's head complete with tusks was carried to the carving table, together with mounds of herons, pheasants and cygnets, and lovely sweet delights like Crustarde Lumbarde and Viaund Royale. Yet nothing seemed to tempt the appetite of poor Bonne who picked at her victuals then left them on her platter.

As the wine flowed and Charles drank more than he should, he found himself staring at her almost continuously, utterly fascinated, and when the minstrels played for dancing in between the first course and the second, it was his mother's hand that guided the boy to his feet, and de Giac himself who charmingly bowed his wife from her seat and into the Count of Ponthieu's arms.

"Well done," said Isabeau softly as the two young people moved away, then gave her lover a wicked smile. "Do you have the stuff?"

"I do, ma Reine. A powerful combination indeed: satyrion, mandrake, hippomanes and cockle-bread."

The Queen glanced in the direction of the youthful couple, dancing well apart, neither catching the other's eye.

"I think our plan is already halfway there. Charles is obviously smitten. Bonne, this new wife of yours, is a very beautiful girl though you must have brought her out. I always thought her insipid when she waited on me."

"Too thin," said de Giac. "Skin and bone. Only a body like yours can excite me, chérie. I am not aroused by such a one as she."

"Then why did you marry her?" asked Isabeau curiously.

"She is an heiress as well you know, and her guardian wanted her off his hands. I have done very well as far as money is concerned. But the girl herself bores me to tears."

"Never mind. We'll soon get rid of her on to Charles."

"And what of our future?"

"We'll speak of that later tonight," the Queen said throatily and was rewarded with a look of sheer lust. "But back to business. Is the potion in liquid form?"

"It is," answered de Giac, and taking a phial from an inner pocket poured half its contents into Bonne's goblet, the other into Charles's.

"There could be only one snag now," he said, as he hid the container away again.

"And what is that?"

"She hardly drinks, that bag of bones."

"Leave it to me. I will propose another toast and she will be obliged to do so."

"And at the end of the evening?"

"You are to take her to his bedchamber and lock her in."

De Giac's predatory smile consumed his face. "And you say we can watch them through your mirror?"

"Oh yes, it was made in Italy and is a spying device. One can see straight through it into the room beyond."

"Excellent," answered Pierre, and under the table slid his hand up the Queen's thigh. "I love watching others."

"I too," she said, and each of them went thrillingly cold at the depths of depravity that both now enjoyed.

But Charles, falling in love by the second with the exquisite little creature whose hand he held as he danced, knew nothing of the base initiation his mother had planned for him, though the wife of the Devil's man, as if some fine-tuned instinct was already at work, surreptitiously glanced

in her husband's direction from time to time, trembling as
she did so.

"What is it, Madame?" asked Charles, speaking to her
for the first time. "Is anything wrong?"

Bonne looked at him properly, also for the first time,
having to tilt her head back to do so as the boy was already
taller than she. She did not notice his homely features, only
his honest eyes, and a little of her terrible fear went away.

"Nothing, Monsieur," she whispered.

"Then why are you shaking?"

"I am cold."

Without being able to help himself, Charles pulled her
closer and, as if he had conjured it, the music changed to
a faster beat and couples began to whirl together. Through
the padding of his jewelled and embroidered doublet, the
Count of Ponthieu could feel the lovely shape of Bonne's
naked breasts, and was aware that he had never known till
now what it was to desire another human being.

"You are so beautiful," he said, feeling gauche, yet wanting to show her in some way that he was falling in love
with her.

"I think my husband is looking at us," Madame de Giac
answered anxiously.

"Let him," blustered Charles, "it is my birthday after all.
I am a Prince of the Blood and may dance with whom I
please."

"But if he becomes angry—"

"Then he will have to answer to me." Charles's tone
altered and his clear eyes searched her face. "You're afraid
of him, aren't you? I do believe you are nervous, Madame."

"Don't be kind to me, please," Bonne replied falteringly.
"If you are I shall cry, here, in public."

"If that blackguard is misusing you," the Count said furiously, "I shall put you under my personal protection."

"But you are only a boy," Madame de Giac answered
tactlessly. "How could you?"

"I am considered important in Anjou," Charles protested, stung to the quick. "And will have more power here
in Paris now that I am fourteen." He looked at Bonne
appraisingly. "And so how old are you, Madame?"

On the lips of that anxious little face a smile hovered
momentarily. "It is supposed to be impolite to ask a woman
such a question, didn't you know that?"

Charles blushed. "I'm sorry, I had forgotten."

Now she *was* smiling. "I forgive you, and the answer is that I am seventeen."

"Then we are practically the same age."

The dance abruptly ended at that point and the boy, unbelievably flushed and excited, bowed his partner back to her seat, to see that Isabeau was once more hauling herself to her feet.

"My dear guests, one and all. My son and I would like to drink your health. Charles, will you join me."

There was no need to ask. Reckless now, the Count looked straight at Bonne as he raised his glass, then drained it in a single swallow. Instantly, as soon as the fluid reached his stomach, everything went black and the boy had to clutch the table for support. Gratefully, he sat down as Pierre de Giac got to his feet.

"On behalf of the guests I will propose an answering toast. To our gracious Queen and her son, Charles, Count of Ponthieu. On behalf of you all I wish him good health, a long life, and a happy birthday."

Nobody queried the fact that he was not an official spokesman nor had even been asked to propose the Count's health. Everyone drank politely and Bonne, too, drained her glass.

Now the momentary faintness had gone, Charles thought he had never had such wonderful wine. He glowed from head to foot, suddenly seeing the world as beautiful, even his mother appearing younger and thinner, her dark eyes brilliant as they had been in the days of his early childhood. As for Bonne, she was loveliness and delicacy personified, leaning forward on the table, smiling at him, no longer self-conscious of the bareness of her breast, which glowed in the candlelight like honey and rubies.

"I love you," murmured Charles, and she smiled all the more.

"It's my birthday," he said out loud, "and I am allowed to eat and drink what I like and make love to the most beautiful women in France."

Everyone laughed politely, for after all the boy was a Valois and obviously drunk, only the Bastard of Orléans frowning at his friend's extraordinary behavior.

"Are you all right?" he said, slipping out of his space

between the two weighty women, and leaning over Charles, pretending to pour him a drink.

"Of course," answered the Count, grinning like a cat.

But he wasn't, as Jean could see at a glance. For the pupils of Charles's eyes were as dilated as if he had been drugged and there was a high bright spot of color on each cheekbone. The Bastard looked round surreptitiously and took in at one sweeping glance the change in Madame de Giac, from frightened waif to alluring woman.

"An aphrodisiac!" he guessed correctly—and not too far to look for the perpetrators of that joke. The Queen and de Giac, quite the two nastiest people in the land, were exchanging sly smiles and secret winks as Charles stood up to dance once more, holding his hand out to Bonne, then grasping her as if she already belonged to him.

"Oh dear," thought Jean, "there goes a lost virginity."

But if Charles was ready for love it was partly the Bastard's fault for giving the boy such graphic descriptions of his own affair with the widow. Helplessly, Jean looked round for an ally but the only other one of Charles's chamberlains who had even noticed what was going on was the Bastard's future father-in-law, who had obviously decided to ignore the Count's odd behavior and instead was gazing at Isabeau as if he would like to ravish her on the spot. Weary of the world's warped deceits, Jean decided to stay as close as he could to his friend without getting in the way of any private matters that might be conducted later in the evening.

The lavish feast went on, the minstrels blew and plucked, the guests became drunk and riotous, and as night wore toward morning, Charles drew Bonne out of sight and kissed her, the first kiss of love he had ever exchanged with a woman, the giving of an unspoken promise for the rest of his life.

"I must make love to you," he said. "Young as I am, I know that you are my chosen woman."

The girl's fear overcame the power of even that most powerful of drugs.

"That can never be," she answered, pulling away from him in alarm. "De Giac would kill me if I were unfaithful to him."

"I would kill *him* first."

"You are a boy, he is an evil man. He knows things, does things, that you and I could never even comprehend."

She turned at that and ran back to the feast, making her way to the high table and taking a seat beside her husband, leaving the place opposite Charles to the anxiously hovering Bastard.

"Why, Bonne!" said de Giac, tongues of flame curling in his scorching blue eyes. "I do hope you are not overtiring yourself. You look exhausted, ma chérie."

"I am perfectly all right," she answered, hanging her head so that she would not have to look at him.

"I promised your guardian that I would cherish you. It is long past your bed time, come."

His fingers on her wrist were like bands of steel and Jean felt a frisson of fear sweep the length of his spine. He watched in horror as Bonne went limp, crumpling like a doll of rags. And then Charles arrived, his face taut and grim as he saw Madame de Giac's plight. Smoothly, the Bastard stood up and placed himself between the girl and his friend.

The great hall was very nearly empty now, only a few of the truly drunk still remaining to watch the capers of Isabeau's fool. The masquers, who had enacted the story of a Knight rescuing a Maiden from a wild man, half beast, half human, had long since gone. The Queen sat motionless in her chair, asleep apparently. An air of sudden somnolence was everywhere and Charles sat down hard, as deflated as the girl with whom he had that evening fallen in love.

"The drug's worn off," thought the Bastard gleefully. "By God's teeth the Devil's man and the fat sow are beaten!"

Almost as if she knew what he had been thinking, Isabeau opened one unblinking black eye and fixed it on Jean. "Take the Count of Ponthieu to bed," she ordered. "The great chamber is already prepared for him, the room next to mine."

"Do you wish to go, Monsieur?" asked the Bastard, deliberately ignoring her.

"I may as well," he answered, looking unhappily at Bonne, who sat with eyes closed and head hanging, fit to collapse.

In the body of the Hall the servants were already stacking the trestle boards as Charles and his Chamberlain made their way to the upstairs chambers, having bidden good-night to the handful of remaining revelers.

"I feel as if I left the earth tonight and have only just returned," said the Count of Ponthieu, as they climbed the stairs.

"I think perhaps your drink was rather strong," Jean replied grimly.

"But it wasn't the wine that made me fall in love," Charles said earnestly.

It was too late at night to reason with the flushed-faced boy, to tell him that however much he cared for Bonne de Giac, she was married to one of the most wicked men in the world and her future was entirely in the hands of fate.

"Come on," said Jean. "It's been a long night."

"What time is it?"

"Almost dawn. There's light in the sky. Here's your room. Now get some rest."

The Count of Ponthieu, shaking slightly from the after-effects of the aphrodisiac, suddenly felt so exhausted that he almost fell into the beautiful bed prepared for him, the air of his chamber full of perfume of the scented candles that burned in brackets attached to the wall, the light just beginning to peep through the mullioned windows. He would have slept, then, at once, had not a noise in the doorway made him sit bolt upright, suddenly afraid.

Bonne stood there, stark naked, her mass of wild dark hair, released from its confining head-dress, her only protection.

"Oh, Mon Dieu!" Charles exclaimed. "What is this?"

She shook her head in a combination of shame and bewilderment. "I don't know. My husband forced me in, said it was my new room. Oh, God help me, am I married to a monster?"

"Yes," said the Count, getting out of bed and going to her, not sure whether he was glad or sorry that he was still partly dressed. "You are. But Bonne my sweetheart, even though I have no good looks my nature is not monstrous. Come here, I will look after you."

He should have been honorable and slept on the floor but Charles could not. Instead he removed what was left of his clothes and the two young people got into bed together, instantly falling asleep, wrapped closely in one another's arms. Strands of Bonne's hair lay across the Count's ugly face transforming it to beauty in the first soft rays of the morning light.

"Christ's blood!" swore de Giac in disgust, looking through the two-way mirror. "They've gone to sleep. I'll whip that girl when I get hold of her."

"Forget them," answered Isabeau, ravenous for coupling as she had now taken a massive dose of Pierre's special love potion. "We'll wake early and watch them then. Come on."

He turned to look at her, saw the quaking heap of flesh and gladly went to oblige her, overjoyed by her obesity.

"Tomorrow will you celebrate a Black Mass with me?" he whispered into her ear. "Will you finally join me and serve my Dark Master?"

"I cannot be certain," quavered the Queen.

"Then *I'll* serve *you* no more," growled her lover, and rolled away.

"Oh please, please," begged Isabeau. "I'll do anything. Just don't stop."

"Good, then," Pierre said triumphantly and rammed into her until she screamed aloud with pleasure.

Just as those two appalling people finally fell asleep, the son of one and the wife of another awoke gently in the early sunshine.

"Oh, Bonne, my Bonne," said Charles, and kissed her.

Then suddenly the transition from boy to man was easy for him and with his body ready for love, Charles's penis entered the joyous place between Bonne's thighs and set up the slow, strong, harshly sweet rhythm that Jean the Bastard had described to him.

It was heavenly for them both as the girl, unafraid at last, raised to him her lips, her breasts, her hips, abandoning shame and moving with Charles as their bodies mingled and merged. Then came the moment when the boy became ruthless, though never like her cruel husband, and slipping a hand beneath her buttocks held Bonne pinioned while he drove his shaft into her rapidly and remorselessly. Then both of them left life for a moment as the power of their shared completion swept them away on a tidal wave of pleasure which finally put them down onto a warm beach of contentment on which they slept once more.

Seventeen

Exactly one week to the day after the Comte de Ponthieu's fourteenth birthday, the Count of Hainault
had arrived in Paris to sign the conditions for the
return of the Dauphin. The Council of France, sitting in
full session in the great chamber in the Hôtel St. Pol, heard
his words in stony silence.

"Monsieur le Dauphin, my son-in-law, will only enter the
gates of Paris if he is accompanied by Jean the Fearless,
Duke of Burgundy."

The *Conseillers* had looked at one another in horror,
knowing full well what such a warning meant. As soon as
that rotting lump of madness known as the King had the
good grace to die, France would fall into Burgundian hands
once more.

There had been a stir as the youthful Count had risen to
his feet. "I say let my brother stay where he is. Paris will
not tolerate the presence of the Duke of Burgundy again.
Tell him that."

It was a brave little speech and the great lords of France
had stared at Charles in surprise.

"That ugly boy is growing up," one had said to another.

"He even looks different. *Cherchez la femme* perhaps."

But these cynical speculations had been brought abruptly
to a halt by a stir at the back of the council chamber. A
door at the top of a short wooden staircase leading to a
platformed landing behind which lay the other rooms in the
King's dwelling, had been thrown rudely wide and Count
Bernard d'Armagnac had appeared in the opening, his savage face almost purple beneath his bristling white hair.

"Arrest that man," he had shouted, pointing a gauntleted

finger towards Hainault. "Put him on a charge of high treason for imprisoning the Dauphin against his will."

That the whole disturbance had been prearranged was
immediately obvious as guards suddenly filled every entrance, rushing towards the Count with weapons drawn so
that the man had temporarily vanished, set upon from all
sides.

"Take him away," Armagnac had shouted, thundering
down the staircase toward the hapless prisoner. "We'll not
brook that kind of blackmailing sedition here."

"Damn you Armagnac," Hainault had shouted back.
"We'll see who comes out of this best. You'll be a dead
man the minute Burgundy enters the city."

"That he'll never do," the Count had answered, removing one of his gauntlets and striking Hainault full in the
face with it. "I'll challenge you to combat hand to hand
before that traitor is ever allowed to return."

The Count of Hainault had turned away, biting his lip to
stop the flow of blood trickling from it, then had been
dragged roughly from the room and on, in manacles, to the
fortress of the Bastille.

But unfortunately that had not been the end of him.
Whether there had been Burgundian sympathizers amongst
the prison guards or whether Hainault had simply bribed
his way out, nobody knew. Yet the fact remained that he
slipped the leash and was gone within twelve hours, back
to Compiègne and his precious son-in-law. In the city of
Paris, Bernard d'Armagnac raged at the Council, the prison
guards and everyone who came within earshot, that a prime
captive had been lost and thus the cause of the Duke of
Burgundy strengthened. But Charles almost felt beyond
caring, caught up as he was in all the tumultuous and rapturous sensations of his very first love affair.

"For God's sake, Monsieur, be careful," said Jean the
Bastard, as they talked on the night of Hainault's escape.

"What do you mean?" Charles answered irritably. "I
love Bonne and always will."

"She is another man's wife, dear fool."

"But he doesn't want her, everyone knows that. He no
longer sleeps with her, in fact he has no interest in his bride
at all."

"I don't entirely believe that."

"Are you inferring Bonne does not tell the truth?"

"No, of course not," Jean replied hastily, more than aware that he was skating on thin ice. "It is de Giac I do not trust. He may say one thing but rest assured he'll mean another. He is one of the most evil beings in the world, surely you do not trust his word?"

But the Count would not see it, blinded by his mad infatuation.

"He is my mother's lover, he adores mountains of blubber. My little sweet is too delicate for him."

"But Charles, think, think, think. Where is it all going to lead? What can possibly be the outcome?"

"She will stay with de Giac until such time as he tires of her and orders her to quit. And then I shall set Bonne up as my mistress and we will have children."

"And do you really think it will be as easy as that? Do you honestly believe that de Giac will calmly tell her to go without causing her pain?"

But it was hopeless, like talking to a piece of masonry, and Jean, from whose spine the chill of apprehension was very rarely absent these days, gave up, for the young man had his own troubles to worry about. Not only was his half-brother, the Duke of Orléans, still a prisoner in London but his future bride's father, another lover of gross bulk apparently, had started an affair with the Queen. The Bastard had temporarily given up all thoughts of his own liaison with the widow in an effort to help his various relations through their current difficulties and diversions.

"I wonder if the Dauphin will come back to Paris now that Hainault is on the run," he said, by way of changing the conversation.

Charles looked at him strangely. "I don't know, but I hope he sees sense soon. I would like to talk to him again before . . ."

"Before what?"

But the Count would not answer, gripped by a presentiment that the prophecy of Nicolas Flamel was about to come true and the days of his brother were nearing their end.

Was it this sense of foreboding that made him dream, as he lay beside Bonne a few nights later, that he was riding behind the Count of Hainault, that he saw the fugitive return to his château at Compiègne, only to be greeted by a grim-faced woman who whispered something to the Count that Charles could not hear? Was it simply his daytime dreads that made him follow Hainault up the stairs in the dream state, only to see Jean the Dauphin inert on a canopied bed, his body, tongue and lips swollen beyond recognition, his poor sad eyes bolting from his head?

"Mon Dieu," Charles heard Hainault exclaim, "what is that terrible rasping noise?"

And, indeed, the room was filled with the sound of Jean's agonized breaths as he fought to get air through his swollen windpipe.

"He's finished," said the long-faced woman, who had come silently to stand beside the Count. "Monsieur le Comte, the Dauphin is dying."

"Oh no!" screamed Hainault. "Oh no, oh no!"

And so screamed Charles, waking in terror, sitting bolt upright and clutching his mistress, his voice reverberating round the tower room in which he and Bonne kept their loving and dangerous trysts, the door safely locked against the outside world.

The arrangements for these illicit meetings teetered on a very knife's edge, everything depending on de Giac announcing in advance that he would be going out for the night. And this, in turn, depended on whether Isabeau was amusing herself with one of her other lovers or had chosen him, for though Pierre himself was happy to have a Roman orgy, his rivals were not.

Though all his sexual activities may be conducted away from home, de Giac's satanic rites were practiced in his own castle, in the dungeons, converted to a chapel for Devil worship. Here no servant or wife dared to tread, and those who came at night to join him in his demonic rituals were never seen, though rumor was rife that Isabeau was one of them, for no hood or mask could adequately disguise that vast body crammed into its wheelchair.

On these sinister occasions, Charles did not call and Bonne, terrified out of her wits, would go to bed and lock the door, praying to her Christian God that her husband would not come and demand she open it at once. If he did so it meant rape and brutality, albeit marital, and the girl would carry her bruises and cuts into her lover's bed, where Charles would kiss each one, rubbing in soothing ointments given him by Guy, and grinding his teeth at his extreme youth and consequent lack of power over people and events.

But this night Bonne was whole, unhurt, and it was she who ministered to Charles, holding him to her beautiful breasts, her nimbus of dark hair falling round his face as she bent over and comforted him like a child.

"Shush, it's all right. You've had a nightmare. I'm here with you."

He calmed down, drawing in a deep breath like a sigh. "I dreamt about the Dauphin, dreamt that he was at his last gasp. Oh Bonne, it was so real I think the dream is going to come true."

"Because of Flamel's prediction?"

"Yes."

"I do not wish death on anyone," answered the girl, snuggling even closer to her boy lover. "But yet I long for the day when you will be King."

Charles smiled in the candlelight. "Because I will be able to give you jewels and gifts?"

The wild hair flew as Bonne shook her head. "You know that's not the reason. It is because you will have the authority to banish de Giac for good so that I can be your *Maîtresse-en-Titre,* seeing you every day of my life."

"That would be wonderful," said the Count and eased down in the bed again, hugging the slight body next to his.

They lay in each other's arms quietly, listening to the noises of that April night: the chant of a distant owl, the light murmur of a spring breeze, the lap and gurgle of the emerald waters of the moat. A nearby nightingale called suddenly, a soaring sensuous sound, surprisingly close, and Bonne whispered, "I wish it could be like this always, you and I together, utterly at peace."

And it was then, as if their innocent happiness had challenged her husband's satanic master, that the drumming of hooves broke the harmony of those gentle rustic sounds.

"De Giac!" exclaimed Bonne, rearing up in alarm, her face suddenly white as ice. "You must go, quickly!"

She was not foolish this young girl, for in deciding on the place for her adulterous meetings she had chosen carefully indeed. A little-used tower room, situated well away from the great hall and living quarters, with two staircases one of which led onto the battlements, had been the chamber elected to give most seclusion and be the easiest to escape from should the necessity arise.

"Hurry," she said now, throwing a shift over her nakedness and pulling a loose robe over that. "Get your clothes on."

But Charles had already struggled into his hose and had one arm in his doublet, shrugging on the other sleeve even while he made for the stairs.

"Wait for me," whispered the girl and, blowing out the candle, was beside him in the darkness, a wraith with moonlit hair, as she led the way up the short spiral and shot back the bolts, then turned the key which held fast the door at the top.

Outside, the moonshine was vivid, and standing in the dark of the tower's shadow Bonne and Charles could see for miles, every leaf clearly etched with shimmering silver. They were afraid to peer too closely over the parapet, for the horseman below was just going out of their line of vision, about to enter the gatehouse guarding the moat, but even that one brief glimpse was enough to tell the silent onlookers that it was not de Giac who returned home early. In that brilliant light the fleur-de-lis emblem on the box of the Queen's *chevaucheur* could be seen distinctly.

"A messenger," whispered Bonne. "I must get back to my bedroom for they'll come to wake me when the servants discover de Giac is out. Wait for me here, my darling."

And with that she breathed a kiss onto his lips and was gone, scurrying along the battlements, then through another door to a staircase which led down to the castle's main dwelling area.

In the moonlight Charles stood alone, feeling the touch of destiny on him, almost knowing what the courier had come to say. From below came the rattle of powerful chains and the groan and crack of the portcullis as it slowly raised in the air, these sounds followed by the distant murmur of voices. In the Count's imagination he could see Bonne, small and anxious, still in her night clothes, receiving the courier in the anteroom, hearing what he had to say in silence, then offering the man food and shelter as was the custom. Soon she would come back to him and nothing would ever be the same again. Almost as if he wished to remember every detail of that moment, the boy walked to the parapet and looked round.

The stars that guided the destiny of mankind were all in their myriad places, some having names that Charles knew. Toward the east, Orion's belt sparkled with all the richness of the wonderful jewels with which that belt was encrusted; the Plough glittered more gorgeously than any earthly counterpart could ever do; the Wolf Star and the Centaurs gleamed as wickedly as their namesakes, shimmering intensely in the clear April sky. Slowly, the Comte de Ponthieu raised his eyes to them and prayed for help in whatever great perils might lie ahead.

And then Bonne was returned, breathless as she came through the door from the tower, something of the spangled firmament in her own eyes. Without saying a word she went down on one knee and Charles knew then that what he had expected was indeed a fact.

"Monsieur," she said, her voice trembling with all her crowding emotions, "the Dauphin is dead, long live the Dauphin."

So the Wheel of Fortune had started to turn, fate had singled out the ugly boy as had been decreed.

"So be it," said Charles. "I will do my best."

Long before the many messengers who were to take to the roads of France during the next few days left for their destinations, two in particular swiftly set out. One, a dark, hard man on a sinewy black horse rode off with secret instructions, sealed with the crest of the Duke of Burgundy himself, making for the Château de Vincennes where Isabeau still held court; the other, a personal servant of Charles de Valois, the Dauphin of France, Duke of both Berri and Touraine, Count of Ponthieu, left at speed for Angers, going to the people whom the boy considered his true parents.

So it was that on 9th April 1417, the two Queens, the hawk and the pouter pigeon, the proud and the profane, read the news of Charles's raising up simultaneously.

Isabeau, of course, already knew. Word had come from Paris within hours that the son she disliked, the plain-featured child who resembled no one, conceived at a time when she had been experimenting with a new aphrodisiac which had demanded instant satisfaction with anyone at hand, was to be the future king. The irony of the situation had struck the Queen forcibly and she had laughed out loud. He could have indeed been the King's son, or that of the Duke of Orléans, equally he could have been fathered by any one of the thirty men with whom she had had intercourse that month.

"Upstart!" she had mouthed, and not known whether to laugh again or cry.

But the letter from Jean the Fearless had put a different complexion on the entire matter. She and the Duke had never, in truth, lost touch with one another, keeping up a clandestine correspondence throughout the years of Jean's exile. They had shared too much in the way of perversion and power ever to break the bond between them. And now he had instructions for her: to lure both Charles and the King to Vincennes so that he, the Duke, could take physical possession of the two of them and thus turn the tables once more on Count Bernard d'Armagnac.

"The Dauphin Jean who was my ally is gone," Burgundy had written. "Now I must forge a new alliance with the Dauphin Charles. Ma chérie, I leave it to you to get them to Vincennes and to let me know as soon as they arrive."

Loving the challenge of a new scheme, Isabeau wheeled her chair to her desk and opening a drawer took out several medicine bottles, and poured herself a good measure of liquid gold. Then she picked up her pen, and started to write a letter to Tanneguy de Chastel, the Provost of Paris, asking him to escort the King from the Hôtel St. Pol to attend a great banquet celebrating the elevation of her third son to the rank of Dauphin.

Similarly, Yolande d'Anjou wrote a letter, sitting at her desk in the room overlooking the river where she and her husband saw petitioners and heard their pleas. But today there was no husband and none had come to seek audience, for the news was out and through the town, both the walled city and the Doutre, that the Duke was seriously ill, that the malignancy which had kept him from the fight at Azincourt had gained ascendancy over their beloved Louis. And it was true. Though she would not admit it even to herself, Yolande knew secretly that the head of the house of Anjou was dying.

But the letter she wrote reflected none of this, containing instead expressions of sadness for the loss of Charles's brother but also words of delight at the fact he was now *the* Monsieur, the heir to the throne, and of reassurance that she would help him in every way possible with the duties that lay before him. This was the true letter of a mother to her son and as such moved Charles to tears on the morning he was due to set out for Vincennes.

It did not occur to the Dauphin even when the Queen's escort, headed by her soldier lover Captain Louis Boisridon, came to fetch him that there was anything suspicious about this visit, in fact Charles was looking forward to it. So, as custom decreed, the Dauphin's escort left the city first, to be followed at a distance by that of the King. Today, the madman was passive, lying on his back in a litter, his person sweet smelling, all the filth and parasites scrubbed away, and it was not until his cavalcade, under the leadership of de Chastel, had reached the half-way point of the journey and caught them up, that Charles realized anything was wrong at all. But to his amazement as the Provost of Paris's men drew alongside those of the Dauphin, Captain Louis and his troops were suddenly set upon and put under arrest.

"No need to worry, Monsieur," said de Chastel smoothly, trotting to the Dauphin's side, bowing, and offering his sword hilt first to show that he meant no harm.

"There's every need," Charles snapped back angrily. "What in the name of God is going on?"

They stared at one another, the olive-skinned soldier and the tall thin boy who had risen overnight to a position of considerable power.

"I'm sorry, Monsieur," de Chastel answered eventually. "I was acting on the direct orders of the Comte d'Armagnac."

"Which were?"

"To arrest the Queen's escort and to take you and His Grace safely back to Paris."

Charles glared at him. "What do you mean 'safely'? We were in no danger."

De Chastel's face hardened. "On the contrary, Monsieur, you and the King were walking straight into a trap."

"What nonsense is this? We were on our way to attend the Queen's banquet."

"You were on your way," answered the Provost shortly, "to certain danger. This morning a messenger with confidential information for the Duke of Burgundy was apprehended not far from Vincennes. The letter he bore stated

that you and the King would be at the château later today
and would be staying for nearly a week. There were plans
afoot to snatch both you and your royal father into Burgundian hands."

Charles stared at him askance. "But who could have
done such a thing? There must be a traitor at Vincennes
who should be stopped immediately."

For the first time in their exchange, de Chastel dropped
his fierce eyes. "Yes, there must," he answered quietly.

"But the letter obviously bore a signature. Whose was it?"

Tanneguy looked up again. "Well, you've come to man's
estate, Monsieur, and so I suppose you should be treated
as such. The turncoat is your mother."

Charles lost color, not so much at Isabeau's perfidy but
more that she had treated him with a friendliness which
had obviously been a sham, a means to an end, making
clear the fact that his mother still had absolutely no love
for him at all. His passionate lips tightened.

"Then I order you in the name of the King to bring the
Queen to Paris to answer that charge."

De Chastel opened his mouth to tell him that that command had already been issued by the Count d'Armagnac,
then hadn't the heart to say to this young creature with its
blood and color up that his wishes really didn't count for
much.

"I'll see to it once, Monsieur," he said, bowing in the
saddle. "You men, escort the King and the Dauphin back
to Paris, you others take the prisoners to the Bastille. Special guard, follow me to Vincennes."

Charles's heart beat faster in his proud young chest. He
had given his first order and it had been instantly obeyed.
Perhaps the thought of ultimate power was not so frightening after all.

"And Monsieur le Provost . . ." he added trying to sound
casual.

"Yes, Monsieur le Dauphin?"

"Be good enough to ask Pierre and Madame de Giac to
accompany the Queen if you would."

"Certainly, Monsieur," answered le Chastel, grinning to
himself as he rode away.

The revenge of Bernard d'Armagnac on a woman who had
come so near to betraying him was terrible. In the name

of the King he confiscated all Isabeau's properties, treasure chests and jewelery. He sent the *Président* of the Dauphin's *chambre de comptes*—his Chancellor of the Exchequer—to disperse the Queen's households and servants and to search for any hidden wealth she might have. This task Jean Louvet, who was in love with Isabeau's fat and who had only a few nights before been in bed with her, undertook with a certain reluctance, until it occurred to him that this was a wonderful way to fill his own coffers without anyone being at all the wiser.

Meanwhile, d'Armagnac drew up plans for the Queen to be exiled, first to Blois and then to Tours, her only campanion the Princess Catherine. He also ordered that her powers of Regency should be taken from her and re-invested in the Dauphin.

"And will all this be in order, Monsieur?" Count Bernard asked, paying lip service to Charles's new-found status.

"It will," the boy replied with dignity. "But I still require to see my mother before she goes. There is something I need to ask her."

And so it was arranged that on the eve of her departure, the Queen should attend him at the Hôtel Tournelles, a private palace which Charles, for reasons best known to himself, preferred to inhabit rather than the Dauphin's official apartments in the Hôtel St. Pol.

That the sight of her would revolt him Charles had already expected, for fat had now completely deformed her. But it was the feeling of utter rejection, the knowledge that her friendly overtures had not held one ounce of genuine affection, that almost made him retch. Isabeau regarded his turning aside from her with an icy and unrelenting glare, almost spitting out her words at him.

"So you find me revolting, do you, you miserable little monster? Well, look to yourself. You have not one ounce of beauty, nor ever will. That de Giac girl is only out for what she can get from you, mark what I say."

Charles gazed at her in horror. "You know about her?"

"Of course I know. So does her husband. We watched you with her, thrusting away, and laughed ourselves sick."

The Dauphin sat down rapidly. "You watched us . . . me and Bonne? How?"

"Through the mirror in my bedchamber. It was made

especially for me in Italy. It is a window to the next door room."

"Mon Dieu!" snarled the boy, rising up again, his face drained but for two flushed patches on his cheeks. "It is you who are the monster, not I. You watched your own child make love, while you did likewise no doubt, floundering in your fat. Begone from my sight! By my own command, for what it is worth, I decree that in exile you be allowed neither food, favor nor fornication. You are ordered to fast, Madame."

He swung away, turning his back on her, so that Isabeau's hiss came from directly behind him as she moved her chair close.

"I swear by God in heaven that you will *never—never* do you hear?—succeed to the throne of France while I live. I'll show you up for the accursed bastard that you are. I'll admit my adultery and rob you of any chance you ever had. By Christ's Holy Blood I would rather see Henry of England take the throne than you get within a mile of it."

Charles spun round again. "And there speaks the traitor that you are. You have been in league with Burgundy all along, he who is our enemy, he who signed a treaty with the English King last autumn and who has declared the French his antagonists. It is the Duke whom you would rather see in my place, and it is to our foes that you are going to sell our poor downtrodden country. Well, you can reckon with me first, Madame. I'll fight you to the end."

She did not answer, ringing a bell for a servant to come and take her away, but meanwhile maneuvering her chair as far as the doorway. There the Queen turned.

"I'll see you dead before you ever become King, you bastard."

"I'll be King," the Dauphin replied, remembering Nicolas Flamel and his fated words. "And it is I who will drive the English out. And you will think of me doing just that when you are old and lonely, Madame."

And with those words he left the room by the further door, feeling her terrible stare rake his back until he had finally gone from his mother's sight.

It was Yolande who closed the Duke of Anjou's eyes for his final long sleep, and it was she who placed his hands across his breast and drew a white cloth over his quiet face before she retired to her own apartments to weep. At the age of forty, the man whom she had married when he had been sixteen years old had been taken from her, and she wept bitterly for him, her greatest friend gone for ever.

Happily, the Duke had lived long enough to know of Charles's elevation and had nodded his head when Yolande had told him of it. And his last words had clearly shown he had more than understood what the Duchess had said. Gripping her hand, Louis had ordered distinctly, "Stop this feud between Armagnac and Burgundy, Yolande. Do whatever is necessary to get the English out. We *must* unite France against the common enemy."

"I will do what I can," she had answered, knowing only too well the hopelessness of the situation.

"Use the boy," he had continued. "Let him be the instrument if necessary."

"I will, I promise," his wife had answered, meaning it.

"Then all's well," whispered the Duke, kissed her hand in farewell, and died without further fuss.

It was very rarely these days that the Duchess's mind turned to Richemont, still a prisoner in England, moved from the Tower of London to Fotheringay Castle because Henry V had not the patience even to see him, despite the entreaties of the Queen Dowager, Richemont's mother Jehanne. But now, when every moment should have been devoted to mourning the dead man who lay in the adjoining chamber, unwanted thoughts of the Earl crept in.

"Both gone," Yolande reflected. "Both the men I loved, in such very different ways, snatched from me."

She wept, then, with self-pity, a rare thing for that fine strong woman, for it seemed to her that she had reached the watershed of her life, the ashes of existence. Yet, intelligent creature that she was, the Duchess knew, even in this state of total depression, that she had the usual two paths of widows: the choice of locking herself away with her memories, a harsh black relict eking out her days until death came for her too, or taking the more difficult road and calling fate to heel, setting herself the task of wrestling with whatever difficulties life might throw her way.

Yet what decision was there really? The new Duke, fourteen-year-old Jade, now Louis III, would need a Council of Regency to see him through the next four years and, miserable though she was, Yolande could not imagine herself allowing anyone else to be appointed Regent. Furthermore, the new Dauphin must be molded into a future king of stature and courage. So, with all these stirring events at hand, it was not possible even to contemplate retiring from the world. With a sigh, Yolande, as she always did when she was deep in thought, went to gaze out the window.

A sharp clear shower was drenching the land, the setting sun still out, throwing great dappled pools of light and shadow on the castle walls and gardens. Over the river arched a double rainbow reminding the Duchess of Dr. Flavigny's Tarot cards and that representing the lovers.

Richemont had come to her in an April night six years earlier and Jehanne had been conceived, but where were those lovers now? A widow and a war prisoner who would probably never meet again. Whatever future lay ahead of her it would seem destined to be one of hard work and struggle with all the softness of love taken from it. And yet the Duchess was still only thirty-seven years of age. With an uncontrollable sob more tears came and both Yolande and the sad sweet evening wept together as the sun finally dipped behind the hills.

Eighteen

Deep down, far away in a drenching sleep, the Dauphin of France dreamed of both his past and the future.

He was a child again, sitting on the lap of Lady du Mesnil, listening to her sing an old French song. Then he was standing in the maze of walkways and dwellings that made up the Hôtel St. Pol, watching and waiting for his beloved sister to come and play with him. And now she was walking toward him, but twined like a creeper round a red-mouthed man whom Charles recognized to his horror as none other than the monstrous murderer of the French nation, Henry V himself.

In despair, the Dauphin called out, "Oh, Catty, don't love him. Please don't."

But it was useless, for her brother knew that the girl was hopelessly besotted, that she would give up her birthright a thousand times just for the chance to lie in the arms of that most brutal enemy of France, longing for the touch of his cold ascetic lips on her strawberry ripe mouth.

The dream changed course and Charles was suddenly a silent spectator, marching with a division of Henry V's army, seeing them put poor Normandy to the sword, marauding and spoiling everything they touched. The fact that Catherine loved such a ruthless, pitiless tyrant made everything more hopeless and the boy felt the taste of ashes in his mouth.

"I hate you, I hate you," the Dauphin moaned in his sleep. "I hate you, Catherine, for betraying me."

The dream altered again and now Charles found himself in a deserted and moonlit field, the landscape harsh and scrubby, the only sign of any human presence a mound of freshly dug earth beside which stood Bonne, her back turned to him, her shift bleached white by the moonshine, her black hair clouding out round her shoulders.

"Oh, darling," called Charles, starting to run toward her. "Oh, Bonne, where have you been hiding?"

She turned to look at him. She had no face, only a grinning skull. She had been dead for weeks.

"Christ," screamed the Dauphin. "Christ protect me!"

And he woke up making the sign of the cross, shivering violently, the bedclothes drenched with the dew of his sweat, and lay thus for a few moments, desperately afraid and disorientated, trying to get his bearings, before finding a tinder and lighting the candle beside his bed only to see the outlines of the Dauphin's chamber in the Hôtel Tournelles emerge from the darkness.

Charles sat up and swung his feet to the floor, trying to slow the racing thoughts which teemed through his brain relentlessly. For in the year since he had become Dauphin of France the situation in the country had deteriorated even further, though through no fault of his.

In the autumn following Charles's elevation, Henry V had landed his troops, once more claiming the right to his bride Catherine, and her dowry. This time he had split his army into four divisions so that Normandy could be conquered systematically. Meanwhile, bored to distraction in her exile in Tours, her lovers, her jewels, her fine gowns all gone, Isabeau had written for help to Jean the Fearless. Hurrying to her rescue at once, he had snatched her from prayer in a convenient convent and transported her to Troyes where, with the full agreement of the English King, Burgundy had set her up as Regent of France.

The Dauphin, while all these ills beset his future kingdom, did his best to lead with what little scope he had. Under the auspices of Yolande he had received the keys to various cities, been stupendously polite to every local dignitary, however boring, spent a few days with Marie then hastily returned to the arms of Bonne, only to find that his future bride had been sent on separately to join him in Paris. Charles had also added several more gentlemen to his household and had begun to sign edicts issued in the name of the King, the boy's well-formed hand with its bold and flourishing signature becoming a familiar sight on state documents.

These days the Dauphin was growing up in every way, the three-year gap between himself and Bonne almost seeming to be reversed, so that he appeared the elder and she the anxious child. This illusion was aided by the fact that the boy had grown taller, though remaining lanky as ever, and his pleasingly husky voice had now become fully mature, charming all those who listened to it. With his lovely eyes alert and his passionate mouth smiling, there were times when even this particularly plain young man could look alive and attractive.

The Dauphin's intimate set of friends—the Bastard, Hardouin de Maillé, his *grand maître,* and Robert le Maçon and Tanneguy de Chastel of the older men—all knew about their royal master's affair with Madame de Giac, and to each one of them, in varying degrees, it gave cause for concern. Knowing her husband's evil reputation, none could understand why the man was not taking his revenge on the young but adulterous lovers, though le Maçon guessed shrewdly that the Devil's man was waiting to see which side would be uppermost in the forthcoming political struggle and then blackmail the Dauphin, should he be the victor, for promotion to the highest position in the land. But in the meantime de Giac, who must have been more than aware of his wife's infidelity, chose to ignore the flagrant affair being conducted beneath his very nose.

Now, sitting on the bed, still shivering slightly, Charles wished Bonne were beside him, that it could be one of the forbidden nights which made his life worthwhile, enriching both his body and soul, or so he made himself believe. But the girl was not and he had little choice but to lie down again and go to sleep and would, indeed, have done so, had not a sudden sound sent him starting up again. Footsteps were pounding up the stone stairs and along the corridor toward his room. Acting almost by reflex, the Dauphin slid rapidly out of bed and pulled on his hose, so that he was at least partly dressed when the door flew open.

Tanneguy de Chastel, the Provost of Paris, stood there, his leathery face pale, his black eyes hot as roasting nuts, while behind him Charles could see Guillaume d'Avagour and his Chancellor, Robert le Maçon.

"For the love of God come at once, Monsieur," said de Chastel urgently. "There is not a second to lose."

"What has happened?" answered Charles, throwing a loose shirt over his shoulders. "Are we under attack?"

"Yes we are, by God. Burgundy has broken through the walls and is entering the city. He'll be after your hide sure as fate. So for Christ's sake don't dawdle."

He was rough, he was peremptory, but nobody cared.

"Where are we going?" asked the Dauphin, breaking into a run to keep up with the others as they hurtled down the staircase and into the great hall where stood the Bastard, his face chalk white.

"There are horses outside," Jean gasped. "We must make for the Bastille. This whole bloody thing's a plot. One of the merchants stole the keys of the St. Germain gate and let the Burgundians in."

"No, no horses," le Maçon ordered, "you'll be spotted a mile off. Go through the gardens. I'll make my own way and join you later."

There was something exciting about such terrible danger, Charles thought, as the four of them slipped out of the Hôtel's terrace door, down the stone steps and into the ink-dark grounds, the smell of night flowers rushing to meet them like a perfumed veil. Beyond the palace the sounds of battle were now distinctly audible, the shouts of men and the scream of horses, the crunching of feet and clash of swords as enemies fought hand to hand. Suddenly only too aware there was a massacre in the city of Paris, Charles turned to the Bastard fearfully.

"Where are the others? Is everybody safe?"

"They're getting out as best they can," Jean answered briefly.

"And Bonne? Where is she?"

The truth was that the Bastard of Orléans had absolutely no idea, having left his own apartments so hurriedly that his livery collar of the Bourbon Porcupine had fallen off on the way. But now he told an expedient lie.

"She and her husband have already quit the city."

"Really?"

"Yes, really. I saw them go myself."

And that could easily be explained away later, should the de Giacs perish in the bloodbath, by saying he must have been mistaken, that his judgement had been impaired by the confusion and panic.

In the darkness the Dauphin blushed, suddenly remembering poor inoffensive little Marie, his hapless fiancée, back at his side since the New Year, hating every minute of court life and mightily suspicious of the delicate and beautiful Madame de Giac.

"And Marie?" he asked. "What about her?"

"Also gone," the Bastard answered, lying again. "Now come on."

Beyond the Hôtel's walls the Bastille, the grim fortress used as a prison by the Council of France and to which Tanneguy de Chastel, as Provost, had immediate right of entrance, threw its towers and turrets like an even darker shadow against an already dark sky. But it was with relief that the royal party, fearing tremendously for the Dauphin's safety, heard its portcullis raise at de Chastel's shouted command and then, even better, lower again behind them, hearing from the guards as they passed through that Robert le Maçon was already inside.

"Monsieur," said the Provost, bowing, a fact which made the Dauphin smile a little, "welcome to the Bastille. My lodgings are at your disposal. May I suggest that you resume your broken sleep while we others plan the best way for you to leave Paris without danger."

"I thank you for the thought," Charles answered at once, "but I would rather be privy to your decision. After all, it is me that is going to have to do the escaping."

It was said so quaintly that everyone laughed and with a great sense of camaraderie the five men, the difference in their ages and rank forgotten, went to the Provost's quarters and sank down several flagons of good wine to raise their spirits and help their thoughts flow more brilliantly. And, so inspired, at about two in the small hours, the escape plan was formulated.

Visiting the prisoners that night and now unable to return to their Abbey were an order of monkish brothers, and it was soon decided that they, out of love for their King and his heir, should surrender their habits to the five gentlemen wishing to leave the city urgently. But then another problem was posed, namely that there was only one horse in the entire fortress and that belonging to Robert le Maçon.

"You must take it, Monsieur," said the Chancellor. "The road to Melun is still clear, or was at the last reconnoitre.

I insist that you go ahead, knowing we will follow as soon as other mounts have been found."

"But I will be leaving you in danger."

Guillaume d'Avagour, silent till now, said, "Monsieur, that really is beside the point. It is *you* not us who are heir to the throne and consequently the one to rally to your side those still loyal to our cause. If harm should befall you I think all our futures would be in the direst peril."

So it was agreed and an hour before dawn Charles, dressed in the robes of a white friar and escorted by a band of fellow hooded monks, all on foot, left Paris by the only gate that had not yet fallen into Burgundian hands. But at the last second the Dauphin turned to Jean the Bastard.

"Bonne and Marie, you are certain they have already left?"

"I assure you of it, Monsieur," answered Jean, crossing himself surreptitiously within the folds of his disguise.

"And all of you will only be an hour behind me?"

"At the most. We will go in search of horses as soon as you have gone."

"Make your way straight to Melun, Monsieur," ordered de Chastel, his voice harsh with strain. "Stop for nobody and nothing. Wait for us there but if we have not come within a day and a night, go to Angers and join the Regent."

"And you?"

"We will find you, never fear."

"God speed," called Robert le Maçon as the boy wheeled in the gateway.

"Au revoir," Charles called back, and with that galloped away from the city of Paris, a city that he was destined not to see again for another nineteen years.

They got out as best they could, the Dauphin's men. Some went in disguise, some blatantly going through the gates. Pierre de Giac gave the Burgundian porter such a terrible look from eyes both wild and frightening that the man, thinking the Devil himself was leaving in the wake of the Armagnacs, let him through without demur.

Some journeyed on foot, amongst them Guy, who limped out dressed as a beggar in the company of the brothers Jean and Hervé du Mesnil, sons of Charles's ex-governess who had now retired to Anjou. They took the guise of lepers and were let out of the city instantly. Others such as Jean Louvet, a fortune's worth of Queen Isabeau's confiscated jewels and coin carried in bags stitched under his saddle and cloak, left importantly, bearing a forged safe conduct apparently signed by Jean the Fearless himself.

Others, again, bribed their way out, the *grand maître* of the Dauphin's household, Hardouin de Maillé, together with Hugues de Noyer, doing just that, giving the gatekeeper more than he could earn in three years in order to go past him. Fortunately the two most senior men, Yolande's previous Seneschal, Pierre de Beauvau, and Charles's confessor, Gérard Machet, were visiting the Regent in Anjou at the time when the sickening massacre of all those suspected of pro-Armagnac leanings took place, and consequently were spared the danger and harsh necessity of escaping from the Burgundian coup.

Yet the hideous reprisals had an oddly beneficial effect on the Dauphin's cause. The administrators of Paris, men of the University, from the judiciary and Parliament, suddenly found themselves not only unemployed but under threat, and abandoned fine houses and all the goods they could not carry with them as they rallied to the side of the true heir of France. Willy-nilly, a proper court was beginning to form itself.

But yet there were three victims unable to make their escape in time. The lunatic King continued to decay in his palace under house arrest, while Marie d'Anjou, given the Dauphin's apartments, was told to keep utterly quiet, an unnecessary instruction in her case. As for Count Bernard d'Armagnac, the focus of so much hatred, he was hurled into the deepest dungeon in the Bastille and left to exist in constant darkness.

The rallying point for all these people who were now suddenly Dauphinists was the town of Charenton, where Tanneguy de Chastel was organizing an army to go on the offensive against the Duke of Burgundy. Yet though his Gentlemen tried to stop Charles, he refused to be left out of the fight and insisted on riding with de Chastel's troops, admitting to the Bastard that he was thoroughly enjoying every minute of it.

But the attempted storming of Paris ended in disaster. The people of the city, taxed beyond endurance by the Count d'Armagnac, and victims of the plague and starva-

tion into the bargain, joined sides with Jean the Fearless
and threw anything that came to hand at the invading force,
who were reluctantly compelled to turn back. With the capital obviously impregnable, the Dauphinists had no choice
but to withdraw to their territories surrounding the rivers
Loire and Cher and set up a rival court and parliament, to
which those who remained loyal now made their way from
all over France.

It had been Bonne's dearest wish to fly straight to Charles's
side, once having escaped the carnage in Paris. Yet de Giac,
safely at his castle near Vincennes, would have none of it.

"Before I go to join the Dauphin I must pay my respects
to his mother," he had announced airily.

"But how can you?" Bonne had asked unwisely. "Surely
you dare not be seen to have a foot in both camps?"

Even while the foolish girl had watched him, Pierre's face
had changed to that of a satyr.

"Why not, ma chérie? I would have thought you to know
all about that situation."

"What do you mean," she had blundered on.

"Surely you understand? For are you not the greatest
living exponent of the art, having a leg in each bed I mean?
Or have you neglected mine so long that you have
forgotten?"

His arm had shot out like a whip and grabbed her cloud
of hair, wrenching her teeth in their sockets.

"What do you have to say to that, whore? Don't you
think it time you fulfilled your marital duties?"

Bonne had been unable to answer, terrified out of her
wits.

"Can't speak, eh? Well, I'll get some sound out of you,
even if I have to work to do it."

He had raped her then, his organ enormous, battering
and hurting until she finally did cry out. But not satisfied
with that, Pierre had gone on to give her a beating, first
with his hands and feet, then his evil tongued whip. Afterwards he had carried the barely conscious girl to the tower
room where she and Charles had made love long ago, then
he had thrown her on the bed.

"Don't worry," Bonne's husband had whispered just before he left her. "I won't abandon you here to die. Not
because I give a damn about that but simply because, my

little sweet, you are far too useful alive. For all I care the Dauphin can get astride you a hundred times a day, and you can do likewise. But tell your ugly boy from me that I will want a reward for being so obliging, and now he is setting up a court of his own I shall soon be asking for it."

De Giac's wife had moaned involuntarily at this and Pierre's voice had sharpened in tone.

"Now be quiet, do you hear, or I might forget my kind offer! If you behave yourself I will send Guy to you, if you don't you can rot. Oh you needn't look so surprised, the creature walked in this morning. He is a spy for the Dauphin of course, otherwise he would have gone straight to Bourges. However, the freak amuses me, so grotesque but such a good singer! He'll make you fit for your lover again."

De Giac had patted his codpiece obscenely. "And I'm certainly fit for mine, for only she knows how to pleasure me." He had blown Bonne a mocking kiss. "Au revoir, my beauty. I'll see you at court."

"I curse you," she had whispered silently, but those were the last coherent thoughts Bonne had as unconsciousness finally relieved all of her burning agony.

The brutal summer of 1418 gave way to autumn and the Dauphin, safe in the beautiful countryside of the Loire Valley, looked with love and delight on the subtle changes in the landscape, the curl of a leaf here, a colder evening there, a certain deepening in the color of the sky. For much as Charles enjoyed the high season and its pleasurably lazy pursuits, he could only feel a sense of relief that this particular year was at last coming toward its end.

Following the coup and bloodbath of May, June had seen the death of Bernard d'Armagnac, dragged into the streets and killed after de Chastel's unsuccessful attempt to re-take the city. Six weeks after that, Queen Isabeau had entered Paris in triumph, the Duke of Burgundy riding beside her carriage, and somewhere in her victory procession, the Devil's man de Giac. Then, with the capital finally in Anglo-Burgundian hands, Henry V had begun a brutal siege at Rouen, a siege in which the people of the town very quickly came to exist on rats and mice alone, while the ten thousand poor souls turned out into the ditch below the city wall because of their weakness consumed their own droppings and one another before they died.

In the teeth of this dire situation, Charles had been pro-claimed Lieutenant-General of France, acting for his imbe-cile father, his task to defend the realm against the Burgundians. It was now up to him, fifteen years old and thrust unexpectedly to the forefront, to unite every loyal Frenchman behind him. And still, just when the Dauphin could do with all the encouragement he could get, there was no sign of his helpmate Bonne.

"You are sure you saw her going from Paris?" Charles asked the Bastard one September evening, repeating the question for about the millionth time since the Burgundian attack.

"I think I did," Jean answered reluctantly. "But I sup-pose in hindsight I could have been mistaken in all that noise and confusion."

"God's Holy Mother!" came the violent reply. "For the first time, uncertainty. Did you see her go or didn't you?"

"I don't think I did," said Jean, suddenly very serious.

"By Christ's blood, I've a mind to dispense with you from my service," hissed the Dauphin. "If there's one thing I cannot tolerate it is a liar."

It was the first argument the two young men had ever had in all their years together and Jean rose to his feet, his dark eyes flashing in his suave and handsome face.

"Well, know then, mon Prince, that I didn't see your affianced bride go either, and that reports reached me only yesterday that the terrible rumors are true. She is still in Paris under house arrest, but I forbore to tell you knowing how desolated you would be."

The heavy sarcasm was not lost on the Dauphin who seemed almost to have forgotten Marie d'Anjou's exis-tence, and he flushed as the Bastard stared at him angrily.

"So you lied to me completely on the night we escaped?"

"Yes, I lied, Monsieur, thinking only that you would not leave the city if Madame de Giac—and Madame Marie of course!—were not safe. I did what I considered best for both your royal self and the future of France." He picked up his jeweled hat from where it lay on a chair. "I take my leave of you, mon Prince, and shall either assume my duties as an ordinary servant or return to Angers."

He swept to the door, bristling with pride and indigna-tion, but the Dauphin made no move to stop him, watching his friend go with a curious expression on his face.

It was beginning to settle on him, like an item of new clothing molding to his shape and growing comfortable, the idea that he was, against all the odds, one day going to be King. And with it had come the realization that no one, however well loved, must take advantage of the thing which the Dauphin represented, nor must anyone be allowed to manipulate, or attempt to do so, the heir to the throne of France. With a humorless smile at the magnitude of his inheritance, Charles crossed to his desk and rang a bell for a servant to attend him, looking out of the window at the fine autumn evening as he did so.

He had never in his life, except perhaps for his two wonderful years at the castle of Angers, lived in greater comfort, for on succeeding to the title of Dauphin, Charles had also become the Duke of both Touraine and Berri, and though the old Duke of Berri may indeed have been senile when he died he had in his day collected round him the most superb art treasures, all of which packed his castle to overflowing. And it was this castle, thoroughly modernized with money loaned by Jean Louvet, that the Dauphin had decided upon as his principal home.

Splendid views over the river Yèvre were his, hunting land and deer, to say nothing of a fine stable of thoroughbred horses. But the boy knew that all this was under threat, that Henry V's ruthless march south would not stop with Normandy and its adjoining territories, that the Englishman would not be happy till the whole of France had bowed the knee to him.

As the servant appeared, Charles wrenched his mind to the present. "Come back in five minutes, if you will. I want you to take a letter to Monsieur the Bastard."

The man bowed and left and Charles, with the flicker of a cunning smile, sat down at the desk. He was about to play a trick that would become typical of his tactics as both Dauphin and King, he was going to punish an unruly Gentleman by forgiving him; the statesmanlike manipulation of his courtiers had begun.

"My dear Jean," he wrote. "As soon as you left the room I realized how greatly I had upset you, so I know you will be anxious to make amends for the lie that angered me, well intended though it undoubtedly was.

"It strikes me that the best way harmony can be restored between us is for you to go on my behalf to Angers, where

I would ask you to inform the Regent of Madame Marie's plight, and ask how best we can work together to bring about her safe return. Secondly, I would beg you to find Madame de Giac for me. No doubt a man as resourceful as her husband would have escaped from Paris and it seems unlikely he would sacrifice anyone as useful to him as his wife. She is probably still at Vincennes which is too near the city for safety in my view. Request the couple to come to Bourges immediately at my express command."

He signed the letter, "Charles le Dauphin" and added a postscript.

"I will not hear of your resignation as my Chamberlain. We have weathered too many storms together for me to accept such a thing."

It was a neat turn of the tables and the Dauphin felt quite pleased with himself as he went to join Hardouin de Maillé for a ride with their hawks, just the two of them alone in the clear crisp evening.

Apropos of nothing in particular—though Charles felt certain it was leading somewhere—the *grand maître* said, "I received a letter from my wife this morning," as they mounted and set off, the birds being placed on their wrists by the falconer.

"Oh?"

"You are aware that she now serves the Duchess Yolande as one of the Regent's ladies."

"Yes."

"Well, she writes to me that Monsieur René is about to leave Anjou, that the Duchess is sending him to Lorraine to take up residence with his future father-in-law. I hope it is not indiscreet of me, Monsieur, but I believe the Regent intends to invite you to visit the boy and say farewell."

The Dauphin smiled. "It *is* indiscreet but I thank you for the news. I shall go if the war permits me."

De Maillé shot him a curious glance. The war, as such, had not moved sufficiently far south to be a daily threat, and yet Charles seemed in a constant state of frustration, itching to get at the enemy. There had also been a chilling incident in July, shortly after the boy had been made Lieutenant-General, which had showed him in a much tougher light than his courtiers had believed possible.

Riding at a discreet distance past the garrison at the castle of Azay-le-Rideau, firmly held in Burgundian hands,

Charles, at the head of a troupe of men, had heard the
soldiers on the battlements hurling insults at him. Phrases
like "Bastard," "Whore's son," and "Shove off, frog face"
had floated on the air, and the Dauphin had gone into an
absolute frenzy. Turning his horse and ordering the charge
himself, Charles and his men had taken the place by assault.
Then the boy had exacted his revenge. The Captain had
been beheaded and every other soldier in the garrison
hanged, nearly three hundred people in all.

It had been a salutary lesson to all who thought him
puny and every one of his Gentlemen, however well they
knew him, had changed their opinion of this white-faced
and implacable creature who would not countenance personal remarks and had no compunction about ordering the
death sentence.

Now, as the leaves of the woods surrounding the castle
crackled beneath their horses' feet and the clear sweet air
of the river blew the feathers on their hats, Hardouin ventured to say, "The war is indeed a pressing problem, Monsieur, but there is the bond of shared childhood between
you and René. I am sure he would like to see you."

Charles did not answer, staring instead at the sky, and
the *maître* wondered if he had heard him. But the Dauphin
was remembering the moment when he had realized for
the first time that René d'Anjou's extraordinary hands had
been those described to him by Nicolas Flamel as belonging
to a future Grand Master of that mystic order which
seemed in some way to have power over the future hopes
of France.

"Then I shall go," Charles answered slowly. "I shall go
on the proviso that I am contacted immediately should the
situation change in any way."

De Maillé hid his twitching lips and answered gravely, "I
will see to it personally, Monsieur."

"Good," replied the Dauphin, and without another word
shot into the woods and out of sight, leaving the *grand
maître* of the household to ponder the fact that a most
mercurial and eccentric young man now held the future of
France in his increasingly capable hands.

Nineteen

Every step of the journey brought back bitter-sweet memories. The last time Yolande had ridden this route she had been pregnant, afraid, shivering with cold. Now, in the warmth of early autumn, the Regent of Anjou's party including the new household of her son René set out, bravely going across country to Lorraine where the boy was finally to take up residence with his affianced bride.

Leading the cavalcade came a large and fearsome contingent of the Duke of Anjou's army, for though Henry V still remained at the siege of Rouen in Normandy he was for ever turning his soulless eyes southwards and no one could afford to travel unprotected. Behind these men-at-arms rode the Regent's own Gentlemen together with those of the Duke of Lorraine, sent especially to escort his future son-in-law to the boy's new home.

Following this sturdy group came the ladies, traveling in decorated wagons, hooded and curtained against the wind and rain, the Duchess and her son side by side in the most luxurious of all. While bringing up the rear, mounted on mules and donkeys, the servants who had been seconded to Prince René from the royal household of Anjou journeyed along cheerfully, whistling and singing as they went. All in all some hundred people made up the brightly dressed procession which wove its way through the great river valley and then on eastwards to the territories which one day would belong to the young prince.

With every slow mile they put behind them, Yolande's spirits lifted. She had left Angers angry and depressed, furious that Charles had not been at Saumur to say goodbye to René or meet Marie, returned by the Duke of Burgundy

to the Duchess like a piece of unwanted baggage, Richemont's brother Jean of Brittany riding as the girl's escort.
It had been Brittany whom Yolande had persuaded to act
as go-between in the delicate negotiations between the
Dauphin and Jean the Fearless, but Richemont's elder
brother had been none too happy when Charles had not
been available to greet his future bride, in view of the fact
the Duke had gone especially to Paris to collect her.

"What the Devil's the matter with that boy?" he had
said to the Regent, throwing his hat onto the floor in disgust. "Has he got another woman? Begging your pardon,
Madame, but I feel with you I am able to speak frankly."

Yolande had tapped her chin thoughtfully. "It's possible
I suppose, perfectly. I shall find out at once."

"Mark my words, that'll be the case," Brittany had answered gloomily. "They're all the same these lads. Think
what a ram my poor wretched Arthur was in his heyday.
Ah well, there won't be much chance of that where he is
now."

Wondering whether she had flinched, the Duchess had
said, "Is he still incarcerated?"

"I fear so. Henry of England will not even treat with me
over him."

Yolande had found herself unable to reply.

Of course the news had come back to her within a few
days that the Dauphin had had a mistress for well over a
year and the Regent's spy had not spared her any of the
details.

"They had been apart for some months, Madame. She
was caught up in the bloodbath in Paris apparently. But
she came back last week and has not left the Dauphin's
side since."

"And the identity of this woman?"

"Bonne de Giac, Madame."

"Ah," Yolande had said thoughtfully, "that explains a
great deal."

Her creature had sighed. "It is said that Monsieur is very
much in love with her."

The Duchess's green eyes had given a wicked flash. "I
see! In view of this I shall keep my daughter here in the
wardship of her brother. And should she be sent for, Madame Marie is not to leave Angers unless I specifically
order it. Return to Bourges and tell the Dauphin that."

"I will, Madame."

But though she had been able to forgive Charles his infidelity, Yolande's anger had really been aroused when the Dauphin had rejected the treaty offered between himself and Jean the Fearless, refusing point blank to go back to Paris, thus throwing Brittany into such a towering fury that he had declined to negotiate further and had walked out of the meeting in a huff.

So it was with all this on her mind that the Duchess had been forced to journey to Lorraine, leaving the matter of the Dauphin and his paramour totally unresolved. But one thought sustained her, with each mile she traveled the child she had not seen since its birth grew nearer, and Alison du May had already been requested to arrange a secret meeting between them.

It had been Michaelmas when they had left Anjou to traverse a land so ravaged by war that crops no longer grew, and it was on St. Luke's Tide that they first caught sight of the walled city of Nancy, its roofs flushed the color of burning wood in the light of the dying October sun.

Any thoughts of this great party staying in the residence of the King and Queen of Sicily—the remote manor in which Jehanne had been born—had been put aside by the sheer weight of its numbers. Only the Ducal Palace could house such a vast retinue and it was to the royal residence that Yolande, her son and her retainers, now made their way.

Having rested and refreshed herself, the Duchess entered the great hall surrounded by her ladies. Her eyes were drawn at once to René, who glittered with the excitement of all the important happenings in his world. Looking beyond her son for the beautiful Alison du May, Yolande saw her standing amongst the Duchess of Lorraine's waiting women, trying discreetly not to be noticed in the general hubbub. But, it never being easy for the irrepressible to be restrained, as Alison dropped into a rigid curtsy at the Regent's approach there was a momentary but definite suggestion of the girl's incredibly naughty grin.

"Yet girl," thought Yolande, "is not quite the right description any more."

For Alison had filled out plumply, mother of sons as she was, though still maintaining the saucy good looks that she would keep till her dying day.

But, annoyingly, fond as they were of one another and longing to renew a friendship that had borne the test of jointly keeping a vital secret over many years, they were unable to get a private word until long after nightfall. The traditional light supper of cakes and ale had been served to Yolande in her apartments, the Regent pleading tiredness and the need to rest before the next day's ceremony of officially handing René into the care of his future father-in-law. So it was that she was actually in bed when there came a light tap at the door and her principal Lady let in Alison du May, the Duke of Lorraine's cherished mistress, now powerful in her own right.

"Ma chérie," said the Duchess fondly, and embraced the girl with a great deal of affection. "You may go," she called to her hovering waiting women. "Madame du May and I have a great deal to catch up on."

There were several raised eyebrows and one or two noses pointed slightly in the air, but Alison had grown quite used to being unpopular with other women and merely smiled serenely until they had left the room. Then she gave another dignified curtsy before rushing to kiss Yolande's hand.

"Ma Reine, you look lovelier than ever. I do not think you will ever grow old."

The Regent shook her head. "You should not say such things."

Alison frowned. "Was it too forward of me? But I was always myself with you, Madame. Must all that change?"

Yolande shook her head and patted a place on the bed for her devoted servant to come and sit beside her. "Of course not. Now, tell me everything that has happened to you. Are you happy? And how are your little boys?"

"Well and wonderful," answered the Duke's mistress, and started to chatter at such speed that the older woman could not help laughing.

It was just as if no time had elapsed at all since Alison had left the castle at Angers to fulfill her more important role, and as the fire died down and the candles guttered it was hard to think that they were not exactly the same two women who together had delivered Jehanne into the world and so successfully concealed her identity.

"A lot has taken place over the years," Yolande said

eventually, "and many things have altered. Tell me, is all arranged for me to see my daughter?"

Alison made a slight face. "To *see,* yes, Madame. But I think it would not be wise for you to talk with her. To this day her parents believe me to be her true mother. I would not like to disillusion such good people."

"And she is still happy with them?"

"Oh, yes, Jehanne knows nothing different. The child leads an ordinary village life. The civil war may have touched the people slightly as it has, indeed, most places. But other than that she is having a simple and unclouded childhood."

"And does she still believe in fairies?"

Alison smiled. "Oh, yes. I believe she goes to visit the Fairies' Tree once a week."

"Where is it?" asked Yolande, indulgently curious about her small daughter's pretty belief.

"In Chesnu Woods. There is a spring there apparently, near the tree. I haven't been to see it but I believe it is a very pretty place."

"Am I to watch her from there?"

"I thought it might be a good idea. We could observe without being observed, if you understand me, ma Reine."

"And if I insist on speaking to her?"

Alison bowed her head. "I am always your loyal servant, Madame, and will abide by any decision you might make."

The Duchess patted her serving woman's hand. "Don't worry, I will take your advice on the matter. After all, it is you who have acted as Jehanne's guardian, not I."

"Then all will be well."

Yolande changed the subject. "As I wrote to you, the political situation in Lorraine still leaves much to be desired."

Madamoiselle du May nodded. "You refer to the enmity between the Duke and his neighbor, your uncle?"

"I most certainly do."

And it was a fact that a great obstacle stood between Yolande and her plan to unite France against Henry V, in the form of the feud between Charles of Lorraine and Louis, Duke and Cardinal of Bar, both uncles of young René. For Lorraine supported the Duke of Burgundy, and the Cardinal, brother to Yolande's mother, did not. It was as simple as that. Yet the stumbling-block lay in the fact that the boy was sole heir to the two men, his future father-in-law and his great-uncle both having named him their successor.

"Nothing must go wrong in the matter of my son's inheritance," Yolande added quietly. "It is essential that he succeeds to both Bar and Lorraine, and unites the provinces behind the Dauphin." Alison gave her a curious look and the Regent said, "I promised my husband on his deathbed that I would do all in my power to end the civil war so that the English invader could be seen off for once and for all."

"Then you may trust me, Madame. The Duke always consults me on important issues and has come to respect my views. Anything I can do to get the murderer of Azincourt off our land will be a pleasure."

Alison said this last so violently that Yolande thought her servant about to spit on the floor as a gesture of her contempt. But the Duke's lady, who had been born a commoner, remembered herself in time.

"Then I may rely on you?" asked the Duchess, smiling.

"As always, ma Reine. I have never forgotten the fact that I owe everything I have in life to you."

In summer the trees of Chesnu woods met and interlaced overhead, allowing through little sunlight, a cavern of mottled green, filled with birdsong, hushed from all other sound. And now in autumn, abounding with great splashes of color—ochres, vermilions and the deep brown of exotic spices—it still retained its silent quality, its mysterious atmosphere. Beneath the feet of the horses, led now as the two women had dismounted, the fallen leaves gave the merest crackle then sunk deeper into the carpet of vegetation which lay there all year long.

Green velvet moss was everywhere, hugging round the roots of trees, growing in vivid knots on the very trunks themselves, clinging to the long skirts that swished over it as their owners progressed further into the forest. Overhead, what could be seen of the sky was the clear, vivid, very pure blue known as mazarine. Bars of golden light splashed through the spaces where the leaves had fallen, lighting the ground with pools of primrose, a glittering gold dust floating in the shafts of sunshine. Dimly in the distance could be heard the splash and trickle of water coming from some eager little brook pushing its way up through the emerald earth.

"I can hear the spring," said Yolande, "are we nearly there?"

"Yes, there's a clearing round the next bend. I think we should leave the horses, it will make it easier to approach quietly."

The Regent nodded agreement and she and Alison, having thrown the reins of their mounts over an oak tree's supporting branches, made their way without speaking further.

The glade, when they finally came to it, was far bigger than the Duchess had imagined. Large and spacious, it had the air of a cathedral, an impression greatly enhanced by the lofty pillar-like trees and the colors shining through them, as dazzling to the eye as stained glass. In the middle of this almost circular clearing stood the Ladies' or Fairies' Tree, the little spring bubbling near by, and two children, one fair, the other dark, playing amongst the leaves, throwing them up into the air in great armfuls, laughing as only pleasantly happy youngsters can.

The Duchess of Anjou froze to her soul, aware that one of these precious imps was her own flesh and blood, yet not sure which. And then the dark child looked over in her direction and the years rolled away. King Juan of Aragon stared out of the child's deep mysterious eyes, while the sunlight gave her cap of dark hair the bluish sheen of a raven's wing, just as his had had. But the body was Yolande's. Already tall for a girl of six, yet lithe as willow, there was an air of strength about the mite that was almost daunting.

"Jehanne," whispered Yolande and it was not a question. Perplexed, the Duchess looked for any similarity between the girl and her father, then saw a dazzling likeness in a flash. As Jehanne turned back to her companion, smiling, Yolande recognized Richemont's beautifully molded cheek bones and strong white teeth.

"She has good looks," she whispered to Alison.

"But doesn't care about them. She's an utter little tomboy."

"Better that than being sickly."

"Oh, she's very far from puny. Her mother told me it's an effort to get her even to sit still."

"If only I could speak to her."

"Better not, Madame. Let her be."

They must have raised their voices slightly for Jehanne once more peered in Yolande's direction, her eyes bright and alert.

"Who's that?" she called out, her peasant's accent and dialect, the *ydioma Francie,* making her mother wince.

Neither of them answered, standing stock still, and Jehanne's companion also stared in their direction, suddenly nervous.

"Do you think it's the fairies?"

"It could be," answered Yolande's daughter boldly.

"Then we'd better run."

"Why?"

"You know why. If they take us away to Fairyland we won't be able to come back for a year and a day, or even seven years. Oh, Jehannette, come on," and the fair-haired child snatched at her friend's hand and started to pull.

With obvious reluctance Jehanne went with her, glancing back over her shoulder, curious and interested, several times before they disappeared from view.

Yolande, like April, smiled and wept. "Jehannette," she said.

"A diminutive for a diminutive. Come, come, ma Reine, do not upset yourself," Alison answered gently.

"Will I ever see her again?" the Duchess asked through her tears.

"Of course you will. I promise it."

"I hope so," the Regent answered. "Only God knows how much I hope so."

Bonne had come back at the end of September, riding into the castle at Tours with the Bastard as her escort. Charles had thought her pale, ill almost, but she had said nothing to him of her ordeal and with the marks on her body now healed, the Dauphin had put her air of sadness down to the terror of escaping from Paris.

Then there had passed an idyllic few weeks, almost like a honeymoon, during which the youthful lovers had spent every waking moment together. But late in November three people had come to the castle who between them had put an end to this enchantment. First, astride her horse, her long skirt kilted as was her defiant wont, came the Regent of Anjou, her daughter riding side saddle on a palfrey several paces behind.

"Oh, mon Dieu!" Charles had exclaimed, looking out of the window of his bedchamber. "It's my mother."

"The Queen?" Bonne had shrieked in alarm, her black hair flying as she rushed to look.

"No, my mother-in-law of Anjou. I call her mother sometimes. It was she who brought me up, so I am deeply attached to her."

But he had not felt quite so attached when the Regent, demanding private audience, had launched a bitter attack about his behavior.

"If there is one thing I will not tolerate, Monsieur, be it from the Dauphin of France or anyone else, it is arrant rudeness. You had written to tell René you would see him before he left, you knew full well that Marie was returning to Anjou. Yet you let both of them down."

"Well, I . . ." Charles began lamely.

"No excuses. My poor daughter was distraught that you were not there to meet her, having been kept a virtual prisoner, remember. And when I inquired the reason why you did not attend her, I learnt that you were too busy with your mistress, Madame de Giac."

The Dauphin had turned the color of a beetroot. "How did you find out?"

"My dear child," Yolande had answered smoothly, "I am a woman of the world as well as Regent of Anjou. I make it my business to keep in touch with everything."

Charles's face had taken on an obstinate look. "I don't want to give her up. I can't help myself, Madame. I am very drawn to de Giac's wife."

"I hold no brief for the man, never fear," the Duchess had replied crisply. "He is a Satanist and a pervert."

"But you feel I have betrayed Marie?"

Yolande's voice had lost its anger. "No, not even that entirely. You are not yet married and there are few young men who go to their marriage bed virgin. No, it is simply that you did not bother with my daughter when she returned from her ordeal. Furthermore, Charles, it was a serious mistake indeed not to sign the proposed treaty with Burgundy and return to Paris with him."

"To be his puppet?" the boy had answered bitterly. "Why, I'd rather be dead. I hate Burgundy with his boots and his spurs and his traitorous ways. I would never sign a treaty with him, never!"

"But one day you might have to."

"What do you mean?"

"While Armagnacs and Burgundians are at each other's throats the door is open wide for Henry of England."

"I know it, I know it well," the Dauphin replied with much feeling.

"Then you must consider peace."

"But, my dear good mother—and that is how I truly think of you—I will not sign with him unless the terms are favorable to *me*. I will never be Burgundy's creature, though no doubt that is my real mother's dearest wish."

Yolande had seen his point at once; nothing, not even the unity of France, would be worth a life of subjugation to Burgundy.

"Yes, I understand that."

"Do you understand about Bonne too?"

"Even about Bonne."

"Does Marie know I have a mistress?"

"I think not," the Regent had answered thoughtfully, "and at the moment I would rather she remained ignorant. You see, Monsieur, in her simple childish way my daughter loves you."

"And I would never hurt her."

"Then after this visit I shall take her back to Angers with me and not bring her to rejoin you until Christmas when, if Madame de Giac is present, you will no doubt be forced to keep her in the background because of the presence of her husband."

"But what of the future?" Charles had asked flatly. "Marie is bound to find out about it one day."

"The future," Yolande had answered with conviction, "must simply take care of itself."

It was not so much fear of reprisals that had made Bonne keep silent about de Giac's terrible and violent treatment of her, but rather fear of what Charles might do if he found out the truth. Just before she had left to join her lover, Pierre had unexpectedly appeared at the castle outside Paris with the unwelcome news that he would be shortly joining his wife at the Dauphin's court.

"And by the way," he had added, giving Bonne his sinister smile, "no ideas about telling your ugly boy what took place between us, because if you do I'll end the relationship as sure as fate."

"How?" she had breathed.

"By telling him you're whoring with another."

It would have been useless and dangerous to argue and Bonne had simply nodded her head.

"And I'll be wanting that favor soon."

"What favor?"

"The payment for letting your affair go on. Au revoir, my pretty. See you at court." And with that the Devil's man had bowed out.

And now, within a day of the arrival of Yolande and Marie, de Giac appeared, making his way by boat over the chilly gray waters of the Loire to the many-towered castle at Tours.

It was obvious at once that he had not seen Yolande for some time as he made a great show of complimenting the Duchess on her appearance, a fact with which an intimidated Bonne had to agree. In her widowhood and nearing forty, the Regent of Anjou was quite the most elegant woman she had ever seen, only Yolande's slightly hawkish look detracting from an otherwise lovely face. Marie, too, flushed with pleasure at seeing Charles again, was improving, and de Giac kissed the girl's hand lingeringly, slightly drawing the skin up between his lips.

"You have a beautiful bride, mon Prince," he called out jovially to the Dauphin, then let his eyes wander deliberately from Marie to Bonne and remain for a moment. There was an uncomfortable pause before Charles answered boldly, "So have you, Monsieur."

This exchange seemed to set the pattern for the rest of the day, the Dauphin and de Giac constantly trading innuendos, a ploy which terrified Bonne, irritated Yolande and entirely escaped poor Marie. But it was at the banquet held in the honor of the Regent and her daughter, and for which Pierre had most fortuitously arrived in time, that feelings began to run high.

As was the custom, the Dauphin sat at the head of the high table with his future mother-in-law and wife on either side of him. Seated next to Yolande was Robert le Maçon, the other dignitaries of the household interspersed down its length, Bonne amongst them, only de Giac finding himself in a lowly position at the far end. This obviously displeased him enormously and his smouldering blue eyes began to blaze as he stared from Charles to his wife and back again.

As always when the great men of the Armagnac cause were gathered together conversation turned to the state of the nation and, before the wine cups were passed round too often, a discussion better suited to the council chamber took place, partly because the much respected Duchess of Anjou was present.

"Some acceptable settlement with Burgundy must be found soon," argued le Maçon sensibly, to which the Lord de Beauvau gave a forceful grunt of assent.

With two such powerful and highly regarded men coming out in favor of a truce, the warlords present held their tongues, and it was left to Louvet, from whose mind thoughts of money were never far away, to say, "It's a pity we can't bribe him."

"No doubt we could," Yolande put in, "but he would want too much, the price would be too high."

"Unless," said de Giac unexpectedly, startling everyone, as so far that evening he quite literally had not spoken a word, "it could be with something other than money."

He was almost universally disliked and also suspected of being a traitor, rumor after rumor reaching the ears of the Armagnacs that the man still enjoyed a liaison with the Queen, but none the less everyone stopped to listen. There was a timbre in de Giac's voice, a hypnotic quality, which made those overhearing it pay attention, whether they liked it or whether they did not. Consequently, the room grew quiet and the Dauphin became aware of the muted buzz of servants' conversation, screened off at the far end of the hall, the scratch of dogs beneath the table, and the crackling explosion of sun-dried logs. Charles suddenly felt most intensely his love for Bonne, his hatred of her husband.

"What do you mean?" he asked.

Now the Satanist was purring, all signs of his earlier anger gone. "They say that every man has his price, Monsieur. Surely even the Duke of Burgundy must be susceptible to some form of douceur."

"He's perverted if that is what you mean," said an unidentifiable voice from one of the lower tables.

"Boys?" asked de Giac softly, but the speaker forbore

to say it was cruelty that fascinated Burgundy, in view of
the many ladies present and listening.

Somebody drunker than the rest, called out, "I should
have thought you would know, Monsieur. After all, you
and the Duke have mutual friends."

It was an unsubtle reference to Isabeau but de Giac, his
earlier mood vanished, simply raised a long thin eyebrow
and let the comment pass.

"Why don't we make a wager on it?" he said, still holding his fellow guests unwillingly captive.

"On what?" asked de Beauvau gruffly.

"On which one of us can first arrange for milord of Burgundy to confer with our royal master, the Dauphin."

"Surely this is too serious a matter for gaming," Yolande
remarked, frowning.

But already a number of voices had made sounds of approval and she could see her opinion would be disregarded.

"Monsieur?" said de Giac, turning to Charles and baring
his teeth in that terrible smile of his.

The two fishes in Charles's soul swam rapidly in opposite
directions. Much as he wanted to re-open negotiations with
the opposing force, anything suggested by his rival was suspect as far as he was concerned. To gain time, he sank his
jaw into his hand and set his lips.

"I will consider it," he said finally. "And promise to let
you know my decision before the end of the night."

Bonne's husband, who had risen when he first spoke,
now sat down again looking well pleased with himself, and
the Regent found she was smiling. It may only have been
an act on Charles's part but he had conveyed an air of
statecraft; her pupil was obviously apt.

"Did I do well to answer that?" murmured the Dauphin,
very low, for her ear alone.

"On consideration, it sounds a reasonable plan. After all
it would get them on their metal. Yet I have never trusted
that man. You did the right thing to delay your reply."

In one of his endearing displays of affection, Charles covered Yolande's hand with his. "My good mother, what
would I do without you? It was once prophesied that a tall
Queen would be one of the women who helped me and
those words have indeed come true."

Yolande's winged eyebrows rose high. "And who foretold all this to you?"

"That I am sworn not to reveal."

"And Madame de Giac, was she part of it?"

"Beauty to my beast," answered Charles, but would say nothing further.

The banquet took its usual long course, followed by singers and masquers and merriment, but during the entertainment the Dauphin suddenly rose from his chair, whispered to his Chancellor that all should continue without him, and left the room. And to the observant Yolande it seemed hardly a coincidence that about five minutes later Hunchback Guy slipped from his place amongst the musicians and also went out.

"A consultation," she thought wryly, and wondered whether to inform Charles that Dr. Flavigny had died since the Dauphin was last in Angers and there was a general call amongst the members of the household for the hunchback to return and take the place for which he had been trained.

"Well?" said Charles, as soon as the door was closed behind the astrologer's back. "Tell me everything that happened to you, right from the start."

"I obtained a post with de Giac easily enough," Guy answered, sitting down, "though I think he suspects me of working for you. And I have also cared for Bonne as best I could. But Monsieur, she is in so much danger. I fear terribly for her safety."

"But why? What could happen to her?"

"Destiny always has two paths as I have told you so often. And Madame de Giac will be safe and well only if you can get her away from her husband."

"But how can I?" asked Charles. "I simply can't take another man's wife and set her up as my mistress, not openly."

"You could always kill him," Guy said simply.

"I might even do that. I hate him enough."

"And it is decreed he could indeed meet death at your hands."

The Dauphin looked uncomfortable. "The thought of the two paths of fate disturbs me. I wish the future were neater than that."

"But if it were, what function would I or any other mystic have? We are here to advise on the best course to take."

"Then what should I do about de Giac's wager?"

"If you decide to take him up on it, you and Burgundy

will most certainly be brought together, but there are great risks involved, for you, for Bonne, for everyone."

"Why for Bonne?"

"I don't know, I simply feel it," Guy replied honestly.

"But good would come of it? Jean the Fearless and I might be reconciled."

"Yes."

"Then I'll do it," answered the Dauphin. "I shall go back and tell de Giac to lay any wager he likes. And say that I, too, shall personally reward the man who can bring the Duke of Burgundy to my table."

"So be it," whispered Guy as his royal master strode from the room, his mind made up.

It was light when Pierre de Giac returned to his chamber, his face white, his eyes dilated, red specks upon his hands. Throwing himself down on the bed he turned to his side, propping his head on his arm, and stared fixedly at Bonne, who slept delicately, as if she were lying in a shell, her ebony hair spread over the lace-covered pillows.

"So," he said softly, "the game's afoot and you, ma chérie, will have your part to play."

The sound of his voice awoke her and she sat up, pulling the sheet to her chin, terrified to see him so close and so ghastly.

"What do you mean? What do you want with me?"

"Not your body you'll be pleased to hear," de Giac answered, grinning. "No, you must keep that young and fresh—in fact you will only be allowed to go to your boy once a week from now on."

"What do you mean?" the frightened girl repeated dazedly.

"That it is you, my pretty, who will be the bait to lure in the mighty Duke. It is you, sweet Bonne, who will become a lady of midnight, driving him mad with your caresses, bringing him to your royal master's side." De Giac sniggered loudly at his own joke. "You are about to become a whore to Jean the Fearless in order to earn your keep."

"I won't," she shrieked. "I will never do such a terrible thing. I would rather be dead."

"Which is precisely what you will be," snarled her husband, grabbing her by the hair and half-wrenching her out of bed, "if you do not do exactly what I say. You have a

straight choice, Madame. You either share your favors between the Dauphin and the duke or you go to your grave."

"You are evil personified," sobbed the wretched girl.
"You are truly a son of the Devil."

"You surprise me with your lack of affection for your
wretched partner," said de Giac, letting go of her so suddenly that Bonne fell onto the floor in a heap of limbs.
"Any woman worth the name would be only too happy to
seduce her lover's enemy in order to bring him round. You
worthless slut, you will not even give your body to help the
cause of France."

"You are deranged," the girl whispered helplessly. "I
shall go to Charles and beg his help to stop you."

"I think not," answered her husband. "I think you will
find by the time you see him again you and Burgundy will
have already tasted the joys of the flesh together. Get
dressed, pretty bitch. We leave in half an hour."

"Where are we going?"

"To find your new lover."

"No, no," his wife cried despairingly.

But de Giac only laughed as he poured some water into
a basin and washed his hands clean of the fresh blood that
still bespattered them.

In the cold dawning during which the Devil's man and his
tragic consort left the castle of Tours by way of the river,
another strange and secretive journey had taken place.
From the château of the Duke of Lorraine, Alison du May
and René d'Anjou, accompanied only by a single bodyguard, had made their way in the semi-darkness out of the
town of Nancy and headed west to where the dukedom
bordered onto that of Bar.

Here, as the sun came up, bloodless in the chill autumn
morning, they had crossed from one territory to the other,
then proceeded at a good pace to the town of Bar, passing
the churches of Notre-Dame and St. Etienne as they made
their way to the upper quarter and the residence of the
Duke and Cardinal himself, the boy's great-uncle, Louis.

Now, still in the shadows of that gloomy morning, René
was ushered into a receiving room where a swirl of crimson
from a high-placed chair told him that his elder relative
already awaited his arrival. The boy bowed as a voice, large
and deep said, "Let me see you."

Very afraid, René stepped forward into a shaft of light, blinding him with its early brightness, and waited.

"Do you know why you have been brought here?" the voice asked.

"No, my Lord."

"Then allow me to tell you the reason. Nicolas Flamel, whose name I am aware you already know, has died, and with his death the Grand Mastership of an ancient and important secret order, the Priory of Sion, has passed back into the hands of our family. For Flamel, whose right it was to name his successor, nominated you as the next Grand Master."

The boy peered out of his spotlight, glimpsing a rustling red robe. "Me? But why? What does it mean? What do I have to do with it?"

"Nothing as yet," the Cardinal answered quietly. "I shall act as your Regent until you come of legal age, but long before that I will initiate you into the secret which the Priory protects. Later today the initial step will be taken and you will be received into the Order of the White Greyhound."

"Which is?"

"A preparation for the higher order. It will be many years before you know everything, René, but as your great-uncle you may trust me to instruct you wisely. Now go to the table, fetch the wine cup that stands there, and drink with me, my nephew, heir and Master as I welcome you solemnly to your great inheritance."

Wishing he knew exactly what was happening and that he could see who spoke to him more clearly, René took a cautious sip of wine.

"One day," the Cardinal went on, "when that fool, your other uncle, the Duke of Lorraine, has left you his territories and I have left you mine, the duchies of Bar and Lorraine will be united again as they should have been long ago."

"But what connection does Nicolas Flamel have with that?" René asked tentatively.

"One of the great ladies of the family, Blanche of Navarre to be precise, was an alchemist and a mystic. She was also Grand Master of the Order you now lead, and when she died left that honor to Flamel, her teacher and friend, because she felt only he was worthy to succeed her."

"So why has it come to me?"

"Because you were considered worthy too."

"But what about Jade ... Louis ... my elder brother?"

"It was Master Flamel's own choice. Yours was the name he gave us."

"But *why*?"

"He spoke of La Pucelle and your role in her story."

"La Pucelle? Who is she?" asked René, feeling himself begin to grow cold.

The crimson robe quivered as the Cardinal shook his head. "I do not know the answer to that but Nicolas Flamel certainly did. He said that you and she must be side-by-side when the appointed time came."

"I feel afraid," said the boy. "That name makes me feel afraid."

The Cardinal stood up in the gloom and René saw the hem of the red robe shiver to the floor of the dais as if it were a scarlet waterfall.

"Fear nothing, my son. God will take you by the hand."

"But I am still only a child. How can I help anybody?"

"The way will be shown you and when the time comes you will know what to do."

"I feel that a great burden has been laid upon me," said the boy, growing even colder. "Do I have the right to refuse this honor?"

"Yes, you have that choice. But it is foretold that you will not, that you will prove to be one of the greatest Grand Masters the Priory has ever known."

"Then why am I so afraid?"

"You fear the unknown as do we all. Yet remember, René, that my hand will guide you until you reach man's estate. I will look after you."

There was silence while the boy drew his dark brows together, thinking that he would like to run away from the entire situation yet already feeling a touch of excitement at such a fraught and dangerous predicament.

"So be it. I accept," he said eventually.

In the gloom the Cardinal went on one knee before him. "Then the heritage of Sion is yours. I offer to God my prayers for you and pay you reverence."

And with that he kissed the boy's small and icy hand.

Twenty

They met in no man's land, a neutral zone, symbolized by a huge and tapestried pavilion, and they met alone. The Dauphin went in first, passing beneath branches specially woven to form an archway, and stood, white-faced, awaiting the arrival of his arch-enemy, that traitor to his people, the Duke of Burgundy. Then, a moment later, Jean the Fearless's bulk blotted out the light in the entrance and the man and boy stood staring at one another, masking their seething emotions with blank eyes, before the Duke finally dropped to his knees at the Lieutenant-General's feet. So it had come at last! The two sides tearing France to shreds, Armagnac and Burgundian, were finally face to face.

At a carefully measured distance from the central pavilion were two others, equally large and imposing, each belonging to one of the opposing factions, their bright banners and flags fluttering crisply in the evening air, beyond them, on separate sides of the field, the tents of the vast retinue of followers.

Each set of courtiers openly vied with the other as to who could be the most gorgeously dressed, while the knights, in their chain mail, glared constantly at their opposing numbers. Page boys, wearing the livery of their various masters, swarmed under the solemn feet of the foregathered lawyers and clerks, garbed in somber black or resplendent purple, adding to the general atmosphere of excitement. It was 8th July 1419, and talk of peace was running wildly through the great encampment in the meadow lands just outside the town of Pouilly.

It had been Bonne de Giac, of course, who had been responsible for this amazing gathering, contrived even more successfully than her husband had imagined possible. That Burgundy would desire and play with such a beautiful little thing he had never had any doubt, but that the depraved old lecher should actually fall in love with her, de Giac had not reckoned on.

But that strangest of things had actually happened. In her very horror and reluctance, in her terrified shrinking away, the Duke had tasted the sweet fruit of the girl's innocence, and had surrendered his heart to her. So it was partly to please Bonne, partly for his own reasons, that he had at long last agreed to meet Charles de Valois, unaware that his mistress was also that of the Dauphin; and in the eyes of the entire Armagnac faction, Pierre de Giac had been seen to have won the wager.

Yet neither of the two men alone in the central pavilion was aware of how cruelly both of them had been maneuvered by the Devil's man, simply remaining frozen as statues while Burgundy murmured honeyed words of allegiance and conciliation.

"Return to Paris with me, mon Prince, and take up your rightful place as your father's Regent."

"France already has a Regent, Lord Duke. You nominated my mother the Queen as such. I am Lieutenant-General of the kingdom."

"I admit my foolishness, Monsieur. It is you who should by rights be acting in Queen Isabeau's place."

"Tell me," said Charles, narrowing his eyes in his still, pale face, "why are you doing this? Are you suddenly afraid of the English King? Do you think he might be a threat even to you?"

It was so acute an observation that Jean the Fearless shifted very slightly where he knelt, and the Dauphin knew he had hit home. His spies had already described to him the very first meeting of Catherine and Henry V, when the Englishman, though obviously dazzled by the French girl's extraordinary beauty, had not let his heart rule his cold and calculating head. His demand for a dowry of eight hundred thousand crowns, the return of the lands conquered by his grandfather Edward III, the Regency of France and, on the death of the mad King, all of France to become part of Henry of England's domains, still held. And this, so the Dauphin had been reliably informed, had made Burgundy, who had also been present, change from a state of unease to one of open hostility, and the marriage talks had ground to a halt.

"Did she fall in love with him?" Charles whispered now, half addressing Jean the Fearless, half not. "Was my sister violently attracted to the Englishman?"

"She was utterly besotted with him," Burgundy answered, equally quietly. "Madame Catherine will stop at nothing in order to marry the man. It is a highly dangerous situation."

"And so you come to me!" said the Dauphin, shaking his head at the irony of the situation. "Then be assured this discussion will be on my terms."

"But you will accompany me to the court at Troyes?"

"Never! I will not trust my person in your hands. If I am to be Regent I shall rule from Bourges."

"That can never be," answered the Duke, and both knew that there lay the stumbling block in their entire negotiations.

Outside the pavilion the eagerly waiting courtiers grew cold as the sun burned its way out of a threatening sky and cruel black clouds amassed on the horizon, and still there was no sound from within.

"Are they speaking?" whispered Tanneguy de Chastel to the Gascon Arnauld Guillaume, Lord of Barbazan, Charles's personal bodyguard who had sworn never to leave the Dauphin's side yet who had mastered to perfection the art of discreetly distancing himself.

"Very little. The Duke keeps repeating that Monsieur must go with him to Troyes."

"And what does he reply?"

"That he will not put himself at the mercy of the man who murdered the Duke d'Orléans and who slit the throats of twenty-five thousand mutineers at Liège, to say nothing of ordering the massacre in Paris."

De Chastel grinned. "Monsieur has been well counselled."

"And is growing up fast."

"Does the Duke still kneel?"

Barbazan's large dark eyes brightened. "Yes, I am delighted to say he does."

"I wonder how long he can keep that up?"

"That we must wait and see."

De Chastel shivered, looking heavenwards as a gust of

wind suddenly blew between the tents, rattling them where they stood.

"There's going to be a storm."

"Yes, in every sense. The Dauphin is adamant."

"Will the Duke concede?"

"I don't think so."

"Then it's stalemate."

And indeed it was, for though Jean the Fearless repeated his demand over and over again, Charles had ceased to listen and had long since let his thoughts wander to Bonne and the fact that these days she always seemed distant, far away, constantly preoccupied and sad.

"Is de Giac being cruel to you?" he would ask.

But his mistress's only answer was a swift smile and a brush of her lips on his before she would whisper, "No more than usual." Actions and words which did nothing to comfort the infatuated Dauphin. Now he forced himself to concentrate as the Duke spoke once more.

"Monsieur, I feel there is little more I can say to you tonight. It must be past midnight and there is obviously a storm brewing. Do I have your permission to rise?"

"You do."

The Duke got shakily to his feet, rubbing his aching knees. "I have knelt before you some five hours, mon Prince. I hope it has done a little good."

"I hope so too," Charles answered swiftly, and bared his teeth in a mirthless grin, as he walked away from the Duke to the entrance and out beneath the woven arch.

"Little toad," hissed Jean the Fearless beneath his breath before he, too, made his way toward the great tent in which he slept.

Like an omen, the sky split with lightning as the two contenders appeared, and there was a simultaneous shout of thunder directly overhead, then the hiss of wind-whipped rain.

"It's a terrible night, Monsieur, come," said the Lord of Barbazan, sheltering the Dauphin with his outstretched cloak.

"How late is it?"

"Nearly one. You have been in conference many hours."

"Well, nothing came of it," Charles answered gloomily, "except for the pleasure of making him stiff with cramp."

"The Duke knelt *throughout*?" the bodyguard asked in surprise.

"He most certainly did."

Barbazan smiled grimly in the darkness. The Dauphin had exacted a boy's revenge and it was only to be hoped that this would not jeopardize the chance of that most urgently needed peaceful settlement.

But he had no time to dwell on this as the Dauphin's servants rushed into the pouring rain to help Charles into his sleeping quarters, bringing the boy food and wine, and assisting Monsieur to get ready for the night. In this small confusion, Barbazan got left behind the throng, and so it was only he who saw a slight figure battling its way through a wind so strong it threatened almost to blow the woman over. Madame de Giac, undeterred by the lateness of the hour and the terrible conditions, was making her way to the Dauphin's tent.

Barbazan, the model of tact, prepared himself to enact his usual ritual, ushering the girl into the royal presence and then, when the time came for them to make love, searching the bedchamber for any hidden assailant before the couple entered and he absented himself with a perfunctory smile, remaining close enough to the door to guard it but far enough away to be out of earshot.

Bowing, the bodyguard waited for Madame de Giac to take his proffered arm, then straightened again as she passed him by, her hood pulled down against the overpowering gale. Staring in astonishment, Barbazan could hardly believe his eyes as he saw the girl cross from the Armagnac camp to that of the Burgundians, making straight for the tent of the Duke himself.

"Christ's wounds," he whispered into the stirring air. "I can hardly believe it. Monsieur's Madame is both traitor and whore it would seem."

But there was no denying what he had only a moment ago seen for himself. Bonne de Giac had entered the sleeping quarters of Jean the Fearless and so far had not reappeared.

"So," thought Barbazan wryly, "my discretion will not be needed tonight after all. Well, well, who would ever have guessed it?"

But on the point of hurrying to tell his young master what he knew, the bodyguard checked himself. If he were to relate everything he had just witnessed not only the peace treaty but the entire future of France might be put at risk. Deciding to keep his own counsel, Barbazan went to attend Monsieur le Dauphin, being able to assure his master with his hand on his heart that tonight he would have an undisturbed night's rest.

But when all was said and done, the Lord of Barbazan need hardly have bothered to keep his secret. Two days after their first meeting, the Dauphin and the Duke strode from the central pavilion, each in a towering rage, and headed immediately for their own camps. Mounting their horses, the two men almost simultaneously ordered the pennants to be raised, signifying departure, thus destroying any hope left that the civil war might be coming to an end. In full cry, the courtiers and the knights mobilized, ready to go, already forming into columns and starting to move forward.

No one, with the possible exception of the bodyguard, could adequately explain what happened next. As if from nowhere, Bonne de Giac suddenly appeared and ran headlong between the two armies, risking her life should one of the great horses, frightened, bolt in her direction.

"Stop!" she shouted. "Stop! Stop! Stop!"

Both the Dauphin and the Duke wheeled to look at her, equally startled, and Barbazan with a sick sensation in the pit of his stomach saw an almost identical look of adoration cross the Dauphin's young and vulnerable features as did those of Burgundy's debauched and raddled old countenance.

"Listen to me," hissed Bonne violently, coming to a halt and standing between them, staring straight in front of her, not looking at either man. "If you love me you will stop this folly and return to the conference table. You *must* make concessions. The future of France is at stake and personal pride should be put aside."

Charles gaped at her, unable to believe that his mistress should remonstrate with him so publicly and there was a stunned silence before Burgundy eventually said, "I am willing to talk further if you are, Monsieur."

But all the while as he dismounted and went back to the great pavilion, this time surrounded by his cheering supporters, a terrible suspicion was beginning to grow in Charles's mind. A suspicion that persisted and magnified throughout the next frantic hour as, swept along by his advisers who, to a man, enjoined the Dauphin to agree, Charles found himself signing a rapidly prepared treaty. A treaty in which Burgundy recognized him as Regent and agreed that it was not necessary, after all, for the Dauphin to be based in Troyes, and Charles, in his turn, forgave the Duke and welcomed him back to France from exile. With his signature the civil war was nominally over but in Charles's heart it was only just beginning.

Why had Bonne not looked at either of them during her extraordinary outburst? Why had Burgundy started to answer her at exactly the same moment as he had? What could have induced her to act in such an uncharacteristic way? The answers all pointed in the same direction and with a terrible reluctance Charles found himself drawn to consider them, as a moth to a flame.

And then, without the need for further thought, everything was made clear. As more and more people crowded into the pavilion, shouting wildly that peace had come at last, Charles glimpsed Bonne standing beside her husband. And as the Dauphin glanced over at her, so did the Duke of Burgundy. What Jean the Fearless was thinking was written on his face for all the world to see, foolish smile followed foolish smile, the beastly old pervert was in love with the same woman as the heir to the throne of France.

The need to act became irresistible. Charles stood up and there was immediate silence.

"This conference is now over. In future both the Duke and I are sworn to keep peace with each other and to make no treaties with the English. Gentlemen, you may feast in celebration but I am going to pray for the souls of all sinners. I bid you adieu."

He shot Bonne a look full of *hauteur*, as only a Valois princeling could, and renounced her without saying a word, dismissing her from his life as surely as if he had told her directly.

He was sixteen, but Charles the Dauphin felt old and beaten as he slowly left the pavilion, ordering even Barbazan to stay where he was, and hearing through its walls the shouts and cheers of his courtiers as he went to his quarters to weep alone.

Twenty-one

The change in the Dauphin after the signing of the Treaty of Pouilly was noticed by everyone with whom he came in contact. The likeable, slightly eccentric boy had vanished overnight and in his place had come a cynical youth, his penchant for manipulating his courtiers turned to a hobby, his selfishness almost to the point of indifference.

The gentlemen of his household—Pierre de Beauvau, Robert le Maçon, Jean Louvet, Hardouin de Maillé, Tanneguy de Chastel, Hugues de Noyer, the Lord of Barbazan and the brothers du Mesnil, to say nothing of the Bastard of Orléans and Hunchback Guy—all knew the reason but not the remedy.

That the love affair between Charles de Valois and Bonne de Giac was over was glaringly obvious to them all but yet there was not one of them, not even the astrologer, who dared approach either party about the matter. Constantly in the background, triumphant that he had succeeded in bringing together the Dauphin and Burgundy, loomed the sinister figure of her husband, eavesdropping on secret conversations, lurking round corners. It was agreed by them all that none should interfere until such time as de Giac left court.

Probably more hurt by Charles's uncaring attitude than any of the others were Jean the Bastard and Guy. It was they who had been his close companions in the early days, it was they who had always done his bidding, and now to feel themselves shut out of his life was a cruel stroke of fate.

"If only he would confide in me," the Bastard complained.

"If only he would consult the stars," Guy replied sadly.

"He does, through Dr. de Thibouville, he who wormed his way in while you were away serving the de Giacs."

"Thibouville is a good astrologer," Guy commented wryly, shrugging a crooked shoulder.

"But only tells Charles the things he wants to hear." The Bastard hesitated, then said, "Be honest with me Guy, how much of this trouble did you foresee when we were all together in Paris?"

"I sincerely believed then—and still do—that unless Bonne can be permanently removed from her husband's side she will one day lose her life."

The Bastard went pale. "But how could we contrive that?"

"Only by killing him."

"And that we dare not risk."

"No, I'm afraid not."

"Is there any chance that Charles and Bonne will be reunited?"

"There is a chance of everything in this life," the astrologer answered seriously. "Remember that in any situation there are always two paths of destiny."

"But which to take?"

"Which indeed."

"But what ought we to do in this particular affair? How can we restore the Dauphin to his old self?"

"We can't," Guy replied quietly. "Yet in September something might well happen which could change the course on which Charles's future is currently set. You and I are powerless to do anything about it. Only he can do that by deciding against a certain course of action."

"And will he?"

"I think not."

Jean's handsome eyes glistened fervently. "What is it that's likely to happen? Come on, Guy, you can trust me."

"Violent death," answered the astrologer, speaking even more softly.

"Whose?" asked the Bastard, all attention.

"That I cannot say."

"You must," Jean answered impatiently. "Whose death?"

Guy lowered his voice even further and almost inaudibly murmured, "The Duke of Burgundy's."

* * *

The mighty province of Provence, surely one of the most beautiful in all France, with its towering mountains and unassailable peaks, its dramatic coastline and vivid sea, its fields of wild lavender and the smell of its flowers, was one of the places that Yolande d'Anjou loved best in the world. For it seemed to her that only here did the sky have a certain magic luminence, a deep blue against which the clouds appeared startlingly white; only in the hills where the villages clung to the feet of the mountains and the purple lavender threw out its amazing smell could one close one's eyes and dream of paradise; only in the warmth of its hyacinth sea could one swim safely out to the point of a bay and gaze for ever at a coastline both majestic and lovely.

The Duchess's favorite residence when she visited her Provençal domains—Anjou had gained Provence as one of its territories many years before—was the bay of La Napoule. For here, on the very edge of the sea itself, stood a castle built in 1387 by the proud family of Villeneuve, who gladly loaned their jewel of a home to the Angevin Regent whenever she came to visit. Many years before there had been a Roman dwelling on this same spot and, after that, the Saracens had built a tower which still stood dominating the bay. But the most irresistible thing about the place was the castle's gardens.

With the song of the sea in her ears and its breath blowing softly on her face, Yolande could walk beneath stately cypresses, down shady paths at the end of which played fountains, sniff the woody smell of pine, the evocative muskiness of sandal trees. Then, if she turned toward the ocean, the Duchess could traverse a great terrace, below which lay the sea itself, foaming in through arches where it turned to pools of jade and purple in the deep shadows.

Beyond the bay, the distant hills were the color of the wild lavender fields inland, the sea bright periwinkle blue on the horizon, pure aquamarine as it came pounding and sucking up to the glittering shore. Of all the places in the world where the Regent of Anjou would like to have spent the rest of her life, then quietly died there, free from the cares of state, the Château de la Napoule was it. But today, as she walked along the sea terrace, a letter in her hand, there was a slight frown on Yolande's face.

She had left Anjou in the fond hope that domestic matters would run smoothly in her absence but now it would appear there was a hitch. The treaty signed between Charles and the Duke was turning out to be a farce, the Burgundian too frightened of the English king to do more than pay lip service to the Dauphin, the Dauphin himself in a strange uncaring mood. In the meantime, the whole of Normandy apart from the island of Mont Saint-Michel, had fallen once again under English domination, and Henry V had returned to England to raise funds from City merchants to allow him to continue his campaign.

But that was not all that gave the Regent cause for anxiety. The writer, the trustworthy Robert le Maçon, without actually specifying why, for it was dangerous to put too much in a letter that could well be intercepted on its journey, hinted strongly that the Dauphin's apparent disinterest in life was serious. And reading between the lines it was easy for Yolande to guess the reason. With a sigh she thought in hindsight that she should have left Marie with Charles and not listened to her daughter's pleas to remain in Anjou where everyone was familiar and kind.

"You are going to have to get used to being with Charles on your own soon," the Duchess had said sternly.

"But not yet, Maman, not yet. He is sleeping with that horrible Madame de Giac, I know it. He will ignore me completely."

"Then it will be up to you to get him away from her. Royal wives must get used to that sort of thing."

But even as she spoke the words, Yolande had known that poor little Marie never could, never would, sparkle in the eyes of men, that her own powerful personality had not been passed on to her child, and that she must treat her daughter with sympathy.

"Very well. I shall let you stay in Angers until my return. But after that you must join your affianced husband and remain with him until you are old enough to be married."

"But Maman—"

"No buts, Marie. Those are my instructions."

Yet now the Duchess knew that she had been wrong, that she should have insisted on Marie remaining at Charles's side so that if his relationship with Bonne foundered—as it obviously had—her daughter could at least have adopted the role of sympathetic listener.

"God's heart, these men!" Yolande exclaimed in exasperation, and thought of Richemont for the first time in months.

Above her head a seagull wheeled and dipped, an arrow of white arcing through a delphinium sky. Looking around her, the Duchess thought with reluctance that one day she must go back in order to resolve all the problems which had relentlessly appeared in her absence.

"But not yet," she said to herself. "Here there is space and tranquillity. I won't return just yet."

Though the summer of 1419 was difficult for everyone at the Dauphin's court, there was one person above all others to whom each hour was a nightmare, each waking moment an actual physical pain. Unhappy beyond belief, brought to the brink of breakdown by all she had had to endure, Bonne de Giac contemplated suicide almost every day. Only one thing kept her alive and that was the thought of revenge; revenge on her vile and wicked husband, revenge on the filthy Duke who pawed her so obscenely, revenge on Charles de Valois who had tossed her to one side without even bothering to discover the reason for her supposed infidelity.

And yet Bonne knew in her more rational moments that when it finally came to it nothing on earth would ever persuade her to actually lay a finger on the Dauphin. Her ugly boy, as her husband so contemptuously referred to Charles, was the only man she had ever loved or ever would. And now to see him turning away from her, cutting her dead whenever they met and crossing the room to avoid her, was the worst kind of torment.

She had tried writing him brief notes, not daring to explain anything in a letter lest they be tampered with, but they had always been returned with the seals unbroken. As hurt as Bonne, though utterly refusing to admit it, even to himself, Charles had one ambition, to freeze his former mistress out of court.

De Giac, meanwhile, continued to take her to Burgundian headquarters to visit the vile lecher; journeys from which she always returned emotionally wrecked. It seemed to the girl that there was no one in the world willing to help her; even the faithful Guy keeping a cautious and obviously discreet distance. Yet it was on just one of those terrible visits which degraded her to little more than a hired whore, that help finally came. As she had left the Duke's apartments at dawning, retching as she walked unescorted down the corridor towards de Giac's bedchamber, a figure had detached itself from the shadows and clapped its hand over her mouth.

"Jeanne, don't be frightened, chérie," it had whispered into her ear. "It's Roger."

At the sound of her real name, for the wretched girl had been born Jeanne de Naillac, tears had flooded Bonne's eyes. It was her own brother who held her so closely. With a great sob of relief she had turned into Roger's arms and wept.

"There's no time for tears," he had said swiftly. "Save them for another occasion. Listen to me and do precisely what I say. The Duke must be persuaded to go to the next conference at Montereau. He's trying to change the location because his Jewish astrologer has warned him of danger lurking there. It is up to you to persuade him otherwise."

"Why?"

"That I won't say. Just do it, Jeanne, for the sake of us all."

She had guessed then, and for the first time in months some color had come to her cheeks. "I'll do it," she said grimly. "I've been de Giac's puppet too long. It's time I acted for myself."

"For you and also for France. Adieu." Roger had kissed her rapidly on the cheek and vanished into the shadows from which he had come.

"For *me*," Bonne had said fiercely, the whole direction of her life changed in a moment. "I'll do it—but for *me*."

In the way of all conspiracies, the meeting was held at midnight. Most of the Dauphin's Gentlemen were present, in company with Guillaume Bataille, Robert de Laire and the Vicomte de Narbonne, old servants of the murdered Duke Louis d'Orléans. Two stalwarts of Anjou, Robert le Maçon and Pierre de Beauvau, stood in the doorway, ready to silence the entire room should a stranger approach. Only the Lord of Barbazan, tonight his duty more to keep the Dauphin at the chessboard than protect him, was absent— but he had sent a message.

"M'Lord the bodyguard asks me to tell you that he has recently refused a so-called *gift* of 500 moutons d'or from the Duke on the grounds that he never took money except from the masters he served."

"Well said," put in de Beauvau.

"One might as well talk to a deaf ass as Burgundy," Tanneguy de Chastel remarked angrily. "While that intractable old fool leads the Burgundians we will never break the deadlock."

"The situation is hopeless," agreed Hardouin de Maillé. "Neither side can make a move. We have reached *impasse*."

"He has to go," said somebody from the shadows in the corner of the room. "If we are to defeat the English, Burgundy must die."

"Wait one moment." Robert le Maçon was speaking from the doorway. "Better the devil you do know than the devil you don't. His son's an aggressive little sod, more likely than ever to ally Burgundy with the English. I feel we shouldn't rush into anything."

"Hear, hear," said Hugues de Noyer, standing close by him.

"He who hesitates is lost," countered de Chastel. "I say we get the swine at Montereau."

There was a subdued but definite murmur of agreement and le Maçon knew that if it came to a show of hands the death sentence had just been passed on the Duke of Burgundy.

"One moment more," he pleaded. "Is it your intention that the Dauphin should be informed?"

There was another, longer, silence.

"He's still a boy," ventured someone.

"Rubbish!" snapped Louvet in return. "He's sixteen and a man. I say let him be told."

"Do we need his consent?"

"No, we act alone. But I believe he should be made aware of the plan."

"For God's sake," shouted le Maçon impatiently. "Monsieur could lose both his kingdom and his reputation through this."

"Oh, shut up, you moaning old woman," replied de Chastel crossly. "How could he possibly do that?"

"Don't think Isabeau will let a lover's murder go un-avenged. She'll fall like a fury on—"

"And that would flatten 'em," interrupted one of the brighter young sparks.

"None the less," de Chastel stated forcibly, "I'm pre-pared to risk the wrath of the monstrous Queen in order to see Burgundy go down."

There was another, louder, cry of assent.

"Then who," asked le Maçon crisply, "will tell the Dauphin?"

"I will," said Jean the Bastard, getting to his feet and speaking for the first time. "I will. And do you know, gen-tlemen, I think he may well be mightily pleased with your decision."

"For avenging the murder of his uncle?" asked the Vi-comte de Narbonne.

"For that and other things," answered Jean, with a secret smile. "For that and others."

To rise in the dawning like a whore and to feel cheapened and degraded and ashen in the mouth; to stand and watch the sun come up and know that only hours before one's poor body had been both used and abused; to look down at oneself and weep bitter tears, were experiences known only too well to Bonne de Giac, born Jeanne de Naillac, who now lived only for the moment when Jean the Fear-less, Duke of Burgundy, would be done to death as merci-lessly as Louis d'Orléans, the man whose slaying he had ordered so callously all those years ago.

"And then, when he's gone," thought poor Bonne, "if only I can make Charles understand that I was forced, driven, compelled to fornicate against my will, we might yet be reunited and the real wrongdoer, my merciless hus-band, be brought to book for his many crimes."

It was a hope that, in Charles's present mood, seemed utterly forlorn and Madame de Giac sighed involuntarily, then jumped as a voice from the bed behind her said, "Why so sad, chérie?"

It was Burgundy, his leathery features, wrinkled and lizard-like in the sharp light, presently contorted into what he imagined to be a kindly expression.

Bonne could not bring herself to answer him. Knowing all that was at stake, aware of her importance in the plot to rid the nation of his unwelcome presence, she still could not say a word but continued to stare out of the small window at the moat below.

"Darling, look at me," his rough voice continued, softened by tenderness whenever he spoke to her.

"How hideous it is," thought Bonne, "that this terrible man, old enough to be my grandfather and with knowledge of every perversion and sin in the world, has actually fallen in love with me, would give me anything I asked for."

Composing her features, she turned to look at him where he lay like a blemish amongst the lace-edged sheets.

"Monsieur?"

"Your back was turned. I thought you did not love me any more."

Again, Bonne could not reply, simply looking down at her feet.

"Come back to bed, there's somebody here who wants to say good morning." She saw his hands moving under the sheets. "Don't disappoint him."

The girl braced herself for what she must do next.

"If I greet him, what will be my reward?" she asked teasingly.

"Anything you care to name," the Duke answered, his breathing quickening and his face growing flushed.

"Will you let me sleep with you every night at Montereau?"

"Montereau? I don't intend to go there. Bonne, hurry! My friend grows impatient."

She undid her shift and let it slip slowly to the floor, watching the purple veins stand out on his face.

"Christ's blood you are so beautiful. Come *on*! My friend is ready to explode."

"If I help him will you let me live as your wife at Montereau?"

"Yes, yes! Just hurry!"

"Say I promise."

"I promise."

"That I shall go to Montereau because it is Bonne's favorite place."

"That I shall go to Montereau because it is ... Ahh!"

He groaned in ecstasy as she slid on top of him and began to ride, slowly at first, then faster and faster. And then she stopped.

The Duke opened his eyes frantically. "Why did you do that?"

"Promise me again about Montereau."

"I swear it."

"Good."

And with that Bonne moved with such a strong rhythm that Burgundy lost any control he had left and was a spent force within seconds. But though he may be utterly in the thrall of his fragile young mistress, Jean the Fearless was not entirely devoid of sense and suspicion.

"Why did you specify Montereau just now?" he asked, sleepily yet sharply enough for all that.

"Because my husband's castle is near there and I have fond memories of it."

And indeed she had, for it was in that place she and Charles had shared nights full of love in the round room of the château's tower.

"And also because your army is camped there and I would like to see the forces of Burgundy in all their might." Bonne snuggled closer to the Duke's body which smelt unwashed and rank. "Why don't you want to go?"

"My astrologer has warned me of a trap. He says if I visit Montereau I run the risk of assassination."

"What, with your entire company camped round the castle? What nonsense! Why, Monsieur, I swear you are as bad as the Dauphin who will not break wind lest he has consulted his soothsayers first."

Bonne felt a sense of true betrayal to Charles as she belittled him but knew she must use every weapon in her armory to persuade the old horror to ignore his advisers.

"That puny runt!" growled Burgundy. "I swear to God he thinks his cod's only use is the passing of water."

How she longed to rend him with her nails and scream in his ear till its drum burst that her sweet lover was ten times the man he was and knew how to please a woman with a single touch.

Controlling herself admirably, Bonne said, "Then you have nothing to fear from him, have you?"

"No," said Jean with sudden determination, "I haven't. What could a pipsqueak like that possibly do to me? You're right! I shall go to Montereau and to hell with any who say me no."

"Mon cher," answered Bonne, silken-tongued. "What a wise decision. As you say, to hell with them."

"And to you," she added inside her head. "To the deepest darkest pit where I hope you burn forever."

The town of Montereau lay to the southeast of Fontainebleau, straddling the river Seine as it flowed away from Paris into the open countryside. Its château being the headquarters of the Duke of Burgundy, the Dauphin, gone there for the conference, had taken up residence in a hostelry while his army, some twenty thousand men in all, had much to the dismay of the citizens occupied the town. There were soldiers everywhere, billeted out, under canvas, sleeping in temporary barracks, and though the local shopkeepers and the brothel were doing well, others cursed at the fierce congestion. On the opposite bank of the Seine stood the castle, towering over the landscape and there, looking somewhat meager in comparison with the Dauphin's vast escort, were camped the three thousand soldiers of the Burgundian army.

The town being thus divided, it had been arranged that the bridge which joined the castle bank and that of the city should be the scene of the meeting, symbolically on neither side, a type of neutral zone, as had been the middle pavilion at Pouilly. However, there had been one or two rather strange arrangements made by the Armagnacs. Two barriers had been erected closing off each end of the bridge so that the center, which had been nominated as the meeting point, could only be reached by means of a wicket gate, an odd concept to say the least.

On the day chosen for Charles and Burgundy to parley, 10th September 1419, several council meetings had taken place in the town, attended by the Dauphin and representatives of the Duke but not by Jean the Fearless himself, and it was not until early evening that Charles finally signified his desire to leave for the rendezvous, noticeably having some kind of altercation with Robert le Maçon, whom the Prince wanted to accompany him but who, on the other hand, tried to hold the Dauphin back. Finally the chestnut Chancellor stayed behind looking extremely woebegone and muttering that his royal master had been ill-advised.

As the figures on the town clock shuffled out to beat the bell five times, the Duke of Burgundy left his castle and rode on to the bridge accompanied by an escort of ten foot soldiers, passing through the first barrier which was guarded by his officers. As he trotted forward so did the Dauphin, Tanneguy de Chastel beside him, and his Gentlemen, including the three past servants of Louis d'Orléans, forming a tight protective group around the heir to the throne.

With a solemn expression on his face, Jean the Fearless rode through the wicket gate, which closed again so quickly behind him that not all his escort were able to get through.

"Why have you done that?" he called out in alarm.

"Because I need to speak to you privately," Charles answered, riding up to where the Duke awaited him, and then dismounting. "Because I need to ask why you still remain an ally of the English, why you have not acted on all that was agreed at Pouilly?"

"Simply because you have not joined your parents at Troyes, Monsieur, and thereby shown *your* goodwill," replied Burgundy curtly. "The day you take your place at the proper court of France, the day you comply with the wishes of the King and Queen, will be the day I break off all ties with Henry of England."

"I shall never again," the Dauphin said through clenched teeth, "subject myself to a life lived at the mercy of my mother. I am a grown man and entitled to my own household."

"Then it is *you*, Monsieur," purred Burgundy smoothly, "who are standing in the way of the alliance against England. It is you who are putting your personal and selfish wishes first."

"That is a lie," cried Charles furiously, "and you know it."

"Yes," said another, unfamiliar voice. "It is not the Dauphin who is the enemy of France but you, Monsieur le Duc. The whole country is at deadlock because of you and now it is time you relinquished your grip."

Looking behind him, the Dauphin saw that the three Orleanists led by the Vicomte de Narbonne, Tanneguy de Chastel following them, had appeared as if by magic.

"Out, Monsieur," commanded Tanneguy briefly, and grabbing Charles beneath the elbow practically threw him from the enclosure just as Robert de Laire seized one of Burgundy's legs and toppled him out of the saddle.

"Don't look round," de Chastel ordered the boy. "It is not fit that you do so."

But the air was full of the sounds of death as the three followers of Louis d'Orléans avenged the murder of their lord.

Guillaume Bataille's voice rang out. "You cut off my master's hand, so I'll cut off yours." And there was the thud of an axe blade on bone followed by a scream of agony which showed that Burgundy was not yet dead.

"Did they have to do that?" gasped a white-faced Charles.

"He was a Satanist," de Chastel answered shortly, "and as such deserves no quarter."

The Dauphin nodded, still panting. "Is it finished now?"

The older man looked back over his shoulder, his face impassive. Jean the Fearless lay in a pool of blood, his head smashed to pieces by axe blows, his severed hand lying, almost casually, at his feet.

"Burgundy will not bother any of us again."

"Thank God, thank God," said Charles, and wept with relief.

"Surely you are not grieving?" de Chastel asked curiously.

"Far from it, believe me. I doubt that there are many who will do that. Except, of course, for Madame de Giac."

It was out! The Dauphin had actually put into words the reason for all his recent unhappiness and by doing so at last removed the embargo which had kept his Gentlemen silent for so long.

De Chastel cleared his throat. "Without her the Duke would not have come to Montereau, you can believe me. She was forced into his bed by her husband, determined to win the wager that he could bring Burgundy to the conference table, and she has been kept there against her will ever since. As soon as her brother told Bonne of the plot to kill the Duke she did everything in her power to help. She is very much sinned against, Monsieur."

Charles turned on him a look of pure astonishment. "But why didn't you tell me all this before?"

"Nobody liked to, mon Prince. Though we all guessed the cause of your distress, none of us, not even the Bastard, thought it our place to interfere. If only you could have mentioned the matter to someone."

"I thought her a vicious whore. I could not bring myself to speak of it because I loved her so much."

De Chastel nodded wisely. "There's no misunderstanding that cannot be unraveled, Monsieur. Though we must leave Montereau at once, I think that as soon as we have returned to Bourges you should see Madame."

"I would like that very much," answered the Dauphin, and gave his old friend and faithful servant a smile that said everything.

They had not spoken to nor looked at one another for two months, a short space of time in reality but one which to lovers as close as Bonne and Charles had seemed an eternity.

When they were at last alone, both having been guests at an informal supper given by Jean Louvet, a supper at which each of the dozen hand-picked guests had received the gift of a small gem, Charles and Bonne's both being a diamond, they stood in silence, resisting the love potion which their host had so thoughtfully mixed with their wine.

"I thought you had betrayed me," the Dauphin said eventually.

"I betrayed myself," Madame de Giac answered bitterly. "My husband told me that if I did not serve the Duke he would tell you I was a whore. That is why I gave in. I wish now that I had refused. I would rather have been put to death than caused you any pain."

"Oh, Bonne!" Charles's voice was choked with emotion. "How you must have suffered."

"It was terrible. I rejoice that the Duke is dead. I felt—and still do—less than the dust beneath your feet when I was forced to—"

"Say no more of it, there is no further need to think such things. It is done and one of these days de Giac will pay for his crimes. But meanwhile we are back together. Oh, ma chère . . ." The Dauphin took both of Bonne's hands in his, ". . . forgive me for not realizing the truth."

She pressed close to him, Louvet's aphrodisiac becoming hard to ignore.

"Of course I forgive you. Oh, darling, cure me of all ills."

He needed no invitation, leading her to his bed, laid with its best silk linen, the pillows a delicate web of lace. Yet despite his period of abstinence, Charles did not hurry himself over his lovemaking, content to lie silently beside Bonne, staring at her naked body in the firelight, rubbing it with scented oils, running his finger over her lips, her nipples, her thighs.

"I want you to promise me something," the Dauphin said finally.

"What is it?"

"That you will never again allow yourself to fall into such a terrible trap. That if de Giac threatens you, you will come straight to me."

"I wish he were dead, too," the girl answered savagely. "I wish that there had been two murders at Montereau, not one."

"I dare not get the reputation of being a butcher," Charles replied thoughtfully. "Living down the death of Burgundy will be bad enough. I must wait before I kill de Giac."

"But no one can prove you were privy to the plot."

"Neither can they prove I wasn't."

Bonne nodded without conviction. "Perhaps."

But now they had spoken enough and the time had come for love. She was soft as a rose, as Charles held her against him, the dews of her body melding with his, the tumbling black hair brushing against his face, the small lissome shape shuddering to receive him.

The Dauphin of France knew then that he would love her for the rest of her days on earth, that Bonne de Giac was more precious to him than anyone else alive.

"Don't ever leave me," he whispered into the firelight.

"Never!" she breathed, floating on a cloud of sensation.

"Forgive me for doubting you."

"I forgive you."

"From now on we will always be together."

"Always," whispered Bonne, and pressed Charles close to her wildly beating heart.

Twenty-two

It had come as something of a relief to Guy when the letter begging the favor of his return to Angers had arrived from the Regent. Her time in Provence very nearly at an end, Yolande having spent the final few months of her stay preparing an Italian campaign for her son Duke Louis III, in which he would not so much reconquer his Neapolitan and Sicilian territories as re-establish himself as their King, the Duchess was at long last making preparations for her return to Anjou.

Laying careful plans, as she always did, the filling of Dr. Flavigny's vacant post had not escaped Yolande's attention to detail and so she had written to Charles, a masterly letter worded in such a way that the Dauphin could hardly have said no to her request without appearing churlish. Rather reluctantly, not wanting to let him go, Charles had had no choice but to call the hunchback into his presence to discuss the matter.

It was the end of August, almost three months since Catherine had married Henry V, now named by the mad King as the heir and successor to the domains of France in place of Charles. The land groaned in agony as the royal bridegroom crunched the dying countryside beneath his heel. The Princess's honeymoon had been one of war and bloodshed, her new husband besieging Sens two days after their wedding, and going on a fortnight later to massacre the citizens of Montereau in vengeance for the murder of the Duke of Burgundy. And, to the utter contempt of her brother, the new Queen had not uttered a single word of protest at any of these outrages.

It was hard to judge which had affected Charles more, his treatment at the hands of his parents, or the marriage of his sister. But whichever, the change in him was marked. At seventeen he had become a man.

His funny face, so plain and sad, had grown fine-boned, honed with a resilience rare in so young a person. The great eyes, once so clear and true, now had suspicion lurking in their depths and he had learned the trick of masking them to the point where they grew dark and mysterious. The Dauphin's body, too, although still lean, at last seemed in proportion, giving an appearance of splendid height, so that he wore clothes well. And these days what clothes they were!

As if in defiance at the lowly status imposed on him, Charles de Valois dressed not so much like a prince of France as a king. He had adopted blue, gold and vermilion as his theme, and these colors were repeated everywhere: in his flags and banners, in the liveries of his pages, on his shields and escutcheons. Gold was draped over the dais on which stood his high chair, giving him a regal glow, and his personal colors were repeated again in his lush velvet gowns and daringly short doublets, cut to reveal splendid and obvious cod pieces. Blue and white feathers cascaded to Charles's shoulder from his various hats and caps, and his best and favorite blue doublet was covered with dazzling gold threads, on the sleeves, picked out in five hundred and sixty-eight pearls, the words, "For the love of my dark lady."

This was his answer to his crazy father and amoral dam, this was his two raised fingers to Henry V. Wars might indeed be won on battlefields, but in the bed and ballroom the "so-called" Dauphin would shine like a god. And, indeed, though not grand enough physically to take on those proportions, the boy shimmered and gleamed like a faun. Glittering hostility, Charles de Valois was now prepared to defend his birthright, if not by force of arms at least by appealing to the mighty lawyers of the world as to whether he could indeed be legally repudiated by his lunatic father's whim.

But at the moment he was not thinking of this, instead scowling at Yolande's letter, realizing that his brilliant guardian, as he always thought of her, had out-maneuvered him once again.

"So," he said abruptly, "they want you back in Angers. Do you want to go?"

Guy hesitated, deeply attached to his friend and master yet on the horns of a dilemma.

"Well?"

"The truth is that part of me longs to return to my twin, the other to stay with you."

But it wasn't all of the truth. The reasons for Guy wanting to leave were rather more complex than that. He was a genuine clairvoyant, a young man who could use almost any medium to channel his enormous gift: astrology, the tarot, the palms of hands, scrying a crystal, all brought him strange and heady visions, some of which he did not understand himself. And to be a court astrologer, to have to advise a master who had become a companion, to see the dreadful peril in which that companion's mistress certainly lay, was more than he could bear. For months now Guy had borne the intolerable burden of censoring everything he said to Charles, telling him only half of what he saw, and it had become too much for him. Let the Dauphin's other two soothsayers, Dr. de Thibouville and Dr. des Phares, water down their facts, he could no longer continue to do so.

"I see. Well, the Regent has put her request in such a way that to refuse would be difficult. I think, with much regret, that I will have to part with you, my friend."

It was said with all Charles's old sincerity, the defiant faun temporarily banished, and Guy felt himself on the point of tears.

"My dear Monsieur," he said, dropping awkwardly to his knees and kissing the Dauphin's hand. "May I indeed call you friend?"

"Of course, we are comrades and always will be. But though it is hard to part you must look upon the Regent's request as a compliment. Obviously she has heard well of you or she would not ask for your return."

From his kneeling position, Guy said, "You *will* be King, mon Prince. Let them rail against you, let them do their worst, the fact remains that the final victory will be yours."

"In my present situation that is somewhat hard to believe."

Guy raised a loyal face. "One is coming who will turn round fate."

"One person alone? What manner of man could that possibly be?"

"Or woman," added Guy so quietly that Charles did not hear. Louder he said, "I do not know, Monsieur, but yet forewarned is forearmed. Have you heard of the prophecies of Marie of Avignon?"

"Yes, of course."

"Read *all* of her words I beg you. Somewhere in them lies the key."

"You mean she has predicted this person who is coming to help me?"

"I believe so, yes."

"Then you must know who it is."

"I don't," answered Guy, laying his hand upon his heart to show he spoke the truth. "I have only been made aware that a being already breathes upon this earth who shall be the savior of France, and that Marie of Avignon has prophesied their coming."

"Then I shall study her writings with care, I promise you," the Dauphin answered thoughtfully.

"If any more is revealed to me I shall inform you of it at once," Guy said anxiously, his funny face strained with the force of his sincerity.

"You must," Charles replied, and sank back into his chair so that the golden cloth over the dais burnished his face. "It is your duty to do so."

The hunchback kissed his master's hand as a token of assent.

"Now go to Angers with my blessing and give my good mother my fondest greetings and respects when you see her. Tell her that I will visit her shortly after her return."

The astrologer rose to his feet and bowed. "May God be with you, Monsieur. I shall ask my brother, Jacques the monk, to pray for you."

The Dauphin nodded. "Do so, do so. I feel in need of every prayer there is."

"Farewell, Master. Keep your faith."

Long after Guy had gone, Charles sat alone in the gathering shadows, his chin sunk into his hand, not moving other than to breathe. He had reached bedrock in the last few months, sick to his soul of defeat and rejection. For, for all his brave show of not caring, the stripping away of his titles, his removal from the line of succession, was eating at him like a canker. If he had had the resources and the manpower nothing would have pleased him more than to have driven Henry V from France with a great show of force.

"And yet I swear by God I'll do it one day!" he whispered into the darkness. "Oh, Christ, have mercy, send help soon."

For the weakness of his position made him vulnerable to hidden enemies, Charles knew it, surrounded by ambitious men as he was. Above all he must survive to be the ultimate winner and in order to do that he had to be one step ahead of everyone else. The manipulation of his courtiers had become more than a game; these days, Charles played chess with real people as the pieces.

With the loss of Guy, one of the only two men he could trust at court was gone. The other, of course, was the Bastard, now married to Louvet's daughter Marie. And it was Louvet, rich as Croesus on other people's money, and pack leader of the most powerful faction at court, who was currently giving the Dauphin cause for concern. Charles had been forced to put a man of his own in to clip the wings of the Chancellor of the *chambre de comptes*. His choice had been Pierre Frotier, a handsome young equerry, now Grand Master of the Equerries, and stylishly clad in furs and gold chains. Louvet, believing the Dauphin to be in love with this dashing creature, had not dared stand in his path, instead inviting the newcomer to join his group. Charles had chuckled to himself and thanked his Italian great-grandfather, Barnabo Visconti, the Tyrant of Milan, for his well-developed streak of cunning.

The ploy, however, had had somewhat unfortunate repercussions. Bonne de Giac, furious as a little wasp, had accused her lover of being bisexual.

"You are as bad as *he* is, who would scruple at nothing."

The Dauphin had pulled her into his lap, laughing till the tears ran.

"Yes, you're right, I am," and he had smothered her with kisses, imitating a monkey.

"Don't, Charles, stop it, I say! What do you mean, you are as bad?"

He had wiped his eyes on his sleeve. "I mean that I will do anything—and I mean *anything*, Bonne—to keep the wolves from closing in. They all believe they have me in their tutelage but the fact is, they don't, none of them. I am playing them at their own game and the weapon I intend to employ is the perpetual setting of a newly found favorite against those already in power."

"So you are not in love with Frotier?"

"I am in love with you and because of that I have revealed to you my secret. Now it is up to you to prove *your* love by telling no one what I have said."

His mistress had looked thoughtful. "What a plotter you are, to be sure. I would never have guessed it. But then, again, perhaps I might have done. You are so different these days, so taut, so blazing. Yes, the more I think about it the more you look an arch-intriguer."

"There is, however," said Charles, almost casually, "one who *is* in love with Frotier."

Bonne had been genuinely surprised. "Oh? Who might that be?"

"De Giac," answered the Dauphin, and had almost fallen out of his chair he had laughed so much.

"No wonder he hardly ever sees me! What a blessed, blessed relief."

"Everyone thinks that all the furs and jewels and horses are given by me. But no such thing. Your hideous husband is besotted with my protégé. They're probably drinking cockerel's blood together at this very moment."

Bonne shook her head in wonderment. "If Henry of England were engaged with you in a battle of wits the future of France would be safe and secure."

Charles had looked suddenly gloomy. "Unfortunately, it is force and force alone that will rid us of the English curse."

"Then let us seek help from others of like mind. Why don't you appeal to the Scots for men?"

"To Scotland," the Dauphin had repeated thoughtfully. "To France's old allies against the English? Henry V holds James of Scotland prisoner, does he not?"

"He most certainly does," Bonne answered with a smile.

"Then," Charles had said, laughing again, "it is high time something was done about it."

Henry of Lancaster had married Catherine of France in June and by high summer, having conquered Sens and wiped out Montereau, he was laying siege to Melun, an Armagnac stronghold if ever there was one, and it was here that two surprises awaited him. Firstly, the location of the town, an island fortress linked by bridges to two walled suburbs lying on either side of the river, made its terrain difficult to say the least.

But the second shock was far worse, for from the flagpoles of the town flew not only the white banners and Porcupine device of the Armagnacs but the Bleeding Heart of Douglas as well. The Scots had risen to defend their old ally, the two nations joined together by their hatred of the English. The Earl of Douglas had sent his army across the sea to aid the Dauphin. Yet the English King only smiled, drawing his blood-red lips up to show long hard teeth.

"It will fall by winter," he had said. "I shall keep my Christmas in Paris."

It would seem he was invincible, it would seem that the destroyer of France could never be beaten—and yet the mills of God were slowly beginning to grind out their inescapable justice. As the King of England's men went down with an epidemic of dysentery, so did he. Nature was doing what the French could not, gnawing out his bowels, but still, and against all the odds, Henry of Lancaster went on, defying even disease in his mania to be master of Paris by the end of 1420.

Now he looked a ghost of what he once had been, thin as a stick through fasting—the only way in his mind to conquer the searing pain—his face white as swan's feathers, the molten eyes and rosy lips set in them, shocking to see. He was ghastly, an upright skeleton, and still the Englishman fought on.

As it must to such an agonized persistence, Melun fell after a siege as terrible and long as that of Rouen, the number of English and French dead shocking to reckon up. Then, in personal agony, only his fanatical zeal keeping him on his feet, Henry V marched the fifty-five miles that lay between him and Paris.

There could be no joy in this victory, for France was destroyed. Without people, without crops, the land barren, still smoking from recent fires, it was not worth the taking, yet that relentless man, that war machine, that King who by now had become slightly deranged, went on to keep his word. He would celebrate Christmas in Paris with his new Queen beside him, his French and English families gathered round. And by this time next year and before death

claimed him, he would have sired an heir to succeed to the
joint kingdoms for which he had so painfully fought.

It was the fall of Paris that finally brought the Duchess
Yolande from her haven in Provence. With the autumn sea
pounding the sands of the bay and its bitter wind whipping
her skirts about her legs, she took her last walk on the
terrace and bade farewell to that most beautiful of castles,
the Château de la Napoule. Messengers had brought her
news that Melun was on the point of capitulating and that
the capital now lay within the sights of Henry of Lancaster.
The time had come for a tremendous effort, she could delay
no longer, what was left of the Dauphin's kingdom must
be put on full alert.

The Regent and her retinue reached Angers in the second week of December and barely had time to organize
their own affairs before they set off again to join the Dauphin who, never settling very long in any of his castles, had
finally decided to keep his Christmas at Bourges. So it was
that they were all together, Charles and his court, the Regent and hers, when the long-awaited news came from
Paris. On 23rd December in the Hôtel St. Pol, ironically
the house in which Charles had been born, his father had
held a *lit-de-justice* and formally disinherited his son, nam-
ing Henry V, who had sat beside him during the ceremony,
as heir and Regent of France.

"So it is done," said Charles bravely, his skin drawn tight
over his cheekbones as he attempted a smile. "I cannot
think for the life of me why they took so long about it."

"The widow of the late Duke of Burgundy was also present, Monsieur. Through her representative, Nicolas Rolin,
she asked that you and your accomplices in her husband's
murder be put in tumbrils and drawn through Paris bearing
lighted tapers, saying that you had wickedly, treacherously
and damnably murdered the Duke of Burgundy through
hatred and without any reasonable cause whatever."

A muscle twitched in the Dauphin's eyelid but he said
nothing.

"There was cause," growled Tanneguy de Chastel.
"There was cause and plenty."

As if he had uncorked a bottle, everyone began to speak
at once and the air was full of the high loud sound of
indignation. Into the babble, Charles spoke.

"We must fight them head on," he shouted. "We must go forth to meet them and engage the Englishman's troops. That must be our answer to charges of willful murder, that must be the reply to my disinheritance. All-out war!"

Yolande could not believe that she was on her feet cheering, that everyone in the room, including poor insipid Marie was shouting, "Oui, oui." The battlecry was up and with it French blood. The Dauphin of France—and there was no one present who at that moment did not believe he was such—was going to head his men into battle, the ugly faun shimmered before them, ready to die if necessary.

"Kill, kill!" they shouted.

"Yes," said Charles of France, "kill or be killed. That is all that is left for us now."

In March 1421, with Henry and his bride returned to England to beg subsidies from the clergy in order to continue the war, Charles rode out at the head of his army. Dressed in full armor and carrying his personal device of a gauntleted hand grasping a naked sword, his squire riding just behind bearing the banner of St. Michael slaying a serpent, the Dauphin looked ready to take on the world and on the 22nd of that month engaged fiercely with the English army, led by Henry V's younger brother Thomas, Duke of Clarence.

The French military might was formidable; the clansmen of Buchan, led by their Earl, had joined with those of Douglas. Thousands strong they marched, playing their bagpipes, the air full of their fearsome skirl. Charles's personal bodyguard was formed by a company of archers led by John Stewart of Darnley, and surrounded by these formidable Scotsmen he charged into battle just outside the town of Baugé.

It was an incredible victory! By midnight Clarence was dead, his standard and those of the other slaughtered consecrated to Notre-Dame-du-Puy, the black madonna to whom Charles had earlier made a pilgrimage. The Earl of Buchan was rewarded for his tremendous part in the affray with the post of Constable of France and a personal gift from Charles, Dr. Germain de Thibouville, the Dauphin's best astrologer now that Guy had left his court.

The triumph tasted like wine and there was no stopping the youthful warrior. With his trusty clansmen surrounding him, Charles besieged and took Chartres, and then marched on toward Paris. But it was here that his luck ran out. Henry of Lancaster, breathing hellfire over the death of his brother, had returned to France, leaving behind in England a pregnant Catherine. With his usual lack of humanity, the English King hanged every Scot he took prisoner and heaped indignation on the hapless James, King of Scotland, whom Henry had recently released from captivity, compelling him to follow the English army as a private knight.

In July, with Henry's troops marching toward them, the sheer weight of numbers of which would most certainly secure them a victory, Charles and his men were forced to withdraw to their own territories. The brief spell of being on the winning side was over.

It was dispiriting for them all, and the birth of a son to Henry V at the end of the year seemed the final bitter pill the Dauphinists must swallow. The Christmas of 1421 was kept quietly with none of the blaze of splendor of the previous occasion, everyone quiet and sad, wondering what the next twelve months could possibly bring them.

With winter past and the green buds of spring bursting forth—the good earth still bravely renewing itself, tormented by warring mankind though it was—destiny once more caught up with the English warlord. The dysentery contracted by Henry V at the siege of Melun had never really been cured, leaving the King in constant pain unless he fasted rigorously. And now at another difficult siege, that of Meaux, where the Bastard of Vaurus, a great bandit of a man flying the banner of the Dauphin, fought tooth and nail to keep the usurper from his gates, Henry was struck down again.

How ironic that it should be when he was stuck in the muds of Meaux, fighting agony at every step, that the English King should hear of the arrival of his son. And what particular act of God decided that Catherine, disobeying Henry's strict instructions, should give birth at Windsor castle, a well-known omen of ill luck for the unfortunate infant? It was at that particular moment, racked with pain and hardly knowing how to conduct himself, that the victor of Azincourt felt for the first time that events were finally turning against him.

Twenty-three

He had resisted marriage to Marie as long as he possibly could but now the Dauphin was cornered. With the arrival of spring, living in as much luxury as the war would allow him, Charles suddenly had no further excuses left.

"The time has come," Yolande had announced firmly, and the Dauphin had known that at long last his freedom was over.

Having arrived with her mother to celebrate the Christmas of 1420, Marie had remained with Charles when the Regent had finally departed for home, leaving a far from easy situation behind her. Naïve and retiring as she might be, the Princess of Anjou was certainly not stupid, and her dislike of Madame de Giac had in its quiet way made life very difficult for the young lovers.

"I know she watches when I come to you," Bonne had whispered in the darkness, guilty for the first time about sinfully sharing Charles's bed.

"I'm sure you are mistaken. Marie retires early. She must be fast asleep by now."

But the young woman knew that her lover was wrong, that a solitary candle burned in the girl's apartments, that there was a rustling behind the door as Bonne, silent and small as a cat, walked past on her way to her paramour's bedroom.

The situation between the two young people had settled into something almost like a marriage, de Giac long since passing up any claim to his wife in return for his high position at court. Added to this, of course, Pierre demanded complete privacy to practice his satanic rites and no questions asked about those who joined him in his unsavory rituals. It did not seem a very high price to pay, and a relationship of live and let live had developed between the cuckolded husband and his wife's royal lover.

Yet now there were other people playing this adulterous game. As Charles grew older and more poised, many young women cast their eyes on him, and he had several times allowed himself to be seduced by Eleanor de Paul of Anjou, a girl so stunningly beautiful that men actually wept in her presence. It had been a weakness of the flesh, no more, for his heart was set on Bonne, but Eleanor kept a voluptuary's bed and the Dauphin had hot blood in his veins, a direct legacy from his lascivious mother.

If his mistress had ever discovered the truth about Madame de Paul, Charles never found out. But something around that time caused Madame de Giac to initiate a new routine, refusing to say when she was coming to visit him, thus making him careful about receiving Eleanor or even being absent. In the midnight darkness Bonne would creep along the corridor, pass by his bodyguards who, to a man, turned a blind eye, and get into bed beside the sleeping Dauphin. Thus he would wake to lovemaking, exciting and excited. As a result Eleanor's nose had been put firmly out of joint, though very occasionally, in the greatest secrecy, she and Charles still shared an illicit night.

But with the arrival of Marie everything had become more difficult to manage and now, with an April marriage looming ahead of him, the Dauphin thought gloomily of the marital duties that he must perform and wondered how he could cut them to the minimum. A plan to make his wife pregnant as often as possible seemed the only solution and Charles, with a certain gritting of his teeth, prepared to make the best of something he had dreaded for years.

The fact that he looked on his betrothed as a sister did not help the situation at all. For the Princess, who had fallen in love with him when she had been little more than a child, now adored him with the ardor often associated with rather plain young women.

"Look at the way Marie is gazing at the Dauphin," whispered Pierre Frotier to de Giac. "I swear if a female could contemplate rape, she's doing so."

"Rubbish," answered the older man. "Such a thought would never enter the head of that little simpleton."

"She's Yolande d'Anjou's daughter, remember. The girl can't be utterly devoid of spirit."

"Mark my words, she's a dunderhead, a perfect partner for a prince. Intelligent women are a bore at the best of times but in a position of power they are even worse."

Frotier giggled audibly and Marie, certain they were talking about her, grew pink with confusion, keenly aware of her lack of physical beauty, devoted to Charles with a child's steadfast loyalty and racked with painful jealousy that he could even countenance affairs with other women.

"If I could only prove to him I am actually and finally grown up, that I could love him as well as any of the rest," she thought miserably as one of the many *damoiselles* in Marie's suite brushed out her hair that night.

And then a plan came, daring and outrageous.

"Tell me," the Princess asked casually, "whereabouts are Madame de Giac's apartments?"

"In the west turret, Madame. Why?"

"I thought I might call on her tomorrow, perhaps play chess."

"But you don't like chess."

"Ah, but I intend to improve my game," Marie answered enigmatically.

And as the castle of Chinon rustled into final sleeping silence, the only sounds the stamp of the watch, the creak of the wicket gate as it cautiously opened for those on late business, the occasional sad moan of a distant hound, the Princess of Anjou rose from her bed and pulled a blue silk robe over her shift. Then, with feet bare on the freezing flagstones, the strewn rushes sharp against her naked toes, Marie made her way to the west turret and threw shut the great bolt that many of the chambers carried on their outside doors. Having done this, pale but very determined, frightened by her own daring and breathing much faster than usual, the Princess stole through the shimmering torchlight to the chamber of the Dauphin of France.

The royal bodyguard of Scots archers—the Lord of Barbazan having gone, taken prisoner at Melun—behaved like true Scotsmen at the extraordinary sight of the Dauphin's affianced bride, clad only in her nightclothes, making her way into her bridegroom's bedchamber, an expression of fierce determination on her face. There was a simultaneous whistle from every one of them and then they shut their eyes, all together, as if they had been rehearsed. But as the inner door closed softly behind her there was a flurry of winks and, naughtily, one or two lewd gestures.

But inside all was sweetness. Charles woke to feel the warmth of a body beside his and bent to kiss its owner's mouth, believing it to be Bonne. It was only when the girl tensed slightly as he brushed her breast with his lips that he became suspicious and put a tinder to the candle that always stood beside his bed.

"Marie!" he exclaimed in horrified astonishment. "What are you doing here? This is all wrong. You must return to your room at once."

For answer she snuggled nearer, putting her hands on either side of his face and once more drawing his reluctant lips to hers, and a miracle took place. The very closeness of her, her very eagerness and longing, conveyed itself to him, and Charles's dread of his bride instantly vanished. The most natural response took place and the Dauphin found himself actually wanting Marie at long last.

"Oh, I love you so very much," she said. "Please take me for your own."

"But we are not married. Such a thing would not be honorable."

Yet the gentleness of her, the sweet smell and touch of her silk soft skin, were weakening his resolve even as Charles paid lip service to acts of integrity. Unable to help himself he drew her close to him—and then came magic! They were wonderful together, like practiced lovers of many years' standing, even the loss of her innocence calm and without distress. In sheer delight at the unexpectedness of such a thing, Charles found unbelievable happiness in the arms of a plain little girl who had obviously been born for love.

"How extraordinary everything is," he said, lost in amazement at the complexities of life. "Oh, Marie, I am truly going to enjoy being married to you."

"And you will pay your respects to the Dauphine regularly?"

"Of course I shall."

"I know you don't love me," Marie whispered softly. "But I have enough for the two of us. It will be a perfect marriage. I shall keep out of the way during the day and we can meet in bed at night."

"It sounds delightful."

"And you won't let Madame de Giac spoil it for us?"

"I don't think she would be capable of it," answered the Dauphin, and kissed his future bride with all the wonderment and joyfulness of new-found love.

In May 1422, Meaux finally surrendered and Henry of England was able, skeletal though he had become, to make his tortured way to Paris to be re-united with his Queen. The King was glad when he saw his Catherine that he had managed to sire her son when he did, for now he was too weak for any such joys. Yet still, like a machine, Henry donned armor once more and marched to Senlis to assist Philippe of Burgundy. How he got as far as Melun nobody ever knew. It was an unbelievable feat of strength and determination.

And then it was over. He was carried back in a litter to the castle of Vincennes, where a girl not yet twenty and a lumbering colossus in a wheelchair awaited him. A few days later the victor of Azincourt slipped into the shadows at the age of thirty-five, and with him went his dreams of conquering the world. The chain-mail fist relinquished its grip and France shuddered with relief. Now things would be different. Now it was up to a babe-in-arms and Henry's brothers, John, Duke of Bedford, the Regent of France, and Humphrey, Duke of Gloucester, Regent of England, to subdue a nation already beginning to take stock of itself.

In the splendor of autumn, the gilded firefly hues heavy on the land, the death of the year starting to show its scarlet signs, Charles the Dauphin, married to Marie that spring, made his way to the great sea port of La Rochelle. And with him, shy, demure, and always in the background, went his new Dauphine.

In the eyes of the world the union was mediocre, run of the mill, but in actuality it was a triumph, exactly what Charles needed. Nervous with people, with no ambition at all to push herself or her point of view, Marie d'Anjou disappeared during the daylight hours to either embroider or sew, but was always ready in her husband's bed at night to share their extraordinary magic. Bonne was furious, the beautiful Eleanor gave up, but the Dauphin's bride, seeking nothing, remained a constant factor in his turbulent life.

"A baby would be nice," she said one day, comfortably, cozily, as one old friend to another. So Charles stopped using his primitive methods of birth control, learned from his friend the Bastard of Orléans, and set about becoming a family man. There was something amazingly sweet about such a thing, and he found this whole new concept of chatting to a reassuring sister figure with whom he could at the same time share sublime sexual experiences, the forbidden feel of them uniquely exciting, quite the most fulfilling of his entire life.

"I suppose I can't compete," said Madame de Giac angrily, looking at her lovely face with its complementary halo of midnight hair in the mirror, and wondering what on earth her lover could see in such a booby of a wife.

"There is no contest," answered Charles lovingly. "You are my mistress, my divine darling. Marie is my friend, a jolly little thing from my childhood."

"Then if that is the case why do you attend her so often in her bedchamber?"

"A husband must perform his conjugal duties," Charles had answered enigmatically, and would be drawn no further.

But everything—his heart, his mind, his body—assured him that his marriage was a good one and though he was not in the least in love with Marie, whatever those words might mean, he would not change his situation for the world.

La Rochelle in the autumn was formidable, the sea a swirling mist until midday then, when the vapors finally rolled away, the expanse of water revealed gray and queasy, a monstrous ocean, yet one that it was the Dauphin's duty to visit. For this was his only great seaport left, the only place where troops from Scotland could land, where the navy of Castille, another friend and ally, could patrol the waves. If this harbor fell into Anglo-Burgundian hands, the cause of the Armagnacs would be finished. But this particular visit seemed worse than usual and Charles had to admit that if it had not been for the nights when he snuggled in Marie's comforting arms, he would have hated every second.

On the 10th October, two months after the death of Henry of England, the Dauphin, gorgeously arrayed in a velvet robe bearing the fleur-de-lis picked out in gold

thread, sitting in a high chair on a raised dais, presided
over a meeting, held on the first floor of the civic assembly
house, of the lawyers, clergy and laymen of La Rochelle.
Ranged in front of him in stalls awaited his attentive audience and Charles, rising to address them, became suddenly
aware of the dignity of his position.

"My Lords, both temporal and spiritual, it gives me great
joy to tell you that our mortal foe . . ." he began, then
stopped abruptly.

As if some mighty justice were being wrought on him,
as if heaven itself were interceding on behalf of his dead
enemy, the entire building began to shake and Charles,
with immense horror, watched as very slowly, like a mum-
mer acting out a slow dance, all movements twice the
length of normal speed, the floor caved in, giving way beneath his very feet. Person after person, screaming horribly,
fell through the abyss which suddenly yawned, and the
chair of state, tottering on the very edge, swung crazily.

"Christ's mercy," shrieked the Dauphin, "what's
happening?"

But there was nobody left to answer as the commotion
beneath, the screams of the injured and dying, swelled to
bursting point.

Trapped as he was, Charles did not know what to do.
He could go neither forward nor back and the only solution
seemed to be to stay motionless, balanced in his chair, peering down into the smoking black hole beneath him where
body was piled upon body, those at the bottom of all lying
so horribly still that their fate was obvious even to his un-
trained eye.

And then the Dauphin must have leaned forward too
far, for the unthinkable happened. His chair swayed, then
overbalanced, and both it and its occupant fell through the
crater, landing with a bone-breaking thud on the squirming
mass of people who wriggled below like worms in a fish-
erman's pot.

Fortunately, help was soon at hand and Charles escaped
with only cuts and bruises to his face and limbs. Yet in his
mind he suffered an irreversible sear. The memory of that
strange event, of the sudden swallowing up of people to
whom he had been speaking only a moment before,
haunting him for the rest of his life.

In the days following this tragic accident, in which several members of the Dauphin's entourage were killed, Marie d'Anjou's triumph became absolute. She may have inherited nothing of her mother's beauty or brilliance but, being a poor conversationalist herself, had long ago mastered the art of being a good listener. And now she not only listened but ministered to Charles's cuts and bruises, standing behind him when the physicians had gone and massaging the Dauphin's neck and shoulders to ease the tensions which came upon him whenever he thought of the disaster. Suddenly, Bonne de Giac, whose sad existence had placed her in the position of taker rather than giver, was nowhere to be seen.

"And to think I dreaded marrying you," Charles would say with cruel honesty. "And now I can't think how I managed before you came."

"You had Bonne," Marie would answer calmly, coming the closest to spite that a kind girl could.

"I still love her."

"She satisfies your need for beauty, that is all."

"She does indeed. But yet this family feeling is so nice. Oh, Marie, what must I do?"

"Continue as you are. You can still see her occasionally."

But the Dauphin knew something that Marie did not, namely that Bonne was beside herself with jealous despair. Charles and his love had become her linchpin, her reason for living, and now that another woman shared his bed she felt unable to endure the personal and public humiliation. For it was the talk of the court that the Dauphin slept in the Dauphine's chamber, a thing unheard of in polite society. Going to disturb his master one night on a matter of some urgency, Tanneguy de Chastel had found Charles's room empty, proof to Bonne if it were needed that her place had been usurped. So beauty alone was not enough it seemed. Yet what mental resources could the wife of a man like Pierre de Giac possibly draw on in order to make her triumph?

All this and more was in poor Bonne's mind as she roamed the corridors of the château at Mehun-sur Yèvre, not far from Bourges, one wet and wind-blown day in late October, winding her pale thin fingers round and round despairingly. To say that the sight of her was distressing was to understate. Madame de Giac looked pitiful, bleached of color and wan, only those who did not like her failing to suffer a stir of pity. Yet, unfortunately for her, it was that very set of people she came across as she turned a corner. The Dauphine and her Ladies were on their way to the sewing room, talking and laughing softly as they went.

"Madame," said Bonne, suddenly rigid, and made a stiff curtsy, back like a rod, as Marie drew close to her.

At the same time the older girl searched the face of the younger for a clue to her power over Charles, but could only see homely features, an incipient double chin, and a pair of limpid brown eyes, not particularly well set and rather short of eyelashes.

Realizing that she was being scrutinized, the Dauphine looked annoyed. "I was always taught that it is rude to stare, Madame de Giac," she whispered, her cheeks flushing.

Bonne said nothing but dropped her gaze to the floor, a solitary tear running down the side of her nose and falling onto her knees, still respectfully bent.

Marie hesitated, frowning, then called, "Ladies, go to your sewing room ahead of me if you would. I shall be delayed a few minutes."

A frisson ran through the maids-of-honor as they guessed that confrontation between the Dauphin's two ladies was imminent, and they went on their way slowly, lingering as long as they could to see if they might overhear anything of the exchange.

But Marie was prepared. "If you would step into my antechamber, Madame de Giac," she said smoothly. "I have such an interesting bale of silk I would like to show you."

Bonne hesitated, almost afraid of the plain little girl who stood so erect in front of her, just for a second having an uncanny resemblance to her mother.

"No, I . . ." she faltered.

"You will like it very much," Marie answered firmly and propelled her victim out of earshot, holding her tightly by the arm.

In the Dauphine's apartments more Ladies loitered and were dismissed, all looking suitably intrigued and excited. And it was only when she had made certain that there was nobody within earshot that the Dauphine finally drew Bonne into a window embrasure, instructing her to be seated on the cushioned sill.

"Now, Madame," Marie began, "let there be no beating about the bush. I think it is high time you and I had a little chat."

Bonne remained mute, wishing that Charles would walk through the door and retrieve the situation. And as if she could read her mind, the Dauphine said, "Monsieur le Dauphin is resting, Madame. There is no fear that he will disturb us."

"What is it you require of me?" Madame de Giac managed at last.

"Very little. I do not even ask you to stop seeing Monsieur. I believe it is *you* in fact who want to say something to *me*."

"I am not conscious of it, Madame," Bonne answered stiffly, regaining a little dignity.

"I am certain," Marie went on regardless, "that you would like me to save your face by keeping away from my own husband. And that, Madame, is something I refuse to do."

"But I love him," answered Bonne, her voice rising above the burst of a sob.

The Dauphine turned on her like a fury, looking anything but the insipid creature who normally made her quiet way about the court.

"Do you think you hold the exclusive rights in love? I also love him and have done for many years. We shared childhood together, we knew one another long before you came on the scene. Monsieur may have his beautiful mistresses, I don't care a fig! For it is I and no other who will always be his boon companion. It is to me he will come home when he is done with his dalliance. So remember that, Madame de Giac, when next you pleasure him in your bed."

Not bothering to fight her tears, Bonne turned on her rival. "Why does he love you, that is what I want to know? What can you possibly offer him that I can't?"

"Safety," Marie replied with certainty. "Beauty, by its very nature, is unreliable. But I, who have none, can be trusted. I am his mother, his sister, his friend, his escape. Whereas you, my dear Madame, represent only challenge and danger."

Again Bonne could not reply, overcome by tears.

"He needs us both," the Dauphine went on, more kindly.

"We are the two halves of a whole. You and Eleanor de Paul along with you."

"It wasn't always like that," Madame de Giac answered brokenheartedly. "Before you came he relied on me to act as his wife."

"Then you must adapt to the new situation, mustn't you?" Marie said with a sweet smile.

It was too much. Bonne could no longer cope with the pressure. Like the leaves that whirled down beyond the window, she fell to the floor, sobbing miserably. For a moment the Dauphine stood looking at her, a plain comfortable girl in charge of a fraught situation, then she dropped to her knees and raised the weeping creature by the shoulders.

"Hush, please, Madame. It is not right that you should grieve so much. If you play the game according to the rules no hurt will come to you."

"You are not married to de Giac," Bonne spat out fiercely. "You are not in the hands of a torturer. You don't know what it is like, Madame la Dauphine, to go in fear of your very life."

Marie looked thoughtful. "No, you are right, I don't. Tell me, Madame, if I promoted you to the rank of principal Maid-of-Honor, demanding your presence, requiring you to be at my constant beck and call, would that guarantee your safety?"

Her husband's mistress looked at her in disbelief. "But why should you do that? You don't even like me?"

"But Monsieur does and that is all that counts. Will you accept the post?"

"I will," answered Bonne, brushing the hair from her eyes and passing her hand over them. "You know I will. And I shall be for ever in your debt as a result."

The uncompromising features of Madame la Dauphine did not reveal that she had already taken into consideration and weighed up this fact.

"Then rise to your feet, please do. It is not seemly that you should grovel."

"I can never thank you enough ..." Bonne began, then stopped as the sound of a commotion broke out from somewhere deep in the castle's heart. There was the scurry of hurrying feet going past the Dauphine's apartments in the direction of her husband's and from somewhere came the voice of Louvet, still the most important man at court, shouting, "What's happening? What's going on?"

"There are riders here from Paris," came the reply. "They have managed to get through the lines and have an urgent message for Monsieur."

"I must go," said Marie practically. "Bonne, wipe your eyes and attend us. And hurry about it."

And with that the Dauphine sped to Charles's bedchamber to find that he had already risen and was being helped to dress by one of his servants.

"Who has arrived?" she asked, not bothering with ceremony.

"I don't know. They say messengers have come from Paris, probably from Bedford himself."

"Umm, perhaps," said Marie, doubting it.

With Henry V dead and laid in his grave, his brother, the Duke of Bedford, Regent of France, now ruled in the capital city, yet it was hard to see why he should be communicating with his deadly enemy the Dauphin.

"Whoever they are from, it is important we receive these men in splendor. Shall I order on your behalf, Monsieur, that the messengers are treated as honored guests until such time as we can see them?"

"No, I am most anxious to know what they have come about. Instruct that they shall be given time to wash off the dust of the road and take refreshment. Say we will give them audience in an hour."

"Very good, Monsieur," answered the Dauphine, and curtsied like a dutiful wife.

But at the appointed time she was agog with interest as four Gentlemen at Arms, wearing the livery of the King of France himself, made a stately entrance into the audience chamber where Charles and she sat on high seats, the rest of the Council gathered round.

Afterwards, Marie d'Anjou supposed she should have guessed their purpose but her mind, like that of most others, was so much taken up with the matter of war that the obvious truly had not occurred to her. And it was clear that it had not done to anyone else either as the spokesman for the four strangers went down on one knee in low obeisance before the Dauphin's chair of state.

"Monsieur," he said, his voice trembling, "we left Paris two days ago and have ridden without stop."

"To tell me what?" asked Charles impatiently.

"To tell you, Majesty, that your royal father has closed his eyes on this world. Monsieur, the King is dead, long live the King."

Charles sprang up, his face scintillating and suddenly white.

"So the prophecy has come true," he gasped almost inaudibly. "I am truly King at last."

There was an intake of breath as everyone present knelt to pay due homage.

"Long live the King," came the chorused shout.

"I thank God for bringing me safely to this moment," answered the boy, and with that swept from the room to be utterly alone with his tumultuous emotions.

Twenty-four

"No," shouted Richemont, "you must not leave me."

He had been dreaming of Yolande, dreaming that the years had never passed and they were together again. But he woke lonely, his fingers reaching to his face to feel for the mutilations which had taken away his perfect looks. They were there of course, just as they had been ever since the moment he had recovered consciousness on the field of Azincourt, just as they had throughout his five-year imprisonment, just as they would be for the rest of his life.

"Christ have mercy," said Richemont softly, and poured himself a flagon of wine.

As ironic fate would have it he had been freed from prison two years before Henry of Lancaster's death, when Gloucester would have ordered his release in any case. Just man though Duke Humphrey was, it was in his best interests to get the great lords of France on England's side, a point of view to which Henry V had eventually come round himself.

"You can go," the English King had said, looking down from his dais at the wounded and filthy prisoner who stood before him.

Richemont had given him a surly glare and eventually said, "On what conditions?"

"How clever of you to guess, my dear brother. Because indeed there *are* two. The first being that you end your allegiance to the Armagnac cause and serve me as ambassador to your brother of Brittany's court. He was supported by English troops during an insurrection by the Penthièvre claimants to his title, and consequently has transferred his loyalty to England."

"And the other?"

Henry V's red mouth had smiled briefly. "It is not so much a condition as a promise. Your mother, the Queen Dowager of England, is under arrest in Pevensey Castle—"

"On what charge?" Richemont had interrupted, not believing what he was hearing.

"Witchcraft," the King had answered, almost casually.

The Earl had been utterly shaken, knowing nothing in his prison cell, not having a notion that his mother was anything but alive and well.

"What dark political plot is this?" he had growled. "I suppose the poor creature made too much of a stir when you threatened the lives of her sons."

"How loyal you are," Henry had said, examining his nails. His tone changed. "But not sufficiently loyal to respect your oath of allegiance to my father. You should have fought at Azincourt with my soldiers, you bloody little traitor."

"Don't give me traitor," Richemont had hurled back. "You who put Frenchmen to the sword in the name of God, pretending He is on your side giving you some divine right to slaughter. It is you who are the traitor, Monsieur. You are the master turncoat of us all. I am not even in the same league."

It was a miracle he had not been marched straight back to his cell, but the English King had merely shrugged a delicate shoulder and curled his crimson lip.

"You sound off like a fart in a thunderstorm, Richmond. Now begone before I change my mind."

The Earl had stood his ground. "You still have not told me the second favor, *brother*." He pointed the word with as much sarcasm as he dared.

"No attempts to rescue your mother. She will be released from Pevensey only when I am assured she does not traffic with demons."

"We'll see about that," Richemont murmured beneath his breath, making an icy bow as best he could in chains.

Henry could not have heard, for that same day the Earl was allowed to have a bath, put on a new suit of clothes and board a boat bound for Brittany, only to find the Duke turning away at the sight of him.

"I know," Richemont had said bitterly. "I left you whole and have come back a monster. In future I will wear a mask."

Duke Jean had rallied, clasping his brother in his arms and kissing him on both wounded cheeks.

"Don't say such terrible things. It was the shock, that's all. You must never hide your face."

But Richemont had been forced to accept that Jean's initial reaction was common to all, everyone who saw him, particularly the women who had once found him so attractive, shuddering when they beheld his mighty scars.

It had been the fact that Marguerite, daughter of the murdered Jean the Fearless and widow of Richemont's friend Louis the Dauphin, did not turn away repulsed, as much as the memory of their night together, not quite lovers, that had made the Earl marry her on 10th October 1423. Marguerite was still very pretty, only in her early twenties, and had so much love for him she hardly seemed to notice that it was not fully reciprocated. For even after the passing of all the years, even after the flowing of so much blood, Richemont's obsession with the Duchess of Anjou, Queen of Sicily, remained.

It was an odd situation, reflected Arthur, wide awake and once more filling his wine cup to the brim. Despite the fact he very rarely thought of Yolande on a conscious level, still she consumed him. A subtle haunting indeed! At night she lay between him and his wife in bed, filling his mind with the remembered scents of her skin, spoiling him for poor Marguerite, who had sought adoration so earnestly from her first husband. But that malicious sprite Louis had loved his best friend Richemont far more than he could ever love his wife and now Marguerite longed to be cherished by her second husband.

"Of course I care for you," the Earl would answer her eternal questions, patting her head absently, his mind far away, almost in limbo.

And so he did—a little.

"Oh God, why did you choose to make me so ugly?" he said aloud now, in a sudden passion of despair.

But there was no answer, only the inexorable feeling that he must work out his destiny for himself, as he stared into the flames that had at last begun to die down to a dull red glow.

*   *   *

Yolande, too, dreamed of the past. She stood in the rain
again and saw a lovely boy walking the parapet of a castle's
battlements, and laughed with him and at him, overcome
with joy merely by watching his youth and beauty. Even
though she was dreaming, the pleasure and excitement of
reliving the moments she had shared with Arthur de Richemont made the Duchess of Anjou smile in her sleep. And
then she sighed and woke, and lay in darkness staring at
the vague outlines of her bed canopy, thinking of what had
happened in the years since he had come back to France.

Yolande had heard of Richemont's injuries almost as
soon as he returned to Brittany, and her immediate instinct
had been to see him, to express her sorrow that such a
grim fate should have befallen him. And then the Duchess
had stopped, quill in hand, and laid her pen back upon the
desk. Almost as if he had walked into the room she had
felt its atmosphere change, had sensed his anguish over the
miles that separated them, and known that the last thing
she must do was sympathize.

"He feels less the man already," she had said to herself,
"far be it from me to add to his humiliation."

And then had come an event which had put Richemont
far from the Duchess's thoughts. On 3rd July 1423, Marie
had given birth to her first child, an ugly little boy who had
been named Louis. Yolande had been in the room, holding
her daughter in her arms, encouraging her to deliver her
baby, as Marie sweated and struggled on the great bed of
state beneath a canopy bearing the fleur-de-lis woven in
gold. Charles and his entourage had moodily stalked the
corridors till the first wailing cry had rung out, then the
young King had rushed to be at Marie's side, smothering
her with kisses.

Not long after that, the Queen-Duchess had been informed that the Earl of Richmond had married the widow
of Louis the Dauphin, and been glad for him. So why had
a strange feeling lurked at the bottom of her stomach when
the news had come? Surely after all this time it could not
be one of resentment? And then the state of the nation had
again absorbed her entire attention and she had thought no
more of it.

Richemont's new wife was also the sister of Duke Philippe of Burgundy, now known as Philippe the Good be-

cause of his leonine attractiveness and habit of throwing
largesse to the scrabbling poor. Unfortunately for the Dauphinists, Philippe had another sister, Anne, and she had
married John of Lancaster, Duke of Bedford, the Regent
of France. Thus a great alliance between Bedford, Burgundy and Brittany had been formed, a triple alliance
whose might in the field seemed destined to doom the new
King's cause irretrievably. At the battle of Cravant in July
1423, Charles's army had been decimated, the cause of
France set back firmly.

And yet there had been a ray of hope from a most unlikely source. Louis the Dauphin's widow had married
again and so, indeed, had the widow of Jean the Dauphin,
the large and ugly Jacqueline, Duchess of Bavaria and
Countess of Hainault, Holland and Zeeland. Jacqueline's
father, the Count of Hainault, furious that his influence had
been diminished to nothing by the death of his son-in-law,
had insisted on Jacqueline's re-marriage, this time to a
cousin and friend of Philippe the Good, namely the Duke
of Brabant.

For such a big ungainly girl, the young widow was obviously as highly charged sexually as her kinswoman, Isabeau,
and had fled the country in horror when her bridegroom,
some whispered through lack of interest, had found himself
incapable of consummating their marriage. In England,
where she had sought sanctuary, Jacqueline had fallen in
love with Henry V's other sibling, Humphrey of Gloucester,
the English Regent, John of Bedford's younger brother.

Humphrey, chivalrous and passionate, a brilliant man,
had been appalled by the fat red-faced girl noisily declaring
her love for him, but had been quite literally forced into
seeking an alliance with the land-owning heiress by his
greedy councilors. As there was little hope of an annulment
of Jacqueline's marriage coming from the Pope recently
elected by the English and the Dutch, she had gone instead
to the Spanish Antipope who, valuing Gloucester's support,
granted her wish. Thus Duke Humphrey, snail-slow with
reluctance, had gone through with the wedding—and ac-
quired enemies as a result! The slighted ex-husband and
his friend Philippe of Burgundy.

Nothing anyone could do or say would remove the conviction from Burgundy's mind that the whole thing was a
deliberate plot to insult and rob him, and that Humphrey's

brother John was not only party to it but partly to blame. The first cracks in the triple alliance had begun. To add insult to Philippe's injury, the gossip had already come from London that Humphrey, hearing that the Roman Pope had declared his marriage bigamous, null and void, had turned to one of his wife's ladies-in-waiting, the golden-haired dark-eyed Eleanor Cobham, for love.

All this and more had been grist to Yolande's mill; the louder Jacqueline complained of her treatment, the louder the Pope thundered about adultery, the better she had liked it. Skillfully, the Duchess of Anjou had painted a portrait for Jean of Brittany in which the triple alliance had split asunder and he had been caught like a hog in middle ground.

Lying in bed, gazing round the vaulted chamber, lit by moonbeams yet deep in shadow, Yolande sighed again for the past and put the present out of her thoughts. It had been many years since she and Richemont had made love in this very room, creating Jehanne out of their long and passionate embraces.

"Why does his memory still fascinate me?" she said out loud, and admitted in a moment of ruthless honesty that she would give almost anything to see the Earl again, all the old anger between them now surely dead and buried.

She rose then, luxuriating in the warmth of that June night, and crossed to her desk, her mind suddenly made up.

"My dear Richemont," Yolande began her letter, and thought of the last she had sent him, telling him to leave without seeing her again.

And it was then, pausing for a moment in the moonlight, that an idea came, cool as a stream, making the Regent's spine prick with the audacity of the notion that had just come into her head.

"I have a matter of supreme urgency I wish to discuss with you," she wrote, then paused again. Letters sent across country were frequently intercepted and yet, without putting anything that could be used by the enemy, she must entice him to come to a secret destination. "So I would very much appreciate it if you joined me in Angers for Whitsuntide on 7th June, Easter having been late this year. In gratitude, your friend, Yolande d'Anjou. Dated this 2nd day of June, 1424."

It was pithy and to the point but it was also intriguing. Knowing the scampish boy that once had been, the Duchess was reasonably certain that the Earl of Richmond would come to her, out of sheer curiosity if nothing else.

Suddenly, she felt that a burden had been lifted, that she was young again and full of the tremulous painful emotions associated with being raw in the world. Going to the mirror, Yolande held her candle high and gazed. Her eyes blazed green fire, her curving mouth was smiling, her cheeks hollow and fine. Youth had, in fact, gone, but she had entered the age of elegance and there was nothing to fear. She was in the forty-fifth year of her life and had become assured and worldly-wise, her loveliness beyond time. In this soft light with her hawk features relaxed, her winged black brows as shapely as they had always been, Yolande d'Anjou was still one of the most exciting women in France.

Richemont was in torment from the moment he got Yolande's letter. After all these years, after going to hell and back again with that agonizing mixture of love and hate, the pain and torment of hope and desire, the Earl admitted to himself that it was only the fact of his gashed face that stood between him and rushing to be at the Duchess's side.

He cared nothing about being married, about any future association between them being adulterous. All he wanted was to see her, to be once more in her presence. And yet he hesitated, staring into the mirror, seeing the way his right eye dipped very slightly where the point of the wounding blade had pierced the skin beneath it, looking with loathing at the criss-cross marks of the gut that had been clumsily sewn in by the English physician desperately trying to put his face back together.

"You hideous monster," he said to his reflection, and did not know whether to laugh or weep at the sheer tragedy of it all.

In the end, Richemont decided to go to her, ordering from his tailors a dozen visors made in different colors to match the new clothes they were hurriedly making, holding on to what was left of his tattered vanity, yet at the same time smiling wryly at his pathetic conceits.

Thus, prepared as best he could, the Earl left Nantes early in the morning of the Feast of Whitsuntide, turning inland to follow the Loire the relatively short distance to

Angers, riding with a safe conduct signed by his brother
the Duke of Brittany, and an accompanying party of two
dozen men. Yet on arrival at the castle in the heat of late
afternoon, Richemont discovered that a shock lay in wait
for him.

"The Queen of Sicily is not in residence, Lord Earl," the
maître-d'hôtel announced, bowing gravely.

"But surely she is expecting me?"

"She asked me to give you this."

And a sealed parchment was put into his gloved fist,
which the Earl broke open impatiently.

Even looking at that long flowing hand was enough to
wipe thirteen years from his mind. He was a youth again,
despairingly in love, being sent away like a disgraced dog
because his mistress preferred Pierre de Giac. Yet now,
having heard so much of that particular man's nefarious
activities, his cruel treatment of his wife, his allegiance to
Satan, Richemont wondered if any of it had been true.

"By Christ's passion, if I learn from her lips that de Giac
lied to me I'll strangle the wretch barehanded," he said
under his breath.

The very thought made sweat start out on him, drenching
his skin, and it was with some difficulty that the Earl
wrested his attention back to the letter he held.

"My dear Richemont," he read, "it is vital that I speak
to you in a place that is utterly secure. I have, therefore,
decided to name our secret meeting place only in a letter
that will be put directly into your hand on your arrival in
Angers.

"My friend, I am asking you to undertake the long and
hazardous journey to Provence, as will I, and go to the
Château de la Napoule situated in the bay of the same
name. A contingent of horsemen are standing by to escort
you to the right destination and bring you safely there. I
beg you to treat the castle of Angers as your own in my
absence. Everything is prepared for you to spend a comfortable night. I trust that you will find yourself able to
comply with this, my strange request. In gratitude, Yolande
d'Anjou."

He was intrigued, there was no denying it. A grin, much
like the one he used to have before he was scarred both
physically and mentally, crept over Richemont's poor
gashed face.

He turned to the *maître-d'hôtel*. "Is there a messenger available to take a letter to my wife at Nantes?"

"The Queen of Sicily had anticipated such a thing, Lord Earl. Even now a rider stands ready with horse saddled and waiting; while parchment wax and inks are already prepared in your chamber."

"So she knew I'd go," said Richemont quizzically.

"Madame the Queen-Duchess hoped that you might," answered the *maître,* and smiled as one man to another over the wiles and ways of powerful women.

It was a journey of unbelievable difficulty and splendor. On the advice of the Captain of the Guard, Richemont's cavalcade avoided the most hazardous routes and followed the Loire as far as Le Puy, then joined another mighty river, the Rhône, turning in along the coast only when they reached that eerie marshland known as the Camargue. It was the end of the month by the time they arrived in Provence and Richemont reckoned that Yolande could only be reaching her destination a mere handful of days ahead of them.

"This had better be worth it," he said grimly, his delight in the escapade just beginning to wear a little thin as the weather grew even hotter.

It was relentless, the sun beating down on them as they passed beyond the fierce mountains to the gentle slopes below, the smell of lavender and flowers heavy on the breeze. Richemont inhaled deeply, stripped to the waist in the saddle, feeling that the foul air of prison had finally gone from his lungs and a part of him had become whole again. With every step of his horse's hooves along that magnificent coastline his heart lifted, and when, late one evening, he caught his first glimpse of the Château de la Napoule, he stared at it as if he had been transported to fairyland and here lay the Queen's bower.

The bay which the castle dominated swept in a huge and glorious curve, distant views of another, equally beautiful, lying just beyond, while two islands off shore caught the light of the dying sun in a sea the color of coral. As for the Château, it almost beggared description. Arriving at twilight and by land as he was, Richemont could see its wooded gardens, its turrets and towers, the Moorish quality of its architecture, smell the scent of its trees and flowers, beneath which constantly lay the smoky aroma of sandalwood. As the porter opened the gates for the cavalcade to pass through, the Earl could only feel glad that Yolande had made him travel such a long and arduous journey in order to see this magical place.

Torches were being lit within the castle and courtyard as the sun slowly dipped out of sight, reflecting in the restless ocean, which was now turning a deep and mysterious blue. Only too conscious of how ugly and disheveled he must appear in contrast to all this beauty, Richemont put a visor over his face as he dismounted.

As was customary, the Earl and his retinue were shown to the guests' lodging to wash, change and take refreshment before joining in the hubbub of castle life. Miserably aware of his disfigurement, Richemont shaved himself carefully before covering his scars with a black mask, matching both his sombre mood and dark clothes. The moment he dreaded was at hand. After years of separation he was to see the woman to whom he had surrendered his virginity, his heart, and then rejected again in a drunken folly. With a heave of his shoulders, the Earl left his chamber and descended to the Château's main living quarters.

She was waiting for him in her receiving room, her back turned, her eyes resting thoughtfully on the seascape beyond the window, as Arthur went quietly in. Just for a moment he stood watching her, then gave a discreet cough, at which Yolande spun round.

She was still beautiful, he thought, with her great eyes glittering in the firelight, her hawk's face softened by her smile. Richemont saw that the Duchess had put on the emerald she had worn when last they met and that it flashed and glinted, as sparkling and alive as she was.

He bowed and said gruffly, "Your servant, ma Reine."

Yolande gave no answering salute but came toward him, stopping only when they stood about a foot apart, staring him fully in the face, her eyes almost level with his own, gazing at her so wretchedly through the holes in his visor.

"Why are you wearing that?" she said eventually.

"I am disfigured, Madame. My face was scarred at Azincourt."

"I know that, but you do not answer my question."

"Very well, if you insist." His voice was harsh. "I am masked because I have no wish to cause you offence."

"How could *you* ever offend *me*?" Yolande answered quietly, and before he could move or protest untied the strings that held the thing in place.

Inside his chest, the Earl's heart died. "I don't want you to see me," he said, wrenching away.

"Why not?"

"I just don't."

"But why?"

"Because, God help me, I'm still in love with you I suppose."

But it was too late. The mask was off and he was revealed, imperfect eye, livid scars, all. Richemont lowered his lids in shame so only felt the long fingers tracing out the line of each gash, slowly and carefully, as if their owner were blind, learning a face.

"The gorge of Verdon."

"What?" said Richemont, opening them again in astonishment.

Yolande was smiling. "You have the map of Provence on your face. This long scar is the gorge of Verdon which is in the mountains of Haute Provence. Quite spectacular! It is very difficult to reach but I shall take you there one day."

He stared at her in astonishment, unable to utter.

"And these two are the bay of Napoule and the bay of Juan. And these ..." her fingers were teasing the Z on his left cheek "... are the winding courses of the Grand Rhône and the Petit Rhône in the Camargue."

Richemont wept silently, the tears splashing down onto her hands.

"And those, drops from the sacred spring of St. Rémy, where the Romans built their baths."

"Oh, stop, stop," he said in a muffled voice. "It is too much to bear."

"What is?"

"The fact that you can *touch* them, that they don't repulse you. Marguerite, poor thing, does not flinch but she has never touched my scars. Never."

"Then I will do more," answered the Duchess Yolande softly, and holding Richemont's face between her hands, drew it close and kissed each livid gash.

The love between them crackled in the air, never dead, never gone, always lurking beneath the surface, rough, raw and wonderful. In a glorious agony, mouth sought mouth as these two incredible people, the giants of their age, drew together once again.

It seemed, then, that the folly of their parting had never taken place, that the wasted years had been but a few moments, and they were picking up their feelings, their intensity of love, one for the other, as if they had never been away. Quite slowly and without rush, they made their way in silence to Yolande's chamber, situated in a far tower that overlooked the waves.

Here, all was clear and blue; the sea and sky beyond the open window; the breath of the ocean, filling the room with its perfume; the bed, hung with blue taffeta; the silk hangings on the wall, woven with soft threads; the rushes on the floor mixed with the blue lavender that came from the fields of Haute Provence.

"There are scars on my chest as well," said Richemont awkwardly.

"Perhaps," answered Yolande, loving him, kissing him, gently undoing his linen shirt, "you are not just a walking likeness of Provence but the entire map of France itself."

Half dressed, the lovers drew one another down onto the bed as if they drowned, down and down beneath the rushing swirling water of the ocean which pounded just beyond the wall. It was the mating of merpeople, of sea creatures, as the Earl of Richmond and the Duchess of Anjou moved into one another rapturously, shapely breast against scarred chest, legs twining like fish tails.

"Never leave me again," breathed Richemont urgently. "Yolande, promise that you will never leave me again."

"Only death will separate us," she answered. "Only that master whom all of us must serve."

Then they spoke no more as passion took them out of the waves and into heaven, beyond the moon to catch the distant stars.

They lay on cushions before the fire after all was done, sharing a wine cup, talking tenderly of nothing, the woman lying in the arms of her lover.

"Tell me one thing," said Richemont, his mouth against the sweep of her dark hair.

"What is it?"

"Why did you send me away without seeing me when I was leaving to join the Armagnacs next day?"

Yolande hesitated momentarily, on the edge of telling him that she had borne him a daughter who was now nearly thirteen years old.

"Well?"

"You were too young to be involved with a married woman and I dreaded scandal."

"And that was the only reason?"

"Yes," lied Yolande. "Why do you ask?"

"I wondered if it had anything to do with Pierre de Giac, that is all."

The Earl felt rather than saw her surprise.

"De Giac? God's mercy, no. Why do you say that?"

"Because he told me it was *he* who spent that night with you."

Yolande did the most reassuring thing in the world and laughed. "With me? That reptile? No indeed. I leave his sort to Isabeau."

Richemont drew her even closer. "Then I was the only one?"

Yolande turned her beautiful eyes on him. "Yes, my love. Only you and my husband in all this time."

"You realized I never stopped loving you?"

The Duchess nodded. "Yes, I knew. Just as I knew that one day we would be re-united."

"And now you are free and I am not."

"Your sad little wife! Poor Marguerite, she has had no love in her life."

"I am as kind to her as I can be when my heart is not hers." Richemont kissed the warm mouth so close to his. "Why did you send for me? Was it simply to seduce me again or was there some other reason?"

Yolande laughed. "How clever of you to guess." Her face changed. "No, there was another purpose but before I tell you of it let me assure you about something. Whatever you answer me, be it yea or nay, my feelings for you will remain unchanged. I swore just now to love you till the end of my days on earth—and I meant it."

"So what is it you want of me? Do you expect me to change sides yet again and join the forces of the new King?"

"Yes," Yolande answered simply. "Yes, I do."

There was a silence which hung heavily between them.

"You put me in an awkward position, Madame. I am bound to both Brittany and Burgundy by ties of blood and marriage. It would be dishonorable to go against such bonds."

Yolande's heart sank, for if the shabby truth be known she had hoped that by going to bed with him she could bring him to her side in more ways than one. Yet the gamble had not come off.

"Your answer is no."

It was not a question just a bald statement of fact.

"It must be. And so I suppose that is that. In the morning you will ask me to take my leave."

She drew away from him, her heavy coil of hair striking his shoulder like a flail.

"How can you be so cruel, so wounding? I told you it was of no consequence. If we are on opposing sides in this war, so be it. It changes nothing."

He dragged her back to him, suddenly rough as blades. "You witch," he said, so close to her that every line of his vicious cuts was clearly visible. "You know I would do anything in the world for you, but this I cannot. A man must have some integrity left. I gave my word that I would serve Henry of England and his allies. I will not renege on that promise."

"Then do not renege on ours. For we have given one, spoken or unspoken."

He kissed her roughly, quivering with intensity. "My beloved enemy, I speak my oath. I will love you all the days of my life. That is my promise to you."

Outside, the cold wind that had caused the fire to be lit banged at the window like a lost soul, the mood within echoing its desolation.

"Then if that is the case let us put all that has been discussed behind us," answered Yolande with great determination. "Otherwise I fear that we may part again—and this time for ever."

But Richemont wasn't thinking about what she was saying, infatuated by Yolande's beautiful proximity, looking through half-closed eyes at her long lean body, stretched to its full length, the firelight shining on its planes and shadows, turning her skin the color of gold.

"I want you," said the Earl. "I swear to God I could not leave you even if I tried."

This lovemaking was carnal, voluptuous, where the other had been romantic. There was a certain desperation to it, engendered by the fact that they had almost argued, almost lost one another when so recently found. The Earl coupled brutally, like a soldier with a hired slut, while Yolande, aroused by such treatment, rediscovered elements in herself long forgotten. "My lovely whore," whispered Richemont as he came to completion.

"You dangerous rake," she answered before she fell back into his arms and died the little death.

They spent four weeks together, destined to be the happiest of their lives. They thought of nothing but themselves, forgetting the English, the war, the fact that they came from opposing sides. Yolande, slightly ashamed that she had even considered using his love for her as a means of persuasion, almost rejoiced that sworn enemies could be so at peace together.

By day they walked the deserted beaches and hills, handfasted and barefoot, swimming without clothes in the warm summer sea, making love beneath the waves and in the roaring surf. By night they dined privately, then went to Yolande's blue chamber, listening to the song of the ocean and the wild high cry of gulls.

At the back of both their minds was the thought that this idyll could not last, that such unqualified bliss could not go on, that the scales must eventually swing. And so it came about, at the end of August, one deceptively calm evening just as the fireball sun quenched itself in the sea.

The clatter of hooves in the courtyard brought no particular alarm, for servants and retainers came and went all day. But within minutes one of Yolande's maids-of-honor had hurried to her side saying that a messenger had arrived with urgent news.

"He will not even wait for refeshment, ma Reine. He says he has a letter for you from the King himself."

"Do you wish me to leave the room? He may have something to impart which is for your ears alone," Richemont asked without irony.

"No, stay. I would rather you did."

He watched as his mistress broke the seal on the rolled

parchment, catching momentarily a glimpse of a flourishing signature, "Charles," then saw her sit down rapidly, her face the color of milk.

"What is it?" he said, going to kneel beside her chair.

"A triumph for you, a tragedy for me," the Duchess answered bitterly. "Charles's army has been hacked to pieces at Verneuil. Bedford himself led the opposing force. Normandy is completely reconquered and we have lost the Constable of France. The Earl of Buchan is dead."

"I don't know what to say."

"Then say nothing. It is better that you don't."

The reality of their situation bore in relentlessly upon them. Where Richemont should, by rights, have raised his wine cup in a toast to the victors. Yolande should have put on mourning for a dead ally. Fate had once again inexorably moved its pawns.

"I think," said the Duchess into the silence, "I would like to be alone for a while. If you will excuse me."

And with that she left the room without looking at him again. Utterly benighted, Richemont followed at a distance, seeing Yolande go on to the sea terrace where she began to pace relentlessly.

The Earl knew, then, what it was to be in pure torment. He loved her so much that her suffering was his too, and seeing her in such distress was more than he could endure.

"Please, my darling, don't," he called, running to her side.

She was not so much weeping as bleeding tears, each one falling with pain from eyes already swollen and red.

"Don't, don't," Richemont cried in agony. "I can't bear to see you like this."

Yolande shook her head. "Leave me alone, I beg you."

"Christ's mercy!" called the Earl to the darkening sky. "What must I do? What shall I do?"

And then he knew without question. Tied by blood and bond he may be to others, but to this woman, his woman, he was tied by something far more powerful.

"Why do you weep?" he asked, his final quest for the truth before he took action. "Is it for the death of Buchan?"

"That and the death of France," Yolande answered harshly. "I swore to my dying husband that I would save this poor country of ours, but by Christ's Holy Blood I have been defeated."

"No," said Richemont violently, "no, no, no. He was my friend, I cannot betray him as well as you. I surrender. I will fight and die for your beloved country. Madame, I give you my services and my life."

She looked at him in astonishment. "But you swore—"

"I know. I take back all I said. It is to you I offer my eternal love and allegiance. Will you take it?"

He dropped on one knee before her, not knowing which was the louder, the roar of the ocean or the pounding of his heart.

Yolande put her hand on his shoulder. "With you by my side I know I can win."

"You can and will."

The words came from nowhere, from a part of her brain where inspiration lay, quiet as the rocks at the bottom of the sea.

"Then I extend to you, Arthur, Earl of Richmond, the sword of the Constable of France. What is your reply?"

He stared at her in blank astonishment. "But I am nothing. A mere soldier. You cannot give me so great an honor."

"Do you accept?" Yolande repeated urgently.

"If I do, it will mean turning my back for ever on my brother of Brittany."

"I think not," the Duchess answered slowly. "It has been in my mind some months now to offer him a prize he will not refuse—in return for his signature on a treaty."

Richemont looked blank and Yolande went on, "My son Jade, Duke Louis III, is twenty-one and not yet wed. I believe your niece Isabella is now of marriageable age—"

Richemont burst out laughing. "She is fifteen and yes, of course Jean will jump at the chance of making her Duchess of Anjou. You cunning minx, Yolande, you incredibly devious schemer."

She smiled. "If Jean breaks with the triple alliance and becomes the King's ally will that ease your path to the top?"

"You know it will, by God's sweet breath you know it will."

The Queen-Duchess wiped away the last of her tears.

"Then stand up, Monsieur Constable, it is not seemly that a man in your exalted position should kneel to me."

"I will, metaphorically speaking of course, be at your feet for the rest of my life."

"So I should hope," answered Yolande, and bent to kiss him as the last rays of the sun lit his scarred but exalted face.

Twenty-five

Beyond the walled suburb of the Doutre, lying across the river from the town of Angers, the Abbey of St. Nicholas lay drenched in the harsh white moonlight of high summer. From the distant fields, above which rose in gentle undulations the hills cradling the city, down to the lake lying below the Abbey's terraced gardens, all was bleached and light, glinting silver where the moon danced upon stretches of water.

It was late, being the hours between Compline and Matins, and a great silence had fallen over the Abbey, a silence which indicated everyone therein slept. Yet in the Abbot's lodging candles burned, for in his parlor, at the desk where those who had administered the Abbey had all sat before him, the Abbot Jacques still lingered, far away in thought.

To have been made Prelate of such a great and important house at the age of twenty-five, as he had, was nothing short of miraculous. And yet doors had opened for Jacques what would not have been considered possible by those beyond the Abbey walls, though amongst the people who knew him there had only been expressed surprise that those all-powerful bodies whose duty is to elect a new Abbot had indeed recognized the youthful monk's outstanding qualities. Yet to onlookers who made a study of faces it would not have seemed so strange.

True goodness and mysticism shone out of the man. From the light, clear blue eyes, as bright and fine as crystals, to the tranquil curve of his sensitive mouth, there was nothing about Jacques that could ever be remotely mistaken for malice or cruelty. The child who had started its days as a street urchin in Paris had grown into a being of exceptional quality.

Strangely, the facts of his early life had not gone against
him when the decision to elect him had been made. Rather,
it had been considered an advantage that he had once been
a creature of the people, knowing what it was to go barefoot and hungry, the victim of occasional beatings and regular fights. Furthermore, it had been remembered that, the
monk swore he had been called, that a vision had appeared
telling him to follow his vocation and enter the cloister. So,
two years earlier, in the summer of 1423, the unusual choice
had been made and Jacques had become the youngest
Abbot not only in Anjou but, undoubtedly, the whole of
France.

It was hot this night when he sat alone, staring into the
shadows, every nerve ending alert, so hot that sleep was
impossible for him. So it was with an almost impatient
movement that Jacques got abruptly to his feet, his black
habit sweeping the flagged floor, and made his way out into
the moonshine to breathe the night air.

The Abbey and its outbuildings were drowned in light,
the cloisters round the great quadrangle, pools of purple
shadow. Moving slowly but steadily, the Abbot's slender
outline threw a huge shadow as he made his way into the
Abbey church, then stopped for a moment to breathe in
the atmosphere of the place. Here, alone, in this half-hour
before midnight, the essence of the building rushed to meet
him; the smell of incense, imbued in the very fabric of the
stone, the altar candles throwing high their small brave
points of flame, the moonbeams casting through the window, lighting the dim interior with silvered shafts.

In the grip of sudden and intense emotion, Jacques left
the collective power of all the prayers that had gone before
him in this dim holy place and sank to his knees where he
was, down on the stone floor, not even bothering to go to
the Abbot's stall. Years ago he had heard a voice while
dusting the Lady Chapel, of all the extraordinary things,
and now the same feeling was upon him that had preceded
that other fateful occasion. Abbot Jacques, dedicated to the
service of God but still a young and vulnerable man for all
his great office, shivered as his spine grew cold and the hair
on his tonsured head seethed with apprehension.

"Lord, what do you want of me?" he asked, simply and
directly, the best way to speak to God in his view, and a
piece of advice he always passed on to the oblates.

The answer came into his head that he must approach the high altar and, like a pilgrim of old, the Abbot made the journey up the nave on his knees, the stone flags warm beneath his skin on this scented summer night. The spear-heads of light on the candles grew higher as he approached and Jacques suddenly felt the presence of something infinitely beyond his understanding. He closed his eyes and prayed for divine guidance.

When the experience was over he wept, so awed by the power of such enormous love and understanding. Yet as Jacques cried he knew that soon he must dry his tears and be strong, that she who was now on her way would need every ounce of the help he could give her. Asking God for His forgiveness even before he did it, Jacques communicated his thoughts to his twin brother, something the boys had practiced almost before they had learned to speak.

"Guy, La Pucelle has started her journey," thought the Abbot hard. "Like the wise men of old, try to find her star."

But there was no time to practice this strange telepathy further. In the distance came the sound of the brothers' tread as they made their way to church to celebrate Matins, the first office of the day. The Abbot rose to his feet to receive them, his fine face radiant, his eyes glowing with light, as the monks filed quietly in to begin the solemn act of worship.

The moment he awoke Guy knew that his brother had just called out to him, sending one of the extraordinary mental messages that by means of the rare bonding known only to identical twins, could pass between the two of them. Yet the content itself was none too clear, though the words "La Pucelle" rang on and on in Guy's mind.

"Jacques, what is it?" the astrologer thought urgently, and went to the window to look out across the river in the direction of St. Nicolas, giving his mental powers a focus as to where they were to go. Yet he was not surprised when there was no response. Judging by the position of the moon, Matins was being celebrated in the Abbey church and the Abbot would be concentrating on spiritual matters, not on a childhood trick. Being the practical person that he was, Guy decided to ride over to St. Nicolas in the daylight hours and try a more conventional means of communication. But meanwhile, on this most exciting of nights, there was much to do.

Throwing a loose robe over his night attire, the hunchback left his bedroom and climbed the spiral staircase to the top of the tower in the castle of Angers, given over by ancient tradition to the current court astrologer. Here, where he had studied long ago with Dr. Flavigny, Guy now had his own consulting room, littered with charts of the heavens and various magical artefacts, not the least of which was the astrologer's glittering crystal, tonight scintillating of its own volition as he approached.

"Be calm," Guy said to it, and knew a thrill of cold apprehension that there was so much alchemy abroad that inanimate objects were picking up the electrical vibrations.

The crystal was icy to his touch, even in the heat of this particular night, and Guy drew in a breath of pure surprise before he stared deeply into its shimmering heart. Then symbols came so quickly that he found himself unable to comprehend them all, even though well aware that he must understand as much as he could to recount to Jacques later.

Guy saw woods and a tree, a spring bubbling near by. Then he glimpsed fairies and children and one little girl in particular. The picture changed and he watched a young female—or could it be a boy?—riding with a band of warriors clad in white, a splayed red cross emblazoned on their surcoats.

"The Templars," breathed Guy in disbelief.

But there was not time for logical thought as the crystal grew dark in the astrologer's hands and, just for a second, the words "La Pucelle" actually appeared. Then the scrying glass started to fade.

"Wait," said the hunchback urgently, "before your power goes tell me one thing. Where is she? Where is La Pucelle?"

Just for a second before it went out like a snuffed candle, the crystal showed a picture of Yolande's second son, René, then it went black.

"René," said Guy thoughtfully. So La Pucelle, whoever she might be, was connected with René d'Anjou in some way. Did that mean she was coming from Lorraine? Or was it hinting at something altogether more subtle? The hunchback's brow creased in concentration as he tried to piece together the various parts of the puzzle.

In the end Guy gave up, knowing that he needed to talk it all out with his twin. Yet he had one devastating flash of clairvoyance before he returned, rather wearily, to his bedchamber. He suddenly knew that in some way René d'Anjou and the Knights Templar were linked.

"But that makes no sense," thought the puzzled astrologer as he blew out his candle. "For the Knights Templar are no more. They have ceased to exist, have been wiped off the face of the earth. They are dead, every one of them."

Yet the vision of that fierce young female riding with a great troop of white mantled men, the splayed red cross identifying them more clearly than anything else ever could, stayed with him until he fell asleep as the moon began to fade.

It was at daybreak that Prince René left the secret meeting of the Priory of Sion and headed for the border between his great-uncle's territory of Bar and his father-in-law's duchy, Lorraine. As always when he had been with the brotherhood, René felt exhausted, as much by the magnitude of the mystery they guarded as the fact that he was the youngest Grand Master, still being only sixteen years of age, that the Priory had ever known. And last night he had acted alone, the Regent Grand Master, his great-uncle the Cardinal, being indisposed and unable to be present.

Amongst all the other weighty matters under discussion there had been much talk of the situation in France and the fact that the Angloys-Françoys, as the alliance between the English and various traitorous French noblemen had come to be known, could yet endanger the Priory itself.

"If all France should fall into the Goddams' hands nothing will be safe," a brother had commented.

The Goddams was a soubriquet for the English soldiers who swore constantly throughout every battle and siege.

"Something must be done to assist the Dauphin," another brother had said.

"The King," René corrected quietly.

"The King, even be he not anointed. I fear if he goes down then so does what is left of the kingdom of France and so do we all."

There had been silence in the shadowy underground meeting place which the brotherhood of the Priory of Sion frequented, and René had looked round the cloaked anonymous figures, simultaneously glad and sorry that such an enormous legacy should have been left to him.

"Is it time perhaps," he said tentatively, "that our military wing was called into action?"

There was a frisson of disapproval and yet, the young Grand Master felt there were some in the room who were with him, perhaps descendants of those who in 1312, when the Order of the Poor Knights of Christ and the Temple of Solomon had been brutally dissolved, had shaved off their beards, put on ordinary clothing and assimilated themselves into the lay population.

"Grand Master," answered the speaker, "though we have vowed to serve you with our lives perhaps such a course might yet be a little extreme. Should we not wait until the Regent has returned to discuss the matter more fully?"

"Indeed we should," answered René, slightly irritated. "But if military action is out of the question there must be another way to help my brother-in-law and childhood friend. I would ask you all to give it your most serious consideration."

So, on this not altogether satisfactory note, the meeting had broken up and the Prince had turned his horse toward Lorraine and the homeward journey.

"There must be a way," he thought as he galloped at some speed, knowing that today was the feast of St. Mary Magdalen, a fast day until evening and one held particularly dear by the Prior of Sion. "But what?"

Born with no natural gift of clairvoyance, the many years of esoteric training which René had already undergone suddenly bore fruit. He was seized with a premonition of change, of things moving in the right direction at last. It also came to the Grand Master that he would be called upon to assist, and soon, on a very grand and positive scale. Heartened, the Prince galloped on, anxious to get to church and pray on this, one of the most important of saints' days in the church's calendar.

She had been fasting since yesterday, as that had been the Eve of the Feast of St. Mary Magdalen. And though there had been no real need for her to deprive herself of food for an extra day, truth to tell she enjoyed the effects of going without; the lightness of mind and body, the strange far-away feeling that set in after sufficient hours of total abstinence had passed, the momentary sensation that she might lose consciousness and fall to the ground.

It was in this state that the girl had come to Chesnu Woods to drink from the spring near the Fairies' Tree, the spring which, so local people claimed, had curative powers. For it seemed to her that this water, surely blessed and pure, might sustain her better, allow her to fast longer, than that from the well outside her father's house.

It was hot this midday and the walk, especially on an empty stomach, had seemed long and arduous. In fact it was good to feel the shade of the trees closing about her like the cool shadows of a cloister. Hearing the tinkling water of the spring gave her a new spurt of energy, though, and she ran forward and knelt down beside it.

Suddenly her legs ached and there was a pain in the girl's chest, while her heart began to thump in a rather erratic and frightening way. Without knowing quite why, she thrust her face into the spring and let the cold water spurt into her eyes.

When she opened them again she was looking directly into the sun, or would have been if something tall, something ringed with light, had not been in her way. She said nothing, too terrified to utter.

A voice boomed. Was it her own calling out in fear, she wondered.

"Jehanne? Are you Jehanne?"

The sound of the spring grew suddenly loud, horribly so, and the next thing she knew she was face down in the ice cold water again. A distant cry was up, "Jehanne, Jehanne, Jehanne."

When she looked once more she could see nothing, blinded by comets of light which shot before her eyes. Then there was darkness as she crashed into oblivion, her last conscious thought that whatever it was that had stood between her and the sun had just now gone away again.

The letter from Alison du May was straight to the point. "Grand Master, I greet you with reverence, and request that you see me immediately upon a matter of considerable interest and importance. I shall attend you in your ante-chamber at dusk. If you could ensure that my audience is a private one I would be greatful."

René was intrigued, his dark face full of questions, as he went at the appointed time to hear what his mother's for-

mer Lady had to say to him that was of such significance
it merited an immediate parley.

Alison was punctual, her bustling form, quite plump and
matronly now that she had given birth to five little bastards,
rustling in importantly. But her beauty was still undoubted,
the red hair as bright as ever, though whether cosmetically
helped René was not quite sure, the silver gray eyes clear,
the skin around them unlined.

Madame du May went on one knee before him and
kissed René's hand, as a supporter of the Order making
her obeisance to the Grand Master of the Priory of Sion
rather than a Prince of the house of Anjou.

"Greetings, Madame," he said, and raised her to her feet.

It had been she who had, years ago when he had first
arrived in Lorraine, taken him to that initial meeting with
his great-uncle Cardinal Louis of Bar, and ever since Alli-
son had been one of that shadowy group of people who
bore allegiance to the Priory of Sion without ever being
privy to its secrets and true designs.

"What is it you have to tell me?" René asked, his amber
eyes twinkling at the look of import on Madame du May's
rounded face.

She paused. "May I sit down, Monsieur?"

"But of course." He indicated a chair, finding it hard to
keep his mobile features under control. For the more serious Alison looked the more he longed to burst out laughing. "Now, my dear lady, how may I help you?"

"Grand Master, it is about my ward."

"Your ward?" René's quizzical black eyebrows shot up,
unaware that Alison even had such a thing.

"Yes. Some years ago I was given guardianship of a love
child, put out for fostering at birth with a family of honest
peasant stock."

"Oh, yes?" the Prince answered cautiously, instantly convinced that Alison was referring to some early mistake of
her own.

"So far the girl has caused no trouble, being brought up
as one of several children and truly believing her foster
parents to be those of her own blood. But now all that has
changed."

"She is in difficulty of some kind?"

Madame du May paused and neatly straightened out a
crease in her full skirt. "Not exactly, Monsieur."

"Then what?"

René would have liked to have asked her to get to the point, to inquire what interest this sixth little bastard of hers could possibly be to him, but for the sake of their long and excellent friendship he just continued to smile.

"Monsieur, she says she has seen a vision, or several to be precise. She says that she has been chosen to save France. That she is the virgin selected by heaven to come to the King's rescue."

"A virgin you say? Does she by any chance live near woods?" asked René, his saturnine face suddenly rapt and attentive.

Alison looked at him sharply. "Yes, she does. She comes from Domrémy, near Chesnu Woods. How did you know?"

René stroked his chin with long, thin fingers. "Because of an ancient prophecy. A woman called Marie d'Avignon long ago predicted the salvation of France by a virgin. Furthermore, according to certain things known privily to my order, Chesnu Woods has been named as the place from which the girl will come."

Alison narrowed her eyes. "Are you serious?"

"Yes, very. It has been so predicted. Now, tell me about her. How old is she?"

"Thirteen."

"Ah! So it could well be the onset of puberty causing her to see and hear these things."

"Quite possibly. She also fasts a great deal, for what reason I do not know."

"Umm. That too could lead to delusions," René answered matter-of-factly. He may well be Grand Master of a strange and mystic society, whose sworn purpose was deliberately shrouded in mystery, but he was at the same time very much a practical young man of the world.

"Indeed it could."

"Is she quite sane?"

"It would appear so. She is really a simple creature at heart. Poor little thing, I feel rather sorry for her."

"How did you get to hear about all this?"

"I visit her parents every few months, give them money for small luxuries for her, that sort of thing. She's told them nothing, by the way, but confessed her secret to a friend, who waylaid me as I left and whispered it in my ear. But

when I taxed the child about it she cried and begged me
to tell no one."

"Why?"

"She thought her voices might go away if they became
publicly known."

"Voices? I understood she saw things as well?"

"She does."

"What?"

"Various saints come to her." Alison's eyes twinkled.
"They speak to her in *ydioma Francie* apparently."

"That's as well," said René, and laughed his hilarious
laugh despite the solemnity of the topic.

"It's an hallucination, isn't it?" said Alison. "I mean
there have been so many of these prophetesses and holy
virgins. She's bound to have heard about them and now
thinks she is one."

"If it weren't for the odd coincidence of Chesnu Woods."
René pressed his fingers together. "Alison, I want to meet
her. Can you arrange it?"

"She's very nervous. She truly thinks this thing—
whatever it is—will stop if it becomes common knowledge."

"Tell her I can help her. That if it really is her mission
to save France she will need assistance."

"I'll try." Alison hesitated. "René you won't exploit her,
will you? She is so pathetically earnest."

"I'll take care of her. I shall treat her with the respect I
would give a sister."

His companion lost color so fast that the Prince wondered if she were going to faint. "What's the matter? Are
you quite well, Madame?" he asked anxiously.

"Yes, yes, of course." Alison fanned herself with her
hand. "Forgive me. It's the heat."

"You're certain?"

Madame du May nodded.

"Then I look forward to hearing news of the meeting
soon. What did you say the girl's name was?"

"She's known as Jehannette to her family and friends
but she's actually called Jehanne."

"Any other name?"

"Darc. Her father is the keeper of the Domrémy cattle
pound."

"Jehannette Darc," said René thoughtfully. "It doesn't
really sound like the saviour of France, does it?"

And with those fateful words the audience between them ended.

The new Constable of France, sworn into office in March 1425, had already made some sweeping changes at court. He had, as part of his inaugural oath, pledged to love, sustain and support those men who surrounded the King: Louvet, Tanneguy de Chastel, Guillaume d'Avagour, Pierre de Giac and his homosexual partner, Pierre Frotier. But three months later they had all been sent into exile with the exception of de Giac and de Chastel, though the last named was shortly to follow his friends. It had been an apparent disaster for Charles as Richemont took the law into his own hands, but after the news of the banishments had been made public he had smiled his glittering smile at Marie and said, "Good."

"You're not sorry?"

"A bit about Tanneguy, he was a friend. But Marie, ma chérie, the rest were all getting too sure of themselves. Why, Louvet practically owned me body and soul I owed him so much money."

"Well, now he's gone," answered the Queen practically, "and we can get The Mirror back."

"Yes," said Charles, and laughed.

"You," commented his wife, "are a cynical little beast," and she tickled his ribs, happier than ever after several years of marriage.

Yet it was all true. With the old wave of courtiers seen off by Richemont another way of life could start, and this one without the worry of owing Louvet a small fortune, the security for which had been Charles's great diamond, nicknamed The Mirror.

"I think you play one lot off against the other," said Marie thoughtfully.

"I have to survive," answered Charles, "and they were trying to swamp me. Anyway Robert le Maçon, who saved my life in Paris, can come back now his enemies are gone. And I am pleased about that."

"Is there anything else behind all this?"

"Possibly that your mother and the Duke of Brittany will soon be meeting with a view to making peace. And he never trusted Louvet, you know."

"Skulduggery indeed! But then of course the Duke and

Richemont are brothers and Richemont would do anything
for my mother." Marie paused. "Why hasn't de Giac been
sent away? Is it because of Bonne?"

"Yes."

"Do you still love her?"

"A little bit."

"Oh, well," Marie answered, sighing.

But it was she who ruled the roost and she knew it.
When Charles was at leisure amongst his courtiers, Marie
would sit on one side of the room, contentedly pregnant,
her baby son playing about her feet, his infant sister bounc-
ing on her mother's lap; meanwhile, on the other would be
Bonne, thin as wire, pale and lovely, obviously envious.
Everyone wondered at the Queen's ability to shine against
such fierce competition, yet shine she did.

The epitome of the contented married man, Charles
would exchange little glances and signals with his wife
throughout the entire evening. Everyone knew by now that
they invariably shared the same bed, and it was said that
Marie had found the one thing she was good at and that it
certainly kept the King at her side. The consensus of opinion was that these days Bonne de Giac was someone more
to be pitied than anything else.

"She's still very beautiful, you see," Charles put in now,
as if to justify himself.

"Beautiful and sad. Poor Bonne. Are you tired,
Monsieur?"

"Very. Hold me close and let me sleep."

"Of course," said Marie, and in the darkness smiled to
herself the sweet small smile of satisfaction.

René d'Anjou did not know quite what he had been expecting of Jehannette Darc but, whatever it might have
been, the first sight of her came as both a surprise and
shock. A tallish girl, about five feet two inches, which was
large compared to other females of her age, she did not
have the skinny body he would have associated with a creature who fasted so often. Rather, Jehannette was stocky,
almost powerful, with a full throat and muscular shoulders
and thighs. René's conscious idea that girls who saw visions
should have blonde hair, be pale and wan, was also firmly
dismissed. This odd little thing had hair black as a rook's
and dark penetrating eyes fringed by a set of thick lashes.

Yet despite her vivid coloring and tanned skin there was nothing really feminine about the child, her breasts as yet undeveloped, her manner boyish and brusque. His practical mind, so often at odds with his mystical training, briefly ran over the possibility that the girl might be one of those creatures whose sexuality remains somewhat dubious throughout the whole of their lives.

"Jehannette?" René said softly, and putting his hand beneath her elbow drew her gently to one side.

It had been arranged by Alison du May that he go to the glade in the Chesnu Woods on a certain appointed day and time and that Jehannette's friend, Blanche, would bring her to meet him there, unbeknownst to the family.

"She'll only come if she thinks you are going to help her," Alison had repeated. "You will be kind to her, won't you René?"

"I shall find out what she believes herself," he had answered, growing very slightly impatient with Madame du May's protective attitude toward the child, "and act accordingly. Does that satisfy you?"

But now he was here, staring the strange young girl directly in the eye, he could sympathize with Alison's mother-hen approach. There was something vulnerable and sad about Jehannette, there could be no doubt of it.

"Show me where the saints come to you," René added gently. "Is it by that spring over there?"

She flushed dark as damask then spoke for the first time. Despite her appearance her voice was feminine enough, low and quiet, but her accent was atrocious and the thought that her visions spoke to her in the local patois had a grin that would not be suppressed crossing René's features before he could stop it.

"You're laughing at me," she said angrily.

"No I'm not, I'm merely smiling," he countered.

The girl looked furious and just for a second, very strangely, in the set of her head, the wing of a brow, René saw a distant resemblance to his own mother, Yolande d'Anjou.

"Don't be angry," he said, "I have come to help you. If you are going to save France you really must trust me, you know."

The dark eyes became positively molten with suspicion. "My visions are not to be mocked. They *have* come to

me, they *did* tell me I must aid the Dauphin and get back
France."

"I don't dispute it for one second," René answered
smoothly. "I am merely questioning whether the voices told
you how?"

Jehannette looked vague. "I can't answer that exactly.
They only said to me that the King should have his kingdom again whether his enemies liked it or not."

René narrowed his gaze very slightly. There could be no
disputing the fact that the girl was sincere, blazingly honest
in fact.

"I hear you fast a lot," he said casually.

Jehannette looked defensive. "Yes, on saints' days."

"And other days as well?"

"Sometimes."

"Why do you do it? Does it help you see your visions
more clearly?"

"In a way." She glared again. "You don't believe me, do
you? You think I imagine things."

"But do *you* think you imagine things?" René answered,
soft as silk.

"I know that I don't. I know my visions are real and are
not demons sent to torment me. I know that my mission is
to save France because they told me so."

"Then that," the Prince replied firmly, "is all that really
matters."

"Is Jehanne mad?" asked Alison later that night as she and
René sat before the fire in her apartments, the Prince having come to report to her on the day's events.

"Not in the sense of being a danger to herself or others,
no. But she is not normal, whatever that might mean."

"I wouldn't have thought normal people ever see visions," Alison answered tartly.

"They don't," René countered. "Normal people don't do
anything a great deal. But Madame, there is no question
of lunacy to be answered here. I went to find out if the girl
is sincere or an attention seeking faker, and the answer is
that she is absolutely genuine. She believes visions come to
her. But whether they do or do not none of us, not even
she, will ever know for certain."

Alison accepted this in silence, unusually sombre, or so
René thought.

"So what are your plans for her?" she asked finally.

"I am going to get her trained."

"As what?"

"A soldier of course."

"A soldier!" Madame du May exclaimed in horror. "A thirteen-year-old girl!"

René had not been raised as Grand Master to no effect. He stood up and loomed over the seated woman.

"Madame, it has been prophesied that a virgin from Chesnu Woods will be the savior of France. Such a virgin has now appeared. Yet there is no conceivable way that this creature, strong though she be, could lead an army, ride a war horse or handle the weapons in common usage. If a miracle is to take place it must be orchestrated and planned."

"What do you mean?"

"Precisely what I say. Full of God's visions she may be but they won't prevent her from getting an aching arse when she rides a cavalry horse."

"René!"

"It's true, Alison. Come along with you." Then the Grand Master paused momentously. "So I am sending her to Scotland to join the only part of the military brotherhood which escaped persecution."

"Jehanne is to become a member of the Knights Templar?"

"Yes, a letter bearing my signature will go with the girl. She will leave early next year when she is fourteen and return to France only when she is fully prepared."

"But what of her parents? What of the girl herself?"

"Next week I shall receive her into l'Ordre de la Fidélité to give her more prestige." His tone became gentle. "Alison, a life as a warrior-nun, a soldier-mystic, will suit her. How can she live as other girls now that this thing, real or imaginary, has happened to her? Let her fulfill the destiny that has been decreed for her."

But Madame du May was still not happy, he could see it in her eyes.

"She's your child, isn't she?" said René, very directly.

"No, she's not, I swear it."

"But there's something unusual about her parentage and you know what it is."

Alison stood up, her plump form settling itself into rigid lines.

"*If* there is—and I'm not admitting it—you can be certain that I will have taken an oath never to reveal the truth, and by that oath I intend to stand until the day I die. All I *will* say is that Jehanne is special and should be treated with respect."

"If she is admitted into one of the most exalted orders in the world I can think of no greater honor."

"But . . ."

René visibly lost his patience. "Enough, Madame. I have made my decision as Grand Master and will brook no further interference. I order you now to make no move to stop Jehanne entering the order."

"I am not bound by your rules," she answered boldly.

"Indeed not. But the Priory of Sion is not without certain powers and influence. I advise you to leave well alone."

And with that he poured himself out of the room, all dark eyes and scowling features, every inch the son of Yolande d'Anjou.

Alison wrung her hands in a torment of indecision. It was her bounden duty to write to Jehanne's mother at once informing her of all the strange and mysterious things that were happening to her bastard daughter. Yet such facts written down would be highly dangerous. A compromise must be found. Eventually, after much heart-searching, Madame du May went to her desk and scratched a terse note to the Queen of Sicily and Duchess of Anjou.

"Madame la Reine: There is much that I would say to you on so many different subjects. I long to see you and talk as once we used. Could we perhaps meet at some point convenient to us both before the ways become too treacherous? I await your reply with much eagerness. Ever your loving servant, Alison du May."

"Oh, please, ma Reine, understand the urgency of this," she said as she put her seal in the wax. "I do not know what to do for the best. Oh, God help me—and also help poor hapless Jehanne to come to no mortal harm in this world."

Twenty-six

The ritual had been long, slow and terrifying, building up to a horrific climax which had both drained and elated the two principal enactors, Pierre de Giac and his handsome new henchman, Gilles de Rais, a young Breton nobleman who had arrived at court in the autumn of 1425, instantly taking the place of the recently banished Pierre Frotier.

The impact of Gilles on de Giac had left the older man gasping. Up to this time he had considered himself the master of all that was evil but now he bowed to a superior. There could be no doubt that de Rais, still only twenty-one when the two men had met, was by far the most wicked creature living. Pierre de Giac had fallen in love with him at once. And with this love had come revelation. Pierre, who had always used animal sacrifices as part of his satanic rituals, now allowed his young companion to persuade him otherwise.

"To please our Dark Master we should have infants to offer, must give him their soft sweet blood to drink. To turn base metal to gold, as I know how to do, the essential ingredients are the hearts, hands and eyes, and above all the blood, of young children. We must have them, Pierre."

"But how? Where do we find such creatures?"

"You can leave that to me."

"But we might be discovered."

"It is worth the risk. For only by human sacrifice does true power come. Why do you think you have risen so high and no higher?"

"I don't know."

"Because you are not pleasing him. Once Satan sees you

are prepared to bow to his demands you will be rewarded in full."

And it was true. No sooner had Gilles de Rais started to procure babies and young boys as terrified participants in the couple's vile practices than de Giac had gone from strength to strength. A woman who satisfied him had finally come into his life, the first since his relationship with the gross Queen Isabeau had ended, and then promotion at court had followed. Much to de Giac's amazement, Charles had made him First Chamberlain, though for what hidden motive Pierre could not tell.

And now, last night, the ultimate sweet rite. A boy and a baby had died while the men had performed unspeakable acts together.

"I wish Isabeau were here," de Giac groaned. "How she would have enjoyed joining in with us."

"Be that as it may, most women are sickening creatures," Gilles had responded. "Particularly that stupid wife of yours. It's high time you got rid of her. At least the widow Catherine is wealthy."

"And fat! Wonderfully, wonderfully fat."

"Yes, she is obscene looking enough, I grant you that. So why don't you marry her? Then her money is yours."

"And Bonne?"

"You'll think of something to do with her."

"Yes," answered de Giac thoughtfully. "I might at that."

The ritual took place at night and lasted until dawn. As soon as darkness fell, the novice was brought into the Chapter House and the doors locked and guarded against intruders. Then, in the dimness, the postulant knelt, waiting for the questioning to begin. This ceremony of initiation, like all others, followed the precise rules laid down for the Poor Knights of Christ and the Temple of Solomon when it was first founded as an Order early in the twelfth century, its origins mysterious and not easy to discover.

It was St. Bernard himself who had helped draw up this code of conduct adopted by the Knights Templar, as the Order later came to be known. The Templars were to cut their hair but not their beards, take a vow of chastity, poverty and obedience, while diet, dress and daily tasks were to be a strange combination of both monastic and military life. Rules for the battlefield were also carefully specified.

An endangered Templar was not allowed to beg for mercy but must fight on to the death. Further, only the Knights Templar were allowed to wear the white surcoats that so distinguished them in battle, the great splayed red cross, adopted by the Knights as an emblem in 1146, emblazoned on their chests.

By the time that the Templars were asked to accompany King Louis VII of France on the Second Crusade they were renowned throughout the world, enormously wealthy landowners, their ranks swelled to thousands, their bravery and arrogance spoken of in hushed tones. They had become a magnificent fighting force, fiercely disciplined, a force which members of every great family in Christendom hastened to join.

By the thirteenth century, the Knights Templar were seen as one of the most powerful groups of people in existence. They had become the primary money handlers of their time, the first bankers; they employed the finest military architects and engineers, the best stonemasons, the most skilled armorers, leather workers and artisans. The Templars had their own group of physicians and surgeons, used Arabic medicines, grew mold extracts with which to treat disease. Not only did they have fighting men, but fleets and ports. They employed Arab secretaries and many were fluent in the language, having learnt it in captivity. The Templars, too, had forged sympathetic links with the Jewish community, with whom they exchanged both financial interests and scholarly thought. They were a crack fighting force who had become internationally all-powerful.

It was obvious that no organization could exist on such a scale without exciting jealousy, greed and fear in the hearts of other rulers, and in 1306 the King of France, Philippe the Fair, finally moved against them. A list of charges was set out, the evidence supplied partly by the King's spies, partly by an ex-Knight who had turned against his Order. And on Friday, 13th October 1307, a dawn raid was made on every Templar holding in France, every knight found arrested, all their goods confiscated. Yet strangely, the fabulous treasure of the Templars was not discovered in this strike or any subsequent search.

Accusations were made, of homosexuality, of anal kisses at the time of initiation, of occultism and infanticide, of blasphemy, of appalling drunkenness. The Templars were

burned, imprisoned and tortured, and in 1312 the Order
was finally dissolved by the Pope, the Grand Master
Jacques de Molay being roasted to death over a slow fire
in March 1314, watching the execution, Philippe the Fair
himself. As the flames engulfed the Grand Master he called
on both the Pope who had decreed the Order finished, and
the King who had used it so cruelly, to join him within a
year at the throne of God to answer for their crimes. Both
had been dead within twelve months.

They had been a mighty and mysterious group, now vanished from the world stage, or so it would appear. Yet to
eliminate such a powerful body entirely was to prove difficult. In England, the Templars escaped terrible punishment
and were given sentences of light penance; in Lorraine, they
simply melted into the local population; in Germany and
Spain, they joined the Teutonic Knights and the Hospital-
lers of Saint John, while in Portugal, the Order was cleared
by public inquiry and merely changed its name to the
Knights of Christ. But in Scotland, at war with the English
at the time, the Papal Bulls dissolving the Order had never
been proclaimed and it was there that Templars from other
lands found refuge, a powerful contingent fighting on the
side of Robert the Bruce at the Battle of Bannockburn in
1314.

But there had been another aspect, another undercur-
rent, in all this. The secret society whose military arm the
Templars had at one time been, the elusive Order of Sion
who, after 1188, went its own way, becoming the Priory of
Sion and leaving the Templars autonomous until their grisly
end, had thrown their full power behind their fellow brotherhood when it was under threat. Behind the scenes, shadowy figures had worked to save both individuals and
property, and, by the time the drama was played out, what
remained of the Knights Templar had owed the Priory of
Sion an immense debt of honor.

And it was because of this debt that on an early autumn
night in 1425, a novitiate knelt in the Chapter House of
the Preceptory of the Templars hidden in the wilderness of
Argyllshire, a clandestine group the existence of which was
known to only very few, and waited to be received.

The candidate, when it first arrived, had come direct with
a letter from the Grand Master of the Priory of Sion himself, yet the Templars' Great Prior had shuddered at what

was being asked of him. A female visionary, a peasant girl who heard voices, who believed she had been chosen to lead the armies of France to victory and drive the English out, had been wished upon him, and he could think of nothing worse.

And yet the creature standing travel-stained in the Prior's Lodging had seemed humble enough, anxious to please, and so obviously sincere that it had been hard, especially in view of the signature on her letter of introduction, to turn her away immediately as he had originally planned.

"It is highly unsuitable that you be sent here," the Prior had said by way of compromise. "This is a man's establishment and we are an Order of fighting monks. For a woman to be amongst us is unthinkable."

"But surely you have all taken the vow of chastity, as will I," she countered. "Therefore I can cause no trouble on that account. Please let me stay. Where else can I be secretly trained to fight?"

"But why should you want to be?" he had asked wearily.

"Because my voices have told me to save France."

"That may be so but you still cannot remain here," the Great Prior had answered forcefully.

It had been early spring when she had arrived, cold and miserably wet, and the Prior had fully intended to send her back as soon as the weather got a little warmer. But somehow in the intervening months, and none of the brotherhood could say quite how it had been done, the girl had made herself useful to him.

Dressed even more like a boy than when she had first appeared, her hair cut short all the way round and acting just as a young male would, she saw to the horses, whistled about the place, cheerful, smiling, and utterly flat-chested. Then one day the girl had mounted one of the great destriers, direct descendants of the French cavalry steeds, and fallen straight off again with a certain amount of cursing.

"Come on, lass," one of the more sympathetic Knights had said, and bleeding though she was, Jehanne—or Johnnie as the Scotsmen had nicknamed her—had remounted.

She had not looked back after that. Whether her saints genuinely inspired her or whether they existed solely in her adolescent mind, as most of the Templars believed, the girl had shown herself an adept and natural horsewoman.

Johnnie's struggle to handle a knight's weapons had at

first been hilarious, uproarious almost, in an Order supposed to maintain a certain amount of silence and decorum. It took her four weeks even to pull the two-handed sword used by the Templars out of its scabbard, each time falling flat on her back, legs in the air. Equally, the great lance had proven too much for her.

"You must build your muscles up," Prior Hugh had bellowed at her. "Eat, run and swim. The weather's getting fine. Outdoors with you."

Even without conceding the fact to himself he knew that she had wormed her way in, that there was something about the girl that made men, monks included, eat out of her hand. Yet sexual power she most certainly did not have; more a friendliness, an openness, an ingenuousness that was utterly irresistible.

"I like her," the Prior had caught himself thinking, and with it had come the hope that the brothers of the Order would not reject her when the time came.

And now that ceremony was at hand. French Jehanne, Johnnie to everyone present, knelt upon the floor of the Chapter House while the Great Prior boomed out his ringing question.

"Brother Knights, do you have objection to this novitiate entering our Order?"

It couldn't have happened had the Knights Templar been as once they were, the most powerful organization alive. But now a group of outcast warrior-monks admitted a young woman, whom most of them suspected of being utterly deluded yet a fascinating character for all that, into their prestigious ranks.

"I swear that I have no marriage partner nor children of my body," said Jehanne, taking the oath. "I swear that I have neither debts nor disease. I vow obedience, poverty and chastity. I vow to protect the secrecy of this Preceptory and its whereabouts with my life, even if I be threatened by torture and death. I ask to become a servant and slave of the Temple. I swear obedience to Almighty God and the Virgin Mary. I pledge my life to France."

It was done. Great Prior Hugh himself draped the famous white mantle round her shoulders. She had entered the exalted ranks of the Knights Templar and now her training proper could begin.

*   *   *

She had known with the unerring instinct of a mistress whose lover has long ago tired of her that only a desperate measure could bring him back to her side, and now Bonne de Giac took the only remedy possible. Instead of shying away from what she had always considered too dangerous a course of action, namely to become pregnant when no longer being ravaged by her husband, she took the chance. Deliberately going to Charles when the time of the month was perfect for conception, Bonne had seduced him into being careless and two moon months later she knew her plan had succeeded. After all their years together as lovers, she at last carried the King's baby.

Standing naked before the mirror, seeing herself as slim as ever, Bonne turned to face him, her black hair whirling out as she moved her head.

"God be praised I am finally with child. Oh, mon chéri, isn't it wonderful?" and she had flung herself into his arms, giving little cries of joy.

It was very difficult for Charles to feel quite as enthusiastic. Since his marriage four years earlier to Marie, who adored being pregnant and surrounded by babies and small noisy children, he had become something of an old hand at fatherhood. In the time since the Queen had become his bride, three infants had been born altogether and now she expected another.

"Why, that's wonderful news," said Charles, with as much feeling as he could muster at the thought of yet another of his seed bearing fruit. "When is the child due?"

"I know little of these things," answered Bonne, fluttering. "But I believe it will be born in March."

"Splendid," answered the young father, thinking to himself that Marie was hoping to produce in February and the times were too close together for comfort. "Quite splendid."

As he said this, Charles caught sight of himself in the mirror and thought that these days he really was looking a regular jackanapes, the sort who spends most of his time in pleasurable pursuits or lying in bed with women begetting babies. As beautifully dressed as ever, his colors of vermilion, blue and gold all about him, he now appeared too worldly for his age, his lifestyle of scheming against his courtiers beginning to show in a certain cunning expression, his overfull love-life giving him a lecherous air.

"I wish they would let me go into battle again," he sighed to himself.

Bonne, thinking he was addressing her, answered. "They all say it's too dangerous. That if you were killed and a child became King that would truly be the end of everything."

"But it's so boring sitting at home, idling my days away, while Richemont rides out with the army."

"Are you bored with me?" she asked petulantly.

"No, of course not. You're beautiful. And I'm pleased about the baby. It is bound to take after you and look quite ravishing."

"What shall I tell Pierre?" Bonne was suddenly serious as she started to dress herself.

"I don't know. Perhaps you should go to bed with him."

She pulled a face. "I couldn't possibly. Anyway he doesn't want me. He's sleeping with that nasty young man Gilles, and has his eye on a fat rich widow into the bargain."

"I'd better promote him again," answered Charles languidly. "That should keep him quiet for a while. Then tell him the child is mine and I will advance him even higher if he acts like a gentleman. He should feel honored the King of France has sired his wife's bastard and there's an end to it."

"Precisely."

But in actuality, Bonne was not as confident as she pretended and said nothing to her husband about the babe she carried, fearing some awful explosion of fury, for all the fact his time was now fully taken up with Gilles de Rais and Catherine de l'Isle-Bouchard, Countess de Tonnerre.

August came and went and eventually the long, slow autumn so famous in the Loire Valley began to show its first fiery fingers. The cultivated fields, where the war had not penetrated, were thickly gold with unharvested corn, from the orchards came the smell of ripening plums and apples. At night, the river shimmered and danced with lights, by noon it hazed over with lingering heat. There were poppy skies in the evening and wild rose at morn, by day the heavens a rich deep blue slowly darkening to wine. A laziness, an air of *fin de siècle* hung over the slumberous countryside, and inside Bonne the child continued to grow.

She knew the precise moment when he guessed. They

had been dining together at home, a thankful rarity these days, and his wife saw de Giac's eyes, their usual frantic shade of burning blue, suddenly alight on her rounding abdomen. An hour later, after consuming great quantities of wine, he confirmed her worst suspicions.

"So here's an interesting situation. Are you putting on weight, ma chérie, or is that a little love child I spy?"

She stood up and tilted her chin defiantly, "I carry the King's child, Monsieur. He has asked me to say that he has amply rewarded you by making you First Chamberlain ..."

"So that was why," de Giac breathed to himself.

"... and that that was only the beginning. If you are good to me and my baby he will promote you higher and higher."

"I see."

De Giac buried his face in his wine cup then, having drained it completely, wiped his mouth with the back of his hand. When he looked at her again, Bonne saw to her horror that his features had completely changed. The demon which lurked just below the surface of his every expression had utterly consumed him. She saw the glint of savagery, the stark white bones of murderous intent.

"Oh, Christ have mercy," she screamed. "Pierre, don't hurt me."

"Hurt you?" he answered, and threw his head back to laugh a laugh that froze her blood. "I'm going to kill you, you faithless whore."

She started to run, but too late. De Giac had already pounced on her and woven the strands of her beautiful hair around his hands.

"A little drink for you and your bastard," he murmured close to her ear, and without looking she knew that he had drawn out one of the many phials he always carried upon him and was emptying something into the cup before he filled it once more with wine.

"Drink!" he said in a terrifying whisper, and forcibly jerking her head back began to pour the fluid into her mouth.

Bonne, trapped as she was, did her best to fight, kicking and punching at him with as much strength as she could summon up. And though she tried to stop herself swallowing, tried to spit out the deadly potion he had mixed for her, at that angle with her head tipped back and held fast, every hair of her head wrenched to the roots, it was impossible to avoid ingesting some of its bitterness.

And all the time he held her in that deadly grip, de Giac repeated the words, "Harlot, whore, slut," as if they were some kind of terrible invocation.

At last the cup was empty and he let her go, watching her as she stood swaying, an expression so evil on his face that Bonne had to close her eyes in order to avoid seeing it.

"So, you're stronger than you look," he said. "What a wonderful breeder you would make, giving birth to bastard after bastard. But what would they say of me, eh? That I wore the cuckold's horns while you sported with your ugly boy. No, never, never!"

He was screaming now and so dangerous his skin had bleached with fury.

"No, that day will never come. You filthy slut, you whore. You'll disgrace me no further."

He yanked once more at her vulnerable hair so that it came out in handfuls as he crashed Bonne to the ground, then dragged her across the stone floor through the scented rushes, out of the dining chamber and across the great hall.

She felt the cold air of night as one of the doors at the back of the château was opened and then the warmth of hay, the comforting smell of horseflesh. So he was throwing her out to sleep with the animals. Bonne could think of far worse fates.

But this pathetic hope was shattered as she was tossed in the air like a broken doll, then plunged beneath de Giac's fastest stallion face downward, her arms wrenched behind her back and pulled round the horse's neck, where they were bound, her feet coming up into the same position, and tied together hard across the horse's rump. She thought she was going to die of pain as every disc in her spine jarred simultaneously. Exposed and tragic, her small round belly hung down, the nearest thing to the ground.

"It's full moon and you're going riding," said de Giac and once again he laughed a wild hyena's laugh, a sound Bonne would not have thought could possibly be human.

They clattered out of the stableyard and the Devil's man immediately applied his spurs so that the capricious beast shot straight into full gallop, the terrified woman beneath it groaning in agony as they headed for the densely forested lands that lay some miles beyond de Giac's château.

Poor little Bonne lost her child about half an hour later, and an hour after that her own small life. She gave it up willingly, knowing there was no one left to love her and nothing left to live for.

With a cold smile on his lips and his maddened eyes glowing in the shadows, de Giac buried his ill-fated wife by moonlight on the edge of a deserted field. Then he desecrated her grave, leaving it unmarked, before he finally turned for home with a song on his lips and a sudden tremendous feeling of being at one, not only with his Dark Master, but also the Devil's most beautiful acolyte, Gilles de Rais.

Twenty-seven

As the winter of 1426 approached and the war, of necessity, came toward its annual close, Georges de la Trémoille left the court of Philippe le Bon, Duke of Burgundy, without having made any progress in his ambassadorial negotiations. With a heavy heart and feelings of frustration caused by the Duke's deliberate obstinacy, the fat man had gladly started the long trek homeward, depressed only that his mission had failed.

A lover of the Queen and a servant of Jean the Fearless, Duke Philippe's father, George's twinkling house-mouse eyes had a way of making him a friend to everyone, particularly when the friendship was to his own advantage. He had fought to Azincourt, been captured and taken to London, but had quickly paid off his ransom and returned to France, shortly afterward marrying Jeanne, the wealthy widow of the Duke of Berri, this at roughly the same time as de Giac's marriage to Bonne.

The convenient death of his wife had been the best stroke of good fortune Georges had ever had. The great riches of the old Duke had by court ruling become his and de la Trémoille's star had gone firmly into the ascendant. During these years of political progress he had also managed to acquire two very valuable allies: the Constable of France, the Earl of Richmond, and the woman whom Georges suspected of meaning more to Arthur than either would admit, the young King's mother-in-law, Yolande d'Anjou. Seeing his potential as a mediator between Charles and Burgundy, the Queen-Duchess and the Constable had appointed Georges their ambassador and sent him without delay on a deputation, the aim of which to woo Philippe back to their side, away from the English.

Such a move was desperately needed. Richemont's brother, Jean of Brittany, had briefly changed allegiance in order to marry his daughter to Yolande's son, Duke Louis, and then, early in 1426, having been defeated by the Duke of Bedford at the Battle of St. Jacques, defected once again and rejoined the triple alliance. The effect of this on Richemont had been disastrous and his brother's betrayal, coupled with the fact that the Constable had been in command at the losing battle, had turned the tide of opinion against the Earl. It was only the combined strength of him and Yolande that was keeping him in his high position as his fat friend Georges had left on this most delicate of missions.

The journey back had not been without incident. After a few miles, de la Trémoille had fallen into the hands of the English and had been forced to part with every bit of his money and all the valuables on his person, only the Duke of Burgundy's signed safe conduct getting him out alive. So it had been with great relief that he had seen the distant towers of the castle at Bourges and crossed the river Yèvre with his party of riders to approach it.

In an odd way, when he recalled events later on, Georges thought he could remember noticing that the King's guards looked different, but at the time he paid no heed, only too gratified to be back and able to shortly go in and warm himself by the fire in the great hall. Handing his horse to an ostler, de la Trémoille hurried inside.

The scene within was one that he never forgot. The great hall was full of the most terrible-looking people; rough oafish men ogled women who had plainly been brought in off the streets, thick with face paint and stinking of unwashed parts, while de Giac's collection of freaks cheered on one of their number who was actually copulating publicly. There seemed nobody there he recognized, but as Georges pushed through the crowd he found to his horror the Admiral de Culant, a friend, lying on the ground being viciously kicked by the Lord de Lignières, one of de Giac's creatures.

"Stop, stop!" de Culant was shrieking as de Lignières's foot went into his stomach over and over again.

He had just had a long and hazardous ride and was also seriously overweight, but Georges did not hesitate. Flying like a cannonball he threw himself at the unsuspecting Lord who toppled beneath the enormous bulk tackling him from

the rear. There was a splintering crunch as the two men
went down together, landing on top of the Admiral who
promptly lost consciousness. The dwarves and freaks, losing
interest at once in their rutting companion, dashed to watch
this latest diversion and screamed shrill encouragement at
de la Trémoille.

"Come on fatty, hit him!"

"Slap him one, big man."

Georges obeyed, ploughing in for all he was worth, until
de Lignières lay in a pool of blood, teeth everywhere but
in his mouth, snarling vengeance with what was left of his
voice.

Dragging his friend to his feet, de la Trémoille exclaimed,
"What the hell is going on here? The place is like a thieves'
bloody kitchen."

But de Culant was too faint to answer and it was only
when he had manhandled him into an antechamber and
sent for wine and water that Georges finally got any sense
from his bruised and battered companion.

"It's de Giac," the Admiral gasped. "He's taken over.
The King is under house arrest, constantly guarded by a
hundred swordsmen. Nobody can get in or out."

"Christ's poor wounds," exclaimed the fat man, deeply
shocked. "How did all this come about?"

"It was while you were away. De Giac took it into his
head to murder his wife—"

"You mean Bonne is dead?"

"Yes, I fear so. Anyway, Charles found out and went
crazy, like a maddened animal. He was just going to have
de Giac put under arrest when there was a coup. Pierre's
troops rounded on the King's and outnumbered them. Robert le Maçon was hauled off as a hostage and not released
until Charles had paid a thousand golden *écus* as ransom.
It is anarchy, Georges, sheer anarchy. De Giac runs this
place like a bandit chief. He'll have you done to death for
saving me. You'd best get out while the going's good."

"Where are the King and Queen?"

"Kept in their apartments. Charles spends most of his
time reading and she occupies herself with the children.
They can't get a letter out. Everything is read and
destroyed."

"Is de Giac totally insane?"

"Oh, yes, he's gone right over the edge. I pity his poor wife."

"You mean he's married again?"

"Yes, the widowed Lady de l'Isle-Bouchard. She was fat when he first wed her but she's hardly eaten since, and is now down to skin and bone."

Even in adversity George's piquant humor flashed. "If that's what he can do perhaps I should marry him as well."

"Don't joke about it," answered the Admiral, mopping his wounds. "De Giac is a pervert. His latest friend is Gilles de Rais, the most evil creature one ever set eyes on."

"Then help must be summoned."

"Yes, it must—and urgently. Go to the stables and take my horse. It's fresh and ready. Strong too," the Admiral added, and chuckled in spite of everything.

"Where's Richemont at the moment?"

"In Angers, helping Yolande defend Anjou. Part of Maine has fallen to the English and she's striving night and day to hold them there. Her great fear is invasion."

"He's not been a very successful Constable so far, has he?" de la Trémoille commented reflectively.

"The great blow was his brother changing sides again. If that hadn't happened I think the Earl might have been able to bring things round."

Georges nodded, taking this in, and would have answered had not a sudden noise in the corridor outside had him springing, light as a cat for such a sizeable fellow, to the far door.

"Will you be all right, my friend? I hate to leave you in such a plight," he whispered from the entrance.

"I think so. But bring help soon for God's sake. Poor Charles, who would have thought this could happen to a King."

"Poor Charles, poor Bonne," answered Georges starkly. "How did she die?"

"The rumor is he tied her to the underside of his horse with her belly dragging along the ground. You see, she was pregnant."

"He's inhuman, vile," de la Trémoille hissed violently. "He should be put down like a mad dog."

"Pray God that happens soon."

"I think it most likely will," the fat man replied with much feeling as he hurried from the room.

*   *   *

Yolande and Richemont had spent a hard summer, fighting
off the English at every turn. John of Bedford, continuing
the policy of his dead brother, was pressing southward,
threatening the Loire and all the lands lying beyond the
mighty river. His entry into Maine, a part of Anjou's many
territorial holdings and the Countdom of Yolande's third
son, Charles, seemed a terrible portent of what might lie
ahead and the Duchess had spared no effort to guard Anjou's borders fiercely. Only now, with the winter of 1426
putting an end to the fighting, could she and her lover afford to relax their vigilance.

There was a further worry to add to the others that beset
the Queen-Duchess at this time. In the autumn of the previous year she had received a strangely worded letter from
Alison du May, and had guessed that it in some way concerned Jehanne. But the meeting that Alison had so earnestly sought had been impossible to arrange in view of the
English advance and the question as to what could be the
matter with her bastard daughter had nagged at the back
of Yolande's mind throughout the entire twelve months.
But short of asking Madame du May to state the trouble
in writing there was little the Duchess could do except wait
until some time in the future when it would be safe to leave
her beleaguered territories.

All in all it had not been a good year for any of them
and it was with much joy that Yolande and Richemont saw
the beginning of December finally arrive, knowing that with
the weather now worsening and the daylight hours growing
short, the war must, perforce, come to a halt till the spring.

"Shall we go to Provence?" Richemont asked, but Yolande shook her head.

"I trust the situation too little to journey so far. I think
we should stay here, or rather I should. When will you
rejoin Marguerite?"

"Just before the Twelve Days. The rest of the time I
shall remain with you, if you will permit me?"

It was all said with ritual politeness but the words hid a
love that still ran savage and raw below the surface. Small
wonder that Yolande's coquettish, "Yes, if you please,
Monsieur," led to a rough kiss from Richemont which, in
turn, led to more which, in their turn, led to Yolande's
bedchamber.

It was in this way that the couple were lying in a calm deep sleep, their first for months without an ear constantly alert for the sound of battle, their lovemaking done, when George de la Trémoille arrived at the castle of Angers in a sweating panic. Shown to the Guests' Lodging and then, some time later, to the Queen-Duchess's antechamber, where Yolande received him graciously, all Georges's suspicions were confirmed when Richemont strolled nonchalantly in some ten minutes later, his scarred face rested, his eyes bright and cheerful, his expression, however, changing abruptly when he saw Georges's obviously distressed condition.

"God's life, what is it, man? You look in dire straits."

"I am, I am," breathed de la Trémoille, gulping down the wine that had been provided for him. "I come from Bourges with grievous news."

"Bourges?" repeated Yolande, rising from her chair. "Why, what's happened?"

"To put it bluntly, Madame, there has been a coup at Court. Pierre de Giac rules by mob law, his swordsmen hold the King and Queen at bay. Ordinary life is paralyzed, letters can neither get in nor out. The entire situation is highly dangerous and volatile."

"De Giac!" growled Richemont. "At the root of every trouble, always de Giac."

And he and Yolande flashed each other a momentary glance which the observant Georges did not miss.

"What's to be done?" said the Queen, looking from one to the other of them in consternation.

"Well, we've got to put a stop to it, that's obvious," Richemont answered without hesitation. "But when?"

"What do you mean?"

"The winter is sealing all of us in, Yolande ..."

De la Trémoille couldn't help but notice the easy use of the Queen-Duchess's Christian name.

"... and we mustn't forget it. If we're to make a move against de Giac we are obliged to wait till next year."

"But what of Charles and Marie? Are they in danger. Monsieur?"

She had turned to Georges who was able to reassure her.

"Certainly not. They are under de Giac's command, that is all. It is not in his interest to harm them." There was a pause and then he added, "Did you know that Madame de

Giac is dead, ma Reine? That it is whispered her husband murdered her?"

"Bonne dead?" Yolande said in horror. "But she was such a close friend to my son-in-law."

"And that's an understatement," thought de la Trémoille irreverently.

Out loud he answered, "Alas she's no one's friend any more. Apparently de Giac slung her belly downward beneath his horse and rode it till she died. She was expecting a child it seems."

"A child!" said Yolande, sitting down again. "Oh, I see."

And she did, everything falling neatly into place. Richemont, too, it appeared, also reached some sort of conclusion about this because he cursed de Giac as only a soldier could.

"Christ's mercy! I'll cut his coillons from his body with my own hand." He turned to look at Yolande, his scarred face wild and livid. "I pray you, Madame, pass the death sentence on him, because it is now high time it was issued. De Giac has sinned long enough in this world. Let him go to the Devil, whom he loves so well, and take his chance in Hell."

"I pronounce it without hesitation," the Duchess answered at once. "Monsieur Constable, Monsieur de la Trémoille, I charge you both with encompassing the death of Pierre de Giac as soon as possible. Give him no quarter or mercy. He showed none to Bonne whose only sin was one that every woman knows."

"Amen, amen," cried Richemont in an ecstasy of revenge. "It shall be done as you desire."

He could not have known that there was now a price on his head and yet, for mysterious reasons of his own, at the end of January 1427, Pierre de Giac ordered that the whole court move from Bourges to the castle of Issoudun, on the river Théols. Here he fortified himself in, making sure that the town gates were locked securely every night at dusk and ordering that no one be allowed admittance without his prior authority. And yet there was one person, other than the captive King, who could overrule that order and it was the one person, because of his involvement in the war, that de Giac had not reckoned with.

So it was a shock when on the evening of 2nd February,

late and in the darkness, the Constable of France himself came to the gates with a small group of men, including the Lord d'Albret, Bonne's brother Roger de Naillac, and Georges de la Trémoille.

"Open up at once," the Earl shouted into the gloom and a second or two later repeated the command as the porter's white and officious face appeared at the wicket.

"You must wait there. I can let no one in without the express orders of Monsieur de Giac himself."

"You'll hang in the morning and on *my* orders," Richemont called back. "Do you not recognize the Constable of France?"

And there was a flurry of movement as the Constable's personal standard was thrust forward and the great chain of office revealed from under Richemont's cloak.

"But—"

"If these gates are not open in the next thirty seconds I'll batter them down and your head with them. Now move, you imbecile son of a whore."

Keys were clanked and the gates flew back so fast that Richemont wondered grimly if the man were trying to set some sort of record. The Constable turned to his group.

"Right, tie him up and relieve him of his duties till morning. The rest of you come with me."

"Where are you going?" whispered Georges.

"To the nearest tavern and then to church. I need to rest and pray before doing what I must."

It was extraordinary to de la Trémoille to watch the scar-faced warrior, once having secured a room in the tavern, settle himself down for a few hours' sleep, the town keys firmly attached to his belt, slumbering calmly through the noise of the roisterers below stairs. Eventually, though, Richemont rose and went straight to the Chapel where he knelt in prayer until d'Albret called that it was after midnight and the Earl, having hastily crossed himself, got to his feet.

Their shoes muffled by cloths, their weapons held in front of them to avoid jangling, the hand-picked group of men went through the town to the castle and there obtained entrance by a little-used door leading into one of the towers. Creeping up the spiral staircase and along the many galleries the silent band of grim-faced conspirators came to the main living quarters and made their way unhesitatingly to the apartments occupied by de Giac, easily identifiable by the strong smell of erotic incense coming from beyond the door.

"Get up at once," bellowed Georges, hammering on the door with his fist. "Get up, Monsieur. Your hour is at hand."

He said this last with great drama, relishing each word, and was rewarded by an oath, a shooting back of the bolts, and the sight of de Giac, stark naked, standing in the doorway. Beyond him, lying on the bed in the same state, could be seen the new Madame de Giac, her figure really very beautiful since her loss of appetite. Every head turned, every jaw sagged, and she snatched the sheets to her chin protectively as ten pairs of eyes looked in her direction simultaneously.

"Mon Dieu!" said Georges softly, while d'Albret, quite involuntarily, gave a low appreciative whistle. Only Richemont remained unmoved, staring at de Giac with a merciless glare.

"I arrest you," he said bluntly.

"On whose authority?"

"My own. Seize him."

The three largest men in the group started forward but Bonne's brother beat them all to it. Rushing up to the Devil's man he heaved his knee straight into de Giac's privy parts and as the man doubled in agony, sliced his hand down onto the back of his neck, then jumped on his erstwhile brother-in-law and began to choke the life from him.

"No," snapped Richemont, "de Naillac, no. He must be tried."

"He has been tried before Heaven."

"I know, I know. But let justice be seen to be done. I want no stain attached to this execution."

They dragged the Satanist from the room, an old cloak covering his blatant nudity, and it was only the fact that one of Richemont's soldiers decided to help himself to de Giac's silver on the way out that caused Madame de Giac, who up till then had remained remarkably calm, to open her mouth in protest. Losing her husband was one thing but being robbed of her valuables was obviously another.

Leaping out of bed, not caring who saw what, she gave

chase to the errant swordsman, shouting, "Stop thief, those were *mine* not his! Return them immediately."

The ancient castle woke in uproar, people hurrying from their rooms to see what was going on, Charles, wearing only a nightshift, coming blearily from his.

"What the Devil!" he exclaimed as Catherine de Giac, stark naked, hurtled past him in pursuit of a struggling figure blanketed by a cloak.

"De Giac's been arrested."

An extraordinary combination of expressions crossed Charles's features.

"On whose authority?" he said, an echo of the victim's earlier words.

"The Lord Constable's."

"It should have been mine," responded the King bitterly. "By God it should have been mine."

Then without another word he marched back into his chamber, banged the door closed, and could be heard shouting and cursing within.

"What on earth is the matter with him?" a shocked de la Trémoille asked Robert le Maçon, still haggard from his recent captivity at the hands of de Giac but doggedly serving his royal master as best he could.

Le Maçon lowered his voice. "These days the King is a confused creature in many ways. Remember his early years and it is not difficult to see why. Sometimes the sheer frustration of his position gets too much for him. Charles has spent weeks, months, plotting his revenge on de Giac. Hidden away in his library he has secretly been formulating plans. And now in walks Richemont, cold as ice, and snatches the villain from under his nose."

"But surely he's grateful?"

"He's grateful all right. It's just that he is sick to his very gut that he didn't have the power to throw de Giac out himself. Do you see?"

"Yes I think so."

"He's twenty-four years old, Georges. He is a married man with children, yet everyone treats him as if he's a babe-in-arms. He is getting into a dangerously stubborn state."

"What can we do?"

"Only hope he gets out of it."

But behind the closed doors of his apartments, Charles

de Valois wept the bitter tears of one who knows stalemate, all the relief that his ordeal at the hands of de Giac was over tempered by his own powerlessness. The agony of Pisces was upon him. A creature with so much to give the world was being netted by a hostile environment. With a feeling of despair, Charles began to swim down to the dark depths below the ocean, regardless of the fact that in the deeps there is no air for a human being to breathe.

They took de Giac out of the city and gave him a summary trial, the verdict of which was a forgone conclusion. Throughout, he scorned the services of a Christian priest but on the eve of execution panicked and asked Richemont to come to him.

"Well?" said the hardened campaigner, remembering how once he had left the castle of Angers at dawn, a boy on his way to war, his heart broken by de Giac's deceit.

"Am I to die in the morning?"

"Yes."

"Then I must keep my pact with Satan or he will be coming for my soul."

"He can have it and welcome."

"Richemont, for the love of God, I don't want to rot in Hell. I promised the Devil my right hand. If he has that then I have kept the bargain and may confess my sins and go shriven to my death. If you have any mercy left, cut off my hand and send me a priest."

"You craven coward," said Richemont contemptuously. "Your entire life has been devoted to demonic arts and now at the end you quail. To Hell with you. I'll not help you."

"Please," said de Giac, clasping his fingers together in supplication. "If I give him what I promised I can keep my soul."

"Why not?" said de la Trémoille, suddenly appearing in the doorway of the cell.

"Because he deserves all he gets."

"Well, I for one owe him this last favor," answered Georges mysteriously, and with that wrenched Pierre's fingers out of the praying position, spread his right arm full length along the floor and hacked the hand off at the wrist with his sword. Blood poured everywhere at the severing of the artery and Richemont turned away in anger.

"Why did you do that?"

"Because tomorrow, when he is dead, his widow, the beautiful Catherine, gives herself—and her jewels by the way—to me. It was the least I could do."

Despite his fury, a grin started to creep over the Earl's features. "God be praised, you don't miss a trick, do you? When did all this intrigue start?"

"From the moment she ran naked into my arms. It was I who gallantly hid her from the eyes of the world whilst taking a good look myself!"

"You never cease to amaze me. Come on, I don't want to watch this creature bleed to death."

But de Giac was still alive in the morning when the town executioners, masked and hooded in black, sewed him into a weighted sack which was thrown unceremoniously into the river Auron.

"The air is suddenly cleaner, isn't it?" said Georges, breathing deeply.

"I hope so," answered Richemont cynically, watching how the last ripple spread out before it finally vanished. "But in my experience there's always another one like de Giac coming up behind."

"How true!" answered de la Trémoille, with twinkling eyes. "My dear friend, how very true."

PART THREE

JEHANNE

Twenty-eight

Autumn began in a blaze of glory: trees like flame, the crisp harsh crack of leaves beneath the feet, skies clear, angel blue, rivers flowing with a cold deep urgent sound. Then came change: frosts by night, the ground white and stiff with rime, skies dark as seal pelts, ominously heavy, rivers starting to freeze in still, silent, currentless pools.

Those who studied weather blew their fingers and pulled up collars, birds sought berries and wild things laid in stores. And yet the snow did not come, instead a constant cruel frost until December when flakes finally fell out of the sky in a blinding mass that brought everything to a standstill. With the claws of winter sunk so deep into the land, the war, which could not be described as raging but rather dragging on interminably, obediently halted at one ferocious stroke from nature.

The town of Vaucouleurs, much like any other small walled city built beside a river, lay deep beneath the drifts, slumbering and silent until, cautiously but determinedly, out came the diggers. Rosy cheeked, hoods pulled down, eyes glistening in the cold, they cheerfully rubbed their hands together then got down to work and slowly the bridge, the gate, the tavern, the brothel—they drew lots as to who should dig out that one—began to emerge from beneath the smooth levels that the heavy fall had caused. Only the castle reared clear, throwing an eerie shadow on the narrow-streeted town that lay, snow filled, below its resplendently high perch.

And yet this work, this shoveling, this battle with the elements, was a relief to every inhabitant. From the smallest toddler, plunging head first into the whiteness, emerging again with quivering lip not sure whether to laugh or cry, to the old men who limped their way to the hostelry leaning heavily upon sticks, the wood almost as knotted and gnarled as they, this wicked white winter was better than the summer when they had all lain under siege at the hands of the Angloys-Françoys.

For from June to November 1428, the enemy had been staring at them across the river and only the gallantry of the townsfolk, under the captaincy of Robert de Baudricourt, who governed the place in the name of Charles of France, had saved them. Thus Vaucouleurs had become the only Valois fortress still holding out to the north-east of the Loire, apart from Montargis, a dire position to be in indeed.

Therefore, this sudden attack from nature, which everyone understood and could reckon with, was preferable by far. In fact there was something satisfying about it all, shoveling and laughing together, putting a hot poker into the wine to mull the dark red liquid, roasting chestnuts, crunching them up with burning tongues and teeth, and spitting and swearing and cursing the Angloys and Françoys until breath ran out.

In the castle, too, there was a sudden mood of contentment. The soldiers who had fought so bravely, glorifying both themselves and their commander, had been down in the streets helping to clear the snow, had been talking to the townsfolk as they worked alongside them, had been eyeing up the young women, who had giggled and colored and brought the fighting men drink and refreshments, or had asked them into their houses to take a sup of ale. After all it was St. Hilary's Day, 13th January, two days into the year of 1429, New Year's Eve falling on the 11th January as it did under the Julian calendar. And on this particular saint's day the ban on marriages, which held good during Advent and the Twelve Days, was lifted until the following Christmas.

So, sitting before the fire in his private chamber, his boots neatly placed side by side in the corner and his toes curling toward the flames, Robert de Baudricourt temporarily put aside his contemplation of the current situation in France—enough to depress anyone—and concentrated instead on enjoying the sheer bone idleness of doing absolutely nothing at all. Other than raising his wine to his lips and grasping the cup in his fingers to prevent it from spilling, he had no other duties; in fact, de Baudricourt had not felt so relaxed since the moment when he had seen the last of the accursed English finally traipse off into the bad weather.

"This is the life!" he said now, and allowed himself the luxury of snoring, something his wife detested, as he hovered between sleeping and wakefulness. Drenched in this wonderful somnolence, stretched out, lazy as a cat, the last thing he wanted was a knock on the door, but that is precisely what came, a cautious tap from someone who obviously knew he was resting and, after a moment or two, a head hesitantly appearing in the crack.

"Captain de Baudricourt, are you asleep?"

"I was," Robert answered tersely.

"Oh, sorry, I'll go."

The head withdrew again but not before the Captain had had time to recognize the craggy features of Simon, his personal servant and general dogsbody, obviously sent to him with a message.

"I'm awake now," de Baudricourt called after him. "What is it you want?"

The head reappeared. "I've been sent from the guard room to tell you that that loopy girl's back."

"God's mercy, what's this?" Robert said irritably. "Come in, man, come in. What loopy girl?"

"The one who came last May, just before the siege. She's here again."

"Not the creature who said she had a mission to save France and must see the Dauphin?"

Simon nodded until the shaggy red curls which grew in a great bush round his granite face flew about. "That's her."

De Baudricourt sunk his head into his hands. "Oh, Christ, what have I done to deserve this? This is supposed to be my day off."

"They tried to get rid of her but she's creating a bit of a scene down there. Says the Lord has told her to be with the Dauphin by mid-Lent so that she can relieve Orléans then take him to be crowned."

The Captain groaned aloud. "I'll give her the Lord, straight up her backside! Tell them I'll be down in a moment."

Simon nodded, tapped his forehead with his forefinger,

said, "There's one born every minute you know," and vanished.

With a great deal of reluctance, the Captain began to pull on his boots.

The girl looked better than when he'd last seen her, he thought when he walked into the castle's guard room some ten minutes later. Then she'd had her hair cut so short de Baudricourt hadn't been able to tell at first exactly what gender she actually was, but now it was long, obviously female, lustrously dark against her red dress.

"Well?" he said coldly.

She glanced at him cautiously yet with direct eye contact, flinching from nothing, and de Baudricourt found himself scrutinizing her closely in the few seconds before she spoke. The creature was over five feet, tall for a woman, and extremely muscular, almost athletic, and her face, though not beautiful, was certainly arresting. Dark, dark eyes, very Spanish-looking, gazed out from beneath thick black brows and lashes, while the hollows and curves of her face would be spectacular when she grew older and had fined down.

"I've come back," she said.

"So I see. Did your father not box your ears hard enough?"

There was silence during which she flushed a little, remembering, no doubt, his advice to her uncle to take the silly chit back to her parents and tell her father to give her a beating.

"Well, didn't he?"

She hung her head momentarily, then suddenly flung it back. "I can't waste time talking about that, Captain de Baudricourt. I have been sent by God, whose instrument and messenger I am. Before mid-Lent the Dauphin will be given help to get rid of his enemies. For, after all, the Dauphin's kingdom really belongs to the Lord and He is tired of foreigners occupying His territories."

"Is He now?" said Robert, a smile beginning to twitch at the corner of his mouth.

"Yes," the girl answered firmly. "Furthermore, Captain, in order that I may fulfill my mission, namely to raise the siege of Orléans and take the Dauphin to be anointed King, I would ask you to give me a horse and escort to lead me to him immediately."

"You're mad," said Robert, sitting down on a stool and

folding his arms on the rough-hewn table. "You are stark staring mad. Now in the name of God, whom you so boldly claim to represent, go away before I tan your hide myself."

"I see you don't believe me."

"No, you silly bitch, I bloody well don't."

"But I am the virgin from God, La Pucelle."

"Really?" said the Captain, and yawned.

"Listen," said the girl, leaning forward on the table so that her eyes were exactly level with his own, "last time I came here you gave me short shrift and sent me packing. Now you're doing it again. But this time I'm not leaving. I am going to stay in this town and will continue to do so until you change your mind. I've got till mid-Lent to get to the Dauphin and neither you, Captain high and mighty de Baudricourt, nor any other mother's son is going to stand in my way. Good day to you."

And she was gone in a flurry of red skirts and swirling hair.

"Well!" said the Captain looking round his astonished guards. "Mettlesome little baggage, isn't she?"

"Extraordinary," said Simon, who had been eavesdropping in the doorway. "Quite a character. Loopy of course, but still a character."

"Lieutenant de Metz," called de Baudricourt to one of his fellow officers who had been standing behind the visitor, watching everything that went on.

"Yes, Captain?"

"Do you remember her name by any chance?"

"I do as it happens. Jehannette Darc."

"Oh, yes, it comes back to me. Well, could you go into the town and find out where Mademoiselle Darc is lodging and suggest to her landlord he moves her on? I don't want her hanging round here making a nuisance of herself till Lent. I really do not."

"But even if he agrees, I can't stop her finding lodgings somewhere else," de Metz pointed out.

"Well, do your best," Robert answered crossly. "The girl is a pain in the arse, not to put too fine a point on it, and I want her out."

"Very good, Monsieur. I'll do what I can."

"Excellent. Now I'm going back to my fireside and my dreams and this time I don't want any interruptions."

"Not even for a messenger from the Lord?" asked Simon irreverently.

"Most definitely not," replied the Captain and, grinning, cuffed his servant's ear.

The visit to Jehannette's landlord went rather badly.

"No, Monsieur," Henri le Royer said firmly. "I'm not turning her out. She is a good girl, a holy girl, and I don't want it on my conscience that I put such a person on the street. Besides, my wife has relatives in Domrémy. What would they say if I forced one of their own out of doors?"

Jean de Metz looked nonplussed. "I know, I know. It's only that the Captain is in one of his moods. He sees her as a potential troublemaker."

"That she isn't. She's in church every morning praying for divine help. Jehannette is as pure as a nun."

"But a fierce nun," answered de Metz, and smiled.

He had let two days pass before calling on le Royer and the snow which had blanketed the town earlier in the week had now subsided into large white mounds, sparkling in the sunshine, slippery paths cut through them to enable the townsfolk to go about their normal business. And sliding down one of these paths toward him as de Metz left le Royer's house came the subject of their conversation, her darned red skirt kilted up inelegantly to help her get along.

"Good morning," Jehannette said cheerfully.

"Good morning," he answered, amused and intrigued simultaneously.

"I've just come from church."

"So I guessed." The soldier drew breath and decided to use his own initiative. "Look, sweetheart," he said, taking her by the arm as if she were a small child, "what are you doing here? It's a waste of time, you know. Isn't the King sure to be pushed out of his kingdom soon and aren't we all going to end up having to be English?"

She stared up at him, directly into his eyes in that strangely disconcerting way of hers. "What is your name, Monsieur?"

"Lieutenant Jean de Metz."

"Monsieur de Metz, as you know I have come here to talk to Captain Robert de Baudricourt to see if he will take me to the King. As you also know, he thinks I am mad and is paying no heed to what I say. But I've got to get to Charles by mid-Lent even if I have to walk there."

"But why?"

The small intense face so close to his underwent a change and Jean gazed in amazement into a pair of eyes radiating light. "Because I am the chosen one, the virgin from the woods who has been prophesied. It is my destiny to save France and, believe me, there is no one else who can do it, neither kings, nor dukes, nor the King's daughter of Scotland ..."

Even in the middle of her flow of words it struck de Metz as odd that a simple peasant should be well informed enough to have even heard of the Scottish princess, but he had no time to think about it.

"... apart from me. I must go to him. I must continue with what I'm doing, because my Lord wants me to."

"What Lord? To whom do you owe fealty?"

"To God. He is my master, Monsieur."

There was a moment of intense silence.

"You really believe it, don't you?" said de Metz finally.

"Of course I do. It's true! My voices told me years ago that I had been chosen, that it was decreed I should be a warrior of France."

Jean couldn't help himself; he roared with laughter. "I've never seen anyone look less like a warrior in my life."

Jehannette frowned. "I know. I hate that. I prefer to wear men's clothes and have short hair. Monsieur, have you any old things which might fit me?"

And with that she put out her hand imploringly and laid it in his. He had never felt anything like it. Magic lay in that touch. Fire and ice shot into him, a charge of power so fierce that he physically jumped.

"Please help me," she said.

Before he knew what he was doing, de Metz was suddenly on his knees in the snow.

"I pay homage to you," said a voice which he recognized with shock as his own. "If the decision is made that you go to France I will accompany you and take you to the King. I swear it before God."

She nodded. "This is well and I thank you. But in the meantime may I borrow some clothes?"

*   *   *

In answer to the impatient ringing of Captain de Baudricourt's bell, Simon's shaggy head appeared in the doorway,
his craggy features lurking just inside the crack as was his
wont.

"About that girl Darc," the Captain said without
preamble.

"Yes, Monsieur?"

"Is she still in town?"

"She is. Lodging with Henri and Catherine le Royer.
They didn't move her on. Wouldn't!"

"Oh, I see. How annoying! What's she up to?"

"Moaning. Telling everyone she's got to get to the Dauphin by mid-Lent, that she has a divine mission, but that
you won't let her."

"Silly bitch."

"She's dressing up like a boy too. Got her hair cut all
short same as she had that first time she came."

"Oh, Mon Dieu!"

"The trouble is they're beginning to believe her. There's
talk in the town that she's the virgin who's been prophesied, the one who's supposed to come from the woods."

De Baudricourt shot him a jaundiced glance. "Superstitious fools."

"Indeed, Captain, but it makes things awkward for you,
doesn't it?"

"What do you mean?"

"Well, if word's getting round she's some kind of prophet
it could show you up in a bad light, if you don't pay her
any attention, that is."

"I see what you mean," the Captain answered, fingering
the pen he was holding, obviously lost in thought. "Would
it be politic to pay the girl a visit, do you think?"

"Good move," answered Simon, nodding his shaggy
head. "Mind you it could be dangerous, she could be a
witch," he added glumly.

"Then I'll take a holy man along," Robert countered.
"In fact to do that might be a very good idea anyway. It
would give the whole thing an air of authority."

"I knew you'd come up with something," answered
Simon, then winked an eye and vanished.

So it was duly in the company of Jean Fournier, parish
priest of Vaucouleurs, garbed ceremonially and wearing a
stole which Fournier had blessed with holy water before he

left the castle's chapel, that de Baudricourt rode down from on high to the bustling little town and sought out the dwelling of Henri le Royer, cartwright.

A small crowd had gathered outside the artisan's door and Jehannette stood just within, wearing a boy's hand-me-downs, the light of the snowlit day shining on her face, giving it no mercy or flattery, simply showing it for what it was, vulnerable, determined, an anxious yet confident little countenance, full of hope and fear as she saw the Captain and the priest dismount.

"If you are a witch or demon of hell approach us not," boomed de Baudricourt theatrically. "For Father Jean wears a vestment blessed with that water which is most abhorrent of all things evil."

"Then I shall kiss it before you enter," answered Jehannette, and stepping into the street, dropped on her knees before the priest and raised a corner of the stole to her lips.

"I think we had better go in," said Fournier solemnly, and drew a murmur from the crowd as he raised the girl to her feet with his own hand. Once inside, he closed the door firmly and rounded on the Captain in rather an accusatory manner. "There is nothing wicked about this child. She could not have touched me had there been."

"You think not?" de Baudricourt answered thoughtfully, stroking his chin.

"I am positive of it, Monsieur. This creature is obviously blameless, without stain."

"I value that opinion." Robert turned to Madame le Royer, who was hovering discreetly in the background, with an air of sudden resolution. "Good woman, may I trespass on your hospitality? I would ask this girl questions in the company of *Messire* Priest."

"Then I shall leave you, Captain, for it is well you have come."

An hour later it was done, and brilliantly at that. Somehow conveying that it was Fournier who had talked him into it, Captain de Baudricourt, already exhibiting the shrewdness and flair that one day would make him both a rich and famous man, suddenly appeared to make up his mind.

"I am convinced," he said heavily, rising to his feet. "*Messire* Priest says he can find naught of evil or harm in you. Therefore, Jehannette Darc, I am going to do my duty and write to the Court to discover their wishes in this matter. If the King is agreeable and wants to meet you, you shall have a horse and men to help you reach him. The die is cast, let what will be, be."

Even as he said the words he was thinking how good they sounded and remembering them for future use.

Jehannette nodded. "God will reward you for this kindness, Monsieur," she said, not humbly but as if it were a fact. "You are doing a great service for France."

"And you are not over-imbued with modesty, my girl,' thought the Captain. Aloud he put on a business-like tone. "The letter will be written and despatched today. I will send for you the moment the reply arrives. Meanwhile contain yourself in patience and prayer."

"I'll do my best," she answered, smiling.

In the hour just before dawn two *chevaucheurs,* the mounted messengers who kept all the regions of France in touch, one with the other, left Vaucouleurs, one heading toward the King's territories, as the Captain had promised Jehannette, the other going in completely the opposite direction toward Nancy. The first had a journey of many miles and much danger ahead of him, the other reached his destination in a couple of hours and was able to return that same day with two letters from Prince René, one for Captain de Baudricourt, the other for the girl who was causing such a stir in the town. But as he rode from the stables, having dined in Nancy, Baudricourt's man saw another *chevaucheur* mounting his horse, also thrusting two parchments into his saddle-bag.

"Going for?" the man from Vaucouleurs called cheerfully.

"To Saumur. These are both for the Queen of Sicily."

The first man nodded, having taken documents to René's mother himself in the past.

"Well, good luck. It's a long haul."

"Thank you. I'll need it."

And with that they parted company.

"She's gone," said Simon from the door crack.

"Who has?"

"Her, the loopy virgin."

"Do you mean Jehannette?"

"I do."

"You're not saying she's taken off on her own, set out to see the Dauphin without my permission?"

The matted hair flew round its owner's head. "No, my Captain, you can relax. Apparently she was sent for."

"What are you talking about, man?" De Baudricourt was thoroughly rattled.

"The Duke of Lorraine wrote and asked her to cure his gout. She took the letter to the priest because she says she can't read or write, though I'm not so sure that that isn't a blind. Anyway, she told Father Jean she doesn't do cures but she'd go despite that. And it was a right good turn out when she went, I can tell you."

"In what way?"

"They'd all clubbed together to get her some new clothes and a horse. She didn't look bad in the gear, though. But just like a boy. Couldn't have told if you hadn't have known. I reckon she's a bit rum."

"Sexually?"

"Not 'arf."

"That's as may be," said the Captain primly, "but it's not our affair. What *is*, is doing the right thing in a tricky situation like this."

"Well, Monsieur, if I am allowed to comment I, personally, myself, think you're handling it a treat. The townspeople are drinking your health because you've sent to Court for instructions, and so is Jean de Metz. You know, I reckon he's a bit sweet on her."

"Go away and mind your own business," answered de Baudricourt irritably. "You're always poking your nose into other people's affairs. You've got no respect, that's your trouble."

"You're right," said Simon, grinning, and went.

So it had happened! The tumultuous thing that Yolande had been expecting for the past two years had taken place. Jehanne had finally made her move.

It had been very difficult at first to accept all that Alison du May had whispered to her when they had eventually caught up with one another four years earlier, in the summer of 1425. That her bastard daughter was seeing visions of saints was hard enough to believe but that René should

have acted on such a thing, sending the child to the last
outpost of the Knights Templar, was unthinkable.

"What does the boy think he's doing?" the distraught
mother had said of the treatment one of her children was
meting out to another.

"Madame, what can I say? You know as do I that René
is the Grand Master. You know the Priory's connection
with the Templars. It is my belief that he intends to use
Jehanne to further their ends at some time in the future."

"Use her? But for what?"

"To fight for France and them I should imagine."

It had been then that the Queen of Sicily, so addressed
since Jade had taken a bride and there was a young Duchess of Anjou, had suddenly seen the potential of the situation as her son had obviously done before her.

She had looked at her Lady and friend most earnestly.
"Tell me, Alison, what *are* these visions Jehanne sees? Is
my poor girl deranged or is the whole thing brought about
because her flux will soon begin?"

"Madame, I don't know the answer," Alison had stated
honestly. "René himself is not sure. What he does think,
though, is that Jehanne herself believes these things. And
that, in his opinion is the most important aspect of the
entire situation."

"Does he know she is his sister?"

"No, ma Reine. I have never betrayed your trust and
never will. He is ignorant of the truth."

"If he had been told I wonder if he would have acted
differently."

"I doubt it somehow. His years of training are his legacy
for life. It is René's sworn duty to act in the best interests
of the Priory of Sion and its secrets and I think he would
put that duty above his ties of blood."

"You have grown into a very wise woman," Yolande had
said thoughtfully.

"It was you who taught me, ma Reine."

After Alison had gone, back to Lorraine and her Duke
and their five unruly sons, Yolande had often thought back
to that conversation, wishing her friend were with her, comforting her and being her confidante throughout the increasingly difficult times. For since the death of Pierre de
Giac, two years earlier, it seemed as if a blight had fallen
on nearly everyone. So much so that the Queen, not a

superstitious woman nor one prone to nervous imaginings, wondered if he had uttered a curse in his weighted sack as it sank down to the bottom of the river, calling on his Dark Master to honor their bargain and serve him at the very last.

Charles had been one of her major worries, continually in a state of total apathy and depression which not even Marie could shake him from. Almost as if to spite Richemont for killing de Giac, the King had quickly made friends with another terrible young man, Le Camus de Vernet, known as de Beaulieu. Terrified that a situation might arise in which Le Camus might also become all-powerful, Richemont had sent in an assassination squad who had killed the youthful Satanist on the riverbank, hacking off his right hand, and tossing the remains into the river. Most tragically, the King had been looking out of the window and had seen the whole thing, and an implacable and furious hatred for the new Constable had grown on the instant.

Then had come revenge. That July of 1427, the Earl of Richmond, without consulting his mistress, had made a terrible mistake. Returning to the battle against the English, he had left Georges de la Trémoille as his deputy at court. Charles had smiled the small cynical smile which nowadays seemed to have become his trade mark.

"Dear cousin, you give him to me and you'll repent of it. I know him better than you do."

And the young King had been proved right. With Yolande away in Provence and Richemont at Chinon with his wife Marguerite, the stage was set for a coup and the treaty between Duke Jean of Brittany and the boy King Henry VI of England was the signal for it to start. The Earl was banished from court and stripped of his Constable's pension by his erstwhile friend de la Trémoille, daily growing fatter and ever more luxuriant. Furious, Richemont had retired to his estates in Parthenay, while Yolande had hurried back to find her work in ruins, her lover gone.

She had nearly panicked then, her mind going round like a mouse on a treadmill. But then the Queen of Sicily had rallied. A storm of weeping and hysteria could do nothing but delay her strike back. She must remain and fight de la Trémoille with every weapon at hand. But the next time she had seen the fat man, Yolande had allowed herself the pleasure of one small insult.

"Gracious, my Lord, with your golden robes and your long beard I half mistook you for some Grand Vizier from the east! But how foolish of me. They, of course, have many wives and a harem and never involve themselves with widows, but then they have no need of other people's money."

De la Trémoille had smiled coldly and Yolande had felt a wave of hatred that someone she and Richemont had looked on as a friend could have treated them so badly.

But one good thing had come out of Georges's new rule. Jean the Bastard, disgraced and sent away from court when his father-in-law, Louvet, had fallen from favor, had come back, as handsome and debonair as ever, ready to fight for his old allegiances. But even he, beloved childhood friend, could do nothing to bring the sparkle of life in to Charles de Valois's eyes.

The winter of 1427 had passed bitterly, Richemont and de la Trémoille both trying to have each other killed. A small band of the Earl's loyal men had crept into Georges's château one night, catching him and the former Madame de Giac *in flagrante delicto*. Creeping up behind the thrusting couple, the assassins had plunged daggers into de la Trémoille's back to no effect, his avoirdupois saving him from harm and the stabs appearing merely as superficial cuts. The attackers had fled, overcome with horror at the fat man's apparent immunity to fatal wounds.

Yolande had remained alone, distressed beyond measure, as Richemont and his Breton troops, fighting back, had taken over Bourges in July 1428. For that crime her lover had been permanently exiled and stripped of office and she had seen him only once more that year, it now being too dangerous for them to meet. The former Constable had come to the Château of the Queen of Sicily in Saumur and there they had made love for what was to be the last time for twelve months.

"Keep faith," Arthur had whispered as they parted. "Stay on the King's Council and be afraid of no one."

"I'll get you back to Charles somehow," Yolande had promised. "There's got to be a way."

"There'll be no way for any of us until he pulls himself together."

"We need a miracle," the Queen had said.

Even as she spoke the words, Yolande was aware of an

idea buzzing at the back of her mind that had not, as yet, taken shape, and in an attempt to crystallize her thoughts the Queen had gone out of doors, walking on the riverbank watching the boat carrying Richemont away from her as it turned into a distant dot before vanishing altogether. Then, and only then, had she known what to do.

A year ago, a brief and coded message from Alison, arriving in the spring of 1428, had informed Yolande d'Anjou that Jehanne had returned home, fully trained and prepared to undertake her mission. Here then, in the shape of her own child, lay the cause to which poor dying France could rally. The Queen had replied at once, "Advise the Grand Master to act and act quickly."

The reply had come back, "Madame, he already has. Jehanne was requested to begin her campaign but was turned back by the commander of her nearest town. Now that town lies under siege and nothing further can be done at present. It is your wish that I apprise René of the true facts about Jehanne?"

Terrified of the consequences should her letter fall into the wrong hands, the Queen of Sicily had answered, "Tell him nothing except that he should continue with his plans. Make it sound as if you express your own views. Do not mention me. I shall not write again."

And then there had been silence as the world plunged into the abyss. Charles, amused and bemused by Georges's large twinkling presence, bowed to his dictatorship; while Bedford, the Regent, sensing the loss of interest in France amongst the English nobles, determined to end the French campaign as quickly as possible by attacking Angers, which he had already claimed as his own personal property. Only at the last minute did he decide to make Orléans the target and Yolande, solitary, with Richemont in exile, drew a breath of relief as on 12th October 1428 the siege of that city began and Angers was thus given a reprieve.

Inside the city, the Orléanists went hungry, and beyond the walls so did the besiegers. Supplies of herrings and "lenten stuff" were conveyed to the English army by a convoy under the command of Sir John Fastolfe, which was savagely ambushed by French soldiers led by Charles, Duke of Bourbon, kinsman of the King. Sir John had defended himself and his wagons nobly and won the Battle of the Herrings as it came to be known. The English had eaten

well, the French had not, and with this subtle blow it had
seemed that the fate of Orléans was irrevocably sealed. Just
like Rouen before it, yet another gallant French city would
have to capitulate rather than starve to death.

Alone in her château in Saumur, Yolande, terrified to
write anything further, sat willing her second son to fetch
Jehanne out of the wings and onto center stage in an attempt to retrieve something from the death throes of an
entire nation.

And now the moment had come at last. In the darkness
of the previous night one of René's messengers had galloped into the courtyard, his letter handed over at once to
Yolande's *grand maître*. With a thudding heart, the Queen
of Sicily had broken the seal and seen Alison's neat hand.
"She is on her way. God grant her strength."

Yolande wept for joy that the child given to her by the
Earl of Richmond had been chosen by God, fate, destiny,
call it what you will, to come to the King's aid and rally
France to her side. She went to the desk and wrote an
immediate reply.

"Say nothing of this to anyone, secrecy is vital. But before Jehanne is sent to Charles—and I will make it my
personal responsibility to see that he agrees to receive
her—I desire you to bring her to me at Saumur."

Twenty-nine

"She's back," said Simon from the doorway. "And she's downstairs."

"Jehannette?"

"Yes. Got a new horse too. Present from the Duke of Lorraine."

"She cured his gout then?"

"No, didn't try. But he still liked her. Apparently told him to give up Madame du May for the sake of his soul, and he just laughed his head off. Cheeky, eh?"

"Very," answered Robert de Baudricourt. "Cheeky and fearless, all rolled into one."

"Any word from the King?"

The Captain shook his head. "No, nothing at all. I only hope the messenger got through."

"Very tricky," answered Simon, pulling a tangled curl. "Swarming with Angloys and Françoys, to say nothing of brigands, that bit of the country. What will you do if you don't get an answer?"

"I'll send someone else," Robert replied. "Somebody who can mingle into the background. Probably yourself."

"No thanks," the servant answered rapidly. "Me, personally, I fall off horses. You'll have to choose a better man."

"Oh, come now," said the Captain, grinning, but the eye at the door crack had rapidly vanished.

So the girl had proved herself a success with the Duke of Lorraine, though small wonder at it with René there, for she had obviously made a great impression on that particular Prince if his letter were anything to go by.

"Please take my advice and help her. According to the Franciscan friars, Jehannette is God's messenger and will put the English archers to flight."

"Franciscan friars! That's a new one," de Baudricourt had muttered to himself.

Yet everything said in defence of the girl was in a way a further worry, for if Charles should write back refusing to see her it could put him, the Captain, in a very awkward position indeed.

"Why me?" Robert asked himself for the millionth time, "why me for such a quandary?"

Then his heart lurched in fright as there came a gentle but firm tap on the door.

"Who is it?" he called.

"Jehannette."

"Come in, come in."

She looked well, he thought, in her funny little suit, a black doublet with twenty aiguillettes secured to trunk hose, a short gray cloak tossed over it, hanging from shoulder to knee.

"You're very smart."

"The townspeople gave it to me. They thought I was dressed too much like a ragamuffin to meet the Duke of Lorraine."

"And so you were."

Robert was trying to keep the conversation light and bantering, not wanting her to ask him about the King's message, but in Jehannette's very next breath out came the dreaded question.

"Have you had a reply from the Dauphin yet?"

"No I'm afraid not. The messenger's journey was both long and hazardous and then, of course, even if he did arrive safely, one can hardly expect the King to come to a decision straight away."

"Why not?" the girl answered angrily, her eyes clouding. "The more he delays the more likely he is to lose the war. He suffered a severe blow at Orléans today and the situation will get worse every hour he keeps me waiting."

"Listen, sauce box," said de Baudricourt, rising purposefully from his desk. "One does not speak about one's King like that. He can keep anyone waiting he chooses. You have no right to give yourself such airs."

"They're not airs," the girl answered bitterly. "I speak the truth as told to me by my voices from the Lord."

"Lord or no Lord there's something mighty suspicious about you," replied the Captain, glinting an eye at her. "I have a friend at the court of Lorraine and he told me all about your interview with the Duke. How, for a peasant girl, you ride like the Devil himself, so much so that Duke Charles gave you a great black horse and said it would suit you better than a village nag, to say nothing of his present of four gold francs to buy necessities. My friend also informs me that you asked the Duke to lend you his son-in-law and some men to lead you into France. Couldn't wait for my reply, could you? What *are* you, Jehannette Darc, that you dare to order your elders and betters about the way you do?"

The dark eyes, looking at him so angrily, suddenly overflowed and the strange little boy figure crumpled as the girl threw herself into a chair in a waterfall of tears.

"I don't want to do it," she said, "but I must. It's my destiny. I was born to save France and thus have no choice."

"You are a very silly, very small, simpleton," answered the Captain, and applied his handkerchief vigorously to her face.

"Don't be angry with me," she said, sniffing and sobbing. "It would make things so much easier if you weren't."

The same childish appeal that had won the heart of Prior Hugh shone from the tragically young countenance.

"I'm not," Robert said in a more gentle voice than he had ever used to her before. "I admire you actually. Whether you be saint or sinner you certainly have a prodigious courage. Now, dry your tears, go back to your lodgings and go to bed. If the King *does* send for you you've got a lot lying ahead. You're going to need all the rest and sleep you can get."

She smiled, such a vulnerable smile, that de Baudricourt added gently, "You're not much more than a child are you?"

"I was seventeen on 6th January."

He shook his head. "You're far too young for all this, you know. Jehannette, please take my advice, given in friendship, and stop now. You really are too small to be a soldier."

A few days later an amazing thing took place. Not only de Baudricourt's rider returned but with him one of the King's own *chevaucheurs,* Colet de Vienne, carrying a box bearing

the fleur-de-lis to denote his royal status and accompanied
by a bodyguard, Richard, a leathery-looking archer.

With hands that shook and sweated, the Captain opened
the sealed parchment they brought, noticing as he broke it
that the device in the wax was not that of Charles de Valois
but his mother-in-law's. The Queen of Sicily herself had
written to answer his request.

"René again!" thought Robert. "There's some thread behind all this. But what?"

He scanned Yolande's fine writing.

"She's to go," he said shortly to the small crowd that
had gathered in the great hall. "The Queen of Sicily asks
on the King's behalf that Jehannette attend them at court."

There was a spontaneous cheer and the Captain, much
to his surprise, found that he was joining in.

"I'll go and fetch her," called Jean de Metz, bright with
pleasure.

"Yes, go and bring her and her few belongings to the
castle. She had better stay here until she is ready to go."

"If this wondrous virgin is going to save Orléans she'll
have to get on with it," put in Colet de Vienne. "There
was a terrible defeat there, the Battle of the Herrings
they're calling it, only last week."

"When exactly?" asked the Captain sharply.

"On Thursday. Why do you ask?"

"Mon Dieu, that was the day she came to see me! The
day she said there had been trouble at Orléans."

"So she really is a mystic!" said the cynical de Vienne.

"Do you know, I'm beginning to think so."

"And will she save us all?"

"Either that or die in the attempt," de Baudricourt answered grimly.

Within the following twenty-four hours all was prepared
for the girl to leave. Jehanne's escort, Bertrand de
Poulengy and his squire Julien de Honecourt, Jean de Metz
and his squire, Julien's brother Jean, were all sworn in,
giving their solemn oath to take Jehannette to the King
and on the journey protect her with their lives if necessary.
De Poulengy, the eldest at thirty, was put in command of
the little band and everyone, including the girl, was told to
take their orders from him.

"But, Captain," he said, as he and de Baudricourt sat
late on the night prior to departure, before the fire, drink-

ing their final drinks. "What do I do about her girlish problems?"

"What do you mean?"

"We will be sleeping rough most of the time. What of her natural functions? We are all men together but a young female is something very different. Supposing she should menstruate?"

Robert shook his head. "The same thought has already occurred to me and I'm afraid I have come up with no answers. All I can say is tell the others to be discreet about what they do and give her time to herself."

"It's a worry."

"It certainly is."

They drank in silence for a few minutes and then de Baudricourt said, "Poor little thing. What a daunting venture."

"She's taking on so much."

"Not to mention a huge and mighty army who wouldn't scruple to kill her."

"I pray it all works well for her."

And so did every inhabitant of Vaucouleurs, by now convinced that the girl really was God's messenger, La Pucelle, as the party set off on the evening of 13th February 1429, their plan to ride all night and sleep during the day to avoid being noticed.

Jehannette wore her one and only suit, a black plumed hat on her head, a sword provided by Robert de Baudricourt in a scabbard at her side.

"I don't know how you're going to handle this," he had said, almost apologetically, as he had passed it to her.

"I'll manage," the girl had replied cheerfully, and something about the way she had taken it from him and buckled the sword on had convinced the Captain that somehow, most strangely, she was used to bearing arms.

"Good luck," he called now as he watched her swing into the saddle aloft the powerful black horse given by the Duke of Lorraine.

"Thank you, Monsieur—for everything." Jehannette turned to go and then impetuously wheeled back and, leaning down low, planted a kiss on his cheek. "You believe in me at last, don't you?"

"Yes," he said, "yes, I do." Suddenly he was blubbing like a babe. "Jehannette . . ."

"Yes?"

"Take care, won't you."

"God will if I don't," she answered, and was gone into the dusk.

"Funny girl," said Simon, right behind him.

"Funny and wonderful," replied the Captain gruffly, and went away to get thoroughly and monumentally drunk.

"He's sweet on her," muttered Simon. But there was no one left to listen for they had all run up the road, going as fast as they could to try and catch a last glimpse of La Pucelle as she started on her magnificent journey. With a shake of his grizzled head, Simon went hastily to join them.

The death of Bonne de Giac, tiring of her though Charles had been, had plunged him into the depths of despair. But, in a way, the killing of her unspeakable husband had had an even more terrible effect. For the King had been plotting, planning, scheming; spending every day of his house arrest perfecting the manner of Pierre de Giac's removal from the world. And then in had walked Richemont, cool as dew, and taken the situation out of Charles's hands.

It had destroyed him; that and no longer being allowed to fight, kept at home because he was too valuable to put at risk. And yet, if truth be told, the King did not particularly like war and skirmishes, preferring by far to play his games of chess with people and pawns. But what had really driven Charles to the depths below the ocean had been the taking away of whatever small, insignificant power he had once possessed. The bright gleaming faun who had called on his loyal men to march with him into battle had not so much been wiped out as transmogrified. A goat now lived where that glittering creature had so superbly dwelled, an ugly goat with a shabby coat and downcast eyes, a goat that had in every sense reached the end of its tether.

As the war had grown in intensity, as the Armagnacs had been beaten back and back, so Charles's soul had shriveled a little more every day. He had undergone the loathsome experience of seeming to stand outside himself, of seeing a powerless King, a laughing-stock of a ruler, losing everything before the ruthless war machine which was the Angloys-Françoys army. And when, even in his own pathetic kingdom, he had been treated like a fool by Pierre de Giac and been unable to avenge himself, something had slipped in his mind.

Then had come the conviction that fate was against him, that the predictions of long ago had been hollow and untrue, probably uttered by a Devil's man in order to fill him with false hope and longings. From there it had not been too great a step to see himself as the butt of destiny, the most inept and tragic King that France was ever to know.

It had been too much for Charles and he had broken on All Souls Day, the day when the dead are especially prayed for. That night, having watched dreary black processions for hour upon hour, the King had risen from his bed and gone into a screaming fit of hysteria, calling upon God either to show His face or leave him in peace, let him just be, let him wallow in the failure that was obviously the evil fairy's gift to him at birth.

Marie had come running, weeping in distress that he had slipped so far away from her. His Gentlemen had appeared only to be driven away by the overwrought Queen.

"I can bear no more," her husband had sobbed, his head in her lap. "I can't go on. I am no longer master of my fate, my soul does not belong to me. I am going to leave this benighted kingdom and go to live in the Dauphiné or away in exile in Scotland or Spain. I am finished, done, I never want to hear the name of France again."

She had not known how to console him. Comfortable little Marie, Charles's safe harbor, his port in a storm, was completely at a loss. Kisses and scolding had both failed equally to rouse him from his terrible depression. It was obvious to everyone, including his wife and her mother, that the boy they had cherished since childhood was suffering a total breakdown.

"What's to be done?" the distraught young woman had said to Yolande.

"Help may yet come."

"What help?" Marie had asked defiantly. "Who can help Charles if I can't?"

"Somebody inspired perhaps."

And after that the Queen of Sicily would say no more.

Rising high above the river, flamboyantly beautiful with its white stonework and dove-gray roofs, the Château of Saumur dominated not only the left bank of the Loire but

also the little town that huddled around its elegant foundations, its emerald rock, as the ramparts were known to the
natives of the town.

Carvings and gargoyles, windows and staircases,
abounded everywhere that the eye could see, for this château, unlike the awesome castle of Angers, was the graceful
country residence of the Dukes of Anjou, their haven, their
idyllic retreat, their place for love and laughter and tournaments. Here, in times of peace, the Dukes came to relax,
to look down at the great waterway below, to leave the
château by the bailey gate and go through the fields to hunt
in the wild woods.

From the bank on which this delightful pile was built, a
bridge spanned the river to an island lying between the two
arms of the Loire which, in turn, housed another bridge
going across to the right bank. And it was here, between
the two bridges, in the district known as the Quartier des
Ponts, that another, smaller, but equally graceful château
stood, virtually surrounded by water, its flower-filled gardens running down to one fork of the river, its imposing
entrance dominating the other. Echoing the Duke's residence, this smaller version also had embellished white stone
and dark slates, and stood three stories high, a fantasy of
towers and turrets and sloping angled roofs decorated with
lavish gargoyle spouts. For this was the home of the Queen
of Sicily, built for Yolande's mother-in-law but extensively
altered and refurbished to suit the younger woman's tastes.

The island château had always been the Queen's retreat,
the place to which she retired to think, to plan, to be private. And it was to this palace, so discreetly hidden from
observers, that Yolande had ordered the King's messenger,
Colet de Vienne, to bring Jehanne, skirting Chinon, taking
the girl away from her planned route.

"She is to see me before ever she is introduced to any
member of the Court, particularly the King," Yolande had
written in her sealed orders, a copy of which had been
given to Bertrand de Poulengy. "It is imperative that I
counsel the child first."

"But why are we not going to Chinon? Why are you
not taking me directly to the Dauphin?" Jehannette had
protested, seeing the road lead off in the opposite direction.

"Because Queen Yolande of Sicily, Prince René's
mother, has asked to meet you first and that is a great

honor," de Vienne had answered firmly. "It was she who wrote giving you permission to come to Court if you remember, so the last thing you must do is be churlish about it."

"But it means yet another delay."

"For a visionary clairvoyante you are remarkably short-sighted," the messenger had answered crisply. "Get the Queen on your side and almost every door will open for you. Just think about that."

And Jehanne, who had been about to say something further, promptly closed her mouth again, obviously doing his bidding. Colet grinned briefly, well aware that he, in his dashing livery, thoroughly overawed her, and very pleased to get the last word with such a thoroughly argumentative little baggage. Yet even he, critical though he was, had to admit that she had behaved impeccably during the journey, sleeping slightly apart from the men, never complaining of discomfort, and traveling amazingly well.

"You've been trained to ride, haven't you?" he had said suspiciously after one particular night when they had covered a distance almost too great for a young female to accomplish.

"I used to get on my father's horses," she had answered casually.

"Don't give me that. No farmhouse nag could prepare you for this kind of feat. We've just covered 65 kilometers in one stint. Only a highly trained cavalry man could manage it."

Jehannette had shrugged her shoulders. "God helps me," she had said.

But Colet had been far from satisfied. He knew a skilled equestrian when he saw one and this peasant girl's riding abilities were quite clearly phenomenal. But he had let her explanation pass, not wanting to upset Jehanne in any way even though his slightly cynical feelings about her had now returned.

That she was sincere in the belief in her voices, de Vienne had no doubt. That the voices came from God rather than her own thoughts and wishes he was not so sure. Looking at her sideways, taking in the strong boyish physique, the tense face filled by the great dark eyes, he thought to himself that this was a very earthy little visionary.

"Tell me, Jehannette," he said matter-of-factly. "When you hear your voices do you also see their owners?"

"Oh, yes," she answered earnestly. "I have seen St. Michael, St. Catherine and St. Margaret. It is they who speak to me."

"Umm!" he thought, saying aloud, "What do they look like?"

"Like us, perfectly normal."

"Then how do you know they are saints?"

"Because they have beautiful crowns, very rich and precious. Anyway, they told me who they were."

"Did they resemble their statues in the church?"

"Very much."

"So that's it," thought Colet. "A highly strung pubescent girl, fasting and prone to hallucinate, imagines things and comes to save France as a result."

Yet that explanation was too facile. For a mere deluded adolescent, Jehannette had remarkable courage and staying power, and none of those interpretations could explain her stunning horsemanship, the ease with which she handled the sword she had been given. Turning it all over in his mind, Colet de Vienne came to a different conclusion, namely that a genuine clairvoyante, a girl of enormous psychic power, had received such forceful intuitions they had given her the confidence to step out of nowhere and proclaim her mission. And that somebody, some hidden person, had utilized this, had had the girl trained as a knight, a training which she had been only too willing to undergo in order to achieve her objective.

"Then let it be hoped that your saints, your voices, will help you to win back France for the Dauphin."

"They will," the girl answered positively. "They will never let me down."

"I pray not," Colet answered, and really meant it.

It was evening, the 21st February 1429, when Bertrand de Poulengy's party of riders eventually arrived beneath the walls of the château of Saumur, pale as a fairy castle in the rapidly fading light, and crossed the bridge to the Quartier des Ponts. In the gloaming they made their way to the town gate of the Château of the Queen of Sicily and traversed the small courtyard beyond, leaving their horses with the ostlers and making their way on foot through the arched entrance. And it was here that the group split up for the first time in eight days, Jehannette being led away by female servants to remove her travel-stained clothes, the men being taken to the guest lodging to eat and rest, awaiting further orders from Yolande d'Anjou.

A dress awaited Jehanne in the chamber which had been prepared for her, a dress of vermilion silk, the most beautiful she had ever seen.

"Madame the Queen asks you to put this on, Mademoiselle."

"But I couldn't, it is far too fine. Can't I wear my ordinary clothes?"

"I think not," answered the lady-in-waiting, specially assigned to serve the extraordinary girl she had been agog to see and about whom, already, there was so much rumor and speculation at court. "It would displease Madame not to comply with her request and, besides, I have been instructed to take your riding outfit away and have it cleaned."

"Then I must obey," the creature answered humbly, and took a sip of the wine that had been put in readiness for her, as if to give her courage.

An hour later Jehanne was ready, washed from head to foot and wearing the red dress, a color that suited her dark appearance well. In fact, thought the Queen's lady, the girl looked quite feminine and attractive, very different from the oddity that had arrived.

"If you will follow me, Madame the Queen has asked that you be taken to a little-used room in the château. This is to maintain the secrecy of your visit."

"I understand," the stranger replied, and went confidently enough through the galleries and down the stairways, making the Lady wonder at the strange mixture of her, the terrible *ydioma* accent, the boyish manner, all combined with an indefinable poise, as if someone had knocked the rough edges off, educated her in certain aspects of behavior and presentation.

"You're not afraid to meet the Queen?" she couldn't help asking, sworn as she was not only to keep this visit secret but to resist questioning the girl in any way.

"I am nervous and yet I am not."

"What does that mean?"

"That God is looking after me so I have no need to be

scared, yet it is still a daunting thing to mix with great men and women."

"I wish you luck in all that you do," answered the Lady simply and withdrew from the small unattached annexe, once the playing room for the Queen of Sicily's children, left empty now that they were grown. With her she took so many extraordinary impressions of a striking young person that she was forced to walk in the gardens for an hour, pitch dark thought it was, to clear her mind.

In the soft candlelight, Jehanne waited, not daring to move, knowing that her moment of destiny was very near and wishing that those voices which pierced her to the heart with their clarity, their profound and incredible messages, would come to her assistance now. But this night they were quiet and it was another voice which said, "Welcome to the Château. Was your journey difficult, ma Pucelle?"

Trained soldier that she was, the girl none the less started violently and peered into the gloom where a figure, clothed entirely in black, moved in the shadows.

"Who are you?" she whispered.

"A friend," came the reply, and Jehanne saw that a Benedictine Abbot stood before her.

She was on her knees before she knew it, grateful that a man of God had been sent to receive her, rather than a proud and sceptical Queen.

"There is no need for that," he answered, raising her up. "It is I who should be kneeling to you. You see, I have awaited your coming many years."

"I don't understand," Jehanne answered honestly.

"I had a vision when I was a boy that spoke to me of La Pucelle. So strong was its impact that I entered the cloister in order to serve you as best I could. Now I have handed the care of the Abbey to my Prior and am prepared to follow wherever you may lead me."

"You have seen them too? The saints?" Jehanne asked, gasping for breath.

"I saw nothing except a light, while a voice spoke inside my head."

"But there was something there?"

"Yes. Why do you ask that?"

"Because there have been moments, Father, when I have wondered, have suffered the sin of doubt, and thought perhaps I imagine it all."

"That could not be," Jacques answered her seriously. "Something, some force has given you the strength to come here. You are inspired, and inspiration in itself is divine."

She was in the presence of good intent and the girl knew it, knew that whatever might lie ahead this young man of God would never hurt or betray her.

"Then I ask you to be my confessor, to stay by my side until the end."

The words slashed like a sword through the air, speaking as they did of fate and finality.

"Bless me," said Jacques, kneeling before her.

"I cannot do that. I am the virgin from the woods, but no more." She hesitated, then said, "Yet that is not all the story, Father. There is something about me I have not told you."

"I know already. You are a Poor Knight of Christ and the Temple. You have been received into that Order."

Jehanne stared at him. "How did you know?"

"If I tell you that you will think it wrong, sinful."

"Nothing is sinful that strives for truth," Jehanne answered.

"My twin brother, as close to me as if he were part of my own flesh, is Astrologer Royal to the Queen of Sicily and it is he who saw you in his scrying glass, riding amongst the Templars."

"It is my mission not only to liberate France but to continue the deeds of the Order. My ultimate goal is to liberate the Tomb of Christ and the Holy Places from the power of Islam. The work of the Templars must go on."

Now Jacques understood the mystery of Jehanne fully. Ordinary peasant she may well have been born—though she seemed to have some air about her that suggested otherwise, yet that made little difference—she had been selected by some powerful person to continue where the Templars had so abruptly and cruelly been forced to finish. The Order, once so strong but now obviously driven underground, was to be revived through La Pucelle.

"Bless me," he begged again, and felt her hand lightly touch his head.

"I do no miracles but I give you my love."

"Then I am content," he said and stayed as he was for a moment, devoutly gazing on this strange dark girl whose eyes lit from within whenever she spoke of what must be done in the future.

And that was how Yolande saw her child for the first time in eleven years, in the act of blessing Abbot Jacques who knelt before her, the shape the two young people made harmonious and beautiful, almost as if an aura of goodness surrounded and glowed about them.

"Jehanne?" she said, and her darling, her love child, turned to look at her with her Spanish eyes, reminding the Queen yet again of King Juan, her father.

With an action that would have been faintly comic in any other circumstances, Jehanne bowed like a boy.

"Aye, I am Jehannette," she said.

"I prefer your grown-up name," answered Yolande and advanced toward her daughter as Jacques moved discreetly away, then through the door, leaving them alone together.

"Do I know you?" said the girl, puzzled. "I feel I do."

"You do and yet you don't. Suffice it to say that I have known you for many, many years."

Jehanne's sudden and very charming smile flashed across her face. "Well, that's not a very long time because I am young yet, as people keep reminding me."

"When one is young," Yolande answered, laughing a little, "one wishes to be older. But when one is old one wishes to be young. There's no pleasing people."

"*You* please me," Jehanne answered, "because you sent for me. That means you have faith in me, and I thank you for it."

"I know you for what you are," the Queen answered, "a pure and honest girl. But there are many at Court whispering that you are otherwise, that you are a witch, or even a common adventuress with whom the King should not associate."

"Who says this?"

"Georges de la Trémoille for one. But enough of that for this evening. Tomorrow I intend to prepare you as fully as I can for all that you will have to contend with at Court, so tonight you shall sleep at the Abbey of St. Hilaire St. Florent, to hide the fact you are in Saumur. But now it is time for the two of us to get to know one another. I would like you and me to sup together privately."

"It is strange but I feel there is no need to get to know you, I believe I am already your friend."

"So you trust me?"

"With my life," answered Jehanne and impulsively, and with no regard for the fact that the woman she was addressing was the Queen of Sicily, she kissed Yolande on the cheek.

Her mother froze beneath that wonderful embrace, not just because of her daughter's glorious proximity but because for the first time she could sense something of her power, her weakness, her strength and her vulnerability.

"Oh, my dear child," she said, and hugged her close, throwing caution to the winds, not behaving as a monarch should at all.

"Are you my friend?" Jehanne asked in that strangely direct and utterly captivating way of hers.

"For ever," answered Yolande, and allowed herself the luxury of joyful tears long, long overdue.

On the morning of 23rd February, after attending mass in Notre-Dame de Nantilly, Jehanne left Saumur for Chinon, trotting in the midst of her escort, dressed in her boy's suit, the beautiful red dress given by Yolande stowed away in her saddle-bag. Watching from a high window in her château, the Queen saw her go, her heart lurching with pride and faltering with fear for the brave little sprite setting out so boldly. But being the woman she was Yolande did not allow herself to sentimentalize, instead going to her private apartments and ordering her Ladies to prepare for a journey.

"Will you be visiting Chinon, ma Reine?"

"I feel confident my son-in-law will ask me to attend him there very soon. But even if he doesn't I shall go in any case. Nothing would keep me from being present when La Pucelle meets him for the first time."

Those words said, the Queen of Sicily went to her writing desk and with a wicked smile, knowing her son to be as great a master of deception as she, Yolande wrote to René, at last free of her self-imposed embargo not to endanger Jehanne by word.

"My dearest Child," she put. "Your wishes and instructions have been carried out and you will be pleased to learn that Jehanne the Maid has left safely for Chinon to see the King. All your efforts have borne fruit for the girl rides and carries her sword as proudly as any Knight of France . . .'

"And let him make of that what he will," Yolande said aloud.

". . . and I feel certain will impress all those with whom she comes in contact, just as she did me. Naturally I will keep you informed of every twist and turn in this, the most fascinating of adventures."

"And if that doesn't bring him hurrying to Court to see for himself I don't know what will," thought the Grand Master's mother.

Incredibly restless, she went to the window and looked out over the river to the tiny Isle de la Poissonnerie, joined to the Quartier des Ponts by a bridge, another small bridge leading from the isle to the right bank.

Everything Yolande could see from her vantage point suddenly seemed very tremulous and fresh; the banks of wild flowers on de la Poissonnerie sharp and colorful in the clear morning light, the wind ruffling the surface of the Loire so that the fishermen had to cast their lines with caution, while the high white sails of boats scudded past like cut-outs beneath the tight-budded willows and the bursting green-gold twigs.

"On such a morning it is right my daughter goes to seek her fortune," the Queen said to herself. "For it will always be remembered that she set out in the spring, a season as vivid as a crocus, just as she is."

A little shower appeared from nowhere and pelted the river with glistening drops.

"Soon there'll be a rainbow,' thought Yolande. 'Yes, I truly believe that soon there will be a rainbow."

Thirty

It was suffocatingly hot, the sheer press of bodies generating a heat that was almost unbearable. Outside, the February night was raw and sharp, the stars whipped to tatters by a bone-freezing wind, but within the hall women grew flushed and faint and great lords dripped sweat, while rank odors rose in abundance from the unwashed majority. Not for a long time could anyone recall seeing such an overpowering throng pack the Salle du Trône in the castle of Chinon, everyone chattering and laughing, loud as monkeys.

At one end of the room a huge fire burned in the stone hearth, devouring the half tree trunks thrown on to it, contributing enormously to the tremendous heat, while along the walls torches held in scones threw wavering lights and smoke and yet more warmth. Between these flambeaux hung majestic arras, some depicting biblical scenes, some mythological, the richness of their colors echoed in the clothes of the courtiers. Velvets and brocades, towering hennins, furs, jewels, everything fine had been brought out for this wildly exciting occasion, the arrival of the virgin from Lorraine, whose presence in Chinon for the last three days had set the whole place in uproar.

The girl about whom everyone was talking, Jehanne la Pucelle as she was generally referred to, had been staying in the hostelry Grand Carroi while the King dithered, torn between de la Trémoille, who said she was either witch or whore, possibly both, and Yolande, for whose advice Charles had sent immediately, and who declared roundly that her son-in-law would be a fool if he did not interview the girl. And meanwhile, his own curiosity was driving him mad.

"Is it possible that this peasant could be our salvation?" Charles had whispered to Marie, not daring to hope.

"Stranger things have happened—at least I think so! Why don't you receive her?"

"Georges says I would be consorting with a hired slut if I do."

"Only because he's afraid of what she might say," Marie answered acutely and in exasperation. "For God's sake, Charles, see the girl at least."

There was a very faint stirring of some of his old spirit and just for a second the faun who had ridden to battle at the head of his troops shimmered a smile at his wife.

"Very well, I will. She shall come tomorrow night. I'll instruct Colet de Vienne to tell her."

And it was as well for Charles that he had made that decision, for the following morning, riding with a large escort which included Abbot Jacques and his brother Guy, the Queen of Sicily appeared with much jingling of harness, the very crispness of her arrival indicating that she had arrived to see the legendary Jehanne, and was not in a mood to take no for an answer.

And now the evening had come, the court packed to the doors, the atmosphere crackling with undisguised excitement, and everyone awaiting the moment when the Monseigneur Comte de Vendôme, who had gone down to the town on horseback, ushered in the virgin from the woods.

Outside the walls of the huge fortress, which was really three castles in one and had two internal moats within its enceinte, the night grew colder, sharp as needles, as out of the bustling town where the houses leaned close to one another, came Jehanne. Following the rough track that wound upward to where the Château sat on a high hill, her black horse picked its way behind that of the priestly Comte, through a thin line of people who had braved the February wind to come and watch her. A child gave a shrill cheer and waved as she passed by—but Jehanne saw nothing except the frosty stars, knowing that tonight irrevocably sealed the rest of her life.

Following her guide, almost in a trance, La Pucelle entered the castle by way of the town gate and made her way past the Fort St. Georges, then over the drawbridge which spanned the first moat and through the archway of the Clock Tower. Now she found herself in the central château, in a great courtyard lit by flickering torches, red-cheeked ostlers at the ready to help her dismount and take her horse. Fear came, black and fathomless, at the sight of it all and just for a second Jehanne stayed where she was, almost as if she would turn her horse and gallop off into the night. But then the noise and light coming from the building lying directly in front of her caught her attention and she knew that she must take this last step if everything prophesied by her voices was to be fulfilled.

"Ready?" said Vendôme, casually, coolly, not wanting to take sides or in any way show favor to this peculiar creature whom he had believed to be a transvestite but who tonight wore a dress of vermilion silk and would have looked feminine were it not for the shortness of her hair.

"Yes, Monseigneur," said Jehanne, and unkilting her skirt slipped out of the saddle and onto the mounting block.

"The King awaits you in there." And the Count pointed to the hive of activity which faced them.

"He and many others to judge by the noise."

"The whole court has turned out to see you. Does that make you nervous?"

"Very. But God will give me strength to cope with it."

"Well, that's as well," Vendôme replied drily.

There were seven steep steps leading up from the court-yard to the first floor salon which reared above their heads, enormous and imposing, its mullioned windows blazing with light. Standing on the very top step was a page, obviously a look-out who, as he saw the couple approach, turned on his heel and rushed within. And as she reached the entrance Jehanne heard the high harsh call of the King's trumpets and realized that they were for her, that the boy had given a secret signal, and that the aim of such a display was probably to make her even more nervous than she already was.

The girl took a step forward then stopped, the sight before her dazed eyes unbelievable, the glitter of jewels, the sumptuous colors of fine materials, the dark svelte sweep of furs, melding into a living tapestry of people. She had never in her life seen anything so rich, so decadent, so totally removed from everything she was herself. And yet there was a fatal fascination about it. Quite unconsciously Jehanne found that she was studying the women, some flaunting high bare breasts, wondering how it could be that

though she and they were all female, the ladies of the court
had elegance and beauty whereas she was tall and muscular, undeniably boyish, far more at ease dressed in men's
clothing. And then she remembered her training as a knight
and dismissed such irrelevant ideas from her mind. Advancing into the room Jehanne gazed round for the Dauphin.

She saw him at once, knew immediately who he was,
even though he had hidden himself away in a group of
courtiers and put another man in his clothes and chair of
state. A silly trick yet one she had more or less expected
as a test of her clairvoyant powers. Smiling unconcernedly,
Jehanne made her way toward him and without hesitation
went down on her knees at his royal feet.

"Sweet Dauphin," she said, "God grant you long life. I
am Jehanne la Pucelle and have come to tell you that you
will be crowned and consecrated at Reims and that day
become the lieutenant of the King of Heaven, who is the
King of France."

Charles stared at her open-mouthed. "But . . ."

Jehanne shook her head slightly. "Do not deny that you
are he born to rule France. That other man may wear your
clothes but he could never wear your crown, sweet Prince."

She had captured his interest completely, she knew it.
"May I speak with you privately, Monsieur?" Jehanne went
on, using her advantage. "There are things I would say that
are for your ears alone."

Charles gazed at her, dumbfounded, and it was several
seconds before he found his voice and answered huskily,
"If you wish it we can withdraw to that recess. Please rise."

She did so, turning her head slightly, and at that moment
had one sweeping glimpse of the room. The courtiers
looked stupefied, unable to credit that their coxcomb King,
the idiotic boy who had not lived up to one grain of his
early promise, had not only made a decision for himself,
but was drawing the peasant girl into a window embrasure,
ordering the guards to clear it of people. The fat man,
whom she was certain must be Georges de la Trémoille,
could be seen seething with fury, his twinkling eyes hard
as pebbles. But Yolande and, most surprisingly, Prince
René, who had obviously traveled from Lorraine expressly
to be present, were both smiling, as were the Abbot
Jacques and his hunchbacked twin.

"Thank you," said Jehanne to her God, her saints, her King, and raised Charles's hand to her lips.

He almost exclaimed aloud, fighting to keep tight control of his emotions, but already there was a pricking of his spine, a stinging behind his eyes, a leap of his soul out of darkness toward the light.

"No one can hear us here," he said, and motioned the girl to sit beside him on the long padded cushion made specially to cover the window's wide stone sill, an extraordinary gesture for a King to make to a peasant.

"Thank you," she said again.

He was trying desperately to study her dispassionately, without feeling, as if she were just another commoner come before him to beg a favor, but it was impossible. Against his will, Charles found himself drawn toward the girl, to such an extent he could do nothing but stare straight into the dark, spellbinding eyes that were gazing at him so candidly.

Like a dying man he saw his life pass before him: he saw all that he had become, a puny midget of a thing fighting for survival, a nothing, a vainglorious puff of wind allowing itself to be ruled by futile creatures, when it should be he who gave the orders, held the reins, issued the commands that would pick his poor bleeding country up from the ground and stand it on its feet once more. Charles saw his shallowness, his attitudinizing, his lack of integrity; saw his lassitude, his depression, the low state into which he had allowed himself to be dragged.

"Who are you?" he whispered.

"She who has come to tell you on behalf of God that you need have no more doubts. That you are the heir of France and as such will be anointed and crowned in Reims Cathedral."

It was impossible to pretend with her and Charles answered bitterly, "But what if I am a bastard? What then? For sometimes in my nightmares I think perhaps that is why my kingdom is slowly being taken from me. Because I am not, after all, its rightful heir and it should indeed go to Catherine's son."

"But even if you are *not* the late King's child," Jehanne answered simply, "then you *are* most certainly the person chosen by God to rule France for Him. My voices told me so. That is why I have been sent to you. To put an end to

the siege of Orléans and ensure that you are anointed with
France's sacred oil. Because that is what God wants."

It was said so positively, with such complete conviction,
such obvious sincerity, that there could be no arguing with
the statement.

"You are certain of this?" Charles answered dazedly.

"I am absolutely sure."

"And these visitations, these voices of yours, how do
they manifest themselves exactly?"

He saw her grow slightly defensive. "Usually three saints
come to me, giving instructions and commands about what
I must do. Though at other times I hear them speak without
actually seeing anything. It is they, acting as God's messengers, who told me I had been chosen to save France."

"But in order to do that, in order to raise the siege of
Orléans, you would have to fight the English. How could
a girl do that? It is a matter for hardened soldiers."

Jehanne made no reply and for once seemed to be
avoiding his eyes, giving Charles the strong impression that
for some reason she did not want to answer. He decided,
for the moment at least, not to press the point.

"How long have these saints been coming?" he asked,
puzzling about what it was that she, who was patently so
open, was suddenly trying to hide.

"Since I was thirteen," she replied, obviously relieved at
the change of subject. "The first time was when I was in
my father's garden, the second happened in the woods. I
picked a flower to remind me of when they first came, and
have kept it since." The girl fished inside her long sleeve
used, in the manner of ladies of the court, as a pocket, and
drew out a faded bloom, long dead and pressed flat.
"Here," she said impulsively, "here, sweet Dauphin, you
can have it if you like."

Charles looked down into the palm of his hand and as
he took in what he held a million comets seemed to burst
inside his brain. For now, at last, all was clear: the prophecy
had not lied. A rose lay there, a faded red rose, and the
voice of Nicolas Flamel rang in his memory as clearly as if
the old man had spoken yesterday.

"Three women will help you. One is a tall queen ..."
Yolande obviously. "... another a virgin bringing a rose ..."
By god's passion what other description could there be for
this glowing child sitting next to him? "... the third will be

beauty to your beast." Poor dead Bonne, rotting some-where in her unmarked grave.

"Oh, God!" said Charles, "Oh God! So you haven't for-saken me! Then be thanked for this great mercy, and for revealing her at last."

For the first time in years the color came into his cheeks and he felt a surge of energy which had him jumping to his feet.

"It's true! You are the virgin with the rose predicted long ago. So you have finally come to me."

"I am indeed your salvation," answered Jehanne, once more kissing his hand. "And to prove it let me tell you things about yourself that you have not yet confided to a living soul. For every night, sweet Dauphin, I know that you pray God to rescue and defend you if the Kingdom of France is truly yours by right but, should it not be so, to allow you to forget you were ever a King and let you go to live in peace in Spain or Scotland."

Charles gazed at her, no longer in astonishment but now in awe.

"Then you are indeed a true visionary for you have just spoken aloud the secrets of my heart."

"By the sign of the rose," answered Jehanne.

It was too much for the overwrought young man listening to her and he started to weep, quietly at first and then more and more emotionally. And as the faint sound of his sobs was heard first by one group of courtiers, then an-other, a silence fell over the entire company gathered in the Salle du Trône in Chinon. There was not a whisper from anywhere except for the crying of the King and the faint breathing of the girl who sat beside him on the win-dow seat, tears dampening her own flushed cheeks as she watched him. Huge in his golden robes, de la Trémoille made to move toward them but was forestalled by the Queen of Sicily, dark as midnight in her deep blue dress, and just as forbidding.

"My Lords and Ladies," she announced in clarion tones, "gentlemen and retainers, the court is cleared. There is no need for any of you to stay. The King would be private with his guest."

"But, Madame ..." boomed Georges, only to find that she was ready for him.

"My son," she said, referring to Charles not René,

"wishes to confer only with La Pucelle, his immediate family and his astrologers. Nobody else should remain except for the Abbot of St. Nicolas and the Astrologer Royal of Anjou. Thank you, Monsieur. Good evening."

And she turned her back. Short of making a public scene, de la Trémoille had no choice open to him. He had been dismissed by a Queen. There was nothing for it but to leave the room with as good a grace as possible.

"And may that see the beginning of his end," Yolande hissed at his departing bulk.

"A pity," said René, watching him go. "He used to be so amusing. But oh, how power corrupts!"

"Richemont said to me shortly after de Giac's execution that there is always another one coming up from somewhere."

"Richemont," René repeated thoughtfully. "Is he still banished?"

"Only while de la Trémoille holds sway. But nothing, not even banishment, will stop the Earl from rallying to Jehanne's call. I'm sure of it."

"She is just what we need if she can summon men such as him."

"Yes," answered Yolande severely, "she is." She turned to look at her son. "Now, are you going to tell Charles the truth about her?"

A look of pure astonishment crossed his raven face. "You know?"

"Of course I know. Alison told me long ago that you had discovered a visionary peasant girl and subsequently sent her for training in the use of arms. Why did you do that, René?"

"Because otherwise she would have ended up dead. God, the saints, simple clairvoyance, her own mind, whatever it is that drives her on, was telling her to go to war against the English. Can you imagine that, Mother? She would have lasted five minutes if she'd been lucky. I *had* to do something and I truly believe in protecting her I also did the best for France."

"Is she a member of the Knights Templar?"

"Yes, she has been received into the Order, the only woman in their entire history. Jehanne has become a fully-fledged warrior-nun."

"Why did you not tell me this before? Why did you try and deceive even me?"

"Because," answered René solemnly, "there are some secrets too deep ever to be revealed. Surely you would agree with that?"

Looking from her bastard daughter to her legitimate son, then back again, Yolande said equally solemnly, "Indeed I do."

The wheel of fortune had finally turned. Everyone who mattered to the newly buoyant Charles agreed with him that Jehanne should be taken seriously. The Astrologer Royal of France, Master Pierre de St. Valérin, concurred with the Astrologer Royal of Anjou, Hunchback Guy, that this was definitely the virgin whose mission was written in the stars, and quoted the predictions of Marie of Avignon that France would be saved by the intercession of an untouched girl. The King's mother-in-law herself announced her willingness to act as Jehanne's sponsor, the Abbot of St. Nicolas declared himself convinced that the miracle had finally taken place. Even Marie abandoned the royal nurseries and had a long conversation with Jehanne, who had been given accommodation in the Tower of Coudray, the place where Jacques de Molay, the last official Grand Master of the Knights Templar, had been kept prisoner, a somewhat grim residence chosen by herself.

Another who flocked to her cause was the young Duke of Alençon, Charles's beautiful brave cousin, whose father had been killed at Azincourt, making the boy a Duke when he was only six, and who had himself been taken prisoner by the English on the field of Verneuil when he had been barely fifteen. For three years the boy had remained locked up in the Fortress of Le Crotoy until his family had managed to raise his vast ransom money, and now he itched to get back into the fight. D'Alençon's attraction to Jehanne was also greatly enhanced by the fact that he adored the supernatural, fascinated by both astrologers and clairvoyants. Once having made her acquaintance, the young Duke spent hours in La Pucelle's company, sitting slavishly at her feet like an adoring dog.

So, with the entire Court either siding with Jehanne or pretending to do so because it was fashionable, it was left to a mere couple of people, Georges de la Trémoille and

Regnault de Chartres, Archbishop of Reims, to make trouble. Arguing in Council that Jehanne might just as well be an envoy of the Devil as of God, they insisted that she should undergo some sort of trial to prove her spiritual allegiance.

Yolande moved against the two decisively. First, she had Jehanne received into the Third Order of St. Francis, knowing the power and piety of the Franciscan movement, inducted by the Mother Superior of the Order of St. Clare, Colette de Corbie herself. Next, she persuaded Charles, only too willing to listen in his present state of jubilation, that if there were indeed to be a trial and a physical examination of Jehanne—this insisted upon by de la Trémoille who declared that if the girl were the Devil's bitch then she most certainly could not be a virgin—it must be undertaken by the preaching orders.

Thinking that he had made his point Georges agreed to this, and it was decided that Jehanne should go to Poitiers where the doctors of law and theology who had left Paris at the time of Burgundy's invasion had set up a rival university.

"How do you feel about going on trial?" Charles asked the girl, alone with her in her bleak tower.

"I object to the delay but not to the inquiry itself. It's just that the longer I leave them at Orléans the worse their situation will get. And, of course, they are now expecting me."

And it was true. Word had reached the beleaguered city that a miraculous virgin had appeared whose avowed intent it was to relieve the siege, and messages came regularly from the Bastard repeatedly asking when the girl was to join him.

"I sympathize with you," Charles answered, thinking seriously about what he was saying. "But Queen Yolande believes the only way to refute those who doubt you is by recourse to theologians."

"Then she must be right for she is a good woman. And besides, my voices will tell me what answers to make."

The King smiled faintly. "Jehanne, I know you are the predicted one, and I believe in you completely ..."

"But?"

"But there is still one thing that worries me. How can you, a seventeen-year-old girl from Domrémy, take command of an army of mercenaries, of rabble, most of them deserving little better than the gallows? How can you convince the hardened generals, especially that devil La Hire, to follow you? And, most of all, how can an innocent virgin possibly engage in physical fighting?"

There was silence, then finally Jehanne put out her hand and said, "Come with me. There is something I have to show you."

Simultaneously apprehensive and mystified, the King followed her down the stone staircase to the room below, the place in which the wretched Templars had eked out their last days before being taken away for execution.

"Here," said Jehanne, and made her way to the northern wall, on which the prisoners had engraved messages in the stone. Charles gazed on the rough plan of a church, a radiant heart, monk's faces, the cross and instruments of the crucifixion, a raised hand.

"There are messages too," added La Pucelle, and her fingers traced out the name J. Molay, scratched above the representation of a stag being hunted down by a hound.

"The last Grand Master of the Templars."

"Not the last. They are still in existence though long ago forced to become an underground stream. I am one of them, sweet Dauphin. You need have no fears for my safety. I am a Poor Knight of Christ."

"But that is not possible."

"It is," said a voice from the arched and vaulted doorway and Charles swung round to see that it was René d'Anjou's lean frame which had suddenly blotted out the light.

"What do you mean?"

For answer, René held up his extraordinary hands, and the disproportionately long little fingers cast their own small shadow.

"Years ago you asked me if I knew a man called Nicolas Flamel and I did not answer you. The reason was that though I knew the name it meant nothing to me at the time. It was only when I went to Lorraine that my great-uncle, the Cardinal of Bar, told me that Flamel had nominated me as the next Grand Master of the Priory of Sion, the secret society who at one time had been the non-military arm of the Knights Templar."

"But why you? A child?"

"That I will never know but, whatever the reason, I be-

came the guardian of the Priory's secrets, one of which
was that many of the Templars remain alive, have gone
underground, and that an entire chapter is active in
Scotland."

"It was to them that I was sent for my training," said
Jehanne. "And it was into that chapter I was finally received as a member of the Order."

So now it was clear. La Pucelle's ability as a horsewoman, spoken of in awed tones by the King's courtiers,
and her incredible strength with the lance, discovered by
the handsome d'Alençon, who liked nothing better than to
take the girl into the tilt-yard to joust, was explained.

"Is the Queen of Sicily aware of all this?"

"Oh, yes," René replied wryly. "My amazing mother
found out, as she always does everything."

"Amazing indeed!"

"I like her," said Jehanne. "You are both very lucky to
be her kin. I envy you that privilege."

The Trial of Poitiers was without doubt a great success,
Jehanne mostly answering the examiners' questions with
patience and humor. Only once did she come near to losing
her temper, shouting out, "In God's name, I have not come
to Poitiers to make proofs—but take me to Orléans, and
I'll show you the sign for which I have been sent."

She had then gone on to make four predictions to the
court of inquiry: that the siege of Orléans would be raised
and the English defeated; that the Dauphin, whom she declared she would not call King until he had been anointed
with sacred oil, would be crowned at Reims; that Paris
would be taken and returned to the King; and that Charles,
Duke of Orléans, would be set free after being a prisoner
of the English for twenty-five years.

"And if these things do not come true, and more, then
you may indeed denigrate me as a false prophet."

But, when all was said and done, they were only words
and Regnault de Chartres, head of the inquiry and no
champion of the girl, an ally of de la Trémoille, persisted
that she should still be physically examined to prove that
she was both female and *virgo intacta*. It was the Queen of
Sicily who was finally nominated for this task, in company
with Madame de Gaucourt, wife of the governor of Orléans, and Lady de Trèves, wife of Robert le Maçon.

Yolande had gone alone into the room where Jehanne lay upon the table, stripped of all her clothing and naked as on the day of her birth, which her mother still remembered as though it were yesterday. Glancing at her daughter, the Queen could see what she already well knew. Jehanne was obviously female, though very small in the breast and packed with sinew and muscle. Yet, on stepping closer, there was indeed on small peculiarity which would not have shown itself in a baby but would have become apparent as the child grew. To her horror, Yolande d'Anjou realized that the lips of her secret parts were joined together by nature and there was no doubt that Jehanne would remain a virgin for the rest of her life.

"Have you menstruated?" the Queen asked abruptly, too shocked to tread delicately.

"No, I am still waiting," answered the girl, blushing wildly, obviously not used to such direct questioning. "Why?"

Yolande thought rapidly, and lied. "Because sometimes athletic girls such as yourself never do."

"Really? It would be helpful not to in my case."

Poor little creature, so innocent and yet so tough. "I feel that perhaps you will be exempt," the Queen said quietly, and then, spontaneously, planted a kiss on her daughter's freshly scrubbed cheek. "Now put on your breeches and I will call in the other ladies."

"But won't they want to look at me as well?"

"Just your top half. I will not let you be embarrassed further."

Nor did she, and it was Yolande's sworn word alone that Jehanne was a true and intact virgin that was given to the court.

"In whom I can say there is manifest no corruption or violence," the Queen concluded her evidence.

"Definitely?" asked Archbishop Regnault de Chartres.

"Definitely," she replied with dignity.

And with that matters were finally done. The hearing retired to deliberate their findings and Jehanne, in the confident hope that they would decide in her favor, dictated a challenge addressed to the King of England and the Duke of Bedford, "who call yourself Regent of France," telling them to leave the city of Orléans or "wait for news of La

Pucelle who will shortly come to see you to your very great loss."

It was a threatening and belligerent letter in which Jehanne described herself as chief of the army, and it was enough to push the tribunal in her favor. On 24th March 1429, she left Poitiers in triumph, the next move to equip her as a fully-fledged knight of France, the indignity of the court hearing behind her.

The armorer's shop in the town of Tours seemed a veritable palace of splendor and excitement to Jehanne, who unashamedly adored weapons and all the accompanying accouterments of war. Filled with the sound of clinking hammers, pieces of armor displayed all about the place, it held as much fascination and charm for her as a merchant's warehouse would for any other girl of her age. La Pucelle stood, half smiling, one foot upon a velvet cushion, being fitted into the leg pieces of the small but extremely special suit of armor that was being made for her, twirling a flower that an admirer had given her in one hand, the fingers of the other resting lightly upon the hilt of her sword, a sword which had indeed been found by truly miraculous means.

Those piercing voices which told her everything that guided her life, had whispered that a sword lay buried in the ground near the altar in the shrine of St. Catherine de Fierbois. When a search party had looked where Jehanne had described, they had indeed found something, an old crusader weapon decorated with five crosses on its blade, extremely rusty but for all that in good condition. An armorer at Chinon had sharpened and cleaned it for her and now she wore the sword constantly, only taking it off when she went to bed. To those who had had any doubts left about the girl's visionary powers, the finding of the sword had been proof positive that Jehanne was a genuine clairvoyant.

"The saboton is not too big for you?" asked the armorer, slipping on one of the foot pieces.

"No, I don't think so." Jehanne stretched her toes inside the metal. "It seems a good fit."

"Then that's well."

He grinned cheerfully, immensely flattered to have been asked to create the girl's entire armor, separate pieces usually being made by different people and then assembled together, and delighted by the fee of 100 *livres tournois* being paid to him by the Queen of Sicily herself.

"In fact I'm very pleased with all of it," Jehanne went on, and looked down at the extraordinary little suit with obvious satisfaction.

"What a warlike creature it is," thought the man, unable to stop himself wondering if such a girl could be absolutely normal.

"You look superbly savage," said a voice from the door, and both Jehanne and the armorer gazed round to see who had come into the shop.

It had become the habit for various young dandies of Tours to follow the miraculous Pucelle around, studying and marking what she was doing and who she was going to see, and it had not been a surprise to either Jehanne or the craftsman to observe a small group of youths watching her through the shop window. But now one of them had detached himself and come in, standing in the doorway, looking at Jehanne with a certain amusement, determined to catch La Pucelle's eye and wink.

It did not need the cry of her voices to warn the girl that she was in the presence of evil, nor the prick of thumbs to tell her that here was wickedness made flesh. So it was very slowly that Jehanne braced herself before staring into the furnace of the stranger's pupils.

The man's smile deepened. "I greet you," he said.

"And I greet you," she answered steadily.

They stood looking at one another, not as a man and a girl, but as two adversaries of old.

"Why have you come?" she said quietly.

"To be at your side," he answered. "For you need me. You have no true meaning unless I accompany you, ma Pucelle."

The armorer, made uncomfortable by the strangeness of their conversation, stood up from his kneeling position at Jehanne's feet.

"Well," he said, rubbing his hands together, "that's that then, I'm glad you're satisfied, Mamzelle."

The girl turned to look at him and he saw that her eyes were far away, not thinking of her armor or his shop or anything remotely to do with reality.

"Thank you," she answered automatically, then gazed once more at the stranger. "Introduce yourself, Monsieur."

He bared his strong white teeth. "Gilles, ma Pucelle. Gilles de Rais. I am a *Maréchal* in the army of which you are so soon to take command."

"I see," answered Jehanne, smiling to herself. "So you will indeed be always by me."

"I will never leave you, you know that."

"Yes, I do."

"Will that be all?" said the armorer, coughing.

Gilles de Rais laughed, a harsh sound. "I think La Pucelle has done with you, yes."

Jehanne took control of the situation, pulling the metal gauntlet from her hand and holding it out to the craftsman.

"You have done well and I am grateful. Pray for me."

"I will," the armorer answered, kissing her fingers.

"And now to battle," said Gilles softly.

"Yes indeed," answered Jehanne, drowning him with her eyes, "now to battle."

Thirty-one

No one who saw La Pucelle set out from Blois to relieve the City of Orléans would ever forget the sight. As a symbol of her purity she rode a white horse, while over her head fluttered a white silk banner depicting the world in God's hand, two angels at His side, the background fleur-de-lis, the words Jhesu Maria written above. Behind Jehanne rode the members of her household: Jean d'Aulon, the squire, Jean Pasquerel, her chaplain; Abbot Jacques, her confessor; two pages, Louis de Contes and Raymond; her two brothers, come especially from Domrémy, and finally two heralds, Ambleville and Guyenne.

Over her silver armor Jehanne wore a short red cloak, her head covered by a hat of crimson felt, her helmet carried by d'Aulon. She had been appointed Chef de Guerre by Charles VII and there was not one of the great soldiers of France who was not now answerable to her.

The entire court had turned out to see La Pucelle go to war: Charles and Marie and their first-born child, six-year-old Dauphin Louis, who waved his little handkerchief to Jehanne; Yolande, openly weeping, her enemies whispering that it was because she had sold her silver and jewels in order to raise enough money to pay the soldiers and buy provisions for the people of Orléans; de la Trémoille who, to his credit, had negotiated at all levels to get La Pucelle extra help, trying to smile; Regnault de Chartres, reluctantly giving the girl blessing. As to the military leaders, they had every one of them either been persuaded or bribed to accept their extraordinary new commander with as much good grace as possible.

The most difficult of all to either impress or win round had

been, without doubt, Captain Etienne de Vignolles, known as
La Hire by the mercenaries, of whom he was one, a man of
such repute that he had kept his men loyal to him throughout
five grueling years of defeat. He was too tough a warrior to
be impressed with talk of God and holy virgins and Yolande
d'Anjou had done the most sensible thing and filled his
pocket with a handsome *douceur*. Now, leaving the lines of
troops, La Hire gave La Pucelle a florid salute and verbally
pledged his allegiance to her. At this, the Marshal de Rais
raised a cheer which was taken up by the ranks. So it was in
the midst of the army's jubilant cries that Jehanne finally rode
out of Blois at the start of her mission.

Still weeping, Yolande d'Anjou turned to go back into
the château.

"My good mother," said Charles following her, "why are
you so sad? Are you not convinced, as I am, that La Pucelle
will lead us to victory?"

"But at what cost to herself?" answered Yolande bitterly.
"She is a child, a seventeen-year-old. How can we do this
to her?"

"Because she is inspired," Charles replied, meaning it.
"This is no ordinary girl going off to fight. This is the
prophesied one, remember that."

But Yolande was too distressed to answer, a strange combination of pride and anguish fighting in her soul. Yet over-
riding those feelings came another, a certainty that events
had now moved too far for the Earl of Richmond, still
banished from court and stripped of office, to be left in
ignorance of the truth. A desperate need to see him, to
confide in him all that was in her over-burdened heart,
overcame the Queen and, as she had done so often in the
past, Yolande sat down to write the Earl a letter.

Then, because she had made up her mind at last, everything had to be done on the instant. Knowing that he was,
after all their years together, still unable to resist her summons, Yolande wrote, "Meet me in two days' time at
Saumur. I must see you on a matter of extreme urgency. I
shall leave Blois at once in order to receive you there."

And then she slept, awaiting his return, as did her daughter, already so many miles away from all who loved her.

What a frenzied dream came to Jehanne that night, camped
beside the great river opposite the Grande Isle aux Boeufs,

within sight of the besieged city of Orléans. What tormented thoughts could have been in her sleeping mind that
she saw herself deserted, leading the assault against the
English alone, her only companion Gilles de Rais, who
rode stark naked beside her.

The dream changed, the battle over, and she and Gilles,
laurel wreaths crowning their heads, played chess, the
board representing the world and the pieces all of humanity. Jehanne drew off her gauntlets and moved the first
pawn, standing to see the board better, noticing that Gilles
was surrounded by children whom he fondled intimately.

"You disgust me," she said.

"But still fascinate you."

And he spoke the truth. He, the most depraved creature
alive, the epitome of wickedness and cruelty, aroused unspeakable emotions within her undefiled and innocent
breast.

"I shall fight you until time runs out."

"That is our destiny, Jehanne. Good and evil inextricably
linked, one unable to exist without the other. That is why
we, the two opposing ends of the scale, must be lovers."

"But we hate one another."

"What difference? Those emotions are so akin that they
are almost indistinguishable."

They played on, a brilliant cruel game, the outcome of
which lay in the balance.

Gilles laughed as he took Jehanne's bishop. "A church-
man! Could you not guess that he would be the first to
topple?"

"God will protect me," answered La Pucelle.

"He did not save His own Son," said Gilles and once
more smiled that terrible beautiful smile of his. "My God,
why hast Thou forsaken me?"

It was then that Jehanne knew real fear. Her great faith
was under attack.

"Love me," whispered her adversary, "love me and I will
relinquish my claim on the world," and de Rais kissed her
naked feet.

"No, I can never be yours."

But even as she said it, Jehanne knew that she must give
herself to him to save mankind, that only by her sacrifice
could evil be put to flight. She flung herself down upon his
bed, seeing her own flesh, white as milk, raked by the

strands of her long ebony hair, the scarlet of her spilled blood fresh upon the linen sheets.

"I am La Pucelle no more," she cried, and wondered as she woke why Gilles wept for her instead of laughed.

Richemont arrived in the dawning of the appointed day, covered with dust and somewhat disgruntled. He had been lying low at his estates in Parthenay, not far from Poitiers, and had ridden by night in order not to attract attention. Now the Earl crossed the bridge leading to the Quartier des Ponts fully masked, a fact that made Yolande, who was watching from the window of the high tower, smile to herself.

And then, unbidden and most certainly unwanted, the Queen suddenly felt her customary self-confidence vanish. It occurred to her harshly that soon she would be in her fiftieth year while Richemont was still in his thirties, and she wondered, frighteningly, if she had gone too far in demanding his presence when he was officially exiled. Flying to her mirror, she rapidly applied paints and brushes then, as an afterthought, fixed the great emerald that matched her eyes to her head-dress before she went downstairs.

The Earl looked tired, she thought, and somewhat older, gray streaks showing in his dark hair and lines visible round his eyes that had not been there eighteen months earlier.

"You are well, Monsieur?" she asked formally.

"Aye, but bored to the bone. What I would not give to be going to Orléans with the rest of the soldiers."

"Then perhaps you should go," she answered quietly.

The Earl looked at her wryly. "And risk imprisonment? No, I could not endure that again."

"I don't think, believe, such a thing would happen. They are desperate for help, for leaders and for men. Nobody would make a move against you, especially if you took orders signed by myself."

"You carry so much weight there?"

"I paid for the army."

He grinned, some of his old look returning to his face. "I might have guessed. You haven't changed, have you baggage? Come and kiss me."

She rushed into his arms, helter skelter. "Oh, thank goodness. A moment ago I thought you no longer loved me."

"Why, in the name of God?" said Richemont, holding her at arm's length, looking into her face.

"Because I am getting old, not in my head but in my body. My flux is leaving me, I have got wrinkles, I have to peer to see things clearly."

He swung her in the air. "You will never change, my Queen. You will remain a girl until the day you die. As for me, my opponent at Azincourt did me an enormous favor."

"What do you mean?"

"He aged me so rapidly that I can never look worse, except perhaps to add a few minor rivers to the map of France!"

She laughed at him. "I have missed you very much."

"And I you."

"Then why not earn Charles's gratitude and go to fight at Orléans? I will take full responsibility."

Richemont stretched himself like a weary cat then, sitting down, began to pull off his riding boots. "I'll think about it when I've had some sleep. It's been a long hard ride."

"I'm sure it has. Will you go to bed straight away?"

"If you'll come with me."

She laughed again, very happy now. "You may go but I will not join you for a while. There is something I must do."

"And what is that?"

"Write to you."

"What are you talking about, sweet and senseless creature? I am here with you. There is no need."

"There is every need. This is a letter I should have written eighteen years ago."

The Earl shook his head, frowning. "Eighteen years?"

"Don't puzzle over it. I will put the parchment on your pillow while you sleep. When you are fully awake read it, then call for me."

He smiled at her lazily. "You need never worry about getting old, you know."

"How do you mean?"

"You are so utterly intriguing, so full of surprises, that time will be far too daunted to cross your threshold."

"I hope so," answered Yolande and kissed him lightly on the cheek.

Thirty-two

When the Duke of Bedford had first besieged the city of Orléans, he had intended that the affair would be quick and bloody, forcing the Orleanists into rapid surrender, but in that his hopes had been dashed. Jean the Bastard, a brilliant soldier, commanded the French troops in a town which was almost impregnable, protected on the south by the mighty river, and on the north, east and west by a series of moats and walls. Unfortunately, at the start of their campaign, the English had taken the suburb of Portereau on the south bank, together with the monastery of the Augustinians and the twin towers of the bridge, Les Tourelles. With the English encamped on the far end, the governor, Raoul de Gaucourt, in conference with the Bastard, had been forced to cut the bridge in half, thus stopping the Angloys-Françoys from simply swarming across.

The Earl of Salisbury, leading the English attack, had been mortally wounded by a shell splinter, fatefully thrown across the river by a boy playing a prank, and the Earl of Suffolk, who had stepped into the command, had decided to reverse Bedford's decision and starve the Orleanists out slowly rather than go into headlong attack. So in that harsh winter as Jehanette Darc had trudged through the snows to Vaucouleurs, Suffolk's troops had spent the time building gigantic forts round Orléans, all connected to one another by trenches and walls.

But now the snows had gone, it was the spring of 1429, and the relieving force had been at Orléans seven days, having arrived on the south bank of the Loire opposite the city on the morning of 28th April.

At first, Jehanne had been furious to discover that the

river lay between her and the main English camp, which stood firmly entrenched outside the city walls. Her voices, most irritatingly as far as the great captains were concerned, had advised her that it was the camp that should be attacked first and, moreover, from the north, an almost impossible feat as the French army was drawn up on the south. That night she had gone to sleep in a terrible mood which had been slightly mollified when the Bastard of Orléans, risking his life beneath English arrow fire, had crossed the Loire by boat especially to meet her.

"Why didn't you let me get straight at Talbot?" La Pucelle had said to him without preamble. "We haven't come here to mess about. We should go straight into battle."

"We can't," he had answered shortly. "We would be wiped out."

"Why?"

"Because our army is too small. No, what is far more important at this stage is that we get the supplies you brought with you into the city."

Jehanne had agreed with bad grace but the following night as soon as darkness fell she had boarded one of the craft in the flotilla that was standing by to take the provisions across the river, determined to see the city at first hand. But fate was against her. A strong north-east wind had made it impossible for the boats to cast off and they had remained stuck fast to the south bank.

In the middle of the tempest, standing wind-blown in the prow of the craft, staring across at the lights of Orléans, Jehanne had suffered the strangest experience. She had imagined that she and de Rais were already there, their souls having flown over the water in the darkness. Together they wandered the streets of the city, watching the gallant occupants going about their business. They walked hand-fast, his wicked eyes turning on her violent looks of adoration. And then he had bent his lips toward hers.

She had wanted to vanish beneath his sensuous mouth, to be sucked into him, to lie and languish in his rotten soul, but one of her voices had called out loudly and she came floundering back, the dream, the astral journey, whatever fantasy it had been, abruptly at an end.

"Girl," demanded the high shrill note, "girl."

"Yes."

"Remove your gauntlets. Whistle for the wind."

She knew at once what was meant, for how many times during her golden childhood, before the visitations came to alter her life so relentlessly, had she seen her father wet his finger and hold it up, whistling the while?

"I'm calling the wind," sweet uncomplicated Jacques Darc would say, and the children had laughed, not believing him.

"Do it now," the piercing voice said again, this time so forcefully that Jehanne had thought her head would burst open with the sound.

Peeling off her gloves she had obeyed, holding a finger high, feeling the north-easter buffet her where she stood, as inconsequential and frail as straw. Behind her in the darkness she had heard the Bastard speak.

"Is the wind going to change?"

She had spun round. "Yes, by God's great mercy, it is. Give it an hour and we'll be across. Every supply will be in by morning."

Black though it was, she had seen his brilliant eyes twinkle. "Did your voices tell you this?"

"Yes, Monsieur Bastard, they did. So do not mock me or them. You will learn that they are always right and are to be respected. Just as I have had to do."

There had been a bitter note in her voice and for the first time Jean had felt sorry for her, up till that moment considering her merely a cocky and bumptious little bitch, full of herself and her own importance.

"They have chosen a hard road for you, these saints of yours."

"Aye," she had answered. "There'll be no peace for me until I go to join them."

"You shouldn't say that."

"Perhaps not, yet it is true none the less."

But, just as she had said, in half an hour the wind had veered round to the west, filling the sails of the flotilla which sailed forthwith. By dawn the supplies had been landed and the city relieved of its immediate problem. Meanwhile the story of Jehanne, the miraculous virgin who could change the direction of the wind, had spread like forest fire but she, perhaps advised by her voices, perhaps knowing that it was sometimes advisable to be unavailable when urgently required, had not spent the night in Orléans but ridden on to Reuilly.

By the next morning she had become a legend. Her continued plea that the army should be moved from the south bank so that the attack could be made from the north, as her saints had directed, had been finally heeded. The English had watched in amazement as the French forces struck camp and appeared to retreat.

That evening, just as darkness was falling, Jehanne had made her entrance into Orléans, riding a white horse, her standard fluttering above her. La Hire had ridden at her side, her personal escort behind and, standing at the gate in order to welcome her, had been the Bastard himself. The English could only look on impotently from the garrison of Les Tourelles as the entire population had turned out, the streets lit by thousands of torches, to cheer the small figure who had ridden triumphantly through the huge crowd which had pressed round her, giving her no room, as they leant forward to touch her or held up their babies to be blessed, and cheered and shouted themselves hoarse.

But that euphoria had abruptly ceased. Within days, Jehanne had been brought to the brink of despair by the constant refusal of the war council to allow her in to their meetings despite all she had done; by the shouted insults of the English soldiers, who told her in no uncertain terms exactly what they would like to do if they caught her, including explicit sexual details, and by the fact that the fight proper had not yet begun.

The Bastard of Orléans, returning exultant from Blois having successfully arranged for the King's private army to join their forces, had led the attack when the first hard skirmish had at last taken place. At midday, while the exhausted Pucelle had been sleeping, a party of citizens and mercenaries had left Orléans by the Burgundy Gate and made their way along the Autun road to the fortress of St. Loup, which lay under the command of the great lord, John Talbot, himself. Fierce fighting had broken out as the English defended their bastille as best they could.

It was then that Jehanne had woken up abruptly, calling out to her page, Louis de Contes, who was in the room with her, "In God's name! My voices have told me I'm about to get to know the English at last." She had rounded on him furiously. "You bloody little boy, you should have woken me. Why did you not tell me that France's blood was being shed?"

Then, getting herself prepared by her squire in tremendous haste, she had shot off on her horse and arrived just in time to see an English counter-attack from the fort of St. Pouair. Shouting encouragement, Jehanne had rallied the flagging French force and after three hours of furious combat St. Loup had been taken and set alight. Yet, despite all that, yet another attempt had been made to keep her out of the council meeting. In a furious temper La Pucelle had burst into the room and only the soothing presence of the Bastard had avoided a monumental confrontation.

"For God's sake," she had protested, her cheeks flushed. "Just because I am young and female there is no need to treat me like an idiot. I implore you, Monsieur Bastard, tell me the plan."

"My dear Jehanne," he had begun soothingly, only to be cut off in mid sentence.

"I fought by your side today, Monsieur. There is no need for you to patronize me."

And with that the angry girl had flounced from the room, racked with sobs.

"I'm going after her. This simply isn't fair," the Bastard had said to no one in particular, and hurried after the small retreating figure.

It was by the riverside that he finally caught up with her and saw to his consternation that La Pucelle was almost hysterical, weeping so wretchedly the air was full of the sound of her sobs.

"Is she ill?" he whispered to La Hire, who stood watching the girl impassively, his arms folded across his chest.

"No. She's just sent a message across to the English who promptly shouted the words 'Armagnac whore' back. They also called you a pimp by the way ..."

The Bastard grinned.

"... so that's got you sorted out. But she's such a funny scrap. Roughs it with the army then cries if someone's rude to her."

Jean smiled quizzically. "When all is said and done, La Hire, she's just a woman at heart."

"Funny scrap!" repeated La Hire, and the Bastard, who had grown to respect and admire the female bundle of energy who was yet so weak in many respects, stepped forward to put his arm round the girl's shoulders.

"I'm all right," she said, pulling away, embarrassed.

"I think you should let the tears go," put in a unfamiliar voice, and the bastard saw to his astonishment that in the darkness a tall figure had joined the group, where they stood on all that was left of the town side of the bridge over the Loire, half a broken arch, the nearest point to the English garrison of Les Tourelles, situated at the southernmost end.

"My Lord de Richemont!" he exclaimed. "What in the name of God are you doing here?"

"I followed the troops coming from Blois and am camped with them to the north." Forestalling any comment, the Earl continued, "Say nothing of my exile. This is the time for all good men and true to rally to their country. I have rejoined the King's army be it legal or not."

But even as he spoke, Jean could see that the scar-faced warrior had eyes for no one but La Pucelle, who was gallantly attempting to control her weeping, wiping her eyes and her nose with her sleeve, just like an urchin.

"Why don't you let it out?" he whispered to her. "You will feel much better if you do."

She gave him one of her challenging looks, obviously thinking that here was yet another seasoned campaigner set on deceiving or belittling her, but the Earl met her gaze steadily and with an extraordinary kind of fervor. Just for a second it occurred to the Bastard of Orléans, quite nonsensically, that they looked alike.

"Only fools cry," she answered.

"Only fools *don't* cry," he countered and taking one of her childlike and blunt hands in his, patted it gently.

"Oh, oh, it's all been such a strain," Jehanne said in a small gruff voice, and then did allow the storm to break and vanished into Richemont's arms, clinging to him desperately. Jean almost felt he was intruding as he watched the Earl stroke the girl's cropped hair, murmuring words of comfort.

"Now, now, sweetheart, it will be all right. You are so brave and have fought so gallantly. Don't worry, I will stay by your side from now on."

And then Richemont, very gently, drew away, knowing that she must have time to regain her dignity, that La Pucelle, who had seen such wondrous visions and heard the voices of the saints, could not be treated quite as any other ordinary girl.

"So now," he said, turning to the Bastard. "I would like to find lodging. I'd prefer to stay here with all my old comrades than go back to the camp."

"My house is yours," answered Jean.

"Then let us go there as soon as convenient, because from tomorrow I have the feeling we shall all be very busy."

"You are game to fight then?" asked the girl, her voice still quavery.

"Game?" replied Richemont, grinning. "Why, that's what I've come for."

"Good, because so have I," and Jehanne squeezed the Earl's arm affectionately, obviously more at ease with him than she had been with anyone since her arrival.

"Then let us address ourselves to the English in the morning."

"After mass," answered Jehanne.

"To which I shall accompany you," said Richemont, and gave a joyous smile.

The twin towers of Les Tourelles stood, heavily fortified and transformed into a garrison for the English army, dominating the south bank and overlooking all that went on in the city. So it was that on the morning of 6th May 1429, the English saw a huge troop of French militia under the leadership of de Villars, Gilles de Rais, La Hire, d'Alençon, Richemont riding with them, follow La Pucelle through the Burgundy Gate, the only entrance to the city left open.

They watched as this great force of mercenaries, most of them Scottish, together with soldiers from the royal army and fighting Bretons, swept down to the riverbank and there attempted to cross on the pontoon that had been put up during the hours of darkness. But this operation took longer than the French anticipated as the makeshift bridge turned out to be too narrow to allow more than a few men to pass over it at any one time.

Eventually, however, English hopes were dashed and the first hundred soldiers managed to land on the south bank where they attacked the fort of St. Jean le Blanc, lying close to the monastery, also an English stronghold. It had been a crushing defeat and what Englishmen survived had run at full pelt into Les Augustins. But from there they had launched a massive counter-attack. Panic had broken

out amongst the French soldiers who, in the face of so
many virulent arrows, had sounded retreat and attempted
to cross back over the pontoon against the tide of the royal
army who were still pressing forward.

It was Jehanne and La Hire, just arriving on the left
bank, who saved this dangerous situation from turning into
a fiasco. Tilting her lance into the charge position, La Pucelle went like a fury toward the English fort. The bugle
call of retreat was changed to attack and with a wild cry
the French troops, as a man, turned and followed her. As
wave after wave of fighting men joined them from the pontoon the strength of the assault force grew, and eventually
Jean de Lorraine, a formidable artilleryman, put an end to
it by smashing the monastery door to smithereens with a
single cannonball.

Like quicksilver, Jehanne slid from the saddle and was
through the gaping archway, planting her standard as she
went.

"Forward in the name of God," she screamed, and behind her tumbled captains, squires, knights, mercenaries,
king's soldiers, all coming in on the attack.

It was a bloodbath. By nightfall what English survivors
there were left had struggled into Les Tourelles, while the
French wounded lay tended by the monks of St. Augustin.
Jehanne, who had herself sustained a minor injury, returned to Orléans in the company of the army leaders, leaving the fighting men to enjoy themselves, consuming the
mountains of food and drink brought to them throughout
the night by the grateful citizens of Orléans, who crossed
by boat regardless of the English menace on the bridge.

And then, her wound cleaned and dressed, her supper
consumed, La Pucelle fell asleep in front of the fire, her
feet on a stool, her face looking very young and childish in
the soft light of the flames.

In the Bastard of Orléans's house, Richemont and his host
were also hurriedly snatching a meal.

"There's to be a council meeting in the governor's place
in an hour. We'd better get a move on," said Jean, gulping
his wine as if it were the last drop he would ever taste.

Richemont swallowed the mouthful he was eating and
gazed at him in surprise. "We? Am I invited then?"

"Not officially, but I'd appreciate your presence."

There was something in his voice that made the Earl look at the Bastard sharply.

"Anything wrong?"

"Not exactly. It's simply a feeling that de Gaucourt is deliberately trying to keep La Pucelle out of things. I don't think he wants her to have any of the glory. It's odd."

"It's not odd at all," snorted his companion. "De Gaucourt is in the pay of de la Trémoille, always has been, so of course he wants to keep her out. It is in the interests of both him and the fat man to belittle her in the eyes of the world."

"Well that must never happen. The girl deserves all the credit due to her. Did you see her today? It was unbelievable. I swear to God she's been trained to fight."

"She has," Richemont answered softly. "Don't ask me how I know but just be assured I do."

"I had guessed as much. But that aside, will you come tonight?"

"I wouldn't miss it for the world."

He was shaking the governor of Orléans as if he were a rat, holding the man by his velvet collar and rattling him about till de Gaucourt's teeth chattered and his eyes started to bulge out of his head.

"You bloody little squirt," hissed Richemont. "I'll see you in Hell before you make one more move against her."

"For God's sake, my Lord," the Bastard pleaded urgently. "Put him down. This is a council of war, not a wrestling match."

"But we *must* attack tomorrow," countered the Earl, reluctantly lowering de Gaucourt to his feet. "Surely you can all see that."

"Our forces are too few," said the Governor's secretary. "We must wait for reinforcements."

"Reinforcements be damned. There were so many of us today we could scarce get over the bridge. For God's sake see sense."

"I'm making a charge against you, Richemont," said de Gaucourt huskily, regaining his voice. "I'll have you clapped in jail for assault."

"No, by God you won't," shouted the Bastard, losing his temper at last. "I'll need every man I can get when I ride to the attack tomorrow."

"There'll be no attack," retorted the governor through drawn lips. "There will be no more fighting till more men and more supplies reach this city."

"Coillons to you," thundered the Earl. "I stand by the Bastard. Come and arrest me if you dare."

And with that he banged the table with his fist until the papers and inkwells jumped, then crashed out through the door, pushing over a chair as he went.

She was still asleep in front of the fire when the messenger from the governor came to tell her that the council had decided to call a halt to the fighting and that because of the superior number of English troops no men-at-arms would be sent out tomorrow. For response Jehanne had simply looked at the man coldly.

"Tell Monsieur Governor from me that I too have had counsel—with my voices. And, you can believe me, the council of the Lord will stand—and yours will come to nothing."

"Leave La Pucelle in peace," commanded the young Abbot, Jehanne's confessor, who many found so frightening with his vivid all-seeing eyes. "She stands in the sight of God which you do not."

Somewhat daunted, the messenger bowed his way out.

"Jacques, are we truly alone?" asked Jehanne.

"We are."

"Then will you hear my confession?"

"I will tomorrow. Before you go to fight."

"Then you may have to hear it twice, for during the day I shall be wounded and will need to prepare my soul for death."

"God's mercy, surely not!"

"Oh, yes. Blood will flow from my body over the breast. Warn Father Pasquerel that he, too, must stay close when that happens."

"I will, ma Pucelle."

"And bless me when I wake, Jacques, for I know I will have more than ever to do."

"I bless you now and then, Jehanne."

And with that the Abbot swiftly bent over her and kissed her suddenly icy cheek.

She rose at three and heard Mass, then rode out of the city in the darkness, ignoring the governor and his protests, and

crossing the Loire by boat. Richemont and the Bastard
were with her and so were all the loyal hearts of Orléans,
determined not to see such bravery fight alone.

At sunrise the battle began and by sunset it was done.
There were four assaults on Les Tourelles each of which
failed, the English sending showers of arrows and cannon-
balls, and pushing down the ladders by which the attacking
force were trying to enter the fort. Shortly after midday
Jehanne came into the sight of an English crossbowman
who deftly planted an arrow between her breastplate and
her neck. On foot at the time, she fell to the ground and
did not get up.

"The Armagnac's whore is dead," came the cry from the
English, and there was an almighty cheer.

Richemont was at her side as quickly as the arrow that
had felled her but not as fast as Gilles de Rais, who was
bent over La Pucelle, pulling the bolt from her breast, sucking out the bad blood. The obscenity of seeing such a man
with Jehanne's liquid on his lips struck the Earl forcibly,
and he practically threw de Rais off the girl's motionless
body.

"Is she dead?" he demanded angrily.

"No, I'm not," answered Jehanne in a whisper, opening
her eyes. "Carry me away and let me recover. We must
not lose the day because of me."

But they nearly did. With La Pucelle gone there was a
lull in the fighting during which the English began to recover themselves, firing repeatedly at the engineers who
were striving to rebuild the bridge with planking from the
Orléans side.

"Should we sound the retreat?" the Bastard asked
Richemont, bright tears rushing down his face.

"No, by God, no. My girl will come back."

It was odd phraseology but Jean ignored it, his tears suddenly dried by the sight of La Pucelle, secured to her horse
but mounted none the less, her standard grasped in her
bloody hand, coming toward them.

"Sound the attack," she gasped.

"But it's nearly dark."

"Do so, Bastard, and we will win. I'm telling you."

Then Jehanne lowered her banner as if it were a lance,
charging toward Les Tourelles shouting, "Forward! Come
on! It's ours!"

The entire might of the French army rallied for the last time and careered after her while the English, under the command of Sir William Glasdale, began to pull up the drawbridge of Les Tourelles, lowered to facilitate their bowmen, in order to save themselves.

"Clasdas! Clasdas!" screamed Jehanne, the nearest she could get to saying his name correctly. "Surrender! You who called me a whore!"

The drawbridge creaked upward, then splintered beneath the weight of all the men standing on it. With a horrible crack it broke in half and Glasdale and many others were suddenly in the Loire, deep and dark in the fading light.

"God have mercy on their souls," Jehanne said, blessing the drowning men, then turned away in floods of tears.

"Amen," said Jacques, and, lifting her from the saddle, held her close to him.

And with those words, the battle of Orléans was won.

Thirty-three

She had not stayed merry-making in the city but had gone straight from the battlefield to Loches where she had found the King amongst his courtiers. Without ado she had gone on one knee before him.

"Orléans is yours, sweet Dauphin. The English withdrew on 8th May. Now you must come with me to Reims for your coronation."

"But it lies in enemy hands."

"Not for much longer," answered Jehanne certainly.

"But what of the Loire? I would see it conquered before I receive the holy oil."

"If you straighten your shoulders I shall get it for you, gentle Prince."

"What did you say?"

"I said stand straight, let the world see your beauty and the victory that is soon to come."

"There is no beauty in me, Jehanne."

"You have the beauty I do. The beauty of God's love and inspiration. Come, sweet Dauphin, and pray with me for a transformation."

And she had led him, without protest, into the château's private chapel.

What happened afterward was, some claimed, a minor miracle, but others recognized it simply as a man regaining his confidence. Charles stood tall, unstooped, his lean body suddenly filling his clothes; the clearwater eyes lost their hunted expression and glittered and shone as they had done in his youth; the long nose flared at the nostrils, sensitive and eager; the full mouth curved upward, the drooping lips a thing of the past.

"Win the campaign of the Loire and I *will* go to Reims with you," he had said.

"It will take two months," Jehanne had answered, nodding at the same time as if someone else were speaking to her.

"Your voices are telling you this?"

"They are, mon Prince."

"Then, for certain, it will happen."

"Prepare yourself mentally and spiritually. And know, Monsieur, that at your coronation I shall carry the banner of my Order. For when I have finished my tasks for you their great work must be resumed."

She had left him then and ridden off with her entourage; shortly afterward had started the succession of messengers arriving daily to keep the King informed of La Pucelle's progress.

It had been phenomenal! On 12th June, the town of Jargeau had surrendered to her, on the 15th, Meung, and on the 17th the citadel of Beaugency. But over this victory there had been a certain amount of controversy regarding the Earl of Richmond, who many said had fought at La Pucelle's side at Orléans—although about this fact there seemed to be a conspiracy of silence—who had suddenly reappeared with his private army and literally saved the day.

Reports on the Beaugency triumph stated that the French troops were about to be caught in a classic battle trap, penned between the castle and the oncoming English force under the leadership of Talbot, still smarting from his trouncing at Orléans, and Sir John Fastolfe, the victor of the Battle of the Herrings. Hopelessly outnumbered, Jehanne's troops had been on the point of retreat when suddenly, out of nowhere it would seem, Richemont had appeared with six hundred men-at-arms and four hundred archers.

Hearing the news, Georges de la Trémoille, who had once been inseparable from the Constable but who had now succumbed completely to an insatiable lust for power, had instantly suspected that the rescue had somehow been pre-arranged between Richemont and Jehanne, that moves were being made to restore the Earl in the King's favor. But there had been no proof of it nor would there ever be and the fat man had simply had no choice but to let the matter drop.

And then, on 18th June, with Richemont as one of her

companions-in-arms, Jehanne had finally avenged Azincourt at the Battle of Patay. Two thousand Englishmen had
fallen that day and, unbelievably, only two French soldiers.
At the end of the battle John Talbot, the English nobleman
and captain who had retreated from Jehanne at Orléans,
had knelt before her and proffered his sword, surrendering
himself to captivity. Sir John Fastolfe, his fellow captain,
had escaped only by reason of having a very fast horse.

When news of that victory reached the fortress of Yen-
ville it surrendered at once, and the English, now in deep
trouble, packed up their things, evacuated the rest of their
forts, and took the long road back to Normandy. The mills
of God were at last beginning to turn their mighty sails.

That night, the night of the victory at Patay, Jehanne
went to give thanks in the cathedral at Orléans, riding in
triumph, her standard bearer walking in front of her. But
on this occasion he did not carry her usual banner depicting
God and the world. Instead there fluttered from his pole a
blue and white flag, written on it the words *Non nobis,
Domine, non nobis sed nomini tuo da gloriam.*

"Give us not glory, God, but give it to your name," trans-
lated one of the onlookers. "But surely that was the motto
of the Knights Templar."

"Aye, and those are their colors. The people, blue, and
the clergy, white."

"Well, well," murmured the Bastard, greeting La Pucelle
with a fond kiss, and thought the rest of his thoughts in
silence.

It was Sunday, 17th July 1429, nine o'clock on a pearl-
misted morning. Very early, shortly after daybreak in fact,
when the haze had hung heavy over the valleys and hills,
six noble lords, the Sires de Boussac, de Graville, and the
olive-skinned Lord de Rais, together with the Sire St. Sévère and the Admiral de Culant, had gone to the Abbey
of St. Remi to fetch the Holy Ampulla to be used in the
King's anointing, which now lay ready in the cathedral's
vestment room, waiting for the ceremony to begin.

As the sun had stolen slowly up over the city of Reims,
the people had come, both great and humble, to pack the
place with their thankful presence. Yet amongst that enormous multitude gathered together in the Cathedral there
were some significant missing faces. The Duke of Burgundy

was not there nor had even bothered to reply to his invitation. Also missing was the Earl of Richmond, much restored in the King's favor thanks to La Pucelle but still not able to come face to face with de la Trémoille. The Queen of Sicily, too, was noticeably absent for mysterious reasons of her own, though nobody could guess what they were. And the Queen of France, brimming with child, had felt unable to undertake the journey. Representing her and her mother, however, were Marie's two brothers: Louis, the jade-eyed Duke of Anjou, and Prince René, smiling his saturnine and secret smile.

Deputizing for the missing lords was Georges de la Trémoille, huge as a pavilion in his flowing robes, his very presence guaranteeing that certain people would not be present. Hating Richemont more than ever for his new friendship with Jehanne, a creature whom Georges considered a freak of nature which should be put down swiftly, preferably for good, the fat man had recently managed to score a sizeable point against his erstwhile friend. Yesterday evening at the pre-coronation Council meeting he had elevated d'Albret, Comte de Dreux, to the position of acting Constable of France, it being *de rigueur* that the Constable be present at the ceremony and Richemont, of course, quite unable to attend.

But now Georges's wandering attention, torn between admiring his own gold tissue clothes and pinching his wife's thigh under her many skirts, a feat not easy to achieve in a cathedral stall, was thoroughly brought back to the grandness of the occasion by the shrill call of the state trumpets.

From the door of the cathedral, walking beneath a blue canopy covered with fleur-de-lis, carried at the four corners by the Maréchal de Boussac, the Admiral de Culant, and the Lords de Rais and de Graville, Charles was making his solemn entrance, clad in a glorious robe of scarlet satin covered with a sleeveless chasuble also sewn with fleur-de-lis, each one stitched in a thousand pearls. In front of the King came d'Albret, bearing the sword of state, unsheathed and upright, while behind him, riding his horse right up to the choir came the Sire de St. Sévère holding the Holy Ampulla, which he would hand from the saddle to Regnault de Chartres, the Archbishop.

In the nave, under the multicolored banners and flags, the congregation stood in two lines, forming a guard of honor, marveling at the man approaching the altar in so magnificent a manner. Slender and graceful, his bare head revealing a cap of russet hair which shone like polished wood in the hazy sunshine, his eyes full of unshed tears, crystal bright, Charles de Valois was scarcely recognizable as the ugly child, the reticent boy, the nervous wreck of only a few months ago.

"A King is born," thought the Bastard of Orléans, and silently burst into tears.

The high bright trumpets sounded again into the sudden awed silence and Jehanne la Pucelle clad in the most noble vestments of cloth of gold and silk, well lined with fur, came slowly down the nave, bearing in her right hand the standard of France. Behind her walked her page, young Louis, carrying the colors of the Knights Templar, a fact which drew a gasp of astonishment from the mighty crowd.

Slowly, but with a sense of purpose and occasion surprising in one so humbly born, she made her way to the altar and knelt down beside Charles on his right, while d'Albret knelt to the left.

The King, now rightful King, not the one who had been so shabbily heralded in Mehun-sur-Yèvre in October 1422, thought as he prayed that his heart might actually burst with the strength of his joy and gratitude, and did not care that he could be seen to openly weep, his tears falling onto the red carpet beneath his knees. Beside him, the strange little thing who had turned his life around and brought him out of the depths, back to humanity, wept also, her sobs audible above the sound of the organ, the choir, and the loud low chant of priests.

Regardless of tradition and ceremony, Charles de Valois turned and, putting out his hand, grasped that of Jehanne Darc, who responded by raising his fingers to her lips and dewing them with her tears. Then, their few private moments over, all three stood, Jehanne and d'Albret one pace behind their sovereign, all of them still as statues, as the five-hour ritual began.

Putting his hand on the gospel, Charles took the solemn oath, swearing to honor and protect both his kingdom and his people.

"In the name of Christ I promise that I will serve ..."

But he was away, dreaming, not thinking so much of the words he was saying as the path he had trodden to get here. In his mind, Charles saw his gross mother, the extraordinary face of Nicolas Flamel, the beauty of Bonne, the power of Yolande, the comforting presence of Marie. But towering over them all, the little girl standing beside him at the altar steps, the virgin knight, the transvestite, the freak, the savage courageous creature who had come out of nowhere and led him to victory.

"... for my country and all my subjects," he said, then looked straight at her to see that she was crying again, or perhaps hadn't stopped.

Charles added an improvisational ending to his oath. "And I promise that for the rest of her mortal days on earth, Jehanne la Pucelle shall—"

And then the most extraordinary thing happened. Before he could complete his sentence, the King's voice was drowned by the frantic sound of a terrified animal. The horse that had brought the Holy Ampulla up to the choir and which was now standing in the cathedral porch suddenly took fright and, rearing up, began to head back down the nave, the squire who had been attending it still clinging to its leading rein. There was a moment of pure pandemonium as members of the congregation seated at the back rose to restrain the frantic animal.

The whole incident could only have lasted two minutes, no more, but it was enough to throw Charles off his stroke and he concluded the oath abruptly, leaving out any further mention of Jehanne, a bad and somehow sinister omen.

But the time had come for the King to receive the regalia of state. The beautiful Duke D'Alençon stepped from the crowd and dubbed Charles a knight, fixing the golden spurs onto his boots; the acting Constable handed him the staff topped with the ivory *main-de-justice*; then the Sire d'Albret ceremoniously gave the sceptre.

And now the ritual was leading toward its climax, the unction, the anointing with the *Sainte Ampoule,* the holy oil believed to hold such supernatural powers that it made the French Kings priests, sacred, capable of curing scrofula by touch. Without this anointing, Charles had only been the Dauphin to Jehanne, and also to a great many others besides.

Bearing the Holy Ampulla, Regnault de Chartres, Archbishop of Reims, motioned Charles to sit on the state throne and then, leaning forward, poured the mystic oil onto the King's head, while the girl briefly closed her eyes in a moment of blissful fulfillment. That done, de Chartres opened the front of Charles's gown and applied sacred oil to his chest, then finally to his hands.

The twelve nobles chosen to place the crown on the King's head closed in a ring around him, arms and hands raised aloft, fingers extended to hold the open crown of *fleurons* high, then slowly lower it onto the monarch's head. The Bishops of Orléans and Sées draped him in a robe of blue cloth, sewn with golden fleur-de-lis and trimmed with ermine. And at that moment, the moment of crowning, everyone, both in and outside the cathedral cried "Noël!" while the trumpets sounded so loudly it seemed the very vaults of the church would crack.

High over the heads of the congregation the twelve peers lifted the throne on which Charles sat so that all the world could see the new King of France, while Jehanne, shaking with sobs, once more knelt at his feet.

"Sweet King, God's will that I raise the siege of Orléans and bring you to the cathedral of Reims for your anointing, so that all should see you are the true King to whom the Kingdom of France belongs, has today been fulfilled."

And with those words she laid the banner of the Knights Templar on the steps of the altar as a tribute.

It was done and they left the cathedral together, Jehanne and Charles, walking side by side through the cheering crowd to the banqueting hall where the coronation feast was to be served. And there she sat beside him, the child of Yolande and Richemont who knew nothing of her antecedents, plied with food and wine which, for once, she took with relish.

"Well?" the Bastard of Orléans said to her, drunk and happy and still occasionally weeping as he was.

"Yes, I am satisfied."

"And your voices?"

He asked that without malice and Jehanne accepted the question as such.

"They are pleased too." She turned her dark eyes on him and he saw in their depths a strange combination of pride and fear, uneasy partners that made the Bastard suddenly anxious for her.

"But something is still wrong?"

"Not wrong exactly, just inexplicable," Jehanne answered quietly.

"What is it?"

"From that day, the day I was wounded, the day that Clasdas drowned, the day of victory at Orléans . . ."

"Yes?"

"My voices changed toward me, they began to address me differently."

"In what way?

"It frightens me, Jean. I don't understand it. For now they are calling me the Daughter of God."

Thirty-four

She was lost in mist, Jehanne was aware of that; drowning in gentle clouds, pale as lilac, deep as gentian. And other people were lost too, she could hear their whispering voices, their words vague and unclear, a constant background of sibilants. The air was full of the smell of flowers and a harp had begun to play, its divine cadences pouring into her ear like drops of crystal, drowning the unnerving whispers, while somewhere a dragon had started to sing. Jehanne raised her sword to stab the beast and realized instantly that it was not a monster but Gilles de Rais, as she had know it would be all along.

The mist vanished, the man assumed his normal shape and, taking Jehanne's hand, led her into a pale pure chapel where he knelt at her feet as if she were one of the sacred images standing in the many niches around the walls.

"Daughter of God," he said, "know that I love you."

"You must not do so," Jehanne heard herself reply.

"Then kill me if I am not necessary to you."

And he pulled open his black satin doublet to reveal the spot where his heart beat.

"I tried to kill you on another occasion but you would not die."

"I will die this time if that is what you want."

La Pucelle broke into tears. "I do not want it, I do not. That is my trouble."

She turned to run, confused by what he was saying and the violet mist closed about her once more, the air heavy with the cloying scent of death, the dragon's song one long continuous scream. With a great cry of terror, the girl woke, shivering and shaking with cold, a prayer on her lips that her saints would return quickly to guide her on the path of righteousness.

They had left her some while ago, those voices of hers, those high persistant tones which could never be ignored, and Jehanne had understood that they were punishing her for disobedience. For she had gone against their advice and in the autumn of 1429 made an attempt to retake Paris for the King without their consent, mounting her attack on a feast day, the birthday of Our Lady. La Pucelle had received an arrow wound in the thigh for her pains and had fallen, hurt, into the fosse, the town ditch, alongside a donkey, where she had remained lying amongst the dung and dirt until one of the Duke d'Alençon's serving men had discovered her and pulled her out, only to be nursed back to health by an overpoweringly attentive Gilles de Rais.

Charles had made Jehanne's wounding his reason for ending the battle and the current campaign and, disbanding his army, had withdrawn to the Loire for the winter. To add to Jehanne's chagrin at this turn of events, the voices had become silent and she had been on her own in every sense, the handsome d'Alençon returning to his wife at the castle of Beaumont, the ardent Gilles, who nowadays could rarely be kept from her company, being sent on a tour of inspection by de la Trémoille.

So she had spent the short dark months kicking her heels, idling her time at court, dressed like a little whore in satins and furs, wishing that her friends would come back and she could once again get down to some fighting. But even more than that, Jehanne had wished those demanding saints would return to blast her eardrums, for better by far to endure their imperious commands, to obey their wishes, than veer about like a rudderless ship. And now it was April, the year being 1430, the start of another decade, a decade during which Jehanne had vowed to see the English off French soil once and for all.

Charles had decided to keep his spring at Sully, the magnificent château of Georges de la Trémoille, created Duke de Sully at the time of the coronation, and the court, including a reluctant and noticeably sulky Pucelle, had moved there with him. She had walked the château's enormous magnificent rooms, bigger by far than anything at Loches or Saumur, comparable indeed to the state apartments at Chinon, and wondered that such a horrid fat man, who did not bother to disguise too heavily the fact of his enmity toward her, should achieve so much. And then, even without her voices, she had remembered God's great and inescapable mills and known that it would only be a matter of time before Georges de la Trémoille went the way of all creatures who create havoc and misery in other people's lives.

But even with these stirring thoughts the stifling atmosphere in that grand and opulent place had eventually become too much for her and one April night, during the hours of darkness, Jehanne had gone forth with her brother Pierre, her squire Jean d'Aulon, and a small company of men-at-arms, once more to take to the roads. She had asked permission of neither her voices nor her King and was, therefore, acting illegally. But then so was Gilles de Rais, promoted to Maréchal of France at the coronation, who had written a coded letter expressing his wish to be at her side again, to get back to some action, and arranging to meet her at Lagny on the 17th April.

And now she woke, cold and terrified, to find she was indeed at that place, within spitting distance of Paris, that she was sleeping rough with her few hundred troops, and that the real-life de Rais, not a dragon but a swarthy-skinned, dark-bearded man with eyes like a falcon's, burnished blue, was leaning over her, staring into her face, saying, "What is wrong, ma Pucelle?"

It was impossible to believe at such a vulnerable moment, lying in her tent, stripped to her hose, legs apart while she slept, that he had not been party to her dream, or to the two others that she had had about him, and in fright Jehanne said, "What do you mean? What are you saying?"

Gilles smiled reassuringly but behind that smile Jehanne saw the face of a tiger.

"I was concerned because you called out in your sleep. I thought perhaps you were having a nightmare."

"You know I was, you know because you were part of it."

He did not try to pretend, instead those liquid blue eyes, bubbling and molten at the core, darkened like a stormy sky.

"So you have let me in at last, ma Pucelle."

She sat up from her ground sheet, every bone in her body aching and dry, staring at him, and Gilles went on,

"I am speaking of how our souls once met, and took up arms against each other in a game of chess."

"Chess?" She felt that she was weakening.

"Aye, Pucelle. Don't you remember?"

How could she forget the whiteness of her body, the blackness of her hair and the crimson of her blood as she surrendered to him that virginity which she had promised her saints to keep in order to honor them?

"That was a dream," she said hotly.

"Was it?" answered Gilles, his mouth close to hers. "When we first met at Tours, in the armorer's shop, you recognized me, knew that we were destined to be together, in love and hate."

Jehanne turned away, unable to bear his proximity a moment longer. "Maréchal de Rais, please leave me. If we are to return to the fight tomorrow I shall need more sleep than this."

The blue falcon eyes glittered. "I will leave you now, ma Pucelle, but never permanently. For I who have had your blood in my mouth have now become part of you."

They entered Melun the next morning, 22nd April, to find that the Burgundian garrison stationed there had evacuated even before the legendary Pucelle arrived. Grateful to have a victory without bloodshed, Jehanne dropped on her knees beside the town moat, and then it happened. Her head was suddenly full of sound, there were bright lights before her eyes.

"Am I forgiven?" she asked.

High as a bell came the reply. "Prepare yourself, Jehanne. Prepare, prepare!"

La Pucelle crossed herself hurriedly, very much afraid.

"For what?"

"For what will inevitably happen."

"Which is?"

"Before the Feast of St. John you will be captured, and so it must be."

La Pucelle found that she was shaking from head to foot.

"You must accept your fate, for God will help you."

"Then I have nothing to fear?"

But there was no reply, the strange burst of sound abruptly at an end.

Jehanne slowly rose to her feet, realizing that up until

this moment she had never had a true sense of danger, had gone into battle in an almost phlegmatic way, certain that nothing could ever stop her or her divine mission. But now an unpleasant realization of her own mortality, her own human frailty, swept over her.

"God give me strength," she murmured, and it seemed to her, then, that one of the voices came back momentarily and said, "Be calm."

She had been in retreat for a week, gone to the chapel of Saint Marguerite, only a short distance from the town of Compiègne, with no one for company except the Abbot Jacques. Jehanne's voices were coming all the time now, telling her that she should take the situation calmly, that her capture was predestined and had to be. But when La Pucelle had asked her saints when and how she was to be taken prisoner they had refused to answer her.

"But Jacques, if I knew I might manage to avoid being caught."

"I think perhaps, ma Pucelle, you should go away now."

"But how can I?" she had asked despairingly. "I believe my voices want me to be a prisoner."

Reluctantly, the bemused girl had left Saint Marguerite and gone straight away to the rescue of nearby Compiègne, under threat of siege from the Burgundians. The Duke's army was already besieging two neighboring towns which controlled the road to Compiègne. Foolishly, blunderingly, Jehanne had offered to go to relieve them.

But as soon as she left, the Governor of Compiègne compelled the King's troops to withdraw and opened the city gates to Jean of Luxemburg, the Duke of Burgundy's captain. Then had come a message from Charles for La Pucelle to disband the militia and return to the Loire immediately.

"You must go," Gilles de Rais had said forcefully. "It is a direct order from the King. It would be tantamount to insurrection if you disobey him."

"Then you go in my place. My duty is with the people of Compiègne."

The great blue eyes had looked at her hard. "There is something about this business I don't trust. I smell a plot here."

"Please, ma Pucelle," put in Jacques. "I beg you to leave

with the Maréchal. Don't endanger yourself any further.
You are being beaten back at every turn."

"But de Flavy has sent a message that Compiègne is
invested on all sides. I can't turn away from that."

"You will if you've an ounce of sense left in that head
of yours." De Rais lowered his voice so that Jacques could
not hear his whispered words. "Jehanne, I beseech you to
come with me. It is not God's will that we should be
separated."

"*You* speak of God?"

"I speak of His mysteries, of which your death might
well be one. Ma Pucelle, you who are my other half, do
not desert me now."

"It is you who are deserting not I."

The falcon's eyes had become incandescent. "No, that is
not true. I am the Maréchal of France. My King has recalled me and I must obey his summons."

"Then goodbye," answered Jehanne, and spurred her
horse away without another word.

"I curse you," screamed Gilles after her departing back.
"I curse you, Daughter of God. May you, who will not love
me as I do you, know pain and death and all that there is
to follow."

A few days later his curse was fulfilled. On 23rd May,
that fateful date in the history of La Pucelle, Jehanne, accompanied by a small band of soldiers and a handful of
her gallant captains, engaged in an attack on Margny, a
Burgundian outpost near the beleaguered town of Compiègne. Strangely, there was no defence, a fact which should
perhaps have warned her of impending disaster. But nobody could have anticipated the enormity of the trap, the
hordes of enemy soldiers who appeared seemingly from
nowhere, surrounding the girl and her tragic little group.

Hopelessly outnumbered, there was only one thing for it,
to make a dash for the walled and moated city and count
on the goodwill of the towns folk to let them in.

"Full retreat," ordered Jehanne, and turned to fight the
enemy every step of the way, waiting till last, watching her
men and Guillaume de Flavy clatter past her and over the
hastily lowered drawbridge.

"Come on, for God's sake!" shrieked Jean d'Aulon, La
Pucelle's squire, in desperation, and grabbed roughly at her
bridle trying to drag her to safety by force.

But it was too late! Even though Jehanne had at last decided to run for her life, the drawbridge was being pulled up in her face.

"Got 'er!" shouted several Burgundian voices together, and then there was no sound but the girl's own scream as the enemy closed in relentlessly from all sides.

Thirty-five

Ten thousand gold crowns was the sum which changed hands between the Duke of Burgundy and the English when he sold Jehanne to them, ransomed as he preferred to put it, in November 1430.

During the middle of that month La Pucelle had been taken from the castle of Beaurevoir, the property of Jean of Luxemburg, brother to Jacquetta, the girl with whom Jehanne's father Richemont had had a fleeting affair, on the first stage of her grim journey to Rouen. Once before La Pucelle had tried to leave the castle, leaping out of the tower window in a despairing attempt to end her life. Fortunately, or perhaps unfortunately, she had fallen into the moat and despite being very gravely hurt had survived to face trial, accused as she was by the English and the University of Paris of both witchcraft and heresy.

With an air of tragic resignation, assured by her voices as she was that it was her duty to be calm whatever happened, that her saints had forgiven her for attempting suicide and that Compiègne would receive help before Martinmas, the wretched girl had gone under heavy escort to be delivered to the people who had sworn that if ever they caught her they would see her burned as a common enchantress.

The news of the sale and of Jehanne's journey to Arras, where she had been put into the custody of Count Pierre Cauchon, Bishop of Beauvais, a man whose implacable hatred of La Pucelle was inexplicable even to those who knew him well, sent a frisson of fear to all those attempting to keep some kind of Christmas in the Loire. Because of it the meeting of the court during the Twelve Days of 1430, everyone by now aware that Jehanne was in Rouen and in mortal danger, became the cover for a hub of political intrigue, as courtiers and soldiers alike puzzled over what was best to be done.

At the heart of the matter stood the King himself; now nearly twenty-nine years of age and saved from nervous collapse by the very girl whose fate everyone was discussing, he had these days become a monarch of considerable substance. For Charles had grown in every way since his coronation at Reims, his slender body filling out to man's estate, his ugly face taking on lines of character, his views on life more cynical yet more rounded, so that now he had no doubts left as to where he was going or what he would have to do to get there.

He had been reunited with Richemont after the battle of Patay, Jehanne herself acting as mediator, extolling the ex-Constable's virtues, speaking of how bravely and selflessly he had fought. Looking at the scarred warrior, the King had made a note to himself that here lay the man of the future, temporarily disgraced because of de la Trémoille's dislike of him but obviously the one to succeed the fat Duke when the other had outlived his usefulness. Yet of Georges's talents at negotiating peace with Burgundy there could be no doubt.

Terrible though it was to admit it, the capture of La Pucelle had in many ways been a diplomatic relief. The campaign conducted just before she had been caught, aimed so hard against Burgundy and his holdings, had been embarrassing to say the least. It had come at a time when discretion and treading carefully were the order of the day and Jehanne's unauthorized attacks had been the last thing the negotiators had wanted. But the fact that she had blundered and blundered badly did not in any way detract from her present terrible plight nor what plans should be made to help her.

The first person to visit the King on Christmas Eve, 5th January, had been his mother-in-law, not waiting even to settle in before she asked for an audience. Half expecting that he might well have a stream of callers, Charles had set aside the great receiving room overlooking the river in which to see them. And it was there in the château of Saumur that Yolande met him, sweeping a dignified straight-backed curtsy, dressed in very dark blue, her skin as white as the snow that threatened to fall from the heavy sky outside.

Charles rose to kiss her, embracing his "Good Mother" on both cheeks, and leading her to a chair by the fire. "Now Madame, how may I help you?" he began, already guessing the reply.

Yolande came straight to the point. "I am here about La Pucelle, Charles. Her trial begins in just a few days' time, or so my informants tell me."

"They are quite right. The first hearing is on the 9th."

"Then what," the Queen asked forcefully, "do you intend to do about it?"

"I have not yet formulated my plans."

"But you are going to try something surely?"

"Yes, of course."

But the truth was that Charles was flummoxed, not knowing how to get out of the dilemma yet keenly aware that action of some sort must be taken.

It was the Bastard of Orléans who later that day suggested a rescue party, an expedition to go into the lands beyond the Seine, to Normandy, to effect some kind of attack on the prison where she was held, snatching the prisoner during the ensuing chaos. But the Maréchal de Rais, also present at the discussion, said he would take no part in such foolishness, that the scheme would most certainly fail, that a small band of men working undercover, posing as guards and bribing their way in, would be far more effective.

By the evening, Charles was exhausted with all the many and varied suggestions, with the unsavory whisperings of Regnault de Chartres that Jehanne had been a cocky little upstart who would never take advice, did everything of her own will, and had got what she deserved; and bored by Georges de la Trémoille constantly assuring him that things really had worked out for the best.

"Well?" he said getting into bed with his safe harbor, his mother figure of a wife, pregnant nine months of the year every year, but with only one surviving son and a horde of daughters to show for it.

Marie shook her head. "No, not well."

"Because of La Pucelle?"

"Yes, of course. You've got to get her out, Monsieur. Or

at least you've got to try. She saved you once, now it's your turn."

"I've decided to give the Bastard money to fund an expedition."

Marie looked dubious. "It might work but it means battles and armies and noisy things. I would have thought secret negotiations would have been better."

"But with whom?"

"Well, who is her principal jailer? Do you know?"

"The Earl of Warwick is governor of Rouen."

"Then you must send an intermediary to him at once. Bargaining for Jehanne's life must begin straight away."

"But what about Bedford? He wants her dead."

"Then the way is clear. You must treat with Warwick."

"But who should I send? The Bastard, de Rais?"

"No, they are both too militant. It should be someone the English know and respect. Someone older."

They both said, "Richemont" together.

"But can I trust him?"

"Charles, he only turned against you when pushed to the limit by old Fatty. And since that one transgression I would have thought he has proved his loyalty a hundredfold. Beside, he seems genuinely fond of Jehanne and I believe would do anything to save her."

"Let me sleep on it," said Charles, blowing out the bedside candle.

"Very well. But I shall want to know your reply in the morning."

"You shall have it. Now, snuggle close. It's snowing outside."

Great with child and comfortable as a feather bed, Marie enveloped him.

"You *will* save Jehanne?" she whispered into the darkness.

"I'll do my best," answered her husband as he drifted off toward sleep.

On 9th January, the day that the court assembled for the start of Jehanne's trial, Arthur de Richemont came to Yolande in the darkness of night. Making his way by water so as not to disturb the sleeping inhabitants of the Queen of Sicily's château in Saumur, he was let in at the River Gate by a drowsy porter, then silently climbed a little-used spiral staircase to the Queen's apartments, to find that though she had sat up to wait for him, Yolande had, at this late hour, fallen asleep in her chair. In normal circumstances he would have woken his mistress with a kiss but the current situation was too desperate for a second to be wasted on niceties. Casting good manners aside, the Earl shook the Queen roughly by the shoulders.

She opened her eyes at once, saying, "I've been asleep. I'm so sorry," then gasped as she took in who it was. "Richemont! You're here already!"

"The king has sent for me. He wants me to undertake a highly delicate mission. To go to Warwick and redeem Jehanne's ransom. Though I've a mind to try Bedford first because of our past connections."

"But has Charles got enough money for that? He told me he was putting all his spare funds into financing an expedition led by the Bastard."

"I have offered to pay," the Earl answered, looking grim. "Why, I'd sell everything I own, even the clothes I stand up in, to see her safe."

Yolande smiled. "Isn't there a proverb about great minds thinking alike? I was going to suggest you went to Rouen and tried to bribe someone in a high place. I even have the money ready, fourteen thousand *livres tournois* . . ."

"But that's a fortune!"

"I pawned the great emerald to a Jew, what else could I do? The rest of my jewels went to pay for Orléans."

Richemont held her close. "Between us we have amassed a king's ransom."

"And is it not worth every sou? Poor Jehanne, my gallant daughter."

"Your lionhearted daughter, *our* brave heart. If only you could have seen her fight. She is better than a brace of sons."

"What a typically masculine remark."

Richemont changed the subject. "Does she really hear those voices she talks about or do they lie in her own imagination?"

"She hears them but whether they are just a product of her mind we will never be certain."

The Earl poured himself a measure of wine from Provence. "Yet she knew that the wind would change at Orléans, in fact some people believe she *did* change it. And she found the hidden sword at Ste. Catherine de Fierbois as if by magic."

"Those two things will go against her if she is to be tried for witchcraft."

Richemont seemed hardly to hear her. "Jehanne left that sword on the altar at St. Denis in Paris as a votive offering, together with a suit of white armor she had won. She took it from a soldier who surrendered to her. But she parted with both things gladly as a gift for the saint."

"Perhaps she shouldn't have done that, perhaps her luck ran out when she gave them away." Yolande clasped her lover by the arm. "Richemont, you will be able to save her, won't you? Do you think your old connection with the Duke of Bedford will be enough to persuade him? Or can the Earl be bribed?"

"I don't know Warwick very well. He might be bribable, he might not. But as far as the Duke is concerned I have a trump card to play."

"And what is that?"

"His mistress, Jacquetta of Luxemburg, was a friend of mine many years ago. I thought I might pay her a visit and see what influence she can bring to bear."

"Anything," Yolande answered despairingly. "Arthur, try anything."

"To save my girl," he answered, his voice intense and his hands shaking, "I would go to Hell and bring out Pierre de Giac."

"Don't say it even in jest," Yolande replied hastily, and crossed herself in terror at the very thought.

The castle of Bouvreuil in Rouen, consisting of seven main towers, one of them much larger than the rest, stood huge and forbidding just beyond the ancient town, a grim and stark dwelling which, none the less, contained as well as the keep and the outbuildings, the royal apartments, the King's *logis* and the Regent's personal suite.

It was to this place that the young Henry VI of England would come when in the city, accompanied by his mother Queen Catherine, who had now recovered from her obsession with Henry V and was living out of wedlock with a handsome Welsh squire, Owen Tudor, to whom she had already borne several sons. And it was in the Chapel Royal of Bouvreuil Castle on 21st February 1431, that Jehanne was finally brought to face her judges and assessors.

Her hair had grown long since she had been in prison but in order for it not to look incongruous with her man's attire, the girl had rolled it *en rond* above her ears. As she stood there, just nineteen years old, dressed like a boy, many of the great men who had come to judge her could hardly credit what they were seeing. If this were the devil's bitch, the arch-enemy, she most certainly had assumed a very young and innocent air with which to deceive them all. Sitting at the very back, his thin face supported by his hand, Henry V's brother, the Regent of France, Duke John of Bedford, could scarcely believe his eyes.

"You must give your name and take the oath," commanded Jean Estivet, the official promoter of the case, the man with overall responsibility for procedure and records.

"A moment," interjected Bishop Cauchon, rising. "Before the prisoner does so there is something that I feel I must draw to the court's attention. As the prisoner has constantly begged and requested that she might hear Mass, I have taken counsel with other wise and prominent persons from whom I have learned that, taking into account the crimes of which she is accused and defamed and also the fact that she insists on wearing male clothing, the request must be refused, and so now I rule."

"So that's it!" thought Bedford. "She's obviously a transvestite and they're going to get her for it."

And staring at the girl before him, her muscular body, her above average height of five foot two, the Duke wondered how long it would be before, tough looking though she was, the prisoner would crack under Cauchon's obvious antipathy toward her.

She hadn't done so by the end of the second day, when the hearing was directed toward Jehanne's voices, suggestions being made that their source was other than divine. Nor did the girl weaken when it was put to her that she had been brought up to hate Burgundians and also to take part in fairy rites, dancing round their tree and searching for them, making garlands, playing in the woods. Bedford, listening, began to believe that the girl certainly was a witch and that her condemnation as such would be perfectly justified. But on Tuesday, 27th February, the Regent felt that the girl had answered more foolishly than with evil intent when questioned about her fasting.

"Have you been fasting all Lent?"

"Is that pertinent to your case?"

"Yes. Truly, it is pertinent to the case."

"Then, yes. Truly, I have always fasted."

"Have you heard your voices since Saturday?"

"Yes. Many times."

"Did you hear them in this room on Saturday?"

"That is *not* pertinent to your case."

"Oh yes it is."

"I did not hear them clearly, and did not hear anything that I can repeat to you before I returned to my room."

"What did they say when you had returned to your room?"

"Answer them boldly!"

Bedford left the session at the day's end with an unfavorable impression, believing by now that the girl was either mad or being deliberately provocative. The sooner the trial was over and they burned the wretched creature the better it would be for them all, he thought as he stripped off his clothes and washed away the smell of the courtroom, anxious not to offend his mistress, the celebrated beauty Jacquetta of Luxemburg, who was currently staying in Rouen and would no doubt be more than anxious to hear his opinion of how the trial was going when he visited her that evening.

The hidden society known as the Priory of Sion, who guarded ancient secrets and who had become the underground stream of that outlawed organization the Knights Templar, were in emergency session, two items of grave news having necessitated the calling of their members together.

On the death of Charles the Hardy, the Duke of Lorraine, early in 1431, Prince René, his son-in-law and designated heir, had received the ducal coronet only to be violently challenged by the late Duke's younger brother, Antoine de Vaudemonte. A fierce battle had ensued at Bugneville at which Antoine, with assistance from the Burgundians, had won the day and René had been both wounded and taken prisoner. Isabella, his distraught wife, had promptly removed herself and her four young children to Charles, begging for René's ransom, but he, having just paid the Bastard two thousand *livres tournois* to meet the cost of the expedition to rescue Jehanne, had been unable to aid her.

"So what can we do to help the Grand Master?" asked one of the Priory members.

"Nothing, I fear," answered the Prior, who stepped into René's role in his absence. "He has been handed over to Phillipe le Bon, who has locked him away at the top of a high and impenetrable tower. Unless his ransom can be found our hands are tied."

"An ironic situation, both he and his protégé incarcerated simultaneously."

"Ironic and dangerous to the underground stream. Let us only hope that La Pucelle betrays nothing if she is put to the test."

"Do you mean torture?" asked somebody else.

"I do," answered the Prior heavily.

"She will reveal no secrets," said yet another man, a grandson of one of the original Poor Knights of the Temple. "She took her vows and will keep them sacred. Jehanne will never let be known the fact that she is a Templar, a full member of the Order."

"But there is someone else who might," said a shadowy figure from the back.

"Who?"

"Alison du May, the late Duke's *other* consort . . ."

There was a ripple of laughter.

". . . is proving dangerous."

"In what way?"

"Drink has been the lady's consolation since the loss of her partner, and in her cups she has been heard to babble and chatter about the origins of La Pucelle. Apparently she is prepared to go to Rouen to reveal the true facts about Jehanne, facts that will get the girl set free."

"But how could revealing the fact that Jehanne is a Poor Knight reprieve her? I would have thought it would make her situation even worse."

"Be that as it may, Prior, Madame du May intends to open her mouth."

"Then it must be closed."

There was a suppressed murmur. "You will visit her in person, beg her to keep silent?"

"I may," answered the Prior ominously, "do even more."

*   *   *

What had been a wonderfully beautiful child had grown into an absolutely stunning woman. At thirty-two, Jacquetta had the loveliness of a pearl, glowing and radiant, a certain bloom added to her fine-boned face, shapeliness to her small but perfect figure, understanding to her violet wild-wood eyes.

"You must be the most perfect creature I have ever seen," exclaimed Richemont, bowled over, remembering with a catch of breath that it had been he who had taken the virginity of this exquisite being.

"That is because you remember me as I used to be," she answered, obviously not afraid to mention their youthful indiscretion.

"You were glorious then, now you beggar description."

"And you, what lies behind that concealing visor of yours?"

"Scars received at Azincourt which I have no intention of revealing in your presence. Beauty like yours must not be sullied by disfigurement."

"I confess that I am intrigued to see you none the less."

"Don't Jacquetta, for I assure you that I am not pleasant to look upon."

"Then if you will not reveal yourself at least tell me why you have come into enemy heartland. I cannot flatter myself after all these years that it was simply to see me."

Richemont laughed. "Had I known how beautiful you are I might have come sooner. But no, there is another reason." He cleared his throat, then said, "I have come about Rouen's most famous prisoner, Jehanne Darc."

Jacquetta looked thoughtful. "Ah yes, of course, I should have guessed. She was held captive at Beaurevoir, you know, the home of my aunt Philippa, Comtess de St. Pol, and I used to see the girl there. At first it was sheer curiosity that took me but eventually I grew to like her."

"Then you don't believe she is a witch?"

"No, I don't. But she is most certainly mystic. Naturally the court have got wind of that and are misconstruing everything she says about the strange voices she hears. I'm afraid John is of like mind with them. He veers between thinking she is downright evil and completely deranged."

Richemont sighed deeply. "And there is no hope of persuading him otherwise?"

Jacquetta moved so close to him he could smell the lingering heady perfume of her hair. "I have been trying and even I have failed." She gave a small reminiscent smile. "Do you remember how I fell in love with him when I was only eleven? Well, I've never changed. My body may have strayed from time to time but my heart most certainly hasn't. And if *I* can do nothing to persuade him ..."

Her voice trailed away and she shrugged her shoulders, the gesture saying more than words.

"A great pity," the Earl answered quietly. "Because I have brought the one thing that even the great Duke of Bedford might appreciate with an army to victual and pay."

"Money?"

"Her ransom. Twenty thousand *livres tournois.*"

"Christ's blood!" exclaimed Jacquetta and whistled like a boy. "Surely Charles de Valois hasn't that kind of money! Whose is it?"

"Six are mine, fourteen have been funded by the Queen of Sicily."

Jacquetta shook her head in wonderment. "It is obvious that you French hold the girl in highest regard. Only a king could demand that kind of fee."

"Then you think Duke John might be interested after all."

"I will most certainly mention it," Jacquetta answered, "who would not?" She moved a fraction closer. "Richemont, do you think for old time's sake ..."

"It had already crossed my mind."

"It would have to be under the terms of strictest secrecy."

"Believe it or not I still love the woman I told you about on that wicked occasion long ago. I will not breathe a word."

"It *was* very wicked but also very wonderful," Jacquetta replied and, stretching upward, kissed him on the mouth. "Are you going to remove your mask?"

"I would prefer not to."

"Then desire and intrigue will run hand in hand."

"Indeed they will," answered Richemont, and let all the savage years slip away from him as he relived the past by sinking down with her onto the cushions by the fire.

It was the only thing that warmed her these days, the fire

from her stomach when it was full of good brandy wine. For though she might indeed never have been legally married to the man she loved, Alison knew she mourned far more than his real widow, the great fat Bavarian hulk who had been only too glad to see the back of Charles the Hardy, that wonderful affectionate amusing man who had come out of the snows to rescue Alison on the night Jehanne had been born, and had stayed in her heart ever since.

"Oh Charles, oh Jehanne!" sobbed Madame du May, and added as an afterthought, "oh René!"

Thinking of the three of them like that almost made Alison sober again as she recalled the old proverb that events, both good and bad, always happen in threes. So, stretching out her arm, the woman who loved each one of that unfortunate trio poured herself another generous helping of brandy wine.

"Mustn't mope," she said aloud. "Must take positive action. There's one of them I *can* help."

"What's that?" asked her principal Lady, equally drunk and slumped forward over the table.

"I'm going to help Jehanne. And I'm going now."

"You can't, Madame, it's nearly dark."

"Nonsense, there are two hours of daylight left at least. Go and give orders for my litter to be prepared. Tell them we're off to Rouen to speak the truth."

But a snore greeted this momentous remark and shaking the woman did no good, rather having the reverse effect as she slumped slowly down the bench seat and finally fell to the floor.

"Servants!" said Alison furiously and, tossing the red hair that had once been so bright and lovely, made her precarious way to the stable block to arrange matters for herself.

Yet when she got there it seemed inebriation ruled everywhere that day, for the principal ostler and his two lads lay sprawled on the cobblestones face downward, and of the other men there was absolutely no sign at all.

"Drunken pigs!" exclaimed the mistress of the house, and hiccoughed loudly.

Weaving dangerously but with a look of fierce determination on her face, Madame du May tottered into the stables, straining her eyes in the hay-sweet gloom.

"Where are you all?" she called. "Somebody come at

once. I have to leave for Rouen. I've got to tell the judges about Jehanne. It's a matter of life or death."

"Death I fear," said a soft voice behind her, and Alison spun round in shock.

"You shouldn't do that," she said angrily. "You could terrify people creeping up on them. I may have to dismiss you from my service."

"Alas, Madame, I fear that will not be possible," the voice answered.

And then two hands with fingers strong as wire were round Alison's throat, constricting and squeezing until she could no longer breathe. It was as well she was drunk and the full horror of what was happening to her was dulled. As well she went quickly, abruptly ending the life that had started in a mean street in Angers and risen to great grandeur. As well her lifeless body was removed and buried so that no one could ever afterward know the awful truth. As well she followed her beloved Duke Charles so swiftly, for an existence without him held no further meaning for Alison du May.

The very thought of coming face to face with John of Lancaster, Duke of Bedford, Regent of France, Richemont's stepbrother, to give him all his many and varied titles, was so daunting after all the intervening years, that the Earl, mighty and seasoned campaigner though he might be, knew a nervous upset of his stomach and found it necessary to visit the garderobe in Jacquetta's grand lodgings several times before the appointed hour came. Finally though, fortified by brandy wine, he settled down, glad that his face was covered by a mask concealing not only his scars but also the depths of his loathing for that most arch of all the enemies of France.

Bedford looked considerably older, the dark hair thick with gray, the hook nose pinched, the full lips, so like his brother Henry V's, surrounded with lines, the intelligent face careworn.

"He's tired," thought Richemont. "He's tired of all this war," and hope suddenly rose in his heart.

"My Lord, it's been a long time," he said carefully, and held out his hand.

"Indeed it has," answered the Duke, and smiled a cynical

smile which started in his eyes then slowly covered the rest of his features.

"And a great deal of blood has flowed."

"Too much, Richemont, too much."

"But that is beside the point. I take it that Madame has told you the reason why I want to see you."

Bedford made much of pouring himself a glass of wine, bending over the jug so that it was impossible to see his face.

"You do realize that my position is difficult, to put it mildly," he said eventually. "The girl is in the hands of an ecclesiastical and Inquisitional court. She is accused of blasphemy, sorcery and heresy, to say nothing of wilfully affecting masculine garb."

"She is still dressing as a boy?"

"She insists on it. And with all these charges against her I really don't see how she can possibly get off."

"Then the matter is simple," Richemont answered boldly. "In return for her ransom money you must enable her to escape."

"What you are suggesting is highly improper."

"But profitable." The Earl drained his wine cup. "My Lord, we are both soldiers. We know the cost of war, know that no exchequer can go on funding men and arms indefinitely. I am offering you twenty thousand *livres tournois* in exchange for the life of a young female. It's a bargain."

"Things would have to be done in such a way that I could not be connected with the affair," Bedford answered slowly.

"There are always solutions to problems," said Richemont softly, his breath quickening at this first ray of hope. "Promise me that you will at least give the matter your consideration."

"I'll go that far, yes."

The two men caught each other's eye and needed to say nothing further.

"I will await your instructions," Richemont replied, and bowed his head to hide the beginning of a smile.

The governor of Rouen, in charge of running the entire city, answerable only to the King and Regent of England, was Richard Beauchamp, Earl of Warwick, who, though not young, was still a lean handsome man with eyes the

color of malachite, eyes which at the present were creased
with amusement.

"He offered you *what*?"

"Twenty thousand *livres tournois*. Double a prince's
ransom."

"They must reckon the witch very highly."

"Obviously." Bedford paused momentarily then said,
"She is that, I suppose? A witch?"

"I imagine so. Why do you ask?"

"Simply because the girl is *virgo intacta*. I know. I saw
it for myself."

"You did *what*?"

"When my wife was examining her for lack of virginity
I looked into the room through the squint. The girl's not
normally made, Richard. She and Satan could never have
known the joys of fornication."

Warwick raised a pointed brow. "Well God damn me! Is
anyone else aware of this?"

"Anne, obviously. And I presume Dr. Delachambre, who
is in charge of the prisoner's welfare."

Warwick put the tips of his fingers together and leant his
chin on them thoughtfully. "What a very interesting slant
on the case."

"Isn't it though. However, that doesn't solve our problem. What are we going to do about Richemont's offer? I
mean we can't let the girl escape, yet to pass up all that
money doesn't bear thinking about."

"There's only one thing for it," answered Warwick, grinning crookedly.

"And that is?"

The Earl glanced round surreptitiously. "Walls have
ears," he said, then, leaning close to his companion and
cupping his hand round his mouth, started to whisper.

Thirty-six

This dream was so vivid she could have sworn it was real. She had been fasting again, partly because she wanted to, partly because she had been ill and food revolted her, and it was hunger and stress that woke her, except, of course, that she was really asleep, simply dreaming she was lying awake.

Throughout her imprisonment in one of the castle towers, her time alone being spent in a small round room, her feet and ankles bound together and attached to a wooden stake, her wrists fettered as well, Jehanne had become convinced that at least one of her voices was actually living in the castle with her. Obviously not in the same cell but somewhere not far away, possibly in the room below hers, possibly in the King's lodging or the Regent's.

"What is your familiar?" they had asked her in court.

"No, my Voice."

"Does it call you the Daughter of God?"

"After Orléans I was called Daughter of God, Daughter of the Church, Daughter of the Great Heart."

"It is sinful to claim to be these things."

"But I *am* from God."

She had felt their coldness, their shuddering away from her, their feeling that if it were so easy for an ordinary person to communicate with the Almighty what need was there for churchmen. With every word she spoke Jehanne was condemning herself and yet her voices assured her that she was doing the right thing and in the end would escape death.

But now she dreamed that an entity stood at the end of her bunk, radiant as moonlight. It was a woman clothed in white, the most beautiful Jehanne had ever seen. Hair the color of molten gold hung loose, flowing to the vision's waist, and eyes like wild violets stared directly at her. Glancing into the corner of the room Jehanne saw that the three English soldiers who shared her cell, reviling her and occasionally forcing her to touch their virile members, only leaving her alone when they escorted her to the garderobe, had somehow all mysteriously vanished.

"Jehanne," said the visitor in French, her accent educated, unlike the other voices.

"Yes."

"Listen carefully to what I have to tell you. Plans have been made for you to escape from prison and when that time comes you must do exactly what you are told. So fear nothing and continue to be brave."

"When will this be? I can't bear any more of this. How much longer do I have to stay locked up here?"

"That I don't know. But whatever happens you may put your trust in the Duke of Bedford."

Even in the moonlight, even though she was dreaming, Jehanne felt there was something vaguely familiar about the beautiful face she regarded so solemnly.

"Madame, do I know you? Are you one of my saints?"

"You must not ask those questions," the stranger replied, smiling to show she was not angry. "Now close your eyes and sleep peacefully."

"God bless you," said Jehanne, starting to cry.

"Shush," said the visitor, and leaning forward gently wiped the girl's face with a fine handkerchief. She was warm to the touch, like a human being.

"*Are* you an angel?" asked Jehanne in sudden disbelief.

"I am what you want me to be. Now go to sleep. We must not speak further."

It was tempting to peep from beneath half-closed lids to see how the beautiful vision dematerialized itself but the vows of obedience she had sworn to her Order still held too strongly to be flouted. Jehanne closed her eyes and when she opened them again saw that everything had returned to normal. John Rys, John Bernard and William Talbot were back on their bunks, apparently fast asleep. Reassured that her visitor must indeed have been of supernatural origin, Jehanne slept calmly for the rest of the night.

*   *   *

Gilles de Rais had rallied his forces. The mission paid for
by Charles and organized by the Bastard had finally fallen
onto the shoulders of the Maréchal, the Duke d'Alençon
and Captain La Hire, who had abandoned their ideas of
secrecy and gone with two armed companies to Louviers,
outside Rouen, and there waited, apparently doing nothing
more harmful than field maneuvers. But during that en-
forced delay Gilles had not known a moment's peace,
under orders not to proceed until the King himself agreed,
yet horribly aware that if somebody didn't act soon La
Pucelle would be destroyed.

During the day, de Rais drank to ease his pain, but at
night he would dream of her, imagining himself ravishing
her white body, corrupting her uncorrupted flesh. He was
on a treadmill of love and death from which there seemed
no escape, besotted with Jehanne's purity, longing to vio-
late it, to make her as depraved as he, yet knowing that to
disturb the balance between them would be impossible.

But now, with her gone, beyond the reach of human help,
such thoughts were pointless, yet continued to come. In
dreams he raped her a thousand times, thrusting in with
wild and savage cries of ecstasy. But he would always wake
with a taste of ashes in his mouth, his body aching and
weak, as exhausted as if all had been reality.

"Jehanne, Jehanne," he would sob in desperation, and
feel his inactivity heavy on him as a yoke, until the day
that Richemont, alone except for an archer, came riding
into their camp.

The three leaders of the expedition rushed to the tent
they used for war council, hastily ordering refreshments to
be brought for the Earl, only delighted that the long-
awaited message had come at last. But in that they were
to be disappointed as Richemont's first words dashed their
hopes.

"Gentlemen, I bring you sealed orders which, I believe,
in effect command you to stay here on detachment. Negotiations are in hand for Jehanne's release and it is felt unwise
that you should make an attack on Rouen at this stage."

There was a moment's silence, then de Rais asked,
"What negotiations are these? From what we have heard
there seems to be little hope left for her."

Richemont's face remained blank. "I am sworn to say no

more. All I can do is assure you that the situation is very far from as grim as it appears."

"A rescue bid, is that it? But how?"

"If I told you that I would be telling too much. You will simply have to take my word for it, de Rais."

"She must not die," the Maréchal burst out violently. "She is too good, too blameless, to be used as a sacrifice."

The Earl turned a fierce look on him, as always inexplicably repulsed by the man. "Do you think I don't know that? She means more to me than I can ever describe. You can believe that I will stop at nothing to see her freed."

De Rais's dislike was written in his pitiless blue eyes. "I'll believe it when I see it."

"And see it you shall—soon."

"Even doves," answered Gilles bitterly, "can be brought to earth by savage hunters."

They had broken her proud spirit at last. After illness, chaining, humiliation, questioning, the insults of her guards, Jehanne la Pucelle had finally reached the point where she could take no more. On Thursday, 24th May 1431, in the cemetery of the Abbey of St. Ouen, where she had been taken to be publicly excommunicated, the girl had surrendered before sentence could be passed. It would seem that her voices and her heavenly visitors had failed her. There had been no rescue attempt and now she was faced with being burned to death. In a faltering tone the fine young creature humbly said that she was a miserable sinner and wanted to obey the church's commands and desires.

They had rushed her back to the castle to prepare a statement for her to sign, and that afternoon she had done so, though strangely not with her name, which she could write perfectly well, but with a circle and a cross which together formed the symbol of the Knights Templar. This done, Bishop Cauchon had repeated the hastily commuted sentence he had passed on her that morning; life imprisonment, eating the bread of suffering and drinking the water of sorrow, and warned that she must from now on accept female dress.

"I will happily do so," the girl had answered, and had put on women's penitential clothes and let down the hair she had worn rolled up above her ears during the trial. And then had come an extraordinary event which had restored

Jehanne's faith in both God and her voices. During the early hours of Trinity Sunday, 27th May, just over a year since the victory of Orléans, they had spoken to her again, telling her she had been wrong to surrender, that God really *had* sent her and that it was not a sin to wear men's clothes. And when in the morning Jehanne had asked her guards to unchain her so that she might visit the garderobe, she had seen a tunic, hose and cap lying at the foot of her bed. In a moment of defiance, knowing that God truly was on her side, she had stripped in privacy and put them on.

It had been the end of her, of course. Bishop Cauchon, obviously acting on information received, had come bustling in and asked her what she thought she was doing. And when Jehanne finally admitted that all she had said and abjured had been because of her fear of the fire and that really she was God's messenger, regretting nothing, she was done for.

In her enormous simplicity it did not occur to her that the clothes had been placed there by an unseen enemy, that it was desirable for her to disobey Cauchon by putting on boy's garb, that it was in the best interests of all concerned for her to die. But, as it was, on Tuesday evening the Bishop, stunned by her disobedience, reconvened her trial in the chapel of the Archbishop's palace.

"Her familiar has returned and told her to defy the court, to put on men's clothing again. These new crimes must be discussed."

A vote was taken and by a majority decision Jehanne's fate was sealed; she was to be handed over to the secular authorities. With indecent haste, the English administration immediately employed workmen to set up a stake and build a low stone barricade round it, this last to keep the pyre from falling in and hastening the end.

But that night, while the builders worked through the hours of darkness, candles burned late in Bouvreuil Castle, and none later than those in the apartments of the Regent, John of Bedford, who sat up till the small hours talking to the Earl of Warwick.

"The poor bitch is asking for the sacraments and I have decided to grant the request."

"But she's been excommunicated."

"Not until they pronounce it officially. It's a loophole and I intend to slide through it. After all, we're taking

Richemont's money for nothing. The least we can do is let the girl have her last wish."

"It bothers you, doesn't it?" said the Earl perceptively. "It's gone against the grain with you to cheat them."

Bedford gave a brief nod of his head. "Yes, it has. And it's not just the fact of taking the ransom. The French are rogues and deserve everything they get. No, it's simply that Jacquetta is so in sympathy with the girl, she really believes her to be spiritual and good."

"The trouble with you, John, is that you're besotted."

"No. The trouble with me is that I think too much."

"Well, stop. The girl's mad, you know it as well as I do. It has all turned out for the best, believe me." Warwick yawned widely. "Well, I'm off to bed. I'll see you in the morning."

"It's morning now."

And it was indeed getting light as a knock came on Bedford's door, the servant standing there informing him that the priests had arrived to see the prisoner.

"Give them my permission to hear her confession and administer the host. And tell me when they have gone, will you."

"Yes, my Lord."

So now he was alone with his conscience, no Warwick murmuring in his ear of how clever they had been to take the enemy's money under false pretences, no Jacquetta telling him that the girl was inspired, divine, and must not be done to death. Throwing open his window, Henry V's brother, tired of war and thinking that perhaps enough was finally enough, came to a momentous decision.

She could not accept that her voices had betrayed her, that she was going to die within the next few hours, for all along Jehanne had believed she would escape, had only surrendered to her judges in a moment of pure weakness, when she had thought about the fire and wondered briefly if her saints had been misleading her. And now it would seem they had, the two priests who had attended her earlier informing her that she was to be taken out and burned that very morning.

So had her whole life been a sham? Had her voices come from inside her head, and had she done and said all she had acting only as a poor deluded fool?

"Oh no!" cried Jehanne. "Oh no!" and stood there in her boy's clothes pulling at her hair and sweating with sheer raw fear.

And that was how the Duke of Bedford found her, collapsed in a heap in the corner of her tower room, her guards finally dismissed, crying like a child.

"Dry your eyes," he said tersely. "We haven't a second to lose."

She looked up fearfully. "Who are you?"

"The Regent of England, about to make an utter fool of himself." The girl stared at him uncomprehendingly, and he went on, "You've been ransomed, child, and as a man of honor I am about to play my part. I am going to get you out. Now shut your mouth, obey me completely, and there may yet be a happy outcome."

She was obviously too bewildered to reply but the girl at least allowed him to help her up from the corner in which she huddled.

"Now listen. This castle is built on the site of a Roman building and beneath runs the aqueduct of Gaalor. The tunnel is big enough to walk along and connects with the well in the room below this one and the well in the Donjon too. It also has a third arm which comes out in the fields. I will give you a candle and tinder and lower you half-way down. Get into the passageway and go to your left. Then it's up to you, you'll have to take your chance. God be on your side."

Jehanne found her voice at last. "Why are you doing this, my Lord?"

"Because Richemont asked me to and once, long ago, we were friends together."

A spiral staircase connected the tower rooms and going down, as she had so many times before while standing trial, Jehanne saw the well in the corner of the lower room, its handle and bucket drawn to the top.

"In you get," said Bedford, "and keep still."

She wheeled to gaze at him and he smiled briefly at the funny little countenance, so tear-stained and vulnerable, thus presented to him.

"God bless you," whispered La Pucelle.

And then the door leading onto the keep was flung open. In the entrance stood Bishop Cauchon, the Earl of Warwick one step behind him. There was a momentary silence during which the world seemed to turn to ice.

"I was bringing the prisoner down personally," said Bedford, the greatest noble in England utterly nonplussed.

"So I see," answered Cauchon pointedly, unable to openly accuse the Regent.

"I thought you might need some assistance," put in Warwick, and looked at the Duke with such an expressionless face that Bedford was never able to tell, from that day to his dying moment, whether the Earl had guessed what he was up to or whether it was all simply a matter of coincidence.

"Here are your penitent's clothes," said the Bishop, thrusting a bundle into Jehanne's hands. "Put them on. Your escort is waiting outside."

She turned to look at Bedford, one last terrible glance, and it broke his heart to say, "I'm sorry, my girl. You are beyond help now."

After it was over, after the bright spirit that had once been Jehanne la Pucelle was no more, it seemed that the square in Rouen still bore the sweet sickly smell of her burning flesh, still echoed with her agonized cries, her final whispered prayer of "Jesus, Jesus, Jesus."

She had died slowly, inch by searing inch, the executioner too nervous to choke her to death with smoke as was the custom. So, without this mercy, Jehanne had burned alive, her fine young limbs, so innocent and blameless, melting into an inferno.

There had been some unrest among the crowd, held back by English soldiers from the place of execution, and it had been noted that the Duke of Bedford absented himself from the ceremony. But only one thing bothered Cauchon, the Bishop of Beauvais, who had sat and watched the entire burning. It had been the look of bewilderment on the face of the accused as she had wept and said the words, "Then was it all a dream?" before she climbed into the fire and vanished forever from the sight of men.

The news reached the French camp at Louviers during the following day, and the three grown men who had fought with La Pucelle broke down and wept when they heard it.

"The murdering cheats," sobbed d'Alençon. "They have

taken both our money and our hope. May they rot for eternity."

"No, don't hate *them*," Gilles had answered in pure pain, "hate the voices that led her to this. Hate her God who let her suffer so."

"You must not speak like that," remonstrated La Hire, but Gilles ignored him.

"Or perhaps He would prefer me to love Him. I wonder how He would like that," de Rais babbled on. "Yes, that's the way. I'll love God and live a life I shall devote entirely to Him, everything I do shall be an act of worship." He burst into a flood of hysterical tears. "Oh Jehanne, Jehanne, how can I live without my soul? They have taken away my other self. In killing you they have also killed me."

And then, to the horror of those watching, the nobleman fell upon the ground and covered his face with the dust and sand thrown up by the hooves of the restless horses, knowing that for the rest of his days on earth he must fulfill his terrible destiny, his only hope turned to ashes, his glimpse of salvation gone.

PART FOUR

�

AGNÈS

Thirty-seven

A cold clear April and the sky blue as periwinkles, the color echoed in the chilly river, still full of last winter's icy currents. Every cloud sharp-edged, white as milk, big as sailing ships, the earth a mass of flowers, the river path yellow with primrose, the trees shimmering silver and green in a lively wind.

This day showers came and went at will, visible as they swept over the hills and down into the river valley, purpling the heavens for a moment then dancing off, throwing rainbows across the watery span behind them. Drenched by their sudden attack, the pale gold sun glistened weakly, casting faint shadows, then vanished behind an indigo cloud round which it threw a splendid nimbus.

Lambs populated the far fields, looking like daisies at that distance, the air full of their bleating, the shout of blackbirds and the high silly bark of the château's dogs, ineffectually chasing a ball in the courtyard below. It was a day of fine rain, wild wind and high excitement as the land welcomed the arrival of spring.

Staring moodily out of the window, not enjoying any of it, thinking the weather dismal and the dogs devoid of brain, stood Louis the Dauphin, first-born child of Marie d'Anjou and Charles de Valois, now aged twenty. The trouble with this particular young man was, put very simply, that where his father was ugly with style, wearing brilliantly colored clothes which gave him a faun-like and gleaming charm, Louis dressed nonchalantly, almost to the point of shabbiness, hiding his features beneath a large hat which he always wore and frankly adored, the only ornament on this unattractive head gear, a brooch depicting the madonna and child.

In looks the Dauphin resembled the very worst of his grandmother Isabeau; inclined to be squat, with black eyes and full lips, his entire face was dominated by an enormous hook nose. It was the Valois trait in caricature, and though the dauphin frequently said that his grandmother—who had died in the Hôtel St. Pol in 1435, alone and friendless, chewing her emeralds to the last—had been nothing but an old whore and that the identity of his grandfather was anybody's guess, it was obvious from that one feature alone that someone of that house had sired the King and thus his son. The only other physical similarity that the Dauphin could be seen to have inherited was his father's long legs, though in Louis they appeared rickety and awkward.

To add to his unprepossessing appearance, the young man had other defects: a speech impediment which made his pronunciation indistinct; a coarseness of manner and a love of eating and drinking which would appear to have been another legacy of Isabeau; and added to all this, and this obviously directly handed down from Queen Venus, a love of women, a sensuality, that was boundless. In his drunker moments the Dauphin declared that horning was his favorite pastime and he would spend all day and all night so employed if he had only half a chance.

He had been married at fourteen, and she a year younger, to Margaret of Scotland, the Scottish King's daughter, and heartily detested his wife from the moment he saw her. She was small, fair, listless and melancholic. She was also, and this was unforgivable, sterile. Every month Louis did his duty and every month Margaret only produced a flux despite the basketfuls of unripe apples and pints of vinegar she consumed in order to help her conceive.

"You are hopeless," the Dauphin would hiss. And his wife would weep and read love poems out loud for consolation.

Perhaps some, if not all, these things could have been forgiven if the boy had had any filial devotion but, as it was, he was in a constant state of rebellion against his father. Not, obviously, of the open traitorous variety but more a dark brooding discontent which had started in his teens and never gone away, and which had actually erupted in a minor rebellion when he had been sixteen years old and spreading his wings.

Charles, with his worldly manner and beautiful clothes, always made Louis feel like a child, a simpleton, his only consolation being that he was the sole heir to the kingdom. For out of the many, many children that Marie had borne the King the only survivors had been daughters. It seemed to the Dauphin that the palaces and châteaux were in a constant state of invasion by an army of little girls who were almost impossible to distinguish one from the other.

To make matters worse even more females were expected at the château of Saumur this very day. Isabella of Lorraine, wife of René, with her daughter Marguerite—the most obnoxious little bitch ever born according to Louis—were coming from Toulouse with their household of Ladies and *damoiselles,* all of them bound to giggle and chatter and generally ruin life. The only consolation in all this was that some of their number would, no doubt, be willing to go to bed with the Dauphin of France and there would be a chance to indulge his greatest pleasure. Turning from the window, Louis surveyed himself in a mirror.

He looked worse than usual, he thought, the bright day showing up his pasty complexion and awful nose, in fact the only good thing he could see about himself were his eyes, which were very clear, shining and alive. He had learned over the years, having no other decent feature, to make them extremely expressive. Sometimes the Dauphin would narrow them, thus looking knowing and shrewd. On other occasions he could make them twinkle and wink, and on others again, glow with passion. Adjusting them now to a steely gaze with which to look straight through his cousin Marguerite, Louis prepared to meet the visitors who he could tell from the thunder of horses' feet were rapidly approaching the château.

From the courtyard below, the building consisting of four wings round a spacious quadrangle, came the sound of the first horsemen clattering on the cobbles and, crossing to the window once more, Louis looked down. Leading the way in was Pierre de Brézé, a member of the King's council since 1437, and a bumptious upstart in the Dauphin's opinion. Tall, muscular, assured, with hair the color of crisp autumn leaves, matching hazel eyes, and a superb speaking voice, Pierre was everything that Louis was not and was soundly hated as a result.

"This visit is going to be disgusting," said the Dauphin

loudly, and pulling his hat down over his eyes braced himself to receive the guests in place of his parents, who were still in one of their winter residences in the Touraine.

"Where's Madame la Dauphine?" he shouted as he made his way from the first floor apartments to the great hall below.

"Resting in her chamber, Monsieur."

"Then get her up. Tell her I want her here. Madame Isabella has arrived."

They were pouring into the hall even as he came down the stairs, Isabella, Marguerite, and what looked like a regiment of retainers. Bowing them in, acting as the King's master of ceremonies, de Brézé smiled and chattered with a flowing good grace which made the Dauphin loathe him all the more.

"Ah, good nephew," called Isabella from the doorway. "How delightful to see you again." And she blew a kiss.

She was an enormously enthusiastic woman who always made an occasion out of an event. Fairly tall, very dark, and extremely overpainted, Isabella waved and shouted a good deal, laughed inordinately at minor jokes, and was good company in small doses.

In comparison with her mother, Marguerite d'Anjou appeared positively mouse-like, but this was merely a superficial impression for Louis knew that the girl was an undoubted brat. Greedy, avaricious, spoilt and demanding, Marguerite played on her good looks for all she was worth. Her eyes, lips and nose were, all three, quite perfectly moulded but her forehead, which she shaved in the fashion of the times, was patently too domed, the only flaw in an otherwise lovely little face. Seeing Louis she surreptitiously raised her thumb to her nose, while he, noticing, shot her a dark glance before putting on a false smile.

"My dear aunt, cousin, how very nice to see you again."

"Louis, so long," gushed Isabella. "And where is Madame?"

"Resting. The Dauphine, alas, suffers with her health."

"A delicate girl indeed," his aunt replied, not concentrating. "King René I fear will not be joining us for quite some while. He sojourns in Italy at present."

"We shall miss him," answered the Dauphin, thinking about the extraordinary turn of fate that had brought his uncle, René, to the throne of Sicily and Naples when Duke

Louis, known to the world as Jade, had died shortly after being thrown from his horse, leaving no child to succeed him.

"Ah, indeed," Isabella replied, and waved gaily at Pierre de Brézé. "Monsieur, come and cheer us all up with your merry presence. Ha, ha, ha."

Barely disguising his thoughts the Dauphin nodded to the newcomer.

"Yes, do come and cheer us. We are so dull without you."

De Brézé extricated himself from the horde of *damoiselles* who were overseeing the portage of all the luggage, and Louis took this opportunity of running an appraising eye over them, deciding which looked likely candidates for a bed romp. There was the pretty one from Anjou whom he had always rather fancied, and a plain one, very earnest looking, who was bound to be flattered and do his bidding. And then the Dauphin stopped short as his eye alighted on a figure in the corner, someone he had never seen before, and someone who set him frankly staring.

A girl stood there, half turned away, a *damoiselle,* utterly new at court and quite the most beautiful creature Louis had seen in his entire life. Hair like polished oak, lustrous and gleaming, was bound up round her head in heavy coils, framing the delicately boned face beneath. A small straight nose, a curving mouth and eyelids like half-moons, lowered and demure, were perfectly placed in a countenance the shade and texture of magnolia leaves.

"Mon Dieu!" exclaimed the admiring young man, then she looked up and he was rendered totally speechless.

The girl's eyes were large, black lashed, a rare shade, a combination of gold and green, clear as Normandy cider. Very fleetingly, just before she looked away, she gave him a tentative smile and made a small curtsy.

As the royal ladies fussed together over their luggage, de Brézé, seeing the direction of the Dauphin's gaze and grinning to himself over Louis's dropped jaw, murmured, "You admire her I see."

"By God's sweet passion, I've never seen anything like it. Who is she?"

"My mistress actually." Pierre tapped his handsome nose. "I know I shouldn't, my wife expecting a child and so on, but I'm afraid I was sorely tempted."

"I don't blame you," answered the Dauphin, wondering why he felt so bitterly disappointed. "What's the lady's name?"

"Agnès Sorel."

"I envy you her, I really do."

"Are you seriously interested, Monsieur?"

"Very."

"Then I'll see what I can do. I don't see Agnès refusing a royal command somehow. It's not in her nature." And de Brézé laughed shortly, a slightly bitter sound.

"You mean you'd share her?"

"If she is willing, I am. I'll sound her out."

Louis, suddenly deciding de Brézé was not as loathsome as he had originally thought, turned on him a beaming look. "You have just risen one hundred percent in my estimation."

"Anything I can do to oblige," said his companion, then laughed and spread his hands.

It being too late for the guests to attend dinner, which was eaten at noon, Louis immediately decided to give a formal supper that evening in his apartments which lay in the château's north wing. Saumur, in fact, did not belong to him, being the property of the Dukes of Anjou, but during René's absences in his other territories the Dauphin frequently stayed as a kind of caretaker, glad to have the excuse to be away from his father and running his own household.

Now, he assumed the role of genial host with ease and threw open his receiving room overlooking the river, setting the musicians to play at one end, the servants to attend the guests at the other. The Dauphin had also taken particular care with his dress that evening, abandoning his battered hat and usual worn gray outfit for a crimson doublet with an embroidered collar. For once, compared with his customary garb, Louis looked reasonably presentable.

Just before dusk the royal ladies and their entourage swept across the courtyard from King René's wing and mounted the elaborate staircase leading to the Dauphin's apartments. Peeping slyly through the window, Louis was gratified to see that the new *damoiselle,* ravishing in deep blue, was climbing the stairs with them, well to the back as her lowly status demanded.

"Monsieur," said de Brézé as she came in, then bowed

and winked, though quite what the Dauphin was meant to read in to that he was not absolutely certain.

The Dauphine, as was her habit, entered listlessly and late, her fair hair woven with ribbons and hung with little veils, hennins having at last gone out of fashion, a lot of jewelry about her neck which only served to make her look pale. She greeted Isabella with polite indifference but immediately went into a huddle with Marguerite, a friend though six years her junior, and could be heard discussing *tendre amour,* part of the tradition of chivalry, in her indifferent French, made all the more difficult to understand by her pronounced Scots accent. Louis, looking in their direction, gave a great roll of his eyes.

The girl, if de Brézé had indeed told her of the Dauphin's *tendresse,* gave absolutely no indication of it, standing, like all good attendants should, behind the chairs of the royal party, now and then exchanging a few words with another *damoiselle,* only glancing up occasionally to take in the scene. As well as beauty she obviously possessed both poise and discretion, excellent attributes for anyone aiming to become a royal mistress.

"Aiming," repeated Louis to himself. "I wonder why I used that word?"

For there was no sign at all that such a thought had even entered Agnès's mind.

"Monsieur." De Brézé was at his elbow.

"Yes?"

"You look bored and we can't have that. May I walk with you, perhaps chatting to a few fellow guests as we go?"

"Why not?" answered Louis cheerfully. "Minstrels, play up. You're too quiet."

But even as they approached, the girl remained passive, almost as if she had either not noticed who was coming toward her or didn't care. Louis felt the slightest tinge of annoyance and wondered whether to walk straight past. But she was too lovely, too arresting, for any such games. He stopped in front of her, made his usual ungainly bow and said to Pierre de Brézé, "Won't you introduce Queen Isabella's latest acquisition to me?"

"Charmed," said de Brézé, the lines round his eyes crinkling suddenly. "Monsieur, may I present Madamoiselle Agnès Sorel?"

She curtsied very deeply and very straight, those intriguing half-moon lids of hers lowered discreetly.

"Your humble servant, Monsieur," she said, and even her voice was pleasing, soft and well modulated, somehow a soothing sound.

"I am captivated," answered Louis, doing his best with his eyes. "Believe me, Mademoiselle."

"Oh I do," she answered, with just the slightest hint of amusement, and looked straight past him.

It struck the unromantic Dauphin that she was like a mermaid, with that gleaming hair and those great golden pupils of hers.

"You are a very pretty young woman," he said awkwardly, and was furious that de Brézé muffled an obvious snort.

Agnès dropped another curtsy, her face expressionless. "Thank you, Monsieur."

"I would like to talk to you further," Louis whispered urgently, trying to drop his voice so that he could not be overheard. "Will you come to my apartments later?"

"No, Monsieur."

"What?"

"I said no Monsieur. I do not visit the rooms of men I do not know, even be the man the highest in the land."

"Then how can I become acquainted?"

"I am staying in the Queen's retinue until she plans to leave, which is some months away. You have until the winter, Monsieur."

He was completely nonplussed, never having had a refusal like this before. "Well, if you think so," the Dauphin stammered out awkwardly.

"I do, Monsieur. Now if you will forgive me I believe the Princess is calling. Au revoir."

He stared after her disconsolately only to see the Dauphine eyeing him narrowly, her conversation with Marguerite obviously at an end. Suddenly rather miserable, Louis went to join her.

"You wanted me?"

"I would like your permission to withdraw, Monsieur. I am feeling a little faint."

"Oh, you're always faint," snapped her husband. "I've never known such a lily-livered creature in all my life. Why can't you be healthy and robust like everybody else?"

"Because I can't," answered Margaret in her terrible French, and started to weep.

"Oh really!" exclaimed the Dauphin at the end of his tether. "You'd better withdraw."

The Dauphine was suddenly all smiles. "Yes, I think I should. I've my apples to eat and my vinegar to drink. You see, I'm trying for a baby," she announced to Marguerite, who had just come over to rejoin them.

Louis's cousin smirked. "I always thought it was the potency of the father that determined these things," she said, then wandered off again.

At night they came back to haunt him and he knew he would never be free of them until the day he died when, or so he most fondly hoped, he might glimpse them again, even if it be only for a short while. Richemont always woke crying after those dreams, his scarred face drenched, his arms reaching out for the space once occupied by Yolande, his ears alert for the sound of Jehanne's battle cry, his heart pounding at double its normal speed.

He would get up then and throw a log on the fire, sitting the rest of the night with his brandy bottle for company, aware that nothing could ever console him for the loss of the two women who had not only touched his heart but conquered it.

The obscene death of his only child had been bad enough to bear, though its effect on the girl's mother had been even more devastating. It was not that Yolande had aged overnight, that would have been too trite and facile a thing to say. It was simply that the fight went out of her, Richemont had been able to mark it visibly. The hawkish features had relaxed and softened, she had ceased to worry about the King and his court, only the fact that the English, against whom she now had an almost fanatical hatred, were still in Normandy, had bothered her at all.

In a way it had almost been a relief to him to watch her settle down to middle age and though the Earl had teased the Queen that she had taken up tapestry work, he had been glad to see her sitting, sewing quietly, instead of concerning herself with matters of state. The death of Jade, that athletic outdoor creature, though it had been riding as he would have wished, had been the final blow to her. Though René had been released from captivity and inherited Anjou, Sicily and Naples with great joy, the Queen Mother had become just that, white-haired and suddenly weary.

She had died in the garden of the Château of the Queen of Sicily. Just a few moments before she had been walking handfast with the Earl, grizzled and grey himself by now. Sitting down on a stone seat to rest, Yolande had turned on him a radiant face, all the youth and beauty magically restored to it.

"I am at peace," she had said. "But very very tired."

"Then rest your head on my shoulder, ma Reine. Take a little nap."

"I will, I will," she had said.

And they had fallen asleep together, two lovers of old, out in the pale November sun. Yet when he had awoken, she had not and, in a sense, at that moment his life had ended with hers.

They had laid Yolande to rest beside her husband in the burial place of the Dukes of Anjou, and Richemont had thrown a single winter rose on her coffin then ridden away before anyone could see him weep. But at night she came to him, lingering beside his pillow, holding him in her cold embrace, waiting for him to join her in eternity.

He woke now, shivering from her touch, and went to stoke the fire, then sat down with his bottle and glass, thinking of all the stirring and strange events that had taken place in France in the twelve years since the burning of Jehanne.

He, Richemont, had become finally reconciled with Charles during the year after her death and had then seen de la Trémoille off once and for all. Oddly, he had almost felt a moment's compassion for the fat man of whom he had once been so fond, hating to see the merry mouse eyes brim with tears. Yet it had to be done for the good of the nation and his removal had seen the end of the old order. The King and the Duke of Burgundy had signed a peace treaty and Richemont, reinstated as Constable of France, had entered Paris in Charles's name. In the following year, 1437, Charles had finally made his state entry into the capital after an absence of nineteen years. The monarch had worn full armor and a hat crowned with fleur-de-lis, riding alone beneath the state canopy, his horse covered with cloth of gold also sewn with the national emblem; a far cry from the boy who had escaped on the only horse left from the oncoming hordes of Jean the Fearless.

After that the wheel of fortune had turned once more. Meaux had fallen into the hands of the Constable, then Pontoise. The English, mourning the death of John of Bedford, who had married his Jacquetta during the final two years of his life, were completely losing heart.

"The only trouble," thought Richemont, drinking his brandy as he reminisced, "was with the universal spider, the Dauphin."

That unpleasant nickname had been given to Louis because of his part in the uprising of the nobles, headed by Jehanne's comrades-in-arms, the Dukes of Bourbon and Alençon. Strangely, the Bastard, whom Charles had named Count of Dunois in gratitude for his services, had joined the rebels for a while, angry that his half-brother Duke Charles of Orléans was *still* a prisoner in England, believing that Charles was leaving him there deliberately. But it was the Dauphin's part in the plot that had been the greatest blow, and the discontented youth had had to crawl to his father, petitioning him with the greatest humility in order to be reinstated in the King's affections.

Of Jehanne's other lieutenant there had been far more terrible news than a mere rebellion. In 1440, Gilles de Rais had been arrested and stood trial, accused, as the indictment read, of "killing 140 or more children, in a manner cruel and inhuman; and that the said Gilles de Rais offered the limbs of these poor innocents to evil spirits; and that both before and after their death, and as they were expiring, he committed upon these children the abominable sin of sodomy, and abused them against nature to satisfy his carnal and damnable passions; and that afterwards he burned in these same places the bodies of these innocents, boys and girls, and had their ashes thrown into his cesspits."

Everyone had reeled at the horror of such crimes and when Gilles de Rais had been first hanged then burned, just as the woman about whom he had had such a strange and inexplicable fixation—though she had not been granted the mercy of the rope—there were some who said he was glad to follow her, that he could not exist without her, that his reign of terror against small and harmless children had been his protest to God and to Satan that she had been taken from him.

Richemont shivered where he sat, drenched with a sudden cold sweat, afraid to dwell on this the most sordid crime ever set on record. Reaching for a woollen wrap that had once belonged to Yolande d'Anjou and still, very faintly, bore a trace of her perfume, he wrapped it about his shoulders, then fell asleep before the fire to dream once more about his two dead loves.

Thirty-eight

The Spider caught the Butterfly on May Day, at least that was how court gossip told the story afterwards. They had all ridden out from the Château of Saumur in a great laughing crowd, heading away from the river towards the forested countryside. The musicians had gone first, playing their flutes and trumpets, wreaths of leaves on their heads, then had followed the Dauphin, dressed in rich blue brocade, his hat abandoned to make way for a leafy crown.

The ladies by tradition wore green, but Agnès had been clever enough to contrast this with a snow white head dress round which she had woven leaves and flowers to enhance her appearance. And this it did to such a stunning effect that nobody could take their eyes off her, the other women stealing covert and jealous glances, the men staring in open admiration, though none more so than Louis, who shook and sweated with the intensity of his feelings. By this stage, having pursued Agnès for four weeks without so much as a kiss, he had convinced himself that he was in love with her, that the constant ache in his loins was prompted by the purest of emotions and sheer crude lust did not enter into the matter.

"You can't keep him waiting much longer," de Brézé had warned. "He might go off the boil and lose interest altogether."

Agnès had given her lover a strange look. "And that wouldn't fit in with your plans, would it?"

Pierre had laughed, slipping one hand inside her bodice and familiarly fondling her breasts. "Ma chérie, it is what we agreed if you remember. We love one another but we

also love money and power; we are children of ambition.
So it is not a question of my plans, they are *our* plans."

He was right. They had decided long ago at Fromenteau,
the château in the Touraine in which Agnès had been born
and where they had first met and become intimate, that
between them they would use the court of France as a
ladder, Pierre relying on his wonderful turn of phrase and
likeable manner, she on her unparalleled loveliness.

"Together we make a deadly but irresistible combination," de Brézé had said, and they had laughed and toasted
one another and the future.

And now her partner had advised submission to the ugliest man in the world, Louis the Dauphin, who could give
them both so much and yet was so truly terrible to contemplate. With a flick of her reins, Agnès moved forward in
the jostling amiable cavalcade drawing slightly closer to her
suitor and thus causing a low buzz of comment from those
near enough to see what she had done. And yet she was
subtle, this nineteen-year-old exquisite, remaining a few
paces behind the Dauphin, not pushing herself any further
until they reached the woods and all of them drew closer
in order to thread their way through the trees.

Louis caught her horse's bridle as Agnès drew level with
him. "No word for me today, Madame?"

"I bid you a happy May morn, Monsieur."

His black eyes glistened. "You know what I mean. I'm
on fire for you. Won't you spare me a few moments conversation in private?"

Agnès lowered her glorious lids. "You are my sovereign,
Sire. I am yours to command."

"Then I order you to let the others go on and to remain
here alone with me. Agnès, if you would give me just one
kiss I swear I would be happy for the rest of my life."

"Is that a command too?"

"Yes it is," the Dauphin answered hotly, and as the last
of the riders went past, spreading out in twos and threes
in their search for branches of blossom, he leaned from his
saddle across the short space dividing them and kissed her
on the mouth. It was pathetic in a way. He wanted her so
much that he could not stop himself from trembling at even
this most mild of embraces.

"Mon Dieu, but I love you!" breathed Louis rapturously,
and leaned over to kiss her again. But she was not there

and, opening his eyes, he saw that Agnès had dismounted and was standing by her horse, looking at him with an expression of some amusement on her face.

"Monsieur, would you not be more comfortable down here?" she said.

It was the first real encouragement he had had and the Dauphin jumped out of the saddle with a will, pulling her into his arms and smothering her lips with his. And then, after a few moments of resistance, Agnès appeared to weaken suddenly and returned his kisses fiercely, running her hands over his body, even fleetingly touching him in his forbidden place.

"Oh God," whispered Louis in ecstasy.

She drew away, blushing. "Monsieur, you have made me forget myself. I apologize humbly."

"But I want it. I want you to do that. I want you to caress me, to kiss me, everywhere."

"And I want it too. Oh, mon Prince, what a fool I've been to keep you at arm's length so long."

He would have taken her there and then, mad with passion, not thinking at all, but now in the ebb and flow of feeling between them it was her turn to draw back once more.

"No, the others are too close by. It isn't safe."

"Oh, Agnès, don't tease me. You are driving me to despair."

"Not for much longer, Monsieur."

"You will come to me tonight?"

"At midnight. How do I find your secret stairway?"

"De Brézé will show you where it is."

It did not strike the Dauphin as ironic that the girl's lover should be the one to escort her to his bed. These were not easy times and in many ways, even at his exalted level, it was every man for himself, with scant room for modesty or impracticalities.

"Till then, Monsieur," said Agnès as he lifted her back onto her saddle. Then she turned and rode off into the woods, a small but smug smile briefly spoiling the perfect features of the beauty who had now most certainly started on the path to wealth and privilege.

"How do you put up with him?" said Marguerite d'Anjou

to her cousin by marriage, Margaret of Scotland. "Doesn't the very look of him freeze the blood in your veins?"

"Yes," sighed the Dauphine, "he is truly hateful. Not in the least like the heroic knights of the romance."

"How could he be?" Marguerite answered. "Nobody as ugly as your husband could ever be heroic. If I were you I'd take a lover."

"I haven't the energy," replied the Scottish girl with yet another sigh. "Just trying to conceive a child by him takes up all my time."

"I pity you, I truly do," Marguerite said sympathetically, and passed her friend an unripe apple, the seventh she had eaten that evening.

They were up late the two of them, the precocious thirteen-year-old and the Dauphin's young wife, discussing chivalry and *tendre amour,* both wishing that they had handsome lovers like those in the stories they enjoyed reading so much.

"There's talk to me marrying the King of England, I believe," Marguerite announced with a note of boredom.

"I know, I've heard the rumors. What do you feel about it?"

"Well, I have no say, of course. But it would certainly mean I could get my hands on some good clothes and jewelry. But as for him, I've been told he's a bit simple. Like his grandfather, the mad king."

The Dauphine looked amazed. "Do you mean that lunacy has been passed down through Queen Catherine to her son?"

"So it's said. But I don't care. I shall simply ignore him."

"But if the madness is hereditary," persisted Margaret gloomily, "what about your children?"

"There are ways round that," the thirteen-year-old replied loftily. "Ways that perhaps you should take."

"What do you mean?"

"That the Dauphin's not potent, that he's got no goodness in him." The girl crossed to the window. "Look over there where he sleeps. He should be here with you now if he wants to beget sons."

She turned away, dropping the silk wall hanging that partly covered the window then rapidly snatching it up again. "Margaret," she said, her voice suddenly changed to an urgent whisper. "Come here, look at this."

The Dauphine hastily tiptoed over and standing side by side the two girls peered down to the courtyard below. Crossing it, then entering the south wing by a little-used door, were a pair of figures who even in the flickering torch light could be easily recognized. Pierre de Brézé and Agnès Sorel were stealthily making their way into the Dauphin's apartments.

"So that's it!" said Marguerite softly. "The Sorel is about to fall into your husband's bed."

"Oh, the horrible creature! How could she?"

"Because she's ambitious, very. She joined my mother's retinue some while ago and has been catching men's eyes ever since. Mind you, I like her. She uses people to get what she wants, an admirable characteristic in my view."

"But what about de Brézé? I thought she was in love with him."

Marguerite frowned. "He's married, of course, though that means nothing. No, she and he are a bit of a puzzle. I've never been able to quite work out their relationship."

"Oh," answered the Dauphine flatly, and suddenly began to cry.

"Please don't," said her cousin, putting her arms round her. "Remember, all the time Louis is with her he won't be bothering you."

"But how am I to become pregnant if he's never in my bed?"

"He's bound to continue to do his duty."

"Once a month! That simply won't be enough. Conception is so difficult, and I just can't face even more sour apples and vinegar."

"And if you use someone else as a sire?"

"Louis would find out, I know he would. And there would be hell to pay."

Marguerite d'Anjou sighed. "What a predicament. Do you think we should consult an astrologer? My late grandmother's hunchback is very good, I believe."

"But he's not here."

"He will come when the King does. Guy belongs to him now."

"Then shall we go to him together?"

"Yes let's," answered Marguerite, and giggled in anticipation.

*   *   *

As a *damoiselle* of Queen Isabella's household, and one low down the scale at that, it wasn't easy to conduct an affair with the son of the King of France and at the same time go about one's duties, particularly as the Dauphin had turned out to be such a demanding lover. For despite his unprepossessing appearance, Louis had an ability to make love all night long almost without pausing. Sometimes, looking at herself in the mirror, the most beautiful girl at court thought that she had become positively pale since their liaison began.

"Late night?" her close friends would ask her, grinning.

"More like an early morning."

"I'm surprised he doesn't speak to his aunt, doesn't take you out of her service."

"But how could he?"

"Well, he *is* the Dauphin."

"Precisely. You need a king to be set up properly."

And yet another thing was bothering Agnès, a thing that hurt her very much, though she was not quite sure what to do about it.

"You don't mind about Louis and me?" she had asked de Brézé as they lay in each other's arms in the heart of the summer forest, the only place where it was safe to meet without word getting back to the Dauphin.

"Mind? Why should I? It's what we both wanted."

"I know what we agreed, I know all that, but I still fail to understand why you're not jealous. Don't you love me at all?"

De Brézé had smiled his bewitching smile, pinching the shapely chin that now trembled with barely suppressed emotion. "I adore you, you are my eternal mystery, my ocean. I could not live without you."

"Then how can you let me go to the Dauphin's bed?"

"Because it is all part of our plan."

There was no shifting him, no way of getting through to him the reality that his indifference wounded her desperately, and that night Agnès, relieved that Louis was due to attend his wife, sat at the dressing table she shared with several of the other young ladies of the household, staring at her reflection and wondering how best to come to terms with the situation.

Her family were members of the minor nobility, the lords of Coudun, neither rich nor poor, their rose-bricked château at Fromenteau in the Touraine modest by some standards but a comfortable home for all that. In fact Agnès could have counted on a reasonable match, an honorable future, if it had not been for the eruption of Pierre de Brézé into her life.

Her father had been a servant of the house of Anjou and so it had been that de Brézé, with his Angevin connections, had come to Fromenteau with a message, and set eyes for the first time on *la belle Agnès*. It had been for her love at once, dramatically, fiercely, surrendering herself and her virginity to the charmer who, married though he had been, had swept into her life so suddenly and altered its course for ever more.

"You'll be a fool to waste yourself here," Pierre had whispered to the fifteen-year-old. "I can get you a position in the household of Queen Isabella. With a beauty like yours, ma chérie, you could go very far indeed."

"But that would mean leaving you."

"One way or another we will have to part from time to time. Surely it would be better for you to be away from home if we are to continue this affair."

His reputation as the finest talker of the day was obviously not undeserved; Agnès had agreed to his suggestion and in the winter of 1442, just after the death of Yolande d'Anjou, had joined the household of Isabella of Lorraine, Queen of Sicily.

But now, now that the airy plans of youth were coming to fruition and she had actually become the mistress of the second highest ranking man in the realm, Agnès was no longer so sure, so certain, that she liked the reality of all their scheming. Because, in truth, she had never ceased to love Pierre de Brézé and the fact that she was sharing her body between him and another made her feel somehow shabby and cheapened.

Sitting before the looking-glass, assessing her faultless beauty with a critical eye, Agnès saw unexpected tears run down her cheeks and suddenly wished that she had started none of it, had remained at home and become respectably married, that she was not so desperately and vulnerably in love with Pierre de Brézé, that Louis the Dauphin might possibly leave her in peace from now on.

As if some humorous sprite had heard the last wish and acted spitefully on it, Louis's obsession with *la belle Agnès*

had increased alarmingly that summer. He felt positively
cheated if she did not spend every night with him and it
was an effort on the part of all concerned to drive him into
the marital bedroom where Margaret, resolutely chewing
green apples, regularly cried her eyes out.

"What shall I do?" Agnès asked her guide and mentor.
"He's getting impossibly demanding."

De Brézé smiled a cynical smile. "Ask him for a diamond
as your birthday gift."

"But that's not till April."

"For New Year then."

"Very well, I will. And as you seem so unconcerned with
my problem, I think it might be best if we parted company,
Monsieur. In future I intend to devote all my time to the
Dauphin."

The fine talker did not reply, too busy winking at her
and smiling a knowing little smile.

"Oh, you are so irritating," said Agnès, and stormed
away.

Strangely, it had not been difficult to stick to her resolve
and the Beauty had thrown herself into her affair with real
zest, pleasing Louis so much that he had indeed started to
shower her with expensive furs and jewels, only demanding
in return that she come to him nightly, like a mare to the
stallion, willing and ready for mating.

In this highly charged atmosphere the summer passed
and as the days began to shorten and the leaves turn color,
Louis at last reached the point where he felt he could no
longer live without Agnès and decided to make her his
official mistress, setting her up in a mansion of her own in
order to visit her frequently and remove her from the hot-
bed of gossip which was court life.

So it was that they were lying in bed one night, planning
the future in rapturous whispers, when there came the sudden stamp of horses in the courtyard below and the sound
of shouting and general clamor. Running to the window,
stark naked in the candlelight, Louis peered out while
Agnès Sorel protectively drew the sheets to her chin.

"God's teeth, I might have guessed," the Dauphin exclaimed savagely.

"What is it?"

"My father's here. Trust him to arrive unexpectedly."

"Oh, let me look. I've never seen the King."

And before he could stop her, *la belle Agnès,* also in the nude, rushed to stand beside him.

In the quadrangle far below, lit by flickering flambeaux, the girl caught a glimpse of a resplendent figure just dismounting from its horse. A scarlet hat and a doublet of black satin of Lucca shone in the light and there was a wink of diamonds from fingers and brooches as it moved.

"Is that him?"

"Yes, the old beast."

"He looks very elegant."

"Like a bloody peacock."

"Oh, shush."

They couldn't have made a detectable sound from that distance nor could the King have noticed a movement in a darkened room but the fact of the matter was that exactly at that moment he looked up, apparently straight at them. Just for a second Agnès stood there, her naked breasts lit by moonlight, and then dived out of sight while Louis, taking a few steps backward, made an obscene gesture at the window.

"Why do you hate him so?" she asked curiously.

"Because he still treats me as a child. Why, I swear he'd disinherit me if he had another son, he thinks I am so juvenile."

"Perhaps you act in a juvenile way sometimes."

Louis shot her a furious glance. "You are my mistress, not my counsellor. I'll thank you to hold your tongue."

"Then I had better go." And Agnès started to put on her clothes.

At once he was all contrition. "No, don't leave me, chérie. I didn't mean it. Please don't get angry."

"I'm not, but I'm leaving none the less. The château will be thronging with people soon and I don't want to be seen coming from your apartments in the morning."

"Are you ashamed?"

"No, not ashamed, merely very discreet," Agnès answered him firmly.

She had a much better opportunity to observe Charles de Valois during the next day's dinner when he and the Queen, the Dauphin and Dauphine, Queen Isabella and Marguerite, and their entire households, sat down to dine in the larger of the two halls. Without appearing to do so, Agnès observed him from beneath her half-moon lids, wondering if he had by any chance seen her on the previous night and if so whether he had guessed her identity.

He was about forty years old, she thought, and, though no doubt considered plain, the King was still a great deal more attractive than his son. But it was his clothes that fascinated Agnès, so elegant and stylish, today clad in a luscious soft green doublet embroidered with the King's device of roses and briars, scarlet hose on his legs, and a hat covered with plumes and silver-gilt ornaments, a far cry from Louis's horrible pilgrim badges. Momentarily forgetting herself the Beauty stared, and was rewarded with a rapid glance in her direction which had her hastily dropping her eyes again.

"Well, well!" thought de Brézé, observing. "I wonder."

But Agnès was still furious with him, not speaking, and had not done so since June.

"Silly girl," thought her lover. "I can see I'll have to have words with her."

From where he sat de Brézé, studied the perfect face yet again, noticing the way Agnès's cheekbones arched and her chin came to a fine and delicate point, how small and straight her nose was, how beautifully placed were the exquisite eyes.

"A rare creature indeed," he thought for the millionth time since he had met her. "A creature that could go to the top of the tree if only she were given half a chance."

But particularly observing the Dauphin that evening in the King's council meeting, de Brézé did just for a moment feel a pang that so lovely a thing as Agnès should be coupling with such a monstrous boy, for tonight Louis looked even grimmer as he scowled and glowered in a great fury.

"What's the matter with him?" Pierre whispered to Jean, the Bastard of Orlèans, Count de Dunois.

"The King has just announced that Monsieur is to lead an expedition against Jean, Count d'Armagnac, and he's none too pleased about it." Dunois gave de Brézé a penetrating look. "Why is he reacting so fiercely? Cherchez la femme?"

Pierre became instantly non-committal. "Possibly, but then you know Monsieur. He changes his affections as other men change their hose. It will be a passing fancy, no doubt."

"Umm," answered the Bastard, unconvinced.

But a thought was growing in de Brézé's mind that was beginning to excite him enormously, a thought that perhaps the Beauty should now aim for the highest prize of all. With great presence of mind, Pierre managed to waylay the Dauphin on his way back to his own apartments, the meeting at an end.

"Monsieur, my compliments. When do you leave on your foray?"

"Officially January. But I shall have to be off in the next few days organizing troops and munitions. De Brézé, I am utterly sick at heart. How am I going to live without her? I swear he has done it on purpose."

"Now, now, Monsieur," Pierre murmured soothingly. "The King's Majesty obviously wanted to give you a chance to prove yourself, that is all." He cleared his throat portentously. "Sire, there is something I have to tell you."

"What is that?"

"The little understanding between myself and *la belle Agnès* that I mentioned to you. I put an end to it as soon as I knew you were interested. Nowadays she and I are merely friends."

"She has told me as much herself but I thank you for saying it, de Brézé."

Pierre nodded. "Now I can be free with you again, thank God."

The Dauphin clapped him on the arm. "You're a good friend to have. I shan't forget what you have done for me."

"Then if you will heed my advice I would attend the Dauphine tonight."

"Why?"

"You don't want to arouse the King's suspicions and if Agnès should come to you . . ."

"You mean he'll have his spies out?"

Pierre shrugged elegantly and spread his hands, saying nothing.

"You're right as usual. Go to her for me, friend, and tell her that we must be careful. But promise her that as soon as I return I'll have her out of this damned court and into her own place."

De Brézé bowed. "At once, Monsieur. Leave it to me."

And he gave such a friendly smile that Louis felt guilty he had ever harbored thoughts of dislike about him.

Agnès was preparing for bed with the other *damoiselles* when a servant's knock disturbed them, and was in two minds whether to go or not when she heard that it was Pierre who was sending for her and not the Dauphin. But eventually, after the retainer had assured her several times it was most urgent, she hurried along to de Brézé's chamber, only to be whisked inside in a conspiratorial manner.

"What do you want?" she asked coldly. "It is most indiscreet of you to see me here."

"Ma chérie, you forget that I am still in love with you, that occasionally passion defies discretion and the longing to be alone with you overcomes everything else."

She knew she was a fool, knew that she must have taken leave of her senses, but the fatal fascination he held for her had never gone away, nor probably ever would. Admonishing herself even as she did it, *la belle Agnès* slid into the arms of Pierre de Brézé and surrendered herself to his kisses while he, with a smile, congratulated himself on keeping her away from the Dauphin as he had promised.

He had noticed her at that first dinner and had wondered straight away if she were the owner of the perfect breasts he had seen so outrageously displayed at his son's window, held there one fraction longer than they ought to be, Charles had thought. Looking over her figure with his worldly eye, the King had made a small wager with himself that she was indeed the girl and had felt a great stir of curiosity tinged with interest. His wretched boy, if the Beauty truly was Louis's mistress, had certainly got himself the loveliest girl in France, in fact the loveliest Charles had ever seen anywhere.

"Maine," he said, calling his brother-in-law Charles of Anjou, Count de Maine, younger brother of Marie and René and the most spoiled pup in the kingdom. "Go and find out what you can about that new girl, that beautiful *damoiselle* in Isabella's train."

The young man smiled an insolent smile, his bright blue eyes knowing. "Interested, Monsieur?"

"I only want to discover whether she's the Dauphin's mistress. But be careful. I want no ruffled feathers."

Maine had swept his hat from his head, bowing. "I am your slave, Sovereign."

"Get out!" said Charles affectionately, and applied the toe of his boot.

A few hours later all the information was his. Her name was Agnès Sorel, she was nineteen and a half years old, she came from the Touraine, was a friend of de Brézé's and, or so it would appear despite a certain conspiracy of silence, was sleeping with the Dauphin.

"He has far better taste than I thought," murmured Charles. "I must make a point of speaking to her."

"On Louis's behalf of course."

"Most certainly," the King answered firmly.

But that was a lie. Even though he would have preferred to deny it even to himself there was a quickening of interest at the very mention of the girl's name. Feeling like a Roman emperor, a lecherous satyr, Charles none the less knew perfectly well that one of these days he would make a point of seeking her out despite his son's prior claim to her affections.

The opportunity, strangely, presented itself of its own accord. The King was out, beyond the château, exercising two of his personal dogs, bracing himself against the brisk autumn weather, snuggling into his furs, when he saw coming toward him his niece Marguerite accompanied by Agnès Sorel, obviously not on particularly good terms with one another, for the Princess stalked several paces in front while the *damoiselle* followed meekly behind, very much the servant.

"Ladies," called Charles, and deliberately stopped right in their path.

Marguerite dropped an informal curtsy, as one relative to another, while Agnès made a low reverence, very stiff and very respectful. Even in that harsh light, bright with the hint of snow, she was absolutely flawless.

"You have finished your walk?" said the King, addressing his niece.

"Yes, Monsieur."

"A pity, I would have asked you to accompany me."

"Alas I must get back and prepare for the Dauphin's farewell banquet."

"Ah yes, of course," Charles answered, smiling, and with that released one of the dogs he was leading and watched it tear off into the distance after a rabbit. "Oh, mon Dieu!"

he exclaimed. "Wretched beast. Can you help me get it back?" And he looked straight at Agnès.

She did not hesitate, pulling her skirts above her trim ankles and taking off at a run, while Marguerite stared after her in a disgruntled manner.

"I'm sorry, mon Roi. I've hurt my foot," she grumbled.

But he had gone too, capering off like a twenty-year-old, leaving the Princess to walk back on her own.

"So!" Marguerite said to herself. "I'll wager the old fool's smitten. God's red blood, that'll put an end to the Dauphin's dirty little games. Margaret will be pleased."

And she went on her way, smirking and humming a little tune to herself, only too anxious to reach the Dauphine's ear and whisper into it.

"The King? The King is interested in the bitch?"

"I'm sure of it. Let's watch points at the feast."

"Oh, yes, what fun!" And poor pale Margaret gave a radiant smile which absolutely transformed her lifeless features.

It was difficult to tell, of course, for with the Dauphin present both the King and the young lady in question were obviously going to be extremely careful, but Marguerite, who already considered herself a tremendous judge both of people and situations, was convinced that the odd look, the occasional little smile, was exchanged, and that it was all highly significant. But what she didn't guess was that Agnès had never been more flustered, that beneath the calm exterior and lowered eyes she was barely keeping a permanent blush at bay.

They had caught the hound up simultaneously and laughed and joked over the naughtiness of wayward animals, Agnès's color rosy and her breath fast with excitement at being so close to the King, yet blaming it on the cold October day and the vigorous run she had just had. Being a man of the world, Charles de Valois had not cheapened himself in any way, merely thanking the girl for her help and asking if she would be present at the feast.

"Yes, I will, Monsieur."

"But of course. You are a friend of the Dauphin are you not?"

"I do have the honor to know him," Agnès answered coolly, hoping to God she was revealing nothing in her face.

"Then my son has great wisdom," Charles has replied.

But now, here, at the banquet, his occasional quick glances in her direction told *la belle Agnès* everything. She had attracted not only the son but the father; the King of France was sexually aroused by her. Further down the table she could feel Pierre de Brézé willing her to look at him but Agnès steadfastly gazed at her plate, planning to lock herself in her room so that there could be no question of sharing the Dauphin's bed on this his last night at court.

Because of her resolve it was an extremely sulky young man who rode off at the head of his column the next morning. His brows drawn together, his black eyes fierce as a bird's, Louis had no smile for anyone, making it obvious that he was as angry with Agnès as he was with his immediate family. Only the Queen, pregnant yet again, got a fleeting grimace that could have been interpreted as a grin as he kissed her goodbye.

"And now for the winter festivities," said the King as his son vanished from sight and the courtiers trooped into the warmth of the château.

"And for love!" whispered Pierre de Brézé to the Bastard of Orléans as they went to stand by the fire.

It was a wonderful wooing because it was done with such charm, such lack of haste, such infinite courtesy and style. In some enormously tactful way the King must have asked Isabella to rearrange her household so that certain of the *damoiselles* were given private rooms and it transpired, naturally, that Agnès Sorel was one of these. And yet, even then, even with her set up in her own luxurious chamber, Charles de Valois did nothing about it.

By this time the girl was in a fervor, infinitely flattered by the admiration of the monarch, yet wondering if he was ever going to make a move, if perhaps he regarded her simply as a friend, or whether out of respect for his wife's condition he was prepared to wait till Marie had given birth. This the Queen finally did on 1st December 1443, and the court groaned at the news that it was yet another girl, the eleventh surviving, the poor woman having been pregnant fifteen times, many of her children sadly dying in infancy.

Christmas came in January with much merriment, Agnès the center of attention when she set a new fashion by weaving a crown of mistletoe and wearing it over loosened hair, the sheen of her long tresses picking up the color of the fires' flames, turning them a deep mysterious red. Yet still the King, who noticed everything, did nothing about his obvious interest, and Agnès began to wonder whether she was regarded merely as a capricious daughter rather than a potential mistress.

She was in a deliberate dream, not allowing herself to think, refusing to have a conscience about Louis, refusing to let de Brézé whisper instructions, concentrating on nothing but her conquest of the King, feeling that she had been challenged, that she was on her mettle, that she must live up to her reputation of the Beauty who could capture any heart. And then came New Year and everything was finally made clear.

It was customary for the Kings of France to give *étrennes,* New Year's Day gifts, ranging from 150 *livres* for the *valets de chambre* to money, robes and jewels for the most highly favored. And there, waiting for Agnès when she woke on that particular morning, was a sealed parchment. Breaking it open, she read, "It is our wish to give your *étrennes* to you personally. Please oblige us by taking supper in our apartments tonight. Charles."

So he had made his move at last; going to her dressing table, Agnès started to prepare. Tops were unscrewed from her gold and silver cosmetic and pomade bottles, her little sticks, jewel-handled, which acted as ear purifiers, tooth picks, tongue scrapers and nail cleaners were applied. Her face and eyes were washed with cold water, her body and hair with hot, scented with exotic perfumes imported from the east.

The choice of outfit was not easy but eventually Agnès decided on a dress of green brocade with half-moons and stars embroidered on it, the sleeves slashed to the wrist so that her arms were visible, the bodice cut revealingly low.

As if he had known what she was wearing, the King was also in green, a complementary shade, the velvet tunic edged with fur, his hose a pale silver gray, while on his feet Charles wore green shoes of Cordovan leather.

"Ah, Agnès," he said, almost in a business like way, as she was ushered into his receiving room. "I am glad you could come. I wanted you to try on this." And between his fingers Charles dangled a diamond, large as a hen's egg, supported on a golden chain.

The Beauty curtsied and took a step forward, holding out her hand for her New Year gift, but the King drew back.

"No. I want to put it round your neck myself."

"That would be a great honor, Monsieur." And she turned so that he could fasten it from behind.

"There is just one further request I would like to make."

"Name it, Monsieur."

"I want to see it displayed as it should be, between your glorious breasts."

Agnès did not answer, merely pulling her dress down a little to rest on her shoulders, and waited for the King to do up the clasp.

"I glimpsed them once in the moonlight," he said dreamily, his voice close to her ear. "And have been enthralled by the sight ever since. They are the most perfect things I have ever seen."

It was his words, his voice, that were seducing her. He had not even kissed or laid a finger on her, yet already she was experiencing thrills of pleasure throughout her entire body. Very slowly, Agnès turned round to face the King.

"They are yours," she said, "as am I, to do with as you wish."

Then in one movement she loosened her laces and her dress cascaded down like a waterfall and lay rippling at her feet like a pool of water. She was naked beneath as was customary, undergarments only being worn by hired women and street walkers, and she heard Charles de Valois's rapid intake of breath as he gazed in wonderment.

"I had expected beauty," he said, "but nothing, *nothing,* like this."

It was the most erotic coupling Agnès had ever known, heightened by the fact that he was her King, that she wore nothing but the great diamond, that he for all his forty years was unbelievably virile and well made, and that the feel of his strong member within brought her to completion so quickly, so satisfyingly, that she could only beg him to repeat what he had done over and over again.

"You were magnificent, mon Roi," she breathed when it was finally ended.

"I satisfy you?"

"Completely."

He did not refer to his son, neither did she, but in the heat of that most exciting night, Charles the King learned that he had nothing to fear from any younger man, that he had become over the years a highly accomplished indeed an inspirational lover, fit for even the most beautiful woman in France.

Thirty-nine

The twilight was as fine as the diamond hung round the neck of Agnès Sorel, glimmering with soft resplendent colors, glorious as that magnificent jewel which rested, animated and alive, a sparkling drop from a fountain caught for ever in microcosm, next to the flawless skin of the most beautiful of the beautiful, as the King now lovingly called his new mistress.

A mist was rising from the Marne when they finally came to anchor, dimming the green woods that swept down to the river's shores. The château on the banks above was a reflection shimmering in the water, its image cut by the prow of their barge, hung with vivid blue, white and vermilion, at odds with the peaceful shades of the dying day. It was hard to think at this quiet hour that the great river so near Paris was the highway of kings and princes, usually covered with merchants' boats, fishermen's craft, single boats plied with one oar. For now the Marne was deserted, the people who lived along its banks gone into their houses, leaving behind them the reflection of the château, its white towers gleaming in the darkening waters.

They went ashore, climbing a hill covered with wild daffodils and vivid clumps of crocus, approaching the fairytale building that rose gracefully above them, seemingly as quiet and deserted as the sleeping river.

"What is this place?" asked Agnès, puzzled, just a little nervous.

"Wait and see," answered Charles, laughing to himself, the lines of his face softened by the delicate light of sunset, his youth returned to him by the love he felt for *la belle Agnès*, his bearing, as proud as once it had been when the glittering boy had ridden to war at the head of his army.

But now the King's pride was in her, this perfect woman who had been given to him in his middle years, so that he had finally become the envy of every red-blooded man in France.

It was twelve months almost to the day since she had first come to Charles's court, for now it was the end of April 1444, Agnès's birthday month, born as she was beneath the sign of the great bull, Taurus. It had been a year in which so much had happened, in which her life had changed so dramatically, from *damoiselle* to the King's mistress, that even thinking about it made her breathless. And yet there were aspects of that year on which she did not like to dwell too greatly; the fact that she had gone from son to father with only the merest struggle of conscience, that Pierre de Brézé—now promoted Seneschal of Anjou and Poitou for services rendered to the Crown—still remained in the background of her life, that she had not cast her lover out as she should have done, that she loved luxury and jewelry, beautiful clothes and furs, that power was beginning to dominate her life.

"This château looks empty," she said now, smiling her special smile. "Look Monsieur, there are no lights on anywhere."

"There'll be enough daylight left for us to see around it."

It was like walking into a dream. White battlemented towers, dark pinnacled roofs and high gleaming skylights stood out against the dark forest lands of the Bois de Vincennes, giving the house a secret and protected air. Below ran the gleaming river, above loomed the trees, while, beyond the battlements, the poppy sky was laced with fine dark fingers of cinnamon.

"It's glorious," said Agnès, "the most beautiful place I have ever seen." And, no longer afraid, she went in through the huge front door which hung, dark and open, awaiting her.

By the time she had walked through the state rooms, seeing herself reflected in a hundred ornate and expensive mirrors, and come again to the bottom of the superbly carved stone staircase, she had guessed the mansion's secret. It was a gift for her, her special birthday present, the personal château she had always wanted to have.

"Oh, Monsieur," she said, and flung herself in gratitude

into the King's arms, kissing the sensuous mouth so near to hers.

"You like it?"

"You know I do."

"And now you are its new and totally lovely owner. So can you guess the château's name?"

"I shan't even try."

"It's Beauté. The château de Beauté. And, therefore, as its châtelaine, you will be known henceforth as the Dame de Beauté."

And Charles laughed with pure pleasure at the fact he had been able to create such a wondrous and imaginative pun.

There was a second's silence before Agnès said, "I am so glad to have Beauté to myself. In fact I cannot think of a better gift. Not just for somewhere for us to be alone together but for another reason as well."

"And what is that?"

She snuggled closer to him. "I don't know whether you will be pleased or angry but the truth is, Monsieur, that I find myself with child. It must have happened during the first few months we were together because I am told the babe will be born this autumn. Your seed has taken root within me. Are you very annoyed?"

She need hardly have bothered to ask. Before her eyes *la belle Agnès* saw Charles de Valois bask in the glory of fathering a child by this most exquisite of creatures.

"Annoyed? I am delighted. For you to bear my baby is the highest compliment you could pay me."

She rubbed against him like a stropping cat. "Oh, Monsieur, you are so kind to me."

He was under her spell instantly, besotted by Agnès's youth and beauty and his own regeneration, as if by osmosis, through being in her company.

"Let me show you the bedroom," he said softly. "I chose the furnishings myself."

"Even the bed?"

"Particularly the bed, which is up there waiting for us."

She ran ahead of him and drew an ecstatic breath as she saw the room, a huge chamber with windows overlooking both the river and the forest, furnished throughout in green and gold, expensive tapestries on the walls, beautiful paintings everywhere, rich silk hangings draping the enormous couch. With the abandonment that Charles so adored in her, arousing him as it did, Agnès flung herself onto the bed and raised her skirts.

"Pretend I am a street girl," she said.

"Oh, you pretty slut," the King answered, as he threw himself down beside her.

Together they traveled straight from Beauté to Paris, the King now having refurbished the Hôtel St. Pol, modernizing and beautifying it, erasing all traces of his hated parents.

When all this building work had been originally undertaken, Agnès Sorel had never been heard of, but since the winter of 1443 further work had been done on the Hôtel, providing the King's mistress with her own spacious apartments. The secrecy and care with which Charles had treated the relationship at first had gone, caution thrown to the winds. It was glaringly obvious from these spacious apartments alone that he was now in the thick of a love affair and that the object of his affections was to be both spoiled and pampered.

Walking into her suite, throwing off her furs, for the April evenings were still sharp and cold, Agnès saw to her astonishment that there were tapestries piled everywhere, thrown over chairs, spread on the rush-covered floor, one particularly enormous work, depicting a hunting scene, even draped over her bed.

"What is this?" she called out, and a second later almost fainted with shock as Louis the Dauphin stepped out from behind an arras, twisting his battered hat in his hands, flushing like a schoolboy.

"Do you like them?"

"Yes, but what are they? Why are you here? What's going on?"

His radiant face dimmed a little. "They are a present for you. I won my campaign and took them from Armagnac's castle of l'Isle-Jourdain. When I arrived at the palace I asked which was your room and brought them straight here." Louis looked round appraisingly. "It's certainly very grand. I presume that is because of me." His voice changed. "Oh, mon Dieu, I have missed you, sweet Agnès. I've had no good horning for months."

She saw with horror that he was already beginning to

undress, removing his doublet, heading for the bed in a purposeful manner.

"What are you doing?"

"Getting ready for a long session, that's what." He stared at her suspiciously. "What's the matter with you? You haven't even kissed me."

"I'm sorry," said Agnès, sitting down, feeling very slightly sick. "I'm afraid I can't do that. While you were away something happened and I had to end our relationship. I have met someone else and am now expecting his child."

Louis stared at her dumbfounded. "What did you say?"

"I am pregnant by another man. Our affair is over. I'm sorry."

As if released from a trance the Dauphin ran toward her and she saw that there were traces of white saliva flecking his lips. "You filthy whore," he screamed, and smashed her so violently round the face that every tooth in her head shook. "You filthy, filthy whore. Tell me his name. Tell me what evil prick has done this to me."

"I can't," she said, flinging up her hands to protect herself. "I can't."

"It's de Brézé, isn't it? The treacherous turd, I should never have trusted him. Well by God I shall seek him out and he shall answer with his life, do you hear me? I shall end his stinking rotten life." And with that the Dauphin ran from the room, weeping uncontrollably.

Agnès crawled to her bed, collapsing on it face down, the mark of the blow already beginning to ache and discolor.

"Oh, God, how I dreaded the day he would return," she murmured into her pillow. "Oh, Holy Mother, please don't let him find out who fathered my child."

But the wish was forlorn and she knew it. A monumental storm was gathering of which she was the eye.

"Let no evil befall the King," she prayed silently, but had the feeling that God was turning a deaf ear to the pleas of such a wanton as she.

"For the love of Christ, Monsieur," gasped the Seneschal, "it wasn't me."

"You're lying, you son of a whore. Who else could it be? The moment my back was turned you couldn't wait to lay her, could you?"

"For God's sake, no," Pierre answered hoarsely, barely able to utter for the Dauphin's long wiry fingers round his throat. "If you kill me you've got the wrong man."

The pressure eased very slightly. "Then who was it?"

"If you let go I'll tell you."

But Louis was in no mood for mercy having ridden from Paris to the Loire in a state bordering on madness, hardly stopping to eat or sleep, covering the distance as if he rode with Satan. Instead of releasing his grip he raised de Brézé in the air, still strangling the man, and proceeded to shake him as a cat does a rabbit. It was only when the Seneschal finally began to turn blue that Louis released him, dropping de Brézé to the ground, seeing him crunch onto the cobbles.

"For Christ's sake what's going on?" said Dunois, the Bastard, coming round the corner and seeing, to his horror, the Dauphin of France doing a very good job of murdering a man. "Monsieur, control yourself, for pity's sake."

Louis turned on him such a tragic face, so tear-stained, so desperately ugly and sad, that Dunois felt a genuine pang of pity.

"She's left me Jean. The bitch Sorel. She's been sleeping with God knows who in my absence and now she carries a child. What am I to do? I love her so much."

"Tell him it wasn't me," gasped de Brézé from the ground. "Please Dunois, clear my name."

There was a horrible silence, the Bastard too afraid to utter a word.

"Why are you both so unwilling to name the man?" asked Louis, looking from one to the other of them. "If it wasn't de Brézé then why are you reluctant to tell me?"

"Please," said Dunois quietly, "let the matter rest, Monsieur. No good will come of asking too many questions."

"But I want to know. I have a right. She was my mistress."

"There are some things better left unsaid."

"But not in this case surely."

"In every case," the Bastard answered firmly.

"You're protecting someone, that much is obvious. But who could be so important to you both that neither of you are prepared to name him?"

And then the light of realization dawned on his face and both men witnessed the Dauphin crease with agony, his features working in pain, tears and sweat coursing simultaneously down his cheeks.

"By Christ's blood, it's *him*. My royal father. That disgusting old whoremonger, may he rot in hell for his crime."

"Please, Monsieur!" begged the Bastard, while de Brézé, feeling that he was safe at last, began shakily to get to his feet.

"Mark this day, Dunois," said Louis, spinning round, only a miracle of self-control keeping him from shaming himself by publicly breaking down. "Because today begins revenge, today begins hatred, today begins my curse on the King."

"Be silent, I implore you," answered Jean in an agony of spirit. "Please, Monsieur, for the sake of your soul, be silent."

Forty

A month after Agnès officially became la Dame de Beauté, a great tournament was held in Lorraine to celebrate the betrothal of René's daughter, Marguerite, to Henry VI of England. Unfortunately the twenty-three-year-old bridegroom was not present, his place being represented by the Earl of Suffolk, but the royal court of France were there in strength, with the exception of the Dauphin who had found it necessary to lead another military expedition, this one to support the Habsburgs against the Swiss.

"Thank God for it," de Brézé whispered to the Bastard. "I don't think I could have stood the strain."

And it was certainly a delicate situation as Agnès, now officially a *damoiselle* in the Queen's household and just beginning to show her pregnancy, accompanied the royal party, much to the amusement of the cynical English.

"No fool like an old fool," Suffolk crowed to his wife, "why, he can hardly keep his hands off her."

"I wonder what the Queen has to say about it," the Countess answered thoughtfully, putting into words what most of the women at court were thinking.

And indeed she had made a point, for Marie, the safe harbor, the King's good-natured mother-wife, was angrier than she had ever been in all of her life. The fact that Agnès was insultingly beautiful and that the Queen through her many pregnancies and a life devoted to child rearing had lost what looks she had, did not help the situation in the least. Furthermore, rumors that Charles had replaced Louis in Agnès's bed had reached her ears once too often for them to be discounted any longer.

"She's a cheap whore and you should be ashamed of

yourself," she stormed. "And whose child is she carrying, that's what I want to know?"

"What do you mean?"

"Is it yours or our son's?"

"Don't make a scene," Charles admonished, "you'll ruin the betrothal party."

"It is you who have ruined it by bringing your strumpet along, not I."

"She is part of your retinue, Marie, and could hardly have been left behind."

"I'll give her my retinue. I shall have the bitch disposed of as soon as we return home."

"You'll do no such thing. No moves will be made against Agnès, do you hear me?"

Marie had looked at him curiously. "You're really in love with her, aren't you?"

"Yes. I'm sorry, I simply can't help myself. But I'm still in love with you too."

"Yes, like an old pet that you've got thoroughly used to, that's all your love amounts to these days. Oh, God, I wish I were dead."

"Why?"

"Because I'm pregnant and so is she. I shall be the laughing-stock of the entire court."

"Not if you behave with dignity, as will I," Charles answered solemnly, but secretly he felt a surge of shaming pride that in the middle years of his life he had publicly become such an undoubted dog, an incredible achievement for such an ugly child as he had been.

Also present with this bickering royal party was Guy, now promoted Astrologer Royal to the King himself. The death of Yolande had released him from service to the house of Anjou, though nominally he had still belonged to René. But the King of Sicily and Duke of Lorraine and Anjou, as René had become, was well staffed with astrologers and had given the hunchback to Charles for a birthday present. So, after many years, the old friends were together once more and at a time when Charles, besotted with Agnès, felt he needed all the amatory advice he could get.

But it was not the King who sat opposite Guy now in the room he had been allocated in the Duke of Lorraine's château in Nancy, but the royal bride herself. Marguerite d'Anjou had come for a consultation before she sailed for England and the unknown life that lay before her.

"My future husband," she said, "is it true he is simple?"

The Astrologer Royal hesitated momentarily, never liking the fact of giving bad news. "You will certainly be the more dominant of the partners," he said eventually.

But Marguerite was vixen sharp. "Then he *is*. Will he go completely insane like his French grandfather or will he just be stupid?"

"He will withdraw from the world. It is you, Princess, who will carry the burden of the kingdom and it is you who must act wisely at all times. There are two roses in this crystal, one white, one red, and with them all the signs of bloody conflict."

"What does that mean?"

"Civil war, somehow connected with roses, will break out in England and you will be involved, heavily at that. Tread with caution always. Do not listen to false advisers. Weigh everything that is said to you with great care."

Marguerite shivered. "It sounds awful—but interesting! Will I have many lovers?"

Guy smiled. "What Queen does not?"

"My aunt Marie for one. It is the King who is the lecher in that relationship. And talking of lechery, how will my friend the Dauphine fare? She would like to have seen you herself but lies ill in bed so asked me to represent her."

The Astrologer's face grew watchful. "I feel Madame should be careful in all that she does."

Marie looked slightly irritated. "You do nothing but issue dire warnings. Surely you can be more specific?"

"Very well. The Dauphine is thinking of playing a dangerous game in order to become pregnant. I believe you know what I mean . . ."

Marguerite blushed, remembering her advice to her cousin to find herself a healthy youth to act as sire to her child.

". . . and this could rebound in her face. The Dauphin is going through a period of hating women. I believe that Margaret of Scotland should beware his wrath."

The Princess of Anjou shivered, suddenly cold. "I will tell her to be on her guard."

"I enjoin you to do so, otherwise her entire future lies under a shadow."

Marguerite stood up, passing him a gold coin. "I thank you, Astrologer. I will think seriously about everything you have had to say. And now may I ask you one final question?"

"Certainly."

"I have heard it said that you knew Jehanne Darc, that your brother once acted as her confessor. Is it true?"

"Yes, it is."

"Then tell me please, what was she like?"

"A strange mixture of things as are most people. But brave and good and honest, a bright flame that can never be put out."

"Why didn't my royal uncle save her?"

"I think he tried but failed."

"Was he sad that she died?"

"He went into retreat at the Abbey of St. Nicolas where my twin was Abbot. I believe they prayed together for many days."

"You said *was*. Is he no longer there?"

"No, he left his post after Jehanne's death and went to Rhodes to become a Knight of St. John of Jerusalem. He believed that her work should somehow be continued so became a warrior-monk in order to play his part."

"That must have been a hard life after the gentleness of an Abbey in Angers."

"He seemed to welcome it," Guy answered sadly. "He was never able to settle back to the monastic existence having once known her."

"She must have been a very powerful person."

"The strange thing was that in many ways she was very weak."

Marguerite shook her head. "I don't understand."

"No," Guy said quietly. "She left behind a great many questions, most of which I believe will never be answered."

In September of the year of Marguerite's betrothal, the Dauphin was wounded at the siege of Lambach, an arrow being shot through his knee, pinning him to his saddle. In an agony of guilt, Charles had written letter after letter begging his son to come home, but the Dauphin preferred to stay away, keeping his own counsel, until the campaign was finally over and there was nothing further left for him to do. Then, very reluctantly and with dread in his heart, Louis had returned to the Loire in the spring of 1445.

He was now a little mad, there could be no doubt of that, the form of his madness an obsessive hatred for his father and Agnès and, even more so, for his wretched wife the tragic Margaret of Scotland. In fact no sooner was Louis through the door at the end of his journey home than he turned on her like a fury.

"You useless cow," he had screamed, throwing the girl violently to the floor. "What cruel fate ever led me to be married to you? You're barren, your dower has never been paid, you cough, you're stupid, melancholic, and recite poetry. Why don't you have the good grace to die?"

"But I've never done anything to harm you," the unhappy creature had sobbed. "I devote my entire life to trying to have a child. It's not my fault if nothing happens."

"Of course it's your fault," Louis had shouted, giving her a swift kick. "For it's certainly not mine. That child the bitch Sorel had last November, I fathered that."

"But you couldn't have done. You and she weren't ... together ... in February. It's the King's."

He had knelt down beside her, his dark eyes narrowed to slits. "You're not to say that word, do you hear? Nobody speaks the name of my royal whoremonger father to me. And if ever you do so again I'll flay you to within one inch of your life."

Poor Margaret had become hysterical at that, shrieking and sobbing so loudly that her principal Lady had come running in, only to find the Dauphine in a state of total collapse.

"You'd better take her to her bed," Louis had said carelessly, peeling himself some fruit. "She's jealous because the royal whore has had a child. Get a doctor to her for the love of God."

It was so cruel, so heartless, that most of the courtiers were sickened by his behavior. But there were those within the whispering gallery who took delight in causing pain and trouble and murmured to the Dauphin that Margaret had been unfaithful while he was away fighting, that she had been trying to find some country boy to act as a stud.

"If she's betrayed me, by God I'll kill her," Louis had said, and there was something about the look on his face, about the wildness in his eyes, that had convinced his set of friends the Dauphin meant everything he said.

Within six months of the death of Yolande d'Anjou, Richemont's legal wife, Marguerite of Burgundy, had followed her to the grave, and the Earl had been left entirely alone to dream of the past. Widowerhood had suited him, had become a way of life he enjoyed, being solitary, to walk by the river when he was at home, free to eat and sleep when he liked, to dream of Yolande and feel her cold hands touch him during the night, to think about his one great love and how different it would all have been if they had married.

But his companions, his comrades in arms, unable to understand that the Earl was perfectly happy, interfered as is the way of the world and, at the great tournament given to celebrate the betrothal of Marguerite d'Anjou, introduced him to Jeanne, younger sister of Charles d'Albret. She was very young, sixteen, blonde, giggling constantly, and she was also very highly sexed, taking a perverted delight in seducing a scar-faced warrior three times as old as she was.

But the dictate of his body, the sexuality of his youth, was still there and a kind of madness overcame Richemont as Jeanne wore him out in her sinful bed. And then came the horrid discovery that she was pregnant and her lust turned to abject despair.

"You've got to marry me. I'll be disgraced," she had wailed.

"But I'm too old for you."

"You should have thought of that before you raped me."

He could have protested, told her that if any raping had been done it was on her side, but the Earl of Richmond acted like a man of honor and married the little slut in a private ceremony. Two months later she was dead, going into premature labor in the autumn of 1444 and ending both her futile life and that of her baby. Richemont had thought that he would never smile again.

But then, returning to the court in the summer of 1445, having besieged and conquered Metz in Lorraine on behalf of the King, he was both pleased and surprised to hear that Jacquetta of Luxemburg's widowed sister Catherine, together with the youngest sister of all, Isabella, were paying Charles a visit. With fond memories of his former mistress, who had tried so desperately hard to save Jehanne, the Earl had looked forward to meeting them.

Much to his surprise, rather than resembling their beautiful sibling, the sisters were not only totally unlike her but also completely different one from the other, Catherine being large, dark and hearty, and Isabella small and redheaded. But the one thing they did have in common with the beautiful Jacquetta, who had consoled herself after John of Bedford's death by marrying Sir Richard Woodville, renowned as the most handsome Englishman of his day, was an acute mind and a ready wit.

Richemont had found himself warming to the jolly Catherine when he had been placed next to her at a banquet, for watching her eat had been an education to him. Unlike many of her contemporaries the widow thoroughly enjoyed her food and made no bones about it, tucking in with relish and eagerly awaiting the next course.

"Aren't you afraid of putting on weight?" the Earl had asked cautiously, knowing that women could be sensitive about such a subject.

"If I do, I do," she had answered philosophically. "I like my victuals too much to give them up. Life's too short for all that nonsense."

Richemont had found himself suddenly laughing, enjoying himself, feeling that a breath of fresh air had come into the room.

"I think you're absolutely right," he had said.

"We've met before," Catherine had gone on, "though I don't suppose you will remember. It was years ago in Brittany, one Christmas when we were all young and gay. I believe you had some kind of liaison with Jacquetta."

"Were you the dark little one with the soulful eyes?"

The widow had laughed uproariously. "Well, I'm still dark at least! But the passing of time has knocked the soulfulness out of me, and as for being little ..."

And she had patted her comfortable girth with a merry grin.

Richemont had found himself laughing once more, and when Catherine had suggested that they ride together the next day had accepted her invitation with remarkable enthusiasm, remarkable in that he had not thought he would ever look forward to a woman's company again.

But to see her riding had been a further revelation.

Plump she might be and hefty her horse, but together woman and beast made a remarkable partnership, and Catherine had taken off like an arrow from a bow, zooming toward the summer woods, jumping obstacles as if they simply didn't exist. By the time the Earl had caught her up, and he was far from a mean horseman himself, Catherine was in full flight, sailing over the brook on her way to the high meadows.

"God's heart," Richemont called after her. "Where did you learn your equestrian skills?"

"Born to it," she shouted cheerfully over her retreating shoulder. "Got on a horse as soon as I could walk. My father always called me the Amazon."

"You're quite a character!" the Earl had shrieked to the black dot in the distance, which had waved its hand then vanished over the horizon.

It had been a strange courtship, not a love match at all, more a series of japes which had had them both laughing at the pure absurdity of their situation. And then had come the night when Richemont had finally grown serious and told Catherine, without mentioning the name, of his forbidden love for a married woman, now long since dead and gone, and how he would never, could never, love like that again.

"Much as I felt for my old thing," the widow had answered.

"You were fond of your husband?"

"I adored him. It was one of those extraordinary occurrences, a chance in a million I suppose. The marriage was arranged yet we fell passionately in love at the very steps of the altar. I can tell you, Richemont, the consummation was memorable! Anyway, we had twenty-five blissful years together—I'm forty-two to save you trying to work it out—and then he went, a candle flame in the breeze. I cried for an entire month. But what's the use? Life must go on."

The words were on his lips before he knew what he was saying. "We should marry for companionship's sake."

"Each other do you mean?"

He hadn't in fact but now that the Lady of Luxemburg came to say it the practicality of the idea struck Richemont forcibly.

"Yes, if you could put up with my scarred face."

"Who's perfect at our age?" Catherine responded sensibly.

"Was that your way of accepting?"

"It certainly was." And she clinked her wine cup against his. "Here's to us," she toasted robustly. "And here's to my sister Isabella and her little intrigue."

"Is there one?"

"Haven't you noticed her and that pretty young man, Maine?"

"Now you come to mention it they do seem quite friendly."

"Friendly? They're thick as thieves. There'll be a double wedding, you mark my words."

And the redoubtable Catherine was right. Charles, Count of Maine, Yolande's third son and the King's kinsman through marriage, who had been angling for a Burgundian heiress and missed his chance through being too dilatory, had decided to cut his losses and marry the ginger dwarf, as he lovingly nicknamed the diminutive redhead who was to become his bride. Thus the stage was set for a great celebration and the King ordered tournaments and jousts, banquets and merrymaking, as he gladly gave permission for both the Constable of France and his spoiled but beloved brother-in-law to be married.

Much to the delight of her female contemporaries, Agnès Sorel immediately conceived following the birth of her daughter, Marie-Marguerite, in November 1444, and went straight from one pregnancy to another, thus temporarily losing her spectacular figure which, in its full glory, was narrow-waisted, slim-hipped, with breasts that would tempt the saints. Yet, despite this silly miscalculation, la Dame de Beauté continued to lead fashion.

Agnès now bought all the cloth for her many sumptuous dresses from Jacques Coeur, a wealthy merchant of Bourges who had his own fleet of ships and imported goods from the great ports of Alexandria, Beirut and Cairo, the Pope having granted him special permission to trade with the infidel. Spices, cloth and jewels were shipped in by the load, and Coeur also exchanged French silver for Arab gold, thus amassing a mighty fortune for himself.

But it was not only her clothes that originated in the warehouses of Coeur, for from him came the fabulous jewelry of Agnès Sorel; her diamonds, her rubies, her pearls with sapphire clasps. In fact it was rumored abroad that la Dame de Beauté now owned more jewels and was richer than the Queen of France herself.

For the weeks of festivities planned to celebrate the two court weddings Agnès, despite the fact she was now six months pregnant, had had nearly two hundred different outfits made and nearly as many veils. Long and transparent, mere gossamer wisps, they floated to the ground from the top of her head, enhancing the lustre and sheen of her polished oak hair, which she wore loosed about her shoulders. There was no woman in the kingdom who could compete with her and as a result la Dame de Beauté was universally loathed.

To mark her disapproval of the public flaunting of her husband's mistress on every conceivable occasion, Marie had made it her habit to stay away from most social gatherings unless her presence was required as a matter of etiquette. So it was that this night she had remained at Tours, the place beside Charles occupied as usual by la Dame de Beauté.

"The King can no longer bear to be parted from her," the Dauphin's chamberlain, Jamet du Tillay, whispered into his master's ear as he poured his wine. "La Dame is beside him at the table, at Council, in his bed."

"Do you think I don't know it," Louis answered fiercely. "She feeds on him like some filthy parasite. And talking of such things, what further news of my wife and her adulterous habits?"

"She's definitely being served by someone or other but her ladies are keeping a conspiracy of silence about who the man actually is."

"You've got to find out," the Dauphin whispered back frantically, breaking into a sweat. "You've got to find out."

He was in a terrible state, almost to be pitied had he not been such an awful young person. Truly believing that the pathetic Margaret, who had ignored Marguerite's advice to find herself a stud and remained steadfastly faithful to her husband, had betrayed him. As a result his cruelty to her of late had reached unbelievable proportions and the Dauphine had now had a complete nervous breakdown, hardly able to walk round, hard put to it to conduct any kind of normal conversation. And this is what led her to be sitting propped up on either side by two gentlemen of the Dauphin's household, unable to be present at the banquet without actual physical support.

"Whore," Louis would hiss at her from time to time. "Adulteress." To which the Dauphine would respond with silent tears followed by a coughing fit, her chronic chest condition obviously aggravated by her nervous debility.

From higher up the table Charles glared angrily toward his son, not quite near enough to hear all that was going on, none the less mouthing the words, "Behave yourself," a fact which sent Louis into a state bordering on frenzy.

Turning to Margaret the Dauphin shouted, "Why don't you go to bed? The sound of your cough is ruining my entire evening."

"I can't help it," she answered pathetically. "I've been on a pilgrimage to try and get it cured."

"To try and get laid more like," Louis answered into a sudden stunned silence.

"What did you say?" roared the King, looking amazingly angry, his eyes hard as rocks.

"Were you waylaid," the Dauphin said brazenly, but nobody laughed at his quick thinking.

"I'll thank you to cherish Madame la Dauphine," Charles shouted furiously, bringing his clenched fist down onto the table. "Go to her now and give her comfort. You're her husband, damn you."

It was the most appalling public outburst and seasoned courtiers, brought up on intrigue and violence, used to such things, were still seen to cringe.

"Very well," answered Louis, his face transformed into a mask of pure loathing. "I will." And leaving his place he went to sit beside the weeping girl, pushing the man on her right out of the way.

"Now, ma chérie," he said, putting his arm round her and pulling her close. "Is your cough tickling you? Here, have a drink." And tipping her head back, the Dauphin poured the contents of his own wine cup down the hapless girl's throat.

Margaret choked and spluttered, unable to cope with so much fluid at a single gulp but, and this was tragic to behold, responded to this mockery of kindness, this sham of husbandly concern, by leaning against the Dauphin weakly and attempting a smile.

"Thank you," she whispered, and then with no warning at all went into a convulsion, a kind of fit, her body completely rigid before she lost consciousness.

There was absolute pandemonium as glasses and plate went flying and Charles hurled his way toward the inert figure of his daughter-in-law.

"Send for Dr. Poitevin," he called to the scurrying courtiers, "and carry Madame to her bed. Musicians, cease your play, the banquet is at an end." He turned to Agnès. "Madame de Beauté, will you attend our daughter?"

"Certainly Monsieur," she answered gravely, and swept a low curtsy before she joined the sad procession carrying the seemingly lifeless Margaret to her own apartments.

Three days later, on 16th August 1445, the twenty-one-year-old Scottish girl was dead, apparently of pneumonia. Dr. Robert Poitevin, who as a young student had been the lover of Richemont's first wife, Marguerite, and who had since become the King's personal physician, was sent for, but could not save the Dauphine, and of a sudden the word poison was on everyone's lips.

"Is it possible?" Charles whispered to Robert on the morrow of poor Margaret's death. "Could our daughter have been murdered?"

Poitevin looked very serious. "Monsieur, Madame always had weak lungs, damaged no doubt by that beastly Scottish climate she came from, and the Dauphine's illness was certainly symptomatic of pneumonia. But ..."

"Yes?"

"She died of suffocation and exhaustion which are also signs of convulsant poison. I am afraid, Monsieur, that the truth will never be known."

"There shall be an inquiry," answered the King. "Just because he is my son there is no need for him to think he is above the law."

The doctor nodded. "You are right, Monsieur. I shall give my opinion honestly and truthfully."

"I am sad, angered and troubled," answered Charles, "and will take my leave within the next hour. Suddenly to be under the same roof as Monsieur le Dauphin is something I no longer want to do."

"You will not attend the funeral?"

"No, let Louis see to that. We have no wish to be present, watching his arrant hypocrisy."

But the Dauphin did not bother even to make a pretence of mourning. As the small coffin was put into the vault beside the other Valois queens, he merely shrugged his shoulders, said, "Our spouse has died of an excess of poetry," then smiled a secretive smile and went on his way.

Forty-one

On the morning of his forty-third birthday, 22nd February 1446, Charles de Valois sat alone in his study in the great castle of Chinon and thought about both the past and the present. Below the walls of the château the little town lay cold in the chilly wind, single pennants of smoke rising from the clustering houses, but here, high up in one of the towers, the world was warm and opulent, the King in his furs, logs on the fire, a hound asleep with its muzzle on its paws.

Only now in these, the middle years of his life, had Charles finally become the person whom Nicolas Flamel had foreseen so long ago in Paris, the King who had brought peace to France. The truce of Tours, signed in 1444, had put an end to the war with the English even though they still remained in Normandy, Maine and Guyenne, and all fighting had now ceased. As to Charles himself, he had found love and contentment with Agnès Sorel, la Dame de Beauté, mother of two of his daughters and quite unquestionably the loveliest woman alive. Thinking about her and his feelings for Agnès, the King could see at last that she had been the prophesied Beauty to his Beast and not Bonne, his tragic mistress whose place of burial had remained hidden from the day of her death to this.

Yet in this great sea of calm, in which his Piscean nature swam with so much joy, there were sadnesses. The fact that Marie rarely spoke to him, had chosen to live in Tours or Amboise, refusing to associate herself with her husband's harlot, as she always referred to *la belle Agnès,* wounded him, though he could fully understand the Queen's feelings. But far worse than that was the ever deteriorating situation between himself and the Dauphin, his only surviving son, whom Charles most strongly suspected of being a poisoner, and yet against whom no proof had been found at the inquiry of October 1445.

The King had been fond of his wisp of a daughter-in-law, felt guilty that he had chosen her for Louis's wife, thus sentencing her to an existence of sheer torment. It had grieved him enormously that she had died saying she had never done wrong to her husband and that she wanted to finish with life; so much anguish to feel at only twenty-one years of age. The King had known on the day Margaret had gone to her death that he would never trust his son again.

Yet he could forget all this when he lay in Agnès's arms, smelling the sweet fragrance of her, the dew of her body nectar, lying between breasts the like of which he had never seen before and which la Dame, now that she was not pregnant, showed through her dresses, driving all men to frenzy. For *la belle Agnès* had openings in the front of her gowns through which either her nipples or indeed an entire bosom were sensationally revealed. Churchmen were horrified, women too old to adopt such a fashion furious, but the King's mistress triumphed. It may not have been a subtle style, she may well have dressed more provocatively than anyone since Charles's own mother, but the fact remained that she had men at her feet, adoring and worshipping.

Even thinking about her made the King glow with happiness and he got up to put another log on the fire, gazing into its sparking heart, seeing pictures, day-dreaming. But the rush of those flames conjured an image he did not want to dwell on at all and he abruptly turned and went to stare out of the tower window.

Far below was the courtyard where Jehanne had dismounted prior to their very first meeting, that small brave oddity who had sacrificed her life for him. Charles had tried his best to save her, though so discreetly that even now blame was laid against him for doing nothing, for letting an innocent go to the stake, a fact which only increased his suffering. And then, of course, there had followed the extraordinary case of the False Pucelle, a woman who had appeared in Metz in 1436 claiming to be Jehanne, saying that she had not been burned but rescued. It had been a confidence trick, of course, but the sex murderer Gilles de Rais had pretended to recognize the girl and had taken up arms with her. In the end the situation had turned from a nuisance to a full-blooded annoyance and Charles had trapped the woman into coming face to face with him in a garden at Orléans where he had denounced her for the impostor she was and forced her to apologize to the Paris *Parlement.*

"A bitch," said Charles to himself and thought again of the real one, of the brave little nun only happy wearing men's clothes, who had never menstruated according to her squire, Jean d'Aulon.

"May I come in, Monsieur?" called a voice from the doorway and, turning quickly, the King saw that the debonair Pierre de Brézé stood there.

"Please do, Seneschal," he answered, glad to have his train of thought interrupted.

"I wanted to convey my birthday greetings to you personally." And Pierre smiled his autumnal smile, charming and amusing as ever.

Charles had never been absolutely sure about him, a niggling suspicion that the man might at one time have been Agnès's lover worrying away at the back of his brain. But to please her he had promoted him, showered Pierre with honors, but never disregarded the fact that de Brézé and the Dauphin were still friends, that it was impossible to trust anyone, not even this eloquent and gracious man who spoke so well in company but who had an irritating habit of contradicting people, even pointing out to his King minor mistakes Charles had made, not an endearing characteristic at the best of times. And now de Brézé overstepped the mark again by pouring himself a glass of wine without asking permission.

"A toast to mothers," said Pierre, raising the cup high. "Always apt on a birthday, don't you agree, Monsieur?"

"Mine," answered Charles wryly, "died of fat, of dropsy, of gout, so enormous she had become semi-paralysed. She was cold and miserable and thoroughly deserved it all. But I drink to her spirit, wherever it may be."

And he swallowed a draught in a single gulp.

"Then I'll toast another mother, more attractive than the last you described. To Agnès, the most beautiful matron in France."

"To Agnès," repeated the King, and wished that the familiar pang of jealousy he felt whenever de Brézé mentioned her name, would go away and cease to torment him.

Richemont could not believe the letter but yet the *chevaucheur* who brought it wore the livery of Georges de la Trémoille, Duke of Sully, and there was no reason to suppose it was a forgery.

"My good Lord Constable," it read. "I whose fate it was to be rescued by you from the wicked clutches of Pierre de Giac send you greeting. Though he has not asked me to contact you I am writing on behalf of Georges de la Trémoille, my husband. Alas the poor man lies dying, disgraced and exiled from court, and yet speaks of you so often, saying despairingly that he would have your forgiveness before he leaves this world for the next. I would ask you, therefore, in the name of Christian charity to put behind you the many wrongs that he did and come to Sully to take your leave of him. If you find it in your heart to grant this, his last request, he will die blessing your name. Your humble servant in gratitude, Catherine de la Trémoille."

"Do you think it is a trap?" Richemont asked his sensible wife, who was munching an apple to keep her going till the next meal.

"Heavens no, deviousness like that is for saints not sinners." Catherine de Richemont looked carefully at the Duchess's writing. "This was penned by someone distressed and hurried, see how her hand was shaking." She pointed at the erratic letters. "No, I think it is genuine and you should go."

"He tried to have me killed several times, you know."

"I expect you did the same to him," his wife retorted roundly, and helped herself to a sweetmeat.

A slow smile crept across the Earl's face. "As a matter of fact you're right."

"Then go and make your peace with him. You'll feel better if you do."

Richemont had left for Sully that day, suddenly all too conscious of the passing of time and the fact that he might arrive too late, that Georges might have left the world unshriven, desperate for a blessing from the man who had once been his closest friend. But, as it was, the pennants and flags flew high above the château, announcing to the people of the little town surrounding it that their Lord was still alive.

Madame de la Trémoille, whom Richemont could clearly picture running naked in hot pursuit of de Giac and the arresting party, loudly demanding not her husband but her silver back, wept as she greeted him.

"My Lord Constable, God will thank you for this. Yet I would beg you to let me warn Georges before you go in. I did not tell him I had written to you in case you refused to come."

So Richemont was left on his own to gaze over the green moat out of which the château, large and formidable, appeared to rise, though it actually stood on a small island. None the less, the impression of strength was overpowering and the Earl found himself reflecting on what a character its owner had been in his day. Thus, he was not quite prepared for the change in Georges when he was finally issued into the Duke's chamber.

The vast stomach still rose high in the air, draped with white sheets, looking like a snow-covered mountain, but the jolly face had sunk away, leaving jowls devoid of fat hanging like empty sacks about the dying man's shaved chin. Yet the eyes were bright in the wasted visage, peeping out as acutely as a rodent's on his final vision of the world.

"Richemont?" he said, just a little uncertainly, and then tried to smile but cried instead.

"Yes, it's me," answered the Earl, controlling his own emotions rigidly.

"Come to take your leave?"

"I never speak of leavetaking while there is life. But I am most certainly here to renew an old friendship, one that was once the best in France."

"Yes, it was that indeed," Georges answered through his tears, and putting out his hand grasped that of Richemont in a tight desperate grip. "My dear man, I beg your forgiveness. I ask you to pardon the sins I committed against you and to let me have your blessing before I go. Once I released Pierre de Giac from his pact with Satan, now I am asking you to release me from my burden of guilt. Will you?"

"Of course," answered the Earl and, kneeling by the bed, put one arm round the fat man's shoulders.

"Then say the words."

"I Arthur, Earl of Richmond, forgive you Georges, Duke of Sully, for any crimes you may have committed against me in either thought or deed. I also give you my blessing as one gentleman of France to another and pray God that he will look with mercy upon your immortal soul."

With a gasp de la Trémoille sank back upon his pillows. "And I Georges," he said faintly, "forgive you for any similar offence and pray not only for your soul but for that of she who has gone before us and whom I will soon see again, the well beloved of Richemont, Yolande d'Anjou."

"My well beloved?" repeated the Earl wonderingly. "So you knew?"

"Oh, yes, I guessed long ago."

"Thank you for keeping my secret."

"No one is entirely evil," Georges answered. And then the housemouse eyes closed and his breathing became slightly shallower. "Send for my wife and the priest," he whispered. "Richemont, farewell." And the pressure on the Earl's hand ceased.

Outside in the coldness of day, Richemont waited alone, staring into the emerald waters, feeling to himself that an era was coming to its end. And when, an hour later, the banners were lowered to half-mast, he wept for the passing of a spirit which, though not that of a good man, was certainly a creature unique.

In order to see the Queen at the time of his birthday Charles had been forced to command a very annoyed and petulant Agnès to stay at Beauté for several days.

"But why should I, Monsieur? After all it is her attitude not mine that prevents Madame and me from meeting."

"Madame is the Queen," Charles had answered with just a hint of acerbity. "She has the right to ignore you if she so wishes."

"Well, I am not pleased about it. I feel I am being shut out of your life."

"That is very silly and extremely childish. Please, Agnès, help me over this."

"Oh, very well," his mistress had answered and had reluctantly left Chinon looking sulky, accompanied by the flamboyant de Brézé, a fact which had given the King considerable disquiet.

Several hours later, dressed in black as was her custom

these days, Marie had arrived with a clutch of little girls, looking about her suspiciously for any sign of the favorite.

"She's not here," whispered the Dauphin as he made his bow. "He's sent the whore packing to make room for you, Madame."

Marie's eyes lit up. "Permanently?"

Louis shook his head. "I fear not."

The Queen pursed her lips. "I thought that would be too much to hope for. But say no more of it, here comes your father."

The King, magnificently dressed in red and silver, came to join them, only for the Dauphin to make an over-elaborate bow and walk away. It was apparent to all that the Universal Spider was plotting something, constantly being caught whispering with his familiars in corridors and corners, but so far no tangible sign of any conspiracy had emerged.

"Marie, ma Reine," said Charles, and kissed his childhood friend, his confidante and wife, on both cheeks.

"I find you well, Monsieur?" she replied with obvious lack of interest, and made a very deep and unnecessarily formal curtsy.

"Never better, chérie, never better."

"Well, I can't say the same for me," Marie answered tartly.

"And why is that?" asked Charles, speaking before he had had time to think.

"I will tell you when we are alone," the Queen stated with great meaning, and her husband inwardly gave a groan.

Throughout the rest of that day they treated one another with a politeness that was positively alarming, their conversation stilted, their smiles artificial, and it wasn't until the evening when they were alone in the King's receiving room, musicians playing softly in a side chamber muting the sound of their voices from any who might think of spying on the royal couple, that Marie finally came to the point.

"I can barely tolerate the existence you have forced upon me," she said angrily. "Why should I, the Queen of France, be forced to live in semi-exile while you parade your half-dressed slut for all the world to see? Why should she not be kept in the background, why does it have to be me?"

"Why does it have to be either of you? Marie, years ago

you accepted Bonne, accepted that I needed beauty in my life. Why can't you accept Agnès now?"

"Because I felt sorry for Madame de Giac, an emotion I most certainly do not have about that other smug bitch."

"But why?"

"Because I don't trust her. She is altogether too powerful and furthermore I am not at all sure she is faithful to you."

"Why do you say that?"

"She is extremely close to de Brézé to say the least. And what about Jacques Coeur?"

"He is a merchant who supplies her with her clothes and jewels. That is all."

Marie glared at him. "Oh, how swiftly you rise in her defense! It is said behind your back that anyone who speaks against her is finished as far as you are concerned."

Charles glared back. "Kings are not concerned with gossip and tittle-tattle, and neither should be Queens. Where is your dignity, Madame?"

"Died of cold when you threw me out of your bed."

"How dare you!" Charles expostulated angrily. "You removed yourself. Don't blame me for your self-inflicted wounds."

"Self-inflicted! What choice did you give me? Damn you, Monsieur, you have ruined my life."

And with that she wept, her middle-aged face, which had not worn well over the years, crumpling.

The King stood helplessly, his hands hanging down by his sides, and then all his old feelings for his childhood friend came rushing back and he knelt down beside her chair, putting one arm round her shoulders. The old magic so long dead, worked again, and they flung against one another in an enormous kiss, their recent anger putting paid to formality and inhibition.

"Mon Dieu!" exclaimed Charles, and tore at his wife's black clothes just as if he were a lusty peasant.

"Not here! The musicians!"

"Come to bed then. Oh, Marie, I love you."

And he did, this was the tragedy of it. In a completely different way, Charles loved both Agnès and Marie simultaneously. But now he was mad to have his wife, pushing her into his bedchamber, taking her where she stood by the bedpost, too excited, his need too urgent, to wait another second. And the Queen, remembering all her old power over him, gave as good as she got, making love to him like a young girl, naked and eager, smothering him with kisses, guiding his vigorous appendage herself. It was a night that neither of them ever forgot and in the dawning, just as the spring birds began to sing, they coupled again, this time in rather a desperate way as if, because the hours of daylight had now returned, the delicate balance of their newfound relationship might once more come under threat.

It was a cold windy sunny March day and on the river Marne the bright sails of the fishing boats dipped and rose, the craft flying along in the breeze, the willow trees on the banks shaking and shivering in a whirl of buds, the golden catkins and the twigs, black from a recent shower, tossing in the air. Gulls wheeled amongst the crows, white wings spread against pitch-dark feathers, and the towers of the Château de Beauté glimmered gold.

In the cabin of her luxurious boat, furnished with rare and beautiful things bought from Jacques Coeur, Agnès Sorel and Pierre de Brézé lay naked, entwined about one another, exquisitely engaged in the most intimate act of all. As always with these two, attracted quite hopelessly to one another and never able to break the spell that lay between them, it was a fine encounter, slow to screaming point but culminating in ecstasy. But then, greedy as children, they were not content and began again, performing the carnal act until darkness fell and it was time to return to the château.

They had moored the boat at a little island, the property of la Dame de Beauté, in order that nobody would guess their secret. But as Pierre rowed back through the darkness Agnès, dressed now, sat silent, trying to come to terms with the fact that she was in love with two men at once. For she *did* love the King, not just as the provider of all good things but because of his sophistication, his charm. The appeal that only a middle-aged man can have for a younger woman was very real as far as she was concerned. And yet Pierre de Brézé, in a way, was the focus of her entire life. He had claimed her virginity and her love at the same time. The idea of giving him up was unthinkable. But, despite that, Agnès Sorel was not devoid of conscience and sometimes squirmed at the enormity of her arrant naughtiness.

In this maze of different emotions there was another factor, too. Jacques Coeur, the dark, intelligent, beautiful merchant prince, also admired and wanted her. Yet his love, thankfully, took a less demanding form than that of the two other men. Half the jewels Agnès owned, including rare and wonderful diamonds, Coeur had given her in exchange for seeing her naked, not touching just looking, walking round and round her where she stood on a podium.

Once she had asked him if he did not want to know her carnally and he had replied that he loved beauty, not sex. And yet the merchant had a wife tucked away somewhere and had fathered children. La Dame had considered it extremely strange. But at least Coeur's love did not tangle her web any further, and for that she was both relieved and thankful.

"You're quiet," said de Brézé, momentarily shipping his oars.

"I'm thinking."

"Of what?"

"The King. Hoping he never finds out about us."

"It's the Dauphin one needs to watch, not his father."

"But he likes you."

"He pretends to, but actually I'm sure he's stirring up trouble."

"Against us?"

"Of course."

It was a sobering thought and it was with downcast eyes and much circumspection that Agnès, having received a message that the Queen had finally left, returned to court in April. De Brézé, of course, had gone ahead of her long since in order not to arouse suspicion, but Agnès was hard put to it not to rush into his arms when she saw him again, suddenly ill at ease, a strange pricking feeling about her spine.

One month later she knew exactly what had caused her premonition, and cursed the fact that she had allowed herself to be sent away so tamely, for the rumor was sweeping court that the Queen was enceinte.

"It happened during the King's birthday celebrations," Agnès overheard one giggling *damoiselle* tell another. "Madame moved back into Monsieur's bedroom and apparently there were high jinks."

"Obviously! My goodness me, I wonder how la Dame de Beauté will take the news."

"She'll be sick in her shoe," answered the other, then they both shrieked mirthfully and moved away.

Agnès stood silently, wondering what to do, unable to consult Pierre who was in Anjou, suddenly feeling totally at a loss. As vulnerable as she was lovely, the girl felt moved to tears by the King's betrayal of her, not giving a thought to her own scandalous behavior. And then she had a moment of inspiration.

"Don't unpack my things," she called to her Ladies. "I've a notion to go to Bourges and see Jacques Coeur."

"But we've only just arrived."

"Then it will be less work for you," answered Agnès, suddenly angry, "if I got straight off again."

The matter of where Marie should be housed was now becoming something of a problem, made all the more difficult by the fact the Astrologer Royal had assured Charles that this latest child, conceived during the wonderful weeks of passion the King and Queen had shared together, was not only fated to be Marie's last but was actually a boy, a boy moreover who would survive, unlike the other little mites, and grow to manhood. Dazed by the news, Charles had consulted every astrologer for miles and they had all come up with the same answer. The Queen of France was going to bear him another son.

"You cannot leave Madame out in the cold, Monsieur," Dr. Robert Poitevin had told the King. "She will be forty-two years old when the infant is born. If you want this to be a successful pregnancy and delivery the Queen must have every care, both mental and physical."

"But Madame will not live under the same roof as *la belle Agnès.*"

"Then *la belle Agnès* must be persuaded to reside elsewhere. After all, she has two wonderful châteaux to choose from."

And it was true, following the birth of Agnès's second child, Charlotte, Charles had given his mistress the Château of Issoudun in Berri, filling it with wonderful tapestries, linen and tablewear, to say nothing of a specially made bed complete with set upon expensive set of lace and satin sheets.

"I'll do my best," Charles had answered gloomily, "but you know what women are like."

"I **know what the** Queen will be like if she is not cherished."

And with **those words** Robert Poitevin had bowed his way out, leaving **the** King to solve the problem for himself.

"Beauty is everything," Jacques Coeur said, gently kissing Agnès's nipples. "Beauty of appearance, beauty of thought, beauty of manners."

She smiled at him in the gentle moonlight, standing naked on her podium, her neck and breasts enhanced by the presence of a single pearl brought from the East, the size of a human eye.

"But you forget yours I think, Monsieur. You promised that you would look at but never fondle me."

"That kiss was a salutation to perfection, that is all. I would never lay my hands on you, ma belle. You are too perfect ever to be touched."

"But I *am* touched and you know it."

Coeur made a very slight face. "I do not wish to think of it. Such things are not aesthetically pleasing."

It occurred to Agnès briefly that the merchant might be homosexual but she discounted this on the grounds that he had a wife and children.

"I came to you for advice not a lecture, my friend. What should I do about the Queen?"

"Accept the situation with grace, ma belle. Let the poor woman return to court. Show the world that you are as beautiful on the inside as you are to behold. Take up residence somewhere near by but not intrusively so. The King will love you all the more for it."

Agnès sighed. "You are right, I know it. I must be seen to have the manners of a princess even if I am not one."

"A charming sentiment." He kissed her navel. "And as a reward you may keep the pearl."

Agnès's hands flew to it and she lifted the precious thing in order to look at it. "But I couldn't, it is far too rare."

"Wear it and say it came from Jacques Coeur, then my fame will spread throughout court and everyone will buy their jewels from me."

"But they do that already."

"Be that as it may, I want you to keep it, *belle Agnès.* Wear the pearl and think of me."

And the strange exquisite would hear no more of it,

merely giving her one more very intimate kiss then sending La Dame de Beauté back to her sovereign lord.

It had been a great relief to all concerned when the King's mistress announced that she would like to live at Loches, at least for the time being. And it had been an even greater relief to the doctors and astrologers when Marie, huge already despite the fact that the pregnancy was only four months advanced, arrived with her suite to settle with Charles at Chinon. Even the Dauphin, who was presently living a life devoted to conspiracies and carnality, was in a happy frame of mind. He was currently sleeping with three ladies at once, some said quite literally so, and this had put a smile back on his ugly face.

In this peaceful atmosphere the Queen bloomed while Agnès remained quietly in the background, and on 1st December 1446 went into a short vigorous labor the result of which was the birth of a large baby boy who, despite the fact he was baptised Charles almost instantly, appeared to have absolutely no intention of dying. His horoscope being cast by Guy, the Astrologer Royal was pleased to inform the King that the boy would both live and love well.

"A Prince after my own heart?"

"Absolutely, Monsieur."

An even greater bonus was that the family tendency to extreme ugliness seemed to have bypassed this baby, who grew very quickly to look like his grandmother, Yolande.

"I love you. You have given me the greatest gift of my life," said Charles to Marie, and really meant it.

And it was then, this remark being repeated to her by one of her many spies, that la Dame de Beauté decided it was time for her to act, that, despite her legendary appearance, her hold on the King was beginning to weaken. Thus, in the middle of December, she set out from Loches announcing her intention of passing her Christmas at court. And everyone awaited her return with bated breath.

"I shall go," said Marie. "I'm not staying here with that little strumpet."

"But you can't journey in this weather. You've only just had a baby. Please, chérie, stay here for my sake."

"Do you promise not to touch her?"

"I promise," answered Charles weakly, and knew he was lying even as he said it.

*   *   *

It was almost as if de Brézé had taken up the challenge on
Agnès's behalf, an extraordinary fact in view of the secret
situation between them. And yet to this brilliant wily man
the situation was highly dangerous. Much as he loved his
glorious protégée, he had no wish to see her influence di-
minish, her power over the King weaken. It was essential
for his own ambitious plans that Agnès remain the royal
favorite, and the fact that the Queen was now high in the
King's esteem did not please the Seneschal at all. Thus he
decided, on la Dame de Beauté's behalf, to win back the King's
passion.

The means chosen was a banquet to end all banquets,
held on Christmas Eve, 5th January, plate and cloth loaned
by Jacques Coeur, jewels bedecking every course, all of
which were prepared by the finest cooks in France. As for
the principal guest, Agnès herself, she was a masterpiece;
dressed in fur-trimmed velvet, scarlet and black, one breast
displayed, white as a gardenia against the lustrous dark
pelt, diamonds in her hair and ears, one vast stone glittering
at her throat. In comparison the poor Queen, only shortly
risen from childbed, looked fat and frumpish and extremely
middle-aged.

During the course of the feast, while this perfect star
shone in her specially prepared firmament, it was obvious
that Charles was as deeply attracted as ever, that the feelings Agnès aroused in him had not gone away and that,
when all was said and done, the birth of Charles of France
had made absolutely no difference.

"If he's like this on Christmas Eve," said one cruel courtier to another as the King rose to dance with *la belle Agnès,*
his whole manner displaying the fact that he was once more
utterly besotted, "what will he be doing by Twelfth Night?"

"Agnès up to the hilt?" asked his companion in a cruel
play on words, for when a fellow courtier was disliked by
de Brézé they only had to be given an "Agnès up to the
hilt," a word from la Dame de Beauté in the King's ear,
and out they went.

Most unfortunately the new mother, suffering with the
usual depression following birth, overheard the entire thing
and retired early from the banquet, scarcely able to fight
off her tears. And seeing the Queen leave, a fact hardly
noticed by the dancing King, seemed to be a signal for

the Dauphin who also left the table and hurried after his distraught mother.

He caught up with her in her own apartments and displayed an unusual amount of tenderness, putting Marie to sit by the fire, bringing her a footstool and a cool towel for her forehead, pouring a glass of Bordeaux wine, known for its curative effect on invalids.

"What has upset you, Madame?"

"What do you think?" sobbed Marie, finally giving way to tears because of Louis's kindness. "It's her, that evil bitch. She's determined to get him back, not that she ever lost him in the first place."

"You should stand up to her, tell her what's what. Why should she be allowed to get away with it? Truly, Maman, if there are any further displays like tonight I would remonstrate with the great whore. And I'll back you up," the Dauphin added hastily as his mother looked doubtful.

"Would you? Would you really speak on my behalf?"

"Nothing would give me greater pleasure," he said, and rolled his dark eyes in a way that was horribly reminiscent of Isabeau when she had been working herself into one of her furies.

Just as the courtier had prophesied, Charles weakened on Twelfth Night and was drunk enough and foolish enough to plant a public kiss on Agnès's lips at the end of a slow sad dance which had brought them close together, but never quite close enough to touch.

"I adore you," he said.

"But what of the Queen?"

"I adore her too. Can you accept that?"

Remembering the lesson taught her by Jacques Coeur, Agnès curtsied and said, "I am but your servant, Monsieur. It is not my place to lay down terms."

And it was then, in total contrast to this scene of great humility, Marie erupted on them like a fury. Leaving her place at the table, making straight for the King's favorite, the Queen stood opposite her, staring into her face.

"I'll thank you not to embrace my husband in front of others, Madame, nor, come to that, in private either."

Agnès turned on her a beautiful mask of pure insolence barely concealed by a look of respect.

"Madame?"

"Don't play innocent with me," retorted Marie, and slapped la Dame so violently round the face that the girl reeled back, clutching her jaw. And what misfortune it was that she fell straight into the grasp of the Dauphin who had come silently to stand behind her.

"You wicked slut," he hissed. "You who have shamed my mother before all."

And with that he hit Agnès too, though not with the flat of his hand but with a clenched fist that truly hurt her. There was an awed silence during which the King pulled the Beauty into his arms protectively.

"Madame, Monsieur," he said, addressing his wife and son, "I would ask to see you in my chamber immediately. Seneschal de Brézé, take la Dame de Beauté to her apartments and fetch Dr. Poitevin to attend her." And with that he strode out.

To poor Marie who had loved Charles so long and so well, the next hour seemed like a nightmare as the King spoke to her and her elder son in a voice that terrified, soft but menacing, never rising to anything above normal conversational tones.

"I will never forgive either of you for what you have done tonight," came the sinister words. "Madame, I suggest that you return to one of your favored residences. Monsieur, it is now time you set up your own establishment as it seems you and I cannot live in peace together under the same roof. I would suggest, therefore, that you go to the Dauphiné and hold yourself ready to join the expedition to Lombardy."

"And when will that take place?"

"I cannot say at this precise moment."

The Dauphin jumped from his chair, his face contorted with rage, his black eyes suspiciously bright.

"Such an expedition might never happen. What you are really doing is sending me into exile, isn't it? Well all I can say is you must love your great whore very much indeed."

"Yes," put in Marie, also rising. "If you are capable of putting her above considerations of family, above blood ties, I hope you get all you deserve. Other than for state occasions I shall not visit you again." And she swept from the room, Louis one pace behind her.

The Dauphin turned in the doorway. "Goodbye, *Father.*

Now that you have another son you obviously have no further need of me."

And with that Louis strode out, leaving the King white and trembling, while the boy shed silent tears of grief. This was to be their last meeting. From that day onward they were never to see one another again. The echoes of the slap the Dauphin had given Agnès, said to reverberate even as far as the Vatican, were to sound in his ears until the day he died.

Forty-two

The conspiracy which the Dauphin had been hatching against Pierre de Brézé while continuing to clasp his hand and call him friend finally came to fruition in the spring of 1448. Planted witnesses and forged letters and a statement by Louis that the Seneschal had tried to poison the King's mind against him, led to disgrace and a case being brought before the *Parlement* in Paris. The King departed for the capital in order to be present during the trial and for this state occasion Marie left her self-imposed exile and journeyed with him. Agnès Sorel, ostensibly on a pilgrimage to St. Geneviève, followed a few days later.

Rumor had reached the citizens of Paris a considerable time ago that the King had a mistress and the good-hearted Queen was out of favor and, as a result, la Dame de Beauté was jeered wherever she went. Nor did the flaunting of her two greyhounds, Carpet and Robin, in white fur coats and jeweled collars, endear her to the hungry crowds.

In the end, in order to keep the peace, Marie had led Agnès onto the balcony of the Hôtel St. Pol and stood beside her to wave. But once inside the state room from which the balcony led, Marie had glowered at Agnès and said to her husband, "I would be obliged, Monsieur, if you never ask me to perform that kind of favor again."

"I am humbled by your kindness," answered Charles, and their eyes had met and in his wife's he had read the fact that she still loved him and would do anything not to see him unpopular with his people.

But this incident, superficial though it might have appeared, was part of fate's intent, simply a stepping-stone on the way toward the final fulfillment of the great destiny of Charles de Valois.

With the King already gone from the room Agnès loitered to give her own thanks, for these days she had grown into a woman of maturity despite her superficial arrogance.

"Madame," she said, and dropped a curtsy that though polite somehow managed to block Marie's way to the door.

"Yes?"

"I wanted to say how grateful I am to you, how I owe you a debt. Is there anything I could do to repay you? I know, believe me, how hard it must have been to stand there beside me and smile as you did."

The Queen looked at her hard-eyed. "The truth is I dislike you intensely, Agnès Sorel. That it is you who have come between me and my happiness. How could I in those circumstances ask any favor?"

Inspired, Agnès said, "Because you could use me, perhaps, as an instrument to achieve ultimate good."

Marie paused, obviously dwelling on this, then eventually came to a decision and spoke.

"Has the King's Majesty ever told you of the night when, as a boy, he was taken to see the Grand Master of the Priory of Sion? And of how it was predicted to him that he would be the one finally to drive the English from our shores?"

"His Majesty has talked of it, yes Madame."

"That prophecy has never been fulfilled. It hangs over him, the last thing between the King and ultimate greatness. Already he is known as the monarch who, aided by Richemont and La Pucelle, brought peace to our country. I believe it ought to be he who should take the final step, who must force the English out of the last of their strongholds and return France to its own people."

"Of course he should, it would grant him a place in history. But how may I help in achieving this?"

"Is it not obvious?" answered Marie bitterly. "It is you he listens to, you whom he adores. Persuade him that the time has come for him to break the truce with the English and invade Normandy. That this one final onslaught can bring him the victory and peace that it is his destiny to achieve." The Queen's voice changed. "I can never pretend to care for you, Madame. In fact I detest you for what you have done to disrupt my family. But achieve this one fine thing and history may look upon *you* with kinder eyes."

Agnès went hot, then cold, a sudden feel of her part in

the King's immortality laying its cold hand on her. Curt-sying again, she raised the Queen's fingers to her lips.

"Madame, I will do my best for I believe you to be right."

"Better to be the mistress of a great King than that of a nonentity?" asked Marie cynically, no illusions left for her.

"Better to be the Queen of an illustrious monarch than one who never left his mark," Agnès rejoined with spirit.

During the next four weeks, while one of the most suave and delightful men of his era was on trial for his life, Agnès in the background constantly assuring the King that de Brézé had never plotted against him, the concept of all that the Queen had said had taken considerable shape in her mind. Was she then, the pampered Beauty, also a pawn of destiny? Was it her role to be the power behind the throne? To turn a good King into a great one?

The more Agnès dwelled on it the more she warmed to the idea. Jehanne had gone forth with sword in hand to free France from the yolk of the English. Might she not achieve as much lying between perfumed sheets, her only weapon her sexuality? She delved deeper into the concept of the mistress as God's chosen instrument, the one who from her pillow whispered that empires should topple, con-tinents be won. By the time that Agnès Sorel had talked the King of France into writing a letter to the *Parlement* speaking of de Brézé's value and the services he had ren-dered in the past and would be likely to do in the future, she had become convinced that it was she, working through Charles, who had stepped into the shoes of Jehanne. If, Agnès wagered to herself, Pierre was cleared of the ridicu-lous charges laid against him then she was definitely the one chosen to see France shake off the last vestiges of enemy occupation.

On 14th May, Agnès having left Paris a tactful four days earlier, de Brézé was acquitted of treason, reinstated a Sen-eschal, then called before the King to receive his pardon and orders for the future.

"Monsieur," he said, going on one knee and covering Charles's hand with grateful kisses. "I owe you my life."

The King smiled wryly. "You owe it to *la belle Agnès*. It was she who convinced me that the charges against you were flimsy and that you were indispensable to my cause. Without her judgement I might perhaps have been a little more cautious. So now it is up to you to prove yourself all over again."

It had been Charles's ploy for years; playing chess with people, setting men on their mettle, pretending to be governed then throwing the would-be manipulator out. But de Brézé, even though he knew the King for the wily fox he was, had been badly frightened and said, "Anything, Sire, name it. What new position do you want me to hold at court?"

"I don't," Charles answered drily. "I have an entirely new line for you to pursue."

"And that is?"

"I want you to prepare for the forthcoming invasion of Normandy."

De Brézé gulped. "What?"

"The invasion of Normandy. Certain factions have been speaking about it for months but it was la Dame de Beauté who finally convinced me that it was not only right but inevitable. So, my dear de Brézé, as you and she are so close I thought it only fair and proper that I hand the planning of the entire exercise over to you." And the King laughed soundlessly.

Pierre remained silent, still kneeling at Charles's feet, wondering if there had been any hidden meaning in that last remark, if the King had received information through his vast network of spies about the exact nature of the relationship between the Seneschal and Agnès Sorel. But obviously nothing further was forthcoming so he merely nodded his head and slowly stood up.

"Consider it done, Majesty. The invasion will be prepared."

"Good, good," answered Charles. He looked up. "By the way, Seneschal, I think it might be for the best if Monsieur le Dauphin remains where he is for the time being, so do not involve him in your scheme."

De Brézé decided to risk all and said, "Will Monsieur be coming back to court?"

"No, not for some considerable while," answered the King with a sigh. "In fact, not in the foreseeable future."

Plans for invasion of the territories held by the English continued to simmer secretly for most of that year, it being both Charles's and de Brézé's idea that some excuse should be made for their taking up the offensive, that they should wait for the English to break the truce and then appear to retaliate.

Agnès, delighted that her scheme had worked, that she had been the one to push the King to the point, encouraged them both, still committing the sin of sharing her body between them, still allowing Jacques Coeur to gaze in wonderment, to put his lips where no one but a lover should. But she justified it all to herself by thinking of the part she had played in putting France on the offensive, itching to boot the occupying English forces out for once and for all.

And in March 1449, the excuse they had been looking for at last came about. The town and castle of Fougères, a French stronghold on the Breton border, was seized by an Aragonese mercenary captain in the pay of the English. A general order, "Prepare for War," was secretly sent out and the French army began to mobilize.

Agnès gave a great ball at Beauté to celebrate the fruition of her plans, the guest of honor the King, at the next strata of society, Pierre de Brézé and Jacques Coeur. As it was spring she threw open all the doors and the visitors saw that below on the river floated decorated boats packed with musicians, the lanterns from each craft reflected in the water. As always at Agnès's feasts the banquet and the entertainment were without equal, but it was generally agreed that the dancing was by far the most splendid part of the evening.

Agnès was led out by the King and the guests gasped that she carried a flaming torch which lit her unearthly beauty and flickered on her scintillating jewelry. But after only a few steps la Dame passed the flambeau to the couple behind her, and so it went round, lighting dancer after dancer, until finally it ended with Agnès again. Then, laughing and lovely, she led a line out into her formal garden and there, in the open air, drunk with exhilaration as much as wine, they all performed the wild hard peasant dances of Provence, the women raised aloft, the men stamping their feet, hands clapping as everyone swung into a circle then went whirling round, fingers joined, till the last chords were played and the fiddlers' bows were silent.

Small wonder that after this excitement certain couples wandered into the discreet darkness of the trees, the King and his mistress amongst them. With the moon coming up over the river throwing a strip of silver that seemed to end at the very feet of the lovers, Charles and Agnès swam naked in the shallow water and then, shivering with cold, went to a little stone summerhouse where a fire blazed. As always when he was with her the King was instantly ready for coupling and, on a caprice, having taken her in the warmth and comfort, afterwards chased la Dame through the trees, watching the play of moonlight and shadow on that most exquisite of bodies, unmarked by childbirth or the passing of years.

Silver gleamed on high round breasts, and on her supple waist and elegant hips, and Agnès's face was transformed to that of a goddess by that most bewitching of lights. A halo of moonshine glittered round the burnished hair, the great eyes sparkled, the sweet lips and straight nose were shadowed gray, the splendid neck had become the stem of a flower, the bloom her perfect silvered face.

"If only I could paint you now," called Charles, and La Dame de Beauté paused beneath the trees, as perfect as a statue, so that he could take one final look at her before she ran, laughing, into the forest.

"It's war at last," said Richemont with the relish of an old battle-scarred warrior. "We are to invade Normandy. I have been called upon to mobilize my army."

"You're looking forward to it," said Catherine. "You men!"

"I don't relish killing, don't accuse me of that, but I've been itching to get at the English for years. They're like bloody squatters up there in the North. High time they went."

"I couldn't agree with you more," his wife said heartily. "So I think I'll be a camp follower for this one. I feel like a damned good ride in any case."

He laughed at her, patting her broad shoulder. "What a woman you are. I'm so glad I met you."

"It suited us both," she said, and bit into a fondant to make her point.

"I'm going to look round my old haunts before I go," the Earl said in a different voice. "Say goodbye to them."

"Why? You're not going to get killed if that's in your mind. I'm far from finished with you yet."

"I might die of natural causes. I'm fifty-six."

"Coillons, Monsieur. You're dug in for a long life."

He grinned at her. "Be that as it may, I'm still off to see them."

"Memories of your old love?"

"Perhaps."

He left his home near Poitiers in the blackness of night and rode hard so that he was at Angers before dawn. Extraordinarily for that time of year there had been a heavy frost and the morning was sharp with both cold and mist, which lay heavy over the fields and river forming lakes that were not really there.

The dark gray ridges of cloud, beyond which the first pink threads of day could just be seen, were a mountain range of the mind. Sheep in the pastures leading down to the Maine walked stiffly on the frozen ground, their breath fluting up in little spirals of vapor, their voices clear in the crisp air, while steam rose from the flanks of Richemont's sweating mount as he entered the castle of Angers through the Country Gate and made his way within.

The fortress was just stirring into life, the smell of fresh bread coming from the bakehouse, a curl of smoke rising from its chimney, the creak of bolts as doors and gates were opened for the day, the sound of feet and voices as the scullions went about their business. Without asking permission, knowing that René was not in residence, Richemont made silently for the Queen's apartments.

How many years had it been since he had walked the battlements in his soft boots and heard her laugh? How many years since they had discovered the joys of each other's body, since they had created the little warrior girl who had died in agony in the flames of Rouen, since he had found he loved Yolande d'Anjou?

Foolishly, because he was far from the seventeen he had been when he had first fallen in love, Richemont climbed onto the balustrade and began to walk along it, balancing precariously. And then somewhere behind him he heard a woman laugh and nearly fell to his death in fright. Somehow steadying himself, Richemont quickly jumped down to the safety of the balcony.

The wooden door leading to the Queen's chamber was open and within the Earl saw the black outline of a woman, standing silently, watching him.

"Yolande?" he whispered.

But as he rushed forward, his arms outstretched to embrace the specter, he saw that it was not his dead lover but her daughter Marie, the Queen of France.

"Madame," he exclaimed, "why are you here?"

"I could ask you the same," she retorted, but he saw that she smiled in the dawning, her plain and careworn face, never as beautiful as her mother's, softened by the gentle light.

The Earl shrugged apologetically, more than a little embarrassed. "I came to look round the scenes of my youth before I went off to war."

"Yes, it has come at last as I had hoped. But will the King win? Will the English finally go?"

Richemont thought carefully about his reply. "This is our great chance. The enemy are tired and have no stomach for it. Yes, it may take us a while but we are going to win."

Marie nodded. "Then everything has been worth it."

"What do you mean?"

"Asking Madame Sorel to talk the King into fighting, humbling myself, it will all have been worthwhile if France is the ultimate victor."

Richemont, curious, said, "Forgive me, Madame, for I know it is not my affair, but yet I long to know the answer. That day in Paris when the crowd booed la Dame de Beauté, why did you lead her onto the balcony and show her friendship?"

For answer, the Queen asked another question. "You were fond of my mother, weren't you?"

"Devoted to her."

"Then you will remember the two proverbs she liked so well. 'Cast thy bread upon the waters' and 'As you sow so shall you reap.'"

"I do, clearly."

"I reaped bitterness after striking la Dame in public. It was I who felt cheapened and degraded, not she. So when it came to the incident in Paris I knew I would cleanse myself of that guilt, reap a good harvest, if I could only help the King by pretending to like her."

"And you cast your bread by asking Agnès to spur him on to fight the English?"

"Precisely. I feel somehow that my mother would have been proud of me for that."

"She would indeed."

There was a moment's pause and then the Queen said, "You were more than fond of her, I believe. In fact I think you were in love with her."

Richemont smiled. "I loved her all my life and still do. That is why I came back here. To see the places where she used to walk and talk."

"You are a good man, Richemont," said Marie. "I wish you well for the rest of your days."

"As I do you, ma Reine," answered the Earl, and kissed the Queen's hand.

Charles declared war on the English on 31st July 1449, and a few days later set off with his army for Normandy. He was too old now to heed advisers who told him not to put himself at risk, and besides there were the Dauphin and young Charles of France to succeed him. With the gleaming smile he reserved for ceremonial occasions, the King excitedly put on armor and rode at the head of his troops, the Constable of France beside him.

In September Coutances, St. Lô and Carentan capitulated to the royal armies, followed next month by Gavray. But in November came the greatest triumph of all when Fougères, Château-Gaillard, Harfleur and the much prized Rouen fell into French hands. December saw Charles capturing Bellême and then, as usual, the winter put paid to fighting and the King's army, well advanced into Normandy, decided to make camp in Rouen and the surrounding area in order to keep their Christmas.

Charles himself chose to stay outside the city in Jumièges, built between the forest and the Seine. For a whim, a caprice, for the sheer novelty of the thing, the monarch elected not to lodge in the nearby mansion house but instead remained in his pavilion. Dressed like an ordinary soldier, enjoying the challenge of living outdoors the King could not remember a time when he had felt more content or in better health, for now he had reached the pinnacle of his entire life.

Inspired by his leadership, his army had marched to the northernmost part of his kingdom to play out the ultimate challenge of his destiny. The prediction of Nicolas Flamel was at long last to be fulfilled; the English were crumbling before his advance, the final confrontation was shortly to take place.

Charles knew now with absolute certainty that he would be remembered for ever as the King who drove the foreign invader from French shores and brought a beleaguered country out of the darkness into the shining light of a thousand new hopes.

On 5th January, which was Christmas Eve, it snowed, the northern climate of Normandy being so much colder. The forest sparkled, covered with a fine powder like icing sugar, the serpentine loops of the Seine shone like frosted glass, while the distant hills hung white as pearls in the misty morning. And into this wintry scene, into this glistening January day, came a sudden cavalcade of riders, the bells on the horses ringing clearly in the thin air, the blues and scarlets of the company like splashes of paint against the whiteness, the wonderful furs of the horsemen lustrous and shining in the clear light.

A sledge was in the middle of this extraordinary entourage and Charles could hardly believe his eyes when he saw who sat there. Covered with pelts, beautiful as ever but absolutely huge with child, was Agnès.

"Mon Dieu," he exclaimed in pure astonishment. "I can scarcely credit it. My very dear girl, what are you doing here?"

La Dame was obviously none too pleased by the shocked expression on the King's face for a frown crossed the exquisite features.

"Aren't you pleased to see me?" she said crossly.

"Of course I am, but frankly bowled over. What induced you to make such a hazardous journey in your condition?"

"Loneliness frankly," Agnès replied acidly. "I was bored to sobs at Loches, sitting on my own wondering what you were up to. So I have come to bring you Christmas cheer, gifts and food and wine." And she indicated another sleigh loaded with all kinds of good things.

In a way it was embarrassing. He had wanted to spend a soldier's Christmas, a man among men, and now here was his mistress, enormous, obviously due to drop her child at any moment. The place would not only be swamped by her prolific presence but overrun with all her chattering retinue, who even now were jumping up and down, blowing their nails, and making a general commotion.

It was Richemont who sorted it out, commandeering the manor house of Mesnil-la-Belle for Agnès's use, making sure that everyone had a bed for the night, pouring the King a swift glass of brandy wine.

"Women!" he whispered. "Such unpredictable creatures."

And Charles had turned on him a look of gratitude that the Earl never forgot.

It was not the sort of Christmas that any one of them had envisaged but for all that went well, Agnès indomitably organizing a banquet and ball in her temporary residence. Yet her condition worried Charles. She was now too big to move round comfortably and seemed somehow feverish and overbright, her beautiful creamy skin slightly flushed and damp-looking.

"You will be careful, won't you," he admonished.

"Oh, shush. This is my fourth child. Believe me I am much happier here than twiddling my thumbs waiting for you to come home. Besides this war was partly my idea, I had to see how it was going."

But then, and most strangely on St. Agnes Day, 21st January, when the sun entered the House of Aquarius, la Dame de Beauté went into labor and aided by Catherine de Richemont, who had accompanied her husband to war, produced a tiny daughter, a scrap of a thing weighing only a few pounds but which none the less survived the birth and lay in its cradle with hands like minute starfish, gazing at the world from sad and solemn eyes. Seeing how weak she was, potions were brought by the monks from the Abbey infirmary to strengthen *la belle Agnès* after her ordeal, but inevitably there was a certain amount of head shaking.

"She was utterly foolish to undertake such a journey in this weather and in her state. There can be no doubt that La Dame has drained herself of energy."

"What do you mean?" asked Charles, overhearing one of these comments. "What are you saying? She is going to get better, isn't she?"

"Of course, Monsieur."

But for some reason Agnès seemed unable to rally after

this fourth birth, though she had borne her other three babies with no difficulty at all.

"Poison," whispered someone, and the rumor was round in a moment that somehow the Dauphin had managed to introduce a deadly substance into Agnès's food.

"That's nonsense," the King's physician assured him. "La Dame has that fever which sometimes affects women after childbirth."

"But the Dauphin swore to strike down all those who had contrived to have him thrown out of his home."

"But how could he have done it? Monsieur is miles away."

"Be that as it may, I still don't trust him. But can she be saved?"

"They are praying for her at the Abbey."

"I didn't bloody well ask that," said Charles, suddenly at breaking point. "I asked if she was going to die. Is she?"

"If you want the truth I will tell it to you. She has a fifty-fifty chance, Monsieur. I have attended women with this condition before and those who have been strong enough have fought it off. But, alas, Madame is weak from that ridiculous journey."

"Oh, Christ," said the King, "oh, Christ and His precious Mother. I can't bear it. She is my great love, my joy in living, please don't let her go."

"Majesty, calm yourself," Poitevin answered gently.

But Charles was beyond listening and rushed to Agnès through the snow, finding her white as a Christmas rose, no life left in her.

"Oh, my darling, my darling," cried the King and threw himself down on the bed beside her and would not leave until the physician and those attending her begged him to give them a few moments alone with la Dame de Beauté. But after they had gone, Charles de Valois crept back into the chamber and stood looking at her. She was completely white and utterly lovely, a marble statue now, a sleeping Beauty.

"Agnès," he whispered, and she opened her glorious lids and looked at him for the last time.

"Au revoir," she whispered, and her voice was light as a flute's.

"Agnès," sobbed the King, "Agnès, don't. I can't live

without you. There is no life for the King without you. I
beg you not to leave me."

But it was no use. She had gone on her great adventure
and the perfect thing whose hand he now ardently kissed
was simply her mortal shell, all that was left of the glorious
being who once had so delighted the hearts of men.

Epilogue

He had lived on, of course he had. He had taught himself too well, trained himself too hard to be an exceptional King, a King who would lead France out of the dark ages into the Renaissance. But it had never been the same again for Charles with la Dame de Beauté gone. Emptiness everywhere. In his many splendid homes, in his bed, in his life.

There had been other little diversions, he couldn't say there had not, but they hadn't amounted to much, a physical dalliance to prove he was still virile, no more. But Marie had never come back to him, even with her rival dead and laid in the grave she had considered their marriage over and done, and had stayed away, keeping her own house and her own counsel.

They had beaten the English completely. By the end of 1450, the year in which Agnès had died, they had thrown them out of Normandy, and by the end of 1453, English resistance in Guyenne had totally collapsed. The rats had fled to Calais, the only place they had left in the entire kingdom of France, and he had become Charles, the Very Victorious, the most successful king France had ever known.

It had been the death of Richemont, his old companion and faithful Constable, that had finally made Charles give in to the bouts of ill health which had struck him from time to time now that peace had come again. He had first been attacked by sickness in 1455 and then, four years later, his leg had become swollen and ulcerated, to say nothing of his mouth. But these inconveniences hadn't stopped him moving about his beautiful châteaux and territories and it was only in the year of 1461 that he had come to Mehun-sur-Yèvre with no further inclination to move on.

"I'm dying," thought Charles, staring up at the ceiling. "That is why I am remembering all this, because I'm dying."

He had had a tooth out two weeks earlier, his jaw and gum terribly inflamed by an abscess and the tooth removed to let it drain. But his mouth had become acutely tender and his digestive tract painful, so much so that he had stopped eating altogether.

"Are you afraid the Dauphin is trying to poison you?" his physician had asked him. "Because I can assure you all this food has been tasted first."

"No," the King had scrawled on a piece of paper, it being far too difficult to talk. "It is just that everything hurts so much."

They had left him alone then, knowing that if he couldn't swallow it would be only a matter of time before he slipped away and now, with the dirge-like prayers of a priest in the background, he supposed he was doing just that.

Louis had not come to visit him, treacherous little toad, and Marie was at Chinon, not forgiving him even in these dire circumstances, though Bonne was in the room, he could see her standing in the corner, small, dark and nervous as usual, and Jehanne had elbowed the priest to one side and was coming to have a closer stare at him.

He shook his head and mimed, "Please don't, I look awful," but La Pucelle merely smiled and stood aside to let la Dame de Beauté get closer.

It was then that Charles had realized what was happening. They had come from whatever extraordinary place they had all gone to and were here to escort him there too. But now they were standing respectfully aside as the Queen of Sicily, Yolande, his good mother, came to join their throng. And, unbelievably, sitting in her wheelchair, Catherine bravely pushing it, Charles saw Isabeau looking quite affable, even winking at him with one of her glittering black eyes.

Before Charles stretched a tunnel, two great fish leaping and playing in the ocean that lay beyond, the sparkle of their silver scales blindingly bright in the brilliant sunshine.

"Come Piscean," they called. "Come back to your element."

And how wonderful it was to take Yolande's hand, Isabeau and Catherine only a step behind, the three younger people running on ahead, then plunge down and down, knowing they were there beside him, into the fathomless blue ocean that so calmly awaited beyond.

Historical Note

It was in the summer of 1988, when visiting the Loire Valley for the first time, that I initially became aware of Charles VII as a person and realized with a certain surprise that he who had possessed, supposedly, the most beautiful woman in the world for a mistress had also been associated with Joan of Arc, or Jehanne as I later came to think of her. The contrast between the voluptuary and the virgin was enough to set me thinking, but when I came to research the King more closely and the rest of the dazzling women in his life were revealed, a book was born.

Yet Charles remains a mystery, an enigma; his two modern biographers, Philippe Erlanger and Malcolm Vale, in direct disagreement as to the character of the man. Erlanger follows the more traditional line put forward by Bernard Shaw in *St. Joan*. "The dauphin is at Chinon, like a rat in a corner, except that he won't fight. We don't even know that he is the dauphin: his mother says he isn't; and she ought to know ..."

But Professor Vale sees Charles not as a craven coward but a complex creature, planning and scheming, manipulating his courtiers to suit his own purpose, letting them 'entangle themselves in the webs that they spun.' And, 'playing for the very highest stakes—his own survival.' And survive the King did to see the English driven back to Calais, an achievement indeed. However history judges Charles de Valois and his extraordinary career it must never be forgotten that it was he who led France out of the Dark Ages towards the Renaissance.

Of the many women involved with the King, the most terrible by far was Charles's mother, Isabeau. A monster in every way, her profligacy knew no bounds. She was the most immoral woman of an immoral age and none of her actions have been exaggerated in this book. Yet if Isabeau lacked any kind of discipline, Yolande d'Anjou was quite the opposite. My admiration is boundless for this remarkable, clever Spanish princess who virtually ruled Anjou single-handed and whose enormous influence over Charles is agreed upon by all who have studied him.

But there can be no doubt that the most interesting of all the King's women was Joan of Arc who signed herself Jehanne and, indeed, is referred to as such in several of the older reference books. As I went from place to place, trying to gain insight into her character, I became convinced that what she did was actually impossible, that no teenager from the backwoods could have ridden the great French war horses, let alone covered the enormous distances that she did every day, nor handled the powerful weapons used by the army at that particular phase of history. Inspired though the girl obviously was this could not, for me, explain her enormous physical strength.

Throughout that research trip I felt there was some hidden thing which would explain all this and I believe I finally found it. A stroke of luck in Saumur, where I was looking for the Château of the Queen of Sicily, led me into the Auberge Reine de Sicile and into conversation with the owner, Monsieur Bernard Juguet. He showed me some original documents, gathered by a Saumur historian, in which is expounded the theory that Jehanne and Yolande d'Anjou had been working together throughout and that Jehanne had actually gone to the Château of the Queen of Sicily in order to be briefed before leaving for Chinon. This historian, too, raised the question of Jehanne's feat of arms but could not explain it.

It was the remarkable book *The Holy Blood and the Holy Grail* which gave me my eventual lead. In this work, the authors prove quite conclusively the existence of a secret society known as the Priory of Sion. This society had close links with the Knights Templar and at the time that Jehanne first appeared on the scene René d'Anjou, Yolande's son, was Grand Master. The connection became apparent. Somebody, somewhere, heard of the visionary virgin and had her specially trained for what lay ahead. The Knights Templar had gone underground but were far from finished. The piece of evidence which finally convinced me was the fact that Jehanne herself raised the standard of the Templars and vowed that their work must continue. Why should a simple rustic from Domrémy do this if she were not, in fact, a member of their order?

Obviously, my researches into Jehanne led me to the "bastardy" theory. Several French historians believe that La Pucelle was not a peasant but a royal bastard, the child of Isabeau and Duke Louis d'Orléans, taken to the country to be brought up for its own safety. The argument is flawed in many ways and the thing I found impossible to believe was that a bright being like Jehanne could have emerged from two such terrible people. If she was anybody's bastard it was far more likely that she came from the house of Anjou, with whom she was always so closely linked, but even this is sheer supposition and cannot be supported by any reasonable evidence, the very nature of the relationship between Yolande and Richemont never having been properly explained. The only odd fact is the complete disappearance of Alison du May, leaving no trace, at the time of Jehanne's trial. Was she removed because she knew too much?

Most of La Pucelle's biographers mention the fact that according to her squire, Jean d'Aulon, the girl never menstruated. This would explain a great deal about how she coped with living amongst and fighting alongside the French army. Dr. Delachambre, who attended Jehanne during the trial, gave more precise medical details which appear to have been the basis for a description given of her by the Abbé Villaret. "Rustic life had fortified her naturally robust body even more. She had only the exterior of her sex, without suffering from any of the infirmities which are characteristic of its weakness. This disposition of the organs would necessarily have made her imagination more active." The author Pierre de Sermoise has concluded from this ambiguous remark that Jehanne suffered from gynandromorphism, a partial pseudo-hermaphroditism in a woman with secondary male sexual characteristics. If he is right many of the unanswered questions about Jehanne would be solved.

Madame de Giac is another figure shrouded in mystery, even French experts not being certain whether she was de

Giac's mother or wife. The facts are that there certainly
was a Madame de Giac, that she was the mistress of the
Duke of Burgundy, that she had a powerful influence over
Charles, that she actually stopped the argument between
Burgundy and the young King by the extraordinary means
of physically stepping between the two departing entou-
rages and sending them back to the conference table. My
portrait of her is based on what shadowy facts there are
available, yet what is certain is that she died in the horrific
way described.

Many writers believe Agnès Sorel to have been not
only the most beautiful woman of her time but also the
most honorable, yet contemporary evidence points another way. The monumental row between Louis and
Charles—they literally never saw one another again after
they parted company in late 1446—begins to make sense
if one gives credence to the theory that Agnès was the
Dauphin's mistress before becoming that of the King. To
quote Malcolm Vale: "If Louis, as well as his father, was
her lover, then she might have been the principal cause
of the estrangement between them." And as for the volatile Pierre de Brézé, to quote a contemporary source,
". . . he keeps himself marvelously well in with the King,
partly by means of Agnès, from whom he has what he
wants." Enough said I think!

Interestingly, Agnès's second daughter, Charlotte, married Jacques de Brézé, Pierre's son. Their son was Louis
de Brézé whose second wife was Diane de Poitiers, the
legendary beauty who became mistress of Henri II. Agnès's eldest girl, Marie-Marguerite, married Olivier de
Coëtivy, the Seneschal of Guyenne, while her third child,
Jeanne, married Antoine de Bueil. Her fourth daughter,
whose birth killed Agnès, survived her mother only six
months.

The Queen, Marie d'Anjou, even today remains in the
background of Charles's life, remembered only for her
large brood of children and her refusal to dabble in political
affairs. My theory that their marriage was a happy one,
bringing the King a curious kind of contentment, is supposition only. Yet the fact remains that Charles of France was
born to the Queen late, the last of fourteen offspring, proving that despite Agnès the sex life of Charles and Marie,
if nothing else, remained active.

As to the rest of the story, reality and fiction are sometimes interwoven, though the facts have been researched as well as they possibly could be. This extraordinary account of those grim and terrible times is as close to the truth as I could make it.

Bibliography

The Holy Blood and the Holy Grail, Michale Baigent, Richard Leigh and Henry Lincoln.

The True Story of the Maid of Orleans, Maurice David-Darnac.

Charles VII et son Mystère, Philippe Erlanger.

Life in Medieval France, Joan Evans.

Operation Shepherdess, André Guérin and Jack Palmer White.

Joan of Arc, John Holland Smith.

Yolande d'Anjou, la Reine des Quatre Royaumes, Jehanne d'Orliac.

Joan of Arc and her Secret Missions, Pierre de Sermoise.

Charles VII, M. G. A. Vale.

Gilles de Rais, A. L. Vincent and Clare Binns.

Bluebeard, Thomas Wilson.

There's an epidemic with 27 million victims. And no visible symptoms.

It's an epidemic of people who can't read.

Believe it or not, 27 million Americans are functionally illiterate, about one adult in five.

The solution to this problem is you... when you join the fight against illiteracy. So call the Coalition for Literacy at toll-free **1-800-228-8813** and volunteer.

Volunteer Against Illiteracy. The only degree you need is a degree of caring.